Elizabeth Laird

ARCADIA

Elizabeth Laird

ARCADIA

MACMILLAN
LONDON

First published 1990 by
MACMILLAN LONDON LIMITED
4 Little Essex Street London WC2R 3LF
and Basingstoke

Associated companies in Auckland, Delhi, Dublin, Gaborone, Hamburg, Harare, Hong Kong, Johannesburg, Kuala Lumpur, Lagos, Manzini, Melbourne, Mexico City, Nairobi, New York, Singapore and Tokyo

ISBN 0-333-53296-1

A CIP catalogue record for this book is available from the British Library

Typeset by Matrix, 21 Russell Street, London WC2
Printed and bound in Great Britain by
WBC Ltd, Bristol and Maesteg

For my mother and her sisters

Acknowledgements

This book could not have been written without the kindness and hospitality of my many aunts, uncles and cousins in every part of New Zealand, who gave me an enormous amount of their time, and helped me with their wide-ranging knowledge of New Zealand history, botany, forestry and bird life. My mother's accounts of her forebears' experiences gave me the original inspiration for this story.

I would also like to thank the staff of the National Maritime Museum, the London Library, the Renfrew District Museum in Paisley, the Turnbull Library in Wellington, the Early Settlers Museum in Dunedin, and most of all Jill Tasker of the New Zealand High Commission Library in London, who kindly read and commented on the manuscript.

My brother, Graham Laird, has given me his enthusiastic support at every stage, and has contributed a great deal from his wide knowledge and experience of ships and sailing.

Chapter One *Edinburgh, 1820*

1

The pale slanting sun of a February afternoon threw long shadows down the grey Edinburgh street, but did not warm the small hunched figure of a woman, who pulled her black shawl tightly round her neck to ward off the bitter east wind as she limped furiously along the frost-rimed pavement of Princes Street.

'Wait till I tell him, wait till he hears about this, Fanny Heriot. You'll be sorry you laughed at me, so you will,' the woman muttered to herself as her plain brown boots tapped unevenly along the flagstones.

The baker's lad, humping a load of oatmeal on the corner, heard her talking to herself and laughed aloud. 'Did you hear that, Wullie?' he called out to the grocer's caddy across the street. 'Yon Aggie Heriot's gone daft at last!'

Taking not the slightest notice, Aggie hurried on, one hand on her painful hip as she struggled up the slope of Frederick Street, turned into George Street and knocked out her characteristic sharp rap on the door of her father's house. It was opened at once by old Jeanie.

'Now whatever has happened to overset you, Mistress Aggie?' she said, peering at Aggie with eyes misted over with a blue film of cataract. 'You look like a thundercloud, so you do.'

A scowl had indeed settled upon Aggie Heriot's forehead. It deepened lines that marked her strong-boned face, from which the dark hair, parted in the middle, was rigorously scraped back into a hard knot at the back of her head. It was the face of a woman of fifty, but Aggie Heriot was no more than thirty years old. A lifetime's battle with the nagging pain of a diseased hip had drawn marked lines of character around her eyes and mouth and had etched on to it a permanent sharpness. Aggie Heriot, who had realised many years ago that she could never be beautiful, had learned to cultivate her plainness with relish.

'Where's my father, Jeanie?' she said, in a surprisingly deep voice. 'Is he still at the shop?'

'Aye, he'll be a while yet,' said the old woman, 'and it's no bad thing, for wee Missie Fanny is up there in the drawing room laughing fit to bust with that fancy body from Glasgow.'

'Indeed!' said Aggie, and Jeanie, for all her blindness, noted a spark of triumph in her brown eyes. 'Then I'd best be up there before more harm is done,' and she stumped across the chequered marble floor to the staircase, leaning on the curved and polished banister as she dragged herself up to the drawing room on the first floor, while Jeanie shuffled down to the kitchen to warn Mrs Fergus to send up the old china for tea, for a storm was brewing upstairs, so it was, and there was no call to put the best service into danger.

Aggie paused for a moment outside the drawing-room door. The house, newly built in the fashionable classical style, was so solid that not a board creaked under her weight, and the heavy mahogany door swung so easily on its hinges that not even the slightest squeak betrayed her presence. She had plenty of time to watch the occupants of the elegant drawing room before they became aware of her.

She could not, in any case, have spoken at once, as the shocking sight that confronted her took her breath away. A fair young woman, dressed in a white muslin gown with a rose-coloured sash, her blonde ringlets tied up in a ribbon on the crown of her head and artfully arranged to cascade over her ears, was sitting on the stool of the grand piano, being passionately kissed by a young man, whose thick black hair was ruffled in a way that could only suggest the work of the young woman's fingers.

'Fanny!' Aggie's voice, for which they were both unprepared, made the couple jump guiltily apart.

'Aggie! I thought you were . . . ' Fanny started to say, her blue eyes wide with horror, then bit her lip and blushed.

'That's right, miss. You thought I was at the Relief Society and likely to be there for another hour or more. You thought you could fool me, you and fine Master Hector here, and make me a laughing stock behind my back with your loose ways. You should be ashamed of yourself, and you will, when Father hears about this!'

'Aggie! You wouldn't – you can't tell Father!' Fanny had spent many hours in front of the looking glass practising the flirtatious effect of her thick-lashed eyes. She now tried out her most piteous expression on her sister.

'Hector and I are going to be married, Aggie,' she wheedled. 'There's no harm in—'

'You're disgusting, Fanny, that's what you are. You've been man mad since you went into long skirts, and you'll throw yourself away on the first pair of pantaloons that will take you.'

The young man, who had been straightening his rather too large cravat in the delicately carved gilt mirror that hung over the fireplace, looked round, his embarrassment turning to annoyance.

'Mistress Agnes,' he said, marching across the pale blue carpet towards her, 'please don't be too hard on your sister. I am to blame. But you must believe that I don't mean any harm. I intend to talk to your father this evening . . . ' he paused, watching for the softening effect that his charm usually worked on middle-aged ladies. Aggie did not so much as blink. 'We rather hoped,' he said, sounding less dignified than he had intended, 'that you would be our friend.'

Aggie shifted the weight from her bad leg. In spite of herself, she was impressed by the fellow's brawn, by his broad, powerful shoulders and serious, decided expression. He was certainly a cut above the last young fool, a poetically minded clerk in the law courts, with adoration in his eyes and ink stains on his fingers. She stood nonplussed, looking momentarily uncertain.

Unfortunately, Fanny, rash and impetuous, broke in. 'Aggie, you can't let us down! If you'll only speak to Father for us he'll come round in the end, you know he will.'

'I? Speak to Father for you? Why ever should I, miss?' Fanny had touched a raw nerve, and Aggie's voice was shrill with renewed anger.

Fanny was puzzled. She had, of course, shocked her strait-laced sister. That was not surprising. It was all the fault of that stupid new carpet that Father had laid down in the hall. It muffled the sound of feet coming up the stairs in a wholly unnecessary way. But Fanny read more than outrage in Aggie's stony face. Something else had happened to upset her.

'You've been talking to those old cats again!' she said, her eyes filling with the easy tears of a spoilt child. 'They're all against me. They're just a parcel of dowdy—'

'If', said Aggie, with awful formality, 'you are speaking of the members of the St Andrew's Ladies' Relief Society, I am pleased to inform you that they consider idle gossip beneath them. I had my information from a much less desirable source. Old Nimmo . . . '

Fanny looked suddenly anxious. Old Nimmo had been her father's chief clerk since Simeon Heriot had established his gunsmith's business in fine new premises on Princes Street, twenty years before. If he had taken his tale to her father, then no one, not even his own daughter, would be able to cast a doubt upon it.

Aggie watched with satisfaction as Fanny dropped ten years from an eighteen-year-old beauty to an eight-year-old miscreant who was scared of a spanking.

'Old Nimmo tells me that he saw you and your fine beau here strolling about in the Meadows this very day, making a display of yourself in the ornamental arbour for all the no-good gossips of Edinburgh to see.

' "Well, well, Mistress Fanny," he says, "and does your sister Aggie not keep a better eye on you than this, larking with a strange body whiles you should be minding your needle at home?"

' "Oh no," says you, flicking your yellow curls about in a hoity-toity fashion, "my sister's too busy on her good works to care a jot for me, and besides, she doesn't mind, and on top of that, she likes Mr Jamieson, and anyway, what does she know about love, being so old and ugly and crippled as she is?" And then,' went on Aggie, her breast heaving and her mouth working, 'yon hairy langshanks *laughed*!' Aggie dashed a furious hand across her eyes, and gazed belligerently at Hector.

Her heaving bosom and shaking forefinger had an unfortunate effect upon Hector Jamieson, whose sense of the comic was too easily tickled. Careless of Mistress Aggie's finer feelings, he threw back his handsome head and laughed again, while Fanny, infected with his mirth, buried her face in the edge of her lawn shawl and sank down once more on the piano stool, in the grip of a helpless fit of giggles.

The slam of the drawing-room door made the chandelier tinkle and the window sashes rattle in their frames, and it brought them both to their senses.

'You've done it now, you silly boy,' said Fanny, pouting. 'Aggie never could stand being laughed at.'

'What do you mean, *I*'ve done it?' demanded Hector. 'You were the one to chatter away to that dusty old clerk of your father's.'

'And how was I to know he'd run to Aggie with his tales?' said Fanny, aggrieved. 'What was the old fool doing anyway down in the Meadows at half past ten o'clock in the morning, I should like to know, when he should have been busy at his ledger?'

'It's all very well, my love,' said Hector, suddenly serious, 'but if Aggie turns your father against me we're done for. You know things have to be decided very soon. I can't dangle about here for ever, trying to turn his mind. I am only waiting for a reply to my letter to Mr Murchison in Calcutta before I set sail, and if we cannot be married before then, heaven alone knows when we may see one another again.'

His seriousness had its effect. Fanny stopped pursing her lips in a coquettish manner and began to bite her forefinger, an ugly childish habit which she had not been able to break.

'You'll have to talk her round.' Hector poked vigorously at the smouldering coals in the fireplace with the toe of his boot. 'And I must get to your father before she can set him further against us. I was intending to call on him after dinner this evening, but now I had better go to him at the shop. Now you go to your sister,

Fanny, and make her your friend again,' and Hector started towards the door.

'Hector!' Fanny seemed suddenly to wake up. She had flirted with so many men for so long and with such success that she had begun to confuse what was real and what was play-acting. She had, she felt sure, meant the promises she had exchanged with Hector, under the exciting influence of the pressure of his arm about her waist, and she had thrilled to the idea of setting off with him for foreign climes, but the glow had faded under the impact of Aggie's irate interruption, and now that Hector was actually about to confront her father, she was suddenly shaken with the enormity of what he was proposing.

She had been able easily enough to imagine herself in India, a queen among her servants, plucking exotic fruits in an Indian garden, tending her peacocks and riding about on an elephant. It was the more immediate problems that puzzled her. How would she face her father's anger? What clothing should she take for the voyage? Would she be obliged to leave her kitten behind? How could she bear to leave her best friend, Minnie Farquarson? Who would look after her when she was ill, as Aggie had always done, the sister who, for all her crotchets, had nursed Fanny devotedly since babyhood?

Finding herself suddenly and unusually speechless, Fanny looked up into Hector's impatient and confident eyes, and wondered, with a shock of fright, what she knew of this stranger who had made such sweeping plans for her future. Hector misunderstood her anxious look, and bent to kiss her cheek.

'You're not to worry, now,' he said with determination. 'I've made up my mind to have you, and not all the fathers in the world can stand in my way. You're mine, Fanny, no matter what they do or say.' And he walked quickly off, down the stairs, and let himself out of the house, leaving Fanny standing, half inspired, half terrified, pleating her sash in and out of her nervous fingers in the sudden realisation that from now on, her life would be quite outside her control.

2

Hector Jamieson, at twenty-seven years old, was very much used to getting his own way. It was not so much his considerable charm that usually won him the day, as his optimistic enthusiasm which swept all along in its path, and before which opposition melted away. The one spoilt child of an unsuccessful lawyer's widow, Hector had endured a youth of genteel poverty, and since his first taste of success at school, he had been determined to go up in the world, to make a fortune, to free himself from the humiliating necessity for patronage and the day-to-day grind of making do. He was a generous spender and a begetter of large plans, and he was looking forward to being rich, entirely confident that this happy state of affairs would soon come about. Four years of boredom studying the law had made him finally rebel against his mother's wish to set him in his father's footsteps, and five years of impatient diligence in his uncle's shipping business had only succeeded in sharpening his urgent ambition. An opening in Calcutta, where, as everyone knew, fortunes were to be made, had come his way, and Hector was prepared to plunge after it with all his heart and soul.

Fanny had erupted unexpectedly into Hector's scheme of things, but he had had to do no more than tie a knot here and let out a tuck there and his plans were easily adapted to accommodate the possibility of marriage. Fanny, Hector had decided on their second meeting at Minnie Farquarson's father's house in Leith, was the woman he would marry, and the decision was no sooner made than he was impatient to bring it about.

Fanny had claimed him utterly. It was not her flirtatiousness which attracted him. That he discounted as a manifestation of her extreme youth. He was too direct and impatient to play such childish games. But he had watched her jump down the last two steps as she ran down the Lawnmarket Stair. He had seen her thrust her way impetuously and with a fine disregard for the baskets of others, to the front of a crowd, in her eagerness to gain the best view of the *Lucy Ann* as she limped into Leith harbour, masts broken and rigging torn from the terrible storm she had endured. He had heard her laugh with loud, unladylike abandon at her friend's good-humoured wit, and he had sensed a response to his own strong passions behind the innocence of her kiss. Her courage, he guessed, would equal his own. She would be up to anything he might ask of her. She would seek out adventures in the same spirit as he might, and when the fortune he would surely win was his, he would pile riches upon her, certain that she would enjoy them with whole-hearted simplicity.

The notion that old Simeon Heriot might not share his confidence in the brilliant future mapped out for his daughter did not for a moment cross Hector's mind as he covered the short distance between the Heriots' new house in George Street and the family's prosperous business in Princes Street.

Simeon Heriot's gun saleroom, which led straight off the newly laid pavement of Princes Street, was the pride of the establishment. No expense had been spared in the arrangement of mahogany showcases, bow-fronted cabinets and leather chairs for the use of those sporting gentlemen who used Heriot's showrooms as much to meet and talk of hunting matters as to spend their money on firearms. A pair of them were thus engaged as Hector strode in through the door.

'... so I lifted my head a moment from the bracken, and bade old Jimmy hold his tongue and mind the dogs, and you'll not believe it, Fergus—' one was earnestly saying to the other, but his sentence was never completed for Hector cut across it.

'I wish to speak with Mr Heriot,' he said shortly to Old Nimmo, who with unnecessary diligence was polishing a gleaming barrel on which no speck of dust had ever dared to land. The old man looked at him sharply, then returned in a deliberate manner to squinting along the metal.

'Aye,' he said, slowly. 'Mebbe you do.'

A snicker of laughter from the sportsmen brought a quick flush to Hector's cheeks.

'Mr Heriot,' he said, slowly and distinctly, as if addressing an imbecile. 'I wish to speak with Mr Heriot.'

Old Nimmo laid the gun back in the velvet-lined case, and lovingly fastened the locks.

'I heard you the first time,' he said. 'But there's a question ye havena answered. Does Mr Heriot wish to speak with you?'

Hector did not deign to reply. He looked quickly about the saleroom, lifted the flap in the counter, passed through it, opened the door that stood behind it, and shut it firmly after him.

'Hey!' called Old Nimmo, spurred suddenly to action. 'Ye canna go through there!' But he was too late. Hector, finding himself in a small passageway, had already opened an imposing door at the end of it, and entered Simeon Heriot's inner sanctum.

The two men who were sitting on either side of a bright coal fire looked up in surprise. Hector glanced at them both, then turned at once to the older man.

'Sir,' he said. 'I have a matter of some urgency to discuss with you.'

Mr Heriot's brows, which were striking enough in repose, snapped together over his beak of a nose.

'Then you'll wait your turn in the saleroom, young man, for I'm engaged on a matter of business with Lord Airlie and I gave clear instructions that I was not to be disturbed.'

The younger man laughed, stood up and picked up his beaver and gloves from the litter of metal parts on the table.

'No, don't disappoint this young firebrand, Heriot,' he said. 'We've agreed on the matter. You'll work out the improvements to the hammer following my drawings, and see if you can effect a greater smoothness in the mechanism. I'll send Tolcher round for it in a fortnight or so. No, don't come with me to the door. Old Nimmo will see me out. It's long enough since I've passed the time of day with him.'

Hector stood back to let Lord Airlie pass him, and turned to see Simeon Heriot struggling to his feet. The old man, with a sturdy disregard for fashion, was wearing the knee breeches and buckled shoes of a former age, and his long hair straggled over his limp cravat, but Hector had no desire to laugh. The severity of Simeon's gaze and the ramrod stiffness of his back brought to Hector a sudden consciousness of his audacity. It had not until now occurred to him that Fanny's father might be anything but delighted with him as a suitor. Now he had disquieting doubts.

'Well?' said Mr Heriot. 'What is this urgent business which has caused you to break up a meeting with an old and valued customer in so unseemly a fashion?'

Hector felt suddenly that the room had grown too warm.

'It is about your daughter, sir,' he said. Nothing, after all, was to be gained by beating about the bush. Simeon's massive eyebrows lifted in surprise.

'I am not aware that you are acquainted with Agnes?' he said.

'Not – not Mistress Agnes,' said Hector, wishing that, after all, he had waited until after dinner to confront the old man, when a pint or two of claret would no doubt have softened his demeanour. Old Simeon was looking more alarming than ever.

'You wish to talk to me about Fanny?' he said. 'For what possible reason should I choose to discuss my younger daughter with you?'

Hector, casting about for a diplomatic way to proceed, found none. 'I wish to marry her, sir,' he said baldly.

For a long moment Simeon Heriot and Hector Jamieson looked at each other. Then Simeon found his voice.

'Then you'll wish in vain, young man,' he said, 'for Fanny has been reared in a decent home, and she'll marry no young blackguard who woos her behind her father's back.'

Hector started forward, his temper touched on the raw.

'That's not fair, sir,' he said quickly. 'I have not courted Miss Fanny behind your back. I haven't had time. We've only been acquainted for a little over two weeks.'

A rare smile creased Simeon Heriot's leathery cheeks, setting off a ripple of unaccustomed wrinkles.

'Two weeks!' he said. 'And how many hours of those two weeks have you spent in my daughter's company?'

'As many as I could spare, sir,' said Hector uncomfortably.

A rusty chuckle emerged briefly from behind the threadbare waistcoat that had covered Simeon Heriot's stomach for the last thirty years.

'And where, pray, did you spend those spare hours?'

'At the house of Mr Farquarson,' said Hector, conveniently forgetting at least two long mornings spent in rapturous wanderings about the braes of Arthur's Seat. 'Nigel Farquarson is an old schoolfellow of mine, and his sister Minnie, as of course you are aware, has the honour to be your daughter's bosom friend.' He breathed a short sigh of relief, confident that these credentials could only be acceptable. Simeon, however, was not impressed.

'Silly squawkers the lot of them,' he grunted, 'and Minnie's the worst of the lot. Bad company, bad company,' and seeming to lose interest in Hector, he sat down heavily once more in his chair, shook his head and looked broodingly down into the fire.

Hector moved round to face him again.

'Sir,' he said desperately, 'however much you may regret the manner in which I have come to know your daughter, I must assure you that I am well able to keep a wife, and that my prospects, believe me, are excellent.'

'Prospects?' The word seemed to irritate Simeon out of his lethargy, and he turned his withered face once more to look at Hector. 'Oh aye, you young men all have prospects nowadays. You're all in a great way in the law courts, taking other men's money off them, and setting up in manufactories, to ruin the old craftsmen and run them out of business. Prospects! I know prospects!' and he spat forcefully into the spittoon by the fire.

Hector, feeling himself to be at a disadvantage standing so tall above the old man, sat down gingerly on the edge of the facing chair, and sought to exercise his charm.

'I share your feelings, sir, naturally, with regard to the law courts and the manufactories. But I am far from being in such a business myself. I am in the house of my uncle, John Jamieson of Vincent Street, Glasgow, and I am shortly to take up a position in a thriving business at Calcutta, where, I am led to believe—'

'Bengal?' There was no mistaking the shocked disapproval in Simeon Heriot's voice. 'You are proposing to take my daughter to Bengal? She'd not last the year, and that's for sure. I haven't lost two wives and brought up two motherless children without learning something about the constitution of women, and I can tell you, young man, India is no place for a woman.' He paused for a moment, as if surprised himself at his unusual loquacity, and then resumed. 'Aggie's mother died of a fever when the child was but ten years old, and Fanny's lasted no more than two. And both with the best doctors of Edinburgh, and that means of the world! Calcutta! Pouf! Fanny! Bengal! The very idea!' and Simeon filled his cheeks and blew the air out again in sharp puffs of exasperation.

'Sir,' said Hector, abandoning his deferential air, and standing up once more to impress upon the old man the force of his determination. 'I have promised to wed your daughter and to cherish her until my dying day, and those promises I intend to keep. You must see—'

'Oh, get you gone, get you gone!' burst out Simeon, his patience quite exhausted. 'Fanny will have none of you, and you'll have none of her, and I'll not sit here, listening to such foolish twaddle when there's business to be done in the shop and my dinner spoiling at home, as like as not. Good day to you, sir, and I'll thank you to keep away from my daughter.' And the old man got to his feet again, marched to the door and slammed it shut behind him, leaving Hector smouldering with helpless rage, unable to relieve his feelings in any more effective way than by smartly kicking the chair that Simeon had vacated, and addressing him under his breath in the most insulting language he could call to mind.

3

Alone in her bedroom Aggie Heriot wept. Unlike Fanny, tears did not enhance her. They did not make her appealing and pathetic. Instead, they reddened her nose, puffed up her eyes and made her angular face look positively harsh. Unlike Fanny also, Aggie did not give way to her grief. She did not fling herself on her bed, indulge in hysterics, or moan and scream in order to attract the attention of anyone who might be passing her bedroom door. Aggie cried stiffly and silently, and made a serious attempt to darn a stocking as she did so.

Fanny's careless words, repeated by Old Nimmo, had angered and hurt her, but it was her sister's laughter that had cut her to the heart. Fanny had joined with her lover to mock Aggie's obvious distress. She had deliberately and cold-heartedly added insult to injury.

Chattering, laughing at me, going on behind my back, Aggie said to herself, her lips moving soundlessly as she went over and over the hurt in her mind. It was the culminating betrayal in a long list of recent grievances that she had to lay at Fanny's door.

Ever since the day when her soft, ineffectual stepmother, wasted by a hideous tumour at her breast, had pointed to the infant Fanny asleep in her cradle and whispered, 'Mind her now, Aggie, for there's little enough her father can do for her, poor bairn,' Aggie had nursed and cherished her little sister with a tenderness of which no one, except Fanny herself, would have believed her to be capable. She had held the chubby baby's hand when she took her first tottering steps along the flags of George

Street, clutching with the other hand at the conveniently positioned iron railings. She had taken her into her own narrow bed to comfort away the terror of her childish nightmares. She had braved the anger of their stern father on Fanny's behalf time and again to beg forgiveness for the little sins of childhood.

Fanny had been such a lovely child that Aggie, taking pride in her prettiness, had spoiled her perhaps more than she should have done. But no sooner was she into her teens than Fanny had begun to show alarming signs of independence. She had tied her sash as tightly as possible under the arms to emphasise her budding breasts, and she had learned to tilt her head provocatively and speak in a high lisping voice through pouting lips in a fashion she rightly supposed to be full of coquetry.

Aggie had at first half admired her sister's talents, which were of a kind she could never hope to command herself. It had seemed a shame to restrain the pretty charms which made old gentlemen unbend towards her so with such fatuous indulgence. But as Fanny advanced further into her teens, her wiles appeared in a more sinister light. Aggie saw that she was bent on entrapping any man who came her way, and that she did not care one jot about what her sister or any other older person might think. Carried away by the intoxication of being her own lovely self, Fanny had become a handful.

Aggie had waited, hoping that her sister's silliness would diminish as she grew older. Fanny was a woman at last, and could now be expected to repay with real friendship the years of Aggie's selfless devotion. But she showed no sign of caring for her sister at all. She would have none of female company as long as there was a man, any man, in the room, who would admire, flirt, whisper behind fans, and play compliments. There had been Alex McNeil and Andy Ferguson, both harmless in their way, but gormless enough too to make them ready for any kind of rowdiness. There had been Walter Jeffreys, Frederick Kerr and Jamie Harrison, and not even wee Rab the apothecary's assistant or old Tom the cobbler had been spared Fanny's sly looks and flirtatious chatter.

'Man-mad, man-mad she is,' Aggie whispered furiously to herself. 'And this smart Glasgow good-for-nothing is worse than the rest of them,' and she tugged at her needle so viciously that the silk thread snapped in her hand, and she had to poke about in her workbox to find a length that matched, impeded by the angry tears that had filled her eyes again.

The darn was only half completed when the click of the front door brought Aggie to her feet.

Father home already, she thought, and the dinner only half cooked, I've no doubt, and me not fit to be seen.

She splashed some water from the pitcher on her washstand on to a towel, and vigorously sponged her eyes. Then, first checking in the mirror that any tendency towards independence in her front hair had been ruthlessly suppressed, she went down the stairs and into the hall to greet her father and take his hat, in the way to which he had grown accustomed.

The hall was empty, but a footstep in the dining room told her that someone was there. She opened the door. Fanny was moving away from the window, and though she moved quickly she was not fast enough to prevent Aggie from noticing the hand snatched away from her bosom as if she had just hidden something inside her dress.

'Aggie!' Fanny came quickly towards her sister, ready and willing to make up the quarrel, but Aggie had seen, through the bright panes of the window, cleaned to a faultless brilliance by Jeanie's tireless hand, a familiar head of black hair disappear along the street and turn swiftly off down Hanover Street, and she drew a hasty conclusion.

'Bringing you letters now, is he?' she burst out furiously. 'How could you lower yourself like this, Fanny, no better than a trollop, a scarlet woman, and before dinner too, and such an unprincipled young man, and laughing at me together, the two of you,' and the tears, which had not been far away, broke out again in regular sobs.

Fanny was appalled. She could barely remember a time when she had seen her sister cry. Aggie had been her mother, her mentor, her friend, her comforter since before she could remember, but never before had she asked for comfort in return. Remorse for what she had done already, and doubts about what she was about to do, made Fanny's voice sharp with anxiety.

'Aggie, don't! Stop it! Aggie, you mustn't cry. I can't bear it. Aggie, you must, you must understand!'

She ran forward to embrace her sister but Hector's unfortunate note, which he had delivered into her hands but five minutes earlier, crackled as she moved. Aggie jumped back as if she had been bitten.

'You deceitful, lying creature! Hiding his letter and trying to get round me! Well, I wash my hands of you, Fanny Heriot, and I hope the Lord will have mercy on you, for I'm very sure Father will not,' and she pressed her handkerchief to her eyes once more as she turned and hobbled out of the room.

No sooner had the door shut behind her than Fanny dragged Hector's letter from its hiding place and began avidly to read it. So desperate was she to know its contents that for a moment the words swam about on the page, and she had to force herself to read slowly and from the beginning.

My love,

I have bad news to give you – your Father does not favour our marriage as he fears for your health in the climate of Bengal. I cannot be angry with him for wishing to cherish you, but since we will both die if we are parted, I fear he is going about it the wrong way.

I have but an hour ago received an urgent message from Mr Murchison's partner in Glasgow. He begs me to go to him at once as he has news of an important nature to impart. I feel sure it can only be an immediate summons to join him at Calcutta, and I am leaving in haste by this evening's mail to discover if I am right. I will send you news as soon as may be possible through Nigel Farquarson at Leith. He is a good fellow and will serve me in any way he can. I fear that I may not again have easy access to your Father's house.

Goodnight, my sweet love, and dream only of
your devoted
Hector

It was not until Fanny had read the letter three or four times that she fully understood it. She had first to recover from the curious lurch of her heart at the daring intimacy of 'My love', and the tenderness of the conclusion. But when at last its message became clear, she was breathless with fright.

Hector could be leaving at any time for Calcutta! And without her! She could imagine only too well the painful scene that must have passed between himself and her father. She had had only a faint hope in any case that Simeon Heriot would accept Hector's suit. And with Hector gone, probably for years, and all correspondence between them forbidden, as it surely would be, all chance of their marriage would be lost.

She waited for the slight feeling of relief that she had expected to come over her, now that the adventure was not to be. But instead she was overtaken by the sudden, powerful recognition that had come upon Hector at their second meeting. He was hers, and she was his, no matter where, no matter how. Her father, her sister, were of no account any longer. Hector was her chosen husband, and come what may, she would be his wife.

4

If Aggie had not succumbed two days later to a bout of fever, which laid her low upon her bed and sent Jeanie up and down the stairs at all times of the day with cups of tea and bowls of broth, and if Simeon Heriot had not been suffering from the misapprehension that since all seemed as usual at home, the person of Master Hector Jamieson must have been dutifully put out of his daughter's mind, Fanny might not have enjoyed an unusual degree of freedom, which enabled her to dream all day of her lover, and to turn over in her mind plans which would have shocked a more lenient moralist than Miss Heriot.

But Aggie did have a fever, and Simeon Heriot did not descend from the Olympian heights of the gunmaking business to delve into the furthest corners of his daughter's mind. Fanny was free to do as she liked.

In the first few days of Aggie's illness, remorse made her as good a nurse as she knew how to be. She dabbed her sister's brow with eau de Cologne, sent for fresh sheets when Aggie's were wet with perspiration and offered to read aloud favourite passages from *Ivanhoe* by the mysterious author of *Waverley*. She even volunteered to undertake Aggie's daily visit to the markets in the Old Town, but on the first morning she came back with a piece of salmon fit only, Jeanie opined, for an alley cat in Aberdeen, and on the second she had forgotten the carrots which Mrs Fergus had requested, but instead had wandered from the vegetable market at the Tron up to the Castle, and had frittered away her money on a pretty bone box which a French prisoner of war had thrust at her through the bars of his prison. 'Because,' said Fanny, 'he looked so thin, and I thought Aggie could keep her thimble in it.' Mrs Fergus had raised her shoulders in despair, and Jeanie had gone to market thereafter.

Aggie, though touched by Fanny's anxiety, was too unwell to bear much company. She wanted to be quiet, she mumbled to Jeanie, and sleep.

'Just keep an eye on Fanny for me,' she said anxiously, in a voice hoarse with coughing. 'Tell her to keep out of mischief.'

Jeanie, who had disapproved of Fanny since the child had been found dancing in front of the looking glass at the age of eleven dressed in her sister's Sunday best costume, and who frequently declared her a naughty baggage destined to end her days in the Cowgate, was only too happy to oblige.

'You're to stay out of mischief, young leddy,' she said severely, 'if you don't want to drive your poor sister to an early grave worrying. And mischief means laddies, and laddies means yon great Glasgow lump with a black mop on his head.'

She peered at Fanny, looking for a reaction, but Fanny affected a gaze of innocent enquiry before which Jeanie could only retire, baffled and suspicious.

'Aye, folly's a bonny dog,' she said, with sinister emphasis, and went off to the kitchen to enjoy an hour of prophetic observations with Mrs Fergus on the doom which would surely befall Miss Fanny, and the dreadful grief and shame that would no doubt overcome her family.

It was four days before the longed-for message came from Minnie Farquarson. It was in the form of a note, written in haste and blotched.

> A certain person has returned from Glasgow and will be awaiting you in Greyfriars Churchyard at 11 this morning. He says to take a chair as secrecy is vital. Your devoted, M. F.

A flush of excitement rushed to Fanny's cheeks. She crushed the note and flung it into the fire, stirring the coals until the paper had been entirely destroyed, then she ran upstairs and scratched at her sister's door.

'I'm away to see Minnie,' she whispered to the motionless figure in the bed. 'Are you comfortable, Aggie? Is there something I can do for you?' She held her breath as she waited for the answer, for the clock stood at a quarter past ten already, but only a grunt came from the pillow, and she sped on to her room to arrange her curls under her best and most fetching bonnet and to pull on a thick cloak for protection against the biting wind.

As a rule Fanny avoided sedan chairs. They were outmoded and stuffy, and often the padding carried all too obvious souvenirs of the previous occupants. She disliked, too, the tough little Highlanders who carried them, their sing-song Gaelic voices and their habit when drunk of abandoning their passenger and engaging in bouts of fighting with whoever obstructed their path. In any case, when she walked out she was accustomed to attract admiring glances from passing gentlemen who were apt to cast appreciative eyes at her small feet, the neatness of her figure and the charm of her face under its fashionable bonnet.

Today, however, was different and Fanny realised with a pang that she would not for much longer be in a position to bask in the approving smiles of strangers. Only one man in future would have the right to all her tender looks.

The chairmen set her down by the gates of Greyfriars Churchyard as the clock on the Tron Church was striking eleven and Fanny, hurrying hastily in, saw Hector waiting for her under the shadow of a broken column.

'Hector!' she cried, and ran towards him, decorum forgotten, expecting the rapturous greeting of an ardent lover after the dreadful separation of four whole days, but Hector, looking hastily round, captured both her hands in his and frowned down at her.

'Be quiet!' he said, sternly. 'Do you want all the world to know we have an assignation?'

Abashed, Fanny started to speak but Hector cut her short.

'Listen to me, my little love,' he said in a gentler voice, and Fanny, impressed by the earnest note in his voice, held her tongue and looked questioningly up into his eyes.

'It was as I supposed. The summons has come for me. I am to leave for Calcutta on the thirtieth.'

'But that is scarcely a week away!' burst out Fanny.

'It is next Thursday,' said Hector calmly. 'I am taking ship from Leith to London aboard the *Lizzy Dee* and will there transfer to the *Thalia*, bound for Calcutta. Mr Murchison has sent me money for the voyage, and letters of introduction to his associates at Cape Town and Bombay. He says his business is growing so fast he has no doubt but that I will soon be in a very fine way to be making excellent opportunities for myself. He says – but look, read his letter for yourself!'

He thrust a bundle of papers into her hands, plunged his own into the deep pockets of his riding coat, and stood back to watch Fanny read, a smile of pleased expectation on his face. Fanny bent her head over the lines of copperplate, but could not make out a word. A great tear dropped on to the page smudging a row of letters, then another, and another. In an instant Hector's arm was about her shoulders, his handkerchief had been applied to her eyes, his hand had forced up her chin and he was looking with bewilderment down into her face.

'Whatever is there here to upset you?' he said, removing the letters from her limp fingers which were threatening to drop them on to a damp and mossy tomb. Fanny stamped her foot with impatience.

'Oh, don't you see?' she said, enraged at his stupidity. 'You're going away for years and years and you'll forget me, and you'll marry a horrid woman in India, and I'll never see you again!' She stopped as the tears threatened to choke her.

'Fanny!' Hector's hand was under her chin again. 'Fanny, you don't think, you can't imagine that I'm leaving for Calcutta without you?'

Fanny's exasperation broke out again. 'How can you tease me so,' she said crossly, 'when you know that Father will never agree?'

'I do know,' said Hector, with a gentleness he rarely displayed, 'and I'm sorry if the idea of an elopement makes you unhappy, my darling, but you and I must never be parted again, and on Thursday of next week we are leaving for India together. Your father will know nothing of it until I have you safe on board.'

'Hector!' The shout with which Fanny launched herself into his arms drove a pair of indignant pigeons fluttering from a neighbouring urn, and caused an aged gardener to look up from sweeping the paths and to regard the couple with sour disapproval, but this time even Hector had abandoned caution as he caught Fanny in a crushing embrace. She was the first to return to earth.

'But how shall I do it? What shall I bring with me? Who is to tell Aggie? Can't you wait at least another week?' She was breathless with excitement.

Hector began to stride up and down the churchyard paths, gesturing firmly with his hands as he always did when making plans, and Fanny, clinging to his arm, had to trot to keep up with him.

'There's no need to worry yourself,' he said. 'I have money for the two of us, and we will have time in London for you to buy your bride clothes and order a trousseau for Calcutta. As for your leaving home, I think you should tell your sister that Minnie has asked you to a musical soirée on Wednesday night at Leith. You have been with her frequently before. And you can say that she asked you to stay until the next day, to prevent a late home-coming through the streets, as there has been so much talk in the newspaper of rowdiness by drunken youths. That will offer an excuse to put up a few necessities in a bag, though you will be obliged to leave most of your things behind. But instead of going home from Minnie's, you will come to me on board the *Lizzy Dee* in Leith. The captain says he must up-anchor soon after midnight to catch the tide, and we will be far out to sea before anyone can know of it.'

Fanny, dizzy with excitement, could only cling to Hector's arm and gasp as his audacious plan unfolded, but when he had finished she was silent for a moment, and then she looked down as a blush crept up her cheeks.

'When – when are we to be married, Hector?' she said in a small voice. A picture had come to her mind, a horrid image of a slut she had seen in the Cowgate grasping with dirty fingers at the sleeves of passing gentlemen, thrusting forward her withered breasts with drunken unsteadiness. Such a fate, she knew, inevitably befell all those who permitted themselves to spend a night in the company of a man outside the married state.

'We will be married at the Farquarsons',' said Hector positively. 'Nigel Farquarson is acquiring the licence and making all the necessary arrangements. We will be man and wife before we go on board.'

Chapter Two *Ayr, 1820*

1

At about the time that Hector and Fanny were plighting their troth in Greyfriars Churchyard, a very different young woman was standing on the pierhead at Ayr, holding a plain woollen plaid close round her shoulders against the stiff sea breeze. The wind tugged at the round bonnet that was tied tightly under her chin and whipped some errant strands of fine mouse-brown hair across her face.

Isobel Kirkwood put up a hand to protect her eyes, for a gritty black dust swirled up from two heavy colliers tied up in the harbour, into whose holds a team of labourers were loading sacks of Ayrshire coals.

A shout from one of the harbour loungers made her turn her head.

'Hey, Angus! Is that not a timber barque coming in from the north-west? Would it be the *Ailsa* maybe?'

A ruddy-complexioned individual who had been standing near Isobel, gazing with seeming concentration at nothing in particular, removed the pipe from his mouth and shouted back, 'Och no, how could it be? The *Ailsa*'s not three weeks out of port, and she was bound for Quebec with a full hold. It'll be the *Martha Blair*, for sure, in from the West Indies.'

Isobel's hand clutched at another fold of her plaid, and she felt her heart miss a beat.

'The *Martha Blair*? Aye, could be, could be. But this one has a funny kind of roll to her that puts me in mind of the *Ailsa* all the same.'

Isobel shook the hair out of her eyes with a quick sweep of the hand. The argument would go on for hours, she knew, each contender sticking to his convictions, marshalling his evidence, parading his vast expertise on the minutiae of the varied shipping that patronised the harbour at Ayr, until the vessel came close enough for its name to be irrefutably legible. That would not be for several hours in this contrary wind and she could not remain here, making a spectacle of herself for the gossips, while the kitchen floor needed sweeping and her invalid mother's wants had to be seen to.

She dragged her eyes unwillingly away from the dancing, distant sails, and ran lightly up the lanes that led to her own narrow close. Mrs Kirkwood's plaintive voice, from the box bed set into the back wall of the small living room, greeted her almost before she had lifted the latch.

'Is that you, girl? Where have you been this hour or more?'

'Just down to the harbour, Mam, to see if there's news of Joseph's ship.'

'Oh aye, the scamp. He'll be home in his own good time, no doubt, when it suits him, no matter his old mother's waiting for her time to come and no one to carry in the water.'

'Mam, that's not fair, and you know it! It's to be his last voyage. He promised you.'

Mrs Kirkwood shifted her head, reproved by her daughter's indignation. She had all her life been a stoical woman, blessed with good health and a kindly tongue, but dying was coming hard to her and her anxiety to have her son home again had added to her newly acquired petulance.

'Well?' she said, plucking at the darned cotton counterpane. 'And was there news?'

'There's a barque sighted,' said Isobel, turning her back on her mother and busying herself with sweeping up the hearth. 'They said it could be the *Martha Blair*.'

'Then you'd best hasten to put all to rights here,' said Mrs Kirkwood, nodding feebly, 'for if Archie Tomlinson's come home with your brother you must be at the quay to greet him, in case yon Elspeth Hastie gets to him first.'

Isobel felt her face redden, but old Mrs Kirkwood was taken with a fit of coughing that left her too spent to look for an answer. And besides there was no need, as Isobel well knew, to fear the likes of Elspeth Hastie. Archie Tomlinson, shipmate to her brother these five years or more, was as true a man as any in Scotland and his promise that had filled her every waking thought these six months or more with a blissful certainty of future happiness could be broken only by . . . She shivered. It did not do, when your man was coming home from the sea, to think of accidents. No word of their mutual dread would be permitted among the knot of women that would be collected on the pierhead in an hour or two from now.

Isobel had no need either of her mother's urging. Her deft hands were at work already, polishing up the brass and copper. By the time the barque, whichever she was, had nudged into place at the quay, the freshly ironed linen would be folded away in the press, the bread would be set to rise and Mrs Kirkwood's broth would be bubbling on the fire. If Joseph were to bring Archie home with him, it would never do for the least curl of dust to be visible on the flagstoned floor.

The wind freshened from the north and combined with a strong incoming tide to hasten the barque's progress to such good effect that Isobel was taken by surprise. She had but washed her face and was, with uncharacteristic thought for her appearance, tying the strings of her bonnet at a fetching angle under her chin when she heard boots flying along the cobbles of the close and a boy's voice calling out to his comrade, 'It's the *Martha Blair*, landed just now! Come away, Walter, down to the quay, and we'll try for a chew of sweet tobacco from the sailors!'

Isobel, her bonnet forgotten, wrenched open the cottage door and went running down towards the sea on winged slippers, lifting her petticoats to prevent herself from tripping, while round and round in her head went the refrain, 'He's home! He's come home!'

She was still a street away from the harbour when the first person she met stopped her in her tracks. Her neighbour, a dark-haired woman's arm about her, was stumbling up the pavement, face white, bonnet askew, eyes turning wildly from side to side. A stone seemed to fall into Isobel's chest. She felt short of breath. The woman's friend caught her eye.

'The *Martha Blair*'s in. She lost a mast off the west of Ireland. Several men are gone. Your brother's safe. I've seen him, just now.'

'Archie Tomlinson?' whispered Isobel.

'I couldn't say for sure.' The neighbour, shaking herself like a sleepwalker on the edge of waking, gave a shuddering cry.

'She's lost her Robert,' mouthed the dark-haired woman over her friend's head and, tightening her grip on the other woman's waist, proceeded on up the street.

Isobel could not for a long time afterwards remember the hours that followed. There had been no words, only Joseph's craggy face searching out where she stood at the back of the knot of women, and his slow shake of the head. Then she had turned and run, away out of the town and into the fields and he had run after her, and it had been hours later, when she had sobbed out the first of her grief on his rough blue sailor's jersey, that brother and sister had gone home together, to parry the curious glances of the neighbours and face their mother's anxious questioning.

It was a week before Isobel could speak at all, and a month before the first genuine smile melted the dreadful hardness which had settled in her face. It was Joseph who caused it. He came home late one evening, bending his tall head under the lintel and shaking the raindrops from his thick reddish hair. Isobel looked up from the stitches she was setting by the light of a single candle, and put her finger to her lips.

'She's gone off but a moment ago,' she whispered, nodding towards the humped figure in the box bed, 'and she's that cranky tonight, I wouldn't have her wake for anything.'

Joseph took off his boots, put them with a sailor's neatness by the door, and with an exaggerated mime of extreme caution tiptoed to the table and lowered his weight carefully on to the second stool. Isobel snatched her sewing away as he laid a wet hand on the table, and quickly pushed underneath it the handkerchief she had earlier been applying to her eyes.

'I've news for you, Izzy,' said Joseph. 'I've been to Mr Forbes today. You wouldn't believe me when I told you I'd not be going back to sea, but it's true. I'm going back to my old trade again. Mr Forbes is setting up a web for me, and taking me back into his loomshop. He says in a year or two . . . '

He broke off. Isobel had let out a squeak of joy that had made old Mrs Kirkwood grunt in her sleep and turn over in her bed, and though Isobel clapped her hand over her mouth to prevent any further exclamations, Joseph could see the huge smile that he thought had gone for ever.

Burning with impatience, Isobel waited until the boards under her mother's mattress had stopped creaking to her restless movements. Then she leant forward.

'Is it true what you're telling me? You'd never joke with me over this, would you, Joseph?'

'Of course it's true. You know fine I would not bear false witness, and I would not joke on a matter as earnest as this. Mind, I don't doubt I'll regret it tomorrow, when the lads are away off down to the harbour and the *Martha Blair*'s riding the swell like the duck she is.'

'But why, Joseph? You couldn't bear your loom before. You couldn't wait to get off and go to sea. It's never for Mam's and my sake? She wouldn't hold you to your promise if you want to go. Don't do it for us, Joseph.'

He shook his head. 'It's not for you, though you need a man right now. It's just that – oh, I couldn't share a berth now with any man but Archie and that's the truth of it!'

She did not trust herself to speak.

'And besides, there's another reason.'

He seemed unable to go on. Isobel looked at him in surprise. She had never known him lost for words before. He shifted his shoulders, as if his clothes were constricting his throat.

'I'm thirty years old, Izzy.'

'I know, I know.'

'You do not. You're but eighteen. But it's time I was thinking of settling down.'

'Oh.'

'Eliza . . . '

'Oh,' she said again.

'I mean to ask her tomorrow.'

The smile had left her face, and the strange weight pressing on her heart, which had lifted for a moment, was crushing her again.

'Do you think she'll have me, Izzy?'

She could not bear the uncertainty, the humility in his usually powerful and confident voice.

'Of course she will. She's been making eyes at you these two years, and . . . '

She stood up abruptly and went across to the hearth, to push aside the kettle whose singing suddenly seemed unbearably irritating. She must not, she told herself savagely, be betrayed into saying anything more. Joseph must never know how she despised Eliza Turner, light of foot, silly of head, weak of arm, and feckless enough to leave her milk to boil over nine days out of ten. How could Joseph, so strong and upright, so faithful and serious of mind, have his head turned by such a foolish creature? How could she respect a love like this, a soft, silly fondness, when she had known such a real, such a perfect . . . She set the kettle down with a snap. She had seen this coming, before ever Joseph went away, and dreaded it.

Suddenly she crossed the room and shook her brother's shoulder.

'Joseph! Let's go away, now! Take me away to sea with you! Let's do as you promised, when you came home from your first trip and I was a wee girl. Let's away to the colonies, to America, or New South Wales, or – or anywhere, and be free, and see the world together! Aunt Jeanie will stay with Mam. We'll leave her in good hands. I just want – oh, I want . . . '

She felt his shoulder shake under her hand and snatched it away. He was chuckling, the sound rumbling deep in his broad chest.

'Och, Izzy, what a girl you are! For a moment there I thought you were in earnest! Go to sea, to the colonies, and leave Mam in her sickness! And here I am, just come home, ready to take up a steady life, as you've all begged me to for years passed, and bring home a wife and all! America! Australia! Why, the last time we went out to sea together, when we crossed to Arran, you mind the time, in the *Peggy Lee*, you were that sick I thought you'd throw your heart over board!'

The spark that had suddenly kindled in Isobel died down as quickly as it had sprung up. She sat down heavily on her stool by the scrubbed table and took up her sewing again.

'When do you plan to marry, Joseph?' she said, in a small flat voice.

He had stood up to remove his jersey and set it by the fire to dry, and he did not notice the change in her expression.

'As soon as she'll have me. Och, but she's a pretty one! And a fine Christian woman too, I doubt not. I observed her close last Sabbath and

I could tell she knew her psalms without reading in the psalter.'

Isobel pursed her lips. She had observed Eliza too, and had seen that although that young lady had indeed not consulted her psalter, she was opening and shutting her mouth at random and had certainly not been singing the words of the psalm, her mind being engaged elsewhere.

'Will you bring Eliza to live here? Or will you look out for another house?'

'Why, she'll come home to us, for sure! What for should I be taking on the expense of another roof? She'll be company for you, Izzy, and give you a hand with Mam. Though I mustn't speak yet as if she's promised to me. Oh, but think of us all together under one roof! It'll be grand! Just grand!'

Isobel snapped off her cotton between taut fingers.

'I hope you're right, Joseph,' she said, and this time he could not miss the dry tone in her voice. She saw his eyes on her, and not wishing to spoil his happiness she forced a wintry smile.

'Eliza Turner and I will get by well enough together,' she said. 'But I've no wish to stay at home for ever and be an old maid in my brother's house, so if you won't take me to America, or even to New South Wales, I'll have to look about me for a husband.'

'Izzy, don't,' he said, distressed by the bitterness in her voice. 'I didn't wish to remind you . . . '

'Don't fret yourself, Joseph. I remember him all the day long, and will do till I die. But marry I must some time or another, and since I can't have Archie, I'll have to make do with whoever comes along. Go to your bed now, before Mam wakes herself properly, and take care you don't fall over your sea-chest as you did last night, for I nearly had the fright of my life thinking there were ghosties in the house.'

She shut her sewing in her sewing box, and knew as she did so that she was shutting her youth away with it.

2

'You'll have to speak out to her, Joseph. I can't stand to see her doing it all day, morning and night. I can't stand it any longer.'

Eliza sat in the cottage's sole armchair by the hearth, expressing fatigue in every line of her lax body. Her hair, which she had not bothered to dress properly today, had lost the girlhood sheen which Joseph had so much admired. It hung limply about her pasty cheeks. Pregnancy did not suit Eliza. She found the least exertion too much to bear, and was taken with fancies which sorely tried her husband, who, after a mere ten months of matrimony, looked more careworn than he had ever done after the most rigorous storms at sea.

The problem, as usual, concerned Isobel. Eliza had not, as her husband had fondly hoped, taken her sister-in-law to her bosom. She had, in fact, lost no time in falling out with her. Isobel was unfeeling. Isobel was managing. Isobel required Eliza to do more than a woman in her delicate situation should undertake. Isobel was too quiet, unfriendly, unused to taking a joke. Isobel looked at her in a way Eliza did not like.

Today the complaint concerned Isobel's unfortunate tic, which, to Joseph's distress, had become increasingly apparent these last few months. His sister had always been nervous. As a child she had chewed her clothing, bitten her nails and twisted tufts of hair around her fingers until it had come out at the roots. One by one, as each ugly habit had been broken, another had taken its place. In her happiness with Archie, she had seemed to put these little manifestations of anxiety behind her, but since Joseph's marriage she had begun involuntarily to jerk her head around, as though starting at a sudden noise.

'Back and forth, back and forth, bobbing her head like a mad woman! It's all for spite, to upset me! The bairn will take ill from it! I feel it shiver when she tosses her head at me like that. I'll not stand for it, Joseph. She'll have to keep out of my sight. It's not right for a woman in my delicate state to see queer things . . . ' and the easy tears set off again along their well-worn paths down her cheeks.

Joseph looked down at his wife in great perplexity. Women were beyond him. He could not get the hang of them. He had lived with other men at close quarters since he had run away to sea as a boy. From the age of nine, on his first man o' war the *Speedy*, he had roughed it with all sorts and conditions of men. He had not liked them all. They had many of them been detestable. But where he had not given his friendship he had rubbed along well enough. Why could the womenfolk not do the same? Why was there this endless brangling and brawling, crying and complaining? It was, he dearly hoped, no more than the foolish fancies brought on by his wife's condition. If it were not, if he were to face a lifetime of . . .

He looked helplessly across towards his mother's bed. She was awake. She rarely spoke now. It was a marvel, everyone said, that she had lasted as long as this, and it was thanks only to Isobel's devoted care. The old woman's mouth was twitching as if she were trying to speak, and Joseph could see her eyes upon him, bright and watchful. Did she wish to warn him? Or to admonish him? Had she advice for him? What was passing through her locked mind?

The eight-day clock on the mantelshelf began the wheezy whirring that signalled the striking of the hour. Joseph seized upon the escape it offered him.

'I must away back to my loom. The beamer's finished setting up my warp for sure, and he'll be looking out for me. Don't trouble Izzy now, Eliza. She has sorrows enough of her own.'

He stood outside the cottage and inhaled deeply. Inside, Eliza was crying noisily. He hesitated, started to turn back, then changed his mind and set off with his long stride down the close to the loomshop. He had been right enough about one thing. His warp would be set up and ready for starching and he must have it stiffened and dried today.

The quiet, regulated industry of the loomshop came as a relief after the emotional storms of the cottage. Joseph's two colleagues and their attendant drawboys acknowledged his arrival with no more than a look or a nod, and Mr Forbes, sitting at his loom and plying his shuttles skilfully among the threads, continued his discussion with the beamer. This lively gentleman had finished his work on Joseph's loom, and was packing his tools away in a capacious bag before starting out for the next loomshop to require his skills. As Joseph entered he was gesticulating, a borrowed poukin pin in hand, in support of his argument.

'I'm telling you, man, Paisley's the place. Your plaids of Ayr are all very fine – ' he met the fulminating eye of Mr Forbes and repeated hastily, '*very* fine, but when you've seen the new patterns! Copied from the Indian, from the old Cashmeres, and Mr Clark told my brother Donald, who works in Paisley as a flower lasher, that finer things you couldn't see, not even in Paris! Paris! Frenchies! It's the French ladies themselves that seek out the work from Paisley by name! Paisley shawls are getting a name for themselves, putting Norwich out of business, I can tell you. The work's snatched off the looms before it's fairly finished, and off to Glasgow and London where the ladies fight over it! Aye, the highest paid work's to be had in Paisley. The pine pattern they call it, like raindrops with curly ends, and all they twirly bits, and squiggles . . . '

'Thank you, Charlie,' said Mr Forbes repressively. 'We are familiar with the Indian patterns. You've been so intent on describing the wonders of Paisley while you've been beaming up Mr Kirkwood's warp that perhaps you have not had a chance to observe Mr Dunbar's loom?'

The third loom, by the furthest wall of the loomshop, was set against the window so that the full light of day was thrown over the weaver's shoulder on to his work. The beamer darted round to look at the delicate pattern that was emerging from the mass of claret, olive, blue and yellow threads.

'Why, Mr Dunbar! This is fine! And you working so quietly in your little corner a body would never know you were there!'

Isaiah Dunbar looked up irritably.

'Just so, just so. Those of us doing the finer work have need of our powers of concentration. Chattering is all very well for some, and amusing enough, I doubt not, but when it comes to the intricate business . . . '

He stopped talking, and with a tut of irritation commanded his diminutive assistant, a child of no more than ten years old, to pay more attention to the lashes or he'd foul the pattern and receive a clout instead of his tea.

The beamer, feeling disapproval in the air, nodded affably to Mr Forbes, winked at Joseph, pulled the nearest drawboy's hair and departed, shutting the loomshop door with a clatter behind him.

'You'd best inspect your loom,' said Mr Forbes drily to Joseph. 'Yon tattler has talked his head off this last hour or more. It's Paisley this and Paisley that till you wonder he can bear to be seen in such a lowly place as Ayr! How a man can work and blether at the same time as he does – but there, the Lord gave some of us wits and some of us tongues, but seldom the two at once.'

Joseph took down from its hook his ample frieze apron and tied it tightly under his armpits. There was no need to respond to Forbes's sally. It was as well, he thought with relief, that women seldom entered the loomshop. Discussions there might be, and arguments in plenty when the work allowed it, but neither Dunbar nor Forbes, for all their failings, had ever shown the least sign of dissolving into tears, or drawing him aside to complain of each other.

The task of mixing the starch and applying it to the web did not tax his ingenuity, and left his thoughts free to work over his vexations. The only good thing to be said for the weaving trade, he thought gloomily, was that it allowed the mind liberty to roam at will while the body was horribly chained to the loom. And there was work indeed for his mind today. How was he to make peace in his house? How could he possibly satisfy both his wife and his sister?

He was working over the dressed warp threads with a goose-quill fan to ensure its drying evenly when raised voices broke in on his abstraction. Mr Forbes's drawboy Tommy had withdrawn his attention from his work at a critical moment in order to tease the poor lark which hung in a cage at the window. The threads of the simple had become tangled. The work had to be interrupted while his master put all to rights. No one knew better than Tommy that Mr Forbes's repeated threats to skelp him and skin him alive were mere bombast, but he was managing in a show of contrition to keep the normally cheeky grin off his rosy face, and looked so comical, with his tuft of red hair poking up through a ragged hole in the crown of his Kilmarnock bonnet, that Joseph chuckled.

'Send the rascal over here, Forbes,' he said. 'He hasn't read his chapter today. I'll take the task of hearkener while my warps are drying.'

The careful neutrality of Tommy's expression broke down into genuine dismay. The daily chapter, that regular scourge of the drawboy's existence, he considered to be a gross infringement of his personal liberties. He scowled at Joseph. He might have got off with a skelping if Mr Kirkwood had not been so busy. Ten to one Mr Forbes would have forgotten his religious obligations, as he did five days out of the seven. Reluctantly, he fetched the loomshop Bible down from the crowded bookshelf by the chimney-piece and opened it. He would rather do an hour at the harness than ten minutes at the book any day.

'Proverbs I believe, Tommy,' his master said, enjoying the boy's discomfiture. 'Chapter twenty-one or thereabouts. As a special favour to you, we'll permit you to read an extra one today. Chapter twenty-two as well, if you please.'

' "The – the king's h-heart is in the hand of the Lord",' began Tommy. ' "As the rivers of water. He turn – turneth it" – oh, what is this one now? "with – wither-so-ever . . ." '

Joseph's attention wandered. His mind was engaged elsewhere, up in the rigging of the *Speedy* where he and Archie had first met, powder monkeys the pair of them. The laughing expression on his friend's face turned in his mind to one of horror. It was not the *Speedy* now. It was the *Martha Blair*. He was yelling to Archie to hang on, hearing the crack of the mast as it went over, the screaming of the men . . .

Tommy's halting voice broke in on him.

' "It – it is better to dwell in a corner of the housetop, than with a b-braw-brawling woman in a wide house." '

Joseph smiled ruefully. Aye, that was true enough. It was the first time for many years that he had been struck by a word from the Good Book. At sea he had never thought of it. Since he had come home his mind had been distracted by other things. Tommy was ploughing on.

' "It is better to dwell in the wild – wilderness than with a . . ." och, sir, Mr Kirkwood, there's no such word as this!'

Joseph looked over his shoulder.

'Contentious, Tommy, contentious. It's a good enough word for its meaning.'

' " . . . in the wilderness than with a contentious and an angry woman." '

True again. Joseph looked down at Tommy's struggling face and smiled. What an odd sight the child was, his breeks inexpertly cut down from a larger size, his jacket too small for him, a wriggling bulge in his pocket betraying the presence of his beloved pet rat. How strange that words of such wisdom should issue from so unpromising a source!

' "By humility, and the fear of the Lord, are riches, and honour, and life," ' read Tommy, soldiering on through his second chapter, and gaining a fluency with each verse.

Joseph's fan remained suspended in mid-air. Riches, honour, and life, and by the fear of the Lord! There was a word for him, all right. The fear of the Lord had not been his chief concern when he had rushed headlong into matrimony. It was the lust of the flesh more like that had led him there. Well, he was paying for it now, and would for years to come. If he had only taken heed sooner! The fear of the Lord! Yes, he had ignored it. He had not followed the prayerful way, the path of grace as his father had forever urged him to do. He watched as Tommy shut the Bible with a snap of relief and marked the place where he had put it back on the shelf. He would make up for lost time. There was no human course of action he could take to resolve his domestic griefs. He had sinned, and he must pay his debts. But he had seen the way forward now. He would seek humility, and the fear of the Lord.

The loomshop door opened, letting in a bright shaft of sunlight across the beaten earth floor. Isobel came in. For a moment her hair was caught in the light and formed a golden aureole round her head.

'I've a message for you, Joseph,' she said shyly.

'Come away in, Mistress Isobel,' said Mr Forbes expansively, his gallantry aroused at the sight of her nervousness. She stepped down into the room and looked about her.

'You've not seen us at our work before?' said Mr Forbes. 'Look about you, my dear. Look about you! We are all men here, you know, not used to females. No pretty knick-knacks, just plain work . . . '

Isaiah Dunbar coughed. 'Not *all* plain work,' he said.

'That's right! Plain and fancy, fancy and plain! Some of us fancy, some of us plain! Oh, don't look at this poor stuff, my dear. Look over there, at Mr Dunbar's new pattern. A shawl as fine as any made in Paisley, I do assure you. Very superior quality. Fit for a queen, or a princess at the very least. You'll not see its like in Ayr.'

Isobel made her way through the scrap ends of threads and cloth across the uneven floor and looked wonderingly at the mass of coloured wools on Isaiah's loom. The emerging pattern made her draw in her breath.

'It's – beautiful,' she said awkwardly, looking with respect at Isaiah. 'You are – you must have a great deal of experience, Mr Dunbar.'

Isaiah was pleased. He liked his qualities to be recognised. He looked Kirkwood's sister over, and approved of what he saw. She was a sensible young female, plainly dressed, nervous in manner perhaps and with an unfortunate disfiguring tic, but she showed good judgement and a proper degree of respect.

Isobel bent to look more closely at the pattern. The thing was quite lovely, the colours rich, the pattern amazingly intricate. She glanced curiously at its maker. She had met Isaiah Dunbar perhaps two or three times before, but he had not hitherto impressed her. He was a slight, delicate-looking man, a little stooped with an ill-developed physique. His hair was thin and grey, and made him look older than his thirty-five years. He was not much given to speech, though Joseph had said he was a good enough fellow, perhaps a little inclined to stand on his dignity, to imagine slights where none were meant and to expect rather too much deference to be given to his opinions, though it was true that no weaver in Ayr could produce better work than Isaiah Dunbar. He was a master craftsman, and more knowledgeable connoisseurs of fine weaving than Isobel had been lost in admiration at the delicacy of his shawls. The common opinion was that Ayr provided too small an arena for his talents, and that he would shortly remove to Paisley where he would be among others of his quality.

Isobel looked up from the swimming masses of orange and red threads and her eyes met Isaiah's. A man whose fingers could create such a lovely thing must have beauty somewhere in his soul. She could see no sign of it in his face. She turned away.

'Eliza says for you to remember to come home early tonight, for you promised to mend the gate to the kailyard before the week was out,' she said softly to her brother. She smiled understandingly at his unresponsive grunt, said a hasty goodbye to Mr Forbes, and slipped out of the loomshop.

Isaiah's drawboy, his hands on the lashes, wondered why his master's shuttles had fallen still. He would have been greatly astonished if he had been able to read the mind of one he considered as ancient as the Romans.

'You could do worse, Isaiah Dunbar,' Isaiah was saying to himself. 'You could do worse. A decent young person, strong, hard-working. Do you credit, I do believe. The Dunbars, Mr and Mrs Dunbar – of Paisley. Aye, it could be. Could be.'

'Kirkwood!' he called out suddenly, surprising himself almost as much as his colleagues. 'Do you care for a game of bowls with me Saturday next?'

3 *Paisley, June 1823*

Isobel sat down at her wheel with a sigh of relief. Peggy McFee, Paisley's most persistent gossip, had taken herself and her tambour frame out of the Dunbars' kitchen at long last, down the steep stair and away down Castle Street. Isobel counted the pirns in the upturned hat by the wheel. Only four done this morning, and Isaiah would need six by tea-time.

The regular whirr and click of the wheel worked soothingly on her as it always did. The peace of her little kitchen closed round her again.

All was neat and tidy, the delf porringers upon the dresser marshalled in an orderly row, the fire irons polished to the sheen of gold, the peacock feathers over the mantelpiece precisely angled over her mother's dear old clock, whose wheezing chime was as familiar and welcome as the voice of a friend.

A coal fell from the fire, spoiling the whiteness of the scrubbed hearthstone. Isobel started up nervously and swept it into the ashes. Order was everything. Absolute tidiness was essential. It was only by conquering outer chaos, only by imposing the strictest discipline on everything around her that her inner turmoil could be kept within bounds, and the demon of despair chained up outside the gates.

A scrabbling at the brilliantly polished window made her turn her head. A scraggy pigeon was strutting on the sill, making a pathetic display of himself for a female, who pecked at her wing unconcernedly on a neighbouring rooftop. At least they were not at the fruit, thought Isobel, and while her practised hands continued their work her eyes travelled past the birds and down into the well-kept yard behind the weaving shop, where rows of turnips and kail sprouted in lines of military stiffness between Isaiah's precious golden sulphur gooseberries and her own blackcurrant bushes.

From below there was a sudden silence. The rumbling of machinery in the weaving shop had stopped. It was dinner-time. The men would be covering up their looms and hanging up their aprons. Isaiah would be up the stairs any moment now and wishful for his dinner. Well, it was all ready. She had only to lift the pot from the fire and fill his plate. Not once in their two years of married life had she kept him waiting for his dinner.

She heard the click of the door that led from the weaving shop into the yard. This was a break in his habits. This was unusual, in a man whose hours were so regular that she could, and did, set the clock by him! A minute later his step came on the stair and he hurried into the room with an unaccustomed air of excitement.

'My pinks are coming into bloom, Isobel! I saw them from the shop window. Two out and three showing colour. Most satisfactory, I am delighted to say. There is a very interesting stripe in the petals, quite a new effect! I believe I may at last put my name to an original variety. It will disappoint Gregson most sorely, for he has been quite disparaging of my methods of breeding. He will not be at all pleased when he hears of this!' Cracking the joints of his thin weaver's hands, and looking not at all put out by the idea of his friend's dissatisfaction, Isaiah took his place at the table and waited placidly for Isobel to serve him.

He did not expect his wife to speak, nor did she. Her quietness was what he most liked in her. She knew her place. She contrived very well with the money at her disposal. She made him comfortable. She kept her distance from the gossips, and did him credit when she walked on his arm to the kirk. She was a thoroughly respectable woman. His marriage was all that he had hoped for. He finished his meal in silence, rose from the table, and took his tall chimney hat from its peg.

'I'm away to see Gregson. If my pinks are through there's no saying but what his are too, though if his have bred as well as mine I shall be astonished.'

When he left the room, Isobel stayed on at her place at the table. She could look out from her seat on the rooftops of Paisley stretching away, and the carefully tended gardens in between. Just now, however, she did not see them. She was revelling in the luxury she allowed herself only once a day, at this time after dinner, when Isaiah had gone out for a smoke and a chat with his fellows before returning to his loom. Now, just for half an hour, she could permit herself to dream. She did not see the waves of green vegetables and fruit bushes under her windows, but instead saw real waves, watery waves, heaving up and down. And she was on a ship, and Joseph and Archie were with her, comrades all, and they were escaping together on a great adventure, away from the narrowness, the pettiness, the sameness of the house above the weaving shop in Castle Street. They were away to the ends of the earth, to distant lands, to a new life, where they would live, feel, face dangers, laugh and talk, wrapped together in companionship and love. Somewhere far, far away, at the end of the voyage, in a place she could not clearly see, there would be a wee house for them where they would be alone but not lonely, free but not afraid.

The clock began its noisy preparations for the striking of the hour and Isobel resolutely turned away from the window. The dream must not go on too long, or the demon despair would snap its chain and leap in and throttle her. She must sip her pleasures slowly as a wise man does his whisky. It was time now to beat the hatches down again, to nail up the dream, one blow of the hammer for each chime of the clock, and to make herself once more into the quiet, obedient wife she so arduously strove to be. The dinner must be cleared away, the pirns wound, the kettle filled for tea, the coals brought up from below.

She was starting down the stairs on this last task when she was surprised by a hammering on the door. She felt almost tempted to hide herself. It could only be Peggy McFee, back again, and she had already spent two hours this morning pouring into Isobel's ears the sorry tale of her husband's unnatural behaviour when elevated with the liquor. Isobel did not feel capable of listening to any more today. She hesitated. The knocker fell again. That was not Peggy's stroke. It was stronger, more insistent, more masculine. Curiosity urged her down the last half-dozen steps.

'Joseph!' The shriek with which she greeted her brother was so out of her usual subdued character that two gossips, standing in the doorway opposite, turned to each other with raised eyebrows. Isobel caught their expressions and shrank back into her passageway.

'Come away in! Come up!' she said, and turned to lead Joseph upstairs.

It was not until they were in her small kitchen with the door shut behind them that Isobel realised Joseph was not alone.

'Why, it is – yes, it must be – Malcolm!' she said, stooping down to a small boy, who stood holding on to his father's breeks with one hand while the thumb of the other was planted firmly in his mouth.

Isobel kissed him, then straightened up and shook her head in disbelief.

'I don't understand, Joseph. I had no idea. Is all well at home? Eliza? The baby?'

He was looking round with admiration at the comfort and orderliness of her kitchen.

'Aye, Izzy, all's well enough, I suppose. How fine you are here! It's a big house and all, and so nicely set up! But you were ever a good housewife.'

She detected a note of dissatisfaction in his voice, but said nothing. She could imagine only too well the sorry state of Eliza's kitchen. Joseph sat down at the table, and Malcolm scrambled up into his lap.

'Joseph, you should have written to tell me. I wish I'd known! There's nothing in the house but bread and cheese and an end of bacon, for it's market day tomorrow, and I've not even a pound of potatoes until then.'

'Never mind your vittles, Izzy. All we need is some milk for the bairn, and a bite of bread and butter. We had dinner early, some cold potatoes and meat I put up for us to eat on the road. I'd have sent word but that I came all of a sudden. Forbes has been on at me for weeks past to fetch some new patterns down to Ayr, for the Paisley shawls are so much in demand now we must follow the new styles or go under. I had the chance of a seat at a moment's notice in Mr Turnbull's carriage, offered out of the blue, and I took it up at once. And Eliza – with the baby you know, wee Jem – oh, but he's a fine lusty fellow, Izzy! He beats his brother with his fists though he's only six months old! – well, Eliza begged me to bring Malcolm with me as she gets tired of him tagging by her skirts all day long, so I took my wee man up with me, and he's been a bonny traveller right enough, have you not, Malcolm?'

The little boy had not yet made up his mind to be acquainted with his aunt. He buried his head in his father's coat and refused to look at her.

Isobel jumped up.

‘Candy! I have a piece of candy here in my dresser,’ she said with a lightness in her voice that her husband would hardly have recognised. She stepped round behind Joseph, opened a drawer, and took out a sticky black ball. Malcolm accepted it doubtfully, held it for a moment in a grubby fist, and only when he felt his elders’ eyes were off him did he slide it surreptitiously into his mouth.

‘Isaiah is . . . ’

‘Eliza said . . . ’

Brother and sister spoke together, and both stopped and laughed awkwardly. Each longed to know of the other’s true state of affairs, but neither dared ask, nor speak of their own.

‘Isaiah’s out at Gregson’s just now,’ said Isobel at last, filling the silence. ‘But you’ll be staying the night with us, will you not, Joseph?’

‘Aye, but I must use my time well today. Mr Turnbull returns to Ayr at noon tomorrow, and if I wish to ride with him I must start my business this afternoon. There’s Thomson in Causeyside Street . . . ’

‘The Causeyside?’ Isobel jumped to her feet. ‘We’d best go now, Joseph, if that’s where you’re bound, for there’s some warehouses put up their shutters after dinner. Just give me a moment to fetch my bonnet and I’ll walk with you, and the wee man and I will take some crumbs to feed the sparrows while you do your business. Will that not be fine, Malcolm?’

The little boy looked at her and nodded solemnly. A trickle of black stickiness running down his chin bore witness to his appreciation of the candy, and once out in the street he permitted Aunt Dunbar to take his hand and jump him over the gutter as a sign that his approval had been fully granted.

Joseph looked sideways at his sister. The painful tic was still in evidence but much reduced from the time when she had first been married. It was now no more than a slight tossing of the head, as if she was trying to shake the hair from her forehead. She looked well enough, bonny even. He could not but admire her neatness, her cleanliness, the fresh smell of the bleaching-green that hung about her well-pressed clothes, the quiet authority with which she restrained young Malcolm’s impulse to throw himself beneath the wheels of a passing dray.

How long was it since he had taken pride in Eliza’s looks? Why, his ring had hardly been on her finger when she had proved herself a slattern. For a time, at least, she had taken pains to tidy herself before she stepped out of doors, but since Jem had been born, six months ago, she had not cared at all for anyone, but had gone abroad in a dirty fichu and torn gown, her bonnet strings unpressed and her face unwashed, making her husband so ashamed he was glad his mother was no longer alive to witness it. Joseph’s remonstrances had produced such shrill recriminations, such tears and rages that he had forborn to comment further. He had quietly set about doing as much as he could for the bairns himself, and on his own account had given up all thought of domestic comfort. He had acquired the habit of spending any time he could spare at the kirk in the company of the elders, among whose number he had recently been proud to count himself. There, under the guidance of an inspirational minister, he had taken to studying the Bible, passing many nights in prayer, and debating with growing knowledge and interest all kinds of theological matters, and in this way he had found the strength to carry the burden of his shrewish wife, and provide for his sons the care which she seemed unable to give them.

Isobel nudged his arm. 'A gentleman's looking at you,' she whispered.

Joseph turned his head. A salesman in a smart black surtout coat, a rose of monstrous size in his buttonhole and a satin hat with a wondrous sheen on his head, was smiling and waving at Joseph with obsequious affability.

Joseph raised his own more battered headpiece.

'Good day to you, sir,' he said cordially.

'Good day to *you*,' said the salesman, rubbing his hands together. 'From Ayr, are we not? A partner of Mr Turnbull, I believe? I could not but observe you stepping out of his coach just half an hour ago. Mr Turnbull is an *old* customer of ours, an excellent customer I should say! Why, we have sold more shawls, and of the best too, to Mr Turnbull than . . . '

Joseph's chuckle interrupted him. 'You'll sell more to him than to me, then,' he said, 'for I'm a weaver, a plain working man, not one of your fine merchants. I make the goods with the sweat of my own hands. Mr Turnbull's an acquaintance of mine, an elder in our kirk at Ayr, as am I, and for friendship's sake he brought me in his carriage, but it's not shawls I want to buy, but pattern books, and if you can inform me where Thomson's . . . '

He got no further. The salesman, who had stiffened at the first part of this speech, had not waited to hear the second. He had spied more hopeful prey at the end of the Causeyside. The afternoon coach from Glasgow had disgorged two likely-looking passengers, men of prosperous mien who could only be in search of merchandise, and he was determined to shepherd them into his own establishment before they were lured into anyone else's. He left Joseph talking to thin air.

Joseph turned back towards Isobel, and so comical was the surprise on his face that she giggled. The laughter transformed her to such a degree that a tall thin young gentleman, dressed in clerical garb, looked twice at her before approaching with hand outstretched.

'Good day to you, Mrs Dunbar,' he said, with the shy eagerness of the young minister who still feels unsure of his standing among his flock.

Isobel blushed. She did not like the minister to come upon her, laughing immoderately in the street.

'Good day, Mr Elliott,' she mumbled, looking down at her shoes. But the minister's attention had passed already to her companion, whose ham-like fist was thrust out in greeting.

'Kirkwood,' said Joseph, introducing himself with confidence, and measuring Mr Elliott with interested eyes. 'I'm Mrs Dunbar's brother.'

Mr Elliott's timidity betrayed him into too much enthusiasm. He rocked forward on the balls of his slender feet.

'Ah, how delightful! A family visit! From Ayr, is it not? I believe Mr Dunbar informed me of your family connections in Ayr? You are most welcome to Paisley, Mr Kirkwood. Very welcome indeed.'

Joseph wrung the young man's white hand.

'Are you acquainted with Mr Murray, sir, our minister at Ayr?'

A slight wariness flitted over Mr Elliott's expressive face. Mr Murray, a theological firebrand, was as famous for his ardour in suppressing the sins of his flock as for the fiery conviction of his sermons, and Mr Elliott, whose own faith followed a quieter, more troubled path, was ill-equipped to deal with the enthusiasms of his colleague's followers.

'Mr Murray,' he said cautiously. He thrust a hand inside his black serge coat, withdrew a large silk handkerchief and mopped his forehead with it. 'Indeed yes, of course.'

'A man of God,' said Joseph. 'The fields of Ayr are white unto the harvest, Mr Elliott, but lo, the Lord hath sent workers into his vineyard.'

Isobel looked at her brother in surprise. She had not known Joseph to be so well versed in the Scriptures. He had always been a faithful member of the kirk, but never as fervent as this. It was, of course, impossible to be too religious, she thought a little doubtfully, but she was not sure if this new way of talking was entirely comfortable.

It was ten minutes before Mr Elliott felt able to raise his hat and retreat. When he had gone Isobel felt a slight constraint. She sought for something to say but before she could think of anything, Joseph burst out with the question he had been burning to ask.

'Is he good to you, Izzy?'

She bent to take Malcolm's hand and began to walk once more along the pavement.

'Och aye, he's a good man enough. He doesn't drink, and he doesn't dice, and he never lays a hand on me in anger. He works hard and regular and puts by for a rainy day. It's only, it's just . . . ' She shook her head.

They walked on in silence.

'Do you remember,' he said, 'before I asked Eliza, when Mam was still alive, and you begged me to take you to the colonies, and I wouldn't listen to you? I've sometimes thought since then that you were in earnest.'

She said nothing. He smiled heavily.

'The devil stopped up my ears that night, Izzy. I've thought and I've thought on it, and I believe the Lord wished for us to go, to seek a new land elsewhere and till the soil for our own food. It was my sinful desires that led me astray.'

She was not used to hearing him speak in such a way and she did not know how to answer him. He smiled down at her.

'Who knows? If the Lord wills it, he may yet find a way. But you'd not wish to go to the colonies now, Izzy, and leave your grand wee house and all?'

Before she could answer him she felt a tug at her hand. Malcolm's feet, dragging ever more slowly along the cobbles, were too weary to take him further.

'Will I carry you, Malcolm?' she said. The child nodded. Isobel took a snowy white handkerchief from her pocket, wiped the last stains from his mouth and hoisted him up to a comfortable riding position on her hip. Joseph watched her admiringly.

'You've a great way with the bairns,' he said. 'Is there no sign yet of . . . '

She blushed and shook her head, and Joseph, berating himself for a clumsy fool, was relieved to find that they had arrived at Mr Thomson's premises, and that the shutters were still down.

Chapter Three

1

On board the East Indiaman 'Thalia'
In the English Channel
18th March 1820

My dearest Minnie,

We are out of Gravesend but a few days aboard the 'Thalia', and pass by the English coast, and it makes me feel so strange that I am leaving all I love, apart from dearest Hector, for such a destination. But I cannot wait to write, even tho' I know not when this letter may be dispatched.

Oh Minnie, however can I thank you for all you have done for us, arranging with your brother for our wedding, and braving the anger of your Papa and mine, and lending me your new silk gown for my wedding dress. I am so grieved that I spilt some wine on the sleeve when I jumped up in that stupid way to clap Hector's grand speech, and I beg you will tell me when you write if Kirsty has got it out.

There was never anything so exciting in my life as our late night nuptials, and your dear face, starting nervously when the door creaked in case it was your father come home early! And how we laughed when it was only Jimmy Coachman come back from the tavern! Then of course our sad farewells. It was long, I assure you, before I raised my eyes from my handkerchief, but Hector at last made me dry them, for he said he would not risk being clapped into prison for abducting a lachrymose and unwilling female! And so we came to Leith.

You can imagine, Minnie, how strange it is to find oneself alone in the company of a man, even one's own dear husband in the intimacy of a ship's cabin, and I will not deny that I felt a great degree of nervousness, but it is odd how soon one becomes accustomed to the wedded state, and now, I own, I live in such happiness I never knew existed, with a tumult of new sensations and feelings as I am sure you too will know when you follow me into married bliss.

(By the by, you must write me all concerning Mr S. . . . ! I will say no more!)

We passed but three nights in London, and all in a whirl of shopping. Hector is determined to present his bride in a fitting manner, and as you know, I could bring nothing from home except my plain bonnet and drab cloak with a bag of the barest necessities for fear of arousing suspicion. Old Jeanie pretends to be blind, but never servant had a sharper eye for all that! The warehouses in London are such as would make you stare, so many fine stuffs and all in the height of fashion, and with such a crowd of people that makes our Edinburgh seem quite deserted. The noise and tumult I cannot describe, and so many vehicles are in the streets you can scarcely pass along them.

Dearest Minnie, I must conclude, for we are summoned to dinner. Captain Blaikie is quite stern as to hours, and I dare not displease him in case I am thrown into irons! Do, if you can, say a kind word to Aggie for me. I do not feel easy about her. As for Papa, I fear he will never forgive me. It makes me low when I think about them, so I try not to think about them at all, though you must not believe, my dearest friend, that you are ever far from the thoughts

of your devoted
Fanny

On board the 'Thalia'
At sea off Madeira
2nd April 1820

My dearest Sister,

I received yours of the 17th here at Madeira where we are forced to stop a week for repairs after buffeting in a heavy sea. It came by the 'Amelia', that is bound for Sydney, that put in here for water, and I was so happy to hear from you I cried for a full hour until Hector told me to stop.

Oh my dearest Aggie, your letter was so kind and forgiving, and you must never reproach yourself for being angry with me that dreadful day. It was not, as you think, your being angry that drove me to run away with Hector, but my real and tender love for him. Oh Aggie, he is all I could dream of in a husband, and you must not think I am unhappy, except in missing you, and in angering Papa, and for a horrid seasickness in the Bay of Biscay. But Hector looked after me as if he was my own good, kind Aggie, and not just a husband.

There is a little dog on board who diverts us greatly. He belongs to Mrs Castle. She is to join her husband in Calcutta. Mr Castle is in a very good silk house, and her stuffs are the finest I have ever seen. And she dines with the best society in Calcutta and tells me how I am to go on there. So you see, I am learning to be a respectable wife. Mr Castle is like Hector, I mean that he came to Calcutta as a young man with few connections, and has made a great fortune. He does such tricks, standing on his hind legs, and pawing at Mrs C's gown, till she says 'Get down sir,' and then the boat rolls and he slides on all fours across the deck, and we all run to catch him. It would be too horrid if he fell overboard and got eaten by the sharks. I mean the dog, of course, not Mr Castle! And he barks so loud at the chickens, which are cooped up on the deck, and give us fresh eggs for breakfast, and the goats whose milk, though rather strong, is a welcome addition to our table.

Hector spends a large part of his time in a study of the Hindoo language, for he means to make his own way among the natives. He has made the acquaintance of an extraordinary man much travelled in the Antipodes, who is returning to New Zealand via Calcutta, and tells of such adventures among the fierce New Zealanders as would make you stare. He has made a fortune in the Southern Oceans in the whaling business, and has taken a great fancy to Hector (which does not surprise me in the least!). He has begged Hector to give up his project of conquering the markets of Bengal, in favour of a life in the fern forests of the Antipodes! So you can see that, if we do not succeed in our present enterprise, we have many more strings to our bow!

Our cabin is so snug you would not believe, for Hector bought a good sofa and cushions and a commodious sea-chest in London, and though crammed into a tiny room we want for nothing, except enough books and drawing paper, for there is a great deal of time and few amusements. In the evenings there is some singing, and Hector sings old Scottish songs in his fine voice, and Captain Blaikie sighs and says he thinks when he hears it of Dundee, and so the evenings pass very gaily. But the ladies retire early before the gentlemen become too merry. All except Hector, of course, who as you must realise is most abstemious as he says no drunkard ever made a fortune.

I will try to send letters at the Cape, dearest Aggie, where I believe we may put in for a few days if the winds are right, but if you do not hear from me, do not imagine that you have been forgotten

by your own loving
Fanny

Calcutta
30th June 1820

Dearest Aggie,

We arrived at Calcutta yesterday and I am in haste to send you a letter by the frigate 'Hellespont' which leaves at noon, to tell you of our safe arrival.

We came up the last part of the Hooghly river at night, and this morning the view of the port burst upon us. But I had no eyes for the hundreds of ships' masts or the hordes of natives upon the burdened wharves or the distant white frontages being wholly overcome by the most disgusting odours of the harbour. There is nothing even in the most dismal lanes of Edinburgh that could prepare the nose for it. Hector looked over the side of the ship into the water, and withdrew his head quickly, looking pale, and when I asked him what was the matter, he said, 'Nothing,' so I started to the rail to see what had affected him so, but he held me back and said I was not to look, for a corpse had attached itself to the anchor chain, and he would not wish me to see such a ghastly spectacle. I know I shock you, dearest Aggie, by saying that I nearly shook off his grasp to run and look, so curious was I, but you will be glad to hear that I am now a model wife, and obeyed Hector in this as I do in everything, or 'in nearly everything', perhaps I should say, for I find that men after all do not always know what is best, in large as in small matters, and sometimes, even Hector owns that I am right, as in the matter of the disappearance of his gold watch chain, which he would blame upon the thieving habits of the lascars, but which, I knew, was a matter of his own carelessness, and so it proved to be, for I made him turn out his chest again before reporting the matter to Captain Blaikie, and there was the chain, fallen into a fold of his shirt, and so a scandal was avoided, which Hector nobly admitted was the result of my superior good sense.

We are putting up at a fine hotel here and will look about us for lodgings in a few days. It is so delightful to be still at last, after the endless motion of the waves. You cannot imagine what a pleasure it is to put a plate down on a table and feel sure that it will stay there!

There is so much bustle in this great city I am all in a whirl, and my head spins with strange words like 'baboo' and 'chowkidar' and 'maidan' which I would explain to you if I could but I cannot. You could never imagine a crowd of such odd appearance as passes constantly beneath my window so that I am forever hanging out to gasp at the antics of a half-clothed pilgrim, or laugh at the pretty ways of the little brown children, or admire the gorgeous retinue of a prince.

I must leave off now for Hector comes up the stairs (I cannot understand how he runs up them two at a time for the heat makes me very indolent, though people say it is nothing at the moment) and he will be whisking me off to view the sights, though I will not go to put on my bonnet until I have sent you, my dear sister,

the fondest love
of your devoted
Fanny

Calcutta
30th July 1820

My dearest Aggie,

I scarcely know where to begin in telling you all our news since my last. We have been so busy setting up our establishment and now I am mistress of a pretty 'bungalow' and upward of twenty servants! Yes, I can see you smile, but it is true, I assure you, and Hector tells me we are in no way extravagant for many of our countrymen have twice the number and only half the means! But he is determined to build up and not spend.

I must laugh when I think how you would stare to see me on my 'verandah' early in the morning, nicely shaded by our own cocoanut palm, instructing my bearers and maids and cooks and gardeners how to go on. Sometimes I wonder why I continue to do it, for they never listen to me, but do it all as they will. And the truth is that I feel less and less inclined to interfere with them, for the heat tires me greatly, and I feel often low and out of sorts. Mrs Murchison tells me that it is only to be expected in my interesting condition, and I am sure you will be pleased to hear that a happy event is expected in the coming year. Do tell Papa, as it may incline him to feel more kindly towards his own naughty Fanny. I own I am sometimes quite miserable when the mails bring no answer to my little messages, and I long for his forgiving heart to embrace me once again.

Oh my dear sister, how I wish you could see my strange Indian home, with its odd collection of furniture (which we acquired from the auctioning of a departed family's goods), and its heavy window screens to protect us from the worst of the heat, and its 'punkah', a kind of ceiling ventilator, which a poor little boy works from outside the house by an ingenious arrangement of ropes and cords.

How I would rejoice to prepare a room for you, and show you how cleverly I can contrive to produce a good dinner and a comfortable day's entertainment! How dearly I would love to show you our mission schools, where I am sure, an excellent work is done among the natives (as you see, I am not entirely given over to frivolity!) and even more, our wonderful Chowringhee, which is, you must know, the Princes Street of Calcutta, tho' altogether grander, I assure you, for the palaces of the old Nabobs would only make you stare. Hector vows that we too will be making a great fortune soon enough, and indeed, I believe him, for he is so clever and good at business that Mr Murchison has already talked of making him a partner in the firm, and Hector is full of ideas for expansion. Mr Murchison only fears that he will not be able to keep Hector long, as he is so energetic, and wishful to do well, and constantly looking about for 'fresh woods and pastures new'.

Mrs Murchison has quite taken me up, and goes with me everywhere. She is very kind and respectable, tho' rather strict, stricter even than my own dear Aggie, and I must own I sometimes feel a little low when I hear of the gaieties of this most amusing city and know that I may not attend them. But Hector assures me I must not exert myself in my present condition, and also to heed Mrs Murchison, for some of the company here is quite wild and a lady's reputation is easily lost.

You can imagine, my dearest sister, how at first I found all around me of the greatest interest, and I would forever ask Mrs Murchison the meaning of the horrid attire of the heathen priests, or the strange sights to be seen at every street corner. But she tells me it is improper to show too much curiosity, and it is better to know nothing about the natives at all, as there is nothing there to elevate the mind. And when I enquired about learning the Hindoo tongue (I know you will laugh when you remember how poorly I worked at my French!) she threw her hands in the air and said I must not, for it can so easily corrupt. Only sometimes I do wonder if Mrs Murchison is quite right in this, and wish for a little more knowledge, so that I could speak to some of the Hindoo ladies of the better class, as they are very pretty and look so kind.

Mrs Murchison tells me daily that my duty is all to Hector, but she need not, for I know it myself, and wish only to be a devoted wife. Only he is so extremely busy at his business, which, as I have already told you (and I hope you will tell dear Papa) prospers exceedingly, so that we will soon be quite rich!

I am sending you in the next mail some of the finest muslin from Mr Murchison's best warehouse. Do not, I beg of you, leave it in a drawer, but have Bessie Nimmo make it up for you into a pretty gown for summer. With it I am putting up an embroidered shawl from Cashmere. It is all made by hand, from the softest wools. I hope the design will please you, so that, whenever you wear it,

you will remember
your ever-loving sister
Fanny

Calcutta
15th January 1821

Dear Sister,

I am pleased to tell you that Fanny was yesterday delivered of a fine girl, whom we have named Justina Agnes. Fanny tells me she bears a strong resemblance to her Aunt Aggie, but I do not see any likeness myself. I am very glad to say that the child is strong and healthy, and in the care of our good Dr Simpson of London University, who has procured an excellent Hindoo nurse.

Fanny goes on well. She has had some suffering but is pulling up now, and we are glad that it is now cool and pleasant in Calcutta, as it is healthier in every way. We are fortunate that our residence is in a good situation, and that no fever has ever struck its inhabitants, for which mercy we pay a larger sum in rent, but it is worth it I assure you.

Fanny begs me to send you her most grateful thanks for the package of books and the coloured ribbons, which arrived most timely and are very fine. She is herself so much more cheerful that her thoughts have turned once more to her own dress which, she tells me, she has 'sadly neglected' in recent months, and she has begged me to find her some plumes for her hat, which I have been unable to procure in our Calcutta warehouses, and so, in trepidation I dare to ask if you will despatch some to her as I am sure you have greater knowledge of these matters than I. In doing so you will earn the lasting gratitude

of your respectful brother
Hector

P.S. Please convey my respects to Mr Heriot, and assure him that his daughter and grand-daughter are going on very well, and that their health is at all times my first concern. H. J.

Calcutta
17th August 1821

Dearest Papa,

Your letter made me so happy, and Baby too, for she sat upon my knee and crowed with joy when Hector read it out. I received also by the same mail the fine lace bonnets and infant clothing put up by dearest Aggie, for which also my thanks.

Baby knows how to be grateful too, I am sure, for she blows big bubbles when she is pleased and she blew an exceedingly great one when I gave her Grandpapa's blessing!

We have had a dull time of it here. The hot weather was most miserable, with Hector in a most painful heat rash, and Baby cross, and nothing to do at home but lie about and try to forget the cruel heat. But now we are all fine again, and the cold weather will soon be here.

Business prospers very well, and we will soon remove to a larger house in a more fashionable position. Hector has purchased our own chaise, and we drive about in fine style. He works with so much determination I am sure he will soon be a great man, but he only smiles when I tease him and tells me business is not a matter for joking, with which you, I am sure, dearest Papa, agree.

In the coming cold weather we look forward to an increase in our amusements, as there are some picnics and musical soirées planned. But believe me, dearest Papa, nothing will give me greater happiness than the assurances of your forgiveness, which you so generously made in your dear letter, and your blessing on my marriage, which has now its own happy issue. The only cloud on my serenity is the knowledge of the pain I have caused you and my dear sister by the clandestine nature of my marriage, but on that head I will be silent, as you have so kindly promised to be for ever more, and in so doing have brought the greatest happiness to

your own
Fanny

Calcutta
7th July 1822

Dear Sir,

I write to inform you of the birth of your grandson, Edward Simeon, whom we have named with due deference to both his paternal and maternal grandfathers. He is a jolly little fellow, and cries loudly, which Fanny assures me is an excellent sign. His sister, who is usually very good and quiet, does not seem delighted at the birth of her brother, but is most jealous, and her tricks to gain our attention away from him are quite amusing! Fanny, I am glad to say, has picked up quickly and seems almost her old self again, looking forward to a more varied life as she tired of the confinement her delicate situation imposed upon her.

On your recommendation I have withdrawn some of my interest in the Indian silk and muslin business. Prices of Indian muslins are not standing up well, and our merchants believe this decline will continue as British stuffs improve in quality. Paris and London no longer look to buy our Cashmere shawls, but to the copies of them made by our own Scottish weavers!

I am most grateful for your advice concerning the advisability of making some investment in an Edinburgh bank, and I agree that it is prudent to spread one's financial net wide, but I have at the moment committed all my available resources to an interesting opportunity in the indigo trade, and have invested through a profitable Calcutta bank a good sum in a shipping venture, so have no funds to spare. But I am assured by all that the prospects for both are excellent. However, I will keep in mind your kind and fatherly advice, and act upon it when the occasion presents itself.

Your obedient etc.
Hector

Calcutta
(Our grand new villa!)
4th December 1822

Dearest Minnie,

How happy I was to hear of your nuptials and do send you and Mr Sinclair my heartfelt congratulations. I can only say that if you are as happy as I, you will be happy indeed. I am only sorry that I do not spend as much time with my husband as I would like, since he is exceedingly busy at his business. He has left Murchison and Co. and has set up a trading house in his own name. Jamieson and Son sounds well, does it not, though I am sure poor little Edward cares nothing for it. He is a sickly little thing, I must own, and I am sure that only the devotion of his nurse, a good, kind native woman named Lakshmee (Justina cannot say it, and as we all have some difficulty, we copy J's babytalk and she is 'Lucky' to all of us!) – oh, I write so fast I lose the thread – ah yes, it is thanks to Lucky that he pulled through a bad fever in the wet weather. My dear, how it rains, you would not believe it. You could as well plunge into the sea as stand out in the rain for both would wet you equally.

I own I am glad to be free of childbearing for a time. It is a weary business. And our society here is so gay that we never want for amusements. At last I am free of that moralising old biddy, Mrs Murchison, whom I was obliged to humour while Hector stayed in her husband's company, but who was forever putting a brake upon my least show of cheerfulness or spirits. Now I ignore her as I please! Only fancy how she stared when she saw me driving out Tuesday last with Mr Murray, a very dashing blade in an indigo house, for she saw us just as Mr Murray was attempting to remove a horrid insect that had dived into my bonnet and became entangled in the ribbons at my neck, at which I laughed merrily, I assure you, as both Mr Murray and the insect tickled me dreadfully, and I laughed the more when I saw her Sunday face. And there was no harm in it, for Hector laughed too when I told him, and said I was ever a naughty puss, and he knew all my wicked wiles, and I was not to make poor Mr Murray die of love, for all he needed was a kind lady 'to practise upon', being so young as he is, at which I slapped his hands and said did he rate my charms so low, as being only worthy for youths to learn from, and he said Mr Murray had better do no more or he would be obliged to call him out, since any man that meddled with his wife, etc. etc. But I will spare you the rest, for when Hector climbs upon his high horse there is nothing to be done but play the meek wife, and say 'Yes, dearest,' and 'No, dearest,' until he climbs down off it again.

How I wish you could be here with us just now, dearest Minnie, for this is the best time of the year, and now that Hector is so rich we are invited everywhere in the grandest style. You would not credit the gorgeousness of some of the balls I have attended, with flocks of servants in the most magnificent liveries, and tables bowing under the weight of roasted peacocks and all kinds of wonderful meats and fruits dressed with such strange species that you could hardly imagine.

But I must hasten to conclude, for we are bidden today to a garden party, and I must don my prettiest gown the better to extend Mr Murray's education, and to annoy Mrs Murchison, and to remind my darling Hector of the value of his prize.

And so I leave you dearest Minnie, and send the fondest love of

your affectionate friend
Fanny

P.S. 'Kenilworth' is perfection! I am so grateful to you for sending it. There are no books to be had at all in Calcutta and I am already besieged by anxious friends wishful to borrow it. Do send me the latest by the same author whenever you can! F. J.

Paisley
July 1826

Dear Brother Kirkwood,

I write to inform you that your sister is delivered safely of a girl. I am thankful that the weary business is over and that she seems to be a good child, not given overmuch to crying. Though naturally I am disappointed in the sex, your sister is content, and is making a recovery, of which I am glad as I do not like the continuous interference of neighbours. Had the child been a boy I would have named him Walter for my father. I have left the choosing of the name to your sister, who inclines towards Margaret, which was, I believe, the name of your mother.

I am sorry to hear that you have left Mr Forbes's weaving shop. Though you have never excelled at the work, it is a sad thing to leave a respectable trade, and one which promises continuous prosperity to us all. Your new master, Mr Turnbull, is a man of good repute, and well known in Paisley, and I am interested to hear that he is expanding his business into agriculture. No doubt the life of the farm will suit your energies better than the finer work of the loom.

Your sister begs me to remember her to her nephews, and to Mrs Kirkwood, and informs you that she will write when her strength is up to it.

I remain yours truly,
Isaiah Dunbar

P.S. When you write again be so good as to put Mr to my name when you back your letter.

Ayr
July 1826

Dear Sister,

Your husband's letter arrived yesterday and brought great joy to us all. I thank God that the babe is sound. As for the name I have enquired of Mr Murray as to its origin. He is a man of great erudition, well versed in the Hebrew and the Greek. He informs me the meaning is 'Pearl', and so I hope she will be a pearl to you, for 'The Kingdom of Heaven is like unto a merchant man, seeking goodly pearls: who, when he had found one pearl of great price, went and sold all that he had and bought it.' Matthew ch. XIII.

As for ourselves, we are well and labour not in vain. My master, Mr Turnbull, does well by me, and though I had never thought, being one as was first bred to the sea and with the loom to my trade for many years, to find myself tilling the soil for my daily bread, I do not doubt but that it is the Lord's will for me. And yet it is a weary thing to plough another man's acres and I own to you, my dear sister, that I have not altogether give up my dream but am putting by for a time when I can see my way clear. I do not speak of it to Eliza for her health is not good. There are many here have gone to the colonies this year past.

The wee boys grow apace. You will see how much a change four years will bring to your own bairn. Young Jem is forever in a pickle and leads us a merry dance, full of mischief as a nest is of birds. It is a hard task to be a father for the spirit of the child must be broke if the devil is not to have his way with him. Malcolm is a good boy and causes no trouble.

I was at Maybole fair and stopped two nights for my master's business, but I wished I had stayed at home for wickedness is terrible to behold. There I met your husband's old friend Gregson on a visit to his brother's widow. He tells me you have still the Indian designs in your Paisley work but much improved, and pattern nearly all over with little plain at the centres. I am thankful God has removed me from such an industry for my great hands are better at harnessing horses than harnessing looms. I am like a Highlander, my fingers are all thumbs. Your Paisley weavers must be men of substance now for Lady Eglinton passed me in her carriage on the Maybole Road and she had about herself a plaid in the Indian Cashmere style but wove by Scots fingers I would be certain of it. And she is a grand lady indeed. If you are indeed going on in a prosperous way I am glad of it for I know, dear sister, that you will be ever mindful that the love of money is the root of all evil, and will not be led astray by lucre, but will give of your substance to the poor and needy who are always with us.

And so I am glad that wee Margaret is come safe among us.

Your affectionate brother,
Joseph Kirkwood

P.S. Gregson informed me that your minister, Mr Elliott, has removed to Edinburgh. I hope for your sake that your new man will be filled with zeal for the Lord.

Chapter Four *Edinburgh, October 1826*

1

'Well, Mistress Heriot, and have you heard the news?'

The speaker's sharp eyes darted between the two other women as her needle continued to plunge in and out of the calico on her lap. The members of the St Andrew's Ladies' Relief Society were at work in Miss Heriot's drawing room preparing for the forthcoming autumn bazaar, the proceeds of which were destined for the deserving destitute of Paisley under the aegis of Mr Elliott.

Aggie and her particular friend, Mrs Euphemia Macfarlane, exchanged glances. Mrs Hamilton's tongue was indiscreet and could be malicious. She would have to be deflected if she became too flagrant, since Mrs Macfarlane's two young girls were at a susceptible age, and their febrile imaginations could all too easily be stirred by unguarded talk.

'What news would that be now, Mrs Hamilton?' said Aggie carefully, raising her eyes from the exquisite lace she was setting on to a child's petticoat.

'I had it from Janet,' Mrs Hamilton pressed on eagerly. 'And I'm surprised your Jeanie did not inform you of it, for I saw them hobnobbing on the corner of Frederick Street, right enough, as I stepped out to replenish my stock of thread.'

'Jeanie knows better than to bring servants' gossip to me,' said Aggie drily, but she might have saved her breath for Mrs Hamilton was fairly bursting with her news.

'Why, it's Mr Elliott, of course. Since he left Paisley and came to be minister at St Andrews not one sign has there been, as you well know, that he was intending to marry, as any young man in his situation should do, I am sure you will agree. And we all know the lengths he has gone to to avoid the wiles of certain persons . . . ' The Misses Macfarlane looked eagerly up from their hemming, but Mrs Hamilton caught the warning in Aggie's frowning eyes and paused. 'But on that head I will say no more, for as you know I was never the one to gossip.'

A giggle from Miss Susan broke the heavy silence which followed this remark. Mrs Hamilton ignored it and sailed on.

'Well, Janet informs me, and I know she is to be trusted for she has never misled me yet, that Mr Elliott was seen only yesterday at noon, meeting a young lady off the coach from Glasgow, and that she wore an exceedingly fetching bonnet all over bows and ribbons, and just wait for this, that he, er, *saluted* her upon the cheek in the warmest and most affectionate manner.'

A quiver ran through the generous person of Mrs Macfarlane, causing the bow in her white muslin cap to tremble and her black taffeta gown to rustle.

'Is that so?' she said, with disappointing mildness.

'Aye,' said Mrs Hamilton avidly, 'and Janet had it from wee Jimmy the stable lad this very morning that he saw Mr Elliott fairly running up the College Wynd from the Cowgate so fast that his coat tails were flying all about him and carrying a parcel in either hand, and that he burst into the house of Mrs Robinson, who takes in lodgers since the death of her husband – you know the house, where the Wynd joins on to the High Street – and he called out loudly, "Ettie, Ettie, come put on your bonnet directly, for I've come to show you the sights of our grand city," and then Jimmy came away being, as he said, mindful of his duties, as I am sure he ought to have been, for a lazier wee rascal I have not ever . . . but never mind all that.'

Mrs Hamilton looked around the room quite out of breath, but her triumph was shortlived, for Mrs Macfarlane let out the gust of mirth she had with difficulty been keeping under control and her two girls gave way to shameless giggles.

'Aye,' said Aggie, relishing her moment. 'That will be Miss Henrietta Elliott, I've no doubt, on her way through to York where she'll be visiting her Aunt Kerr. She takes the opportunity to stop in Edinburgh for a day or two, for it's been nigh on a year since she's seen her brother. Mr Elliott himself informed me of the circumstances of her visit when he called upon me yesterday to settle the arrangements for the bazaar. His health, you know, has caused his family some concern, for he near worked himself to death in Paisley ministering to the poor in those fever-ridden, unwholesome weaver hovels.'

A red flush spread up Mrs Hamilton's scrawny neck and settled upon her bony cheeks.

'I'm sure *you*'re mighty pleased it's only his sister, Mistress Heriot,' she said waspishly, 'so fond of the minister yourself as you are.'

Aggie's mouth, severe to the point of sternness in repose, broke into a smile of surprising sweetness. Mrs Hamilton was closer to the mark than she knew, for Aggie watched over the red-fisted, earnest young minister with a tenderness of which only her closest friend would have believed her capable, but her concern was so far from the romantic adoration of which Mrs Hamilton suspected her that the arrow went wide of its mark.

The arrival of Jeanie with a tray of refreshments brought a welcome interval to the conversation, and it was not until the Misses Macfarlane had their plates well filled with buttered scones and their seniors were provided with their favourite plum cake that conversation again became possible.

'Have you heard from India at all now, Aggie?' said Mrs Macfarlane. 'Has poor Fanny recovered yet from the sad loss of the wee boy, James, was it not?'

Aggie brightened. 'I have indeed heard, my dear Effie. In fact, I was on the point of telling you Fanny's news before . . . ' Aggie looked over towards Mrs Hamilton but forbore to punish her further. 'It's wonderful indeed, for Fanny has so far recovered from her bereavement that she is fit enough for anything, and Mr Hector Jamieson has decided that there is too great a risk in keeping Justina and wee Edward in Calcutta with so many putrid fevers about, and he's fixed on it that Fanny should come home with them for a visit to Edinburgh! She must have left Calcutta' – she fumbled in the pocket of her apron, drew a letter from it, and searched about for the place – 'aye, here it is. She must have left Calcutta three weeks ago, and she'll be with us here at home before the New Year!'

Four cups of tea remained suspended in mid-air as the ladies took in this remarkable information. Aggie had finished with a little air of defiance, for the scandal of Fanny's runaway marriage was still fresh in many minds, and she was grateful that Mrs Hamilton was momentarily too subdued to be spiteful.

Mrs Macfarlane beamed with whole-hearted delight as she shook a crumb off her ample skirt. She had not herself known Fanny, having moved to George Street shortly after Fanny's flight to India, but in the six ensuing years she had become fond of the outwardly formidable Miss Heriot, shrewdly appreciating the courage, loyalty and capacity for affection which that lady so carefully hid from the eyes of the world. A visit from Fanny and her children would, she knew, make Aggie happy, so it made her happy too.

'Well, well, that is great news to be sure,' she said. 'And no doubt the bairns will be as excited as can be to see their Aunt Heriot for the first time, so faithful as you've been, Aggie, sending them toys and books and clothes these last four years and more.'

The two Macfarlane girls had been whispering together and now could contain their curiosity no longer.

'Mrs Jamieson is very rich, is she not, Mistress Heriot?' blurted out Miss Susan, ignoring the frowns of her mother.

'Will she bring her black servants with her do you think?' joined in Miss Bessie, 'and her jewels and her silken gowns and everything?'

Mrs Hamilton interrupted them. 'I'm sure Mrs Jamieson will be most careful to present a restrained appearance,' she said, her voice as sour as vinegar, 'since she will naturally wish to silence any references to . . . '

Once more, a glance at Miss Heriot's face effectively silenced her. Aggie's scowl was, indeed, so terrible that Mrs Hamilton was quite alarmed. She bent to feel for her reticule, lost amid the folds of her dress, then stuffed into it her needle, scissors, thimble and thread.

'You'll excuse me, I'm sure, dear Mistress Heriot, if I slip away now, for I've a sick cousin to visit in the Lawnmarket before the day is quite over,' and quickly arranging her scarf over her arms she hurried to the door, calculating that she would have time, before her husband could reasonably expect her to be home, to call upon at least three ladies who would find the news of Fanny's forthcoming return as deeply interesting as she did herself.

It was late when the Macfarlane ladies at last followed her example, and for once Aggie was pleased to close the door behind her friend. She wanted time to think, to relish Fanny's letter, and to dwell upon all the delights of the forthcoming visit. She called Jeanie to clear away the tray, then unbuttoned the boots that pinched her ankles, swollen as they were with arthritis, and sat in the gathering dark.

There would be no recriminations. The hurt of Fanny's marriage was entirely forgotten, smoothed away by years of affectionate letters and the pain of absence. Among their acquaintance there would naturally be some return of the talk of six years ago, and Aggie would have to do what she could to ease the way for Fanny. At least there would be no difficulty with Father. Age had wondrously softened him, and besides, the regular accounts from India, with the reports of new grandchildren and new business successes, had entirely reconciled him to Hector. He would probably spoil dear little Justina and dear little Teddy abominably.

The lamplighter passed down the street outside, but Aggie sat on, dreaming of the days they would spend together, of the treats she would provide for the little ones, and trying to conjure up in her mind's eye the forms of the two children she had never seen.

An idea had come to her so daring it fairly took her breath away. Calcutta was no place for bairns, the whole world knew that. And now that poor little Jamie had succumbed to its unwholesome climate, could not Fanny be persuaded, perhaps, to leave her two surviving ones behind when she went back, as she surely would, to her place by Hector's side? This big house had been so empty since Fanny had gone, the rooms on the top floor cried out to be used. The nursery would be at the front. It would be no big thing to send a man from the gun shop to fix bars to the windows. Then the sunny room at the back would make a fine schoolroom. She would need, in due course, to think of desks, a bookshelf, and dimity curtains in a fresh print. She had the very stuff put by. They would need a nursery maid, of course, and a governess in the fulness of time . . .

The click of the front door roused her. She hastily buttoned her boots and hobbled down the stairs.

'Father, oh, Father, I've a letter from India arrived this morning. Such news! Our Fanny's coming home and the bairns are coming with her.'

2

December 1826

'Teddy pushed me!'

'I didn't!'

'You did!'

'Didn't!'

'Did! Ow!'

Edward burst into a howl of pain and rage as Justina's sharp little finger and thumb bit into the tender flesh of his arm.

'Mama! Mama! Justy pinched me!'

Justina watched Edward's anguished tears with satisfaction.

'Teddy's a baby, Teddy's a baby,' she chanted triumphantly.

Fanny wearily turned her head away from the vista of rolling hills outside the window of the postchaise and looked at her two brawling children with disgust. It had been a hideously exhausting journey from London. The past four days cooped up in the jolting postchaise and the three uncomfortable nights in overcrowded inns had seemed more like a week, in spite of the huge sums of money she had disbursed on private parlours and superior horses, which, even with her new wealth, she had found exorbitant.

She leant back on the squabs, arching her back to relieve the tightness of her stays, of which the steel ribs were becoming hourly less comfortable. She had given up trying to quell the children, who were now scuffling on the dusty seat of the chaise beside her over a disputed ball. In all her life, she had never wished for anyone as intensely as she wished for Lucky, the children's adored ayah, who had steadfastly refused every inducement to accompany her charges overseas. A hasty replacement had been found in Calcutta, a lazy, slatternly English girl. In a spurt of anger, Fanny had turned her off in London, deciding that she could very well manage the children herself for the rest of the journey to Edinburgh. She had also (rashly, she now decided) postponed the hiring of her own maid until they should reach home, and so found herself accompanied only by the two hired postboys, who were wholly engaged in driving the lumbering vehicle and of no use at all in entertaining the children.

On the first day, full of her usual optimistic high spirits, Fanny had quite enjoyed herself. Unused to the company of her children, she had been amused by their games. She had had the forethought to buy a Noah's Ark in London, and it had, for a while, amused her almost as much as Edward and Justina. They had mewed, roared, hissed and bellowed like three children, instead of a mother and two. But after the first day the toy had begun to pall, and then Fanny had been at her wit's end to keep them happy, telling stories, singing until her throat ached and trying to recall how to make the cat's cradle for the benefit of Justina's agile fingers. The hours had dragged endlessly, and every return to the postchaise, after a stop for refreshments or for an overnight rest, had seen the little party become increasingly bedraggled and irritable.

Both children were crying now in earnest. Fanny pulled out a tin of barley sugar from behind a cushion.

'You can each have a piece if you promise to be good, and stop fighting, and sit up, and stop crying, and behave yourselves,' she said, without conviction.

The children reached out grimy hands and took the bribe. They stared at each other for a moment with deep hostility, but the fight had, in any case, worn itself out. Justina returned to her doll and began to croon to it in a sing-song voice. Edward felt among the remarkable collection of objects in his pocket, drew out a stone and a stub of pencil, and began an elaborate game, in which the stone became the chaise and the pencil by turns a postboy, a highwayman, and Edward himself. Relieved, Fanny turned back to the window.

It was nearly dark when, at last, the creaking vehicle, mud splashed high up its yellow panels, pulled up at the door of the Heriot house in George Street but Fanny herself was no longer tired. She had passed the last half-hour glued to the window in a state of glorious anticipation.

'Look, children! There's Arthur's Seat, where we used to go for picnics! I'll take you there when the weather turns fine again. And here's Calton Hill, where we roll our eggs on Easter Day, and do you not see the city there, Auld Reekie itself, rising up to the Castle? And look! Look! Princes Street! You'll see Grandfather's shop in a moment. No, we're turning up Frederick Street already! See? Who's that old dame in the antiquated hat? Lord, it's Mrs Wilkes, still alive after all these years! And this is George Street at last! We're here! We've arrived! Oh, stop, stop the horses here! This is the very house!'

Fanny had tumbled out of the coach before the steps had been let down and was hammering on the great door of her father's house while the coachman had as yet scarcely persuaded the horses to stand still.

The brass knocker flew out of her hand as the door was wrenched open from the inside. Aggie, trembling with excitement, saw a strange woman, taller than the old Fanny, who though travel-stained was dressed with a mature elegance. The eager, pretty face was still there, but it was more subtle now, warmer, less avid, more humorous.

Fanny, dazzled by the bright light within, saw her own unchanged Aggie, in what appeared to be the same black, high-necked gown, her hair as severe as ever under its plain cap, but her face softened and warmed with the indulgent smile that Fanny, of all people, had reason to know so well.

Old Mr Heriot, tottering forth from his study, supported by Jeanie's tremulous arm, saw dimly a lovely woman, which part of his wavering mind knew to be Fanny, who had done something wrong some years ago, he could not remember what, but who now seemed miraculously to be his own Janet come back from the dead. And then old Simeon saw no more, but staggered, and Jeanie's loud cry startled the sisters out of their tearful embrace and they rushed to support his weight as he threatened to topple over entirely.

It was a long time before either of them could think of anything but the blue tinge around Simeon's mouth, the lolling head, as he lay back in the chair hastily dragged out from a corner of the wide hall, the eyes obstinately closed in unconsciousness. Smelling salts were fetched, feathers burned, but all in vain. The postboys who, in haste to finish their own journey at a convivial tavern, had been unconcernedly uncording and bringing in a great pile of trunks, dressing cases and packages from the roof and rear of the chaise, were diverted into carrying the inert form of Mr Heriot up the stairs to his bedchamber, where Aggie and Fanny worked together to untie his neck cloth, remove his outer clothing and discuss in agitated whispers what kind of turn this could be, while Jeanie clapped her bonnet on her head, wrapped her cloak around her and ran for the doctor.

Dr Brown, who lived near, and was mercifully at home, had arrived and ushered the sisters firmly out of their father's bedchamber before another thought had a chance to enter their heads. It came to them both simultaneously.

'The bairns!' said Aggie.

'The children!' said Fanny, and with Aggie struggling behind she ran down the stairs and into the street, her breath making puffs of white ether in the frosty December air.

The last and heaviest of the trunks was being lowered from the top of the vehicle, the door of which still gaped open, on to the straining back of the man below, but of the children there was no sign. Fanny's heart missed a beat.

'Teddy! Justina!' she called, and dodging past the laden postboy she thrust her head into the chaise.

The two children were sitting close together with their legs crossed like two little Indians, their mother's wrap around their shivering shoulders, their eyes dark apprehensive pools in their small white faces.

A laugh, half exasperated, half amused, broke from Fanny.

'You silly wee things,' she said. 'Whatever are you doing, sitting here in the dark alone? Why didn't you come away into the house?'

The children said nothing. Fanny shivered. It was too cold to stand about in the street, coaxing these ridiculous infants out of their fears.

'Justy said—' began Edward, but he was silenced by a dig from his sister's sharp elbow, and a stream of Hindustani.

Fanny sighed impatiently. 'I've told you before, Justina, I won't have you speaking that language any more. You've to forget all that now. You're good Scots Christian children, not Indian heathens. Whatever will people say?'

She realised that her careless question had gone home. In the dim shadowy light that penetrated the cavernous interior of the chaise, she sensed the children's tension increase.

'What is this? Are you scared of what they'll think of you? Why, your auntie's just dying to see you, and so will your grandfather be when he – when he's well enough. Now you just come along out of here before you catch your deaths of cold,' and reaching into the coach, Fanny grasped each child firmly by the hand and dragged them into their grandfather's house, shutting out the bitter night air with a click as she smartly closed the door.

The door had, in fact, been open for so long, as the men had been bringing in the trunks, that it was scarcely warmer inside than out. The children sheltered behind their mother's full skirts and at first Aggie, crossing the hall in agitation, did not perceive them. Fanny turned, clucking with exasperation.

'Children, for goodness' sake, you'd think there were tigers waiting for you. Come out, will you now, and kiss your aunt!'

Nothing happened. Then Justina, recognising with the superior sense of her five years the folly of postponing the inevitable any longer, stepped shyly forth and permitted the alarming lady, who had sunk awkwardly to her knees in the middle of the vast sea of chequered black and white marble that covered the hall floor, to put her arms around her and give her a hug and a kiss. Experiencing for the first time the unique odour of camphor, peppermint and perspiration that clung to Aunt Heriot's clothing, she planted a dutiful kiss upon that lady's cheek.

'Och, the wee soul,' said Aunt Heriot. 'And now, where's Teddy?'

The sound of his own name on the lips of this stranger proved too much for poor Edward to bear. As Fanny thrust him forward, he opened his mouth, screwed his fists into his eyes, and began to bawl.

Aggie knelt and gazed at him. He was filthy, terrified and exhausted. His short jacket was awry, his collar askew, and a damp stain was spreading in the front of his high-buttoned nankeen trousers. Slowly his tears abated. His hands fell from his eyes and he looked at her. She smiled at him, and opened her arms. He walked into them, and leaped straight into her heart, where he would reign for ever more.

3 *June 1832*

'Will you just look at this now, Mistress Heriot?' said Jeanie with disgust, holding up a boy's shirt from which a button had been torn, leaving a gaping rent down the front.

'Aye, well, he's just a wee boy,' said Aggie indulgently. Jeanie peered at her mistress with eyes sharp enough for all her blindness.

'He's a boy, right enough, but none so wee. Ten years old next month, and growing like the plagues of Egypt.'

'Well, well, Jeanie, they're all the same, though I've not known a boy like him for his love of all the beasties of creation. Mr Elliott's a naturalist himself and even he has not seen before some of the wee beetles that Teddy's found for his collection. "A remarkable knowledge for his age," he says,' and Aggie could not disguise the note of pride in her voice.

Jeanie sniffed but forbore to comment. She had no great opinion of any creature which boasted more than four legs or less than two. She made way for Aggie, who moved a pile of laundered chemises along to the end of the scrubbed kitchen table, and began to inspect her niece's stays. Jeanie looked over her shoulder.

'Look at these eyes, half pulled out,' she said with a disapproving cluck. 'Twelve years old and tightlacing already, or would be if she could manage it herself. "Will you pull my laces for me, Jeanie," she says to me the other day, "for Aunt won't do it, and I'll never be able to go abroad with Ellie showing such a nasty, common thick waist as this." "Then you'll stay at home, Miss," says I, "for I'll not interfere with the Lord's work. If he'd a wanted you split in two, he'd a' created you in separate pieces." '

Aggie grunted an acknowledgement but had ceased to listen. Jeanie's tongue ran along well-worn tracks and needed little response. She picked up a large cotton nightgown, shook it out of its folds and examined it critically.

'The old master'll no be wanting nightgowns where he's gone, God rest him,' remarked Jeanie with ghoulish satisfaction. 'It's a shame, though, for the stuff's good and barely worn.'

'It'll cut down fine for Teddy,' said Aggie happily, seeing an elegant solution to the problem of disposing of Simeon Heriot's effects, while at the same time exercising her talents as a needlewoman. It would be an economy too, for one to whom thrift was second nature – not that economy was absolutely necessary, for Hector, growing richer by the month in Calcutta, sent regular and handsome sums to pay for his children's upkeep, and Simeon Heriot, a canny businessman to the last, had invested his property wisely. The sale of the business after his death a year ago had also gone unexpectedly well, ensuring for Aggie a secure and comfortable future.

She added a worn petticoat, a second torn shirt and a holed stocking to her mending pile and, leaving Jeanie to set the flat irons by the fire in preparation for an afternoon's steamy labour, she limped up the kitchen stairs and crossed the hall to the small parlour, whose window provided the best light for close work. She sat down in a high-backed chair, drew her sewing towards her and threaded a needle. Really, she thought contentedly, looking over the task before her, there was hardly time for anything these days, so busy was she with her multitude of duties, overseeing the children's lessons, attending their catechism, settling their differences, regulating their meals, seeing that they were turned out presentable to the critical eyes of their friends and neighbours.

Such funny wee bodies they were too, their angers so fierce, their woes so deep, their joys so tremendous. She was hard put to it sometimes to know how to act for the best. She needed the judgement of a Solomon to arbitrate in their quarrels and know when chastisement was due. Though she kept to a strict enough routine her heart inclined her to leniency, especially where Teddy was concerned. He was so thin and earnest, so shy and easily upset, so ridiculously passionate about the aquaria, the forest of sprouting seeds, the sketches of wild birds and the cases of desiccated insects that had made the children's old nursery a positive hazard to all who dared enter it. Justina was a more difficult child, polite, certainly, but with a face that could close like a trap, locking its own secrets inside. She devoted passionate attention to all matters of dress and decorum, anxious to impress those she considered her social superiors wherever and whenever she could.

It was hard enough to be an aunt, thought Aggie, so maybe the Lord had known best when he had spared her from motherhood. The love of a parent must be so much greater than that she felt herself, though she could hardly believe it possible. She could scarcely bear to think of the suffering poor Fanny must constantly endure, separated from her darlings. Not even the five years that had passed since she had left her children in her sister's care could, Aggie felt sure, have been enough to ease the pain of that wretched parting.

She snipped off her finished thread and reached for the reel. Her eye fell on a letter, lying open on the table. She picked it up, and read it.

Dearest Mama and Papa,

I was very happy to receive your kind letter of 16th March and am sorry to hear that Baby is cross. I have sent her a bib I have knitted though there is a mistake in the pattern I fear thatt is why it is not quite right. Aunt has bought me a fine new gown and pink ribbons and it is prettier by far than Ettie's we are to go to Princes Street tomorrow to purchase shoes as my feet grow greatly this year. Teddy has broke my doll though he says it is an accident I do not see how a doll can fall from a window unless it is thrown. J'apprends le français et je suis très diligente. Aunt Heriot says I may have the necklet of seed pearls you wore when you were a little girl if you will send your permission for she has it put by in her jewel case so please may I, dearest Mama?

Goodbye and au revoir and adieu, and farewell
from your own affectionate
Justina

Aggie, smiling over this epistle, was startled by a sudden rat-tat on the front door.

Mr Elliott here already, she thought, and me but half ready for him!

She jumped awkwardly to her feet, and by the time Jeanie, called from the nether regions below, had answered the summons, had relieved Mr Elliott of his hat and gloves, had permitted herself an acid comment on the minister's unseemly air of haste and had ushered him into the parlour, Aggie's deft fingers had organised the heaps of clothing on the table into orderly piles and she was tying a neat bow in the length of white tape that bound the last of them.

'Excellent, excellent,' said Mr Elliott breathlessly. He had taken the last hundred yards to the top of Hanover Street at a speed that hardly accorded with the dignity of his cloth. 'I can assure you, Mistress Heriot, that your charity will cheer many a poor wretch. If you could but see the misery . . . ' He shook his head.

'Aye, well, it's little enough we can do for the poor souls,' said Aggie comfortably, 'and if there's stuff here can keep the bairns warm, they're welcome to it. If it was heathens in India now, or the poor savages in the jungle, you could understand it better, but to think of them so near! And respectable families, you said, used to the finer things of life, cast down by the slump. Trade's a fickle thing, Mr Elliott, when all's said.'

'It's worse when disease follows depression, Mistress Heriot, for there's little a working man can do when he's struck by the cholera.'

Aggie nodded and laid a hand on one of her bundles. 'You'll be weighed down with things to carry over there, I've no doubt, after the fine plea you made on Sunday last?'

Mr Elliott smiled ruefully and shook his head.

'As to my being weighed down, I'm afraid it is far from the case. Mrs Macfarlane, indeed, has put up an excellent supply of shirts and stockings as well as a pair of good, serviceable blankets, but I fear that some of our number have weakened in their zeal. A most unfortunate report has been circulated, pointing to the enslavement to strong drink of some of the poorest Paisley families, and try as I might to point out that Mr Armstrong, who distributes our charitable collections, takes the greatest pains to ensure that only the honest and industrious among the destitute benefit from our efforts, I fear I have not been quite able to satisfy them.'

Aggie, listening to this speech with growing indignation, could hardly wait for the end of it.

'That Hamilton woman again!' she burst out wrathfully. 'Too mean to part with so much as an inch of candle herself and so ungenerous she must needs stop others giving too! I'll show her!' And with a brusque, 'Wait here, Mr Elliott, for I'll not keep you a moment,' she hobbled to the door and stumped up the stairs, muttering fiercely to herself.

She was back moments later, carrying a large bundle awkwardly in her arms. 'You've to mind now,' she said, thrusting it into the minister's arms, 'and give it to some poor shivering soul who's too cold to sleep well o' nights, for I heard you tell how there's some decent folk over there that have been reduced to selling their very furniture when there's others not two miles from here who'll not think twice before they spend a fortune on a bonnet.'

Fleeing from this awful sarcasm Mr Elliott took himself off, and Aggie stood at the window and nodded with satisfaction as she watched him bobbing along the street, encumbered by his load of bundles. Then she turned back to her unfinished mending and chuckled aloud. She would, she felt sure, derive great amusement from the expressions of puzzlement and dismay that would pour forth from old Jeanie when she discovered that the feather-stuffed quilt was unaccountably missing from her mistress's bed.

The candle was guttering low in its battered brass candlestick the next evening, but the two men sitting over their supper in the draughty dining room of a Paisley manse had no thought of retiring early.

'Man, it's good to see you again,' said Andrew Elliott, spreading butter enthusiastically on a slice of coarse bread. 'If you only knew how I miss it all – you, the simple fare, the old kirk with its rough walls and hard seats, and those battered old tin sconces. The best families parading in their finery on the Sabbath morn, and the poor ones singing lustily at the back. My new kirk in Edinburgh, for all its gas brackets and varnished pews and tinted glass, does not give me half the welcome I received from the weaving folk of Paisley. Then, here, you have the chance to do some real good, to bring relief where there is no other source of aid . . . '

'Man, there's poverty enough in Edinburgh,' said his friend drily.

'Oh, aye, right enough, but in the New Town, where my kirk is, we're awful rich, Peter, awful grand and rich. It goes hard with my conscience sometimes.'

The Reverend Peter Armstrong pushed the fair hair out of his eyes and grinned. 'That's the old Andrew talking, right enough. You should have been a missionary, my dear fellow. I can see you quite plainly, making a meal for a party of hungry cannibals with the greatest goodwill in the world. "Come, come, my good sirs," you'd say, "there's precious little meat on that foot. Take the other as well, and an arm and a leg if you fancy it. Objection? What possible objection could I have if you are hungry and I have flesh to spare?" '

He pushed his chair back, still chuckling, and reaching for a fresh candle from the sideboard, lit it and stuck it on top of the melted remains of the old one. Andrew Elliott, looking up at his friend, watched the laughter die out of his face.

'You wanted to hear all our Paisley news – well, I wish for your sake it was more cheerful. The trade is changing and since every man, woman and child in Paisley lives by the loom, it takes but a small flutter in the market for plaids and shawls and the like to shake us all to the foundations. There's more men coming into the business every year and the power looms are taking them out of their own weaving shops into the factories. The wages can only go down. You'd never know, to see the fame the Paisley shawls have acquired hither and yon, that it will soon be only the best of the weavers who will earn a decent day's wages. Oh, there's few reduced to begging in the streets. They're too proud for that. The most of them struggle along with a little less than before, but it takes only a small tap of fortune and they are down. And when they're down, they're down! There's children blue with cold, women dressed in rags scarcely whole enough to preserve the common decencies, men too sick from working seventeen hours out of the twenty-four in damp and freezing weaving sheds to feed their families. It's horrible, Andrew. And they say we are but seeing the beginning. It will get to be much worse before it's better, if indeed the industry ever does improve again. And what can we do, what can I do, except give out maybe a blanket here or a few shillings there? Yes, Marie, what is it?'

Mr Elliott looked round to see a small wizened face that had poked itself round the door of the dining room. The little maidservant slid through the half-opened door and stood twisting her apron in her red hands as she carefully rehearsed her message.

'Please, sir, it's Mrs Dunbar took bad with a fainting fit and Mr Dunbar in a taking and no money to send for the doctor and the wee girls without their supper and no bed to lay Mrs Dunbar in for they sent the blankets to the pawnshop on Thursday last.' The child stopped and frowned, trying to recall the rest of the message. 'And Mrs Denny next door says it's maybe her heart and she'll want you to say a prayer with her in case she doesn't last the night,' she finished triumphantly.

'Dunbar?' Mr Elliott's brows came together in an effort of remembrance. 'It surely can't be Isaiah's family? Why, I knew them well. Fine people. A highly skilled weaver. Regular at the kirk and a good, respectable woman. Many's the pleasant visit I've made to Isobel's little kitchen.'

'It's Isaiah Dunbar's wife right enough,' said Mr Armstrong grimly. 'I told you, Andrew, some folks have come to a standstill here, and since Isaiah fell out of work last winter when the cholera struck the house he's had no chance of finding it again. His health is delicate and he's been six months away from his loom. They had savings, I don't doubt, but they'll be long spent. I've watched them go down and down but never a complaint have I heard from them. Isaiah would call for help soon enough, but Isobel has more pride in her than any woman rightly should. She must be bad if she's let them send for me.'

Mr Elliott grasped the candlestick and led the way out into the narrow hallway.

'I'm coming with you, Peter,' he said. 'Just hold on till I fetch a bundle I've set somewhere down here.'

Mr Armstrong laughed. 'I'll not try to gainsay you. I'm not such a fool as to waste my breath. But mind you don't catch another low fever. Paisley's nearly killed you once already and if it succeeds this time I'll have your pretty sister to reckon with. I'd rather stand up to a wild bull than face her fury again!'

4

Drizzle had set in and Mr Elliott grunted as he buttoned his worn coat closely up to the neck and clasped his bundles to his chest to ward off the rain. Cloud had obscured the moon but Mr Armstrong, displaying an impressive knowledge of the maze of lanes that ran between the close-packed houses of Paisley, led the way unerringly to a low front door over which hung a straggling edge of ill-kept thatch.

'Surely this is not the place?' said Mr Elliott, peering round him in the dark. 'I remember a broader street, a sturdier door, two storeys surely, and was not the roof tiled?'

'It's as I told you.' Mr Armstrong's hand was already raised to knock on the door. 'The condition of the family has greatly altered and for the worse. After Isaiah took the cholera they could not keep up with the rental and had to remove to this low district. Isaiah was right, I am sure, to avoid falling into debt. He was ever a man to pay his way. But since his health has broken down he cannot undertake the big pieces, fine craftsman though he is, and work of any kind is harder to find in such a place as this.' He rapped on the door, and the thin pane of wood rattled in its frame beneath his knuckles.

The door swung open on a rusty hinge into black nothingness. Startled, the two men looked into an empty room. Mr Elliott shuddered. How could the door have opened of its own accord? But then in the gloom his eye detected a fluttering movement of something pale poking out from behind the door just above the level of his knee. It was a tiny child, a girl, no more than two or three years old. Even in the darkness the two big men could feel her fear, could sense the terror in the dark pools that were her eyes and the tension in the thin body as she shrank away from them.

Mr Elliott, seeing himself momentarily through her eyes as a frightening black shape against the sky, folded his lanky legs at the knee and crouched down to her level.

'Jessie! It must be little Jessie! Your father wrote to inform me of your birth!'

The great eyes regarded him for a second, then, as suddenly as a mouse darts into its hole, the child turned and whisked away across the small bare room. A door at the far end opened. The faint ray of a tallow candle flickered through the opening and the two men heard murmuring voices.

Mr Elliott, following his confident friend into the house, was seized with a familiar pang of doubt. What had he to say to these people? Was not his very person, well fed and warmly clothed, a reproach to them? What right had he to witness their grief and degradation? What words could he say that could possibly bring them relief? Then he felt the weight of Aggie's packages in his arms and was comforted. Tonight, at least, he had something useful to give. It only remained to make the gift acceptable.

The second room of the cottage was so small that the few people in it gave an impression of uncomfortable crowding. A rickety chair, a table, on which stood the sole candlestick, and a bare wooden bedstead constituted the sole furnishings. Seeing the empty bed Mr Elliott feared for a moment that they had come too late, and then he saw the box bed, carpentered into an alcove in the wall, and the wretched, drawn face of Isobel Dunbar, who lay shivering under a single worn sheet.

Isaiah started up from the chair when he saw the visitors approaching and shook hands with them both. Mr Elliott was struck by the nervous rapidity of his movements. He had been used to the pallor, the supple, delicate fingers, the hunched shoulders and the poor bodily physique of the weaving folk but never before had these impressed him so forcibly. Surely Isaiah had not seemed so old, so broken, so careworn when last he had seen him? He could scarcely recognise in this gaunt ragged figure the respectable artisan of six years ago who had been used to ushering his neatly dressed family into their pew with pride and dignity.

'Mr Armstrong! Good of you to come, sir. And Mr Elliott! Well, well, this is a surprise indeed. Though sorry I am that you should see us come to this. You would never have thought when last you saw us to find the Dunbars in such misery. Why, only yesterday I was obliged to take to the pawnshop Isobel's clock that she had from her mother to buy vittles for the evening, though cook them I could not until Mrs Denny showed me the way of it.'

Mr Armstrong disengaged himself from Isaiah's clutching hand, and turning his back on the monologue – which, as he well knew, would not cease until it had finished a comprehensive account of all the family's disasters – he turned to the sick woman, knelt on the floor beside her and gently took her hand in his.

'You've not sent Meg for the doctor?'

Isobel Dunbar compressed her lips but did not answer. Mr Armstrong turned over the hand that lay weakly in his and examined the fingernails. He had long since ceased urging his flock to call in the services of a profession whose fees they could not pay and whose prescribed remedies they could not afford to buy, but an interest in natural science had encouraged him to extend his own knowledge of medicine and his pronouncements on medical matters were increasingly welcomed by the needy among his congregation.

'When did you last eat a decent meal?'

Isobel turned her head to look at her husband. She was too weak to talk against his loud voice, now embarked on a catalogue of woe to the listening Mr Elliott. Mr Armstrong frowned but Isaiah was unaware of all but his own tale. He did not even notice the insistent hand of his older daughter Meg, tugging at his tattered sleeve, until her voice grew more shrill than his. 'Da! Da!'

'Whist now, Meg, what is it? Can you not see I'm busy with Mr Elliott?'

Meg pulled her father down so she could whisper in his ear. Isaiah listened, then straightened up and laughed with embarrassment.

'What is it? What's the matter?' said Mr Elliott, bursting out in his anxiety to be of some assistance.

'She's a mite hungry, that's all,' said Isaiah. 'She's wishful to know if there's to be any supper tonight.'

A relieved smile crossed Mr Elliott's face.

'That there is, Meg,' he said. He set down the smaller bundle which he had until now held awkwardly in front of him like a barricade between his heart and the sadness in the room.

Aggie's knots had been well made and by the time the cloth wrapping had fallen away the two Dunbar children had conquered their shyness and, brave with hunger, had crept up to stand one on each side of their visitor, their eyes growing rounder as each treasure was uncovered.

Mr Elliott, filled with a sudden gaiety, had made himself the master of ceremonies.

'A knife, Meg, and a plate or two!' he called out, and the child scampered off, the prospect of a meal filling her with sudden unaccustomed energy.

Isaiah's eyes had brightened, too, at the sight of three large loaves, a pound of butter, two pounds of cheese, a poke of tea and a large piece of bacon, and he exclaimed with pleasure as he turned one of the glass jars to inspect its contents.

'Conserves! Mr Elliott, this is a feast indeed! You will not believe how long it is since we enjoyed such fare as this at our table!' And hastily removing the knife from his daughter's grasp, he began enthusiastically to slice the bread, then spread himself a generous helping of butter and jam and began to eat, while his daughters watched him, their hearts in their eyes.

Mr Armstrong, surveying this scene from his place by Isobel's bed, turned to look at the woman. She was struggling with a strong emotion. Was it relief? Shame? Pity? He spoke in a low voice.

'You've starved yourself and the bairns to feed him, haven't you now? There's little enough that's wrong with you, I know well, except that want of food has nearly brought your overtaxed system to the point of breakdown.'

He stood up, and, looking tall and forbidding in the small room, marched the three steps it took him to reach the table.

'Mr Dunbar,' he said, so sternly that Isaiah jumped and then froze, the hand holding the bread motionless in mid-air. 'Have you no thought for your wife and bairns? There's naught wrong with Mistress Isobel that a few hearty meals cannot mend. Have you not seen that she's been starving herself to save every morsel for you?' He shook his head, and the heavy fair hair flopped over his high forehead. 'For shame, sir, to eat before your family are fed!'

A flush mounted Isaiah's cheeks and he laid his bread down on the table. Meg's and Jessie's eyes followed it with rapturous interest as their father turned reproachful eyes on his wife.

'Is this true, Isobel?' he said, in an aggrieved tone. 'Have you indeed wilfully brought yourself to this pass, which has caused me so much worry and distress? I had no idea of this, no idea at all,' and he shook his head sorrowfully over the folly of his wife.

Mr Armstrong sighed with exasperation, then, hastily preparing a plateful of food, he took it across to Isobel, while Mr Elliott, spurred into action, cut bread and spread it generously for the children.

'Eat, woman!' commanded Mr Armstrong. 'But go slowly, or I fear your system will rebel.'

For a long moment Isobel's eyes held his. He saw her lips form the words, 'No charity,' but no sound issued from them. In answer he lifted his brawny arm and pointed to the children, who were eating with passionate desperation, concentrating with the whole of their small beings on each mouthful.

'You're a foolish, proud, stiff-necked, obstinate, remarkable woman, Isobel Dunbar,' said Mr Armstrong, 'and I wish you could have known my mother. You would have dealt well with each other.'

Isaiah had lifted a hand in wavering protest at the first part of this speech, not quite liking to hear even the minister address his wife in such round terms, but he was saved the necessity of interfering by a faint though unmistakable chuckle from his wife.

'Aye,' said Mr Armstrong, watching with satisfaction the tinge of colour that had returned to his patient's waxen face. 'And you have the gift of laughter too. Now then . . . ' and he presented the plate to her again.

Mr Elliott, watching the feline delicacy with which, even in the grip of starvation, Isobel Dunbar ate each mouthful, was overcome with admiration for his masterful friend. How knowing Peter was! How well he understood these people's characters and feelings! How useful was his practical knowledge of sickness and remedies! How woefully he himself would have handled this affair! Why, he would not even have remembered to unwrap the parcel of food if little Meg had not so timely intervened.

The thought of Aggie's food parcel reminded him of the other that lay still tied up on the floor. But Isaiah, while still eating, had begun once again to enumerate his woes, motivated by a need to justify himself.

'A man must eat if he is to work, Mr Elliott. A man must have the strength for it. My family would starve indeed if I were to fall sick. In these hard times the webster's work, you know, lies in going out to seek webs for the loom as much as in plying the shuttles. Why, only today I have tramped nigh on five miles to seek a commission. And I can boast a little success. Yes indeed, you have come upon us at our lowest ebb, I do assure you. I have taken on a large piece of work, too large, I fear, for the price I am to be paid for it but we cannot choose in these trying days. I will be at the loom again tomorrow and with industry and patience we may yet raise ourselves to our former happy state. But it's a bitter reflection to me, Mr Elliott, bitter indeed, that our government cares nothing for our sufferings. They bring in foreign goods at prices that will ruin us! French silk! Indian muslins! Aye, even from the heathen East it comes, cheap, poor cloth, not half so fine as ours. And who is growing rich on all that? Not the poor heathen weavers, I'll be bound. No, it's the same the world over, the agents, the merchants, yes, they're the ones! You know how they say,

'Tis strange the agents live so well
Or take such very hearty slices
Since every weaver here can tell
Their only aim is breaking prices

'Breaking prices! That's it, Mr Elliott, breaking prices!'

Mr Elliot, only half listening, watched Mr Armstrong take up his hat from the floor beside the bed. The visit was coming to an end. Mr Armstrong laid his hand on Isaiah's thin shoulder.

'She's to eat, mind. She's to rest and eat. I'll call again tomorrow. She'll soon be right again. But she needs to be warmer than this! Feel her hands, Mr Dunbar! She'll take a fever in this cold!'

Mr Elliott, seeing his chance, cleared his throat and bent awkwardly to untie Aggie's remaining bundle.

'I beg you will accept – that is – I have been asked to pass on . . . ' he stopped, unable to meet Isobel's stony eyes. Mr Armstrong removed the beautiful soft quilt from his friend's arms and laid it over Isobel's emaciated form.

'You are not taking it for yourself, Mrs Dunbar,' he said, and the gentleness in his voice brought a lump to Mr Elliott's throat, 'but because if you do allow yourself to sicken further, and to die, you will leave two motherless children defenceless in this world. Your first duty is to them. You are accepting this quilt for their sake, not for your own.'

Isobel's eyes closed wearily as she permitted herself to relax.

'Yes,' she breathed in a faint whisper, and Mr Elliott could almost see the delicious warmth that had begun to flood through the fingers that had drawn the quilt up to her neck.

Out once more in the street, the two ministers stood for a moment, bracing themselves for the walk through dismal, stinking lanes that lay between them and the haven of the manse.

'Peter, you managed so well,' burst out Mr Elliott. 'You understand these people, better, I fear, than ever I will.'

Mr Armstrong took his friend by the elbow and steered him off into the night.

'As to that, I hope I am mistaken. I hope I have understood wrong in this case. Isobel will recover just now if she's provided with food and kept warm, and we can see to that. But I believe her heart to be affected. She'll not live to make old bones. Those wee girls will be motherless before they're grown, I've no doubt of it.'

He was not to know that Jessie had opened the door a crack to watch the marvellous visitors depart and that his words, half understood, had buried themselves deep in her mind as she scampered back to the cramped box bed to snuggle under the wondrous quilt beside her mother's peacefully sleeping form.

Chapter Five

1

Calcutta
6th November 1836

Dearest Sister,

I write with the best and happiest of news for our son was born a week ago today. We have named him Adam, and truly I think he deserves it for he is the first man to us all here. Bessie (we must call her 'Baby' no longer) loves him fondly, and hangs over his little white cot dangling her own old rattle to amuse him, but to no avail for Adam stares at her with great solemnity for all the world like his papa staring at a shipment of muslins.

You would not believe, indeed, how like his father he is. The resemblance is quite strange. Even Hector remarks upon it and I believe that little Adam has stolen Papa's heart in a new way, for Hector, as you know, is not the man to take much heed of babies. But Adam is so strong and so lusty and so black-haired and cries so loud, I believe Hector sees himself in the cradle again, and so he might.

I am relieved indeed that the birth this time passed off so quick and well (though it is ever a frightening and painful business) that I am hardly pulled down at all, and feel that in one or two weeks I shall be quite my old self again. I shall need all my strength then, however, for Hector has decided that our increased family (and his own increasing consequence!) merits a larger residence and we are to remove to a new bungalow recently built in a fine part of town in, I am assured, a salubrious position and with a superior system of drainage. It already looks very handsome though scarce finished yet. The ceilings of the principal rooms are quite twenty feet high, and besides the drawing room and dining room there is a study for Hector, numerous serving rooms and several good bedrooms and dressing rooms, the whole surrounded by a handsome and ample verandah, very necessary in this climate. We will have to increase our establishment and must have,

I believe, quite thirty or forty servants, though that is not at all out of the way here, and you must not believe that we are at all extravagant!

Bessie pulls me by the sleeve to send her love to Aunt Heriot and her big brother and sister, who are great heroes with her, though she has never yet seen them. She comes on very fast, and is a little like Teddy at that age, forever in a day dream of her own.

I am so happy to hear your good reports of my two great children. Justina writes me a very proper letter, spelled quite right too, though of course it should be, for I forget she is now almost sixteen years of age! Pray have her likeness taken, dearest Aggie, and charge it to Hector's account, for I would dearly love to see how she looks in her first grown-up dresses! Teddy too seems in good heart, though he writes only of mosses and caterpillars.

Dear, good, kind Aggie, how can I ever repay you for your great goodness to my children? I should say our children, for you have indeed been a true mother to them, more than I.

Hector is as ever at his godowns, but sends, I am sure, his affectionate regards, as I do my love.

Fanny

Edinburgh
June 1837

Dearest Mama and Papa,

I do hope that you and dearest Bessie and Baby are well, as we are here. We are all in a bother as Aunt has taken rooms in North Berwick for the whole of July as she has been told that the air will improve Teddy, who, she fears, will fall into a consumption as he is so thin and has grown so tall this year. But of course she has written to you on this already.

I am sure there is nothing at all wrong with Teddy for he makes as much noise and mess as ever, and I am sure I do not wish to go to North Berwick for it is devoid of all interesting company and Ellie is to stay all summer long in Edinburgh. For myself, a daily walk in Princes Street Gardens is all the fresh air I require and keeps me in perfect health.

You must know that I have persuaded Aunt Heriot at last to purchase a key to the gardens and I am so glad she has done so for all the fashionable people walk there now. It has quite overtaken the Meadows. As we were going along yesterday Ellie introduced me to Lady Craig, who is related to the sister-in-law of Ellie's papa, whose own cousin is a lord. So you see, though the key cost three guineas it was not money ill-spent.

I was wearing my best morning gown with the big puffed sleeves

I wrote of to you before, and had besides a new muslin frill and was very thankful I had not worn my old grey gown. Lady Craig was very gracious and said we were bonny young ladies and she hoped she would meet us again.

Please kiss the little ones for me and remind them of their loving sister,

and your affectionate daughter,
Justina

P.S. Aunt desires me to ask for Bessie's foot size as she is working a pair of velvet slippers for her. She will add to it an extra size to allow for growth.

Paisley
January 1838

Dear Mr Elliott,

I received yours this day and was glad to hear of your welfare. We are all well, thank God, though Meg has just got out of the pox. She is on the better way now. Your friend Mr Armstrong is removing to Glasgow as I doubt not he has already informed you. He will be sorely missed by the folk of Paisley for he has been well liked for his charity and his sermons.

Trade is good and you will not find us again in the sorry state when last you visited. There are some as may not do well from the great demand for Paisley wares but they are not the skilled men, though the Irish are coming in too many for our prosperity. I am glad to say my health keeps up well and the bad time after the cholera is all forgot as we are back again in our old good house in Castle Street and the loom is not idle more than seven hours out of the twenty-four, though we do not forget how quick good fortune can turn to ill.

You ask for news of Mrs Dunbar. She is quite well, I am sure, and makes no complaint, and the girls grow fast. Meg is now twelve years old and setting her stitches well. Jessie is six and minds her book.

As you request I will convey your greetings to your old friends of the connection, and hoping this finds you in good health and spirits, I remain, sir,

Your obedient
Isaiah Dunbar

Paisley
March 1838

Dear Brother,

Your last was wrote in such haste I could hardly decipher your meaning, but I beg you will not concern yourself unduly. Your Jem came safe enough to me last evening, and though he does not talk overmuch I understood that he had taken great offence and had thought to run away to sea. I am so glad he came to me first, as you guessed he might. He was in great indignation over the money for he says he never was a thief and he never knew where you kept your savings and so could not have taken a penny from them. I told him you had wrote to me that you found the sovereign after all, rolled under the bed, and so had accused him wrongly. He was sorry for the hard words he spoke and I truly believe he is wishful to come home and is giving up his idea of the sea. I spoke to him of his chances and what he could do at home, but all he would say was he never wished to work in a weaving shop, and he is not minded to be a drawboy any more, and if he is driven to it he will bolt again. I do not believe him to be a wicked boy, Joseph, only headstrong, and he is but fifteen years old after all. He says he likes to be out of doors and not cooped up in a cramped, dark place. Is there not some shepherding work to be had near home, for I do believe it might suit him best?

I have spoken to the boy of his mother, and his duty to her, and he says her weakness is so much greater and she cannot stand to have him near her for she is so easily tired. I am sorry Eliza's health is so poor and hope she will not long be so enfeebled.

Jem says he will go home tomorrow and so I promised to write so that you will not greet him in anger.

Please write me if you find a good place for him, and not in the weaving trade.

Your loving sister,
Isobel

P.S. He is a good boy, I am sure of it. Do not forget that you ran away yourself when you were much younger, and were fighting Boney at his age. Do not be too hard on him, brother.

Ayr
March 1838

Dear Sister,

Jem came home safe yesterday, and I was mindful of your advice and did not speak harshly to him except to remind him of his duty to honour his father and his mother. I am glad that the boy came to you and thank you for looking after him so well. I do not know what you have said to him but he appears thoughtful and chastened in his demeanour. I have told him I would not make him stay in the loomshop. He has been drawboy these three years or more and no master has been satisfied with him. I believe you are right, that it is better to let him follow his natural inclinations. I have mentioned the matter to Mr Turnbull, my master. He does not have a place for a shepherd, but he will speak to Lord Eglinton's steward. Lord Eglinton has enclosed a good deal of land hereabouts for sheep and Mr Turnbull says he may have a place for a strong lad.

I am glad to hear from your husband's last that you are going on in a good way. You will not forget the bad times after the cholera, I am sure, and I thank the Lord for his goodness that you have bread on your table and plenty in your house again. When you can, put a little by, week by week, as I do in my 'colonial fund'.

Your affectionate brother,
Joseph

Edinburgh
June 1838

Dear Father

I received your letter with great interest and was most fascinated to learn of your expedition to Assam with Mama. My own memories of India are now so faint I can recall only little of our bungalow and the garden, though I do remember a great pot that stood upon the steps leading up to the verandah with a large flowering bush that grew in it, which our gardener watered every evening, for I used to wait till our ayah's back was turned and make mud pies in the softened soil.

I am truly grateful for the honour you do me of looking forward to my joining you in the business, and I am only afraid that I may after all not measure up to your expectations. My career at the High School has, as you remarked, now come to an end, and I am glad to report to you, dear Father, that I have been awarded a gold medal for my studies in Greek and Natural History. It is this which gives me courage to formulate my request, for you will see that I have worked hard and will continue to do so.

Dearest Papa, I would be so glad if I could postpone my coming to India for a few years yet and take up my studies once more at the university. My tutor, Mr Laws, has been so kind as to assure me that my work at Edinburgh High School has indicated a good career at the university and my own inclination to study further has made me earnestly desire to study under Professor Jamieson (can he be a family connection, I wonder?) who holds classes in Natural History at the Faculty of Medicine. He has already encouraged me to inscribe my name for the first year of studies, and that I have done so will not, I hope, lead to your displeasure, as there has not been time to seek permission from you in Calcutta before the closing date required by the university.

I do hope you will look favourably upon this request, dear Papa, and beg you to pass on my affectionate salutes to Mama and the little ones.

Your respectful son,
Edward

Dear Brother,

I write in haste to add a postscript to Teddy's letter. I do believe it is best for him to remain in Edinburgh for the time being as I am not quite happy about his lungs. Although it is June he still has not altogether thrown off the cough that clung to him all winter, and Dr Brown agrees with me that the climate of India could only be injurious to his health.

The dear boy has covered himself with glory at the High School and does, I believe, most earnestly wish to try his wings in a wider scientific sphere and I am afraid that to deny him the occasion to do so will lead to great dissatisfaction. Do not, I beg you, consider his remaining with me an obstacle. You know how devoted I am to both my nephew and niece.

I greatly look forward to receiving your decision on this matter, and, in expectation of your complaisant answer, remain, my dear Hector,

your affectionate sister,
Aggie

Calcutta
September 1838

My dear Edward,

I will not conceal from you my disappointment in hearing that you wish to defer the start of your career in Hector Jamieson and Sons. It is the dearest wish of my heart to see both yourself and your brother Adam (who bids fair to become a fine businessman by the charm he throws over us all) working beside me in our offices. However, I see that your glorious career at school (on which I must and do congratulate you) has turned your head towards less practical matters, and I believe I must succumb to the wishes of yourself and the pleas of your aunt and allow you a time of study at the university.

I own it has been a great sorrow to me that we have been apart for the large part of your youth, as I feel sadly we are almost strangers. Now that you have reached manhood I feel sure that we can look forward to that interesting friendship so dear between father and son. It is not, I am sad to say, a bond which I could enjoy with my own father, who died before I reached mature years, so it is all the more to be looked forward to. I had hoped very much to see you soon in the bosom of your family here in Calcutta, but I suppose I must acquiesce in the delay.

Your aunt writes with some anxiety about your constitution. She has, of course, suffered from a painful complaint all her life and so is perhaps liable to look for sickness where there is none. Do not, I beg of you Edward, allow her to turn yours into a hypochondriacal nature, forever concerned with flannel underwear, overheated systems, palpitations and such nonsense. I can honestly say that I have never suffered a day's ill health in my life. I do not even know what it is to have the headache (save on some youthful occasions when I had imbibed too freely!) and I put it all down to a good hearty diet with plenty of red meat, a great deal of healthful exercise of the most vigorous kind, such as climbing, running, sparring and the like. You will find swimming in the sea even at the coldest times of the year most invigorating. I am sure you have too much sense to let your Aunt mollycoddle you.

Your mother sends you her fondest love, as also do I, and I add to it

the blessing of
your loving Father

P.S. I cannot tell whether or not your Professor Jamieson is a family connection for I have never heard of the fellow.

Calcutta
27th February 1839

My dearest Aggie,

I write in such agitation as I am sure you will hardly be able to read this scrawl. I have the most dreadful, the saddest news to break to you, for yesterday morning, about 5 o'clock, my darling angel Adam breathed his last. He was not yet three years old!

He had played so happily as usual with his little hobbyhorse until only on Tuesday, but as evening came he looked flushed and feverish. I sent at once for the doctor, who diagnosed a dysentery and applied leeches. His fever was so bad and so sudden! We covered his poor little abdomen and aching head with cold towels but the little darling's sufferings were so horrible. He started up and cried out 'Mama!' and then 'Papa!' Hector sat with him all through the night.

On Wednesday he seemed a little better, and took some gruel and milk-and-water. But our reviving hopes were utterly dashed, for on Wednesday night the fever came on even stronger, and he was raving, 'Oh, Bessie, where's my hobby horse? Lucky! Sing, Lucky!' and more in Hindustani. Towards dawn the crisis came and I held him in my arms as he breathed his last.

Hector is almost distracted, he paces up and down on the verandah and does not go to his office. He was never so when poor little James was taken from us, but he had such a special love for darling Adam, and I did too. Oh, the anguish of it, dearest Aggie, to see my darling's cot empty and to listen in vain for his laughter in the morning! I suppose I must be thankful that God has spared him perhaps, from a life of suffering, who knows, but to take such a merry, blessed little soul – at least I must thank God he will never know such grief as mine.

6 o'clock

I open this letter to add yet more to your grief, for my sweet little Bessie now sickens with the fever. She has but now gone off to sleep and is lying so hot and restless I hardly dare send the quill across the paper for fear the scratching will rouse her. I will fumigate these pages and send them by tomorrow's early mail, with whatever news that God may send to follow by the next.

In haste and deepest sorrow
your own sister,
Fanny

P.S. Break the news as gently as may be to Justina and Teddy who, though they never saw their brother, yet sent him so many loving messages that I am sure this news will afflict them greatly.

Calcutta
6th March 1839

Dearest Aggie,

You will, I know, as well as Teddy and Justina, be waiting eagerly for news and oh! how I wish I could, by telling you it was good, make it so! But I cannot. Indeed, I can hardly bear to write of it, for after days of suffering and struggling, my dearest little darling was carried off and we laid her poor little body beside her two brothers on Friday last.

I have not been able to write before, being so wholly distraught with grief. Our great house now seems so strange and empty, its lofty rooms echoing sadly to nothing more than the plaintive cry of darling Bessie's talking bird. I have not yet been able to enter the sad, deserted nursery, even the sight of the empty chairs at the breakfast table being enough to overcome me. It is strange how much more nearly the loss of these little ones has affected me than the sad death of poor little James, years ago. Perhaps with these younger ones I have been a less giddy mother, being older, and it is certain that they occupied more of my time and my cares than ever did Justina and Teddy at their age.

Oh, Aggie, now that my babies are gone, my grown up children are the dearest objects of my life, and I long to clasp them once more in my arms! I feel I can no longer stay here, where every sight and sound recalls my sad loss. Oh cruel, cruel India! I have myself such an excellent constitution and have never suffered, but there seem to be more fevers than usual of late, and the newspapers of Calcutta are full of the saddest notices, taking many columns. So many little ones gone! And young ones in their prime! How glad I am that dearest Teddy did not obey his father's wishes and come here (though Hector was in a great rage about it at the time) for only think if he had been lost too!

I long for Edinburgh and my old home, the delicate colours and sharp air of Scotland. Oh, how tired I am of the endless clamour, the gaudy brilliance and the sickly perfumes of the East! For so long it has thrilled and delighted me but now it only reminds me of the happiness that is over.

You, my dearest Aggie, who have been a mother to two of my children, will, I know, share with me in this deepest of all sorrows, and remember in your prayers,

your despairing
Fanny

Calcutta
August 1839

My dear Sister,

I write to inform you that we have at last settled upon a date for our return from India. We are embarking from Calcutta on board the 'Emily' on the 2nd November and are due in Tilbury in the new year. I had until a month ago settled only upon a short visit to Europe, but our decision is now made to quit India entirely and to remove with all our effects to our home climes. Fanny, I regret to say, is not yet herself, though she has plucked up wonderfully since the sad loss of our little ones, but she is of such an energetic and sanguine nature that she does not long remain moping and inactive. She has conceived such an urgent and unanswerable desire to leave India for ever that I have had to bow to it, not unwillingly, however, for I have a most capable agent in charge of my affairs here, and have indeed been for some time considering the advantages of opening an office in London to further my business interests at that end.

I have, therefore, taken the lease of a very good house at Enfield, near London. It is the family home of a fellow merchant at present residing in Calcutta, and, after a visit to you and to our old haunts in Edinburgh, Fanny and I will be taking up residence there in the early part of next year.

I owe you too much, my dear sister, to ask any more favours of you, but I do beg that you will give us the pleasure of your company at Enfield. We will, of course, be hoping to introduce Justina a little into society, in which, I flatter myself, I can now take my place, as my endeavours to make a fortune in India have not been entirely unsuccessful. If she is only half as pretty as her mama was at her age, I make no doubt she will conquer many hearts. Of Edward we must talk further. You know, of course, that I wish him to cease postponing the issue and to take his rightful place by my side in the business, but as his letters refer only to such absurdities as his 'Andromeda polifolia' and his 'Erica ciliaris' (no more nor less, I believe, than varieties of heather, which he has, not to my astonishment, discovered on his wanderings about the Pentland Hills), I fear I may have to exert the authority of a father to bring him to a sense of his duty.

I will, of course, my dear sister, acquaint you with any further developments in our arrangements, and I take this opportunity to inform you once again how deeply in your debt Fanny and I believe ourselves to be. It is my fervent hope that, relieved of your responsibilities, in our new family home in Enfield, you will be able to enjoy, at last, some respite from your years of devotion, where I assure you, you will enjoy the warmest gratitude

of your respectful brother,
Hector

Chapter Six *Edinburgh, 1840*

1

'So you see, my dear Edward, the chances of naturalising such a tender subject, even in the most sheltered spot of these gardens, are slim indeed.'

The speaker, a portly man of uncertain years, from whose rubicund nose a pince-nez constantly threatened to fall, smiled up at his companion, a tall, slender, gangling youth, whose deep interest in the subject was betrayed by his tendency to stumble unseeing over obstacles in his path and by the enthusiastic gestures of his long thin arms, which narrowly missed slicing off the buds of more than one rare azalea.

'No, but sir, Mr Jamieson,' said Edward, 'you yourself explained just now in your lecture that by the artificial regulation of heat and light and a constant flow of humidity, we can simulate conditions of the hottest jungles upon earth.'

Professor Jamieson seemed to lose interest in the subject. He stopped in a spot conveniently sheltered from the sharp east wind by one of the exotic trees in which the Botanical Gardens abounded, and withdrew a cracked clay pipe from an interior pocket. As he stuffed it with tobacco and felt for his box of lucifers, he regarded Edward steadily through his pince-nez, till that youth, embarrassed, turned and looked away down an avenue of young trees. When the pipe was drawing to his satisfaction, Professor Jamieson walked on and Edward followed him, shooting sidelong glances at his teacher. The professor's pipe-smoking was a cause of great mirth among his irreverent students, for his parsimony was well known. Reluctant to spend good money on new pipes, he would re-use his old ones even when the stems were broken, and as they grew shorter and shorter, his smoking grew more and more dangerous so that he had even, on occasion, been known to set light to his whiskers.

'I wonder now, Edward, have you thought of what you wish to do when you have completed your course of studies?'

'Yes, sir. That is, I would like most of all to continue at the university, employed in some branch of botanical research, but . . . '

'So you've thought of that already? Excellent. I had hoped you were enthusiastic enough to continue. I have already put your name forward in connection with a possible appointment. You have the makings of an excellent scientist, sir. An excellent scientist.'

A blush mounted Edward's stem-like neck and suffused his open, unguarded face.

'Thank you, thank you indeed, sir,' he stammered, 'but . . . '

'But what, man? Surely there can be no obstacle?'

'My father, sir, is hourly expected home from India. I have not seen him since I was a small child. He has built up a great – I mean, I believe he has large commercial interests. He wants me to – I am his only son, sir.'

Professor Jamieson frowned and the pince-nez, finally dislodged, fell the length of the cord and bounced against his waistcoat.

'Ah, my boy, you need say no more. I understand perfectly. It's a shame, a great shame. I suppose there is no possibility . . . ? But no, it is a splendid opportunity for you, wealth, travel, responsibility. And yet, are you perhaps quite suited to . . . ?'

'No!' burst out Edward, threatening with his vehemence to decapitate a nascent ceanothus. 'I am quite sure I am unfit for a commercial life, sir, as I have never cared for muslin or calico or such things. I cannot look forward to the drudgery of the counting house and the company of clerks after the interest and freedom of — oh, sir, if you could only speak to my father, tell him of my ambitions, of my skills and talents even!'

'No, no.' Professor Jamieson's pipe, ignored for too long by its owner, had gone out, and he stuffed it back into a hidden recess in his clothing. 'It's your battle, my dear Edward, and you must fight it alone. But do not disappoint your father, my boy. Remember, while he has been toiling long years in all the heat and inconvenience of India, building up his empire, he has no doubt been planning and thinking chiefly of you and your welfare.'

Edward's mood as he made his way home up the unsympathetic stone pavements of Leith Walk was hardly cheerful. His heart pounded at the delightful prospect of seeing his beautiful, exciting, perfumed mother, so different from poor dear Aunt Heriot. From her he expected nothing but tenderness, sympathy and the old careless gaiety he remembered so well. But his father – the very thought of that distant, martial figure made his pulses race with fright. To the infant Teddy he had been a giant, in fact as well as in imagination, for Edward had reached only half-way up his thighs. His father had been peremptory, impatient of weakness, demanding instant obedience. And yet there had been times (Edward could dimly remember them) when Papa had crawled on the floor with Edward laughing uproariously upon his back, playing elephants, hunting a shrieking Justina, who, in delicious terror, had hidden herself among Mama's skirts.

Of course, that was all old history now. It was no longer a question of Papa and little Teddy, but Hector Jamieson and Son, partners in a great commercial enterprise. The professor was right, thought Edward. He could not disappoint his father. He would have to keep his botanical interests for his leisure time. Perhaps one day when he had proved himself in the business, he could take the subject up again.

He turned into George Street and was rooted to the spot. A yellow-bodied chaise stood outside his aunt's house. It was piled high on top with a multitude of trunks and boxes. Edward saw again, in his mind's eye, the draughty, dusty vehicle in which, fourteen years ago, he and his sister had shivered in the dark and cold, too frightened to follow Mama into the big, forbidding house.

A man who had been paying off the postillion turned, and with a lurch of his heart Edward knew it was his father. Surely, though, he was a much smaller man than his father had been? Unconsciously, Edward straightened up to his full height. I shall be able to look down on him, he thought with satisfaction. He took a few steps forward, unsure of how to approach. Hector turned. His face lit up with recognition, the full red mouth opened in a smile over the strong white teeth, and he started down the road towards Edward. A thrill of joy, so sharp that it almost hurt, pierced Edward's vulnerable heart. He loves me! He remembers me! We will be friends! was all he had time to think, for a burly figure rushed past him and flung itself into Hector's embrace.

'Nigel! Nigel Farquarson, by all that's wonderful! You old rascal, it's a joy to see your face again. We have but this moment alighted from the coach! I've not even stepped into the house yet! And to see you straight off! It's a great welcome home, it is that!'

'Hector! Man, it's wonderful to see you. Come, let's to the tavern and drink to your return!'

'Hold on, Nigel, I haven't seen my son and daughter, or paid my respects to Miss Heriot. The tavern will have to wait.'

'Oh aye, of course, of course. Miss Heriot's ever the same, a good body. Your girl's a bonny wee thing and no mistake, as neat as a pin and as fond of a title as your great English ladies. She'll catch her lord, I doubt not, before she's done. You've a fine son too, Hector, a clever lad. A mite too timorous and fond of his books, maybe.'

'Aye, Nigel, so I've heard. I've come home to make a man of him.'

Edward, head high, marched straight up to the two men, passed them without a glance, and went trembling on down the street, unnoticed by his father.

'I'll go to the tavern myself,' he muttered, 'and take a drink and be late for supper and put Aunt in a fuss. That'll teach them who's a man and who is not.'

He turned the corner into Frederick Street and almost collided with Jeanie, whose old arms were straining under the weight of a basket laden with provisions.

'Master Teddy? Oh, aye, 'tis you indeed, now I look close. And it's a fine thing I've caught you, for you can carry this load for me, and your ma and pa are just now come home, and your ma dying for a sight of you. And to think I might have missed you! The house all in a bother and Mrs Fergus with not a thing to give them for supper and they with their fine foreign ways, used to all they hordes of heathen servants being so rich and all as they are now. And when I think of yon black-headed great daftie coming after Mistress Fanny – but there, it's all long since awa now, and he's not the one to bear a grudge for the poor welcome he once got from me, for he comes straight out with a great laugh.

' "Ho, 'tis Jeanie," he says. "Well, well, Jeanie, you're single yet, I see?"

' "Aye," says I, "and I'll not give up my single life for all the double ones I ever saw," and he laughs right out in that impudent way of his, tossing his black curls about.

' "Where's yon son of mine?" he says. "Where's ma wee Teddy?"

' "He's nane so wee sir," says I, "and like to surprise you yet, for he's a great big handsome laddy and the first genius this family's seen since I've been in service to it these last fifty years and more." '

'Och, Jeanie, you're a grand soul,' said Edward, his mood shifting again, and he astonished himself as much as her by kissing her roundly on her withered cheek. Suddenly he could wait not a moment longer to see his parents. He thrust the basket back into Jeanie's arms, sprinted up George Street and pounded on the knocker of the front door, which had but a minute earlier closed behind his father.

It opened at once, and Hector and Edward stood face to face.

'My boy,' said Hector, and Edward's heart burst with relief as he heard the break in his father's voice and felt the muscular arms tremble as they closed round him. 'My son.' At that moment, as his father's unruly black hair tickled his cheek, Edward's ambition to succeed Professor Jamieson with another of his own name in the Chair of Botany faded and was gone. His father, after all, loved him. He would not let his father down.

Hector stood back, and holding Edward at arm's length scrutinised his son's face. Edward, nervous again and dreading criticism, felt his dignity shrivel and his muscles shrink but he stood his ground and looked his father squarely in the face. In doing so he realised with surprise that Hector was as nervous as he, shy even, and that the direct brown eyes, so used to obedience, were asking for approval as well.

Again, Hector was the first to move. He put one arm around Edward's shoulders and drew him towards the stairs.

'Come up and see your mother,' he said, then putting his mouth close to Edward's ear he whispered, 'and don't be surprised if she starts to squawk. She's a remarkable woman, the best in the world, in fact, but you know what females are!' and digging his son in the ribs, he winked at him.

Edward, taken aback by this man-to-man camaraderie, so different from the severity he had feared, and at the same time gratified and embarrassed by his father's assumption that he was well versed in the ways of women, could do no more than blush and stammer till they reached the door of the drawing room.

He then had cause to be grateful to Hector for his warning for Fanny, looking thin and pale and quite unlike her old careless light-hearted self, no sooner saw him than she jumped up from the low chair by the fire where she had been holding Justina's hands in her own, and burst out crying. As Edward went forward into her embrace, Hector stood and watched from the door of the room, seeing not this lanky over-sensitive stripling, whom he barely remembered as a child, but Adam as he would have been at eighteen years old, bold, black-haired and dashing. He stifled a sigh, and went forward towards his family saying cheerfully, 'Well, the Jamiesons are reunited at last and I'll see to it that we're never parted again.'

Chapter Seven *Enfield, 1840*

1

The branches of the great beech tree swayed gently in the breeze that fanned the cheeks of the two ladies who sat underneath it, their dresses forming islands of frothy white muslin in the cool green shade. Fanny, accustomed to an afternoon siesta, dozed over her book. She had kicked off her slippers and her feet rested on a footstool, placed in front of her cushioned seat by an attentive footman. She felt entitled to her rest, for after an early luncheon Justina had urged her to drive about the hot and dusty lanes of Middlesex from one large house to another, leaving three cards in the hands of each stately butler, a ceremony which Fanny found boring and exhausting but which her daughter, with her passion for correctness and formality, would not allow her to neglect.

In spite of the sultry heat, Justina resisted sleep. She sat upright on her chair, snipping, stitching and threading needles with brightly coloured silk. She had, on only her third Sunday attendance at Enfield Parish Church, received the most gratifying attentions from Lady Dunstable, widow of an eminent baronet, whose excellent breeding, long family history and far-reaching aristocratic connections, along with a certain natural hauteur, had made her the most notable personage in the society of the immediate neighbourhood. Lady Dunstable, unbending in the most remarkable manner to the unknown daughter of a mere merchant, had said, 'Ah, Miss Jamieson, I am always on the search for clever young fingers, as I have no doubt yours are. Our bazaar, you know, raises much needed money for the poor, and I am sure you will be able to help us with some fine embroidery or fancy work. Can I persuade you to join us on the day to sell our small endeavours, if your mama will allow?'

Justina, dazzled by this condescension, and conscious of the gratifyingly jealous gasps of the Misses Cobley who, on an afternoon call only the day before, had regaled her with stories of Lady Dunstable's legendary pride, would have been less pleased if she had overheard the noble lady's remarks to her thirty-year-old son, the twelfth baronet, as their phaeton clattered away from the lych gate at a smart trot.

'The father's a nabob, Andrew. There's no doubt about it. Letty Marchmont's brother in Bengal assured her that his fortune is fabulous, and likely to increase. Vulgar, of course, but the girl's young enough to be trained and looks biddable. There's a chance for you there, if only you will seize it. If you do not manage something of the sort, we will be forced to practise the strictest economies.'

Justina held her work out at arms' length and studied it critically. 'As a present for a gentleman,' her pattern book had said, 'a black satin letter-case is most useful. A cluster of dog roses, embroidered with shaded silks, will make an excellent finish.' Justina had embarked on the article as a suitable present for Papa but Lady Dunstable's invitation had changed all that. She intended her work to outshine the best endeavours of the parish's foremost ladies and for the first time she was grateful for Aunt Heriot's strict tutelage, which had made of her a first-class needlewoman.

A bee, tossed by a gust of breeze out of the heady embrace of a cabbage rose, bumbled past Fanny's chair and Justina, distracted, turned to look at her mother. Fanny's hair, still a fine pale blonde, was escaping in wayward curls from under her lace cap and her bustle was bunched awkwardly to one side. Justina looked away with displeasure. Her mother, so long admired from afar, had proved to be a disappointment to her. Mama lacked refinement. She had been at first subdued on her return from India, still bowed under the weight of tragedy, but setting up house in Enfield, and the visits and parties that had ensued, had quite revived her spirits. She had become noisily cheerful, unrestrained, careless of what people might think. She did not notice when her bonnet was askew. She laughed too much. She did not enquire about people's birth and breeding before she gave them her friendship. She preferred to have jolly, cheerful people about her, she said, than bores with long noses and long names. Justina sighed and plunged her needle into the heart of a budding rose.

In the distance a door opened and across the shimmering expanse of close-mown grass that separated the old beech from the terrace running along the side of the house Justina saw three figures approaching. The first, a stiff, small woman in a black gown, was undoubtedly Aunt Heriot. The last, a dignified personage carrying a jug and some glasses on a tray, was Jackson, the butler, but the apparition between them, young, good-looking and made to appear even taller than nature had intended by the magnificence of his Guards' uniform, could only be the military son of their nearest neighbours, in whose praise the Misses Cobley had been most eloquent.

'Mama!' hissed Justina. 'Wake up! We have a visitor!'

Fanny snorted, opened her eyes and moved her head lazily. Then, like a cat, she stretched herself delicately, shook the hair from her eyes, resettled herself in her chair so that her bustle regained its correct shape and her skirts were prettily arranged, and smiled. The impact of her smile hit the captain full in the face as he came to a halt beside her chair.

'Why, it must be Captain Blake,' purred Fanny. 'How delightful.'

'Blakeney, ma'am,' corrected the gentleman, bending over Fanny's outstretched hand. Then, ignoring with a visible effort the frankly inviting gleam in Fanny's eyes, he turned to Justina.

'Oh, fair, fair picture! Beauty and virtue combined with charming industry! Present me, ma'am!'

Justina looked startled but Fanny giggled.

'My daughter, sir, is unaccustomed to such flights of fancy.'

'Divine modesty!' The captain smiled down at Justina through handsome moustachios in a way that would have caused the Fanny of twenty years ago to squeal with delight. To her surprise, however, Justina's eyes remained primly set upon her work, and as soon as Captain Blakeney moved aside to accept a glass of lemonade from the tray which Jackson was offering him, she gathered up her work in one deft movement and slipped from her seat.

'Pray take my chair, Aunt,' she said, turning her back on the captain. 'It's the most comfortable, I believe.'

Aggie lowered herself gratefully on to the cushioned seat with much creaking of stays and rustling of starched petticoats.

'Thank you, dearie,' she said.

Her aunt's voice, as always uncompromisingly Scots, sounded positively outlandish now to Justina's sensitive ears. She herself was working on her own speech to such good effect that she would soon be taken by everyone for a perfect English miss. Aggie beckoned to Jackson, who served her a glass of lemonade.

'It's certain sure I need to take the weight off my feet, for there's more to do in yon great rambling rabbit-warren' – she pointed an accusing finger at the façade of Bushy House, whose long graceful windows, capped with white pediments, rose in three tiers from the grey stone terrace – 'than ever mortal woman could accomplish, for all the grand English servants there are about the place.'

Justina's face assumed an expression of distant amusement, as one who smiles indulgently at the prattling of a child, but Fanny laughed out loud.

'Come on now, Aggie, you've not had so much fun for years. You've organised us all down to the last kerchief. I heard you this morning, showing Cook your way of making the strawberries into jam, and telling that saucy little thing – Annie, is it not? – to wear fewer petticoats, and sending Jobson back to the kitchen garden for a better basketful of peas.

Was that before you informed Mrs Jolly of the rent in the drawing-room curtain, or was it afterwards?'

Everyone, including Aggie, laughed and even Jackson's lips could be seen to twitch. It was the general opinion in the servants' hall that while Mrs Jamieson was a soft touch, too easy by half and spoiled by all those heathens she'd had about her for so long, the old Scots tartar was the real thing, and though anyone could see she wasn't used to living in the grand style, no one could tell her much about housekeeping. A terror she was, and no mistake, with eyes in the back of her head, but good-hearted all the same as several youthful housemaids, in possession of Aggie's sovereign remedy for the spots, had reason to testify.

Captain Blakeney, laughing with the others and relishing the informality of his hostess, looked curiously at the sisters. His mother, intrigued by her new neighbours, by the exotic allure of their Indian past and the conflicting accounts circulating in the neighbourhood of their fabulous riches, had urged him to call.

'If they are possible, I'll visit myself. As a matter of fact, Frank, I'll probably call anyway, for I'm bored to death since your sister was married, and there are two young people I believe. The girl is quite pretty, so Maria Dunstable says in that odious patronising way of hers. She, of course, is desperate to catch an heiress for her stick of a son. I'm sure you would only be doing the girl a kindness, Frank dear, if you were to cut him out, for there's not a woman alive who could bear to be made love to by such a prosy old bore.'

Frank Blakeney reflected, as he listened to Aggie's humorous expostulation and Fanny's teasing chatter, that his new neighbours were certainly possible. Miss Jamieson was, as he had expected, no more than a dull, prim miss, scarcely out of the schoolroom and quite unworthy of gallant attentions. But Miss Heriot, with her sharp Scots practicality and dry eccentricities, would delight his mother, and as for Mrs Jamieson, she possessed just the kind of warm, ripe beauty which he himself most admired. He looked forward to a delightful and innocent flirtation with her, which, he knew for sure having noted well the practised flutter of her eyelashes, she would enjoy as much as he would, and which he also felt sure, would cause great annoyance to his fond mama, who was clearly scheming to entrap him into a tedious marriage with the insipid heiress.

Fifteen minutes and no more was the prescribed length of time for a first call and Captain Blakeney did not presume to overstay his welcome. Fanny watched his retreating figure with pleasure, noticing the cut of his scarlet tunic and the powerful stride of his long legs as he made his way across the grass to the stables. Then, suddenly, she came to her senses. This was not India, where in the heady atmosphere of Calcutta she had been free to flirt with any young officer who came her way. It would be fatally easy, she knew, to entrap Justina's suitors in her own coils, a temptation she must in future try hard to resist. This was England, after all, and by all accounts a stricter and more puritanical country than the one she had left twenty years ago. She must accept that she was now a matron with a grown-up daughter to establish. She really must learn to be more dignified.

She turned a little guiltily to Justina, ready to forgo her own interest in the dashing captain in order to encourage her daughter's, but she was astonished to see that Justina, far from watching Captain Blakeney's elegant retreat, was calmly proceeding with her sewing, giving all her attention to a stray thread that needed trimming.

'Upon my word, miss,' said Fanny sharply, 'you're mighty cool when such a handsome young fellow comes to call. Why, when I was your age, and a young officer was about, I . . . '

Aggie gave Fanny a reproving frown, no different from many she had administered to her impetuous younger sister years ago.

'You were very correct, Justina dear,' she said, 'quite the young lady, in fact. I see you've learned well the lesson that Ellie Hamilton's mother was at such pains to teach you.'

'Which lesson, Aunt Heriot?' Justina's head assumed a defensive tilt as her practised ear detected a certain dryness in Aggie's tone.

'Is Captain Blakeney not a fine enough gentleman for the rich Miss Jamieson?' said Aggie, this time with unmistakable irony.

'How can you say such a thing, Aunt?' said Justina, looking flustered. 'It's just that, that . . . '

'What, pray?' said Fanny, sitting upright and staring at her daughter with frank disapproval.

'Well, if you must know,' said Justina desperately, 'Miss Cobley says the Blakeneys are not much thought of in society in Enfield. Why, Mrs Blakeney's father was a poor curate and her sister is married to a nobody, a grocer in the city, and old Mr Blakeney himself . . . '

'Oho!' An angry flush was rising in Fanny's cheeks. 'A nobody, eh? Only a grocer is he? And who do you think you are, madam? Was your grandpa a duke or an earl or a laird even? No, he was not! He made guns for gentlemen in a perfectly ordinary shop, and greatly respected he was, too. But let's not talk about him any more in case the dreadful secret gets out.'

'Oh, Mama!' burst out Justina. 'You don't understand!'

'Of course I understand. You've had your head so stuffed with lords and ladies and all that society nonsense you're ashamed of your own family. We're none of us high and mighty enough for you now, are we? Why, your poor father's nothing but a merchant, even though he has made a fortune, and as for your brother . . . '

Fanny stopped, shocked by her own display of temper. She had tried to ignore the fact but there was no denying it. The daughter she had so looked forward to making her friend had disappointed her. Instead of growing up into a gay, happy young girl in whose youth she had hoped to relive her own, Justina had become a dry, dull creature, concerned only with ranks and titles, caring more for pedigrees than for good, hearty cheer. It's her generation, I suppose, thought Fanny, trying to find excuses. They all seem so earnest and proper and ambitious nowadays. Young people don't seem to know how to enjoy themselves now, as we used to. She sat back in her chair, determined not to provoke a quarrel, and deliberately lowered her voice.

'What is it you want, then, if the likes of Captain Blakeney are not for you? I take it you do wish for a husband?'

'Yes, of course, Mama.' Justina, too, though flushed, was clearly determined to retain her self-control.

'Are you looking for a title, perhaps?'

'Yes.'

The bluntness of Justina's answer shocked Fanny but did not surprise her. She opened her mouth to answer, but faintly from the front of the house came the sound of carriage wheels and horses' hooves crunching on the great circular sweep of gravel that led up to the white pillared portico of the front door.

'Your father and Teddy are home from the city,' she said, and she jumped up from her seat, threw open her parasol and started across the lawn towards the house, glad to leave the conversation behind her.

The hall of the house was pleasantly cool and dim after the glare of the summer afternoon outside. Hector was laying his hat down upon a highly polished mahogany table on which a bowl of full-blown roses, artfully arranged, perfumed the air with their sweet heavy scent.

'Fanny!' Hector's arm went round her waist and he sought her lips for his homecoming kiss, but Fanny put her hands on his chest and pushed him away.

'Ugh! You smell of the city! Fusty offices and unwashed clerks, and tobacco and club-house beef!'

'Mama! How can you!' Edward, half-way up the wide panelled staircase, turned to laugh down at his parents. 'You know he has common tastes and eats nothing but tripe and trotters which he snatches up between one engagement and the next. You'll never make a great man out of him, for all he's a nabob.'

'Grr! Rascal!' Hector flung a glove expertly in Edward's direction, but his undutiful son caught it and, aiming carefully, caused it to land neatly on the Benares brass tray set out for the purpose on the hall table.

'At least I know how to behave like a gentleman, Father,' he mocked, and ran lightly on up the stairs to his room where, delighted to have his day's work behind him, he planned to divest himself of his hated city clothes, don an old tweed jacket and some comfortable breeks and spend a happy hour or two botanising down by the stream where he had already found two remarkable specimens of a rare balsam.

'He seems in spirits,' said Fanny, thankful that at least one of her children was capable of laughter.

'Oh, aye, he's fine. I'll not make a great businessman of him, but he's a good lad for all that,' said Hector, massaging his elbow. 'Lord, how that coach jolts. The road's in a terrible state, though it's quick enough into the city, I'll admit. I was shaken to pieces up Winchmore Hill, the more so as that fine son of yours persuaded Tom Coachman to pass him the reins and teach him to drive the horses. I shall have to invest in a chaise with sounder springs and I can see that young sir will be after me for a sporting curricle in no time at all.'

Looking not at all put out at the idea of indulging any extravagant wish his son might have, Hector pushed open the library door and looked about for the newspaper. He found it at last flung down on a chair, away from its appointed place on the table.

'My little puss has been reading the society columns again, I see,' he said indulgently. 'I never knew a child for such nonsense.'

Fanny's brow creased and she bit at her forefinger.

'Yes,' she said, 'and I really believe, Hector, that it's gone too far. You'll have to speak to her about her ridiculous notions. Why, only this afternoon . . . '

'Nonsense.' Hector, scanning the city columns, barely listened to his wife. 'She's very young, my dear. She'll fall in love just like you did and marry a fine young man, I'm sure of it. And that puts me in mind of something else. Direct Jackson to lay two extra covers at the table tonight. I've invited young Higgs and his friend Mitchell from the bank to dine with us this evening. They're excellent young men, full of fun, ambitious, too, and thoroughly fond of Teddy, laughing at him about his birds and flowers you know, but in a good kind way. I like to see all the young people laugh together and enjoy themselves. It'll bring some pink to Puss's pale little cheeks, bring her out of herself a bit.'

Fanny tossed her head. 'Put her out, more likely,' she said drily. 'Young madam's got her eye on bigger fish than small fry from a counting house, and she won't put herself to the bother of entertaining a pair of city clerks, not even to please her dear papa.'

2

As Hector Jamieson descended the staircase to the expectant hush that hung over the ground floor of his house, he was a happy man. He wandered with unusual lack of purpose from one elegantly furnished room into another. The hectic bustle of the day had been succeeded by an unnatural calm. The sawing and hammering of the carpenter, erecting stands for the vast numbers of vases that lined the ballroom, the toings and froings of gardeners with baskets of flowers to fill them, the stately procession of Jackson and his myrmidons from kitchens to dining room bearing heaped trays of crystal, dazzling white napery and gleaming silver – all this was over and the house was ready for the ball. Only a faint clatter of pans from the kitchens below informed Hector that last-minute preparations were still in progress.

He drew his heavy gold watch (one of the few items he had inherited from his father) from the pocket of his silver brocade waistcoat. The guests would arrive at any moment. Hector turned into the drawing room and surveyed himself in the handsome mirror that ornamented the chimney breast. He could not prevent the smile of triumph and satisfaction that creased his cheeks. He had achieved everything he had set out to do. Fortune, family, good standing in society – all were his. He had returned from India determined to enjoy the fruits of twenty years of unremitting labour, and now, on this evening of Fanny's first grand ball when his pretty daughter was to be formally presented to the society of Middlesex, he was conscious of a deep sense of fulfilment.

He had had some uncomfortable moments in the past year or two. The death of his son Adam had caused him to feel the only passionate grief he had ever known. Fanny's subsequent depression had profoundly disturbed him. He had feared for a while that she would never be herself again. The transfer of his business to a partner in Calcutta had caused him some uneasiness and a real pang of regret. Then, too, the characters of his children had come as a not entirely welcome surprise. Justina, though he took pride in her well-bred manners and girlish prettiness, had nothing of her mother's exuberant charm. Somehow, although he had become sentimentally attached to her, he did not feel that he knew her as a father could expect to know a daughter. And then there was Edward. At the thought of his son, Hector turned away from the mirror and walked over to the long windows that opened out on to the terrace. It was a warm June evening and the scent of honeysuckle wafted into the room from the trellis by the conservatory. The lawn, interrupted only by the one great beech tree, sloped smoothly down to a willow lined stream beyond which a series of lush pastures separated the property from the straggling village of Enfield, from whose cottages the smoke of kitchen fires rose into the setting sun.

I must look about soon and buy a property of my own, thought Hector. It will be of all things what Teddy would like best.

He could not deny that Edward had at first been a greater disappointment even than Justina. For a long time he had not been able to shake off the fancy of Adam's grown-up shadow, underlining every deficiency of his living son. But slowly, Edward had quite won his father's heart. He was so unworldly, so good-hearted, so enthusiastic. He was like a colt unbroken to hard discipline, still full of fits and starts. He was so touchingly dedicated to his scientific pursuits. Hector had reluctantly accepted the fact that Edward was not blessed with his own mercantile genius. But then, with judicious handling and a careful selection of managers to run the business, he would not have to follow too closely in his father's footsteps. He would be rich enough to set up as a country gentleman, living in comfort and security, pursuing his butterflies and herons to his heart's content. It was not what Hector had hoped for but he knew enough of men to bow to the inevitable. There was no use in pushing the boy when his heart was elsewhere. Edward tried hard enough. Hector could not fault him there. But he lacked the passionate drive, the interest in money, the joy of getting the better of lesser men, the delight in taking risks, which was the life blood of the true entrepreneur.

'Hello, Father. Is my necktie straight?'

Hector turned. Edward stood at his elbow. His fair hair was brushed forward over his high forehead. His tight-waisted blue coat was open over a gorgeous pale gold waistcoat, cream-coloured trousers covered his long legs, and the pumps on his restless feet were perfectly clean and shiny. With a shock, Hector recognised for the first time that his son was a good-looking young man, could even be called handsome. His features were expressive and finely chiselled. His shoulders and arms, though slender, showed unexpected muscle under the fine cloth of his new dress coat. His expression, when not studious, could break into a smile of unexpected sweetness and his blue eyes, dancing with excitement as they now were, were disconcertingly like his mother's.

Hector tweaked an end of Edward's necktie into place and looked his son up and down with approval.

'Magnificent, upon my word,' he said. 'You'll break hearts tonight, I've no doubt of it.'

Edward blushed with pleasure. The adoration he felt for his father was in no small part due to the delight he experienced in being treated confidentially, man to man. In all his life he had known nothing like it. To Aunt Heriot he would ever be a little boy, to be wrapped in cotton wool and protected from the east wind. To his professors in Edinburgh he had been but a student, promising perhaps, but definitely no equal. But Hector had never, by look or word, relegated him to childhood. Far from begging him not to risk a tumble from a nervous horse, as Aggie would have done, Hector had assumed that Edward was only too eager to make up for a lamentable lack of equestrian education, and had bought him a spirited hunter with no more than a careless instruction to take a few lessons from Purvis, the head groom, and avoid breaking his neck. On their daily journeys into the city Hector talked to his son as to a respected colleague on such matters as the price of calico in Manchester, the advantages of one method of processing indigo over another, the relative excellence of the Chinese and Indian climates for the production of tea, and the problems of shipping and warehousing posed by the ever more congested docks that served the Pool of London. Edward, nodding and attempting to look wise, was flattered by these conversations, but not particularly edified. Try as he might, he ended up bored and puzzled, and though Hector patiently answered his faltering questions, Edward often felt that a cleverer fellow would not have needed to ask them.

But it was when his father looked sly and confidential and teased him about young ladies that Edward felt most flattered and delightfully confused. For a young man of eighteen years he had been singularly free of interest in females. Indeed, thanks perhaps to too great an exposure to his sister's feminine preoccupations he had avoided girls as much as he could, despising their gigglings and whisperings, their silly panics at the sight of a spider and their equally silly ecstasies over a common overblown rose. But when Hector spoke of women Edward saw a new world opening up before him, a world in which men were men, forthright, commanding, reassuring, and in which women, far from treating him as a little boy, as Aunt Heriot and Justina had always done, would revere and respect him, look up to him, obey him and seek to please him in every way. Edward did not quite see how he would ever be able to step into this role, but he watched his father with his mother, and though he often suspected that Mama was more managing and less compliant than Father fondly believed, he pushed these thoughts to the back of his mind and was content to share such crumbs of male authority as his father occasionally dropped in his path.

The orchestra had arrived and through the open windows of the ballroom, from which the green silk curtains were looped back, came a medley of discordant notes from the musicians tuning their instruments. The sound sent a wave of excitement through Edward's slim body.

'Where's Mama, and Justy? Aren't they down yet? They'll be late!'

'Your aunt insists on seeing to their final toilet herself. I heard her. She said, "Ye'll appear like decent Christians if I have anything to say in the matter, and not like these English scarlet women of Babylon." '

Edward burst out laughing.

'I can just hear her! And of course she'll be in a plain black gown as usual. I'll be surprised if she's not taken for the housekeeper and asked to provide second helpings from the jellies.'

Hector pretended to look severe.

'She's a grand woman, son, and don't you forget it. Mind, you should have seen her face when she caught me kissing your mama before we ran off together. Thunder! Aye, and lightning, too.'

Still laughing, Hector and Edward went out into the hall and were in time to see Fanny and Justina, curled, frilled, beribboned and scented from nodding curls to shining slippers, float down the staircase in twin clouds of rustling silk.

'My dear!' Hector started forward, his arms outstretched, but whether towards his wife or his daughter even he seemed undecided. In spite of the eighteen years that separated them it was indeed impossible to say which of them presented the most compelling appearance. Fanny's was without doubt the loveliest face but Justina's was certainly the prettiest dress. Cut low across the bosom, her neck and shoulders rose smoothly above the white material, her skin seductively soft and covered with the bloom of youth and health. Her waist, tightlaced to a mere eighteen inches, was encircled by a sash of delicate shell-pink satin, below which her ivory silk skirts, decorated with embroidered wreaths of palest pink roses, billowed out in a soft ball about her, upheld by an invisible mass of petticoats. Her fair hair, parted demurely in the centre, was tied in an arrangement of rosebuds from which her artfully engineered ringlets fell in charming profusion. The importance of the occasion, the consciousness of her own prettiness and the admiration in her father's face added the crowning touch of animation which brought a glow to her skin and a sparkle to her eyes overcoming, for once, the prudery and primness which normally so irritated her brother. Edward was so impressed he actually clapped his hands.

'By Jove, Justy, you look capital!' he said. 'I might even dance with you myself if you ask me nicely.'

Justina ignored him, bent her head sideways with a graceful gesture to offer her cheek to her father's kiss, and tripped into the drawing room, swinging her hips from side to side with quite unaccustomed boldness as she enjoyed the delicious sensation of her first ball gown.

'Well done,' said Hector, offering Fanny his arm. 'Very fine indeed.'

'Are you complimenting me on my own dress or on your daughter's?' said Fanny, looking up at him provocatively from under the fashionable arcade she wore on her hair, which, daringly substituted for the more conventional matron's cap, consisted of no more than three or four wires round which were twined a clever confection of lace and ribbons.

'Can you ask, my dear?' said Hector, pinching her cheek. 'That shade of blue suits you to perfection. I shall be forced to keep an eye on you for the entire evening or young Blakeney will be taking more than his fair share of the dances. You will make poor little Justina jealous, you know, with your shocking flirtations.'

'You're right,' said Fanny seriously, 'and believe me, Hector, I do try to behave, but you know how it is, particularly when it's a case of military uniforms which take a most unfair advantage.'

'I do know how it is, Fanny,' said Hector, 'and if I did not I would either have shot dead half the population of Calcutta, or strangled you, my dear, many years ago, for if you had ever entertained one of your young men seriously, or allowed any of them to—'

'Hector, how *could* you?' Fanny turned a shocked face to her husband and squeezed his arm affectionately. 'If only you knew how many delightful propositions I have turned down for your sake . . . !'

Hector's laughter burst out with a sudden crack.

'My dear, you are a baggage,' he said. 'And now we had better take up our positions to receive our guests for I fancy I hear the sound of the first arrivals.'

3

The ball at Bushy House was all that its guests had expected and more. Even the gentlemen, who had come to assess the wealth and standing of their new neighbour, to look him over and calculate his character and his fortune, were well satisfied. Hector's wealth had assumed legendary proportions in the gossip of the neighbourhood. The notables wished to assure themselves that he was a proper person to receive, neither too vulgar to be exposed to their ladies, nor too proud to be approached for financial support on the numerous local projects on which they were engaged. On the whole they were pleased. Hector's gold watch chain might be a trifle too massive, his waistcoat too loud and his geniality a little too effusive, but his energy and directness were well noted.

'A request for the restoration fund of the church tower might not perhaps be . . . ?' the Reverend Mr Endersleigh murmured into the inclined ear of Sir Horace Harper, as they stood under a showy portrait of their hostess on which the varnish had as yet scarcely had time to dry.

'An excellent idea.' The portly knight bowed to a flock of young ladies who passed by in a giggling mass of ribbons, flowers and feathers, and made a mental note to call on Mr Jamieson at the earliest opportunity before

George Endersleigh could dip his fingers too deep into this promising source of revenue, in order to interest the nabob in Lady Harper's pet scheme for the establishment of a Foundling Hospital in Barnet.

The band struck up. The young ladies were descended upon by a mass of would-be partners and the group scattered as each belle floated off in a pretty swirl of petticoats to tap out on the smooth floor of the ballroom the fashionable rhythm of the polka. Sir Horace frowned. Why was his Letty the one girl to be left unpartnered? He had seen her shake her head at all requests. Surely she could not wish to remain a wallflower? Then his face cleared. He noticed young Edward Jamieson standing uncertainly by the window looking enviously at the dancers, too shy to seek a partner for himself. Sir Horace smiled approvingly as he watched Letty, with an air of innocent hesitancy, move along the wall of the ballroom towards the window, her head turned towards the dancers so that she could not be supposed to see where she was going. He nearly laughed aloud at the start she gave when she collided with the embarrassed Edward, who had attempted in vain to shrink back into the wall to avoid her. He watched with delight as Letty hung her head, looked shy, then provoked, then coy, and finally triumphant as Edward gingerly led her out to join the other dancers.

Women are devils, thought Sir Horace feelingly. The poor fellow never had a chance. He felt a momentary compassion for Edward but suppressed it and went off in high good humour to look for a glass of wine, calculating the size of the settlement that Hector Jamieson would be likely to provide when his son found himself a bride.

The dance over, Edward thankfully led Letty back to the chairs that lined the ballroom. He had painstakingly learned the steps of the waltz, the polka and the country dances which Justina had forced him to practise with her but he had never before been in such close proximity to a young lady – and one, moreover, who clearly regarded him with such a predatory eye. The end of the dance had come as a great relief and he looked about for an excuse to make off for the company of Messrs Higgs and Mitchell, which would, he knew, be a good deal less strenuous.

Miss Letty, however, was a formidable huntress, and she was not to be easily detached from her prey.

'Your garden is so pretty, Mr Jamieson,' she said with a sentimental sigh, rising from her chair and looking out of the window, from which, in the gathering darkness, there was still a partial view of cosseted shrubs and flower beds. 'I am so interested in botanical pursuits.'

'Really?' Edward looked at Miss Harper properly for the first time. Perhaps, after all, there were some females in the world capable of sensible conversation.

'Yes, indeed.' Letty sensed her advantage and pursued it. 'I have such a charming book at home that explains the language of flowers. So pretty, don't you think? And quite historical, too. Red clover, you know, means industry and cowslips are for pensiveness. Mama laughed at me when she saw I carried pinks in my bouquet tonight for their meaning is so very . . . '

She stopped and looked up coquettishly. To her vexation Edward was no longer listening. His eyes had wandered over to a pair of tiresome city clerks who were unmistakably beckoning to him. Letty mentally kicked Harriet Cobley, whose information regarding Edward's interest in flowers had been so misleading. She had wondered at the time if it was not a strange pursuit for a rich young man. She thought quickly. Had not Harriet mentioned birds, too? She would risk it. It was her last chance.

'Are you fond of birds, Mr Jamieson?' She had had no time to think up a more subtle approach to the subject.

Edward brought his eyes reluctantly back to her and nodded. He was not willing to be fooled a second time.

'Ye-es,' he said cautiously.

'Then you must have been most interested to hear of the pair of nightingales who are nesting by the stream beyond your garden.' It was a flash of inspiration.

'Nightingales?' There was no doubt that her ruse had succeeded.

'Yes. Old Jobson your gardener, you know, informed our Peterson of the circumstance. I do believe, do not you, that there is no lovelier sound in all the world than the song of the nightingale?'

'Yes, of course.' Edward was intrigued. 'It's very strange, for Jobson said nothing to me of it, and I have spent some time by the stream listening out for evening birdsong and have never yet heard a nightingale.'

'Perhaps the weather was not fine enough.' Letty was beginning to find the need for spontaneous invention exhausting. 'I believe they sing best on fine nights such as this.'

'Aye, perhaps so,' said Edward politely. With a practised movement, Letty flicked into her hand the fan that dangled from her gloved wrist, opened it, and waved it languorously back and forth in front of her face.

'It's so very warm in here,' she murmured.

'Allow me to fetch you a glass of lemonade?' said Edward, seeing a chance of escape.

'No – that is, thank you very much, but I would prefer to enjoy a moment or two of fresh air. Would you be so kind – perhaps the terrace . . . ?'

There was no help for it. Edward forbore to look towards his friends, who were witnessing his discomfort with unmistakable signs of mirth, and followed his companion with as much good grace as a dog dragged from its bone on the end of a lead.

The evening was so fine and sultry that the air was almost warmer outside than in. Edward passed a gloved finger between his collar and his neck, conscious of the stickiness the heat was engendering, and as he turned his head he caught sight of a figure standing in the shadow of a tree.

'Why – is that you? Yes, it is! Jobson!'

The gardener reluctantly came forward, expecting a rebuke. He had not been able to resist the lure of the music and the sight of the grand company through the windows of the ballroom but he was very much afraid that he had overstepped the mark. Then he recognised Edward and relaxed. Young Mr Jamieson was a nice enough lad, full of questions and knowing most of the answers, too. He and Jobson had spent many hours in discussion over this plant or that, and Jobson had to admit he had learned a thing or two.

'Just the man I need,' said Edward happily. 'Do tell me, where are the nightingales nesting?'

He stepped forward to the edge of the terrace and leant over the lichened stone parapet to talk to the gardener.

'Nightingales, sir? I ain't seen nor heard of no nightingales this year, nor last either come to that.'

'Why, Miss Harper told me that you told Peterson there was a pair nesting down by the stream.'

'Told you that, did she?' Jobson chuckled. 'Aye, maybe she did, but it weren't no nightingales she was wishful to find in the wood, if you take my meaning, sir. Oh, I'm sorry, I'm sure, sir. I didn't mean – goodnight, sir.' And Jobson, aware by the stiffness that had set upon Edward's face that he had gone too far, retreated, and melted into the gloaming along the path that led to his cottage.

Edward turned to find that the terrace was empty. Letty, as soon as Jobson had appeared, had fled the field, and when Edward returned to the ballroom she was twirling about on the arm of Captain Blakeney, who, while hovering near Fanny, had been peremptorily ordered to do his duty.

'For,' said Fanny, 'she looks as if she'd swallowed a fly, and I'm too busy to cheer her up myself.'

Fanny was not exaggerating. She had been delightfully busy for the entire evening. She had the unusual knack of enjoying her own parties, being able, once the preparations had all been made, to stop worrying about the excellence of the supper or the arrangement of the furniture or the correct precedence due to her guests. She radiated excitement and pleasure and it was to this that the undoubted success of the evening was due. She had the happy skill of putting everyone at their ease. She was kind and complimentary to young girls in the throes of shyness, she was good-humoured and confiding with matrons of her own age, she was attentive to the weakness of the old. She flattered and cajoled men of middle age, who thought she was 'an extraordinary woman, sir, a remarkably fine woman', and she ordered their callow sons about with so many flirtatious looks and smiles that they rushed to do her bidding and came back for more.

Of the few people who did not respond to Fanny's exuberant style, Justina was the most critical. She could not but feel that a woman of thirty-eight was too old to behave so girlishly. She could not bear to see her mother peep out from behind her fan, or rap young men on the shoulders, or make outrageous demands with the inappropriate arrogance of a reigning beauty. She could not understand how Papa could endure it and she hated to see how Mama flirted with him even more boldly than with the others. She wished with all her heart that Fanny had chosen a duller shade of silk than the shimmering blue which fixed every eye upon her when she whisked her skirts around to the music of the waltz, clapped her hands with immoderate pleasure when the dance was over and looked around eagerly for another partner.

Justina herself did not find her pulses racing at the sound of the orchestra, nor did she feel intoxicated by the compliments she received. Her moment of greatest pleasure was due to the distinguishing degree of attention she received from Lady Dunstable.

'My dear,' said that lady affably, sailing up to Justina in a full rig of purple tarlatan and towing Sir Andrew behind her. 'How charming you look! Yes, indeed. A most delightful gown, and quite appropriate too for a coming-out ball. Sir Andrew admired your good taste when he first entered the room.'

Justina, overcome by this condescension, did not raise her eyes to Sir Andrew's face, which was fortunate, for, appalled by his mother's blatant lie, the baronet had set his jaw and assumed the appearance of a waxwork.

'Ah!' Lady Dunstable feigned a start of surprise. 'My good friend Mrs Cobley signals to me, I see. I must go and speak to the poor soul for she so greatly appreciates any little attention it is in one's power to give.'

Quelling with a look any urge Sir Andrew might have had to follow her, Lady Dunstable tacked round the edge of the room towards Mrs Cobley who was enjoying a quiet tête-à-tête with Hector and who watched Lady Dunstable's approach with misgiving.

Left to rely on his own resources, Sir Andrew was tongue-tied. Ever since reaching manhood he had suffered from the unfortunate misapprehension that every unwed female he met had designs upon him. So sure was he of his own worth, the nobility of his name, the antiquity of his title and the correctness of his personal appearance that he had cultivated a manner of conversation with females that was designed to depress pretension and nip any hopes in the bud. It had become such a habit with him that he hardly knew how to dispense with it when the need arose to make himself charming. Unlike his mother he was not convinced that Justina would make him a suitable bride, but he had agreed to look her over, and now, as he stood awkwardly beside her, he was uncertain how to proceed.

Justina did not help him. She was minding her manners very carefully. She shared Sir Andrew's view of his own importance. His correct, dignified deportment and the splendour of his family were exactly in the style that pleased her most. She did not want to spoil everything by a forward attempt to initiate a conversation which she felt was the prerogative of the gentleman.

They might have stood there for ever in silence if Mr Higgs, a little too merry from the effects of Hector's wine, had not rushed past them bursting with laughter, and if Mr Mitchell, even merrier and in hot pursuit, had not stumbled over a nearby chair and spilt some champagne from the glass he held aloft down the skirt of Sir Andrew's impeccable dark grey coat. His apologies were curtly accepted and Mr Mitchell retired abashed, but not for long, for a minute later peals of laughter could be heard from the next room where Mr Mitchell was busy impersonating the outraged Sir Andrew to the delight of Mr Higgs and Edward.

'Oh, how disgraceful, however came they to . . . Oh, I am so sorry.' Justina's evident vexation mollified Sir Andrew, and he unbent a little.

'It's nothing. Just a little wine. It won't show when it has dried out, I'm sure.'

'No, but to be so rowdy and rough . . . '

'I fear' – Sir Andrew allowed himself to smile stiffly – 'that the young man has imbibed too freely.'

'Inebriation of any degree is disgusting to me,' said Justina firmly, pursing her lips primly.

Sir Andrew looked at her with approval. Here, after all, was a woman of sense. He made a conversational effort.

'I suppose you experienced a good deal of that kind of thing in Calcutta?'

'Calcutta? Oh no, sir. I left India when I was still a small child. I have lived all my life with my aunt in Edinburgh.'

'Edinburgh!' Sir Andrew was pleased. There was a steadiness, a respectability, a solidity about Edinburgh which suited him better than the worryingly exotic ideas which India brought to mind. He could pursue the topic of Edinburgh.

'I have very few acquaintance in Scotland, except for Muir of Inveresk – Sir Jonathan Muir. An old family, I believe.'

'I – I am afraid I do not know them.' Justina was regretful. 'But you see I was confined to the schoolroom in Edinburgh, and my aunt, of course, has been an invalid for years and has not been in the habit of going out much in society.'

Guiltily she looked about the room. Aggie was sitting in placid conversation with Mrs Blakeney, with whom she had struck up an unlikely friendship. She looked in such perfect health that Justina dropped her eyes to her posy of rosebuds and hoped that Sir Andrew would not notice the blush that had accompaniied the lie. He did, but thought her heightened colour was caused by a natural excitement at receiving so much distinguishing attention from himself, and he admired the demure way in which she continued to study her flowers. He was conscious of a faint stirring of interest in his breast. It was not in his nature to move quickly. In fact, he had never acted on impulse in the whole of his life. At the same time, he felt that his domineering mother had not been entirely mistaken in directing his attention towards Miss Jamieson. Had there been no fortune, of course, he would not have felt the slightest interest in her, but in the circumstances . . .

He swallowed and executed an awkward bow.

'I fear I am too sedate to be considered the liveliest of partners, but would you do me the honour, Miss Jamieson, of accompanying me through the quadrille?'

4 *Christmas Day 1840*

Fanny shivered as she led the party of ladies across the wide hall from the dining room to the drawing room and pulled her wrap over her shoulders, which her evening dress, following the dictates of fashion, left uncomfortably bare. After years of the luxurious warmth of India she could not reconcile herself to the English climate. She had acquired a large selection of fleecy shawls and scarves which she would wrap around herself whenever she felt the cold, but discard as soon as she was comfortable again in the vague but inaccurate belief that they gave her the appearance of a poor old dame. As she could never recall where she had left them, it was a constant occupation of her maids, footmen and housekeeper, as well as her son and husband, to find one and bring it to her whenever her sensitive flesh felt the prickle of goose bumps. Justina was not asked to perform this service for her, for since her mother's favourite paisleys and cashmeres had sunk out of fashion this year she could not bear to connive in what she considered a shocking lapse of taste. Her mother, she felt, should resign herself to the cold like everyone else.

Fanny could not, in fact, complain that the hall was ill-heated, for a roaring log fire burned in the fireplace, above which hung an elaborate motto worked with green leaves on white paper, surrounded by a pretty wreath of holly, yew and laurel. It read:

Kind hearts can make December blithe as May
And in each morrow find another day.

It was the fruit of several hours' work by Justina, who had taken it upon herself to see that no doorway, looking glass or picture frame had been left unfestooned with garlands of greenery, had burned her fingers dipping peas in sealing wax to make up for an unseasonal lack of holly berries and had even, in spite of Edward's ribald laughter, constructed a kissing bough from which several oranges dangled dangerously, threatening to drop on the heads of anyone rash enough to pass beneath.

'Very festive, Puss,' Hector had said abstractedly. Business was engrossing him at present. He had not realised how difficult it would be to keep in communication with his interests in India and several unsatisfactory letters from his agent had caused him some uneasiness.

'Charming, my love,' Fanny had said approvingly, pleased to see Justina for once in the grip of an enthusiasm.

Edward was more forthright. 'Oho! We all know who you want to kiss, Justy. Though how anyone could stand the touch of such a dry stick as your wee Andy . . . ' and had been forced to apologise when his witticism had reduced Justina to tears. He could not understand what had overcome her these days. She was so tense and moody, dreaming around the place one moment, and flying out at him the next.

Aggie alone had made no comment on the mass of greenery that had invaded the house. While glancing through a newspaper she had come upon a description of the Christmas festivities at Windsor, in which evergreen decorations were a prominent feature. 'We have no doubt', the paper had concluded, 'that aspirants to fashion will increase their efforts to "deck the halls" in imitation of our young Sovereign and her merry court.' Aggie had needed no further explanation.

Jackson, waiting to open the drawing-room door for the ladies, swayed on the balls of his feet. The servants' dining table had groaned with a Christmas dinner only slightly less sumptuous than their master's, and Jackson had still not overcome the effects of hare soup, boiled turbot, roast beef, boiled turkey, mashed potatoes, broccoli, plum pudding, mince pies and raspberry trifle, assisted by a pint or two of claret and a free post-prandial indulgence in Hector's second best port wine. Fanny pretended not to notice and Mrs Blakeney, who was complimenting Justina on the happy effect of snow she had achieved by painting holly leaves with glue and dredging them with flour, saw nothing amiss, but Aggie, following on behind, was less forbearing.

'Jackson,' she said, eyeing him severely, 'you're drunk.'

'Yes, madam.' Jackson rashly attempted a bow and staggered.

'Go and drink some coffee, man, and mind you're sober before you bring in the tea, or you'll rattle the best china all to pieces.'

Mrs Blakeney laughed as the drawing-room door clicked shut behind the departing butler.

'Miss Heriot, you are too much!'

Aggie looked at her with mild surprise.

'Mind you're sober before you bring in the tea!' Mrs Blakeney's imitation of Aggie's Scots voice was so good that everyone laughed, and Aggie herself smiled, not at all put out. She limped over to a high-backed chair set beside a table on which her sewing was lying ready. Christmas Day or no, there were flounces to be mended and hems to be stitched and while she worked she would enjoy listening to Mrs Blakeney and Fanny rattling on, laughing and gossiping with unrestrained wit over the foibles of their neighbours, while Justina delivered an almost correct rendering of a Beethoven sonata on the piano.

It was not long before the sound of male voices and laughter in the hall informed the ladies that the gentlemen were about to join them. Hector did not enjoy sitting long over his port and Edward had no taste for wine. Mr Higgs, who, at the advanced age of nineteen, believed he could hold his drink as well as anyone, had not been given the opportunity to prove it, and Captain Blakeney, whose head was harder than most, had proved it too often to need to do so again.

The door opened and at once the atmosphere changed. Justina stopped playing in mid-phrase and shut the piano. Mrs Blakeney smiled encouragingly at Edward. She had taken a fancy to him and enjoyed listening to his enthusiasms. His endless talk of caddis fly larvae and great diving beetles put her so much in mind of how Frank had been at a younger age when he was forever bombarding her with military information and begging her to tell him whom she considered to be the most brilliant of Wellington's generals.

Fanny smiled at Hector and said, 'Here you are at last. Now we can all be merry again.' She had long since abandoned her flirtation with Frank Blakeney. The families had become too good friends for such nonsense, and once Mrs Blakeney, drawn by the informal gaiety of the Jamieson household, had formed the habit of dining regularly at Bushy House with her son, the play-acting had become too absurd to be sustained.

Edward wandered over to the fireplace and noticed suddenly a battered box on a small rosewood table beside his mother's sofa.

'Why, it's our old game of goose!' he said. 'Come and look at this, Justy. The board's here, and all the counters and the die! Where did it come from?'

'I came upon it in a box I unpacked only last week,' said Aggie, 'and I put it by for a suitable occasion. Do you remember how you pulled your sister's hair when she used to win?'

Edward laughed. 'I'll pull it again if she wins tonight. Come on, Justy. Do play with me.'

He looked so eager and youthful that even Justina smiled. In any case, she could not resist the lure of the shabby old box, and as Edward laid out the board and set out the counters, she drew up a chair and rolled the die, while Aggie, well satisfied with the results of her forethought, nodded and smiled over her sewing with such a softened expression on her face that few would have recognised in her the crabby old maid of fifteen years earlier.

Edward's shout of triumph at the end of the game set off a regular tournament.

'I'll beat you all!' he cried, his face flushed with pleasure. 'Come on, Frank, you next,' and in quick succession Captain Blakeney, Mr Higgs and Mrs Blakeney went down before the roll of the die. Hector, though, had better luck. He trounced Edward's counters off the board, and then Fanny beat Hector, Mr Higgs triumphed over Fanny, and Aggie came out last and best, the winner over Mr Higgs.

The success of the game gave everyone a taste for more. Mr Higgs, looking suddenly more like the schoolboy he had recently been than the young man about town to which he aspired, proposed to amuse the company with his cunning card tricks but his voice went unheard in the general demand for dumb crambo and after the team of four ladies had finished their whispering by the piano and the four gentlemen, at the far end of the drawing room by the conservatory door, had completed their arrangements, the acting began.

It was the ladies' task to guess a word rhyming with 'feel'. Aggie, with a scowl and gestures of ludicrous fearfulness, began the game, tiptoeing to the mantelpiece and furtively tucking into her reticule a gold-rimmed miniature of Simeon Heriot that was displayed on a miniature gilt easel.

'Steal! Steal!' yelled Frank Blakeney and Edward in unison and their booings and whistlings told the ladies their guess was wrong.

It was unfortunate that Justina's turn came next. She had just arranged herself on her knees on the floor in a dumbshow of the word 'kneel' and to add to the picture had clasped her hands before her in an attitude of prayer, when the drawing-room door opened.

'Sir Andrew Dunstable,' said Jackson, bowing himself out again with too obvious carefulness.

Justina scrambled to her feet, blushing furiously. She and Sir Andrew had agreed, in one of the many self-congratulatory conversations they had enjoyed over the last few months, that games of all kinds, except perhaps the superior forms of card games and such intellectual diversions as chess, acrostics and so forth, were infantile and vulgar. She could have wept with mortification as he stepped into the room. The resulting change of temperature was immediately noticeable. The game ceased, the hilarity was at an end. There was an almost audible groan from Edward.

Fanny stepped into the breach. She did not care for Sir Andrew but she understood that Justina's heart was set upon him and she did not wish to stand in her daughter's way.

'Sir Andrew, how charming of you to call! You have come just in time for some music. Mrs Blakeney was about to favour us with one of her German songs.'

Mrs Blakeney looked startled and shook her head so vehemently that the ribbons of her cap fluttered across her cheek.

'No, no, I assure you. It is Miss Jamieson who must do the honours.'

'That's right, Puss,' said Hector heartily, who sensed Justina's discomfort but was unable to fathom the ins and outs of it all. 'Cheer us all up now with one of your merry songs.'

Justina walked across to the piano and began to look about for her music. She took her time, waiting for her cheeks to cool and her hands to stop their trembling. She saw Sir Andrew as a being from a higher world, a world of refinement, of elegance, of quiet good breeding and subtle nuance, from which her family's low behaviour threatened for ever to bar her. She fumbled uncertainly about, then turned to find Aggie at her elbow. Her aunt directed one look at Justina's face and said, loudly enough for the whole room to hear, 'Your music isn't here, child. I found it myself this morning in the breakfast room. I believe Jackson placed it on top of the bureau. Sir Andrew, would you be kind enough to help Miss Jamieson? The shelf is too high for her to reach.'

Aggie's calm tone soothed Justina for a moment, until she understood what her aunt was saying. To send her out of the room alone with Sir Andrew was as good as inviting a proposal. If Sir Andrew was intending to declare himself, he had been offered a perfect opportunity. But Aunt Heriot was making a dreadful mistake. After the exhibition of levity he had witnessed, Sir Andrew must be disgusted. To leave the room with him and return unengaged would be to expose herself to a dreadful humiliation. Justina opened her mouth to protest but Aggie propelled her firmly towards the door. There was no help for it. Sir Andrew had obediently stepped forward and was holding it open for her. Justina, her heart thumping, walked past him, and Aggie shut the door with a click behind them.

Edward, who had been holding his breath until his face was almost purple, let it go with a wail of mirth, which he had the good sense to muffle in a cushion. The rest of the company sat in silence for a moment, awed by Miss Heriot's masterful tactics, and Fanny smiled a little anxiously at her husband. Hector jumped to his feet.

'We can't sit here like fools, waiting for, waiting for . . . ' he said, marching to the piano. 'I'll sing to you all myself since no one else will.'

He opened the piano, struck a couple of chords and cleared his throat. Then, in a good, ringing baritone, he began:

'The dusky night rides down the sky
And ushers in the morn,
The hounds—'

'Oh, not that old hunting song, Father,' interrupted Edward, who was still in the grip of a rollicking tide of laughter at his would-be brother-in-law's expense. 'Something more lovey-dovey to put him in the mood! Something to give him a hint, you know!'

'Teddy!' Aggie frowned at her nephew. She had seen real anguish in Justina's face and was herself on tenterhooks for her niece, but Hector winked at his son, ran his fingers expertly up and down the keys, and began again.

'Here's to the maiden of bashful fifteen
Now to the widow of fifty,
Here's to the flaunting, extravagant quean—'

'Hector!' This time it was Fanny who broke in, though her voice could hardly be heard above whoops of laughter from her undutiful son, Mr Higgs and even Captain Blakeney, who had become similarly affected.

'Sing something more tender, more soulful . . . '

'Oh, very well.' Hector found a new chord and began to sing again.

He had a fine voice and a good ear, and the familiar words of 'Drink to me only with thine eyes' passed through the drawing-room door and penetrated as far as the breakfast room, where they were ignored by Sir Andrew, who was indeed casting his careful soul before the deeply gratified Justina.

Some hours later, when the house had settled down at last, the embarrassed Sir Andrew had been assured of Hector's blessing, glasses of champagne had been drunk and the future bride and groom kissed and congratulated till both were exhausted, Fanny and Hector found themselves alone at last in their bedchamber.

'I do hope it will turn out well,' said Fanny doubtfully, sitting in front of her looking glass and unpinning her back hair. She had sent her maid off early for a Christmas visit to her family and was, for once, forced to undress herself.

'I feel sure of it.' Hector spoke with more confidence than he felt. Sir Andrew was not only an unlikeable fellow, he was also, thought Hector, a poor businessman. Hector's discreet enquiries into the Dunstable family's financial position had not reassured him about Sir Andrew's practical abilities and he would have opposed the match if Justina had not been so set on it.

'What can she see in the fellow?' wondered Fanny. 'He's so cheerless and stiff.'

'He's steady though,' said Hector comfortingly. 'Justina will never have to fear that he'll mistreat her, or embroil her in a scandal, or show too much interest in another woman.'

'No, indeed!' Fanny laughed bitterly. 'I feel sure he would have shown no interest in her if it had not been for the lure of handsome settlements.'

Hector frowned. 'He expressed himself very properly on that head and you know, Fanny, although perhaps he started out with her fortune in mind, I do believe he really loves her. Only a man in love could have made such a dreadful business of asking for her hand, dwelling on the difference in their ages, you know, and assuring me of how he hoped he knew how to make her happy. He was in a sweat of apprehension in case I withheld my permission. I felt quite sorry for the fellow.'

'Yes, Hector, but . . . '

'No buts, Fanny. We must make up our minds to welcome him into the family, or Puss will never forgive us. She's a funny little thing and I do believe that Dunstable will suit her very well.'

Fanny removed the last pin and her hair cascaded down over her shoulders. She shook it back.

'Well, you are right of course, but I'm sure I can't think where she gets her nature from, for she's as unlike both of us as can be.'

Hector chuckled.

'It's my fault, I believe. You never met my mother, Fanny, but she had just the look of Miss Prunes and Prisms. It was Hector this and Hector that and manners and reputations and gentility until I ran shouting from the house.'

'I can't believe you had a mother as bad as Justina,' said Fanny, looking appreciatively at her husband over her shoulder as he loosened his cravat and released his shirt studs in readiness for bed, 'for a more reckless, impolite, bold and impossible creature I never met in all my life.'

'Well, at any rate miss never got her primness from you,' said Hector, and Fanny, laughing, got to her feet and allowed her dress to fall to the floor, then danced teasingly across to the washstand raising her mass of petticoats to display a pretty pair of ankles.

'And my mother, I'm sure, would never have shown off her limbs in such a shameless way, even to her husband, any more than Justina will to hers,' said Hector, catching Fanny round the waist and working with practised fingers to untie the laces which bound her stays.

Chapter Eight *London, September 1841*

1

Hector was prey to a sense of unease. He could not quite locate its origin. It had come upon him when the negotiations for Justina's marriage settlements had obliged him to transfer a considerable amount of capital from Calcutta to London where it could more easily be administered by the inexperienced Sir Andrew. Hector had resolutely put aside his dislike of his son-in-law and had settled upon the couple a sum of money that even Lady Dunstable thought generous, and Hector's banking associates considered positively prodigal.

It was not that there had been any untoward delay or even any reluctance on the part of Mr Pluckton, his Calcutta manager, to forward the money, but Hector's sixth sense, one of the most formidable weapons in his capitalist's armoury, stirred with suspicion and he began to watch out for indications in every mail he received that might tell him the true state of affairs.

The arrangement of Justina's financial future also brought him to an uncomfortable realisation that his fortune, though very great, was too specific. He had built it up through an acute study of the movements of prices and commodities in the Calcutta market. An instinct, which could amount almost to inspiration, for predicting the seasonal fluctuations in the prices of such items as indigo, jute and bales of Surat had served him brilliantly. He had invested his gains carefully and in Mr Pluckton he felt sure he had found a diligent and honest manager to administer his affairs in his absence, but his investments were all in India, and all of them were to some degree or other dependent on such unpredictables as monsoons, the rise and fall of the floodwaters of the Brahmaputra, and the steadiness or otherwise of the Bank of Bengal.

Preoccupied with settling his family into Enfield, and with grasping the complexities presented by the very different commercial world of London, Hector had allowed his financial acumen to be temporarily dulled. It was time, he decided, once again to take matters firmly into his own hands. The irritating lapse of time between decisions in London and their implementation in Calcutta worked greatly to the detriment of his affairs. Pluckton, it had to be said, lacked initiative. He was too apt to wait months for instructions from London, which, when they finally arrived, were out of date and inappropriate. The solution was simple. The bulk of his Calcutta interests must be sold off and with the huge sums at his disposal Hector would then be in a good position to invest money on a wider scale at home, in the new railway schemes, for example, or in the interesting wool market so rapidly developing in New South Wales.

Although he had not been long in London, Hector's circle of business acquaintance was already a wide one. It was made up of men who, like himself, had spent years of their youth in the great mercantile enterprises of the East. Such men could discuss intelligently the cost in rupees of a maund of indigo or the likely effect of the late arrival of the monsoon on the crop. They could happily speculate over a glass of brandy on the possible fall of the interest on shares in the Bombay Bank to below 24 per cent, or wonder at the stagnation in the cotton market owing to the late arrival of the mail ships.

Chief among these friends was the portly figure of Mr Herbert Dickson, whose knowledge of money matters was far-reaching and whose hints on future developments Hector had come to respect.

It was early on a September afternoon, a few months after Justina's wedding, that Hector saw Mr Dickson attempting to cross the grossly congested thoroughfare of Cornhill and waved genially to him. Mr Dickson, risking life and limb between a lumbering stage coach and a curricle drawn by two temperamental horses, changed his course in mid-street and plunged across to where Hector was standing. Hector found his hand enfolded in a pudgy paw and his elbow grasped as he was steered along the street to a tavern.

'Jamieson! My dear fellow! You are of all men the one I most hoped to meet today. I have a scheme to propose to you. But first we must get out of this infernal bustle!'

In the smoke-filled interior of the tavern Mr Dickson, breathing heavily, lost no time in explaining himself.

'My dear Jamieson, I have the most interesting proposition for you, if only you can turn your mind away from your damned Calcutta wares for a space! I saw that fellow Wakefield again yesterday. You have not heard of him? He is forever on the subject of colonisation and now he has a bee in his bonnet about New Zealand. No, don't frown at me like that. My information is good, I assure you. He has formed a company and invites investors. I thought of you at once, for a principal commodity is likely to be flax and with your experience of jute . . . '

Hector smiled and resigned himself to the tirade he knew would follow. He had sat many times in taverns being canvassed by Dickson for this new idea or that, the certainty of putting money into steamships, the sheer necessity of investing in China tea, the absolute folly of ignoring Baltic furs, and although he had never yet succumbed to Dickson's eloquence, he had to admit that he had sometimes regretted it. Today, however, Dickson was more than ever enthusiastic.

'You must see, Jamieson, the position of New Zealand, surrounded by great sea-fisheries, within easy distance of Australia and the Dutch Indies, opens up the most exciting possibilities. And the country abounds with natural resources. The harbours are excellent and with no shortage of pure water. There is, I believe, an inexhaustible supply of timber of the best kind for shipbuilding and the flax I spoke of grows nowhere else, and is of first-grade quality, Wakefield says. The supply of whales is unlimited and the potential in oil quite incalculable. Then, too, the climate is most healthy. Enough to make youths of us all again, I hear. I almost feel tempted – but Minerva would never hear of it. And the native population is small and by no means entirely hostile. Wakefield believes, as do I, that eventually the islands are likely to form the natural centre of a new maritime network comprising the Polynesian Archipelago, Van Dieman's Land – but I will not go on. You shall see for yourself. Come with me.'

He rose to his feet, his knees creaking a little as they adjusted themselves to carrying his weight, and hurried Hector out into the street. Hector began to disengage himself but Dickson tightened his grasp on his sleeve.

'No, no, you shall come with me. There is a great to-do down in Blackwall today. A colony is to set off for New Zealand and the ships are tied up and ready to leave. Only the best kind of emigrants, I am told, or "improvers" as they call themselves, and they are to survey and settle the land. You must judge for yourself what kind of an enterprise it is and how much enthusiasm is felt for it. Prices will rise, Jamieson, they will rise. The shares will be a great hit, I am sure of it. I am only giving you a hint out of friendship, you know, for I have no advantage to gain from it.'

Still speaking, Mr Dickson propelled Hector into a hackney cab and gave directions for Blackwall. Hector, unusually passive, allowed himself to be carried along on the wave of enthusiasm. He had no pressing calls to make, the day was fine, the thought of his papers bored him and in spite of himself he was intrigued. Dickson's enthusiasm had come at an opportune moment. He had been considering diverting some funds to other ventures. The opportunity to begin had been presented to him. He stepped out of the cab at Blackwall ready to be impressed.

Hector was no stranger to the docks. He seldom needed to leave his comfortable premises in Cheapside for the windy flats of the Isle of Dogs but something in the endless movement and roar of the great quays, with their black chimneys, forests of masts and towering hulls, drew him frequently back. It was here, only here, that it all made sense, the rows of figures in his ledgers, the sheaves of paper passed from clerk to clerk, the rates of interest, bonds, shares, speculations. Down here, in the greatest docks in the world, the figures became facts. As he stumbled over stacks of cork and bins of sulphur and wrinkled his nose against the stench of half-cured hides and horns, sniffed appreciatively the aroma of tobacco or coffee, and covered his ears to protect them from the deafening roar of chains, loosed of their weight, rattling back up to the towering wheels of cranes high in the warehouses, his blood raced with the thrill of commerce. His heart pounded in time with the chants of the dockmen who, their faces blue with indigo, laboured in gangs at the great capstans to winch the ships to their berths. The riches of the earth, wrested from it by the labour of millions of men, lay all about him. The very stones he trod on were sticky with the sugar oozing from a thousand casks.

Hector had once or twice brought Edward here but the visits had not been a success. He had found himself expostulating, arms flung out, more vehemently than he intended in his effort to convey the excitement of it all to a boy who watched with horrified concern the miserable labour of the dockmen treading the crane wheels and yawned at news of developments in the Indian tea trade which set Hector's pulses racing.

Today there was no need to penetrate behind the massive walls that guarded the great West India Dock. The ships bound for New Zealand were already loaded and moored out in the Thames off Blackwall. A crowd of investors, relatives and onlookers was gathered on the jetty and Dickson, his bulk a distinct advantage, surged into the thick of it to sound off a barrage of questions.

Hector did not follow him. His mood had changed. He no longer wished to talk about whale oil and ships' spars. Dickson had told him enough to rouse his interest. He would certainly make an investment in the New Zealand Company. It had all the indications of a great commercial success.

He leant on the river wall and looked out across the Thames. Behind him, to the west, the roar of the city came to him in a confused hubbub, a compound of hooves, hammers and machines, of cries, barks and whinnyings, of metal-rimmed wheels thundering over cobble stones and machines clattering in workshops and factories. In front of him the river curved away to the east, through meadows lush with deep grass in which cows grazed contentedly. Masts bright with flags and sails crowded up and down the waterway, seeming to pass through the very fields.

The rotten, salty smell of the river made him restless. He had an urgent desire to be young and free again, to go off and make his fortune, untrammelled by retinues of clerks and hordes of servants, untied by a great house and a round of balls and parties. He looked at the two ships lying at anchor in the river. Sailors were busy in the rigging. Small parties of emigrants strolled about the deck, the women in dark, serviceable dresses, the men in hardwearing working clothes. One man, hatless and bearded, leant on the rail amidships, and waved. Hector waved back, conscious of a pang of envy. Tomorrow the ship would be slipping down the Thames with the tide, out to Gravesend and away to sea, bound for uncharted waters and an unexplored land.

He turned away and looked about for Dickson. He had no business to be wasting time in idle daydreams. He had already been too long away from Cheapside. There was no knowing what nonsense Teddy and the clerks would be up to in his absence.

2 *Paisley, November 1841*

'Stop! Oh, Pa, what is it?'

Jessie Dunbar clutched convulsively at her father's arm and almost made him stumble.

'Hold your peace, child,' said Isaiah, irritably shaking her off. 'It's only a horse, can't you see that?'

Jessie gave a shuddering sigh. Pa was right of course. It was only a horse, though the grey shadow looming suddenly out of the dawn mist had seemed at first so unearthly that she had thought it must be something much, much worse. She stepped aside to avoid the trickle of water running down the channel gouged by the rain in the centre of the steep lane and plodded on up the hill.

There was no doubt but that the country was a strange place, she thought, and not at all as she had imagined it. In all her eleven years she had only once before been beyond the outskirts of Paisley, and that was to go with Ma and Meg on the carrier's cart to Ayr to visit Uncle and Aunt Kirkwood. It had been so long ago she could scarcely remember it. She lifted her skirt and edged her way round a muddy puddle. She must not get her best kirk clothes splashed with dirt before they even arrived at the farm.

It was hard, she thought, to believe that the great day had come at last, so long had she waited and hoped for it. Last year at Martinmas her father had promised her that she might walk with him to the Holmes's farm to bring the cow home to be slaughtered, but on the day itself she had had a cold in the head and Ma had made her stay at home. All last night she had lain awake, dreading that a sudden cough or fever would strike her, but nothing had happened and her father had called her as he had promised an hour before dawn. She could not have slept in any case. To walk away out of Paisley, away out of town, far into the country, was the most exciting thing she had ever done in her life.

They were nearly at the top of the rise now and Jessie could hear her father's breath coming fast and heavy. Isaiah was not used to travelling long distances on foot and his annual November expedition to the farm had become increasingly bothersome. If it were not for long habit and custom, which it was not in his nature to break, he would dispense quite happily with the Martinmas feast, when the freshly slain meat was enjoyed in abundance and the salted remains put up for the winter. After all, it was not as if they had a great family of boys to feed. There was only Meg, with the finicky appetite of a miss of fifteen, and little Jessie who, though always hungry, was obliged to make do with a child's portion. As for himself, he had never cared for salt meat and his own digestion was delicate. Rich food of any kind was abhorrent to him. He suspected that Isobel gave away a large proportion of the Martinmas cow to the beggars who were forever at her door. In their own days of financial ruin – now, thank God, no more than a painful memory – the Dunbars had preferred to starve rather than beg from their neighbours. He, for one, could not see why Isobel should be so soft on the feckless and unfortunate.

A shaft of sunlight, piercing through the mist, distracted him from his gloomy thoughts. He looked round for his daughter. She was some way behind him, sitting on a stone beneath a dripping leafless tree, removing her shoes.

'Come on, child!' he called. 'Make haste or we'll never reach the farm today!'

She rose quickly, tied the laces of her cumbersome shoes together and hung them round her neck. They bobbed heavily against her thin chest with each step but she was glad that her feet were free of them. Ma had made her promise to wear them, at least as far as the first fields, but she had said nothing about the country lanes. The hated straight shoes, designed to fit either right or left foot, chafed her unbearably and she never wore them if she could help it.

'I'm coming, Pa,' she called to her father's unresponsive back. He did not answer. He had resumed his steady pace, his bowed back and thin legs looking even to her eyes frail in this sturdy landscape.

Isaiah shook his head. It had not been his idea to bring his daughter. He had been overruled by his wife, too fond of getting her own way in such matters, and too softhearted to withstand the child's insistent pleading. It would not be his fault if she returned home over-weary and lame and he would not take responsibility for it. He had told her plainly that she must look after herself on the way and he meant to stand by his word.

Jessie, her feet comfortably bare at last, started after him. Her spirits were rising with the mist and the sharp sunlight, glinting off the wet grass and sparkling hedgerows, was suffusing her whole being with happiness. There were so many strange sounds in the country! She could not get used to the absence of cartwheels rumbling on cobbles and the endless clatter of looms and yet it was not silent here. Nearby a blackbird was singing on the topmost branch of a windblown thorn tree, while far away sheep bleated on the hillsides. There was so much to see, too. She could not simply walk past every enticing novelty, like the huge spider's web hung with dewdrops, as fine as any of Mrs Gregson's best lace, or the family of rabbits grazing nervously on the road's verge. Unwilling to startle them, she tiptoed carefully past.

'Hurry up, Jessie, will you?' her father called from away down the road, causing the rabbits to bolt for the cover of the hedge. She ran to catch him up, and, oblivious to his frowns, tucked her hand into the crook of his arm.

'Did you see the robin, Pa? And the rosehips? I could pick some for Ma, to make a syrup with.'

'There's no time, no time,' said Isaiah. 'Now walk with me and hold your tongue. Save your breath for the next steep hill.'

It was five hours before the farm was reached and long before then Jessie had fallen silent, from inclination as much as paternal discouragement. Her feet were blistered, her bones ached and she was dreadfully hungry.

'Will you look at the child, now?' said Mrs Holmes, the farmer's wife, by way of greeting, and taking Jessie's hand she led her through the farmyard, where two speckled calves were drinking milk from pails and a cluster of wriggling piglets were fighting for places at their mother's teats. In the cavernous kitchen she indicated the settle by the fire, and placed in one of Jessie's hands a large slice of bread, and in the other a beaker brimming with creamy milk.

'The men are away to fetch your cow,' she said comfortably, 'and if you'll just wait awhile till I turn my bannocks I'll find you a basin of warm water so you can soak your poor wee feet. Look at the state of them! It's a good thing Mr Holmes has it planned to take the cart into Paisley this afternoon, for you and your pa can ride with him and tie the cow up behind.'

Jessie gave a sigh of pleasure, plunged her face once more into the milk, then raised it and licked off the moustache of cream she had acquired. The miles home on her sore feet had been troubling her mind. She could relax now and enjoy the rest of her day out.

By the time Isaiah and Mr Holmes returned, leading a soft-eyed brindled cow on a halter, Jessie had decided that heaven could be no improvement on the Holmes's farm. She had played with a basket of kittens, taken a turn at the butter churn and stroked the velvety nose of a colt in its stall.

Everything here was nicer than at home. Mrs Holmes was so chatty whereas Ma was always quiet. Mrs Holmes's dresser was encumbered with an interesting clutter of odds and ends – mousetraps and candlesticks and cracked china and handleless knives – whereas in Ma's kitchen no item was ever allowed to stray from its allotted place. Mrs Holmes was so big and full of good humour, so ready to enjoy a mouthful of cake or a good laugh at the follies of her neighbours. Ma was quiet and laughed rarely, and when she spoke she was often sharp, bidding Jessie not to soil her apron, or to mind and wipe her feet on the mat. Here, the door was forever banging open as the lads brought in pails of milk, or one of the giggling daughters went out to collect the eggs or feed the ducks. Isobel's door remained shut tight against the world and was opened reluctantly only to a known and select few.

'Eh, but Jessie here's a friendly wee thing,' said Mrs Holmes approvingly to Isaiah, as he sat at the table with a mug of tea, while the farmer put the horse to the cart ready for the journey home. Isaiah frowned with surprise. Jessie was teased at home for her shyness and dislike of speaking to strangers.

'What have you been up to?' he said to her accusingly, but before she could answer, Mr Holmes poked his head through the top half of the two-tiered door that led out to the barnyard.

'We'd best start off while the light holds,' he said, and Isaiah thought no more of his daughter's unusual behaviour but told her to hurry up and put the kitten back in its basket, and thank Mrs Holmes for the good fare, and to come now and not keep them all waiting.

It did not occur to Jessie until they were more than half way home that the pretty little cow, who trotted with such docility behind the cart, slipping a little in the mud and shaking her head in vain attempts to free herself from the unaccustomed halter, was destined to die that very evening. Jessie had been sitting with her back to her father and Mr Holmes, who conversed together on the driver's seat on matters political and economical, and she was busy smiling at the cow and trying to draw the animal's attention when the idea suddenly came to her that she was little better than a murderess, aiding and abetting an execution. She looked at the poor creature, who flicked her ears innocently back, then in distress she scrambled on to the driver's seat beside her father and sat for the rest of the journey resolutely refusing to turn round again and shivering guiltily every time the cow mooed or snickered through its soft nostrils.

Isobel was waiting anxiously for their return. She had not quite liked to see Jessie go off on such a long walk and she was afraid the returning miles might have over-taxed her. She would have gone with her, but had not felt confident of her own strength. She was so often breathless these days, and had a tightness in her chest that was greatly increased by any undue exertion. In her relief at seeing her she kissed her little daughter with an unusual display of affection and was surprised to receive a rapturous hug in return.

'Oh, Ma, it was lovely, and the spiders' webs like lace, and the piglets and all. And oh, Ma, can't we keep her, the little cow? You won't kill her, surely, Ma? It's so cruel!'

Isobel peeled the small arms away from her neck more roughly than she had intended. She was afraid of her own tender feelings. She too hated the killing of the cow. She could not bear to look into its trusting eyes before it died, or see them filmed over with death afterwards. Every year she reproved herself for her weakness and steeled herself for the task.

'None of your foolishness, now,' she said abruptly. 'Mr Gregson's here already to see the job done. It's more than your father and I can manage alone. Run away up to the kitchen and ask him to step down to the shop, for we've cleared a space by the looms there, and bring down the knives and the bowls I've laid ready on the table.'

In the little bedroom up the steep stair which Jessie shared with her sister Meg, there was a cupboard beside the unused grate. In all the years of her childhood it had been more than a cupboard to Jessie. Sometimes a ship, sometimes a little house, sometimes a shop, it had always been a haven, a safe place, a retreat from Meg's teasing and her mother's irritability. She crept into it now and sat knotting a handkerchief round her fingers. It had been so beautiful today! Her heart had rushed up from the grass with the startled thrush and bounded across the newly ploughed fields with the racing hare. She could still feel in her mouth the crumbling perfection of Mrs Holmes's gingerbread and taste the rich fullness of milk warm from the cow. There she was, back at it again. The cow! Try as she might she could not take her mind away from the slaughter even now going on below, the cruelty of her parents, the lost liveliness of its hooves, the tasselled tail that would never swish again. She rocked backwards and forwards as the handkerchief went round and round her fingers. She must think of something else, anything else!

From down below she heard a knocking at the street door. She cocked her head and listened. Meg was with her embroidery frame over at Mrs Brown's. She'd not be back for some time yet and the others were all too busy carrying out foul murder in the weaving shop to answer knocks at the door. Reluctantly, Jessie crawled out of her cupboard. The knocker sounded again. She ran downstairs and opened the door. She had expected something special on this day of days, she knew not what. It might be a shepherd with a crook, perhaps, or a dairy maid with a great round of cheese, or at the very least the minister with his tall black hat.

It was the postman. She took the proffered letter, shut the door hastily to discourage encroaching remarks, as her mother was wont to do, and looked at the letter doubtfully. A call from the postman was an event. News important enough for a letter must be news indeed. Jessie turned the small square of folded paper over in her hands. Her mother and father would not thank her for keeping it from them, no matter what business they were engaged in. She stepped along the passageway and stopped outside the door of the weaving shop.

No wonder they had not heard the postman! Voices were raised in exclamation and command and she could hear the swish of a blade sharpening on steel followed by grunts of effort. She pushed open the door and went in.

Mr Gregson was not adept at butchery and his annual endeavours at Martinmas had not significantly improved his skill. To Jessie's horrified eyes the weaving shop was a shambles. Blood seemed to be everywhere. The oil lamp, normally suspended over her father's loom but now hanging over a wide area of space behind it, gleamed luridly on red splashes on the whitewashed walls, smears on her mother's apron, smudges on her father's arms and face and worst of all on Mr Gregson's hands which were red up to the wrists and dripped blood from the fingers.

Unnoticed, Jessie let go of the door and slipped round the loom. Now she could see the cow. It was no longer an animal but a thing, a misshapen, distorted lump of flesh, a bloody mass of mangled limbs. Mr Gregson, who had peeled away from its rump a large flap of hide, was slicing collops of meat with a long bladed knife and laying them upon newspapers set about the floor, which were already soaked with blood. Isobel was bending over the animal's neck, a bowl filling with blood in her hands, while Isaiah cut into the flesh to encourage more to flow.

'The bowl's full,' said Isobel. 'Take it and set it down.'

Mr Gregson sat back on his heels and wiped the sweat from his forehead with a gory sleeve.

'Don't waste it, mind,' he said cheerfully. 'There's more blood in this beastie than I've seen in a long time and great puddings it'll make, that's for sure.'

Isobel pursed her lips. Distaste for blood and disapproval of waste warred in her. As usual, sense won the battle over sentiment.

'Take the bowl, will you,' she urged her husband, who was standing motionless.

Isaiah took it from her and as he turned into the light, Jessie saw his face. It wore an expression she had never seen before. It frightened her. She grasped hold of the upright post of the loom. Her father was staring at her mother, his face red, his eyes protruding. His hands trembled so that the blood in the bowl shivered and threatened to spill out of the side. Isobel sighed with exasperation, took it from him and set it down. Isaiah glanced towards his friend but Mr Gregson had his back turned and was engrossed in severing a leg joint at the shoulder. Isaiah took a step forwards, his sparse lank hair bobbing over his pale forehead and caught his wife by the waist.

'Stop that now,' she said sharply, and pushed at him.

Mr Gregson made a final cut and held up a great joint of meat.

'Why, Jessie,' he said, catching sight of the child. 'Have you come to see what's for supper?'

Isaiah let go of his wife abruptly and, turning his back on them all, went across to where the knives were laid out and began to sharpen them on the steel. Isobel, who had frowned when she saw her daughter, noticed how pale the child was and her expression softened.

'What is it, my lass?' she said.

Silently Jessie held out the letter. Isobel looked at the frank and the strong black writing of the direction, wiped her hands on her apron and unfolded the single sheet of paper. She read slowly and deliberately. Jessie, watching her closely, could not decide whether she was reading good news or bad.

Isobel came to the end, folded the paper again and handed it back to Jessie who took it with care, unwilling to touch the red smears left by Isobel's fingers.

'Well?' said Isaiah impatiently, picking up another knife. 'What is it?'

'It's from Joseph,' said Isobel in an expressionless voice. 'Eliza's dead, poor soul.'

3

Eliza's death was the first bereavement Jessie had ever experienced in the family and she was surprised how much enjoyment resulted from it. She acquired at once a new dress and, though it was black, it was the nicest she could remember owning, for it was the first she had ever had new from the dressmaker and not handed down from Meg. She had expected lamentations and sighs, of the exuberant kind Mrs George had produced over the demise of her dissolute brother Henry, but although Isobel had appeared grave during the mourning visits she had received and shaken her head sadly whenever Aunt Kirkwood's name was mentioned, she had actually been unusually merry since the sad news had arrived and had even been full of a secret excitement, which betrayed itself in a quickness of movement, a lessening of her habitual tiredness and a tendency to hum old songs about the kitchen.

In spite of Isobel's happier mood, the Martinmas dinner was not a success. Jessie could not remember when the feast had been so lacking in jollity. It was a great occasion in the Dunbar household for it was the only time in the year that Isobel, an excellent cook, prepared a grand dinner for invited guests. The company never varied. Mr and Mrs Gregson, as a token of gratitude for his aid in the slaughter of the cow, were always bidden to the banquet and, when they had all done, Willy McFadden, the simpleton from Craighead, was sat down by the hearth out of the way and a capacious napkin was tied round his neck. He ate pieces of beef with a spoon out of a great bowl that he held carefully on his knee, and he stared long and earnestly at Isobel, until she bade him kindly to watch what he was doing, for the gravy was dribbling down his chin.

Mr Gregson, on this annual occasion, usually paid for his supper by the sparkle of his conversation and the rendition of popular songs in a ringing bass voice. He was well supplied with a fund of stories and liked to air provoking opinions for the pleasure of animating his old friend Isaiah, but tonight his manner was subdued and his voice was flat. Not even Meg's timid request for music, when the dishes had all been cleared away and Isobel was filling the clay pipes at the fire, would draw a response from him.

'Would you not, Mr Gregson? Just a verse or two of "My Nannie O!" It was so fine when you sang it to us last year,' she said, blushing at her own boldness.

Mr Gregson took a pull at his glass of whisky and shook his head.

'I cannot sing tonight, my dear,' he said, 'for there's no knowing but that this will be the last Martinmas we'll ever sit down to together,' and he shook his fleshy jowl impressively.

Isaiah puffed at his pipe. 'For the feckless, maybe,' he said complacently. 'Times are bad, we all know that. But for those of us who have had the forethought to put a little by to tide us over until trade recovers . . . ' He smiled, as if enjoying a secret pleasure. 'You have no cause to talk as if we all faced ruin. Last Martinmas? That is all nonsense. Why, I have already spoken with Holmes for next year's cow.'

Jessie thought of the calves sucking at their pail and shivered.

'Next year's cow,' repeated Mr Gregson, sighing heavily. 'Aye, well, there's some as lives in happy ignorance of the true state of affairs, Dunbar, but I had not thought you were of their number.'

'Now, Sandy,' said Mrs Gregson, laying a warning hand on her husband's sleeve. 'Don't start, not this evening, not . . . '

He brushed her hand aside and leant forward towards Isaiah, stabbing his finger in the air to reinforce his point.

'Can you not read the signs, man? This is not like the last depression when you took the cholera and had to remove from Castle Street. That was but a small dip in the trade but even then you had to sell everything and came almost to ruin. There's worse, much worse to hand. Paisley is dying, Isaiah, and we must see to it that we do not die with it.'

Isaiah blew out his cheeks complacently and expelled a puff of smoke.

'For the plain work, I grant you, there's a downturn in the trade. You are right there, right enough. Patterson and Kerr and men of their stamp are all going to the wall I hear. But they are not the true craftsmen. There will never be a lack of demand for our work. Why, the new patterns have come direct from Paris! The loveliest things. Wait, now, till I show you.'

He stood up from the table, ignoring his friend's head shakings, and took from a chest under the window a carefully folded shawl.

'Here, Isobel, take the end of it,' he said, 'and mind that it does not get spotted with grease for I'm expecting Mr Shaw to give me a fine price for it.'

'Fine price!' muttered Mr Gregson, but Isaiah did not hear. He was absorbed in handling the lovely material, stroking its soft surface of silk and cashmere with his long sensitive fingers.

In the candlelight the brilliant colours of the shawl seemed to glow even more deeply than by day. On a background of rich claret, sinuous arrangements of drooping teardrops were interlaced with a mass of intricate flowers and leaves, so perfectly woven that not the tiniest irregularity could be detected, nor the hint of a warp thread appeared on the surface between the tight packed wefts. Jessie put out a timid finger and felt it. It was the softest, most supple thing she had ever touched. She withdrew her hand quickly before she could be reproved. No one had noticed her. Even Mr Gregson was distracted from his depression.

'Eh, Isaiah, I would say that's the finest you've done,' he said. 'This effect, now, on the outer border' – he pointed to the strip of riotous vines that ran around the edge of the shawl – 'the pattern is from Thomson's, is it not? But there's something here, in the arrangement of the corners . . . '

'My own design!' burst out Isaiah eagerly. 'I have improved on Thomson's not a little in the corners. Even though they bring their ideas from Paris, the weaver who works the stuff knows best how to make it all neat.' He took the end of the shawl from Isobel's hands and began to fold it again. 'Oh, aye, I'll get a good price for this one, never mind your talk of depression and all.'

'You'll be fortunate to get a price at all.'

Mr Gregson was of such a naturally optimistic and convivial turn of mind that this pronouncement, made with due heaviness, had a great impact upon his hearers.

'Rubbish, man,' said Isaiah testily. 'Why, I have worked on this for months. Shaw knows its real value. He . . . '

'Have you seen Shaw in the last few days?'

'No, but he is forever at his warehouse in Causeyside . . . '

A cackle from the fireside startled them and made them all turn their heads.

'Shaw! Gone! Run off! Tam Shaw! No more!' Willy McFadden's cracked voice rose in a parody of song. 'The weaving is a trade that never can fail, As lang's we need a cloot to keep anither hale, Sae let us aye be merry—'

'Well sung, Willy, well sung,' Isobel broke in, taking the empty bowl from the man's hands and patting him repressively on the shoulder.

But Willy, once aroused, was not easily silenced. 'Tam Shaw! Tam Tyrie! Tam Shaw! No more! Wee Tam Tyrie, He jumped in the firie, The fire was ower hot, He jumped in the pot . . . '

'That's enough now, Willy,' said Isobel kindly, seeing the poor man beginning to wave his arms and knowing that his excitement, if it was not checked, could mount alarmingly. 'Give me your napkin, now, and you can have an apple. Then you must be off home or your auntie will skelp you.'

Willy McFadden stumbled to his feet and held out his hands. Isobel put an apple in one and a biscuit in the other. Then she put another apple in his pocket and led him downstairs. 'Away to your house, now,' the silent party upstairs heard her say. Then the latch fell and they heard the rustle of her black skirts on the stair.

'What does Willy McFadden know about anything?' Isaiah said irritably. 'A seven months' child and touched in the head since birth.'

'It's true enough and sorry I am to be the one to bring such bad tidings.' Mr Gregson passed his finished pipe to Isobel and she handed him another. 'I thought you knew. Shaw has absconded, taking his money with him and his debts are such that he's ruined several smaller men. It was all over the close this morning.'

'I have not been out today.' Isaiah's face, naturally pale, had whitened further.

'Gone to America, so they say, far out of reach of the law.'

'But he owes me – I have been promised . . . '

'You might as well whistle for the wind.'

Isaiah looked down at the shawl, still on his knee, and a little colour returned to his face.

'Well, well,' he said, 'so one rascal goes but there are scores of others. I need not fear to take my work to any wholesaler. I am well known, they have vied for my—'

'Wait.' Mr Gregson withdrew from the recesses of his coat a folded journal and laid it on the table.

'What is this folly?' said Isaiah testily.

'Folly it is indeed,' said his friend solemnly. He turned the leaves, and under his strong workman's hands the fashion plates, depicting ladies with impossibly tiny feet and improbably narrow waists, looked incongruous and outlandish.

'Here! Here's the place!' He stabbed at a paragraph with a forefinger, held the paper up to the candle and read aloud.

' "Our correspondent in Paris announces the ascendancy of a charming new style for promenades. The mantelet is now greatly to be preferred over the humbler shawl. These delightful confections of tarlatan or tulle are trimmed with lace and ribbon of the newest shades in clement weather, or made of heavier velvet with a fur edging for snowy days. Our fashionable ladies are packing away their shawls, which have for so long held sway, or donating them to their country cousins. We can predict that this season not one 'cashmere' or 'paisley' will be seen amongst any who aspire to the realms of *à la modalité*." '

Silence greeted the conclusion of this piece, broken at length by the soft chime of the clock on the mantelshelf. Jessie looked up at it. Her father had bought it only last year and set it in its place above the fire with due ceremony. It had not, Jessie knew, pleased her mother, though she could never understand why. A memory stirred faintly in Jessie's mind of another clock, long since gone, and another time, when she had been dreadfully cold and there had been nothing to eat. They had lived in a bad house, where there had been no garden and no gooseberry bushes. And one night two men had come to the house, great tall men all dressed in black, and when they had gone one of them had said a word, a bad word, that had frightened her very much. What was it? She would call it to mind directly. Aye, that was it – 'motherless'. He had looked at her and then he had said 'motherless'. And there was an expression now on her father's face and a pinched, weary, pained look on her mother's, that somehow reminded her of that time.

* * *

The next day, and the day after that, a strange calm ruled over the Dunbar household. Isaiah's loom was still. It was as if he had been deaf and blind these last months while his lovely shawl was in the making, but now that the full scale of the economic disaster had penetrated his mind his collapse was all the greater. He ran feverishly from one man to another, seeking news, looking for reassurance, trying to sell his work. Everywhere he met the same gloom, the same woeful forecasts of utter hopelessness, the same stories of bankruptcies, evictions and seizures. It was as if the town of Paisley, so prosperous and bustling a year ago, had been visited by the plague.

'I would – I would murder them, shoot them, hang them,' he burst out to Isobel one afternoon as she scrubbed her kitchen table to an effulgent whiteness. She had abandoned the wheel at which she normally sat for the better part of the day. With the loom idle, and likely to remain so, what point was there in preparing thread for it?

'Who do you wish to murder, husband?' she asked coolly.

'Those fine ladies, those whores, those Jezebels, who spurn the work of an honest man for all they bits of French trumpery! I'd like to give them fashion, so I would! The shawl's a decent, modest garment to cover the body and warm it, and display the beauty of a craftsman's work. Who are they, the harlots, the—'

'Mind your tongue,' said Isobel curtly. She looked meaningfully towards Jessie who, under her mother's strict tutelage, was rubbing lard into flour for the covering of a pie.

Isaiah glowered at his daughter.

'Get me a cup of tea, girl,' he said, 'and I'll away to the end of the close to seek for news.'

At the close mouth the hectic conversation of his fellows, Chartists to a man, was more to his taste just now than the silences of his wife, which he had once so deeply appreciated. He could not understand Isobel. The gravity of their situation had not appeared to have affected her. She went on calmly with her daily tasks and several times he had surprised her singing. She had received more than one letter from her brother, too, and had not disclosed their contents to him. Still, he supposed her lack of concern was not surprising. Women could not be expected to grasp the immensity of a situation such as this. Matters of business were men's work, after all.

He drank his tea quickly and set his cup down, but before he could start down the stairs he heard the hinge of the front door creak and Meg's voice, high with excitement, 'Come up, Uncle! Ma's here, I know, and Pa too, maybe.'

Joseph, entering the room on Meg's heels, seemed to fill the small kitchen. To his sister's eyes he appeared to have grown. He stood with his head high and there was a boldness, a courage, a confidence in his eyes she had not seen there for twenty years. It was almost as if the young sailor, Archie's friend, stood before her again.

That's what Eliza did to him, she thought fiercely, and unconsciously clenched her fists.

Isaiah took his brother-in-law's hand in greeting but his smile was sour.

'You're remarkably cheerful for a man who's newly widowed and who's come to a house that's staring ruin in the face,' he said waspishly.

Joseph ignored his bitterness and embraced his sister.

'Poor Eliza is with the Lord in a better land above,' he said calmly. 'I will not mourn for her, for her burden was weary and she laid it down gladly. And as for you, brother' – he pulled a paper from his packet, and put it down on the dry end of Isobel's table – 'your sufferings can be ended if you wish it. You need not sink into poverty and destitution, as I fear so many of your townsfolk may. I have come to propose a scheme to you, to unite our families, I and my boys, you and your daughters, in a great venture to which the Lord has led me through many hours of prayer and supplication.'

He pointed to the large black lettering and Isaiah read, with starting eyes: 'The New Zealand Company announces the sailing of the passenger ship the *New Zealand*, a barque of 455 tons, under the command of Captain C. H. Worth, to depart from Greenock, July 1842, bound for Port Nicholson and the Colony of Nelson, in New Zealand. Cabin accommodation and steerage. Assisted passages for selected emigrants.'

Isaiah looked uncomprehendingly at his wife and saw her face alight with excitement and hope. His brows twitched together in a frown. He took a step backwards and shook his head violently.

'Oh, no, no! You're crazed, the pair of you! I'll starve first. You'll not get me aboard an emigrant ship, not even if you bind and gag me first. We'll not do it, Joseph, and that's my last word.'

Chapter Nine *Enfield, February 1842*

1

Fanny sat bolt upright in her drawing room and her hand, gripping the wooden scroll that decorated the end of the sofa arm, showed white at the knuckles.

'Why, Hector, what can you mean? You cannot be serious! Explain it again. I do not understand.'

The strain of the last few weeks was evident on Hector's ravaged face. He had lost the corpulence which the good life of Enfield had added to his person. He strode restlessly up and down the room, refusing to meet his wife's eyes. Edward stood by the mantelpiece, his stomach tight with sympathy for his father and pity for his mother.

'I tell you, Fanny, I have done everything that could be done. Had I known what kind of man Pluckton would turn out to be – the folly! The damned stupidity – I can hardly contemplate it. If he had been my worst enemy he could not more successfully have brought about my ruin.'

'The man's dead, Hector,' said Aggie quietly. 'You should not speak ill of him.'

'That's the worst of it!' Hector's voice was bitter. 'To take his own life when he had ruined mine was the crowning act of idiocy! How was I to know that he had become a slave to strong drink? I have seen him down his bottle like every other man in Calcutta but I never saw the signs that his character was about to be so altered. His wild speculations, his lack of judgement, the lies he has told – he has squandered everything! My credit is ruined. I am left with nothing, after all those years of patient effort, lost, gone, in a few mad, wild months . . . !'

The colour had left Fanny's face as she absorbed the import of Hector's speech. Her blue eyes formed deep pools in the whiteness.

'Do you mean, Hector, that we have no money any more?'

'None! Oh, a thousand pounds or so which I have already invested here, a few trivial bonds, in this company or that, but our fortune is quite, quite lost!'

'Justina's portion?' Aggie's voice was still quite calm.

'Oh, that is safe enough. I made sure of tying it up so tight that Andrew could not play fast and loose with it. I never thought that I would be the one to . . . '

Fanny felt a kind of numbness. Her mind moved slowly as the implications began to dawn upon her.

'The house! We will have to leave the house and pay off the servants – pay! Have we money for that, Hector?'

'Oh aye, we won't cheat the servants, my dear. We'll find the money for that, never fear.'

'But the furniture, and the order for new curtains, and the party – I have already sent out the invitations! A cottage! We must find a cottage. A few neat rooms, a vegetable plot . . . '

'There's no call to be talking of cottages, Fanny,' Hector broke in roughly. 'We're off to India again. I did it once and I can do it again. There are new opportunities to be had. Why, I believe that tea is now grown in Assam. The Chinese monopoly has been broken and . . . '

'No!' Fanny's vehemence brought all eyes back to her again. 'I cannot, I will not bear it, Hector. I am warning you, I will not go back to India. The memories, the anguish – you may think I have recovered but not one day passes that I do not think . . . To return to scenes so sad, so melancholy, I will not, I cannot do it.'

'Then I must go alone, my dear.' Hector had stopped his restless march. He dropped on to the sofa beside his wife and took her hands in his.

'No! No!' Fanny snatched her hands away, and beat them on her lap. 'We will not be parted again, we promised each other. You cannot break your word. And then, only think of it Hector, to start again, to be a poor man when you are used to being so rich! To endure the pity of the Murchisons, and the contempt of every jumped up planter! It could not be borne. How they would talk! Hector, it is not to be thought of.'

It was as if Fanny had delivered the coup de grâce. Until this moment, only the prospect of returning to Calcutta and burying himself in the work he understood so well had carried Hector through the anguish of the last week. As the mails had come in, and the rumours had flown about, as the evidence had grown in the piles of paper under his hand, he had sustained himself only by planning his return to the scenes of his early successes. He had built one calculation on another. A contact here, a judicious loan there – he had believed it might be done. But Fanny's realism had swept all that away. He saw immediately that she was right. The world would have only contempt for a failure. He had seen it already in the lowered eyes and evasive conversations of his erstwhile friends in the city. Calcutta would not open its doors to him again. No credit would be extended to a man who had crashed with such spectacular speed and from so great a height. As the last rung in the ladder of hope snapped beneath him, Hector buried his face in his hands and gave way to despair.

If he had raised it again at that moment he would have been surprised. The colour had returned to Fanny's cheeks. Earlier in the afternoon she had taken to her sofa with the headache, an affliction which had increasingly beset her since Justina's marriage. But now the pain was forgotten. She jumped to her feet and took Hector's place, walking resolutely, with a swish of her petticoats, up and down from the long windows to the door and back again.

'The wine merchant. The order must be cancelled immediately. Teddy, go to Jackson and – no, wait. We must plan first. Take some paper and sit down at my secretaire. A list. We'll make a list of the tasks to be done. The wine merchant first. Write it down, Teddy. What an excellent thing that I forgot to order last week, and was so vexed, too, with Jackson for failing to remind me!

'Mme Dupuis. Write "dressmaker" if you cannot spell the name, Teddy, for I have sent for an opera cape from Paris and the order must be countermanded at once if we are to forestall a large bill. The party. Yes. An indisposition I think will cover that. We will write the notes after supper. You will help me, Teddy. As to the servants – how much money are we to have, Hector? Will there be enough to retain a housekeeper? And Jackson, perhaps?'

Hector groaned, grasped his hair in both hands, and shook his bowed head without raising his eyes.

Edward turned round, straining the spindly chair that served Fanny's little desk, an elaborate concoction of ornamental marquetry and veneers designed for the composition of billets doux and society invitations.

'There is almost nothing left, Mama,' he said, looking at his mother with admiration as the energy which she had lacked in recent months visibly surged through her again. 'Father has several creditors he is obliged to settle with. We cannot hope to remain here or keep a carriage or . . . '

Fanny looked sharply at her son for a moment and then smiled at him, satisfied. Teddy did not seem at all disturbed by the drastic change in his prospects. Unlike his sister, he had never set much store by the family's meteoric rise to fortune. He had seen it, as much as anything, as an impediment, coming between himself and his studies. He had no social aspirations. He did not care about wealth or power. He had no expensive tastes. He had dutifully ridden the horse his father had bought for him and he had certainly enjoyed taking the reins of the carriage from time to time, but he had no real passion for equestrian pursuits. He was happiest poking about in hedgerows and sifting through the slime at the bottom of ponds in search of natural phenomena. He had seen his father's fortune rise and fall with perfect equanimity. Fanny need have no fears on Teddy's account. She turned her mind back to the question in hand.

'The house must be given up at once,' she said positively. 'There is no doubt of that. But where are we to go?'

'Justy and Andrew are nearby, of course,' said Edward doubtfully.

The suggestion found no favour with Fanny. She dismissed it.

'Impossible. To receive patronage from the Dunstables would be more than any of us could bear. And besides, think of Justina's feelings. She would be mortified. No, we must leave Enfield, and the sooner the better.'

She looked about the drawing room with a calculating eye as if already assessing the returns to be had at auction on the dozens of expensive trifles that littered the room.

'Will you stop blethering about cottages and Justina and the like?' Aggie was scowling ferociously but she did not fool Fanny, who saw the fierce delight her sister felt, not on account of Hector's downfall, but for the chance it gave her to show her love in a practical way. 'You'll pack up and come home with me like sensible bodies.' Aggie's voice was gruff with emotion. 'It's your home as much as mine, Fanny Jamieson, for it belonged to our father and there's room enough there for an army. And if it's money that's worrying you, you know fine that the gun business sold for more . . . '

'Impossible!' Hector had roused himself and was frowning at Aggie under his black brows with a glare every bit as dreadful as the one she bent on him. 'Take money from a woman! How could I? It's out of the question, sister, and I'll thank you not to mention such a thing again. Your father very properly left his house and his money to you in its entirety in the confident and, it would seem, mistaken belief that I would be able to provide for Fanny and the children. I'll not touch a penny of it.'

Aggie sniffed. 'You're a proud man, Hector, and hot-headed too, and if you're going to take that line with me there's little enough I can do to make you change your mind, for all I think you're a fool. But hospitality's another matter altogether and there's no reason on earth why you should not return to Edinburgh with me, or at least Fanny and Teddy, while you look about you for a new fortune to make, for I've been eating my head off at your expense this last year or more and you have no business to refuse me if I invite you in return,' and Aggie looked so belligerent that Hector almost smiled.

'Yes, well, perhaps for a time at least, until I see my way to establishing – you are very good, Aggie.'

Fanny listened to this exchange with exasperation.

'Return to Edinburgh? Are you mad? I would sooner die! Receive the condolences of the Hamilton woman and watch the smiles as I pass down Princes Street? Oh, I don't mean to hurt you, Aggie — ' she sat down on a chair beside her sister and shook her arm. 'I know you would be happy for us to make our home with you and for a short time I could bear it, at least until my gowns needed turning and my bonnets are out of fashion. But then – oh no! I could not remain for ever in Edinburgh, growing shabbier by the day!'

Disappointment made Aggie cross. She had, in Hector's downfall, seen her own liberation. She had become aware during these last few weeks of a homesickness for Edinburgh. With Justina safely wed, the purpose seemed to have gone out of the social round of Middlesex. In any case, she missed her comfortable gossips with Mrs Macfarlane and she worried in case Mr Elliott was in need of her assistance. She had felt torn between her family and her home and the prospect of uniting them permanently had filled her with happiness.

'You've no choice but to emigrate then,' she said abruptly, and instantly regretted it as she saw the idea take root.

'Emigration!' Fanny repeated thoughtfully.

'No, no, I was not serious,' said Aggie hastily, appalled at the thought that she might be taken seriously. Travel beyond the British Isles had always seemed to her to be the most foolhardy activity. She had never ceased to give thanks that Fanny had returned unscathed from her death-defying voyages across the treacherous oceans to and from India. But she was too late. The word had been said. Edward had leaped up from the desk, almost overturning the inkstand.

'America!' he burst out, his eyes blazing with excitement. 'Only think of it, Mama, the prairies, the forests – oh, I would like nothing better than to go to America!'

Her head on one side, Fanny considered the New World. A picture came into her mind of a white-pillared plantation, a field of labouring darkies, and a shed full of bales of cotton. She dismissed it. It was too like India.

'No,' she said at last. 'The climate would not do for me. It is too hot. And you need money, you know, to buy a plantation. They are not to be had for nothing.'

'Not the south,' said Edward, still on fire with excitement. 'The north, where there are beavers and bears and unexplored forests, and oh, Mama, just think of the Wild West!'

The Wild West found no more favour with Fanny than the Deep South. 'Yes, dear,' she said practically, 'but your father would have to work you know, and cities are where he does best. I fancy you would not enjoy the life of New York or Boston without some money to set us up, for we know nobody there and, besides, the snow in winter is enough to freeze you in your bed.'

The heat and cold had disposed of America, and Fanny fell silent for a moment. She sat down again beside Hector and put her hand on his arm. He had sunk into a lethargy. His eyes seemed to have receded into his head. His hands were planted motionless on his knees. He roused himself and looked at Fanny. She was flushed and prettier than ever, her face only slightly less excited than her son's. It sent a pang to Hector's heart and he clenched his teeth in distress.

'Don't, Hector. Don't look so discouraged. We have it all planned. We are to emigrate, you know, only not to America, on account of the heat and the cold. It only remains to settle on a suitable country.'

'New South Wales!' Edward was radiant at the prospect. He had never been so excited in his life. If a messenger had arrived at that moment with the news that Hector's fortune had been miraculously restored, he would have been thoroughly disappointed.

'The Antipodes! Well, that is a good idea, Teddy. There are sheep, I believe, and Hector would soon have a great understanding of wool.'

Aggie looked from her sister to her nephew in dismay. She could not bear to hear the way their talk was going. What could Fanny be thinking of, encouraging Teddy in such wild ideas? She had to admire her sister's fortitude, of course. She was taking the shock remarkably well. Perhaps it was the shock that could account for it. Perhaps Fanny had become unhinged. This talk of emigration could only be explained by insanity. Fanny would surely not be joking at such a time as this.

Aggie was right. Fanny was not joking, but neither was she losing her wits. She had understood almost at once the magnitude of the disaster that had overcome her family. It was as if, over the last few weeks of tension, while she had been watching Hector become ever more distraught, she had been unconsciously preparing herself for it. The strange thing was that now the blow had fallen, she felt above all a sense of relief. No doubt, later on, she would become regretful. She would resent the loss of her ball gowns and feel the lack of her carriage. But now she felt only how good it would be to be active again. The dawdling life of Enfield had not suited her at all. She was sick and tired of making endless calls, conversing politely with ladies who had never been further from home than Brighton or Harrogate, deferring to Lady Dunstable at every social gathering in order to please Justina. She did not even have the distraction of the flirtations she had found so amusing in Calcutta. The stuffy society of Middlesex did not understand that kind of thing, and in any case it seemed ridiculous in the mother of a grown-up son and daughter.

Fanny had been bored and a violent change in her circumstances could only bring a welcome stimulus. She did not, after all, she thought, enjoy being a grand lady as much as she had expected. For one thing, she was acutely aware of the sneers of half the women she met, who did not bother to hide the contempt they felt for a family so newly raised from obscurity to wealth. For another, she did not enjoy the responsibilities of the great lady. It was not in her nature to patronise her inferiors. She was distressed by the poverty of the cottagers she felt obliged to visit, but she did not feel competent to offer them advice or suggest remedies for their manifold diseases. And she did not like running bazaars. The thought of travelling, to a country far away from the petty snobberies and trivialities of England, was like a window opening through which she might fly to freedom, as she had once flown from her father's house to India. The very idea made her feel young again. The happiest time of her life had, after all, been those early years in Calcutta, before the cares of a great fortune pressed down so heavily on Hector's spirits.

Hector, his eyes still fixed on his wife, took courage. She was magnificent, his Fanny, equal to everything. He remembered how he had once had to hold her back as she struggled to evade his grip and look over the rail of the East Indiaman at the grisly corpse caught in the anchor chain on the Hooghly. All her life she had run to meet every challenge, eyes sparkling, hands outstretched. She would run to meet this one and, if he was not careful, she would leave him behind.

Another picture came to his mind. He saw again the emigrant ship, bound for New Zealand, and the groups of men and women, determined, energetic, confident, walking about the deck of the ship. It was an idea. Certainly, it was an idea . . .

The door opened and Jackson entered, carrying a silver tea-tray on which a Wedgwood service was laid out on a cloth of Nottingham lace. Fanny looked at it and broke into a peal of laughter.

'You may take the tray away, Jackson. We're much too poor to drink out of such fine cups now. It will be only common earthenware in the future, I'm afraid.'

2 — *April 1842*

'Excuse *me*, ma'am.' The auctioneer, stepping over a rolled-up Turkish carpet between Fanny and a crate of china, spoke in a voice of unctuous deference. He had attended many households at times such as these and had scant sympathy for financial failure, but he knew that a little oil applied all round was good for business, and, by adding more items to the forthcoming sale, could help to increase his commission.

'Oh, Mr Smedley, is that you?' Fanny was working her way through a sheaf of receipts that had long lain forgotten at the back of her desk. 'You must take a look at these figures to get some idea of the true value of the clocks, china, ornaments and so on. The pair of Egyptian vases, for example, are very good. I paid more than fifty guineas for them.'

Mr Smedley smiled consolingly.

'And very lovely they are too, ma'am, just such as I would choose to have in my small home if they were not quite so large. But sadly, you know how it is, the fashion changes and we must not expect more than five pounds for the pair.'

He passed on quickly, not wishing to be caught in a conversation that would, he knew only too well, bring satisfaction to neither party, and left Fanny to her scribbled lists. She sighed, gathered up the receipts and dropped them in a heap on the table. Mr Smedley was quite right. She had attended countless sales in Calcutta of the effects of people departing hastily for home and she knew only too well how cheap things were to be got at auction. She had herself profited many times from the circumstance in her early days, when she and Hector were living on his meagre salary from Murchison's. It was a good thing, she thought practically, that Aggie had brought her up to be thrifty, for, though she had happily squandered Hector's money while it was there for the spending, the old habits had never quite been forgotten and now they were needed she found it only natural to reduce her table to a nourishing minimum, to cut down to a skeleton staff of three servants in the few weeks that remained to them at Enfield, to shut off those rooms of the house that were not in general use and to take stock of her clothing in order to see what might be altered for the voyage and the unknown life ahead.

Surprisingly, it was Aggie who seemed least able to adapt her mind to the change of situation. She lived in a turmoil of sympathy for her sister's family and dread of the forthcoming parting. Her own income, invested by her canny father, had been derisory in relation to the Jamieson fortune but now it seemed indecently large to Aggie. She had repeatedly begged Hector to take over the capital and, after accepting that she could not change his mind, had spent hours in puzzling over the income, saving every penny she could to spend on comforts for Fanny and Edward on the terrifying voyage to which they were looking forward with such astonishing sangfroid.

Fanny had to keep a constant watch over her sister. She had accepted the gift of a warm, fleece-lined cloak, which, she agreed, would be most useful both at sea and on land, but she had remonstrated over the five flannel petticoats which she had found surreptitiously packed at the bottom of a sea-chest, and she had objected even more when Aggie had produced supplies of potted meats, preserved by an ingenious arrangement of sealed tins.

'We are not quite reduced to common emigrants, Aggie dear,' she laughed at her sister. 'Hector is to arrange cabin accommodation for us and the food on board is excellent, I am told. The New Zealand Company is not at all like those dreadful Australian and American runs, forever skimping on the passengers' fare. Hector has inspected some of the ships, you know, at Blackwall, and he says they are more comfortable in every way than the old East Indiamen. The diet will be very adequate, I am sure, and I will put by some raspberry vinegar and ginger beer powder and such like to add to the water for it is never drinkable on its own after the first week or two.'

Aggie had been forced to bow to Fanny's superior knowledge of travel. She had sat tightlipped on a chair, placed out of the way by a condescending clerk in Mounery's, the emigrant outfitters in Fenchurch Street, while Fanny haggled over cabin furniture, sea bedding and tin chests for the hold and laid out some of her carefully counted sovereigns on marine soap for salt water use, a cabin candle lamp and a metal washbasin.

As the days had passed and the nightmare had begun to take shape, Aggie had become more and more obsessed with the details of making and mending, and as she stitched at canvas linen bags for cabin use and flannel linings to stays, she began to conceive in her mind a plan so daring it almost took her breath away. Parting with Teddy, and with Fanny and Hector too, of course, was too painful to be borne. If she let them go off to New Zealand without her, she would never see them again. Even if they survived the storms, icebergs and ferocious whales (Aggie had seen a print of such creatures at the moment of capture and had disapproved of the species at once), they would surely succumb to the clubs and spears of the Maoris. Even if, by some miracle, they outlived all these terrors, they would never, she felt sure, risk the journey home once the move had been made.

Their minds had been made up. She had given up trying to change them. The only answer, then, was for her to go with them. A cold terror in the pit of her stomach rejected this idea when it first occurred to her, but, unbidden, the thought returned, not once but again and again until Aggie began to feel carried away in its grip. She was not ready, yet, to share the idea with anyone else but quietly, secretly, she began to amass her own piles of felt petticoats and cotton chemises. There would be time enough to broach the subject, she felt sure, once she had returned to Edinburgh with Teddy and Fanny. Hector would be remaining behind in London to see to the shipping of the patent hand mills and steel ploughs he was taking with him as the basis for the new trade empire he hoped to build. He would embark at Gravesend at the end of June and make the sea journey to Greenock, where the ship would take on board its load of hardy Scottish emigrants, who would be travelling steerage, and Fanny and Teddy in the cabin accommodation.

With her secret locked in her breast, Aggie had even, for the first time in her life, resorted to cunning. When Hector had brought home a printed handbill describing the *New Zealand*, on which he proposed to embark his family, Aggie, while pretending to make a note of the cabin dimensions for the purpose of seeing whether Fanny's old sea-chest would fit, had surreptitiously noted down the address of the Scottish agents, Andrew Mercer, Son and Co. of Greenock, and had even sent off a letter enquiring in a roundabout way into the availability of further cabins suitable for single ladies.

Fanny, working from dawn to dusk at the dismantling of the Bushy House home and the preparations for the voyage, had seen nothing amiss with her sister, beyond a slight increase in her normal acidity. She had, in the first rush of enthusiasm, decided to part with everything. Pictures, books, furniture, silver, china – all would go under the hammer. But now, at the last minute, aware of Mr Smedley's thinly veiled contempt, she was having second thoughts. A few items, just one or two, particularly those whose purchase dated from the early years of her marriage, might surely be saved? After all, if Hector was proposing to fill up half the hold with his horrid mills and ploughs and winnowing machines, surely she could take one crate of silver, and a few pieces of china, if carefully packed? Pictures, too, cut out of their frames and rolled in green silk, took up very little space and would survive the journey well if only the salt water did not get at them. And it would be such a shame to leave behind all her comforts, such as her new feather pillows, which were so conducive to a hearty sleep.

Wandering from room to room, ever aware of the ubiquitous Mr Smedley, Fanny came to a stop before the small piano in her boudoir. So many happy hours she had spent here, playing her favourite airs and accompanying Hector as they read through the latest book of German songs. She put out her hand to stroke the silk-like ebony and straightened the brass candle brackets on the handsome front panels. She had always preferred the softer tone of this dear little instrument to the louder, showier sound of the grand piano in the drawing room. Come to think of it, it had been the first item she had bought in those heady early days in England, when she had spent with a free hand in every London warehouse.

She sat down and ran her fingers over the keys, then sprang up suddenly as her eye caught the auctioneer's ticket laid on the top. No, Mr Smedley would not have this! She could forgo her silly desk with the lid that did not shut properly and the gothic chairs which she had never really admired, but this little piano was truly hers and, by hook or by crook, she would take it with her. They would need music in New Zealand more than they had ever needed it at home. Fanny bent down and played a jig, then straightened up at the sound of the door opening behind her. Sir Andrew came into the room.

'Why, Andrew, how kind of you to call so early. You have come for the bundle of old clothing, I am sure, that Lady Dunstable wished me to . . . '

'No – yes, that is, of course I can take it if you have it ready.' Sir Andrew's lean face looked perturbed and his punctilious manners had for once deserted him. 'I called, in fact, to see Mr Jamieson, on a matter of some – but I suppose . . . '

'Oh, Hector is in town, as ever, hunting about for bargains in his ridiculous agricultural warehouses. You know we are soon to be quite rich again, when he has turned all his ploughs and suchlike into a good profit.'

Sir Andrew's frown was prompted by a combination of emotions: distaste for the mention of profit, disappointment at finding Hector away from home, and disapproval of Fanny's levity.

'I hardly think that now' – he waved a newspaper in front of Fanny's eyes – 'when Mr Jamieson hears what I have to tell him, this project of New Zealand will go any further.'

Fanny raised her eyebrows. 'Why, Andrew, what can you mean? Whatever could stop our departure now? Our passage is all arranged with the New Zealand Company. Hector has bought shares in the colony of Nelson. Did he not tell you? We have actually fixed on the site for our new home, or at least, it will be fixed as soon as the land is properly surveyed, in the town that is to be built. There is a handsome harbour and a charming vista across the Cook Strait. You see I have learned all the names. The climate, we are told, is—'

She stopped, checked by an impatient movement of Sir Andrew's arm.

'Do not go on, I beg you, ma'am. When you hear what I have to tell Mr Jamieson—'

'Yes, but why can you not tell me, Andrew? What has happened? Has the company gone bankrupt? Heavens! What a shocking thought! Our last few pounds! Andrew, do not tease me, tell me what it is at once.'

Sir Andrew had been accustomed to receiving orders from powerful women all his life and he was no match for Fanny. He hemmed and hawed for a moment or two, muttered, 'I wish Mr Jamieson were here,' and 'I wish I knew what to do for the best,' and finally, seeing the spark in Fanny's eyes turn from impatience to real irritation, he pulled out *The Times* once more and said, in solemn and portentous tones, 'You must imagine my feelings when I read in the newspaper an account of one Joshua Newburn, a young man who has recently escaped after being nine years a prisoner of the Maoris. He even underwent the appalling disfigurement of tattooing, which I believe is a common practice among that unhappy people. His sufferings, wandering half naked through forests of fern which chafed and lacerated his skin, the appalling barbarities he witnessed, slices of scarce dead enemies being cut off and devoured, eyes pulled out— ' he held the newspaper out of reach of Fanny's outstretched hand. 'No, no, I assure you, it is not suitable for the eyes of a delicate female. Such horrid scenes, such dangers, I had no idea – surely you cannot now, in the light of this, have the temerity to venture all in such a wild place?'

Fanny, unable to bear the pomposity of her son-in-law any longer, burst out laughing.

'What? Is that all? I thought you had something dreadful to tell me. I should scold you, Andrew, for giving me such a fright over nothing. Your poor Mr Newburn no doubt has had his sufferings, but there is nothing to fear, in a general way, from the native population. They have lived peacefully side by side with whalers and such ruffians for years and will be all the happier to meet with good law-abiding settlers like ourselves. Why, in India, if I told you of the frightful practices of persons with whom one never came into contact, thugee, you know, and the punishments inflicted on themselves by the holy men . . . '

She saw Sir Andrew blench at the thought of hearing such things from a lady and took pity on him.

'No, Andrew, you must understand. We are seasoned travellers and not to be put off by such blown up accounts of horrors and disasters. Why, I daresay you are more likely to suffer death at the hand of an honest English footpad than we are to fall foul of the Maori. Now do, I beg you, take the bundle and tell your mama . . . '

'But that is not all!' Sir Andrew's agitation reduced his voice to an undignified squeak. 'I have come across such reports of Port Nicholson which must give you pause for thought.'

He pulled another tattered newspaper from the large pocket in the skirt of his coat and searched for the place. 'Ah yes.' He cleared his throat. ' "We sailed safely through Cook Strait but a hurricane blew us a hundred miles out to sea." ' He stopped, and looked meaningfully at Fanny. 'You see the dangers of navigation in those turbulent waters?' He waited for an answer, but received only a shrug. ' "Provisions here are dear, pork and potatoes scarce, fresh butter at three shillings a pound, eggs six shillings a dozen . . . emigrants who left London last year still do not have their allotment of land . . . affairs gloomy . . . all here disappointed . . . not a road commenced, not a house built . . . one day intense cold and rain, the next a broiling sun . . . " You see how you have been misinformed! You cannot, surely, contemplate removing to such a desolate – without any of the comforts of – fraught with so many . . . ' His perturbation rendering him at last speechless, Sir Andrew stopped talking and stood helplessly waving his newspaper in the air.

Fanny gently removed it from his grasp.

'Now, Andrew,' she said, in the tones of one speaking to a child, 'you are not to get into such a taking. I could show you a dozen reports of quite a different nature from those you have brought me. Bad news is always sensational, you know, and is the first to be reported in the newspaper. Why, I laugh when I read the horrors that are written about life in Calcutta, which I know from my own experience to be perfectly safe and ordinary. You really must have a little more faith in Hector, my dear. I have followed him blindly since I was nothing but a girl and he has never led me into a scrape yet.'

Sir Andrew, lacking Fanny's adoring trust in her husband, shook his head and sighed.

'Justina has been so brave,' he said, and Fanny was touched to hear the tenderness in his voice. 'She is so young, so newly reunited with her parents. I fear that this parting will cause her much anguish of mind. I could not bear to see her unhappy.'

He smiled at Fanny for the first time, and shook his head as if disclaiming his own weakness. It had, indeed, taken him by surprise. He had astonished himself, and greatly annoyed old Lady Dunstable, by falling deeply in love with his young wife. Justina's hero worship had touched him to the heart. Her efforts to please him and her reverence for his lightest word had broken through his customary arrogance. Her belief in his strength of character and in the infallibility of his opinions had aroused in him depths which he never knew he possessed. He had even found the will to stand up to his mother, who now thought twice before attempting to bully her daughter-in-law.

Fanny, watching the progress of the young couple, had been half irritated, half amused. On the one hand it was comforting to know that Justina's marriage seemed set fair for happiness. She could leave her daughter with a clear conscience, safe in the knowledge that she had settled happily into her new home. On the other hand, it was galling to find that Sir Andrew was now the authority on every matter, and that the narrow, cautious Dunstable view of the world had swept aside the broader, bolder outlook of the Jamiesons. 'Sir Andrew thinks' and 'Sir Andrew says' were now the prelude to every sentence Justina uttered, and Fanny was heartily sick of them. Her own view of her son-in-law had not changed. She was glad to know that he had a heart to lose, but she still thought him a dry stick, dull to the point of tediousness in speech and woefully timorous in action. However, she could not let him go, so miserable as he looked, without a word of comfort.

She patted his arm and pulling a document off a pile of newspapers still to be disposed of, pressed it into his hand.

'You will find this more instructional, believe me, than the exaggerated accounts in the newspapers, which are notoriously unreliable. Now, do go home, Andrew, and read to Justina how excellent the climate is, and how plentiful the food, and how splendid the prospects for people of energy. And don't, I beg of you, forget to take the bundle to Lady Dunstable for I must get it out of my way today.'

The quickness in her voice told Sir Andrew that the interview was over. Fanny had lost interest in him and he would get no further with her today. Dejectedly he turned to go. Fanny, relieved that he was at last taking himself off, felt nevertheless moved by his genuine concern.

'There's one thing I'm sure of in all this business,' she said to his retreating back, and he turned at the door to hear her out. 'We're leaving Justina in the best possible hands. I know you'll look after her better than anyone else could have done and she'll be happier in your family even than in her own.'

Sir Andrew's face broke into a smile of unusual warmth and, as she heard his footsteps echo down the now uncarpeted floor of the hall, Fanny reflected on the strange circumstance that she and her son-in-law had never understood each other so well as at the time of their parting.

3 *Edinburgh, July 1842*

Rumour, ever rife among the grimy small-fry of Edinburgh's New Town, had predicted a bustle at the Heriot house in George Street, and for once it proved accurate. The gang of crossing sweepers, caddies and stable lads, watching from the other side of the street, were rewarded with the sight of a hired carriage being loaded with a multitude of boxes and trunks by a sweating jarvey and even more interesting glimpses of tearful females through the half-closed front door.

'Yon's Mrs Fergus, the cook. She's awful wild with her ladle, that she is. Clout you round the lugs, she will, if you even so much as request a bit of her baking.'

'There's old Jeanie, blind as a bat. She's away to her sister's in Fife, I heard my ma tell.'

'Aye, and she's a right fountain of tears today. Go on, Jimmy, lend her your shimmy for a hanky.'

The boys were deflected for a moment as they mocked young Jim, whose shirt, filthier even than those of the others, was rent from neck to hem in two places. They turned back to gape as the front door opened wider and Miss Heriot emerged.

'Hey, watch out! Here she comes!' The young watcher had good reason to be careful. Aggie was feared for her sharpness over such misdemeanours as dropping bundles, stepping on skirts or failing to sweep a proper crossing through the horsy mire of the thoroughfare, but she was also known for the generosity of her payments when such jobs had been properly performed and was therefore an awesome figure.

'There she goes, aye, there's the old dragon herself, away to Americy.'

'She never is! It's Australia. My mam told my pa.'

'You're wrong then, the both of you. It's the other one, the new one, New-something-land.'

'Newfoundland, I bet you.'

'New-lost-land, more like.'

The row of urchins bent double in appreciation of this witticism, then wee Jock straightened up suddenly as inspiration struck.

'New Zealand! That's the one! Where there's awful fierce savages and man-eating lions.'

'Lions! I wadna go there for . . . '

'It's not the lions I'm afraid of. It's the giant crocodiles and the gorillas and the poisonous snakes with bodies as thick as a man's and as long as Princes Street.'

'They are not!'

'They are! Well, Hanover Street, anyway.'

'Go on, I don't believe you.'

'St Stephen's Street then, and that's the truth.'

'You're daft.'

'I am not! You're the one who's daft!'

'I'll show you what I think of you, so there!'

The meeting degenerated in the usual way and the knot of tussling boys was dispersed by a few judicious cracks of the whip from the jarvey, who had earlier taken exception to some of their cheekier sallies and was pleased with the chance to get his revenge. The children straggled away unwillingly back to their tasks, and the coachman, grunting as he straightened out the cricks in his back, which had buckled under the weight of Miss Heriot's emigration outfit, went back into the house in search of another trunk.

Inside the hall, the emotions both of the assembled travellers and those about to be left behind were running high. Of them all, Fanny was the calmest. She had left this house too often to feel the pangs as keenly as the others, and, though she knew that it was, in all probability, for the last time, she had her mind already fixed on the journey ahead, on the reunion with Hector on board ship and on the need to ensure that her party arrived in Greenock in good order and with plenty of time to load their baggage for if the wind was fair Captain Worth would not wait, even for his cabin passengers.

She had surprised herself, these last few weeks, by thoroughly enjoying the prospect of leaving the pampered life of Enfield for the rigours of a wild new world. Her headaches had miraculously disappeared. She was up early each morning, no longer tempted to linger over the lavish breakfast that a maid had been used to bring her, piping hot from the hands of an expert chef. The old elasticity had returned to her step. Instead of collapsing with exhaustion at the end of a languid afternoon, spent sipping tea and exchanging gossip in exquisitely furnished drawing rooms, she found herself still full of energy at ten o'clock at night, after a day spent packing and stitching, clearing out closets and writing a pile of letters.

There had, of course, been painful partings. Mrs Blakeney had spoken quite affectingly. She had, she said, been so inspired by the Jamieson family's enterprise that she was quite infected by the bug of emigration. If it were not for Frank, so happy in his military pursuits, she might almost feel inclined to join them. But then, of course, Fanny would wish her to stay behind and be a friend to Justina, who was losing her entire family at a stroke. Justina had thanked Mrs Blakeney very properly for her kind sentiments but it was clear to everyone that the stroke was falling less cruelly than might be expected. The society of Enfield had remarked on her fortitude with surprise and admiration but Fanny herself had not been astonished at her daughter's calm acceptance of the parting.

After all, she said to herself philosophically, we have not been together very long. It's Aggie who has known her since childhood and they never struck up a very close friendship. And then . . . She did not quite wish to formulate the thoughts that followed but found she could not help herself. She's still ashamed of us, I suppose, with our cheery, old-fashioned ways, and now she's won her ambition and made herself a lady, she'd only find us an embarrassment, living so close as we have been. I'm sure that within a year from now she'll have quite forgotten that her papa started from nowhere and made his fortune in trade and she'll have invented a whole crowd of high-flown relations for herself. She stopped, upset by the bitterness of her train of ideas and feeling a little guilty in case she had failed her daughter in some way, but then she thought, well, when she's my age maybe, with children of her own, she'll see there's other things in life besides grand names and titles and think of us fondly and wish we were near her.

The idea saddened her and she had bustled about more vigorously for a while, until Aggie's sensational announcement had thrust Justina quite out of her mind.

'Aggie! My dear sister! You cannot mean it! You cannot be serious! Think of your terror of the sea, and of your painful hip! You would be undertaking a great deal, more than you realise, I am sure of it. The cramped accommodation, the extremes of heat and cold, the disgusting condition of the drinking water. Of course, it would be wonderful for us to have you with us, but are you sure . . . ?'

But Aggie had been adamant. Her mind was made up and to New Zealand she would go. Now, though, as she stood in the hall of her old home and gave her final instructions to the women who had served her all her life, she felt almost faint with the impossibility of what she was about to do. There had been no time, no time at all, to see to the sale of the house and the auctioning of her effects. She had been obliged to leave everything to the good offices of Mr Elliott and Mrs Macfarlane, whose insistent offers of help she had reluctantly accepted.

'It's the least I can do, Mistress Heriot, after all the many kindnesses you have shown to me,' Mr Elliott had said, smiling down at her, still gawky and boyish despite the patch of thinness on his crown. He was here now, superintending the loading, keeping an eye on the bewildered Jeanie, whose emotions threatened at any moment to overwhelm her, and engaging in last-minute banter with his old friend Teddy, who was too excited to be of any use but kept racing up and down the stairs like an ill-trained puppy, in search of a set of drawing pads and pencils with which he intended to immortalise his discoveries in the fern forests of New Zealand, or a reference work on the habits of molluscs without which he could not possibly put to sea.

The moment of parting came at last. The final box was strapped on, the last embrace given and received. The crowd of friends and well-wishers standing about the front door watched as Aggie locked it behind her and placed the key with a trembling hand into the outstretched palm of Mr Elliott, then marched, grim faced, across the pavement and into the waiting coach. They gave a ragged cheer as the coachman flicked the leader with his whip and the horses, straining to take the weight of the heavily loaded vehicle, shambled into an unwilling trot. The urchins, who had reassembled for the departure, cantered after it, calling out as rudely as they dared, vying with each other in naughtiness, emboldened by the certain knowledge that Mistress Heriot would never come back to scold them.

At the doorstep Mrs Hamilton turned to Mrs Macfarlane and a smirk crossed her face.

'Well, she's making a terrible mistake, and that's for sure, and I put it all down to the bad influence of that flighty sister of hers. Easy come, easy go, that's the story of money and fortune hunters. You mark my words, Mrs Macfarlane, Aggie Heriot will live to rue the day.'

But Mrs Macfarlane did not answer. She was paying silent tribute from the bottom of her heart, not to Fanny, waving triumphantly and benevolently to friend and foe alike, nor to young Edward, jauntily shouting out his farewells from his seat on the roof beside the coachman, but to the courage she had seen in the white, set face of Aggie, who had taken her place in the coach dry-eyed, and had sat bolt upright, staring straight before her, refusing to turn and look back to her old home and the friends of her entire lifetime as the coach rattled away across the cobble stones.

Chapter Ten *Paisley, July 1842*

1

As the Jamiesons' coach lumbered out of Costorphine on its way to Glasgow, a squall of rain which wetted Edward's fustian coat passed westwards and the tail end of it caused Joseph Kirkwood and his two sons, trudging up a steep brae, to pull their caps down over their ears and button up their coats.

The shower had spent itself by the time the three men reached the top of the rise and they shook the drops out of their eyes and stood for a moment, awed by the magnificence of the panorama in front of them.

Immediately below lay the close-packed chimneys of Paisley, bisected by the silver thread of the White Cart River, while to the east lay the dense mass of Glasgow, its streets and squares as sharply defined as on a map in the clear air that had followed the rain. To the north and west lay the ever-widening Clyde, dotted by hundreds of ships, to whose very edge the Highlands seemed to roll down in a tumbling mass of hills, from the far rugged peaks of Argyll to the nearer ridges of Cowall.

The sight moved Joseph to shake his grizzled head.

'It's a bonny land, true enough, but the Lord knows how great a sorrow is hid in yon fair cities.'

Malcolm sighed in sympathy but young Jem, not given to introspection, had seen a field of fat ewes grazing on the slopes of the brae, and was casting a professional eye across them. His two border collies, which customarily ran like lean, silent shadows at his heels, had flopped down panting at the roadside but they followed their master's gaze and trotted over to sit expectantly on their haunches beside him, ready to round the sheep up, separate them out or herd them through the gate at the slightest word of command.

'I hope the *New Zealand* is bigger than yon wee tubs,' said Malcolm apprehensively, not liking the sight of any of the craft that were plying up and down the river beyond the spires of Paisley. Joseph, putting up a hand against the bright sunlight that had succeeded the rain, raked the firth with a sailor's eye.

'There's no great tonnage comes up this far. The sandbanks are treacherous further east than Greenock and the channel's awful hard to navigate. She'll do us fine, the *New Zealand*, for all she's but a Blackwall frigate. She's no great size but she'll be easy to manage in a heavy sea. I mind fine, on the *Speedy* . . . '

His sons exchanged undutiful glances. Their father's garrulity was increasing with his age and he was inclined to dwell at ever increasing length upon his youthful adventures at sea. 'Of course a great boy like you can carry this small sack of coals!' he would say. 'Why, when I was but nine I was heaving cannon across a deck slippery with men's blood. A powder monkey's life . . . ' And, 'What do you mean, you're afraid to scramble down this wee ladder? When I was five years younger than you I was up the rigging in a storm with a rope's end beating at my legs.' The very words 'on the *Speedy*' were enough to send the boys off to occupy themselves elsewhere, and their father, well aware of it, would sometimes avail himself of them with a twinkle in his eye, to drive Malcolm back to sorting threads and Jem off to mind Lord Eglinton's flocks.

Once again, the words worked their magic.

'We'd best get on, Father, before the rain comes on again,' said Malcolm hastily, gripping in his fine artisan's hands the handles of the cart while Jem whistled up Bess and Tam, who had allowed themselves to be distracted by a rabbit hole.

'Did Auntie not expect us yesterday?' Jem asked quickly, as they set off again down the hill, with the transparent intention of keeping his father's mind off past glories. He had been too careless. Joseph turned a shocked face towards him.

'She'd never have looked for us on the Sabbath Day. Have you forgotten already how Mr Murray preached yesterday on the twenty-third psalm and assured us of the prayers of the connection?'

The fact had, indeed, slipped Jem's mind. The past few weeks had passed in such a turmoil that he had hardly known one day from the next. Since his mother's death six months ago, the world seemed to have stood on its head. His horizons, which had until now been confined to the rich pastureland of Lord Eglinton's acres and the occasional seascape beyond, had broadened to embrace the entire world. His mother had hardly been buried when his father had withdrawn a heavy stocking from under his bed and explained to his sons the future he had in mind for them. Malcolm, always timid, had needed much reassurance and Jem had been surprised at how gentle Father had been with him. There was no doubt of the outcome, of course. Malcolm would always be guided by a stronger spirit. As for Jem, he had needed no encouragement. It was in fact the only time he could remember that he and his father had been in complete accord. Once assured that his beloved dogs might emigrate too, Jem was ready to be off at once, the sooner the better, his blood racing with excitement. Joseph had seen it with delight. It was the first time he had worked harmoniously with his son and he harboured hopes that the boy was learning at long last to tread the path of humility.

'How did you persuade my uncle, Father?' said Malcolm. 'I wouldn't have thought he would take easily to a change as great as this. Weaving is everything to him, I've heard you say it often enough yourself.'

'Aye, and weaving's dead, or dying,' said Joseph.

'But things may change again and the Paisley work come back to its old popularity,' said Malcolm doubtfully. 'Fashion is aye a fickle thing . . . '

'Maybe, maybe,' said Joseph heavily, 'but the old craft's going and men as can't see it will go under. It's machine oil will replace human sweat and metal fingers will do the work of flesh and blood.'

'You mean the power looms?' said Malcolm. He had joined in such a discussion a hundred times with his fellow weavers at the close mouth and, unlike his father, had found himself in tune with the opinions of the most conservative. 'No, but, Father, the novelty will soon wear off and they'll break down, and the costs – the investment . . . '

Jem was not interested in this discussion.

'Father,' he interrupted, 'you have not told us. How did you fix it with my uncle?'

'I did not fix anything.' Joseph's tone was reproving. 'The Lord wrought in his heart and led him to see the wisdom of removing from his old place of abode. And besides, things have come to such a pass in Paisley that they face starvation else. I've heard such tales . . . '

They all fell silent, each wondering what they might soon see in the streets of a town whose present fate was sending shudders of dismay through the whole of Scotland.

A puff of wind, blowing from the north, brought a tang of salt to Joseph's nostrils. He raised his head and sniffed it appreciatively. It did not do to be forever brooding over the misery all about. He was leaving it for ever, a free man at last. The years with Eliza had been – well, the Lord had not seen fit to bless him with a healthy wife and the poor soul had caused him more cares than – but she was safe at last, at rest, and he might now live like a man again, fulfil the dream that had sustained him through so many weary years, leave another to plough Mr Turnbull's furrows, wake again to the sound of running feet on decks overhead and shin up the ropes to the yard arm – no, perhaps not that. He must not forget his fifty-one years. There were younger men to sail the boat. It would be his task to look after his family, to protect them and sustain them with the strength that God had given him on the voyage and to guide and encourage them once they had arrived.

It had not, in fact, been easy to persuade Isaiah to join him in the venture, in spite of the pressure he was under from his wife.

'Emigrate? To New Zealand? Joseph, you do not know what you are saying! The terrible distance, and the work – you know I am not fit for it. I know no craft but weaving so how can I be expected to – to hack down forests, defend myself against wild animals and – and . . . ' His knowledge of the world beyond Paisley being sketchy, these objections soon ran out. He tried again.

'No, but, brother, are you mad? Isobel, her health would never stand it, and as for the bairns . . . ' He indicated Meg, whose eyes were still fixed industriously on her tambour frame, her fingers racing to achieve the day's tally of work, and little Jessie, who sat, her gaze intent on her uncle's face, one hand clutching at the ends of the ragged shawl that scarcely covered her thin shoulders. She waited until her elders paused, then dared to ask the question that had been burning within her.

'Are there piglets in New Zealand, Uncle?'

'Aye, my lassie, and plenty of them.'

'Calves?'

'Aye.'

'Cream on the milk?'

'For sure.'

'And – and . . . ' she sought about for the loveliest thing she had ever seen. 'Spiders' webs?'

The leather that was Joseph's skin wrinkled as his eyes smiled from beneath jutting, bushy brows at his small niece.

'I couldn't say for sure about the webs,' he said, with a scrupulous regard for truth, 'but there's plenty of good things to eat, heaps of pork running with fat, and tatties, and great big fishes swimming about in the rivers, and plump fowl, and . . . '

Food had been scarce in the Dunbar household since Martinmas, for Isobel, scraping together every penny she could for the great adventure, had fed her family sparingly and on the simplest victuals. The idea of pork and tatties was so appealing that Jessie closed her eyes for a moment, almost believing she could smell them. She jumped off her stool and stood beside her uncle.

'I'm coming with you,' she said firmly. 'I can manage fine without the spiders.'

The big man picked the child up, surprised by how easily he could lift her, and set her on his knee. Jessie did not speak again. She sat still, her hands tight clenched on her lap, her forehead wrinkled thoughtfully under the fine, mouse-brown hair that fell below her shoulders, her solemn brown eyes so full of desire and a kind of desperate courage that Isobel dabbed her own with a corner of her apron when she saw them.

His whole family now working against him, Isaiah had not been able to hold out for long. He had at last seen the sense of the idea, though he had brought Joseph's patience near to straining point with his endless landlubber's haverings, his querulous questions and complaints.

The iron-bound wheel of the handcart was ringing now on the cobbled streets of Paisley and before long Malcolm dropped the handles gratefully outside his aunt's small cottage. The three men had fallen silent once they had entered the town. This was not the place they remembered from a couple of years ago, when a column of smoke had risen from every chimney and the streets had been full of a happy bustle, drowning out even the clack of the thousand looms at work behind each pair of well-washed windows. Jem had turned away, sickened, at the sight of a woman, too emaciated to move, who sat listlessly by a wall, her half-clad infant crawling in the filth beside her, and Malcolm had stared straight ahead, afraid of seeing worse, while Joseph shook his head in sympathy and had had to be restrained by both his sons from giving away the coat from his own back to a destitute weaver, who sat hunched in his doorway racked by a tremendous cough.

The sight of her brawny nephews brought a flush of pleasure to the pale cheeks of Isobel Dunbar. They looked so strong and well fed, so rosy-cheeked and cheerful, so like their rock-like father. The very sight of them gave her confidence and she was able to ladle out the porridge and buttermilk that constituted their frugal supper with more gaiety than she had felt for years.

'So, brother,' she said, pushing a wisp of hair off her blue-veined forehead, 'it's off to sea again for you, only this time you'll not be content until you've dragged your whole family off with you.'

'Well,' Joseph solemnly shook his head. 'The fact of the matter is, if you really wish to know, I was that feared to go to sea again I had to have my wee sister with me to give me courage. I could not bear to face all they monsters, and horrible big waves, and scaly beasties with hundreds of rows of teeth, and tempests, and slimy things with dozens of arms and legs, and—'

'Joseph, will you stop your nonsense now!' said Isobel sharply, casting an anxious glance towards her husband, who was looking grave and pulling nervously at his whiskers. Joseph was a terror for the jokes and teases, and Isaiah, poor soul, had not a shred of humour in him while his fears, once roused, were not easily stilled.

'Sea monsters! Well, brother, I do not at all like the sound of that. I thought you had told us quite clearly that there was no danger to be feared from the creatures of the deep, but if indeed . . . '

'Och no,' broke in Jem hastily. 'It's but one of Father's jokes, Uncle.'

'Jokes!' Isaiah looked puzzled and shook his head. 'Aye, well, I was never a great one for the jokes.'

Jessie, passing behind the box on which her father sat with a plate of porridge in his hand, stifled a giggle, then looked down anxiously to check that she had not spilled any on her wonderful new clothes. The responsibility of them was weighing on her, dulling the edge of the deep sense of satisfaction she had felt since, earlier in the day, her mother had stripped her of her old, ill-fitting garments, had bathed her skinny little body from head to foot and dressed her in a new pair of stays, a dazzling white cotton petticoat, a new brown dress, with a neckerchief about her shoulders, black worsted stockings and, wonder of wonders, an actual pair of right and left shoes, a little large about the toes and heels perhaps but the finest things she had ever owned. She had stuck out her feet to gaze at them long and wonderingly, admiring the clever way they were shaped differently to fit each foot. Isobel had sat back on her heels to view her little daughter.

'You look grand. Just grand.'

Jessie was unused to considering her own appearance but now she felt suddenly curious.

'Am I pretty, Mam?'

Isobel, still kneeling, put her arms round Jessie and pulled her into a rare embrace.

'You're as pretty as – as a rosebud,' she said awkwardly. She had never been a demonstrative woman but Jessie in her finery had touched her.

The child stood perfectly still. She was not accustomed to showing her feelings. They lived and grew deep within her and were seldom shared. Her mother's words struck into her heart and the joy they gave birth to filled her whole being. Isobel, watching, saw only a glow in her dark eyes and a flush mount her cheek. She had struggled to her feet, checked a moment to fight an attack of breathlessness and went on sorting cotton reels and needles in the sewing box that would accompany her on the voyage, while Jessie tiptoed about the house, hugging herself with joy yet fearful of scratching her shoes or creasing her gown.

Emigration was a wonderful thing, she thought. It made you rich at once. Never before had she seen money spent on such a scale. The trunks and boxes which now lay about the otherwise empty cottage were filled to overflowing with such items as nightdresses, caps, gowns, bonnets, cloaks and shawls for herself, her mother and Meg, and fustian jackets, duck trousers, Guernsey shirts and caps for her father, all as nearly new as made no difference. It was necessary, Uncle Joseph had said, to fit themselves out completely according to the recommendations of the New Zealand Company and the lists with which they had been issued had been scrutinised and followed to the letter. Towels, sheets, tablecloths, blankets, bolsters and counterpanes had all been reverently laid in a series of sea-chests, while pride of place on the top was given to the treasured feathered quilt which Mr Elliott had brought, a gift from heaven, at the time of their greatest need. An empty crate stood ready to receive the cups, plates, knives, forks and cooking pots which would be bestowed in them after supper. On Joseph's advice, too, a barrel of oatmeal, some potatoes and flour had been purchased, to add to the basic diet of ship's biscuits and salt meat which would be provided on the voyage, while Joseph himself had put up a supply of rice, tea, sugar, treacle and allspice.

The colossal expenditure involved had sent Isaiah into a frenzy of worry. He was never happy unless he could save a little for 'a rainy day', and even when his children had had to go hungry to bed, he had never allowed Isobel to borrow from the money put by for the rent. It had taken some time for the idea to sink in that there was no point in saving for the rent if the rent would never again have to be paid, nor was there any point in clinging on to items of furniture when they could not be taken abroad. It was Isobel who had had to manage everything, and by dint of persuading her husband to part with his savings, realising all their remaining assets, extracting £2. 10s. repayment from the landlord for the six months that had been paid in advance and accepting (without Isaiah's knowledge) a generous sum from Joseph's secret hoard, she had done very creditably. The family would set out well equipped and respectable. She could do no more.

The meal over, Jem slipped away from the 'table' (made from two chests put together and covered with a tablecloth) and, pulling a malodorous package from the top of a bundle, laid out an unappetising mess in the corner of the room, on which Bess and Tam fell ravenously. Their snufflings roused Isaiah from his brooding.

'You're never taking your dogs to New Zealand?'

'That I am, Uncle,' Jem said, bracing himself for criticism.

'How will they eat? You'll no be feeding them on sea-water?'

Malcolm laughed a little sourly.

'You'll never get Jem to part from his dogs, Uncle. If he could not take them with him, he would not go at all.'

'Aye, but who's to pay for their victualling, and where are they to be stowed?' Isaiah's indignation was growing.

'Oh, you don't know the half of what this lad of mine will do for these hairy creatures.' Joseph's voice expressed a mixture of pride and exasperation.

Jem leaped to his own defence. 'I'll need them in New Zealand, Father, you know that. If I'm to work as a shepherd I'll be lost without my dogs. And besides, Bess is a good strong breeder and if I can sell the pups it will be worth what I've paid for their passage.'

'Paid?' Isaiah squealed. 'The waste! To squander money on lifting dogs half-way around the world! I never heard . . . '

'Whisht, man,' Joseph broke in peaceably. 'It was Lord Eglinton who paid.'

'Lord Eglinton?'

'Aye. He's a great one for the shooting, with all his grand friends and relations, and when they're after partridges and pheasants and such like there's not a man on the estate but has to drop his work and get out to beat. Well, my fine lord has a friend he wants to impress – Lord Hamsey or some such, was it not, Jimmy?' Jem nodded and tried to look modest. Joseph chuckled. 'You'll never believe what daft ideas these noble lords cooked up between them.' He looked round the circle of faces, lit up by the last rays of the late evening summer sun that filtered through the crooked panes of glass in the single window of the cottage. 'A wager! Sinful nonsense, but there's lords for you. Five hundred pounds of good money that would keep a family of weavers for years, to be paid to the man who could slaughter most birds in a day. "Take your pick of my men to be your loader," says Lord Eglinton, laughing up his sleeve. "Oh," puffs Lord Hamsey, "I'll take your head gamekeeper, for he should know the business right enough." "Fine, fine," says Lord Eglinton, and he sends for our Jimmy, knowing as he does that there's not a man in Ayrshire can load a gun so fast. "There's ten sovereigns in it for you and a suit of sporting clothes to take with you on this crazy emigration adventure of yours," says my lord, "if we bag the most birds," and he had a bargain, so he did, for ten sovereigns was nothing compared to the five hundred pounds he won from Lord Hamsey,' and Joseph, who at the time had spoken out strongly and at length against the wickedness of wagers, and the immoral behaviour of the aristocracy in general and Lord Eglinton in particular, laughed again at the thought of Jem's skill, which, in the euphoria he felt in his new-found happiness with his son, now outweighed all else in his memory.

'Ten sovereigns!' Isaiah's eyes were round as he contemplated the hero of the tale. Then he pursed his lips. 'It's as they say, a fool and his money are soon parted, and why you should choose to spend ten sovereigns on naught but a pair of . . . '

'But he didn't, husband,' put in Isobel, smiling at her nephew. 'He gave four of them to his father, to help with the expense of the outfitting, didn't you Jem?'

The virtuous aura that surrounded Jem disgusted Malcolm. He looked across the room towards Meg, the quiet one of the family, the one he most approved of and was relieved to see that, far from gazing at Jem with the fatuous admiration that energetic lad aroused in most female breasts, Meg shared her father's disapproval and was looking at the dogs in the corner with distaste. Malcolm followed her glance. Jessie, while everyone had been listening to Joseph's story, had been cautiously approaching them and was now bending over Tam, watching him with interest while he ate, one tentative hand stretched out to stroke his rough black coat.

'No! Stop it! Don't touch him, Jessie!' Jem's sharp voice made her start back, and Tam and Bess, thinking the command was for them, flattened themselves on the floor and laid their long snouts between their front paws, swivelling their eyes round towards their master in the fear that rebuke would be followed with chastisement.

'Don't fondle them, for goodness' sake. They're not lap dogs.' Anxiety had made Jem speak more roughly than he meant to, for he was afraid that Tam might turn and maul the small hand.

'They'll give you a mighty nip if you do,' said Malcolm with satisfaction, glad to see Jem's star a little on the wane.

'Savage, are they?' Isaiah's face was lengthening again.

'Of course they're not savage,' burst out Jem, enraged at the insult. 'But you should never interfere with a dog when he's feeding. Any fool knows that.'

Jessie crept back to her place, shrivelled with embarrassment. She had been half inclined to place her handsome cousin on a pedestal. But he had fallen from grace before he had had time to acquire it.

In the silence that followed, Joseph cleared his throat.

'Before we go to our rest, let us seek a word from the Good Book.' He directed Malcolm with a nod to a box in the corner of the room, and Malcolm extracted from it a well-worn Bible and laid it on his father's knee. Joseph opened it, looked down the page and smiled.

'The Lord has directed my eyes,' he said, 'and sent us a word of comfort meet for the occasion.' He began to read in a deep, resonant voice, allowing the words to roll off his tongue and pausing majestically between the verses.

' "Ho, everyone that thirsteth, come ye to the waters, and he that hath no money; come ye, buy, and eat; yea, come, buy wine and milk without money and without price. Wherefore do ye spend money for that which is not bread? and your labour for that which satisfieth not?" '

Isaiah shot a meaningful look at Jem and seemed about to speak, but Isobel nudged him into silence.

' "Hearken diligently unto me, and eat ye that which is good, and let your soul delight itself in fatness." '

A sigh broke from Jessie and her mind, fluttering down from the lofty heights at which she had been trying to keep it, conjured up a picture of delicious things to eat, such as she had but rarely tasted and of which she so often dreamed. She came back to reality with a start as her uncle's voice, so strong you could almost lean on it, poured out words she hardly understood but which filled her with a feeling almost akin to ecstasy.

'"For ye shall go out with joy, and be led forth with peace: the mountains and the hills shall break forth before you into singing, and all the trees of the field shall clap their hands. Instead of the thorn shall come up the fir tree, and instead of the briar shall come up the myrtle tree: and it shall be to the Lord for a name, for an everlasting sign that shall not be cut off."'

No one cared to break in on the silence that followed the reading, until Isobel, seeing the words 'Let us pray' forming on her brother's lips, forestalled him. Joseph's prayers were capable of lasting for upwards of forty minutes and she for one was conscious of the tasks that had to be done before the family could lie down and sleep.

'Isaiah, will you pronounce a blessing on us?' she said quickly, and when her husband's 'Amen' had sounded she rose to her feet and busied herself about the bare cottage, directing her daughters to wash and pack the utensils and her nephews to lay out bedding on the floor. When all was done, the Kirkwoods and Dunbars lay down to rest, the young to sleep peacefully, the older ones to toss and turn, fearful of the momentous day about to dawn.

2

Isobel, struggling up the gangway, gasped for breath and dropped the canvas bag she was carrying. Meg was directly behind her. She was jerked to a halt, and leant forward to look at her mother.

'Is something wrong, Ma? You look awful pale.'

'No, no, I'm fine. Just give me a moment to catch my breath.'

Behind them, the crowd of men and women pressing up on to the ship craned their necks to see what was causing the stoppage.

'Will you get along there, for goodness' sake?'

'What's stopping them now?'

'You keep your hands to yourself, you Irish bogtrotter!'

Joseph Kirkwood thrust his load into Jem's already straining arms, pushed his sister gently aside, and picked up her bag. The stream of humanity moved forward under a wheeling arc of gulls screaming overhead.

Once on deck, Joseph looked about appreciatively. The ship was small but it was in good order. He noticed approvingly the neatness of the rigging and the cleanliness of the scrubbed boards. The first mate had spotted a frayed rope end and was directing a sailor aloft to whip it. Joseph grinned reminiscently at the bark in the officer's voice and the alacrity of the sailor's response. Just so, on the *Speedy* . . . But he had no time for that now. His family had gone on ahead of him and had already disappeared down the companionway to the emigrants' quarters on the between deck below. He could hear Isaiah's voice raised in complaint.

Joseph sighed, shifted the bag on to his shoulder and nimbly lowered it and himself down the ladder-like stair to the dark interior of the ship. Even he, used as he was to the rigours of life at sea, felt his heart sink as he surveyed the scene within.

The between deck, which was to house the steerage passengers for the next five or six months, was a broad, low space running the whole breadth and length of the ship. A long table ran down the middle, with fixed benches at each side. Jutting out from each curved wall were double tiers of bunks, joined together with no space in between, so that the only way their occupants could enter them was by plunging in head first, or worming their bodies in after their feet.

'There must be some mistake. This cannot be correct.'

Joseph's heart sank still further at the sound of his brother-in-law's high, complaining voice as he pushed his way through the mass of bags, bundles and people between the benches and the bunk ends. Isaiah turned to him, overwrought.

'It appears that our entire accommodation is to consist of no more than two small bunks, one for myself and Isobel above' – he indicated with disgust the cavity six feet long and three feet wide by his head, separated from its neighbours on either side by no more than a low wooden wall, two feet high – 'and this is for the girls here below.' He peered into the dark narrow hole at his feet only to meet the delighted face of Jessie.

'It's our own dear wee bed, Meg,' Jessie called out, peering round her father's legs to where her sister, appalled, was standing gazing at a couple of barefoot Highland women who, amid excited Gaelic chatter, were unpacking an odoriferous bundle of cheeses and laying them on the table.

'Aye, well, it's cramped enough,' said Joseph peaceably, 'but that's sea life for you. And no doubt we'll get along well enough when we're acquainted with our neighbours.' He had no time for more.

'What are you doing here, man? Where's your wife and bairns?'

A small man in an officer's uniform was frowning up at him.

'My wife's with the Lord,' said Joseph, 'and my sons are here behind me.'

'Then you've no business in the married quarters,' said the officer briskly. 'Away forrard with you. That's where the single men are berthed.'

Joseph drew himself up smartly. 'Aye aye, sir.'

The officer's eyes twinkled. 'An old sailor, are you?'

'Royal Navy, sir.' Joseph did not attempt to disguise the pride in his voice.

'A man o' war's man? Very good.'

The officer looked him up and down. This was just the kind of fellow he needed, strong, sober, humorous, used to the sea and to the ways of young men.

'What's your name?'

'Kirkwood, sir.'

'Well, Mr Kirkwood, I'll be grateful for your help. I've thirty young rascals penned up in the single men's berths, and all of them dying to get at the grog and at the young ladies in their quarters astern. I could use a man like you to help me keep them in check. Turner's my name, Frank Turner, ship's surgeon.' The surgeon held out his hand. Joseph shook it, picked up his gear once more and began to lead Jem and Malcolm to their quarters, Tam and Bess clinging to their master's heels.

'No, but this is too much!' Isaiah's querulous voice rose high above the clamour of the 'tween deck. The surgeon turned. Isaiah's confidence began to ooze out of him under Mr Turner's eye, from which the twinkle had departed, leaving it fishy and cold.

'Human beings cannot be expected to sleep like this, herded together, married people, with no privacy. There's men and women all jumbled up. Why, the common decencies . . . ! '

'Take the example of your good wife,' interrupted the surgeon, 'and make the best of it,' and clambering over a hodge-podge of belongings left stranded in the walkway, he was gone.

Isobel had indeed been making the best of it. She had taken in at a glance the hideously cramped space allotted to them, had hung her bonnet on a convenient peg, had unpacked a selection of eating utensils and disposed them in the plate racks below the table, and was now busying herself with the bed, on which she was arranging the bedding. Something about her calm acceptance infuriated her husband.

'Isobel, this is impossible! Have you not thought? We are to be cooped up here for maybe five or six months, like animals! And if there are storms how are we to survive the tossing about in such a small space? Oh, how I wish I had never consented to this terrible plan! It was not my idea, I was against it from the first. And the people . . . ! '

He looked about him with disgust. On the bunk next to his an old woman was cradling a young one in her arms, sobbing aloud at the prospect of the imminent and final parting, while the young husband looked on uneasily. Further down a brother and sister stood in tender isolation, oblivious of the racket around them, saying goodbye to each other for ever. All around him were faces charged with the most profound emotion, some tight shut against threatening tears, others openly abandoned to grief. Some sought relief from their feelings in outbursts of irritability, others sat motionless, withdrawn, dejected, gazing at the floor, incapable of comprehending the fate that had overtaken them. Only the children seemed unconcerned. They wriggled between legs, squirmed in and out of their own and each others' bunks, jumped off tables and benches and swarmed up and down the hatchway to and from the deck above as carefree as monkeys.

Isobel's face was pale but set. Not by a tremor did she betray the pain that was eating at her inside her chest, the terror she felt for her daughters on the dreadful adventure ahead, the anguish at being parted for ever from her home, the exasperation her husband aroused in her. Only her voice was a little harsher than usual.

'And what is the alternative, Isaiah? Are you wishful to return to Paisley and starve? Or have you some other scheme in mind to keep us all fed and clothed?'

Isaiah bit his lip and turned away.

'Go and seek out Joseph,' said Isobel more kindly. 'He'll tell us how to make the best of things, I doubt not.'

The thought of his brother-in-law's cheery optimism depressed Isaiah still further. He pushed through to the hatchway and climbed up on deck. Jessie, who had been exploring every crevice of the ship, skipped up to him.

'Isn't it beautiful, Pa? Isn't it just the bonniest ship you ever did see?'

Isaiah looked down into his small daughter's rapturous face, and in spite of himself, he smiled. He had never had much time for his little girl, so busy had he always been at his loom, but even he could not fail to remark the new bloom of hope and happiness on her face. Her cheeks were pinker already. Holding her hand, he made for the steps leading up to the raised poop deck in the stern of the ship. Jessie tugged him back.

'No, no, Pa, we're not allowed up there. I tried myself just now, and a big man all over gold braid told me it wasn't for the likes of us. It's just the cabin folks can go up there, and they don't come on to the ship till the steerage quarters are all filled up.'

Jessie darted off again, the ends of her shawl flying, and Isaiah leant over the side of the ship to watch the bustle on the quay below. The emigrants had all embarked now, and the cabin passengers were arriving by carriage on the quayside. Preparations for the sailing were going ahead. A group of departing relatives, who had made their last farewells, were straggling down the gangway, many convulsed in tears, looking back fondly at their loved ones who stood along the rail beside Isaiah, waving handkerchiefs and caps. A German band had assembled and the men were tuning up their instruments. A last-minute consignment of bulging sacks was being loaded from a dray on to the backs of a line of dockers, who were running them up on board.

The carriage parties were clustered in conversation. One poor young lady seemed almost overcome with emotion, and was being supported on the arm of her stiff-backed father. Nearby, in another family group, a middle-aged woman, dressed in black, was preparing to mount the gangway. When she moved, Isaiah could see that she walked with a limp. The sight of her comforted him. If a lame woman imagined that she had prospects in New Zealand, then perhaps he, with his lack of primary skills, would also find his place. Then he saw her companions and shook his head. The handsome woman and the two men with her, one middle-aged and black-headed, the other young and too slender to be used to physical labour, were obviously wealthy. They were dressed in expensive, fashionable clothes, and the assurance with which they moved spoke of the confidence of wealth. They were not of his kind, dependent on their own muscle power for their bread. He hoped very much that there were not too many of their sort going off to the new land, people fit for nothing but to live on the sweat of others. Why, it was just such ladies as that one with the saucy yellow curls who had decreed Paisley shawls unfashionable and condemned him and his ilk to poverty and exile. Isaiah found that his fists were clenched and he turned away. He had no desire to see them saunter on board and take up the pleasant space of the poop deck from which his little Jessie had been so unceremoniously evicted. He would go forrard and look for Joseph, as Isobel had suggested. Perhaps his brother-in-law would have some influence with the officers, to get them an extra berth, or at least a change of position, nearer the main hatchway perhaps, where the air was fresher. There was no point in rejoining Isobel. If Isaiah knew his wife, she would by now have found out, in her quiet way, the names of half the families in the 'tween deck, and would be sitting down with some of the women, making practical arrangements for the disposal of their bags and bundles in the tiny locker spaces under the lower bunks.

3

Jessie woke with a start and wondered for a moment where she was. Meg's arm was digging into her side and her face was pressed uncomfortably close to the board that separated her from the three little Wilson boys who shared the bunk alongside. Instantly, recognition came. She was on board the *New Zealand*! They had eaten their first meal and slept their first night! The rolling of the boat, the creaking and straining of the timbers told her that they must be already far out to sea. She imagined them slipping away all through the night, the Captain nobly alone at the helm, the ship striking out into the ocean, miles already from the quayside at Greenock, where she had watched that sudden, horrible gap widen between the ship's wooden side and the granite of the quay wall with an indescribable feeling of excitement, intensified by the music of the German band blaring out 'Rule Britannia' and the cries and groans of people wrenched for ever away from their loved ones. Even now the ship might be passing some far-flung tropical island, or riding between giant whales, or steering towards an iceberg!

Unable to contain her excitement any longer, Jessie wriggled out of her bunk feet first, careful not to waken Meg, and stood perplexed in her nightgown, not knowing how to proceed. It had seemed so odd, last night, undressing in front of all these strangers. Never before had she imagined doing such a thing, appearing in her shift before such unknown people as Mr Wilson, who with his wife slept inches away from her parents, or the uncouth Highland party opposite, whose melancholy singing had kept her awake till late in the night. There had been such contortions, repeated the length of the great open room, behind improvised screens held up by spouses, as women had struggled out of their voluminous petticoats into their nightgowns, and men had exchanged their trousers and jackets for nightshirts. One bold rude family, from Glasgow she had no doubt at all, had called out in a ribald way so coarse and rude that Pa had had to speak to them, and several people had laughed and teased her afterwards. She, Jessie, had thought it all wonderful fun, but she supposed Pa was right and it was all very shocking and not to be borne by decent folks.

She crept along to the hook where her day clothes hung and began to dress herself, draping her skinny little body modestly as she did so in case she had wakened any other sleeper who might even now be watching her. But the noise of the ship was on her side. It muffled all but the loudest sounds. She could hear now the running of feet overhead, no doubt the sailors preparing for what must be a storm. The groaning and creaking of the timbers was growing louder.

The main hatchway had already been thrown open. Perhaps it was the noise of it banging on the deck, that had first aroused her. She climbed up the steep steps, gulping gratefully the fresh air that smelled so good after the frowstiness below, and looked eagerly about for the great ocean. It was not there! Instead, all around, were the green hills of Scotland, reflected in the brilliant early morning light in the clear waters of the Clyde. And Greenock itself was but a mile or two back, still in sight.

Disappointed, Jessie stood on tiptoe on a coil of rope and leant over the rail to look down into the water. It was so deep and dark and cold down there! The thought of it made her shiver. Small waves slapped along the coppered hull of the ship, whipped up by the south-westerly wind which blew up the Clyde, opposing the *New Zealand*'s progress.

A shout behind her made Jessie turn quickly. The sailors were bustling about, snapping to the command of an angry-looking man in a blue cap. One of them ran towards her and ordered her sharply off the coil of rope. Jessie obeyed, abashed, as the man leaped on to the rigging above her head and began to swarm up it. She stared up at him open-mouthed, astonished by his daring. Another went up after him and another. Jessie stepped back to get a better view, and collided with a coop lashed to the rail of the boat. A squawk from within startled her. She dropped to her knees to look inside and found herself face to face with a hen, whose red comb flopped to and fro as it pecked crossly at the bars. Delighted, Jessie laughed aloud. How could she not have noticed it yesterday? Why, here, in a lifeboat, were half a dozen or more sheep, and here, beyond the chickens, was a cage full of piglets who, roused by a roll of the ship, which had just gone about on a new tack, were squealing and trampling about their restricted living space.

A door leading to the cabin quarters directly below the poop deck opened and a young man came out. Jessie, feeling shy and nervous in case she had somehow penetrated into regions banned to steerage passengers, backed away, and then turned and ran back to her berth below, where the rest of her family was beginning to stir.

Edward did not notice her. He had woken in his tiny cot in the small cabin next to his parents', convinced from the rolling motion and the creaking of the timbers that the ship must already be well out to sea. Excitement and curiosity had pulled him out of bed. He had flung on his clothes and come out on deck to look around, only to be disappointed. The ship was still within sight of Greenock! Surely they must have travelled further since last night, when the boatswain had piped 'All hands up anchor', and the sails had risen to the wind as the ship had begun to creep away from the shore?

A movement above made him raise his eyes. Good heavens! The audacity of those men aloft! The very thought of shinning up to those swaying heights made Edward feel sick. Come to think of it, the motion of the ship was already having an unfortunate effect on him. He thought that perhaps, after all, he might not join his parents and his aunt in the cuddy for breakfast.

The door behind him opened and Hector stepped out, clad in a gorgeous dressing gown, a relic of former affluence.

'There you are, my boy. Bad news, I'm afraid. Your Aunt Heriot has passed a most wretched night. Even this slight swell has made her horribly sick, and I will have to ask Mr Turner to put up a composing draught for her. I doubt if she'll keep it down. I don't like the look of her at all. If she's started to heave in a flat calm such as this, Heaven knows what the Atlantic storms will do for her!'

'Is this a flat calm, Father?' Edward asked nervously.

Hector laughed. 'Well, not precisely. You won't know what that is until we hit the doldrums where the smallest motion of the boat comes as a relief. But this rough? No! A little choppy perhaps, but nothing that a hearty breakfast of kidneys and bacon won't put to rights.'

Breakfast was to be the least of Edward's trials that day. The wind freshened as the vessel, mindful of sandbanks, inched down the estuary and the waves mounted. By midday he was far from well. Dinner, a rich repast of pork, currant jelly, roast duck with boiled ham, pickles, carrots, peas, tart, plum pudding and strawberries, proceeded without him. He had taken to his berth and was convinced that only death could ease his sufferings.

On the far side of the planking that divided his cabin from the next, Aggie lay similarly afflicted. For her though, the case was far, far worse. She had spent a miserable night, at first numb with the shock of leaving her homeland, and then engulfed in the keenest misery of regret for all that she was leaving behind. By dint of prayer and sheer strength of mind, she had subdued her emotions to a containable level, only to be overcome, as the night hours wore on, by a horrible antipathy to the motion of the ship, which, before five a.m., marked by a clamour of bells somewhere too near at hand, had caused her to lose her supper, and by the time the rest of the family was stirring, had made her lose all interest in anything but the pitching and rolling from which there was no respite. Added to that, the unaccustomed smallness of her cot had made her lie awkwardly, and the ensuing strain had touched up the old pain in her hip. To be so wretched so soon, with Greenock still in sight, made Aggie's heart fail at the idea of the rigours to come.

'I can do it, I can survive it,' she muttered to herself, thinking of Edward, but as the day wore on, and her sickness increased so greatly that nothing, not Dr Turner's draught, nor even a sip of water stayed down, her resolution began to weaken and she could answer Fanny's compassionate enquiries with no more than a moan of agony.

By evening Fanny was seriously concerned. She herself was used to spending a few days of discomfort at the outset of the voyage before finding her sea-legs, but she had never experienced the intensity of illness from which her sister was suffering.

'If she's this bad now,' she said to Hector, as they sat in the padded seats that lined the walls of the cuddy, a pleasant room reserved for the daytime use of the cabin passengers, 'how will she be when we reach the

Bay of Biscay? Or even worse, the gales in the Southern Ocean?'

Hector raised his eyes from his book. The inactivity of shipboard life always irked him. He had made it his practice to put the time to good use, and his river journeys in India had been occupied in the study of the Hindustani language. True to form, he was now embarked on the small library he had acquired before leaving London, and the first day out was not too soon to begin. He could not, however, ignore the anxiety in Fanny's voice.

'There's no need to put yourself in a fuss,' he said, frowning. Illness of any kind was abhorrent to him. He had never suffered from it himself, and he believed a little effort and plenty of physical exercise were all that was needed to overcome any unease of mind or body. 'She should get up and walk about the deck. It never fails to remedy sea-sickness.'

'Get up? Walk about? Good heavens, Hector, you have no idea what you are saying. Her legs would not for a moment support her.'

'What does Turner say?' said Hector impatiently.

'He is seriously concerned. He says her constitution is such that sickness of this intensity is not easily shaken off, and may recur at any time in the course of the journey. He is not convinced of the wisdom of her continuing with us.'

'What?' Hector's interest was now fully transferred from his page to his wife's face.

'He proposes to send her ashore with the pilot at Cumbrae. You know the pilot goes off there tomorrow morning, if these adverse winds permit us to reach that far, and that will be the last chance for her to disembark before the Cape.'

'But this is preposterous!' Hector flung down his book, rose to his feet and sat down again suddenly, unbalanced by a roll to starboard. 'After the preparations she has made, her house for sale, her affairs wound up . . . '

'Yes, but you know, Hector, I have been thinking that, after all, it is not so bad. Her house is not sold yet, it is just put in the hands of Mr Elliott, who cannot have proceeded far with it. And there was no time to complete her business arrangements. I am convinced that they could all be unwound again.'

'Do you wish her to go home, then?'

'I – I'm not sure.' Fanny blushed, and looked down. 'I own I do sometimes wish for a little more time to myself, a little less of her company when I could be enjoying yours alone. It is selfish, perhaps, after all she has done for us and all she has given up to accompany us, but I cannot forget how she disapproves of me sometimes, and – oh no, of course I do not wish to say farewell for ever, as this would mean, but we will need all our strength and health on this venture, and if Aggie's is to be seriously impaired by the voyage, as Dr Turner fears it may be, I do not see how we are to carry the burden.'

Hector rose to his feet again, this time more steadily, and leant over to peer out of a porthole. The island of Cumbrae was already in sight, at a distance, but slowly approaching.

'You are right,' he said positively. 'She must at least be given the chance to make this decision, as it so closely affects her health. I will speak to her myself.'

Twenty minutes later, his head appeared again round the brilliantly varnished door of the cuddy.

'You had better come and pack up her things, for I see that you are quite right. She is too ill even to stand.'

The dawn of the next morning was their second at sea but to Aggie it seemed an eternity since she had hobbled up the gangway. Later, she knew, she would be overwhelmed by despair, shame at her weakness and an endless sorrow for the family she was leaving, a sorrow as deep as bereavement. Now she felt nothing but a passionate longing to stand on *terra firma* once again. Her cabin trunk had been quickly repacked. In her two days on board there had hardly been time to disturb its contents. The chests and trunks in the hold were another matter. Captain Worth had shaken his head and pursed his lips at the idea of disturbing the careful stowage below, when every man was needed aloft to manoeuvre the ship out to sea, and Aggie, becoming agitated, had disclaimed any desire to retrieve them.

'There's nothing in them that could be of use to me at home,' she had whispered, the word 'home' ringing sweetly in her ears. 'And there's a whole lot you'll find handy out there, clothing, and books, and utensils and such like. Take them, for goodness' sake, Fanny, and don't argue about it. In any case I couldn't stand to see them all again. They would only remind me of . . . ' and tears had poured down her cheeks.

It was a sad party that collected at the rail as the steps were let down into the pilot's cutter. He was an uncommunicative man, used to such occurrences. Indeed, he hardly ever left an emigrant ship without one such passenger, who had had a change of heart at the final moment, or at the very least without a bundle of last tear-stained letters. He preferred to keep his own counsel, and Aggie, too wretched to speak, was glad of it. As the little boat pulled away from the great one, she had, in any case, only one thought on her mind – how to live through the next hour of agony until this terrible rolling ceased.

The last glimpse that Hector, Fanny and Edward had of her was to haunt Fanny, at least, for a long time. She seemed diminished, her usual ramrod straightness bowed down, her strength, upon which they had all been used to lean, reduced to nothing, as she sat, pathetic and suddenly old, surrounded by her belongings in the cutter. They turned away from the rail when it was too far away to be easily seen any more, and Hector put his arm round the shoulders of his weeping wife.

'She was right to go, and she'll be happy enough once she's settled back in George Street.'

And Edward, who had some small inkling of the central place he held in his aunt's heart, vowed to himself, 'I'll write to her regularly as long as I live. I won't forget her, poor Aunt.'

Later that day, as they sat on the poop deck enjoying the warmth of the afternoon sun, Edward's sickness already forgotten, they could not know that miles away, on a promontory on the island in the distance, a small figure stood, and had stood for many hours, shading her face against the light, watching with her heart in her eyes as the ship's sails grew smaller and smaller, shrank to no more than a dot and finally disappeared over the far southern horizon.

Chapter Eleven *August 1842*

1

'Is this all right, Meg?' Jessie passed a stained chemise to her sister, who held it for a moment against her cheek to aid the detection of dampness.

'Aye, that's dry enough. Be careful of the drawers, though. They were lying next to that wee leaky place on the deck and I doubt they're dry enough.'

The two sisters were kneeling by a box, which had been withdrawn from the hold so that they could stow away the last month's accumulation of dirty linen from the canvas bags they were allowed to keep by them on the 'tween deck, and extract enough clean clothes to last until Captain Worth announced the next change. All around them on the deck, boxes and chests were lying open, and women were sorting and folding, checking for any dampness that would quickly turn to mildew and then to rot in a carelessly packed chest.

A shadow fell across the nightgown that Meg was holding up for inspection. She looked up to see Dr Turner standing over her. He had been everywhere this morning, exhorting cleanliness, advising on the waterproofing of boxes, in case sea-water penetrated into the hold, and encouraging those reluctant to wash to be more particular for the general welfare of all the occupants of the ship.

'How's your mother today?'

'A wee bit tired, I think.' Meg had been surprised when her mother had remained in bed these last two days, for it was unlike her to give way to idleness, but she had seen no cause for concern. 'Will she be obliged to get up this afternoon? I think she'd prefer to rest.'

Meg had seen Dr Turner's ruthless methods with lie-abeds. He was quite capable of hosing them out of their cots, if they did not get out on deck for the daily doses of fresh air they needed. It was ten shillings he'd be paid for every one he landed alive, he said, and by God, he intended to make sure he got his money. Few of the emigrants needed his encouragement to keep themselves active and busy. They were all hardy folk, used to accomplishing more than a day's work in the twenty-four hours, and few of them had ever had the opportunity to cultivate habits of laziness.

At Isobel's bedside, however, Dr Turner had become gentle. He had spoken quietly to her for a while, held her pulse and listened to her chest. There had been no threats of punishment if she remained in bed.

'No, no,' he said, in answer to Meg's question. 'She'll not need to stir. She needs to rest, poor woman. You're a good pair of girls and you can take care of everything, see to your father's victualling and so on, I doubt not. There's a decent soul next to you, Mrs Wilson is it? She can help with your provisions, and prepare your puddings and pies for the galley, I'm sure.'

A confused medley of shouts and stampings from behind the barrier dividing the single men's deckspace from that of the women and families caused the doctor to raise his head, and when it was repeated, he hurried astern to see what was to do. Infringements of the ship's strict discipline, of course, would be dealt with by the captain, but the responsibility for the welfare of all aboard was his, and he had been ceaselessly at work to promote it, arranging amusements, setting up concerts, organising a circulating library from a pool of passengers' books, and overseeing a daily round of exercise, children's classes and religious services that gave a semblance of normality and routine to the cramped life on board. The single men were ever the greatest threat to order, and he had come to rely more and more on the sense and strength of Joseph Kirkwood for keeping them in check.

Now, however, as he darted between the boxes and heaps of clothing that littered the boards of the deck, he could see that trouble of some kind had broken out. So far on the voyage nothing very serious had occurred. A rude fellow had insisted upon playing his flute during evening prayers, and when asked to desist, had pulled the first mate's nose, but had apologised after a reprimand from the captain, and another, who had refused to wash himself, had been deposited in a tub on deck and scrubbed by his hilarious shipmates within an inch of his life.

The noise had quietened by the time Dr Turner reached the stern deck, and he found himself among a crowd standing in silence, eyes turned upwards to the rigging, where two figures could be seen shinning up like squirrels towards the top of the mast.

'Go it, Jem, my shilling's on you!' came from several throats.

'Come on, man! Faster than that, damn you, or you'll ruin me!'

Among the crowd stood Joseph Kirkwood, white-faced with distress.

'Silly young fools! If I'd known what was afoot . . . '

'Come on, now.' Dr Turner was not inclined to take a serious view of the matter. 'They're fine young fellows, used to tree climbing I daresay, and unlikely to fall. Why, you yourself, in your sea-faring days, must often have— '

'No, no, you do not understand. It's not one of our lads up there with my Jem, it's the young scientific gentleman from the cuddy!'

'What!' The colour ebbed from the surgeon's rosy cheeks and he peered upwards to where the two pairs of legs were already high aloft. 'How came this about? What was he doing on this deck?'

'He's been here many times, looking out for dolphins and such like, which he says he can observe more easily than from the poop. Awful set on creatures, he is, and a nice lad, friendly, not at all proud or grand like some cuddy folks. Tells you everything you want to know and a great deal more besides about the beasties of the water.'

Joseph was looking increasingly grim. 'Seems some folks aren't content to learn of the wonders of God's creation,' he said, raising his voice till it was audible among the crowd of young men staring raptly up into the rigging. One or two began to shift their feet and look uncomfortable. 'They must needs tease a man for his knowledge, and make out he's no better than a female with all his book learning, and bully and jeer till he's stung to take up a foolish wager to see who can get up the mast quickest. Gambling on it! Aye,' Joseph shook his head sorrowfully, 'it's my own fault. I should never have let my lad take the ten sovereigns from Lord Eglinton. He's learned once to come by money dishonestly, and he's away up there, teaching another poor young soul to do the same thing.'

Dr Turner was hardly listening. The consequences of an accident occurring to Edward were working strongly upon his mind. He would have to suffer the reproaches of the parents, the rage of the captain, and the repercussions of this most regrettable lapse of discipline for the rest of the voyage. It would be intolerable. In any case, he liked young Edward. Their shared interest in natural history had led to some of the pleasantest hours he had ever spent at sea. It was not usual to travel with persons so enthusiastic and so well informed. It would be tragic if anything should happen to the boy. He could not think how he could have been induced to undertake anything so foolhardy. He must have been goaded beyond endurance. Why, the lad had confided several times to the doctor that, having no head for heights, he could hardly bear to see the men go up the rigging and that when, in heavy seas, they raced to obey the order 'Lay aloft and furl!' and had to stand out at the extremities of the spars so that they were dipped into the ocean every time the great masts swung over, he could not bring himself to go out on deck for fear of seeing them fall. The thought of being bullied up the rigging, as he had seen the boatswain bully the young apprentices, had, he admitted, actually given him nightmares on more than one occasion.

A gasp rose from the circle of upturned faces, and Dr Turner felt a tightening in his stomach. He could not quite see what was happening, the belly of the main topsail obscured his view, but he could sense that something had gone wrong. He strained his eyes to look. His instinct had not misled him. Something was seriously amiss.

Edward had been lashed to a most uncharacteristic rage by the mockery of the crowd of bored young men on the foredeck. His sunny nature normally ensured him a welcome wherever he went, but he had not found it among the dour young men travelling steerage in the bows of the ship. They had taken exception from the first to his white scholar's hands, so different from their own reddened, calloused ones. They could not understand what he was about when he lifted buckets of water on to the deck and waxed enthusiastic over small wriggly things that no sensible man would waste his time with. In any case, they did not enjoy the intrusion of a gentleman into their company. It made them uneasy and spoiled their fun. Of them all, Jem Kirkwood had most taken against Edward. He had no desire to be reminded of his years of servitude with a fine lord, who cared nothing for ordinary folks and spent his money like a fool. There was, too, the unaccountable behaviour of Tam and Bess, who had recognised in Edward a rare kindred spirit, and who had adopted the annoying habit of thumping their feathery tails on the boards whenever he appeared on the foredeck.

The ribbing he had received, gentle at first and then more unpleasant, had reminded Edward of his early days in Scotland, when he had struggled so hard, with his chi-chi accent and Indian ways, to make himself acceptable to his Edinburgh peers. When the breaking point came, it was hardly Jem Kirkwood's voice he heard, goading him up the rigging, but the cries of a dozen children, whose taunts he had never forgotten. He had seen red before his eyes, and blinded by all but the desire to show these louts that he did not want for bravery, he had raced at the rigging as if it were a deadly enemy, and begun to climb, hand over fist, heart hammering so violently he was all but deafened, so maddened that he was high above the deck, nearly level with the top of the fore topsail, even well ahead of Jem, who has heavier and more cautious, before he had time to think.

But as his head began to clear, and the immediate impulse wore off, the old terror of heights began to clutch at him, churning his stomach. The crowd below saw him falter. He felt rather than heard their gasp. Sheer courage was all that now drove him on. Those fools down there, who thought the antics of a handful of cockroaches with their legs torn off more interesting than the wonderful divings of the dolphins about the bow wave, would not have the pleasure of seeing him fail. If only he could control this absurd trembling in his limbs! If only his hands would stop sweating!

At that moment the wind, that had been blowing strongly from astern, shifted. Edward had until now had the wind at his back, and had been aided by the tilt of the ship, but he now found himself on the lee side, attempting to climb an overhang, while the wind clawed at him, pulling him away from the shrouds which now jutted out over him. He looked down. There was nothing between him and the cold blue swell far, far below. A gust tearing through the rigging caused him to shift his position. His feet slipped from the ratlines which, like rungs in a ladder, had been his footholds. He was now hanging helplessly by the arms. The wind went round again, and the great mast righted itself. Edward, desperate to find a more secure hold before it swayed again, lunged for the fore topsail yard, the thick wooden spar from which the sail depended. He touched it, but his hands, clammy with sweat, slipped on the smooth surface of the wood. He fell.

He felt rather than heard himself scream. Falling, scrabbling wildly in the air, he clutched at the nearest object and his hands caught hold of the footrope which ran under the yard. He clung to it desperately. His hands held firm, but his body dangled helplessly in space. Now, terror had him tight in its grip. Death would come soon, as soon as his hands, no longer able to bear his weight, lost their hold on the footrope, from which even now the freshening wind seemed to be trying to dislodge them. He would be smashed to pieces on the deck below, or, if the ship was listing again at the time of his fall, he would drown in the cruel immensity of the ocean that stretched from horizon to horizon. He would greet the final moment, when it came, almost with relief.

Below, the crowd of young men moaned as each movement of the ship threatened to dislodge the slim figure from its tenuous hold so far aloft. But now they had more to watch. At the moment of Edward's fall Joseph Kirkwood had bent to remove his boots, and in an instant, before the doctor could catch hold of him, he had started up the rigging. It was thirty years since he had last done such a thing, but he had moved instinctively, without a thought for what the intervening time might have done to his skills. By now the whole ship with the exception of the crew, busy in the hold, seemed to have become aware of what was happening above their heads, and they held their breath as Joseph reached the yard and edged his way along it, his bare feet gripping the foot rope.

Jessie's face had become perfectly white.

'It's Uncle Joseph,' she said in a hoarse whisper. 'And the young gentleman from the cuddy. And that's Jem up yonder, way up high, near the top! Look!' and she took her sister's wrist in a tight grip which Meg was too terrified to feel.

At that moment, as the ship heeled even further, a convulsion ran through Edward's body. The sudden appearance of Joseph near at hand had reawakened hope, but paradoxically his terror had redoubled. He tried to strengthen his grip on the foot rope but felt his arms cracking under his weight. Below, necks craned to watch. Why had the older man stopped moving? What was he doing now? Why didn't he hurry? Surely the young one could not hang on much longer?

They were too far below to hear Joseph's low, level voice as he calmed the panic-stricken boy.

'Now listen to me, laddie. You've to do exactly as I say or I'll beat the living daylights out of you when we're back down there on deck. You'll start by shifting your left hand towards me along the foot rope. You'll do it now.'

Edward heard the voice as if it came from far away. His brain commanded his hand to obey. The hand did not move.

'You'll do it now.' Joseph's voice was inexorable. 'You'll move it on the count of three or I'll tear you limb from limb with my own hands. One, two . . . '

Edward jerked his left hand along the rope and the sickening swing of his body over empty space threatened to bring a faintness that would mean the end.

'Now your right hand. Move it, you landlubber, or I'll . . . One, two . . . '

The right hand moved. A communal sigh rose from the watchers below. Jessie's fingers relaxed a little, and Meg automatically rubbed the bruise they had left on her arm.

'Your left hand again. Now!'

The hard voice whipped the boy into obedience. Mesmerised, he forced his hands to follow Joseph's feet as they worked back along the rope. Six more lurches, and he was within reach of the mast. Joseph's iron fist caught him about the waist, and half fainting, sick with horror, Edward clung to him.

'Now down, hand over fist, one, two! Do it!'

Edward gathered up the last shreds of his courage and controlled with a hideous effort the trembling in his limbs. A cheer almost rocked the boat as the men reached the deck, and Edward slid to the boards in a dead faint at Joseph's feet. Jem, whose triumphant ascent to the top had passed unnoticed, had sheepishly scrambled down the other side, and resisted the temptation to flee to his berth. There was nothing to be gained by hiding. There was nowhere he could run to. He could not escape the lash of his father's tongue. It was better to stand and take it straight away.

Joseph's voice, when it came, was quiet. He glared round the group of shamefaced young men, and not one of them looked him in the eye.

'There's different kinds of courage,' he said. 'There's the kind that comes from living an outdoor life, and being used to hardship, and rejoicing in your own strength. Then there's the other kind, that pushes the body beyond what it can do and makes it go on in the face of fear. That's the courage of the soul. And this young gentleman, whom you have nearly killed, has that courage in rare abundance, silly young fool that he is.'

He looked down at Edward, who was now struggling to rise to his feet as the smelling salts held under his nose by the deeply thankful doctor brought him back to consciousness.

'And then,' Joseph's voice went on inexorably, 'there's several kinds of cowardice.' He seemed about to say more, but his eyes, travelling round the group, found Jem and halted. When he spoke again, his voice held withering scorn.

'As for you, the next time you gamble I know fine it'll be because you wish to see your father die of shame.' And Jem, white-faced and sick in his stomach, turned away to hide the trembling of his lip.

2

Unlike Hector, who took a secret delight in Edward's escapade, Captain Worth was inclined to take a serious view of the affair, and he clapped young Jem Kirkwood into irons for three days. It was more difficult to punish Edward. What was viewed as a crime in persons travelling steerage was inclined to be laughed off as high spirits in a young gentleman from the poop deck. However, Captain Worth was a fair man, and he confined Edward to his cabin for three days as well.

The sentence did not drag heavily on Edward. In fact, he was relieved to be sharing something of Jem's misfortune. He bore that young man no ill-will. On the contrary, he had begun to see, on reflecting on the matter in the solitude of his cabin, that a kind of resentment had been brewing up for some time. He could understand that Jem, who seemed a prickly, uncomfortable sort of fellow, might be jealous when some of the single young men, whose unacknowledged leader Jem seemed to have become, had on occasion left Jem standing in order to listen to Edward's discourse on the habits of the barnacle, or shared an interest in a passing school of whales. Edward disliked the thought of anyone being made uncomfortable on his account and he could not but feel for Jem. He bribed the cabin steward to put up a plateful of delicacies such as Jem, on a diet of bread and water, might be expected to enjoy, and sent them off with a note.

Congratulations on getting all the way to the top! I fear I haven't the head for it. Sorry they treated you so severe. Hope these few morsels will help to alleviate your sufferings!

Jem did not respond to this missive. Indeed, it only added to his depression. He was not a malicious young man and, though he had certainly wished to take Edward down a peg, he had not intended to kill him, as everyone seemed to suppose. He himself had been itching to have a go at the mast ever since he had boarded the ship. How was he to know that my fine young sir would make such a sorry business of it?

Jem did not know why it was but Edward irritated him profoundly. Why could he not stay on the poop deck with the grand folk, instead of poking his nose in where he had no business to be? Why could he not keep his soft cajoling ways for people of his own kind? Jem was not vain exactly, although he was not unaware of his own good looks and physical prowess and the effect these had on his fellows, male and female alike, but he could not help noticing that Edward had a superior power to attract people. It was not so much that Edward was classically handsome, for he was not, and his muscles had not yet developed the rugged fullness of manhood, but he had such wiry strength and grace in his movements, so much charm in his manner and such friendliness of spirit that few could resist him. Edward would have overcome more quickly the suspicions the young men on the foredeck harboured for anyone who talked and dressed like a gentleman, if Jem had not used his influence to whip up feelings against him.

For all his brooding, Jem could not untangle the web of envy, shame and resentment in which he was trapped. He only knew he had come out badly from the whole affair. No one had remarked on his successful ascent of the mast. They had left him alone, to smart under Joseph's public rebuke. Later, his father's exhortations to 'take the burden to the Lord in prayer, and lay it down, and beseech his forgiveness' had only made matters worse. Lying hour after hour in his airless prison, Jem had gathered up his feelings in one festering burden and laid them down upon Edward. A wordless hatred had been born. When Edward's letter came, Jem screwed it up and threw it away with an oath. In spite of his hunger, he was not tempted to touch the food. He gave it to his dogs.

On the third and last dawn of the young men's imprisonment, Jessie woke in her sleep, suffocating in a kind of terror. She lay for a while, trying to convince herself that she had only had a bad dream, but the panic did not leave her. She wriggled out of bed to seek comfort from her mother. It was almost dark in the 'tween deck, but she could see, in the pale early morning light flickering in through one of the sidelights left open to encourage a passage of fresh air, Isobel's hand dangling over the end of the bunk. Jessie wanted to take it, to press her cheek against it, but she hesitated. Ma did not like to be roused from her sleep without good cause. Besides, Jessie did not know quite what it was, there was something strange about her mother's hand. It was surely not usually as pale as this, white as marble almost? And the fingers seemed to stand out so straight, so strained.

As gently as she could, Jessie put out a fingertip to touch Isobel's hand. It was quite cold. The feel of it frightened her, and she grasped at it more roughly. The fingers were hard and stiff. A sob welled up in Jessie's chest. She half climbed into her parents' bunk. Her mother was lying on her face. With trembling fingers, Jessie stroked her hair. She had never felt hair so chill.

'Ma,' she whispered. 'Shall I put my own blanket round you? You're awful cold, Ma.' Isobel made no movement.

'Ma,' she said more urgently. 'I need you, Ma! I'd not disturb you else! Please wake up! Ma! Ma!'

She tugged at her mother, careless now of angering her, desperate for an answer, for any response at all. The ship lurched, and Isobel's body rolled over. Her eyes were shut, her lips drawn up in a slight smile. She looked so peaceful and happy, as if she was enjoying a beautiful dream, as if she had recognised someone she loved, that Jessie felt reassured, and bent to kiss her cheek. But the touch of Isobel's skin set a panic rising in her. Something was wrong, she knew it. Her mother's cheek was stone cold, and hard, and deadly pale. Deadly! Dead!

Jessie's scream roused her father and sister, but did not disturb many others. The steerage passengers had become used to hearing all around them the most intimate noises of the night. Grunts of pleasure, coughings, snorings, the wails of teething infants and the squeals of those overrun by rats had become the regular background to sleep. A few drowsy faces peered out of dark holes, dimly saw the child in her white nightgown, her mouth open in a frozen agony, and went back to their slumbers. The nightmares of other people's bairns were no concern of theirs.

It was Isaiah's choking cries that woke everyone, and it was Mrs Wilson, the kind neighbour in the next bunk, who sent for Dr Turner. Still in his nightshirt, he came at once and tut-tutted in sympathy but he showed no surprise. He sat Isaiah down on the bench at the central table, and enlisted the help of Mrs Wilson. In a few moments, Isobel's poor body, wrapped in a sheet, had been pulled unceremoniously from its berth and transported to the female's hospital cabin.

The news spread down the length of the ship. The hatchway was opened. Passengers struggled into their clothes, and stood about in sympathetic knots, talking quietly about the dead woman, wondering out loud about possible infection, and tactfully looking away from Isaiah's showy display of grief and from the pathetic sight of Meg clasped in Mrs Wilson's motherly arms.

No one noticed that Jessie was not there. She had slipped like a shadow behind the men who carried her mother, with no more ceremony than if she had been a sack of coals, away to the hospital, and she had hidden behind the door of the small cabin. She stayed there motionless, and when Dr Turner had gone off to dress himself, she crept up to where her mother's body, defeated at last by exhaustion, was laid out on the white cot, the strands of thin, dark hair tossed haphazardly about on the pillow as if she had been turning restlessly in her sleep.

'Ma!' whispered Jessie. 'Ma!'

She could not believe that Isobel would not hear her. She sat back on her heels, quite still, listening. If she was quiet enough, perhaps she would catch a faint whisper from her mother's soul, which might still be hovering somewhere nearby. No word came. She waited for a while, then she leant forward and studied her mother's face. Her expression had changed. In the act of moving her body, her features had been rearranged. The peaceful smiling mouth was now turned down at the corners. Why did she look so stern, forbidding even? Was she angry? Had she, Jessie, done anything wrong? Was it her fault that Ma had gone? She could not think of anything in particular. Ma had not said anything cross, anyway. Jessie had snuggled in beside her for a moment or two last night before going to her own bunk with Meg, and Ma had weakly patted her hair and said, 'A good wee girlie, my own wee girl,' in a kind of voice that almost sounded as if she might be crying. She had been sad, but she had not been angry.

Was Ma angry with Daddy then, or Meg? She did not think so. And then a new fear stole into Jessie's mind. Perhaps, she thought, Ma was angry with God for making her die. And if God knew she was angry, as he would, since he knew everything, then perhaps she wouldn't be allowed into heaven, and she would have to go to that other place that Jessie so hated to hear about when Uncle Joseph preached one of his fiery sermons. She broke into an anxious prayer.

'She's not really angry, God,' she whispered. 'You mustn't be cross with her. It's just that she didn't want to die and leave me. Don't take any notice if she says anything a wee bit sharp. She doesn't really mean it. She speaks to me very cross sometimes but it's only her way.'

She waited, hoping for a sign, studying Isobel's face anxiously for a return of the lovely smile that might show that God was being kind to her. She was kneeling up against the bunk, so lost in her thoughts that she heard nothing, when Dr Turner at last returned. He was a kind man and the sight of her anxious white face wrung his heart. He bent down, picked up Isobel's nightcap which had fallen to the floor, and put it in Jessie's hands. Then he lifted her to her feet and led her out of the room.

'Motherless,' she said.

'What was that, child?' The doctor bent his head to her level to catch her soft voice.

'I'm motherless,' she said, experimentally.

'Don't you worry, now,' he said kindly. 'You've a fine sister and a good father to take care of you, and your uncle and cousins on the ship too.'

'I know,' said Jessie.

The doctor cast around for something else to say. 'Your mother was a fine woman, God rest her soul. She must have suffered greatly, but she's in a better place by far now, a spirit of light and air with the blessed angels.'

Jessie frowned at him. 'How do you know?' she said.

Dr Turner was shocked. 'She was a good Christian woman,' he said uncertainly. He was not accustomed to looking beyond the words he always used in comforting the bereaved. They rose automatically to his lips and he had not considered their precise meaning for many years. He quickened his pace down the long passageway that led between bunks and tables from his hospital to the Dunbars' berth, and turned to say a last word to Jessie. She was no longer to be seen. She had slipped behind the crowd of weeping women, and had bolted into the dark recesses of her parents' now empty bed, where she was rocking to and fro, nursing her pain, clasping Isobel's quilt tightly in her arms, while silent tears of terror and anguish streamed down her cheeks.

3

News of a death in the steerage reached the cabin passengers at breakfast. It dimmed the joviality with which Edward had been welcomed back to the fold.

'Poor creature,' sighed Fanny. She had attended funerals at sea in the past and they always had a lowering effect on her.

'Does she leave a family?' asked Hector, helping himself to another rasher of ham. He was more inclined to take it as a matter of course. A few deaths on the long voyage were, after all, to be expected, and he had never met the woman.

'Two daughters,' said Dr Turner, shaking his head. Inured as he was to the melancholy aspects of his profession, he was always depressed by a death. He had liked Isobel Dunbar, and he was not looking forward to reading the funeral service after breakfast. A thought struck him. He turned to Edward. 'By the by, she was the sister of Joseph Kirkwood, who did you the honour of saving your life.'

'Really?' Fanny broke in with a warm rush of feeling. 'Then we must do all we can for the poor souls. A collection for the widower and the children – the funeral – I was not thinking of attending, but in that case of course – Teddy, you should certainly pay your respects. It is only what they would expect.'

She sat back and fanned herself. After the pleasant days and balmy nights of the first part of the voyage, the ship was now becalmed in the doldrums, and the heat was oppressive.

Edward prepared himself for the sad little service with mixed feelings. On the one hand, he was curious. A funeral would certainly be interesting. He had never attended one before, and at sea it would have a special kind of significance. Then, too, after five weeks' voyaging any event was a welcome break in the routine of shipboard life. On the other hand, he felt shy at the thought of coming face to face with the single men again. His escapade up the mast had left him feeling foolish. He was not concerned with the opinions of the other passengers. He had never spoken to any of them, and he did not suppose they had noticed the incident. He had only watched them from the relative space and comfort of the poop as they went about their business on the crowded main deck, taking their loaves and puddings to the galley to be baked, or collecting hot water from the cook for their tea. He had enjoyed watching the children play, and had thought rather wistfully how jolly some of the family groups appeared to be, as they chatted or sang together or read aloud, but he had not actually spoken to anyone, and he had no idea that the adventure of the 'young scientific gentleman' had been the main subject of conversation for days past, that his good looks were generally admired by the women and his daring universally respected by the men.

By ten o'clock, all was ready for the ceremony. The air was still. Later in the day it would no doubt be stiflingly hot, but the sun had not yet climbed high enough to be intolerable. The sails flapped uselessly about the mast. There was not wind enough to fill them. At any other time in the voyage the superstitious sailors would frown at anyone careless enough to whistle. It was tempting providence to blow up a gale. But now anyone who pleased might whistle for a wind, and as loudly as they wished.

Just now, however, no one was tempted to whistle. For this solemn occasion every soul on board had assembled on the deck. For once, the single men from the forequarters and the single women from the stern were allowed to mix with the family groups. They stood in silence, eyes lowered, and made a path for Isaiah, Meg and Jessie, who were led by the surgeon to stand by the rail where Isobel's body had been made ready for its final committal.

Edward, standing bareheaded beside his parents, could not remove his eyes from the bundle that rested on the rail, supported at one end by two sailors. Only the outline of Isobel's body was visible. It had been laid on a plank with weights attached to the feet, and the whole had been stitched into canvas by the sailmaker, who had been summoned to his grisly task as soon as the death had been made known. A Union Jack lay over it, adding a touch of gaudy incongruity.

Edward dragged his eyes away. He was dreading the moment when the sailors would upend the body and it would fall into the ocean. What would happen to it then? He supposed that fish, or sharks, or . . . He turned his mind away from the thought and looked towards the family. The husband was shading his eyes with his hand and leaning on the shoulder of his brother-in-law. It was difficult to imagine two men more different, the one so strong, the other so weak. The elder daughter stood with her two cousins and one of them, Jem's brother, Edward supposed, supported her with his arm. The little girl he could hardly see. She was wedged between her father and her uncle, cramming herself between them as a small, terrified crab might flatten itself into a crevice in the rock.

Dr Turner's voice rose high over the assembled heads. He did not read well, but the words were too beautiful to be diminished by his thin, reedy voice.

'As for man, his days are as grass; as the flower of the field, so he flourisheth. For the wind passeth over it, and it is gone; and the place thereof shall know it no more.'

The short ceremony was soon nearly over. The sailors seemed to be bracing themselves to lift the bier, when Joseph Kirkwood stepped forward.

'Let us pray,' he said.

Edward shot a look at the captain and saw a frown cross his face. In these all but windless seas it was necessary to be constantly on the alert to brace the yards round to catch every catspaw of wind. But even he, anxious as he was to return his men to their duties, could not resist the spell of the Scotsman's deep voice. It rose and fell, in the rich cadences of the Old Testament, exhorting, pitying, reassuring, blessing. When he finished, in less time than the embarrassed Jem had feared, there was a moment of silence as handkerchiefs were surreptitiously applied to eyes and noses.

Dr Turner turned a page in his prayer book. The moment had come.

'We have entrusted our sister Isobel Dunbar to God's merciful keeping and we now commit her body to the deep.'

The flag was twitched off. The canvas-covered bundle was exposed in all its pathetic simplicity. The sailors heaved it up. It seemed for a moment alive, as if Isobel was herself leaping voluntarily over the side, and every ear was strained, through the sound of Dr Turner's voice reading of the 'sure and certain hope of the resurrection', to catch the splash as the body hit the sluggish swell and sank into its depths.

At the moment that it disappeared, Jessie started forward. Her father was too wrapped in his own self-pity to notice but Meg shot out a restraining hand. The movement attracted Edward's attention. He became aware of the child for the first time. He saw her open her mouth and braced himself for the scream that seemed to be forming in it, but heard her only whisper, 'No! No!'

Then Mrs Wilson, sobbing quietly, took her by the hand and led her below.

As the mourners dispersed, the ship seemed to shake itself back into life. The mate, galvanised into action, barked out a string of orders. It was as if the words of the psalm, evoking the passing wind, had indeed called it up. A breeze could now be felt.

'Square the yards!' roared the mate.

Feet thundered across the deck.

'Now then, the main tack!'

'Aye, aye, sir!'

The shanty that poured forth from the sailors as they tugged and heaved on the yards had more bravado in it than usual, as if they wished to shake off the gloom of the preceding hour. Edward looked back at them enviously as he went to the cuddy to fetch a book. He intended to spend the morning reading on the poop deck, determined to enjoy the freedom he had been denied for three tiresome days, but once he had settled down in a shady spot he found his concentration was lacking. He could not remove from his mind the expression he had seen on the child's face. Her wordless scream had contained a purer pain than the loudest cries could have expressed.

Luncheon was a subdued occasion. Only Hector appeared on form. He had been struck by the bearing of Joseph Kirkwood and, though he had not paid attention to the words of the prayer, he had been impressed with their strength, and the effect they had had on the assembled company.

'Yes, indeed,' said Dr Turner, in answer to his question. 'A remarkable man, I believe. An old man o' war's man, you know. Joined as a child of nine, running away from unsympathetic parents, I suppose. He was actually a prisoner of war under Boney, taken at the battle of Corunna, and how he managed to escape and return home is a mystery. He refuses to speak of it, a strange reticence in a man who will talk of his days before the mast until the sun sets. He has a natural authority with the young men. I do not know what I should do without him, for they are a sturdy bunch and ripe for any mischief, penned in as they are in cramped quarters. Cleanliness, you may imagine, is not their chief virtue, and it's as much as I can do to make them pay heed to the common decencies, but Mr Kirkwood commands their respect and they will do for him what they would never do for me. A religious man, of course, in your true Scots way. A Presbyterian through and through. There's no infringement of the Sabbath forrard, I can assure you.'

Hector's capitalistic talents had been without a natural outlet for many months but they had by no means withered away. He saw in Joseph Kirkwood an opportunity, material he could harness – to their mutual benefit, of course – to the rebuilding of his fortunes.

'Is he already engaged on some specific employment in the new colony?' he asked, twirling his glass so that the wine swirled about in circles. 'He is very much the kind of man I would like to employ on my own acquisition of land.'

Edward stiffened with embarrassment. He could not have explained why, exactly, but he felt his father's cast of mind to be out of tune with the spirit of this adventure. To his parents, the 'emigrants' in the steerage were persons of an inferior class, suitable labourers for the 'colonists' of the poop deck to employ. But Edward's few encounters forrard had already done much to erode this idea. After the funeral he had warmed to the friendly greetings as the men had crowded round him. Only Jem had hung back, and had afforded him no more than a stiff nod.

It appeared that, after all, he had become something of a hero. Two or three expressed admiration for his daring, and confessed that they would never have had the pluck. They had begged him to attend the 'ball' they planned to hold during the course of tomorrow evening. There was a fellow from Kilmarnock who played excellently well on the fiddle and they intended to dance away the long hours after supper. No females could be present, of course, but they could promise him a jolly evening all the same. Edward had accepted this invitation with enthusiasm. He thought of their unpretentious friendliness now as he listened to his father. Hector's assumption that he was born to rule while Joseph and his ilk would be happy to serve struck his son as crude.

In spite of the breeze the afternoon was unpleasantly hot, and it was not until the early dark of a tropical night had fallen that Edward went out again on deck to breathe the cooler air. A radiant moon was rising out of the sea, sending a shaft of light spinning across the water. A flying fish rose out of a wave and splashed back into it, leaving an aureole of luminous drops behind as the phosphorescent spray glittered in the darkness. Edward leant over the rail, entranced. He had never before seen this curious phenomenon to such spectacular effect. The display was repeated again and again, sending puffs of light, like fireworks, into the air as the flying fish rose and fell.

A movement below on the main deck caught his eye. He looked down. A small figure was crouched behind a hen coop, hidden from the sight of anyone on the main deck, but visible to him on the poop. He looked more closely. It was the little girl whose face had moved him so strangely that morning. Edward was not used to children, but his heart was stirred. She was so still, so waif-like, as she sat huddled by the rail, peering out to sea. He ran down the companionway and perched beside her on a coop, ignoring the flutterings from within.

Jessie turned towards him. Her face was bleached to a whiteness even greater that her normal pallor by the moonlight. Edward waited. He was used to the ways of wild animals. He knew how to give them time, time to accept his presence, his smell, his sympathetic nearness. Jessie turned away from him to look back out to sea, but Edward knew she was aware of him, testing herself against the quality of his silence to see if she could trust him, as a tree climber feels his way along a doubtful branch.

She spoke at last.

'Will it talk?' she said, so quietly that he had to lean forward to catch the words.

'Will what talk?' He kept his voice gentle, for fear of frightening her.

'The spirit on the sea.'

He was not even tempted to laugh.

'It's not a spirit. The light is produced by phosphorescence in the water. What did you think it was?'

This matter of fact speech seemed to give the child confidence.

'I thought – Dr Turner said Ma was a spirit of light and air now and I was afraid she hadn't been able to get out of the sack they stitched her up in before they put her in the sea. I saw all that light on the water and I thought it was her.'

'Did you want it to be her?'

She turned reproachful eyes upon him.

'Of course not. Would you like to see your mother shaken about like that, all alone, trying to get out of the water?'

'No, I suppose not.'

Jessie frowned with concentration. In the strange white light the pure outline of her face, with its delicate bones and frame of fine silky hair had an unearthly beauty.

'I suppose she must have got out in time. Maybe she did, and she's safely up there with God.'

'I'm sure she is.'

Edward's calmness, his lack of effusion, seemed to reassure her more than Dr Turner's glib phrases had done.

'What was that stuff again?'

'What stuff?'

'That thing you said was making the light.'

'Phosphorescence.'

'How does it work?'

Edward cleared his throat, and embarked on an explanation. He did not make allowances for the youth of his listener or her lack of education. He spoke fluently and at length. Jessie listened with rapt attention, her arms clasped about her knees. At last he stopped, realising that he must have been far out of the child's depth, but to his surprise she smiled at him, suddenly and warmly.

'I like that sort of thing,' she said, 'when there's a real explanation and people tell you things. It stops you getting daft ideas.'

And that, thought Edward, as he threaded his way back to his cabin, past the coils of rope and tackle that littered tne deck, was as good a justification of scientific study as any he had ever heard.

Chapter Twelve *Tasman Bay, November 1842*

1

It seemed to Fanny that the clock was unaccountably standing still. Time had ceased to have any meaning for her. For days past the mountains of New Zealand had been visible, growing out of the sea. They had frightened her. Their massive shoulders and snowy crests had been so forbidding, so rugged, and seemingly devoid of any prospect for settlement. Yesterday, she had stood for hours at the rail of the poop deck, plaiting and unplaiting the fringe of her shawl in nervous fingers, scanning the horizon. She was but vaguely aware of the mass of emigrants on the lower deck below who, like her, strained to pick out the features of their new land, and formed restless knots in which rumours and speculation ran riot.

Fanny had at last returned to her cabin, and this morning she had been unwilling to go out on deck again. She knew she ought to prepare herself for landing, to write up her journal, pack away her cabin comforts and furbish up her land clothes, but she felt lethargic, unwilling to start on the larger tasks and unable to finish the smaller ones. The ship, which had so recently felt like a prison, was now more like a haven, tight, safe; predictable. Its routines had become the natural rhythms of her life. Here she had been fed, housed and told what to do for five long months. She had grown used to it. The responsibility of arranging her life herself seemed now too great to bear. The privations and discomforts of the voyage, the terrors of the storms and the boredom of the calms were all now forgotten, and she was reluctant for it to end.

In any case, she reflected, looking at herself critically in the salt-spotted mirror that Hector had hung up for her on the cabin wall, she had changed so much in her time at sea that she was hardly fit to be seen. As the weeks had passed, the veneer of the fashionable lady had slipped from her. Her best hat, worn to impress the captain and ship's officers on the first Sunday at sea, had blown overboard within sight of the Isle of Man. During an after-dinner stroll on deck in the Bay of Biscay, a freshening of the breeze had wrapped the end of her rose-silk, lace-trimmed mantelet round a rough end of rigging, and Hector, trying to disengage it, had ripped it. Even her trunks, packed away below, had not escaped unharmed. One in particular, containing her most delicate things, had inadvertently been placed close to a leak in the timbers, and by the time the damage had been discovered, most of its contents were rotten with mould.

Fanny had been left with only her plainest clothes and had even found herself obliged to dig into Aggie's almost forgotten chests. She had at first hardly been able to show her face in the drab gowns which Aggie had put by, but as Hector had declared she was as pretty as ever, and as, whatever she wore, Captain Worth continued to doff his cap to her with unabated gallantry, she had soon reconciled herself to looking a fright and had set about cheering up Aggie's plain dresses with a bunch of ribbons here and a fringe of lace there.

She put up a hand to tuck a lock of hair into place and noticed a fresh stain on the sleeve of her gown. There would be no time to deal with it now. A brisk wind had been at work all morning and the *New Zealand*, which had rounded Separation Point soon after dawn, was beating up the coast of Tasman Bay at a fine speed.

Somehow, she did not know why, Fanny could not bring herself to go on deck to join Edward, who had been in a ferment of excitement for days. She did not wish to face the worst – not yet, at any rate. She plumped down upon her bunk, which was cleverly transformed into a sofa during the day. An awful apprehension sent waves of goose pimples up and down her arms and she began to chew at her forefinger.

For a year now she had held in her mind's eye a vague but enticing image of a rustic cottage, surrounded by a garden stocked with fruit trees and picturesque flowers, from which Hector, with his usual energy, would sally forth each day to make another fortune, leaving her to engage in delightful efforts at housekeeping, baking, feeding chickens, churning and sewing with a song ever ready on her lips. But at the sight of the actual mountains, trees, beaches, stones and masses of driftwood, the dream burst and was gone.

The voice of the mate, shouting an order overhead, intruded upon Fanny's misery. She gave herself a mental shake, then felt a powerful sense of Aggie's presence. She could almost hear her sister's gruff voice saying, 'This will never do, my girl, sulking on your bed when there's things to be done!' The thought of it made her smile. She jumped to her feet, and with stiffened resolution opened the door of the cabin and went out on deck.

The low cloud of early morning had vanished. The sunlight made her blink and then gasp with delight as she looked about her. The sea was now no longer a rolling, restless enemy, but a gentle expanse of rippling water, reflecting the tenderest blue from the clear sky above, while the rim of hills about the vast bay, though steep, were friendlier than the mountains beyond.

With a sense of shock Fanny realised that their destination was much nearer than she had thought. She could make out ahead a number of ships riding at anchor and even a few buildings set on a beach behind what appeared to be a small wooded island. A pair of canoes, manned no doubt by Maoris (though at this distance she was unable to make them out clearly) was making progress towards an inlet some way along the coast. Fanny stared at them curiously, then she looked about the deck behind her. Where was Hector? Why was he not here, at this of all times, to share her apprehensions and conjectures? For a long time she stood, gripping the rail of the deck, as the land slid nearer.

She turned her head at last at the sound of a splashing of oars, half expecting to see a war canoe full of native warriors in battle regalia, and had only time to take in the unexceptional sight of a pair of weatherbeaten oarsmen and a stocky passenger in a blue shirt, before Edward, breathless with exhilaration, was by her side.

'It's the pilot, Mama, come to guide us into Nelson Haven, but they must wait until high water which won't be until noon, and Captain Worth says we may get the men – only think, Mama, they are whalers! – to take us back with them ashore! Father's been with the captain, studying the charts. He sent me to tell you. Will you come?'

An uncharacteristic wave of panic washed over Fanny. Her urge to cling to the ship increased. She could not bear to leave the security of her little cabin. She opened her mouth to say that she was not ready, her traps were not packed, she was wearing the wrong gown, but then she saw the blaze of excitement in her son's eyes and, in spite of herself, her heart leaped up to respond to it. She gave the startled Edward a tremulous hug, gathered up her skirts and ran across the deck, calling out, 'My blue bonnet, my blue bonnet! I will not set foot in my new country without my blue bonnet!'

An hour later, sitting in the stern of the little boat, sweating from the heat of the mid-morning sun, Hector's eyes were scanning the scene ahead. They feasted on the unaccustomed sights of land, on the woods with their subtle shades of green, so restful after months of monochrome sea and sky, and he could not but smile at Edward who, unable to keep still, twisted and turned, pointing out every new sight to his parents and plying the labouring whalers with questions. But to Hector's unspoken dismay the beach which they were approaching looked unpromising. He could see little of the thriving colony on which he had set such hopes. A curious low bank of boulders stretched away to his left for miles up the coast, forming the sea wall of a long inner lagoon. The oarsmen were ignoring the narrow channel which led into the haven between the end of the boulder bank and a wooded island, but instead were making for an open stretch of shore on which had been rolled pell-mell a dispiriting collection of maritime junk – rusting ships' cannon, broken barrels and splintered spars. A fair number of people were congregated singly or in knots on the beach, or were bustling around the few makeshift houses built in a crevice on the side of the hill, consisting of no more than half a dozen rough sheds and a tent near the summit of the ridge.

Fanny voiced his thoughts. 'I must say, Hector, it seems a strange place to build a town. No level land and nowhere for proper streets to go.'

One of the whalers laughed and directed a stream of tobacco juice over the edge of the boat.

'That ain't no town, lady. That's the port. Nelson town's on the other side of them hills. Course, it's not London exactly, nor Liverpool neither, as you'll soon find out when you try to walk around in them fancy shoes.'

Hector frowned. He was not used to hearing his wife spoken to in quite such tones by a member of the lower classes. If one of his people in Calcutta or London had addressed Fanny with such lack of ceremony he would have given the fellow a sharp reminder. But it would not do to start off here on the wrong foot. He had read somewhere of the democratic style of the New World, where every Jack was as good as his master. He would have to feel his way, learn how things were done. The men looked friendly enough – well disposed, even. Probably no disrespect had been meant.

The bottom of the boat scraped on the beach, and at once a group of onlookers began shouting across the narrow strip of water.

'Are you off the *New Zealand*?'

'Have you suffered many losses?'

'Is there one Sarah Drewitt on board?'

'Have you any news of the *Mary Ann*?'

'Do you bring mails from London?'

Edward, unable to sit a moment longer, had bent to untie his boots and now, holding them aloft, he jumped out of the boat into the shallow water and ran barefoot, splashing and laughing, on to the beach. At once his hands were grasped and his arms pumped by a dozen work-stained fists, and intoxicated by the warmth of the welcome, and euphoric from the sweet clean air he was drawing at last into his lungs after the stenches of the ship, he executed a hornpipe. Then, mad with excitement, he rushed to the person nearest him (a sailor wobbly with drink) and embraced him, to the laughs and clappings of the watching crowd.

Fanny was grateful for the diversion he had made. She had weighed up the choice of plunging into the couple of feet of water and wading ashore, which promised certain ruin to her skirts and shoes, against the offer of a ride on the back of one of the whalers, which had been made with an unmistakable leer. Averting her eyes from Hector, who was already engaged in untying his shoelaces, she had accepted the ride, climbed upon the man's arched back, and so she landed, breathless, hatless and laughing, to be greeted by a shower of questions and exclamations of welcome, while a kindly colonist retrieved her blue bonnet from the water.

The sensation of standing once more on solid ground was so strange that Edward rocked on his feet. What could be happening? The beach seemed to heave up and down beneath him! Could this be an earthquake, such as he had been led to believe were almost daily occurrences in this strange country? The thought excited him still further. He could not stand still here while his parents engaged in interminable greetings, back slappings and conversations with their new compatriots. He must explore at once. The stones and drift of seaweed growing near the beach had looked strangely similar to any one might see at home. He had somehow imagined more bizarre shapes than these, more exotic lines, more diverse colours in the sea. But he could see, rising away in the distance, a range of hills covered with a forest which he longed to explore. And nearer at hand, on the steep rise in front of him, grew a strange assortment of dark green trees whose tufty, tight-growing foliage was unlike any on an English hillside. Its dull green mass was spangled with the brighter crowns of tall tree ferns, which stood out against it like giant stranded star-fish.

Edward bent down and replaced his boots, then, unable to wait any longer for his parents, he began to run up the path that led to the summit of the small ridge, desperate to see beyond it.

At the top he paused, and gasped in surprise as well as for breath. Spread out at the foot of the downs on which he stood was a stretch of level land running down to mud flats near the water's edge. It was covered with waving ferns through which paths and tracks were cut in swathes, and was intersected by a winding river. A few clumps of trees were dotted about as well as some larger wooded areas, and the strangest collection of dwellings sprouted from the scrub. Here and there a finished wooden house stood proudly forth, boasting two storeys, glazed windows and covered verandahs, but much commoner were crude huts with a brick chimney stack at one end and a mass of fern thatching for a roof. Below him he could quite clearly make out a group of tents and fern shelters, with a fireplace in the centre of the ring, over which a cauldron was suspended from a tripod.

In the middle of the plain, which lay in a bowl of thickly forested hills, a low mound formed the focus of the embryo town and it was plain that here, in the large wooden hut erected upon it towards which a long line of people was streaming, was the heart of the new settlement.

Edward's spirits, already high, rose higher still. It was all so cheerful, so informal, so wonderfully incomplete. He had been afraid that they would arrive too late for the real fun of pioneering, that they would be obliged to move straight into a comfortable house instead of enjoying all the delightful inconveniences of the camping life, for some months at least. He was afraid it would all be too organised, too tame, too finished. But he need not have worried. This would be a real adventure. He gulped down more lungfuls of balmy air, so warm, so scented with the almost forgotten smells of land, vegetation, sunbaked earth and fragrant flowers. The wind, a constant and annoying companion at sea, had dropped here to a slight playful breeze which riffled across the fern, lying golden in the brilliant sunshine. And then the sounds were so new, so refreshing! In place of the creaking of timbers, the whistling of wind through ropes and sails and the splashing and roaring of the waves, there was a distant shouting of human voices, the industrious ringing of a hammer, the barking of a dog, the cackling of geese, the gentle murmuring of leaves in the scrubby bushes around him, and a haunting, fluting birdsong whose like he had never heard before.

As he stood still to listen, the sound of voices close behind came to him and he turned. His parents, together with a new acquaintance, were climbing up the hill behind him. Edward felt a rush of affection and sympathy for them. They were middle-aged, old almost! In a few years his father would be fifty! Why, Edward could see him pausing to take breath though the path was so easy to climb. How brave they had been to take such a drastic step as this! How vulnerable they appeared! All at once, Edward felt sober again and ten years older. He was filled with tenderness for his mother and father. This was a country for young men and his parents would need to lean on him when their energies began to fail. Edward squared his shoulders, and ran lightly back down the slope to meet them.

'By all that's wonderful!' Hector was saying to his companion. 'You mean you actually know old Dickson of Cornhill? It's hard to credit that a man can travel half-way round the world and find one with friends in common! It was Dickson persuaded me to put money into the New Zealand Company. He is the cause of our coming here. I know him well – I have done for years.'

Mr Townshend, dressed in serviceable moleskin trousers, a strange low-crowned hat and the ubiquitous blue shirt of the colonists, and looking as unlike the city businessman he had once been as a songthrush looks like a crow, smiled a little abstractedly at this remark and gave an imperceptible shake of the head.

'I hope our friend has not persuaded you to set up in trade in the colony,' he said. 'Business has been poor here, very poor indeed. I could name you several bankrupts in the last two months. Ironmongery is selling for less than it will fetch in London, I am told. We are overrun with merchants and mechanics, and in desperate need of capitalists, farmers, you know, to bring the land into production.'

Hector stopped for a moment and looked at Mr Townshend in some consternation. This was not the kind of news he wished to hear, five minutes into his new life. He made a mental review of the agricultural implements at present in the hold of the *New Zealand* on which he had set such hopes. Then he saw Mr Townshend's enquiring gaze, smiled and set off up the hill again. It would be bad policy to lay his cards too soon upon the table. He knew enough of business not to believe the word of the first person he encountered. But bankrupts! The word rang unpleasantly in his ears.

Five minutes more brought them to the top of the rise, and the panorama burst upon them.

'Oh! It's beautiful! Beautiful!' cried Fanny, and she turned, flushed with exercise and vibrant with exhilaration, to Hector. 'Could you have imagined such a scene, Hector? The air so pure and good, and the weather so warm and sunny! And those charming woods, and neat little valleys, and the splendid mountains, and the rude huts . . . ! Why, it almost puts one in mind of Switzerland!'

Edward burst out laughing.

'Switzerland, Mama? Surely you have never set foot in Switzerland?'

Fanny gave her son a little push, and he had to prevent himself from falling into a large clump of spiky flax.

'Don't be tiresome, Teddy,' she said, laughing with him. 'Lithographs and prints, you know, mountains, romantic grandeur – though of course, nowhere near as lovely as *this*!'

Mr Townshend beamed at her. A resident of some six months' standing, he felt himself already to be an old-timer, and Fanny's praise made him glow with proprietorial pride.

'Aye, Mrs Jamieson, that's the spirit,' he declared. 'You'll be a most welcome addition to our small community, most welcome indeed. You will be amazed, I am sure, at how much is already achieved. Our own newspaper, the *Nelson Advertiser*, already in circulation, regular Sunday worship, a circulating library – why, we have even established the Nelson Literary and Scientific Institution! Musical evenings, balls, an excellent hotel—'

'An hotel!' Fanny broke in. 'Hector, we must reserve rooms immediately. I will not spend another night in that close little cabin on board ship! I must and shall sleep in comfort on my first night in New Zealand! We can return tomorrow to pack up and bring off our trunks when the ship is fast in the haven.'

The thought of the spaciousness of a real bedroom, and, in particular, the joy of fresh water for her bath, seemed to go to Fanny's head like wine. She grasped Edward's arm and began actually to skip down the hill, leaving Hector and Mr Townshend first to smile at each other in amusement, and then to follow more slowly, plunged deep into conversation in which such subjects as the current rents chargeable for prime town sections, the going price for good quality ploughs, the relative fertility of fern and bush land, the cost of hiring labour, the difficulties of draining swamps and the temper of the local Maori population followed thick and fast upon each other.

2

Jessie sat on a convenient hummock outside the emigrants' barracks and crooned a lullaby to her doll. It had been whittled for her out of a piece of driftwood by cousin Jem, and Jessie's lonely heart had seized upon it. She wrapped it in her mother's old shawl, tenderly stroked its rough wooden cheek, and slept with it cradled in her arms. This morning, still tasting with satisfaction the hearty breakfast she had devoured, she was filled with a solemn, secret joy. They had been three days in New Zealand already, and she had never yet been cold or famished. She had supposed that the life on board was but an interlude between the old misery of Paisley and a new misery to come. She had assumed that Nelson, too, would be a warren of close, sooty streets, that their new home would be like every other she had known, a cramped dwelling above a cold weaver's shed in which she would soon be penned up once more in servitude to her father's irritable commands.

She jumped to her feet. They were bare again. The right and left shoes in which she had taken such pride were too small already. Her poor mother would hardly have recognised her little daughter now. Five months of plentiful food, fresh air, adequate sleep and relief from stunting drudgery had made her grow almost as tall as any other twelve-year-old. Her wrists now stuck out inches beyond her sleeves, and her skirts were ridiculously short. But Jessie was too full of other considerations to care about how she looked. There was so much to see in this wonderful new place, there were so many strange birds to chase and hills to climb, so many beaches to play on and children to observe. She had not yet made friends with any of them. She was not used to being with others of her age. She had never before played with anyone but Meg.

Jessie lifted her eyes from her doll and let them rest vacantly for a moment on the sparkling water of the bay beyond the mud flats. Meg was so different now, boring and strict and grown up. She was forever telling Jessie to comb her hair and wash her face, and not let people think she was a poor slum child. She was so strange, too, whenever Malcolm was nearby, as he was almost all the time. She was always smiling, and looking down, and giggling. Jessie had never known Meg be so silly. Why didn't she want to play cat's cradle any more, or throw five stones like they had been used to do on board ship?

Joseph Kirkwood, blinking as he came out of the barracks into the strong spring sunlight, smiled at the sight of Jessie wrapped in thought. She was a dear child on whom the Lord had bestowed a strange, ardent spirit, as ripe for great suffering as great joy. Just so might his own wee girl have been, had she lived. What grave thoughts were running now behind those serious brown eyes? If he could help it, she would have no cause to worry. He was glad to shoulder the burdens of his poor dead sister. There was no looking to Isaiah, in any case. Isobel's death had unmanned him completely. He had declared his health and spirits quite broken down, and now leant on his brother Joseph for support.

Joseph shook his massive grizzled head. Things did not look as hopeful here as the bright sunshine would make one believe. The soil of Nelson was in general poor, there was no doubt of that. He had listened to other men talking, to Tom Cox from Shropshire, and the Devon man, Billy Hodgkin. They had all confirmed his own view, that the company had misled the emigrants; they could not provide the land they had promised, in the Nelson colony at least; there was too little flat, fertile land, too many steep hills covered with dense bush on which not even a sheep could be run for many years to come, and too many labourers with not enough capital to employ them. There were dozens of clerks, tailors and bakers but hardly any men who understood the land, and cattle, and the raising of crops. He thanked God for the years he had spent as a farm worker in Mr Turnbull's employ. At the time he had doubted God's providence, and counted those years a bitter waste, but he saw now, with a lift of the heart, that they had had a purpose indeed, divinely foreordained. If his faith had been too weak to see it then, it would be stronger now. He would not, like so many others, eat the bread of idleness, taking wages from the New Zealand Company in return for a show of work. He would hire out the skills of himself and his sons, and till the soil and raise up crops for the hungry and, in the Lord's own time, perhaps he could hope to be rewarded with a piece of land of his own, whose title would bear his name and which he could pass on to his son and his son's son.

The thought of grandchildren brought his mind full circle back to

Jessie. There was no doubt that Malcolm had made his choice. It would not be long, he felt sure, before he presented Meg as his bride. Perhaps, in the fullness of time, Jem and Jessie . . . But it was too soon to think such things, with the child still playing with her doll.

He patted Jessie's unkempt hair and the girl jumped with surprise.

'I'd give a penny for your thoughts,' he said, smiling broadly.

'No, you wouldn't, Uncle Joseph. You haven't a penny to spare, and besides, you'd deem it a sinful waste of money,' said Jessie, whose liberties with their censorious father never ceased to astonish her cousins. 'And anyway,' she added, 'sixpence wouldn't buy them.'

Joseph laughed, then, afraid of seeming too indulgent, assumed a serious expression.

'Aye, well, as long as your thoughts are true, and pure, and honest, and of good report,' he said, and started off down the track. Jessie darted after him.

'Where are you going, Uncle? Can I come too?'

'I'm off to look for work, and for a place where we can build our own wee house,' said Joseph, and he made no objection when the child tucked her hand under his arm and skipped along beside him.

To Jessie, darting here and there to chase a quail which started up from the track, or to watch a group of men constructing a whare, as she had learned to call the strange fern huts, the town of Nelson was no more than a hodge podge of makeshift dwellings, separated by stretches of scrubby growth. But to Hector, who had come out with Edward and Fanny to inspect the town acre selected for him, it rose in the imagination as handsome buildings and fine streets, whose outlines were already clearly marked with surveyor's lines and pegs.

'Our frontage is to be on Nile Street,' he was remarking to Fanny. 'Does it not sound well? Townshend and some of the fellows I met at Miller's Tavern have shown me an outline of how the town is to look. The names of the streets and squares will be connected with Admiral Nelson, you know, like Hardy, Collingwood, St Vincent, Trafalgar and so forth. It will be most elegant, I assure you! We can construct our town house here on this very spot, with a fine prospect either way, and I am assured of being able to let the remaining part of our street frontage at twelve shilling the foot or more per annum, which is bound to increase, you may be sure, as the colony prospers and expands.'

'Build our own house, Father?' said Edward doubtfully. 'Do you mean we are to do it ourselves? But how? We have no knowledge of bricks, or wood, or nails, or things of that kind.'

'Silly boy.' Fanny tapped her son affectionately on the shoulder.

'Your father did not mean we are to do the actual work. There are builders, carpenters, people of that sort, who will do it for us.'

'Well, as to that, my love,' said Hector a little defiantly, 'I believe Teddy and I may very well work on the house ourselves. We will need expert help of course, but I do not see why we should be obliged to pay exorbitant sums to others when we have nothing better to do with our time. Everyone here works at such things, you know. It is considered quite the thing. We are in a new kind of life, after all. Pioneers are obliged to turn their hands to anything.'

Fanny laughed.

'What do you find so funny in that?' said Hector, relieved.

'I was thinking of Justina's face if she could see her family now,' said Fanny. 'But you are quite right, Hector. It is just that I have not quite got used to being a colonist. Of course we are to try everything ourselves, and I do not see why we should leave it a day longer. Why, you and Teddy between you will have a snug little cottage ready in no time at all. I only ask that you make room for my dear piano. And I shall lay out the garden. I shall put my cabbages here' – she ran to a clump of toi-toi rushes and swung out her arms, then moved across to another – 'and my radishes here. Then we will construct a shed for the cow *here*, and a coop for the chickens beyond it!'

She turned back triumphantly to her menfolk, but they were no longer listening to her. Hector was pacing out the frontage of the site he had chosen for the house, while Edward plied him with questions about the best proportions for bedrooms and urged him to give proper consideration to the sanitary arrangements.

Fanny looked past them. Dotted about on the flat land that was destined soon to be covered with streets and houses a dozen colourful scenes were being enacted. Here came a gang of labourers on their way to construct a road. A bullock cart driver, drunk already although it was scarcely eleven o'clock in the morning, was steering his beasts erratically along the track to the port. A woman was chasing a goose that had escaped from its pen. She was running along behind it, skirts flying, arms outstretched, while the bird, its wings flapping noisily, cackled down the track just out of reach. A Maori woman, her face tattooed but her clothes in the European style, was accompanying her English husband to the New Zealand Company offices in a stately promenade.

Fanny stared at her curiously. As an Englishwoman in India, she had been expected to keep her distance from the native peoples. In any case, the great variety of castes, races, religions and sects was confusing. One hardly knew where to start. The saddhu with his painted face, the maharaja on his elephant, the baboo with his spectacles on his nose, and the fierce, turbaned Pathan inhabited a world so diverse that she had given up all attempts to understand it. But here it was different. The native New Zealanders seemed open and easy to converse with. They were so friendly and welcoming that it was impossible to ignore them. Their fondness for newcomers, their hearty laughter and cheerful greetings could only evoke smiles and handshakes in return. Fanny had already exchanged pleasantries with a group of men dressed only in mats and blankets hung about the shoulders, whose outward ferocity was belied by the gentleness of their manners. Then, too, Mr Townshend had informed Hector, many of them had embraced the Christian faith, and showed great strictness in such matters as Sabbath observance, so that one could not but feel comfortable with them.

Somehow, Fanny did not know how it was, everyone in this strange place, Maori or European, seemed larger, more definite than the people at home. There were no grey, shapeless forms, gaunt with hunger and grimed with soot, who slipped past on crowded streets and were instantly forgotten, such as she had always been used to in Edinburgh or London. Here, everyone was noticed and remarked upon, everyone was a 'character'. There were, of course, some prominent in Nelson's infant society who would have been extraordinary anywhere. Fanny had known many such in Calcutta, men of corpulent build, huge digestions, prodigious thirsts, brilliant conversation and capricious temper, whose like had flourished in the heyday of the Regency. But even the less spectacular were somehow larger than their equivalents at home. The men of letters seemed more brilliant, the old soldiers more valiant, the religious more spiritual, the reformers more determined, the drunken more bestial. The most ordinary people, thought Fanny, seemed to have some extra force inside them. Working men walked with a different gait, devoid of the old European deference, while the sons of English lords had shed their debilitating disdain, donned corduroy breeches, and dug their own gardens with a will. Women, even ladies, strode about, and ran, and swung their arms energetically, rejoicing in the free use of their limbs in a way that Fanny had found at first a little shocking. Young people seemed to glow with a kind of radiance, an impression created, perhaps, by the warm golden tan their skins had all acquired, so different from the fashionable pallor of England. But it was the children most of all who had come into their own. They ran wild and free, out of school, unharnessed to work, scrambling through ferns and up trees, dirty, scratched, rude, eternally ravenous, endlessly happy, like the little girl she now saw approaching, swinging on the arm of a tall, grizzled man.

'Why, Hector,' Fanny called out suddenly. 'Is that not Kirkwood, from off the *New Zealand*?'

Hector raised his head from his calculations and stared down the track.

'Indeed it is,' he said, and leaving Fanny standing, and Edward flushing with embarrassment, he strode up to Joseph.

'Kirkwood, is it not? Off the *New Zealand*?'

'Aye.' Joseph looked at Hector curiously, but without, Hector noticed, the respectful attention he was used to receiving from working men. It put him on his mettle.

'Kirkwood, I have not properly thanked you for your prompt action in rescuing my son from his foolish escapade in the rigging.'

A smile creased Joseph's cheeks.

'Oh aye, young Master Edward. A fine lad for all that.'

'Yes – well – my wife and I are truly in your debt.'

'Oh, not at all, not at all. It was my own son led him astray with a foolish wager, when he should have known better than to follow the devil's promptings.'

'Yes, indeed, of course, but it was not only on that subject I wished to speak with you. I am in need of workers, Kirkwood. I have first to build my house here in the town, on this section where we are standing, but I intend to move out as soon as possible to the acres that have been selected for me up the valley of the Maitai. I have not as yet had a chance to see them for myself, but I shall commence a farming operation there until such time as conditions for trade improve. But the land is heavily wooded, I believe, covered with "bush" as the term is here, and there is a vast amount to be done even before our first crops can be sown.'

Joseph's eyes had not left Hector's face and under the directness of his gaze, which seemed to be measuring him against some hidden yardstick, Hector felt himself to be on trial. He thrust his hands into his pockets, smiled, and said with the frankness which had for so long disarmed so many, 'I do not disguise from you that I've no knowledge of the land. I've been a merchant all my life, in Bengal for the most part. I can tell you all you wish to know of the prices of indigo or jute on the Calcutta trading floors, or I could have done a year or so ago, but my hands have never held an axe or lifted a spade. And yet we have to make a start. There's no living to be had in Nelson except from the land and I propose, with the help of my wife and son, to build us up to prosperity again.'

To his relief, Joseph's stern face cracked open in a smile. 'And with the help of God, Mr Jamieson, you'll not forget the help of God,' he said, nodding his head. 'And indeed, it's God who has answered my prayer again, for I set out this morning with the intention of seeking honest work and I'm offered it by the first man I meet. But before I accept your offer I must tell you, sir, that the Lord did not lead me and mine half way around the world to set our feet under other men's tables. It seems just now as if that's the way it must be, but our labour brings with it certain conditions.'

Hector, too startled to speak, waited for him to go on.

'We're a family, Mr Jamieson, and we're not to be separated. I've a strong back and a good pair of hands, as have my sons, but my brother's a delicate man. If you take one you'll have to take us all. If you rent us a piece of land of our own to work, that we can buy fair and square in our own time and at an honest price, in return you'll get an honest day's labour from us all. I speak for myself and my elder boy especially. I cannot be sure of Jem, for he'll be away to find a flock to tend as soon as he can. There are the wee girls too, Meg and Jessie, and they can give Mrs Jamieson a hand at the churn and with the chickens. As for my brother-in-law . . . ' Joseph stopped and scratched his head. 'I doubt you'll have a use for one who has no temperament for aught else but weaving, but there's no dog so old he cannot learn new tricks.'

Hector, listening to these comprehensive plans for the staffing of his future establishment, felt out of his depth. Joseph Kirkwood seemed so sure of what he wanted, so confident of Hector's acquiescence. Hector felt obliged to exert himself to gain the upper hand.

'Aye, well, we can come to some accommodation, I am sure, along the lines you suggest. Our first task, until we are ready to move, is to start on our town house. Where *you* are to stay . . . '

'With your permission, Mr Jamieson, we'll build a wee place of our own on the end of your section, one of these bothies, or whares, or whatever they're called. It will take us no time at all and we'll be free of the barracks, which I am wishful for, seeing as how the language and the drinking and the breaking of the Sabbath is not at all a fit example for the young ones. Today would not be too soon for us to make a start. Would it be convenient, now, for us to position ourselves by yon hummock, towards the corner post?'

'Oh, yes, well, certainly, there can be no objection, I'm sure.'

Hector sensed himself borne along on a strong tide and felt the need to withdraw in order to recruit his forces. 'We'll leave you now, for I've business to discuss with the surveyors. Shall we meet again tomorrow? At noon?'

'Aye, noon will be a grand time,' said Joseph equably.

'At, shall we say, Miller's Tavern?'

'A tavern! Now surely, Mr Jamieson, you're not a drinking man?'

'No, of course, I mean . . . '

'Are you an abstainer?'

Hector recovered his composure with an effort.

'I tell you frankly, Kirkwood, I am not, but I hate drunkenness and will not tolerate it in my family. I believe strong drink to be at the root of much human suffering. I mention Miller's Tavern as a useful meeting place, a landmark we may both easily find. It forms a popular centre, I believe, where a good deal of business is daily transacted. We will be able, I am sure, to enquire there about the price of timber and bricks, and where they are to be got. I will meet you outside Miller's at noon tomorrow. Good day to you.'

Hector had thrust out his jaw during this speech, and at the conclusion of it he grasped Fanny by the elbow and steered her rapidly away before Joseph could further undermine his authority. This little triumph pleased him.

'I fancy we have a good man there, my love. Hardworking, I am sure, and honest to a fault. He is not a type one often meets with, quite a personality in fact. He puts one in mind of an Old Testament prophet, does he not, with his white hair and his stern eye and his continual references to Scripture? He may need some careful handling but I know how to go about it, and I believe he will answer our purpose very well.'

Edward had retreated from Hector and Joseph's conversation. He would have liked to speak to Mr Kirkwood, to resume the shipboard friendship, but he was afraid, desperately afraid, that Father was being – he didn't quite know what – too grand, perhaps, or masterful, or worldly. During the long months at sea Edward had listened many times to Joseph's stories of his adventures as a boy in Nelson's navy. They had fascinated him, horrified him, shaken him, but never bored him. He had conceived a liking and respect for the man which would have surprised Joseph Kirkwood's own sons. Edward now stood in a quandary, not wishing to stand with his father but afraid of seeming proud by hanging back. Then his eye fell on Jessie.

Jessie too had been struck with embarrassment. When she had seen the young scientific gentleman standing there by the track as she and Uncle Joseph approached, something had happened to her, she could not say what it was. She remembered with amazement what a child she had been on the ship when this glorious being had explained about phos – phos – whatever it was called. How had she been able to speak to him? How had she been able to lift her eyes to his face? They were at the moment riveted to a point just below his knees where the legs of his corduroy trousers (carefully packed, had she but known it, by the devoted Aggie) dropped to a pair of heavy boots, of a finer quality than any Jessie had seen except on Mr Armstrong. What was the matter with her? She could not pull her eyes from those boots! And now he was talking to her! She recognised his voice, cheerful, friendly, but with such an accent! Why had it not struck her before? It was like a minister, or a dominie, or a laird even. What was he saying?

'Hello, little girl. How do you like your new country then?'

Little girl! Why did everyone call her that? She wasn't such a little girl now. She had grown inches – feet almost – since they'd left home. She was almost thirteen! She was practically grown-up! Jessie felt suddenly flamingly conscious of her looks. Why had she not listened to Meg? Why had she not dragged a comb through her tangled hair this morning, or at least washed her face? How silly she must look, with her arms so long and her pinafore so crumpled! When was someone going to buy her a new pair of shoes and a decent shawl? All at once she hated Edward. He had done something dreadful to her. He was making her feel stupid and poor and – and ugly! Yes! That was it! She was ugly, ugly, ugly!

'I'm not a little girl and I like it fine,' she blurted out, and losing her nerve she turned and raced back to the shelter of the emigrant barracks, leaving her doll lying forgotten in the dust. Edward watched her, wondering what he had done to cause her sudden flight, and thinking that never before had he seen a human being so closely resemble a fawn, startled from its covering of bracken.

3

Nile Street, Nelson
24th December 1842

My dearest Aggie,

It is Christmas Eve, and as I take up my pen to write I confess to a heart confused between delighted anticipation at the jollifications of tomorrow, and a lowering depression when I think of all that is dear and good that we have left behind.

You cannot conceive, my dear Aggie, the joy and comfort your letters have brought me! I run to enquire of the mails on every ship, and on receiving your first two, off the *Scotia*, via Sydney, became positively ill with weeping, until dear Hector, who is more strong-minded than I, threatened to douse me in the charming stream that runs close to our section of land.

I cannot at all understand how you can say 'I have nothing of interest to tell you' in every second line! You must know that the smallest detail from Home is manna from Heaven to us poor 'jimmygrants'. How eagerly I devoured your account of your return to George Street, so often pictured by us all! How thankful we must be that the sale of the house and its contents had not been effected before our departure, and that the fire at your neighbours had been so speedily put out before it could spread to your own roof. Had it not, you would have been homeless indeed! How I laughed when I read of poor Jeanie's terror at seeing you, presuming you to be a spirit rose again, and mistaking your deck bonnet for an unearthly aura! She is too blind and infirm to be of service now and it is just like you, my dear sister, to offer a home and your own loving care for the years that are left to her.

I am sure you would open your eyes to see me now, for I am sitting in my own little parlour, which, though rudely finished, promises to be all that is delightful when once there is glass in the window frames and a complete set of boards upon the floor! A few small matters, such as a roof that will keep out the rain, have not yet been attended to, but Hector assures me that when once the shingles are in place I will be able to put away the arrangement of buckets and bowls that I have cleverly contrived to catch the drops, and sit in perfect comfort. As for furniture, you would be surprised, I am sure, at how well a packing case serves as table, bench and closet in turn. But we are not for ever to be reduced to such shifts, for in four or five weeks from now we will be able to 'settle in', unpack our home comforts, and be ready to face the world. We will then be fine indeed, for we will have, on either side of the front door, two handsome apartments with a corridor running through to the rear. The kitchen and laundry arrangements will be behind the main house, for in these wooden constructions the danger of fire is too great to allow of a hearth being built below stairs, as at home. (I need not dwell on the dangers of fire to you!) Upstairs we have planned three good-sized rooms and a smaller one which will serve as Hector's dressing room for the present. The whole is to be surrounded by a delightful verandah, very necessary, I do assure you, in this country of brilliant sunlight! Indeed, I shall have to guard against the fading of rugs and materials as scrupulously as in Bengal. However, there is no need to worry about that at present, for not a curtain, nor chair cover, nor sheet of wall-paper is yet unpacked.

I wish I could convey to you some impression of our daily life, but it is impossible, for we are living in a way quite unlike any I have known before. I have never until now found myself obliged to wring the neck of a chicken, lay my small clothes over a bush to dry, or boil a pot of soup over a camp fire in the open air, but these are now everyday occurrences, and I fancy I am becoming quite an expert at living the simple life.

You must know that Meg and Jessie, the two Dunbar waifs I wrote of, have proved their worth as good, willing creatures, though untaught in all but the arts of cookery (as well as the remoter reaches of the Old Testament!) in which their mother, poor dead soul, seems to have trained them well. There is not one of our acquaintance but would stare to see us, the strangest mistress and the most unlikely maids, upon our knees, by the stream, a-washing of our linen all together! We live for ever with suds upon our aprons and smuts upon our noses.

Do not, I beg of you, however, receive the impression that we have forgotten all the arts of elegance. On the contrary, we enjoy the most delightful intercourse with our fellow colonists, and it is no uncommon thing to find us, when the morning's labour is done, setting forth across flax and fern to pay a polite call to a windowless hut, and, perched on a tree stump for a seat, enjoy a conversation that would not shame the drawing room of a duchess over a refreshing drink of tea from a chipped enamel vessel!

But I must close as Hector stands by me with his hand held out for my letter, hoping to catch the mails for Port Nicholson, so I will say no more, but conclude in breathless haste with a fond embrace from your affectionate,

Fanny

Nelson
4th January 1843

Dear Dickson,

Receiv'd yours of 2nd September this day and was glad to learn of the latest news tho' by the time this reaches you it will already be as dead as the Greeks.

I am happy to inform you of our safe landing. We are now quite snug in our own house, which wants but some finishing touches to bring it to a reasonable condition of comfort. I must apprise you, however, that the situation here is by no means as I had supposed it to be. Your forecasts for business, I am afraid, erred on the optimistic side. I had hoped to set up my warehouse, and ship out such tools and machinery as would find a good market amongst those engaged in bringing the land into production, but the market is at present poor, the farmers too few, and the merchants too numerous.

I have therefore decided to take possession of my suburban acres as quickly as possible, and will commence the work of clearing the bush and planting. All opinion agrees that this is the first task to be completed and everyone of us must turn to. I own I am not a little put out by this turn of events and had hoped ere this to send you a firm order for goods, but with patience my objective may yet be achieved and I perceive that I must willy-nilly try my hand at farming.

Fortune has favoured us in one respect, however: we have been allotted an excellent section, within a few miles of the settlement, up a fertile valley well-watered by a delightful brook that promises excellent prospects both for livestock and arable production. Labour, though not cheap, is plentiful.

I cannot recommend the climate and landscape of New Zealand too highly: it has the most invigorating effect upon the system. Fevers and colds are of the past, and the vigour of all is a tribute to the good air and pure water. The natives have as yet belied their somewhat fearsome reputation. They have a natural dignity, sobriety and friendliness, and are on excellent terms with the 'pakeha', as they call us Europeans. I have held conversation with some few of them, and I believe we have little to fear from that quarter.

I hope you will be able to read this vile scrawl. The lack of a desk and chair and the unfamiliar necessity of writing on my knee have proved detrimental to the legibility

of your obedient,
Hector Jamieson

Nelson
21st January 1843

Dear Professor Jamieson,

I have long promised myself the pleasure of sending you an account of some of the wonders of New Zealand in the hopes that the interest of what I have to describe will excuse my temerity in opening the correspondence. I wish only that I was possessed of a more expert pen with which to convey to you the beauty of the lofty hills that rise in places almost sheer from the sea, and are covered with dense woods to the very summits, the fascination of the countless (to me unfamiliar) species of plants, and the charms of the multitudes of singing birds, whose calls are so much more lively than those of their drabber British cousins.

The delightful warmth of the climate has produced a richness of forest growth which I have as yet scarce had time to investigate. Massive trunks of our great giants, known here by the local names of 'rimu' and 'totara' (the former a kind of pine, the latter with foliage resembling a yew), as well as many kinds of evergreen beech, sprout from a rich dark earth, while a mass of orchids and ferns of every description suspend from their lofty heights, the whole intertwined in a maze of twisting vines in almost tropical profusion.

I am enclosing a sketch of a strange little fern of an unusual climbing habit, which I think must interest you. I have not seen its like in a published work. I am also sending you some seeds of a palm-like tree, the heart of which tastes somewhat like a cabbage and is much prized by the Maori as a source of food. I hope it will afford you some interest and amusement.

Would you be kind enough to forward to me a copy of the article on Alpine flora, of which you spoke at our final meeting? I hope before the year is past to visit our Antipodean peaks and would like to be well prepared.

In the meantime, please be assured, dear sir, of the gratitude and respectful memories of

your former pupil
Edward Jamieson

Nelson
January 1843

To the Members of the Congregation of the Lord's People in Irvine, in the County of Ayrshire, Scotland

Dear Brothers and Sisters in the Lord,

I received yours of June last with a heart full of thankfulness for the great mercies our Heavenly Father has seen fit to bestow upon us. The past years have indeed tried and tested our people almost to their limits, but the Lord is gracious and will not try us beyond what we are able. Brother Macneil writes that all of our congregation has banded together to give of their substance to the poorest among you and for this I thank God.

As for ourselves, we rejoice in the fullness of God's goodness. We have passed through the perils of the deep and, lo, the Lord was with us alway. He saw fit to take from us my poor sister Dunbar, whose mortal remains have found a watery home but whose soul has reached a spiritual one, even in the bosom of Abraham. 'For this corruptible must put on incorruption, and this mortal must put on immortality.' I Cor. 15, v. 53. We have wept, and we have been comforted.

This is indeed a fair land and none goes hungry here. When bought in quantity, flour is at 2d. the pound, sugar at 2$^{1}/_{2}$d. the pound, butter at 3s., black tea, 3d. the pound. Pork plentiful, no shortage of fish or fowl. Potatoes, carrots, cabbages, peas and beans. Little reward for those who seek it at other men's hands, but work in plenty for those who look to take the wilderness by their own exertions. Excellent climate. Most natives well-disposed and many have accepted the Gospel. Worship regular, but no kirk erected as yet. Few unattached females. Men who emigrate should first marry. Little disease. No famine.

And yet, in spite of all that is good, we see on all sides the wickedness of man. Drunkenness is rife and the Sabbath held in low regard, especially among the English. I have myself had occasion to reprove whistlers, card players, singers of lewd songs and some bent on walking for pleasure on the Sabbath, on various occasions, but their hearts will not be touched. They take refuge in slanders and mockeries. Happy am I that in no more than two weeks' time we will remove from this city of corruption to the purer air of the untamed bush, to the section bought by Mr Hector Jamieson, in whose employ we currently find ourselves, there to build a cabin from the simple materials God will provide and to wrest our living from the earth.

Brothers and sisters, I end my epistle by exhorting you to remember us in your prayers, as we remember you. We will not meet again until we come to Glory and the Lord gathers us unto himself, in that Land where there will be no weeping or wailing or gnashing of teeth. Until that time comes, may the Grace of the Lord be with us all.

Joseph Kirkwood

Nile Street, Nelson
January 1844

My dearest Child,

Since my last sent via the Elise so much has occurred I scarce know how to write to you. We have made such progress that you would hardly recognise, in the respected citizens of Nelson, the regular scarecrows who stepped from the vessel but ten weeks ago! I believe even Lady Dunstable would not be ashamed of the connection now!!

There must, however, be little time for self-congratulation, for your dear Papa has but to complete one scheme than the next takes possession of his mind. We are about to abandon our new home, whose timbers are but scarce settled into place, and will soon be leaving even the rudimentary comforts of Nelson for the absolute rusticity of the Maitai Valley, where our farming operation is to commence.

You must not imagine us, my dear Child, in some desert waste, for the Maitai is a charming spot, a veritable Arcadia, lush with verdant growth and resounding the day long to the glorious music of our feathered friends.

Your Papa has already gone up, with Teddy and the Kirkwood men (who are excellent people indeed) to construct a rude abode, and when the last stalks of thatch are securely tied, they will come into town to fetch us (myself, with old Isaiah and the two Dunbar girls), and our necessaries by bullock cart to the country.

The house here, which stands out well among its simpler neighbours, has already been let to an aspiring young colonist and his hopeful brood, and we must resign ourselves, for a year or two at least, to the delights of a rustic idyll, to earthen floors, open hearth cooking, and rooms of the smallest dimensions.

I will not disguise from you, my dear child, a certain dread at thus abandoning civilisation entirely and assuming the mantle of the true pioneer, but neither can I deny that it is a wonderful adventure, such as few women of my kind are ever likely to undergo, and I confess that I feel not a little excited, rather as one might before departing on a voyage into unexplored seas.

As I am sure you will understand, your letters are the greatest comfort to us all. I feel sure we can soon expect a fine batch from you, for we have received only two since our arrival, and those both rather short. We are delighted to hear you are going on so well, and only sorry that poor Sir Andrew has been plagued with Lumbago.

You will, of course, convey all that is proper to Lady Dunstable, and do not forget to embrace my dear Mrs Blakeney on my behalf, while remembering ever the fond affection,

of your loving
Mama

George Street, Edinburgh
16th May 1843

My dear Fanny,

Your mails arrived this morning and gave me much pleasure and interest in reading of all your doings, especially the arrangements of your new house which sounds more commodious than I had thought. I cannot imagine how you can manage with the rain coming in through the roof, though by now I suppose it is all fixed. I do hope above all else that you have chosen a healthy situation and not too near the stream where you say you do your laundry. Teddy was used as a child to be afflicted with a putrid throat in wet conditions and you should guard against any damp in the house.

You say news from me is like manna to the Israelites but I find it hard to scrape about for anything likely to interest you. You must know that Effie Macfarlane has come to my aid in the matter of servants. Mrs Fergus has been happy enough to take up her old position in the kitchen, not being suited in her new place, and I have a new maid now, whose mother is in service to Effie. She is named Lily Gray and is but seventeen. I had not thought to have so young a person to train, but the child is a little simple, and though good in practical matters, especially where a regular timetable is set up that she can easily follow, she has but few mental abilities and is very nervous. Kindness and firm direction are all she needs, I believe, and I have already seen an improvement in her. I have hopes that she will make a useful and happy servant and we will rub along well enough, I don't doubt.

I am charged with a message for Teddy from his old friend Mr Elliott, who begs me to write that in the manse last Sabbath morn he saw a large black spider with bright yellow legs. Thinking he had come upon a natural phenomenon he pursued it, but on closer observation had to conclude that the animal had wandered into a pot of paint left uncovered by the workmen. I was glad to see him in better spirits. He has for some months past been paying his addresses to Miss Alison Fyne. I have often wished to see him married but this young woman I cannot approve. She is feeble. I cannot abide a languishing woman. Effie Macfarlane informs me that her soporific manner is due to a consumption. I am sorry for it, if it is true, but I wish that she will not communicate any infection to poor Mr Elliott who would be better with another sort of wife altogether.

I suppose now that we are looking forward to our summer, you are making preparations for the winter. It seems strange and unnatural to me. I am sending in this mail some pairs of stout gloves for you all which I hope will not arrive too late to preserve you from chilblains should your south winds blow too strong.

God bless you all, my dear Fanny,
Your loving sister,
Agnes Heriot

4

Duddingston,
April 1843

Edward lay on his back on the damp loamy floor of the bush and waited for the sense of overwhelming fatigue to lift, and for enough energy to flow back into his limbs to enable him to walk home. Overhead the fern fronds, sprouting in wheels from tall spongy trunks, shifted and shimmered in ever-changing hypnotic patterns of sharply splintered sunlight. He felt his eyes closing and forced them open. Once asleep he would be dead to the world for ten hours or more. He had never experienced sleep as he knew it here, the deep, dead sleep of total exhaustion. He had never known hunger like this either. It tore at him at three-hourly intervals, and Fanny's enthusiastically but atrociously baked bread and half-roasted pork were never enough to satisfy it.

A rustling in the undergrowth made him cautiously turn his head. A green, owl-like face was protruding from behind a clump of lacy ferns, while a bright beady eye watched him unwinkingly from above a sharply curved beak. Edward held his breath. Reassured, the kakapo strutted cautiously across the glade and disappeared into the bush once more. The bird had broken the spell. The short rest had given Edward the strength he needed. He stretched and sat up.

Then he heard footsteps. They were not those of his father or any of the Kirkwoods. They were quick, light, confident. He stood up, assailed by a sudden spurt of fear. It was three months since they had come to Duddingston, as Hector, in honour of the loch by whose muddy waters he had first set eyes on Fanny, had named his new estate. In that time they had seen few Maori, and had had no unfriendly encounters, but Hector had come back from his last visit to Nelson with a long face and tales of unrest over at Wairau, where the warlike leader Rangihaeata was disputing the New Zealand Company's claim that it had a right to survey the land.

The footsteps came nearer and a couple of young Maori men appeared. In spite of his fright, Edward could not but stare at their appearance. The taller one wore a pair of sailor's trousers and a battered wide-awake hat, while a cloak of flax partially covered his bare torso. His companion, older and stouter, was clad in a grass skirt over which hung the tails of an old woollen shirt. Yet despite their strange miscellany of garments, the men were striking, dignified, intimidating. Edward noticed that a musket rested on the older man's shoulder.

He forced a smile to his lips. He had not seen these two men before. He knew the few Maori who lived on this stretch of the Maitai. They had come to see his father several times, and had spent hours in amicable conversation. Hector had employed some of them to help clear the first acre of land, and build the primitive homestead. But these men looked different, more purposeful, more watchful. Was the musket only for the purpose of hunting pig, or could it have a more sinister meaning? Edward took a step backwards. He sought about for the only Maori words he knew.

'*Haere mai*,' he said.

The men did not move. Edward took another step backwards and grasped at the berry-covered branch that his right hand had encountered. Instantly the men reacted. Their faces, tattooed in intricate spirals of blue, became violently contorted. Their mouths opened, their tongues shot out, their eyes rolled in their heads. Edward, too terrified to move, stood rooted to the spot. Was this the beginning of one of the war dances he had heard so much about? The taller Maori was now patting his stomach and bending double. Surely it could mean only one thing? They were planning to kill him and eat him! He must escape, at once! He could run, he knew the tracks well, he had a chance. But before he could gather himself for flight, the older man stepped up to him, took his hand and shook it off the branch of berries. Now what was he doing? The Maori seemed to be engaged in some kind of dumbshow. He was pretending to eat the berries, then rolling his eyes in a mime of pain, shooting out his tongue in a graphic display of vomiting, then doubling himself over his stomach, in mock agony.

Of course! Edward let out his breath. The berries he had been touching were poisonous tutus. The men were warning him not to eat them. They were friendly! In his huge relief, Edward began to laugh shakily. The men good-humouredly joined in with him. They clapped him on the shoulder, went through the mime once more, doubled up with mirth this time rather than with pain, then, wiping their streaming eyes, they set off again with their fast efficient gait down the overgrown bush track.

Edward followed them. He had to go home. There was no putting it off any longer, even though his heart sank at the reception he would get. It had all been his fault, he knew that quite well. If he had driven those stakes properly into the ground, Primrose would never have pushed her way across the fence and ambled off into the bush. It would have to be Primrose, he thought with a sigh, the only one of the three precious cows to be in calf. It was hardly surprising that Father had been furious, and had told him to go out and hunt for the beast and not come home until she was found. Hector's scorn had burned in him all through this fruitless day of anxious listening for movement in the thick bush, of hopeless hunting for Primrose's tracks. He had spent nine hours scrambling through the dense undergrowth, losing himself a dozen times, disentangling his clothes from the maddening prickles of the bush lawyer vines, climbing over fallen trees, black and slippery with decay. There had been a few redeeming moments. Edward's pocket book, which he kept permanently in an inside pouch of his jacket, contained the leaves of two new varieties of fern, which he was sure he had not seen illustrated in Mr Cunningham's notes on the flora of New Zealand, and on the back page there was a hasty sketch of a bird Edward had not sighted before, a large, wingless creature with a long curving beak which he had startled from the hollow at the base of a vast tree. But even these precious finds had hardly been worth the misery of the day.

The afternoon sun was low now. Almost faint with hunger, Edward emerged at last into the clearing which, after three months of back-breaking work, was beginning to show positive signs of human habitation.

A flat area near the river had been cleared first, and several large tree trunks lay where they had fallen, their stumps still bright and raw from the bite of the axe. A mantling of grass now covered the cleared soil, peppered with the wild flowers of home whose seeds had come uninvited in the bag of English grass seeds that Hector had bought in Nelson. Near the shingled bank of the river stood the Kirkwoods' simple hut. It consisted of no more than the upright trunks of a few dozen tree ferns rammed into the ground to make four square walls, and was thatched with rushes gathered from a swampy patch near the river. For all its simplicity, it displayed the neat work of Joseph Kirkwood's old sailor's hands.

A few hundred yards away the land rose to a small outcrop, and it was here that Hector had chosen to build his homestead with its back to the bush that rose up the hill behind. Just below the house an area had been fenced off, and in it stood two – no, three cows and a calf! Primrose had been recovered, and had given birth! And the fence had been expertly mended! Edward flushed with irritation. He could have done it perfectly well himself this morning, but Hector had not listened to him. He had made it quite plain that he was not to be trusted with such a responsibility. Jem would make a better job of it.

The sight of the small, two-roomed cottage at the edge of the clearing usually lifted Edward's spirits when he came home to it in the evening. It had been such fun building it with Father and the Kirkwoods in those first extraordinary weeks. Even tonight Edward's eye ran over the clay-daubed walls and low hanging roof and rested on the edging over the door where, he felt, he had made a particularly fine job of trimming the raupo thatch. Vegetables were already sprouting in the well-dug plot beside it, where Isaiah, a gardener of many years' experience, had found his métier. His delicate weaver's fingers had no difficulty in pricking out seedlings and constructing netting to keep away the voracious ducks, who had a predilection for the fresh young growth. Isaiah was a master, too, of the true gardener's pessimism, informing anyone who would listen that the carrots might look bonny enough but there was no saying what was going on below the ground, and he had little doubt that the beans would never ripen before the winter months came on.

Edward arrived at the door and pushed it open. In the gloom within he could barely make out the eight people sitting round the table, which was no more than a couple of planks nailed to the stumps of two great totara trees which had previously occupied the site.

'Teddy! At last!' Fanny jumped up from her place near the big open chimney that ran along almost the entire length of the cottage's end wall and came round the table to greet her son. 'Your face! My dear, it is a positive patchwork!' She touched his cheek, criss-crossed with deep scratches, and Edward flinched. 'My poor boy, you are cut to pieces! Sit down and I will wash the blood off directly.'

Edward, whose eyes were becoming accustomed to the dim light that penetrated into the small room through the calico which covered the window openings, became aware of a derisory stare from Jem. He pushed his mother aside.

'Please, Mama, it's nothing. Let it be. What's in the pot? I've had nothing to eat all day.'

Jessie had already slipped from her place to the great black camp oven that stood on stubby iron feet in the embers of the fire, and was ladling a portion of stew into a bowl. She sliced a hunk of bread and put it in front of him. Edward fell upon it.

'You've travelled a mile or two the day,' said Joseph Kirkwood conversationally, kindly filling the silence which emanated from Hector.

'That I have,' Edward's speech was muffled through the wad of bread in his cheek. 'I see that Primrose is back and has calved! How was she found?'

'Jem had the good sense to search for her upstream,' said Hector irritably. 'She was already calving and it was as well it was Jem who found her, for I doubt you would have had any idea how to assist.'

Edward flushed again and bent over his soup. It was so unfair! He had not been brought up as a shepherd! How could he be expected to know about such things? The good understanding he had once enjoyed with his father seemed to be evaporating by the day. Hector was so morose, so moody, so angry all the time! In this new life the only things that seemed to count were strong arms, a good aim with an axe, and a back that could carry the load of an ox. It was not Edward's fault that his build was wiry rather than massive, and that his strength was his brain, not his brawn. He kept his eyes lowered to his plate as one by one the other men wiped their mouths and stood up, filling the small room with their bulk. There was still an hour of daylight left, and they had plenty of work to do on their own few acres below their cottage, which they were assiduously clearing and planting for their own benefit.

'Well now, Mr Jamieson, we'll be away to our place,' said Joseph, looking down at his master. Hector was not a short man, but Joseph could give him two inches at least. 'I doubt but you'll be wanting to start tree felling again in the morning.'

'Yes, indeed.' Hector sounded testy. Joseph was never less than scrupulously courteous and consulted Hector on every matter, but it was plain to all who made the decisions. There was no doubting that Joseph was more master of Duddingston than Hector.

The latch of the door clicked shut behind them. Meg and Jessie began to clear away, taking the dishes to the outhouse that served as a kitchen, a canvas shelter held up with poles behind the cottage. Edward ran the last piece of bread round the empty earthenware bowl relishing the tastiness of the stew. Whoever had been the cook tonight, it had not been his mother. Meg or Jessie must have concocted this rich, meaty gravy, seasoned with he knew not what herbs from Isaiah's newly sprouting patch. He shot a glance at his father, then looked away again. A thundercloud had settled on Hector's brow. Surely he was not still in a rage over one faulty fence post? Edward slipped off the upturned packing case that had done duty as a seat, and went to his mother.

'I'm away to my bed, Mama. I can hardly stand,' he said. He pecked Fanny hastily on the cheek, mumbled goodnight in the direction of his father, and let himself out of the cottage to the lean-to shelter at the side, in which a simple wooden bed had been constructed for him.

He did not, however, fall asleep at once as he had expected to do. He was disturbed by the sound of his parents' voices. They were punctuated by a swishing, thumping sound which he could not at first recognise. Then he remembered, and smiled to himself in the semi-darkness. Fanny had vowed this morning that today she would learn to make butter in the new churn she had acquired in Nelson. He had left her this morning, sitting at the table, her chin in her hands, frowning at a manual which she had propped up against a pot of wild clematis flowers he had gathered for her the day before. No wonder supper had been so good! Fanny had been otherwise engaged. Then his smile faded as he caught Hector's words.

'I don't know what's to be done with the boy, Fanny. Oh, he means well, I know, but he is so impractical. Dreamy, vague, irresponsible! Ten to one he was watching some tiresome bird or other when he was meant to be fixing those fence posts. Jem and Malcolm can achieve twice as much useful work in the space of an hour as he can manage in a day. I cannot even trust him with a commission to town. You remember how it was last week – he went to Nelson to acquire flour and tea and nails, and he quite forgot the nails because, said he, he had fallen in with Dr Monro who had much of interest to tell him regarding a forthcoming meeting of his precious Scientific Institution!'

'Yes, but, Hector,' said Fanny in a reasonable voice, slightly short of breath with her exertions, 'Teddy has not been brought up to this life after all. He has no practical experience. He has been educated to be a gentleman. You must give him time, my dear. He so much wants to please you, I am sure of that. After all, we none of us expected to be living in quite such a pioneering way.'

Edward heard rapid footsteps, and knew that his father was marching up and down in agitation.

'Oh, my love, don't, please! Don't remind me of it!' Edward sat up, struck by the pain in Hector's voice. 'When I think how I have brought you down to this – this hovel, how brave you are, how I have failed you! If you knew how I weep over your blistered hands and your pretty gowns all torn! You deserve so much, much more than this!'

The swishing stopped. Fanny spoke.

'Hector, have you gone quite out of your mind? You don't understand the first thing about it. You must understand, you *must* believe me, Hector, I have never been happier in my life! To be so healthy, so hungry, to sleep so well . . . I have never known anything like it! I have lost ten years at least, I feel so young again. That dawdling, suffocating life at Enfield did not suit me at all. Try as I might to behave myself, no one really approved of me. Those stupid English ladies courted us only for our money, except my dear Maria Blakeney of course. No, no, Hector, I have found out, for the first time, what I can do! You have no idea how it sets me up in my own estimation. I am not a poor creature, dependent on others after all! I am even half in love with this absurd little cottage, though the floor is only beaten earth, and I confess I am looking forward to our proper homestead when at last we find the time and the money to build it.'

The swishing started up again and the pacing stopped. A faint whiff of tobacco crept through the ill-fitting boards of the lean-to. Fanny's tactics had worked. Hector had calmed himself and had lit a cheroot.

'As to that, Fanny, we may well make a start next spring, six months or so from now. We've made grand progress so far and I bless the day I made a bargain with the Kirkwoods! We'll have nigh on fifty acres sown by October, and with the rents from the house on the Nile Street section we could break even next year and perhaps even show a profit the year after. I take great courage from the healthy calf Primrose has produced. We must look into the possibility of increasing our little herd. Why, in two or three years' time, with a good income from the farm, I might put Kirkwood in as manager and we could go back to Nelson to start up what I always intended to do, a proper import business. After all, Fanny, with my contacts in London and Calcutta . . . Fanny? Are you listening to me? Fanny!'

Edward, his curiosity aroused, slipped off his bed, opened the door, and poked his tousled head through the gap to see his mother, flushed and laughing, push the curls away from her damp brow and jump up and down in triumph.

'Hector!' she shouted. 'Hector! I've done it! I've made it! It's butter, Hector, our first real pat of butter from our very own cow!'

Edward, seeing the emotion on his father's face, the admiration, pity, shame and love, was reassured. He was not the only cause of his father's altered moods. He sensed for a moment the depth of Hector's misery and took courage from it. Then he quietly withdrew his head and shut his door as Hector pulled Fanny into a rough, choking embrace.

5

'That's right, lads, take the strain now! He-eave!'

Grunts issued from the throats of the five straining men as the Kirkwoods and Jamiesons together levered the massive trunk of a felled totara tree another couple of inches towards the waiting sawpit in the small bush clearing. They straightened their backs momentarily, then bent to their task again.

'Careful, now! Take it gently! It must not overshoot the mark! Malcolm, go beyond the pit, lad, and make sure the spikes are well hammered in.'

Another heave, another groaning strain and the great log was eased over the hole in the ground. It rocked for a moment against the spikes, then settled back into place and was still.

The men surveyed it with satisfaction. It had taken hours of digging to excavate the pit, over six feet deep and twelve feet long, a little longer than the log which now lay on the pair of crossbeams along the length of the pit.

'It's a grand trunk,' said Edward, patting it enthusiastically.

'Ay, we'll get some sturdy planks from it, I've no doubt,' said Joseph. 'Now, Mr Jamieson, if you have the saw these lads can test their skills on it, unless they have forgotten the trick of it.'

'I'll go underneath,' said Edward, slipping into the narrow space between the head of the pit and the end of the log. He and the Kirkwoods had the previous week paid a visit to Mr Baigent's sawpit at the Brook, where the Somerset sawyer had obligingly devoted an afternoon to demonstrating his techniques. They had learned how to site the pit, how to handle the massive logs, how to arrange the trunks on the crossbeams over the trench and secure them firmly in place with an arrangement of chocks and pegs, and they had each taken a turn at handling the long saw from both above and below. Edward, too anxious to prove himself equal to the task, had not found it easy to master the demanding techniques required and it was Jem, taking the more skilled position of top-notcher above the log, who had earned Mr Baigent's praise. To Edward's lot would fall the duller but physically more exhausting task of standing in the pit and thrusting the saw up to his colleague above and he was anxious to demonstrate to his father that he had the will and energy for the job.

He looked up through the crack between the log and the edge of the pit. Jem was taking the top end of the saw. He was holding it firmly with the cross handle, and lowering it into position for the first cut. Without a word, he handed the removable cross handle down to Edward, who fitted it on with a sudden sense of nervousness.

'Ready below?' called out Jem.

'I'm ready!' shouted Edward, bracing his legs to grasp the saw as it bit down through the wood, and to steer it up again, in place for the second cut. He heard a cheer from the men watching above as the saw began to travel with painful slowness through the dense trunk, but then he sensed that they had moved away and he gritted his teeth for the tedious, aching hours of work that lay ahead.

Within a few minutes the world had reduced itself to nothing beyond a numbing rhythm, the steady grating as the saw plunged down through the wood, the swish as he threw it back up again and the thud as the handle struck on the bark. At the end of half an hour the sweat was running into Edward's eyes and his shoulders were aching with fatigue. After fifteen more minutes his hands were blistering and his back cracking with the strain. After five minutes more thirst was beginning to torment him.

'Jem!' he called up, as he thrust the saw upwards. 'Shall we take a break? I'm desperate for water!'

The only answer was a grunt as the saw ate down again towards him with a vicious hiss. Edward felt anger pump suddenly through him in answer to the hatred he sensed from above. All right! If that was how it was to be, if Jem was going to push him, to make a trial of endurance, he'd be damned if he'd be the one to weaken! Let the oaf see who would give in first! He sent the saw shooting upwards in a rush of hostility, and relished in his mind's eye the expression of grim satisfaction that he rightly imagined had settled on Jem's sullen face.

The minutes passed. They worked on together, linked by the thin serrated edge of metal, every thrust of the saw an attack, every scream of its biting teeth an insult. Edward's world was now bounded by pain, by the wrenching of strained muscles, the throb of each gasping breath, the stinging of raw flesh on his hands. The pounding of his heart was so loud it blotted out lesser sounds. He did not hear in time the ominous cracking as the crossbeam that held the log suspended over his head began to creak under the strain imposed on it by the two maddened sawyers.

'Jem! Stop, man!' He heard Joseph's voice, edged with urgency, only dimly through his blood-congested ears, as he sent the saw shooting up again. It faltered for a second, as Jem too heard his father, then shot down again with juddering force, but Edward had let go of the handle, he had seen what Jem had not, the split widening in the crossbeam, the fracturing ends pulling apart from each other as it bowed under the terrible weight of the log. He stood motionless for a precious second as his brain took in the horror, then saw that he must escape, at once, to the far end of the pit where the other beam held good. But his way was barred by the saw which Jem had slammed home, and he dared not thrust it up again for fear of hastening the crash. Gingerly he crept underneath it, bent double and began to scramble to the far end of the pit, but he was not quick enough. He heard the beam tear apart, and then there was no sound but a terrible scream as the end of the tree trunk crashed down on to his right foot, crushing the bones like matchsticks, and in the instant before he lost consciousness he knew that the scream came from his own lungs.

His faint was cruelly short. Seconds later he was awake again, and panic engulfed him.

'Help me! Father! Help me! I'm caught!' he tried to shout, but he could hear only that same high, wild screaming. Then, through his terror, he heard running feet and shouts. The light was blocked out as a row of faces peered down on him. His father spoke.

'Teddy? Where are you hurt? Can you not wriggle free? Answer me, Teddy, for God's sake!' The anguish in Hector's voice pushed Edward out of his panic on to a shaky foothold of courage. He spoke through gritted teeth.

'I'm still alive, Father, if that's what you mean, but my foot's trapped. The trunk's lying on my foot. It's all smashed up, Father, I can feel that, I can't . . . '

'Don't move, son, we're going to get you out of there. We're thinking just now of how we can do it. It's too heavy for just the few of us. You'll have to wait now, Teddy, while we think of a way.'

Edward's courage struggled upwards on to another, firmer notch. His voice was steadier. He could even attempt a joke.

'Don't worry, Father, I'll wait. I've no plans to go anywhere just now.'

Hector withdrew his face from the crack, and Joseph turned his eyes away from the horror written on it. Hector had seen the unnatural angle of Edward's leg and the ankle, looking so vulnerable and frail, disappearing under the huge sawn end of the trunk.

'What are we waiting for?' he burst out furiously. 'We must lift it off him! You, Jem, Malcolm . . . ' his voice tailed away. There was no room for more than one man down there and one man, however strong, could no more lift the end of the trunk than hoist an elephant aloft.

'We must haul it off him!' shouted Hector frantically. 'What are you standing there for, you great blockheads! Get the timber drug, the chains! Aye, that's it, we'll attach the end of the trunk to the chains and heave it out . . . '

'And crush him further,' burst out Jem. Joseph ignored them all. He was, he knew, the only one capable of rescuing Edward. Carefully, with a deliberation that maddened Hector, who was almost dancing with impatience beside the pit, he lay down and peered under the slanting trunk, measuring with his eyes, judging, considering. Only then, when he had made his decision, did he permit himself to look into Edward's anguished face, at the teeth biting the lower lip, at the pinioned body rocking with pain.

'I see how it is, lad,' he said with calm cheerfulness, which brought a slight easing of the tension ribbing the muscles that held Edward's jaw clamped shut. 'We must dig your foot out.'

He got to his feet and began to issue orders.

'Malcolm, haul out the spikes. We'll hammer them in under the end of the log to stop it falling deeper on to the foot when we dig. Jem, run to the house and fetch Isaiah's spade. Tell him to saddle Flighty and be away to Nelson as fast as he can for Dr Monro. Then bring the spade here. Run, lad! Mr Jamieson, do you wish to inform your wife? I doubt she'd desire to be the first to know. Good, Malcolm, pass me yon spike and the mallet. Hurry, man!'

Hector had shaken his head at the mention of Fanny. There would be time enough to distress her later when poor Teddy had been freed. There was no need to bring her to this dreadful scene just now.

'I'll climb in there and be with him,' he said, preparing to slide into the pit from the far end under the diagonally tilting log. 'I can comfort him maybe . . . '

Joseph took his arm urgently.

'No, sir, you canna do that,' he said in a low voice. 'There's no small danger. The beam at the far end has been weakened by the jerk this one gave when it split. If that goes as well we'd never get the pair of you out alive.' He grabbed the spike held out to him by Malcolm and scrambled down into the open end of the pit on the far side of the log from Edward.

'Listen, laddie,' he said. 'I'm driving in a wedge on each side under the log, then we'll dig down under your foot to draw it out. You might feel the blows a bit, but it'll not be long now. We're starting to get you out, and you'll be fine in just a wee while. The mallet now, Malcolm!'

Edward stuffed his fist into his mouth to muffle a moan of pain. The first blow of the hammer on the wedge vibrated through the trunk and sharpened even further the agony that was already well-nigh unbearable. He would not scream again. He would not, could not give Jem the satisfaction of hearing him scream again.

Edward did not realise that Jem was no longer there. He was tearing across the cleared acres towards the homestead as if a demon were at his heels.

'It wasn't my fault! Not my fault!' The words echoed round and round in his mind as his feet pounded along the uneven ground. He would be blamed, he knew that. His father would preach and shake his head and . . . His feelings boiled within him and emerged, as they always did, in anger, so that his face as he raced around the end of the cottage and almost cannoned into Fanny was so thunderous that she recoiled, clutching to her chest the great pan full of chicken feed she had been taking to the hens.

'Good heavens, Jem, how you startled me! Whatever is amiss?'

'Accident!' said Jem tersely, gasping for want of breath. 'Edward in the sawpit. Need a spade. Send my uncle for Dr Monro.'

The colour had ebbed out of Fanny's face, leaving it grey and aged.

'A spade? They are burying him! He's dead!' Her eyes staring, she fell back to lean against the cottage wall for support.

'No, no! His foot's caught under the tree. We must dig it out.' Jem was recovering his breath, and a rough pity came over him as he saw Fanny's distress. 'He'll do fine, my father says, there's no vital part of him hurt, no danger to his life, but we must get him out and that's why I've come for the spade and my father says the doctor'll need to be sent for to see to his foot. My uncle's to go into Nelson on Flighty. They're afraid the bones are crushed.'

The colour had crept back to Fanny's face during the first part of this speech, the longest she had ever heard from Jem, only to flee again in the second. She gazed wordlessly at Jem for a long moment, then clutched at the most comprehensible part of his story.

'Send Isaiah into Nelson? Has your father gone mad? Isaiah can never make Flighty go faster than an amble. I'll go for Dr Monro myself. Jessie! Meg! Come here! Meg, tell your father to saddle Flighty, and Jessie, get brandy and tear up my old petticoat to make bandages. A stretcher! We must contrive to bring him home somehow! You will have to see to that. I must go at once for the doctor. Crushed! The bones crushed! Child, what are you staring at me like that for?'

Jessie tried to hide the trembling of her hands beneath her apron.

'Is it Edward? Oh, what has happened? Is he . . . is he . . . ?'

'His foot's hurt, crushed, Jem says.' The need for urgent practical action took precedence over the anxiety that was gnawing at Fanny. There would be time for all that later when she had done everything she could to help Teddy. She put down the chicken feed, and shooed her white-faced maidservants away. 'What are you standing there for? Hurry! Do as I say!'

The hour that followed the accident was the longest in Hector's life. He waited in agony for Jem to return, silently reproaching him for dawdling until he saw the lad racing back into the clearing, Isaiah's spade in his hand.

'Has your father gone for the doctor?' he broke out impatiently.

'No, the missus would go herself.'

'What? Fanny has ridden to Nelson on Flighty? But he's too strong for her! She's not used to him! He'll throw her when he kicks up at the flat!'

'She said he'll only amble for my uncle,' Jem mumbled, morbidly sensitive to the suggestion of further blame being laid at his door.

A moan from the pit made both men turn. A final blow from Joseph's mallet had driven the second wedge home, causing the great log to rock, and grind itself further into Edward's foot.

'The spade, you have it?' Joseph reached up his sinewy arms and bent once more to work. 'Bear up, laddie, we're doing fine now. We'll have you out in no time.' His voice expressed a confidence he was far from feeling. It was as ticklish a job as any he had engaged upon before. It was worse even than that time in France, when he and his fellows in the chain-gang of English prisoners had been digging in the great sewers of Paris and his friend Christmas Halliday had been buried under a sudden mass of earth and stones from a fall in the tunnel roof. He withstood the temptation to stop his work and climb out of the pit to check on the other crossbeam at the far end. If, as he suspected, that one was about to break too, then . . . He jerked his mind away from the thought of it. If that happened, it would be almost impossible to get the lad out alive.

The spade had now excavated a hole under the giant trunk, and an injudicious thrust had jarred it against the foot, which Joseph could now see. He felt his stomach turn at the shriek of agony from Edward, muffled as the boy clamped his hand over his mouth. Joseph had seen courage before, many times, and he saluted it now. There were a hundred scenes he had witnessed in his brutal boyhood at sea, battles, wounds, headless torsos, frightful gushings of blood and splintered ends of bone, that still haunted him from time to time in his dreams. He had hoped never to witness the maiming of a young man again. It seemed now, with the tenderness of middle age, so much more dreadful, so senseless, so needlessly tragic, than it had done in his youth.

He shut his mind against further thoughts and steeled himself to probe round the bloody boot, to free it from the earth and stones in which it was embedded. Then he looked up. His ears had caught another sound. The second beam was weakening. At any moment it would crash down and drop the whole weight of the trunk on to Edward's body. He dropped his spade and began to clamber frantically out of the pit.

'My God!' Hector had now seen the second crossbeam settling in the centre. 'The other beam! It's going! It's . . . '

'Is his foot free yet, Father?' Jem spoke urgently.

Joseph was pulling now on Malcolm's proffered arm as he struggled out of the pit.

'Aye, it is. Wait now, till I'm up out of here. I'll go in the other end and drag him clear.'

He had not finished speaking when Jem moved. Before anyone had a chance to see what he was doing, he had darted to the end of the pit where the log was still held on the slowly sagging crossbeam, had slipped underneath it and was in the trench with Edward.

'Come on, you,' he said savagely. 'You've to get the hell out of here.' He slid his hands under Edward's armpits and began to heave. 'Come on, damn you! Come on!'

At the first jerk on his shoulders, which bounced the smashed foot out of the ground, Edward fainted. Jem had always regarded him as a flimsy kind of fellow, but he found now that Edward was surprisingly heavy. The shoulders he was hauling over the uneven ground of the pit floor were muscular and hard. Unconscious, Edward was a dead weight.

The crossbeam creaked again. Fresh beads of sweat started out of Jem's forehead. Then, with a last tremendous heave, he felt the end of the pit against his back. Hands were plucking at him from above.

'Get out, man, quick, for God's sake! It's going!' Malcolm was almost yelling at him.

Jem ignored his brother, ducked his head, hoisted Edward in his arms and thrust his body upwards where the three waiting men were straining to receive it. But the open space at the end of the log was so confined that he could not easily manoeuvre in it. As Edward's inert body was hauled upwards, his knee caught the end of the log a glancing blow. It was the *coup de grâce*. As Edward was dragged clear, the beam gave way with a juddering sigh. Jem flung himself against the end wall of the pit. He was in the nick of time. The trunk, crashing down, missed his head but scraped down his back, ripping his shirt and tearing off a sheet of skin. He hardly noticed the pain. He jumped on to the fallen log, clambered shakily out of the pit, and then fell on his knees and vomited.

Chapter Thirteen *Nelson, June 1843*

1

'What is it, son? Is your leg paining you?'

Fanny's seat in the bullock cart faced backwards and gave her a good view of Edward who was riding behind on Flighty. The horse had swerved to avoid a quail, which rose cackling out of a clump of fern, and Edward's face had paled with the jolting. Fanny was looking unusually charming in a flowered silk dress with billowing sleeves which peeped out from under a cashmere shawl, but Edward turned his head and pretended not to hear her. It was the kind of question he had learned to dread. Of course his foot hurt, damnably. Or rather, not his foot, which Dr Monro had severed at the ankle two months previously, but the place where his foot had been. That, he felt bitterly, was the cruellest part of it. It was bad enough coping with the pain of the stump and the twinges in his knee, still mending after its dislocation, but worst of all was the aching, tearing sensation he still felt in his foot, a foot that was no longer there. Dr Monro had assured him it was commonplace; that amputated limbs were not so easily got rid of; that in time the pains would lessen and he would walk again without a crutch – do everything, or nearly everything, that he had been able to do before.

'Why,' he had said, with well-meaning jocularity, 'I have seen men with peg-legs run up the rigging in a storm,' and had wondered why his patient had shuddered so violently.

Edward reined in his horse and turned to let the walking men catch up with him. The three Kirkwoods and Isaiah, though almost always silent, were better company just now than his solicitous parents, while Meg and Jessie, who were riding with them in the cart and were dressed up so that he hardly recognised them, had no time for anyone but each other that day. They did nothing but whisper and giggle together. Brides, he conceded, were entitled to a certain amount of silliness on their wedding day, but he for one would be glad when Meg and Malcolm had tied the knot, when the feast back at home, that had taken so many days of preparation, had all been consumed, and they could get back to normal. Not that there was any normality for him now, he thought bitterly, crippled as he was.

The little cavalcade turned the corner and the town of Nelson lay before them. It was only eight months since Edward had first seen it but he could hardly believe the changes such a short time had wrought. Brick and wooden houses lined many of the principal streets in place of the old rush whares, which were fast disappearing. Fourteen hostelries had now opened their doors, while a coffee house in Trafalgar Square catered for abstainers.

The scene was beautiful enough to make most travellers gasp. All around lay gentle hills, falling almost to the town, beyond which to the north sparkling sunlight played on the brilliant blue bay. A fair number of sails dotted its surface, a lumbering whaler in from the Sound, a couple of small schooners and cutters that now plied regularly across the Strait, and a pair of Maori canoes, slicing through the water, laden with provisions for their 'pa', as they called their stockaded village. With a pang, Edward made out in the distance a small Deal boat that was pulling away from a heavily laden brig. The pilot was disembarking. He heard the farewell boom of its cannon, watched it veer away, catch wind and start beating its way northward up Tasman Bay to the Strait, and he knew it was bound for home.

A sudden wave of longing swept over him, for the old house in Edinburgh, the rational conversation of his fellow students, the comforts of an old-established city, the pleasures of a well-stocked table and a decently made suit of clothes, but above all, the bliss of running and walking, of racing upstairs two at a time and jumping over obstacles – joys he had never appreciated before, but which, now that they were lost to him for ever, he knew to be infinitely precious. There was nothing in this country for him, he thought. It had given him nothing as yet. It had only taken from him. And now, on this supposedly happy day, when the Duddingston household was given over to celebration, he would be the outsider, unable even to walk unaided into the Ebenezer Chapel, whose new brick edifice they were now approaching, unable to join the hilarious throng around the bridal couple, or stand with the other men at the breakfast laid out at home, or join in the reels and strathspeys that would crown the day's celebrations. Worst of all, he would have to put up with the veiled glances of pity from everyone he met.

The gig pulled up in front of the chapel. A tall figure came out through the door and strode forward to greet the occupants, but Joseph Kirkwood, hurrying round to greet him before Hector had laid down the reins, was the first to take his hand.

'Mr Watson, sir, we are greatly obliged to you! A pleasure it is, sir, for this unguided flock to welcome one of your calling here among us, and on such a happy occasion too!'

The minister beamed and bent his head in acknowledgement. He was thoroughly enjoying his peripatetic life in this splendid new country. Wherever he went, from one settlement to another, he was sure of a rapturous greeting from its inevitable community of Scots people, who, starved of the regular ministrations of the Presbyterian Church, saved up their weddings, baptisms and above all their hospitality, and gratefully lavished all upon him whenever he appeared.

Hector handed Meg down from the gig. She stood shyly, on show for the first time in her borrowed plumage. Now, at eighteen years old, she was as pretty as she would ever be. Years of poor nourishment had left her shorter, perhaps, than nature had intended, but the bloom of health that New Zealand had shed over her covered any deficiency. Her dark straight hair was swept away from her face and disappeared under a charming ivory-coloured bonnet, drawn from one of Fanny's trunks and refurbished by her skilful fingers. Meg peeped out from under it now, not daring to look at her bridegroom, questioning Fanny with her eyes.

She had conceived a boundless admiration and fondness for her mistress. Never before had she met a person so generous, so happy, so prone to laughter. She had been struck dumb when Fanny had opened her chests, drawn out bonnets, scarves, pieces of lace and fleecy shawls in order to deck the bride. There had even been a frivolously trimmed parasol – 'For after all,' Fanny had laughed, 'June is winter time here, and it will serve to keep a shower off your bonnet if it should happen to rain on the day.'

The idea of a wedding at Duddingston had acted on Fanny like a heady wine, an antidote to all the anguish of the weeks since the accident. The memory of the amputation performed on the table in the cottage, the sweating face of Dr Monro, the drunken mumblings of Teddy, half insensible on brandy, and the weeks of pain that followed it, would take, she was sure, many years to fade. She had thrown herself with zest into the wedding plans, brought forward by the visit of the minister, and now, as she critically examined her two maids, who gazed back at her anxious for approval, she felt a rush of maternal love for them such as Justina, with her finicky, superior ways, had never aroused in her. Then she heard Edward's voice, harsh, through clenched teeth, 'I have my crutch, thank you, I have no need of an arm to lean on,' and her heart sank again.

There was a fair crowd inside the chapel, a few shipboard friends, some of the lads from the fo'c'sle, there to see poor Kirkwood meet his fate, kind Mrs Wilson, who had been the Dunbars' constant companion on the *New Zealand*, and a couple of near neighbours from the Maitai sections. The bridegroom, looking uncomfortable in a highpointed collar and a new coat (a wedding gift from Hector), walked timidly to the front accompanied by his brother, whose dark, forbidding good looks caused a stir in at least two maiden breasts. All eyes, however, were soon covertly observing poor young Mr Jamieson, the fame of whose accident had spread far and wide. He looked different, whispered those who had been privileged to know him before. It was not surprising, seeing as how the poor young man had been crippled, after all, but what a shame that he had turned so proud, so cold-looking, when by all accounts he had been such a pleasant, friendly young man!

A bustle at the porch announced the entrance of the bride, leaning on her father's arm. Isaiah, for once in his life, was satisfied. He had contrived very well, he thought. He had established one daughter creditably with a steady husband, and there was another brother for Jessie, should she have the good sense to take him. As for himself, the air of the place certainly seemed to suit him. He felt better than he had for many years. The climate was pleasant, one could not deny it, and he had no serious complaint to make about the food. Isobel, he was sure, would have managed better than Mrs Jamieson. He could never understand why she had laughed when the calf got loose and trampled his young carrots, or when a family of rats nibbled up his store of peas. Isobel would have taken a properly serious view of such matters, and made sure his own feelings and comfort were consulted. She would not have allowed the milk to boil over or the joints of meat to burn. She would have made sure that the oven was properly alight before setting in her bread, and she would never have gone off to pick flowers for the table before seeing to the hens.

On the other hand, he had to admit that there was always plenty of food, however badly cooked, on Fanny's table. He did feel, sometimes, that his efforts in the vegetable garden were insufficiently appreciated. Mr Jamieson never listened to his advice as he did to Joseph's. But, on the whole, he felt he had done well in fending for his family in the New World. He was glad he had thought of this scheme of emigration. He only wished Isobel was here to give praise where it was due.

'Dearly beloved brethren . . .' The minister's sonorous voice rang round the chapel. The wedding began.

Edward's mind wandered. His eyes followed a fly as it dived in and out of a solid-looking shaft of light beaming in from one of the newly glazed windows. It flitted aimlessly for a while, then collided with a spray of violets that Fanny had deftly arranged round the poke of Jessie's bonnet. There was something in those tensed shoulders, half turned away from him, that held Edward's gaze. What a strange child she was! Only she was hardly a child any longer. She had turned thirteen and sometimes seemed almost a grown woman. He watched her smooth her sleeve with one gloved hand. She was as fine as fivepence today. Fanny had enjoyed dressing her up as much as her sister. Her new clothes had changed her.

She never cared much for her appearance at home, as far as Edward could perceive. Her dress was always plain and carelessly put on. Her fine silky hair, mouse brown but shot through with sudden gleams of reddy gold, was forever blowing untidily about her face. She never walked but ran everywhere, darting eagerly, a kind of suppressed excitement underlying all her movements.

Twang! Joseph Kirkwood struck his knee with a tuning fork, found the note, hummed it loudly, and led off the singing in his rich bass voice. The cadences of the psalm rose and fell. Edward looked down at his psalter, read a few lines ahead and allowed his gaze to wander back to Jessie. Her head was turned towards him now. He could see the little face inside that ridiculous poke. Why had he never noticed before how pretty she was? No, pretty was not the right word. She was not pretty, she was – intense. That was it. Intense. Her face was small and pale, her chin delicately pointed, her nose a little snubbed, but her eyes, slightly slanting, were pools of deep brown, reflecting in their depths every change of mood, every surge of laughter, every shadow of uncertainty or grief. Just now they were preoccupied. He willed her to turn further and look at him, but instead she bent her head once more to her book. He could not help noticing as she did so the natural grace of the head perfectly poised on its frail neck.

The fly fell out of the violet and passed on towards the bridegroom, then zigzagged away from him and buzzed off through the chapel's open door, carrying Edward's thoughts with it.

Fanny's face might now be sunburnt, her hands reddened with work and her feet more accustomed to clogs than to slippers, but she had not lost her zest for a party. A lucky chance to purchase twenty ells of calico going cheap at Mr Sclander's store on her last visit to Nelson, had given her the idea of fixing up a bower beside the cottage which would shelter the wedding guests should the weather prove inclement. She had set Malcolm and his father to work and they had managed very creditably, even taking pride in their structure once it was formed. Tree ferns, plucked entire from the ground, formed the supporting poles, their waving crowns making a pretty mass over a line of packing cases which, fronted with swags of greenery and decorated with tasteful arrangements of leaves, did duty as tables. These were laden with jellies and pies, the work of Meg's hands. Trained by her mother in an interlude of relative prosperity before the last famine had struck Paisley, Meg had developed a natural turn for cooking, and she had insisted on doing the work herself, not wanting her mistress to expose her culinary shortcomings to the guests.

Fanny had been much exercised over the question of music, wanting perhaps a reel or two to liven up the affair, and had discussed with Hector the possibility of conveying to Duddingston her dear piano, still standing unopened in the Nelson town house. She had broached the matter tentatively with Joseph Kirkwood, not sure if dancing would come within the acceptable limits of his stern notions of propriety. To her surprise, he was pleased with the idea.

'There's nae prohibition from dancing in the Bible, Mistress Jamieson,' he said, and she was sure his eyes twinkled at her. 'Did not David dance before the Lord?'

Hector, however, coming in upon them, had declared his opposition to bringing up the piano. The cost would be too great and, besides, there was no room for it in the cottage. Fanny, hearing a testy note in his voice, had felt it wise to change the subject. The matter had been unexpectedly resolved by Malcolm. Looking at his boots, he had mumbled a name to his father, and Joseph's face had brightened at it.

'Archie Wilson! Aye, the very man. He's a handy one with the fiddle and will suit our purpose fine. And besides, he's a God-fearing young man and will forbear the singing of worldly songs. Marriage is aye a difficult enough business without inviting the devil to the marriage feast!' And as he shook his head and heaved a sigh, Fanny, catching Hector's eye, had stifled a giggle.

Now, as the returning caravan of horses and pedestrians breasted the rise above the Maitai and came within sight of the cottage in the clearing, a buzz of appreciation was heard. The homestead was indeed a pretty sight. The slanting winter sun warmed the deep greens of the surrounding bush and the brighter green of the newly sown grass and picked out the whitewashed walls of the little house, from whose chimney a spiral of woodsmoke welcomed the party.

Mr Townshend, invited on impulse by Hector as he had passed them in the town, took hold of his host's elbow.

'My, but you've done well, Jamieson, and in such a short time too! So many acres of bush already cleared, and the soil is good, I can see that from how excellently your grass grows. You were lucky in your selection, my dear sir, lucky indeed. Fernland now is proving a disappointment to the farmer. The roots, you know, are so hard to remove, and the land is exhausted before planting even begins. But this is a fine place! A good rich bush soil. And a snug cottage! I doubt you'll be planning a fine wooden house here before many months are passed. Another year or two of hardship and struggle and your work will be repaid. Cows, I see. Aye, very good. And your vegetables do you credit. Timber plentiful, of course. You have your own sawpit? Oh, I beg your pardon, I am so clumsy, I should not have mentioned – a tragic accident, sir. Tragic. But the young man in full health, and Monro tells me an artificial foot can be strapped on when the healing is complete so the poor fellow will walk comfortably at least.'

Mrs Wilson had attached herself to the two Dunbar girls, and though the air was not warm the exertion of the walk had made her perspire, and she fanned herself energetically as she approached the bower.

'Oh, Lord, I never did see anything half so pretty! And Meg so clever to make all these patties! It does me good to see it and so it would your dear mother, I'm sure. It's easy to see you've done well for yourselves, girls, so bonny and grown so tall as you are, and your poor father too. There's them as should take your example, sitting about in Nelson waiting for the Company to feed them, moaning and groaning about how there ain't no work to be found. Work! There's work been done out here, as I can tell, and so I shall say to everyone,' and Mrs Wilson sank gratefully on to a bench set down in the bower by the table, and watched hungrily while Jessie filled her a plateful of food and poured her a glass of fresh lemonade.

Unassisted by alcohol, the party was, nonetheless, merry. The guests' gratifying interest in the infant farming operation took a considerable time to satisfy. Everyone admired the cattle, exclaimed over the dairy arrangements and made favourable comparisons with other nascent establishments until Hector began to feel more cheerful than he had done for many months. He felt the justice of their praise. He *had* worked hard. They all had. He had taken risks and made sacrifices. His mind bumped painfully against the greatest of them and he looked about for Edward. Where was the boy? He heard a burst of laughter from the circle of young men, in the centre of which Mr Jack Sturgis was giving his famous imitation of a barking dog. No doubt, he thought uneasily, Teddy was somewhere among them.

Jessie had noticed Edward's disappearance. Her quick eyes had seen him flush up at some question from one of their Maitai neighbours, and then, filled with pain for him, she had watched him bend to pick up his crutch, slip through the sheets of calico that formed the backdrop of the bower and hobble away into the bush, in which even the birds, on this winter afternoon, seemed unusually hushed. She waited for a quarter of an hour, pouring out lemonade and filling plates with wedges of pie and slices of Fanny's most successful batch of cheese, then she slipped through the curtain and ran across the path that wound its way in through the great wall of trees.

The sun was low now and dusk would soon be gathering everything into its shadows. Jessie shivered and pulled her shawl closer around her shoulders. Frost was in the air. She disentangled her billowing skirt from a vine, and wished for her own workaday clothes. Pretty gowns were fine, she thought, but not when things needed to be done. She plunged on without hesitation. She knew where to look for Edward. He had shown her once, before the accident, his favourite spot in the bush. It was a rocky hollow in which a spring welled up among beds of the softest mosses and delicate ferns fringed the stream that ran from it. He had dragged a fallen branch to the edge of the water, had shown Jessie the sketches of ferns he had made there, and told her the names of the wild birds which had peered at them through the fronds.

She burst into the hollow suddenly, coming upon it earlier than she had intended, and Edward turned on her savagely.

'What do you want? Get out of here! Can't you leave me alone?'

Jessie drew out of a fold in her shawl an apple and a piece of cake loosely wrapped in a napkin. She surveyed it sadly.

'It's all crumbs now,' she said. 'I picked a nice piece out for you. You'd have missed it, you see, as they were eating it so fast.'

Edward ignored her outstretched hand.

'Didn't you hear me? I want to be alone! It's no use to persuade me to go back there. I won't do it!'

'Oh, no,' said Jessie mildly. 'I didn't think you would. It's not the kind of party you'd like, I suppose. Not very grand and clever folk, I mean.'

Edward frowned at her.

'Grand? As if I cared for that!' Absentmindedly he took a morsel of cake from her hand and put it in his mouth. Jessie said nothing. 'It's not grandness I'm bothered about, you silly wee thing.'

'Oh,' said Jessie, and waited.

'It's just that . . . that . . .'

A weka, finding its customary drinking place overcrowded, called harshly nearby.

'You'd never understand!' burst out Edward.

Still Jessie said nothing.

'It's the way they look at me, thinking, wondering, being sorry. But it's worse than that. It's feeling useless! Good for nothing! Helpless! All the talk is of clearing bush and sowing and fencing and building. How can I do any of that now? How can I help my father when I can't even walk? It was different at home, in Scotland. You could live in different ways, work with your mind maybe. But here a cripple's useless! What can I do, little Jessie, tell me that? What am I going to do?'

Jessie frowned with concentration. In spite of himself, Edward was amused. It was as if the absurd child actually believed she could find a way to help him.

'Your carving is very good,' she said tentatively. He was disappointed. Somehow, he had not known why, he had hoped for something from her, but his carving! The idea was ridiculous. He had entertained himself during his convalescence whittling at odd pieces of wood, making shelf ends for Fanny, a pipe rack for Hector, even a looking-glass frame crowned with a lopsided lovers' knot for the happy couple. He dismissed them with a shrug.

'Oh, that! No, no, I can't make my way in the world with a knife, Jessie. Did you ever go to Edinburgh?'

The suddenness of the question startled her. She shook her head.

'Then you'll not have seen old Jimmy Anderson in Carruthers Close. Lost his foot at Trafalgar and all he can do is whittle away at bits of wood. He stumps up and down the High Street and says, "Twa bawbees, mister, for a birdie," and people look at his birdies and say, "That's no bird, Jimmy, it hasna any wings," and he touches his forehead all simple like, and says, "It's three bawbees if you wish for ane with the wings." No, Jessie, I'll not be a carver for a living.'

Jessie had not paid attention to the end of this sardonic speech. She was thinking hard again, twisting her shawl in her hands.

'There's your drawings of birds and beasties,' she said. 'Could you not sell those to people?'

Edward smiled at her innocence.

'I'm no great shakes as an artist. My sketches have interest only to the scientist. I could not give them away.'

'Well, then,' she persevered, 'why can you not make them into a book? Folks are always wanting books, and I haven't seen any with tree ferns and the like in them.'

This time Edward did not smile.

'Jessie, you little wretch! You've guessed my secret. There is nothing I would like better, one day, than to publish something on the flora and fauna of the bush. But there is my livelihood to earn! I'll not sit and eat my bread at home while the others work, and not make a penny towards my keep! It's too much to bear!'

Jessie was still wrestling with the problem.

'It's dominies and ministers as write books at home,' she said doggedly. 'You've no mind to be a minister—'

'I should say not,' Edward hastily interrupted.

'But they'll be needing dominies in Nelson when the school opens and that will be soon, I'm sure, for I heard my uncle say to your father . . .'

'Jessie!' Edward stood motionless, as the idea caught hold. A teacher of science! Why, oh, why, had he not thought of it before? It was of all things what he would like best, crippled or no. He thought of the best of his old preceptors at the High School in Edinburgh, of their wry humour, their enthusiasm, their learning. He could, he could indeed, think of being a schoolmaster!

Forgetting his stump for a moment, he took a step towards Jessie, and stumbled. He put out his arms to steady himself and found that he was holding her. The sensation of her silky hair on his chin, the smell of her skin, the softness of her body pierced him with its sweetness. Then he released her, and hiding his embarrassment bent to retrieve his crutch.

'We'd best be getting back to the party,' he said gruffly, but she, her heart bounding uncomfortably in her chest, had flitted ahead of him away down the path. He hobbled after her reluctantly. He was afraid that his absence had been remarked, and he felt powerless to divert enquiries. He need not have worried. When he emerged unnoticed from the shelter of the trees he found the entire party gathered around a man who was hitching his foam-flecked mare to a fence post. His words barely made sense.

'Yes, man, it's as I'm telling you. Captain Wakefield and at least a dozen others. All massacred, tomahawked, over at the Wairau. That Maori rascal Rangihaeata has his blood up. He's after every pakeha he can find. The Maori are everywhere in a state of readiness. No one is safe, I tell you. My instructions are to inform all in the outlying sections to come into the town for safety. We're fortifying the hill with a stockade, and bringing in as many ships' cannon as we can muster. Every man is needed. The talk in the pas is of nothing but war.'

2 *July 1843*

'Phew, man, this is heavy work!'

The speaker straightened his back with a sigh and leant on his spade. He was a young man, no more than six or seven and twenty, but beside Jem Kirkwood, who was stolidly plunging his spade into the bottom of the ditch and heaving its contents on to the rampart six feet above, he was puny.

'Are you a man, or an engine, or what?' he went on, in aggrieved tones. 'If you're trying to dig your way home to Scotland you'll never make it. There's easier ways to get there. Lord, but I could drink the Severn dry!'

Jem said nothing. Mr Lowson, looking up, caught sight of the stern figure of Mr Tuckett the surveyor, who was parading along the ramparts surrounding Church Hill, supervising the construction of the fortifications which a panic-stricken colony was hastily erecting. He picked up his spade again and made a pretence of working.

Jem smiled sourly. He had no respect for the army of labourers who kicked their heels at the New Zealand Company's expense, performing the tasks set them as slowly as they could for as much pay as they could wheedle out of their masters. Not even fear was enough to put blood in their veins. They had come scurrying in from their desultory road-building operation fast enough when news of the killing of Captain Wakefield and a dozen of his party in the Wairau had reached the infant town, but when no club-waving warriors had appeared in Nelson itself they had lost interest in the hard work of making the town defensible and had spent the better part of their days clustered round the taverns, drinking away their unearned wages and describing with pot-valiant eloquence the punishment they would inflict on any savages daring enough to cross their path.

Jem bent for another spadeful of earth and sent it spinning aloft. Tam, dozing as near his master as he could get, was struck on the nose by a flying pebble, yelped and skulked to a safer distance where he flopped down again, ignoring a nuzzle from Bess. Jem frowned as they disappeared from view. Though he had got a good price for all three pups from Bess's litter, his dogs were a constant worry to him. It was well over a year now since they had worked a flock of sheep and he was no nearer his own goal of running them with a flock of his own. This stupid business with the Maori was yet another setback. Why should a few grimacing cannibals be allowed to stand in the way of civilised people? They deserved to be clubbed down themselves in revenge, the whole treacherous bunch of them. Then perhaps the colony could settle its land problems and he could begin to see his way to fulfilling his ambition.

The imposing figure of Mr Tuckett receded. Mr Lowson leant on his spade once more and echoed Jem's thoughts.

'A good licking, that's what they deserve. Hang and quarter the lot of them, that's what I say. They've got the right idea over there in New South Wales. You know old Hoppy Bob, that was took ill over that bad ale last evening? Well, he tells me as how the squatters go after the blacks with guns and . . .'

'What's this foolishness?'

Mr Lowson jumped and looked round. Joseph Kirkwood stood behind him, and glowered down upon him. The young man's slack muscles looked pathetic beside Joseph's work-hardened physique but he straightened himself to look Joseph in the face.

'Foolishness it is not, Mr Kirkwood,' he said, intending to show confidence but sounding cocky instead. 'The natives should be punished, taught a lesson. Everyone knows that.'

'Oh, aye,' said Joseph sarcastically, taking the spade from Mr Lowson's limp hands and plying it with skill. 'You've all a great desire to kill the

Maoris, never mind that they were defending themselves from unlawful arrest, and protecting their land from those who would take it unfairly.'

'Pa!' For once, Jem found the courage to disagree with Joseph. 'The land was bought, you know that fine, and the men they killed were prisoners, and their bodies all cut up! Murdering savages – nothing better than . . .'

'God is not mocked,' said Joseph gravely, shaking his massive head. 'Whatsoever a man soweth, that shall he also reap. The colony has sown the wind, and it may yet reap a whirlwind. The Maoris were paid naught but a few guns and jackets and spades and the like for the Wairau, and there is doubt that the land was rightfully sold. Oh aye, I see what you're about to say. "Thou shalt not kill," and true enough it is, they were in the wrong to do it, but it was a bunch of warriors who did the business and not the people we have dealings with. You know yourself we've received nothing but goodness from them on the Jamieson section, and wild talk of savages and thrashings and the like directed towards men who have already received the Gospel of Christ I will not hear.'

'You've been talking with that cowardly Tuckett,' muttered Jem, but his father was no longer listening. He had seen Edward in the distance, hobbling away from a group of sawyers working on staves for a defensive palisade. The boy's leg was not ready yet for a peg. He depended still on a crutch and Joseph's face softened as he sensed the pain the lad was trying to conceal, and saw the pride with which he shook off a solicitous enquiry. Unaware of Jem's eyes on him, he had no inkling of the torment of jealousy raging in that young man's head, of the bitter question that ran round in his mind – why can he not look so at me, his own son?

Edward, trying to balance himself sufficiently to work a saw, had been shaken with horror as memory struck him. Just so had his arms been pumping seconds before the beam cracked. Just so had the blade sounded, grinding through the wood. He felt a stab of pain from his lost foot and muttered, 'I'll be away now,' to the nearest man, who had been watching him with loathsome compassion. Then he picked up his crutch and made off down the hill towards his father's Nile Street house. He stood for a moment at the rough gate that opened on to the rudimentary garden. A fence had been erected around it to keep passing cattle away from the vegetable patch, and the house had already lost its early rawness and acquired a settled look. The kauri pine walls had been painted white and curtains hung in the windows. The tenants had obligingly agreed, for a reduction in the rental, to house the landlord and his family for the duration of the scare but quarters were cramped, and Edward, disliking company at present, knew there was no escape from it here.

His foot hurt damnably and his temper hurt, too. He would not, could not stay another hour in this place! He was of no use here. In the state of alarm in which the colony had been thrown only muscle power mattered. He could not bear to be lumped with the women and children, nor could he ply a saw with the men.

A plan had been forming in his head since early morning. Fanny, fretful at being torn from Duddingston, from her churn, her cows and her new bread oven, whose intricacies she was beginning to master, had burst out at the breakfast table, 'Really, Hector, I do not believe in all these panics and rumoured attacks! I am sure it is a great deal of nonsense and we will come to no harm at home. That odious Rangihaeata and his villains have all gone off to the North Island and we have nothing to fear, I know, from the Maori in the Maitai. We have always been on the friendliest of terms. Think how they advised us when we were building the house! You would scarcely have found such excellent vines for the wattles had not Tame showed you how to use the supplejack, and Tangirau had not been so obliging in keeping us stocked with fresh pork. I hardly know how I could have kept a full table without him. Can you truthfully see either of them or any of their kinsmen cutting our throats? And now the cows have not been milked for days, and Primrose no doubt will have found a new way to escape through the fencing as she always does, and the pigs will be trampling up Isaiah's spinach. Oh, Hector, I want to go home!'

Edward had silently echoed her wish and had been considering all morning how he might fulfil it. There was no chance that Hector would give his consent to a return to Duddingston and no chance either that Fanny would leave Nelson without it. But why could not he slip away alone and see to the cows, and protect the place against marauders? No one then could accuse him of uselessness. The danger, he was sure, was negligible and in any case there was Hector's gun, still in its place in the corner by the fire. Hector had been chiding himself only this morning for leaving it there, in the haste of departure, where it could so easily be lifted by a hostile Maori. As for the talk of forthcoming rape, murder and arson that was circulating in the taverns, he was sure it was untrue and if it were, what did it matter? For himself he did not care. He would rather go out in a blaze, protecting his father's property, outnumbered by a horde of enemies, than sit here to be fussed over in Nelson, an object of pity and contempt. It only remained to provide himself with a horse and even here there was no difficulty. Mr Latymer Montmorency, a gentleman of capital but little determination, had found his nerves unable to sustain the strain of the present unease and had decided to remove to Auckland. Kind Mr Townshend had tipped Edward the wink that Montmorency's grey mare, mild-mannered and easy for a lame man to handle, was for sale at a knock-down price. The opportunity was too good to miss, for horses were still a rarity in the settlement, and Edward had only to present Mr Montmorency with the few sovereigns he required, which as it happened were already jingling in his pocket, and Ladybird, complete with saddle and bridle, would be his.

It was not until Edward had ridden the couple of miles on his new acquisition along the curve of the river as it wound between the wooded hills of the Maitai valley, and had come within sight of the track that led up to the Duddingston section that the first twinge of uneasiness affected him. It had been so good to be free of other people and the track had looked so peaceful on this perfectly ordinary afternoon. But now, as he saw the smokeless chimney and heard a piece of the calico tenting which had formed part of the marriage bower flapping in the breeze, he felt a chill. The place looked so bare, so cheerless. He had been looking forward to some solitude, a time to be alone, to think, to escape from the solicitude of others, but now he felt suddenly desolate. It was not, he told himself, that he was frightened. He felt only how pleasant a friendly welcome would have been at this home-coming.

He hitched Ladybird to a fence post and ran his eyes over the cows. They were all there, thank goodness, and strangely enough they looked quite contented. Their udders were full, certainly, but hardly straining. Only Cowslip looked in need of immediate attention. He would attempt to milk her directly, as soon as he had seen that all was well inside the house. It would not be easy. The cow was temperamental enough at the best of times, and even Jem had been known to swear at her, but no one would be there to see him, to comment, or smile, or look away, or offer to do it for him. He would take his time, use cunning, plan the whole thing carefully, and prove to himself that he was not entirely useless.

He lifted the latch on the cottage door and went inside. A cursory glance showed him that all was in order. No one seemed to have been there since the family had rushed away from the place on the night of the wedding, or, if they had, they had put everything back in its place. And yet, on second thoughts, he was not sure, he could not say why, he felt uneasy. Was everything the same? Had not the settle by the fire been moved to an unusual angle? And surely the door of the clothes press had not been left to swing open in that untidy way?

There was a creak above his head and Edward stiffened. Was that the wind, blowing through the thatch at a loose board, or could someone be hiding up there? He started towards the ladder which ran up into the roof space, in which Meg and Jessie normally slept, then thought better of it and turned to the fireplace to pick up Hector's gun. It was not there.

Edward felt the hair prickle on his scalp. He had not expected this. A troop of warriors, charging at the house with war-cries, he would have taken in his stride. A hidden, armed stranger inside the house was another matter. A board creaked again. The silence was suddenly unbearable. Rashly, without a thought for the consequence, Edward called out, in as commanding tones as he could muster, 'Come on out, you rascal! I know you're armed and so am I. Come down quietly and I'll spare my shot.'

There was no doubt of it now. He heard a scrape on the boards as if a box or chest were being pushed aside, then footsteps cautiously approached the hole in the ceiling. To his consternation he saw not a pair of feet, nor a face, but the barrel of his father's gun, pointing at him. Edward looked wildly round the dim little room and caught up a pewter candlestick that stood near his hand on the table. He rapped it twice, hoping that it would sound, to frightened ears, like the priming of a pistol. He was not prepared for the reaction. A staggering explosion crashed from the end of the barrel and the shock sent him reeling backwards. For a moment he thought he had been hit, then he realised that the bullet had embedded itself in the table top, a mere foot from where he had been standing. He began to laugh shakily.

'You damned fool, you've spent your ammunition and now I have you at my mercy. Come down and surrender before I come up and shoot you.'

Even to his own ears the words sounded hollow but they had the desired effect. Two bare feet appeared through the hole, followed by legs clad in a pair of Hector's corduroy trousers. To his relief, Edward saw that the feet, though grimed with dirt, were those of a white man. He was not dealing single-handed with a vengeful Maori horde, skilled in battle, but with a common thief, a runaway sailor no doubt, whose like were forever skulking about the outlying sections, begging a crust of bread or pilfering from the vegetable garden. So that was why the cows had been milked! Jack Tar, whoever he was, had been helping himself. The Jamiesons could be grateful to him for that, at least.

The man dropped the last few rungs to the ground, turned to face Edward, saw in the gloom a ferocious man pointing a sinister metal object at him, darted to the door and was gone. Edward, hopping after him, saw no more than a tattered sailor's jacket, a mop of dingy hair and a pair of racing feet before the bush swallowed him up.

Edward leant against the doorpost. To his chagrin, he found that he was shaking. He sank down on a seat by the table. The fellow had given him a proper fright. At the moment of the explosion, made louder no doubt by the confined space, he had believed himself to be lost. In that instant he had been pierced through with a sudden, unspeakable anguish, a desperate desire to live. He was not, after all, ready to die! He felt uplifted, raised to euphoria. He had been unarmed against an armed desperado, and he had seen the fellow off! He was not such a weakling after all. And above all, he was alive! Life was suddenly infinitely dear, a treasure that had almost slipped from his grasp but had then been unaccountably returned to him. It was as if his life had started all over again. He was aware of the beating of his heart, of the breath coming in and out of his lungs. Maimed or not, he could still feel, he could still act, he could still think.

He wished he could run after that confounded fellow to thank him. Why, only half an hour ago he had been sunk in despair, but now the future was once again filled with hope. Now the outlines were clearer, less fanciful, more solidly grounded in his own capabilities than they had ever been before.

He had earlier imagined himself succeeding, in the course of time, to his father's position. He had seen himself the master of an estate, first at Enfield, then, on a lesser scale, at Duddingston. He had looked forward to a life enriched with gentlemanly pursuits, the leisurely study of science, a learned correspondence with his old professors at home, the congenial society of friends. Now, he knew, he must rely only upon himself, upon his own strength and skills. Little Jessie Dunbar had given him a clue. He would follow it up at the first opportunity. The only school as yet to be built in Nelson was for rudimentary instruction in the three Rs. He could hardly work in a dame school. Very well, he would go further afield. He would enquire in Auckland, in Wellington, even in New South Wales if need be. He would take his future into his own hands. One day he would have a home of his own, provided by his own exertions, with no aid from his father. He might even marry and have children.

At the idea of a wife a vague outline appeared in his mind, a picture of a woman sitting opposite him at a well-spread table. He could imagine her form, graceful, small, peaceful. But her face eluded him. He tried to bring it to mind, and saw only the open, flirtatious, sparkling face of his mother, laughing up at him as Fanny laughed at Hector. No, that was wrong. A woman like that was not right for him. Her colours were too bold, too bright, too obvious. He would desire someone more restful, deeper, more subtle, a woman who would inspire him, confide in him, an ally, a friend, a – a mate.

A plaintive mooing from Cowslip interrupted his thoughts. It was time he saw to her before the early night of winter fell. He got up to fetch the pail and milking stool. A thought still nagged at him. It was as if a curtain hung between his inner vision and a revelation. A few moments more and he might have been able to draw it aside and see the face opposite him at the table. He might have known her, and claimed her. But now the moment was past. The partial vision was already disappearing.

He limped to the door, but as he approached it he heard Ladybird whinny outside, and fear rushed back, made all the greater by his new determination to live. Who could be coming at this time of day? Perhaps the runaway was returning to finish him off, or maybe the Maori had really come for him this time. He opened the door a crack and peered out. Hector was tying Flighty's reins beside those of Ladybird. Edward flung the door open and waited for him to speak.

Hector looked up and met his eyes. The lonely ride from Nelson had frightened him and worsened his temper. He had prepared speech after speech to throw at Edward. He was infuriated by his son's folly, baffled by his remoteness and grief-stricken by the lost friendship between them. His feelings had welled up in angry accusations, but at the sight of Edward's stern, calm face and confident bearing he paused.

'Good evening, Father.' There was a new note in Edward's voice. It silenced Hector. 'It's as well I came back. A confounded runaway had taken up his quarters in the house and I had to chase him off. He had armed himself with your gun, and discharged a round of shot into the table. It's damaged, I'm afraid, but no lasting harm is done. We should be grateful to him, in fact. He's been milking the cows.'

Hector strode towards him. 'You young fool,' he said curtly. 'What the devil do you mean by it, riding out here on your own without permission?'

'Permission, Father?' Edward's voice was cool. 'I beg your pardon. I did not imagine I needed your permission to ride my own horse to my own home.'

Hector was jolted out of his anger. So the boy had found a spirit of independence, had he? He had grown up all of a sudden! It was not before time. It was to be seen if he had learned enough sense to match his new maturity. Hector marshalled himself for a response that would blend friendliness with a due measure of reproof, but Edward cut in first.

'Will you come in, Father? We can talk more comfortably inside. I have been thinking about my future, and I would like to inform you of my plans.'

Chapter Fourteen *Duddingston, December 1843*

1

Jem staggered, stubbed his toe on a stone, and cursed. His dogs, uncritical shadows of his every movement, halted on the muddy track and scratched themselves as they waited for him to continue on his erratic progress home to Duddingston.

'Yer damned stupid . . .' Jem lifted his other foot to kick the offending stone, missed and almost went sprawling, but he righted himself and, slightly sobered, kept on along the path.

The track from Nelson to Duddingston came out of the bush directly by the Kirkwoods' whare, and Jem stood still, rocking on his feet, at the sight of his father, who was sitting on a tree stump cutting strips of leather from a worn-out boot with his clasp knife. Joseph lifted his head, took a long look at his son, and bent to his task again. Jem walked carefully towards him, steadying himself with a hand against the wall of the new fern whare they had all built for Malcolm and his bride.

'Wha're you doing, Father?'

Joseph did not answer.

'He's cutting up his boots,' said Jem, nodding sagely towards an invisible audience. 'Aye, the poor old fool's gone mad at last and he's cutting up his boots. Next he'll start on his breeks, and then his sark, and then he'll be stark naked altogether!' This struck him as hilariously funny, and he lurched about, hiccuping and laughing.

'I'm making hinges for your brother's door,' said Joseph quietly, 'but if you were a few years younger it's a strap for your own sinful back I'd be making,' and he shook his head.

Jem held himself straight with an effort and wagged a finger at his father.

'Si'ful, you call it! Si'ful! It's not me that's si'ful, it's you, and him, and them, and all they . . .'

'Son, Jimmy,' said Joseph at last, 'you're far gone down the road to wickedness, but remember the prodigal son, who repented and came to his father . . .'

'Proliga', progidal, prock . . .' Jem gave up the effort to arrange the tiresome consonants in the correct order, and settled for an easier word. ' "Repent!" he says. "Repent!" Who are you calling on to repent, yer miserable old hiroprite!' He shook his head in puzzlement, aware that this word, too, had somehow escaped him, then he returned to his theme.

'It's not me that should repent! It's you should repent! You can't tell me about no prody son. I know him, that one, I know! His father loved him, so he did. His father kissed him, so he did. He killed the facked, the fatted calf, aye, the fatted calf. When did you ever fat a calf for me, eh? Eh?'

The calmness with which Joseph had returned to his piece of leather began to have its effect on Jem. He stood for a moment, glowering at him, shaking his fist in a weak gesture of defiance, then a thought occurred to him. He belched.

'You can go to hell, you old bugger,' he said, laughing at his own temerity. 'Aye, go to hell,' he said again, savouring the unaccustomed pleasure of saying out loud words he had so often used under his breath. 'You can go to hell because I'm going to hell.'

Joseph's head came up again with a jerk, and Jem nodded triumphantly.

'Aye, I'm going to hell all right,' he said. 'There's jobs for me to go to, new masters who'll feed me and pay me. There's men needed in the Waimea, and I'm going to hell over there, and you can go to hell, too. Mr Jenkins is taking me on, and the dogs, and I'm going tomorrow. I'm going to h—'

'Jem!' The authority in Joseph's voice cut off the rambling voice at once. Jem stood suddenly still, and his eyes were fixed on his father's. For a long moment they stared at each other, then Jem's eyes dropped.

'You'll go nowhere, son,' said Joseph at last. 'You'll stay here, with me and your brother. You'll do your work and keep off the drink, and leave your blaspheming ways. I'm not letting go. You're not fit to leave me. You're not able to face the temptations of the world. I'm not letting you go.'

Tears welled up in Jem's eyes and made courses through the dust that covered his cheeks. His head fell and he shook it helplessly.

'You'd best be after your dogs,' said Joseph, bending over his work again as calmly as if the exchange had never taken place. 'Look! They're away off towards the bush and if they fall foul of the traps Malcolm's been setting for kiwis and wekas and the like there's no saying if they'll be injured or not.'

'Oh, damn you! Damn you!' burst out Jem, and turning away from his father he started towards the far edge of the clearing, vainly trying to school his lips to form the whistle that always brought his dogs to heel.

* * *

It had been a busy day at Duddingston. The recent hot weather had instilled in Fanny's mind the notion that moths were bound to have been at work in the various trunks and boxes stored above the rafters in the small attic in which, since Meg's marriage, Jessie now slept alone. She had decided on a grand turn-out, and the bushes and fences near the homestead had, since mid-morning, been festooned with a collection of blankets, shawls and clothing of all kinds in which, fortunately, not one silky cocoon had so far been discovered.

Jessie had come to her own trunk last of all, and at Fanny's insistence had carried its contents out into the open, to be shaken out and exposed to the most rigorous scrutiny. Almost the last item to see the light of day was Isobel's quilt, which had been packed at the bottom.

'Don't lay this one on the fence now, Jessie,' Meg instructed her sister. 'There's nails in it might tear it.'

Jessie looked round. In the shade of a pleasantly spreading native beech, which had been left to grow undisturbed on a knoll beside the house, Edward had set himself up to work at a makeshift table. The many letters he had sent off in search of employment had not as yet resulted in an acceptable offer, and he was devoting his remaining time at Duddingston to drawing up his botanical finds. On the table beside him lay sheets of best quality paper from his precious store from home, already covered with drawings in his own delicate hand, and weighted down with pebbles in case a gust of wind should blow them about.

Jessie's eyes flitted past a scraggy shrub and some clumps of tussocky grass and settled on a bush within a few feet of Edward's table. It was the very place! She would not disturb him, of course, but if he did happen to raise his eyes from his work, she would not mind looking at what he was doing.

To her satisfaction, Edward looked up as she approached and smiled at her.

'Still busy?' he asked. His eye travelled over the quilt she held in her arms. It struck a faint chord of memory in his mind, but he did not bother to pursue the idea. 'You look as if you were carrying the crown jewels,' he said teasingly, as Jessie laid the quilt across the bush with meticulous care.

'It belonged to my mother,' she said.

Edward frowned and looked at it again. Something was not quite right. There was something about the quilt and Jessie's mother that did not fall into place. Jessie saw the frown and her heart sank. Somehow she had erred, and the thought saddened her. She found it impossible to mention her mother to anyone but Edward, but with him it was easy and natural to do so. Perhaps, after all, he did not like the subject either and she would have to guard her tongue in future. She gave the corner of the quilt a final twitch, then left it and stepped up to the table, looking for a change of subject.

'I wish I could draw as nice as you,' she said wistfully, looking down at the papers that were spread about him.

Edward smiled. 'Perhaps you can,' he said, 'only you've never tried.'

'Yes, but . . .' She hesitated, trying to find the precise words to convey her feelings. 'I wouldn't see everything you see, all the little veiny things on the leaves, and the long stalk things that stick out of the middle of the flowers, and the way they all grow just like you've drawn it out of the stem.'

Edward smiled again. He had been at work on his drawings all day, spurred on by a letter he had received from Professor Jamieson. '. . . and so publication of your finds in a forthcoming number of a Botanical Journal in which I have an interest would be a possibility . . .' It had needed only this one sentence to raise his spirits to something near their old optimism and he had been engaged at his drawing and note-taking every hour he could spare from those farm duties which, with his limited mobility, he was still able to carry out.

Jessie's eyes wandered respectfully across the pages and Edward, following her gaze, felt flattered. He was not used to an appreciative audience. Fanny was inclined to praise him with uncritical indulgence, rather as one would a child with its first formed letters, and Hector, though he had become more tolerant since the accident, still betrayed the opinion that scientific pursuits were for those incapable of more useful forms of activity. Edward basked in Jessie's admiration. He waited for a final compliment, after which she would doubtless go back to her household tasks.

Instead she asked a question. 'Why don't ferns have flowers?'

'You've noticed that, have you?' Edward was pleased.

'Oh, yes. I've looked often and often for them, and wondered what they would be like, what colour, you know, and how big. But I've never found any.'

'Ferns don't need flowers,' said Edward carelessly. 'They reproduce in a different way.'

'What do you mean?' said Jessie.

Edward felt as a walker might feel who unexpectedly finds himself sinking into marshy ground.

'Plants grow from seeds, do they not?' he said, progressing warily.

'Aye.'

'You see, it's the flowers that make the seeds.'

'How?'

'You wouldn't understand.'

'I might.'

'Well – at the base of every flower is an . . .' Edward faltered, then went bravely on. 'An ovary. Inside it are ovules.'

'Do you mean seeds?' asked Jessie helpfully. 'And they grow big and get ripe? Is that it?'

'Not quite,' said Edward, in whose breast notions of propriety and a respect for scientific accuracy fought a brief battle. Propriety lost.

'First they have to be ferti – they have to mingle with the pollen.'

'I don't quite see . . .'

'Pollen has to – er – enter each ovule, or it cannot ripen into a seed.'

Jessie's eyes were wide with fascination.

'How does that happen?'

The warmth seemed to be affecting Edward. Beads of perspiration had broken out on his forehead and on the palms of his hands. It had not before occurred to him that the reproduction of plants could be construed as in any way improper or embarrassing, but now, faced with Jessie's wide-eyed innocence, his mind skating desperately round the words 'male', 'female', 'fertilisation' and 'sexual', he knew himself to be blushing. His feet were, however, stuck in the quagmire, and though it threatened to become a quicksand, he had no choice but to flounder on.

'Bees or other insects collect nectar from flowers, and then they, um, they rub their legs against the anthers' – he was drawing a rough explanatory sketch for her on a discarded piece of paper – 'and then they fly to another flower and the pollen from the first one gets on to the stigma of the second one, and then it, well, it penetrates the ovary, and enters the ovules, and only then can they develop into seeds.'

He sat back with relief. He was safe again. But Jessie's curiosity was not satisfied.

'Why does the seed need pollen to make it grow? Why can't it do it by itself?'

'Oh,' said Edward carelessly, his guard down, 'all creatures need two parents, a mother and a fa . . .'

He stopped in consternation, perceiving where this line of argument could lead him. Perplexity had settled once more on Jessie's brow. Edward, conscious that he was being dragged into an ever deeper morass, cast rapidly about for a way out. Fortunately Jessie's eye fell once more to the table, and the conversation came back full circle to its starting point.

'I wish I could draw as nice as you,' she said.

'Try it! Try now!' said Edward, seizing the proffered escape route. He pulled a fresh sheet of paper out of his portfolio, laid in front of it the simplest frond from the collection on the table, rose from his seat and offered it to Jessie with a flourish. Her eyes darted back towards the cottage but Fanny and Meg were out of sight inside, engaged on packing clothes away once more with a plentiful supply of mothballs. She felt dizzy with nerves.

'I couldn't,' she said breathlessly. 'I'd only spoil your beautiful paper.'

Edward, however, was not to be gainsaid. A sudden zeal had taken hold of him. Why should not this untutored child learn something of science? Curiosity sparkled in her brown eyes and her questions proved that she was intelligent. If he was to start his own educational establishment run on modern scientific lines, as he planned one day to do, what was to prevent him from trying out a few of his notions on this willing pupil, who was so conveniently to hand? Edward looked at Jessie speculatively and his voice changed. It became deeper, more authoritative, the voice of one who would brook no dissent.

'Sit down,' he said.

To her own surprise, Jessie did so.

'Pick up the pen. Look at the frond. Study it. Count the indentations along the side. Notice its length. Follow with your eyes the pattern on the veins. When you are ready, begin to draw.'

Panic seized Jessie. She was not to know that Edward was rendering, as faithfully as memory allowed, the tones of Mr Gibbs, his first science master, whose personality had imprinted itself forcibly upon the minds of his pupils. She looked up at him, too afraid to speak.

'Don't say anything,' he said firmly. 'Start at the stem. Dip your pen in the ink now. Draw it. Now.'

Jessie, holding the pen in too tight a grip, and mastered by a will that was suddenly so much stronger than hers, obeyed. Her pen made its first mark on the paper and spluttered. Her work-roughened fingers trembled and stopped moving.

'The first line is the hardest. And now it is made, there is no going back. You must continue.'

Slowly, cautiously, the pen travelled across the paper. It accomplished the first indentation without mishap. Jessie let out a long breath and drew another. Edward, standing beside her, said nothing. He was willing her to succeed, his mind forcing hers to concentrate.

Unnoticed, two black shapes raced past them. Tam and Bess were off hunting in the bush. A distant exchange of men's voices, too faint to be recognised, passed unheard.

The drawing was finished. It was the first Jessie had ever done. She surveyed it, her head on one side. It was of course nothing like the masterpieces that Edward seemed to produce so effortlessly, but she could not help but be a little pleased with parts of it. The tip of the frond in particular, she thought, was not altogether bad. Alight with the pleasure of accomplishing something new, but apprehensive of criticism, she turned to her mentor. He was not looking at her. He was watching Jem, who was stumbling round the edge of a newly sprouting patch of wheat towards them. Her drawing forgotten, Jessie scrambled to her feet. She had taken liberties! She had forgotten herself! She had been too familiar! She braced herself for a rebuke in her cousin's customarily curt manner. It did not come. Instead Jem stood silent, looking from one to the other through sodden eyes. Then he directed his wavering footsteps up to the table, and putting both hands under its edge, braced his legs to send it toppling over.

It was only the intoxicated deliberateness of Jem's movements that saved weeks of Edward's work from ending, torn and muddied, on the ground, but they were slow enough to allow Edward time to snatch up the inkwell and, with a deft throw, to flick the contents into Jem's face. Jem stood for a moment, shocked, then he bellowed, but Edward had had time to dodge, as nimbly as his wooden foot allowed, from behind the table and was now intent on drawing Jem's ire away from Jessie and the precious papers. Jem lumbered towards him, fist balled for a punch. Edward raised his own, but as Jem came within fighting reach, he slipped and fell forwards, and what had begun as an attack ended in an embrace as he clutched Edward for support then slid to his knees where he remained, wiping ink messily from his nose and eyes with his frayed cuff, and crying with self-pity.

Edward looked down at him with exasperation.

'Confound you, you fool,' he said. 'Get up, for goodness' sake, and go home and sleep it off.'

Jem sank down further, and seemed about to topple over altogether when his elbow was roughly grasped and he was hauled to his feet. His father had come.

Edward smiled with relief. 'Oh, I am so glad you are here,' he said, trying to make light of the affair. 'You'll know what to do with the silly fellow. I fear he has imbibed too freely, and needs to cool off for an hour or so.'

Joseph did not answer and Edward said no more but watched as Joseph supported his son back down the path to their whare. A sound behind him made him turn. Jessie, white-faced, was trying to gather up her quilt in unsteady hands. Edward saw that a corner of it was caught on a twig and went to release it. Jessie, watching him, saw him stand suddenly still, looking down at the pattern on the material. She waited, puzzled, not wishing to interrupt him. After a long moment he said, in a wondering voice, 'How came your mother by this quilt?'

Sensitive to every inflection in his voice, she could detect no censure, only curiosity, and her heart lifted. He had not minded her mentioning Ma, after all. It was something else that had vexed him earlier.

'I don't – I can't remember,' she said, but then, unbidden, a picture came to her mind. 'Or perhaps – yes, I know it was in one of the bad times, the worst perhaps, when Pa had no work and we were hungry. And there was a man, or maybe two. Very tall and in black clothes, ministers, it could be. And Ma was ill and cold and they wrapped her in it, and afterwards she said it saved her life. So when she was on the ship, you know, and very weak in the last days, I used to tuck it round her, right up to her chin, because I thought, I believed it would . . . But it didn't.'

Her voice ended in a whisper and Edward, folding up his end of the quilt and laying it in her arms, saw again the child he had first noticed, watching her mother's body arc through the air and down into the cold, grey sea.

He touched her cheek with his finger. 'Your drawing is good, for a first attempt,' he said. 'I shall give you a lesson every day, when there is time and opportunity, and if you work hard you shall have your own notebook with empty pages in it, to make your own studies of natural history.'

As Jessie ran back to the cottage, she felt so light her feet seemed scarcely to touch the ground but Edward did not watch her go. He was back once more in Aggie's austere bedchamber, his head bowed, his hands held behind his back, his pride in his new pair of scissors in ruins about him. He heard again his aunt's voice rolling over his head. 'Don't you know it's naughty to cut at good things with scissors, Teddy? You have spoilt my best quilt, and how I am to mend it I do not know, for the corner is quite ruined and I am sure I have not a piece in my workbox to patch it with. Look at it, child. Look at it! Whatever can have possessed you? You will go to bed now, at once, and forgo your supper.'

2 *September 1844*

Fanny was for once alone in her little house. The Kirkwoods were working over by the creek today. The land they had so arduously cleared on the higher part of the slopes above the river valley was already green with a new growth of English grasses, which would next year be fit to feed the growing herd of cattle. The next task was to clear the lower paddocks of the poisonous tutu, which had already brought to a conclusion the eventful life of Primrose, a cow whom not the stoutest fence had seemed able to contain. As for the Dunbars, Isaiah was out tending his precious rows of seedlings while Jessie and Meg were busy with the linen and Fanny's home-made cakes of brown soap at the stream that ran behind the house. Hector had ridden into Nelson at first light.

Fanny was listless today. She had woken unrefreshed, her night cap askew and her nightdress rucked up under her arms, a sure sign that she had passed a restless night. She felt a depression weighing down upon her, almost as real as a physical burden. What was it that made her so low today?

The kettle on its chain above the fire stopped its singing and began to hiss and steam. Fanny got up to make herself some tea. She should not be dawdling inside on this fine spring day, when a hundred tasks stood waiting. The dough for tomorrow's bread should be already kneaded and set by the fire to rise, she should be separating the milk, or mending the rent in Hector's shirt, or sweeping from the corners of the room the huge quantity of litter that mysteriously collected in them. Instead she stood, uncertain, too low to bestir herself. Her eye fell on a letter, tucked behind the candlestick on the mantelshelf.

Justina! A picture came to Fanny's mind, an orderly room full of handsome, polished furniture, a room scented with beeswax and lavender, decorated with porcelain ornaments and hung with silk, in which people of leisure, enlivened with the music of a well-tuned pianoforte, set themselves to charm, men of distinction to discourse and instruct while women of fashion plied their needles with artistry and their tongues with wit. She was homesick. Oh, how she was homesick!

She sank down on the crude bench beside the rough-surfaced table, her drab skirt trailing on the beaten earth of the floor, and rested her head in her hands.

For a while she luxuriated in her loss, dwelling on every phrase in Justina's letter. 'A ball at Hurst Court . . . ' 'Mrs Blakeney not pleased with the new chintz covers to her drawing-room chairs – the stuff is good but the pattern does not suit . . . ' 'a pretty gown of finest silk with rose-pink ribbons knotted in the new fashion much admired by Sir Andrew . . . ' 'the most elegant chaise imaginable, dark green without and the prettiest pale blue within, and my own sweet team of chestnuts . . . '

How had it come about that she, the beautiful, the admired Fanny Jamieson, was condemned to a life of drudgery in this mean hut, worse than any lodging of her father's poorest servant, her hands red with work, her clothes indistinguishable from the most wretched Scots goodwife? A tui somewhere near at hand was pouring heavenly music from its tufted throat. Usually she loved to hear it. Today she would cheerfully have throttled it.

'Why are there no proper birds here?' she said aloud. 'No thrushes, or blackbirds, or robins?'

The sound of her own voice startled her out of her daydream. This was no way to go on! She must think of all they had achieved at Duddingston, count her blessings, forget her woes. She began to recite the litany of successes that she often used to lull herself to sleep at night. 'Twenty acres cleared and sown,' she chanted, 'seventy pounds of butter sold, ten cows and four calves, two sows with litters, fifty pounds earned from the vegetables, a new cookhouse, plans drawn up for the new homestead, rents increasing from the town section . . .'

Her voice tailed off. What did it all mean? What did anything mean, when all she wanted to do was buy a new gown and order a frivolous hat from a smart French milliner? How had she been happy here for so long? How had she been able to take satisfaction in a pile of turnips or a round of freshly made cheese? The very thought of them disgusted her now. She longed only for the sight of a well-dressed man, complete with snowy linen, pomaded locks and a decently cut coat who would charm her with the high polish on his boots and the sophisticated flow of his conversation.

The latch of the door lifted. Fanny looked up, and in spite of herself she smiled. In the place of the perfect gentleman she had been dreaming of she saw the grizzled head, weather-beaten features and sweat-stained shirt of Joseph Kirkwood.

He came in, ducking under the lintel, and stood in front of her, holding his hat before him in both hands.

'I'm wishful to speak with you, Mistress Jamieson.'

From his face Fanny could see that he had something of importance on his mind. She felt a shiver of unease. In the last two years she had come more and more to rely on the old Scotsman. Indeed, they had formed something of an alliance. Together they had made plans, consulted over details, and supervised the young people, tacitly circumnavigating Hector whenever it proved necessary. It was a strange friendship between an ill-assorted pair, but Joseph, who on first acquaintance had disapproved of the mistress's worldliness, had since been more than once impressed by her courage, and touched by her whole-hearted goodness to his motherless nieces and her kindness towards his wayward son. At the same time his own sense of humour, which not even his stern morality had been able to suppress, would be forever bubbling up to meet her own, and though he sometimes had to take himself to task for untoward hilarity after the two of them had laughed together at some absurdity, he could not but feel a kindness for her.

On Fanny's part the friendship went still deeper. She had never forgotten the debt she owed Joseph for rescuing Edward from his peril up the mast, but since then she had come to rely on him more than she would have wished. It was quite evident to her that it was Joseph Kirkwood they had to thank for the success of Duddingston. While all around them the colonists of Nelson floundered in a morass of disappointed expectations, poor farming practices and terror of the Maori, Joseph had quietly steered their barque through the choppy waters and had brought them to a real prospect of prosperity.

But now, looking up at him, Fanny read a new trouble in his face.

'Sit down, Joseph,' she said, 'and tell me what's behind that Friday face of yours.'

Joseph sighed, sat down, and laid his giant fists on the table. He looked down at them for a moment, then rubbed his stubbled chin.

'I'll not beat about the bush, Mistress Jamieson,' he said at last. 'You ken fine I wouldn't want to leave you and Mr Jamieson for no good cause at all, but I believe the time has come for our ways to part.'

Fanny's heart missed a beat and the weight that had lain on her all morning pressed heavier still.

'It's not for myself I'm wishful to make the move,' said Joseph, keeping his eyes glued to the sewing basket which lay on the floor by Fanny's skirt, 'but for the young ones. I didna bring them half way round the world without I had a clear idea of God's purposes for us, and now I believe they are to be fulfilled.' He lifted his eyes to Fanny's face, and she saw that they were shining.

'You've heard tell of the new settlement, Mistress Jamieson, the New Edinburgh scheme? It's fixed upon at last, way down in the south. There's a grand harbour they tell me, at Otago or thereabouts, and the land is fine, better by far than here. And there's no danger to be feared either, for the natives are but few, and those who are there have no mind to turn the settlers away. The land's bought fair and square with money instead of all they blankets and muskets and the like, so there's no doubt but that it will be settled fast. But the best of it is this, Mistress Jamieson – it's to be a colony of the Free Church of Scotland! God-fearing men, all of them! There's to be a good Scots kirk where the word of the Lord will be given to his people, Sunday by Sunday, and a school where the children will be trained up in the way that they should go. It's where I want to take my Jem, Mistress Jamieson, for I'm that grieved at the company he keeps hereabouts, the wildness of it, the drunkenness and swearing, and if I can but take him to a better place I know the Lord will work in his poor rebellious heart.'

His rugged face looked so sad that Fanny would have liked to touch his hand in sympathy. At the same time, she was irritated by his blindness. She had long wanted to talk to Joseph about his son, to advise him to be easier on the lad, to show him the love he craved, love which would work with natural ease the changes his father longed for, while the harshness which soured Jem's temper threatened to make him a stranger for ever. It was strange, she thought, how so kind and good a man could be so unyielding with his own son. She had never been able to speak to Joseph of it. She could not now. She could think of nothing but the dreadfulness of the news. Joseph was leaving! All the Kirkwoods and the Dunbars would go! She and Hector would be left to struggle on at Duddingston alone!

'But the girls! Meg! Jessie!' she blurted out. 'The baby is due soon, in three months at any rate. How can Meg manage alone, so far from civilisation? You cannot surely take her in such a delicate condition into the wilderness?'

Joseph smiled. 'I have no fear for Meg or for the bairn,' he said serenely. 'There's babies come into the world every day, and she's a strong little woman enough. The Lord will uphold her when her time is come.'

Fanny shook her head in exasperation over this masculine unconcern.

'Her first confinement!' she said. 'It is not to be thought of! A motherless girl, and so young! You cannot leave until the child is born.'

Joseph stood up. He had never allowed the opinions of others, especially of females, to affect the handling of his own affairs and he would not allow it now.

'I'm giving you two months' notice, Mistress Jamieson,' he said. 'You'll find good hired help in Nelson, I doubt not. There's as many good fish in the sea as ever came out of it and men there are in plenty seeking honest employment. The worst of the work is done now and you will reap your reward. Duddingston's set fair on its feet and you'll do now without us.'

'But how do you propose to live?' exclaimed Fanny. 'There's nothing further south but bush and mountains and a few deserted whaling stations. It is the most complete wilderness!'

'The Lord will provide,' said Joseph calmly, 'and in any case, we will provision ourselves with flour and other such necessaries enough for a year or two. There's a new Promised Land awaits us in the south, and I'm not the man to hear the call and turn aside. We've all of us saved the most of what we've earned these past two years and now we can hope to buy a piece of land of our own, among our own people, a godly people!'

Fanny sat in silence as Joseph took his leave. She was stunned by the blow. This morning she had suffered a cruel sense of loss. She had not known then how much greater it was soon to be. She had been stripped of everything, her wealth, her luxurious home, her clothes, her servants, her youthful looks. She had lost her sister and her daughter. She had struggled to start afresh and with the labour of her own hands had made a home, simple enough but full of comfort and cheer for her husband, her son and her servants. Now even this was to be taken from her. Her son had been gone half a year already, away to Wellington to tutor someone else's children, her servants were leaving all at once, men and maids alike, and as for her husband – here Fanny paused, and then allowed herself to face the truth she had for months past been pushing away from her.

Things had changed between Hector and herself, she knew not quite how. In all the past years of their married life he had been the master, the leader, the provider. She had relied upon him for everything. It had never crossed her mind that she should concern herself with his business affairs. Money had always been there for the asking. Her task had been to spend it. But now, since leaving England, all that had changed. Fanny had begun to ask questions, tentatively at first, but with growing confidence. In the beginning Hector had laughed at her. It was not necessary for her, he said as he pinched her chin, to strain those pretty eyes over columns of dull figures. She should leave such things to men, who naturally understood them.

Slowly, however, as the farming operation had developed and Fanny's butter money had become an important source of income, Hector had fallen into the way of talking over the business side of things with her. Fanny had made some puzzling discoveries. There was a rashness, a false optimism in Hector's schemes which dismayed her. She had discounted her fears at first as irrational. Hector must know best. She must be wrong. She would suspend judgement until she understood more. But gradually the conviction grew upon her that Hector was too impulsive, faulty in his judgement, too prone to trust a good fellow he had met in a tavern, too easily persuaded to part with his money.

The seed of doubt, once sown, grew with frightening rapidity. Hector had made his Indian fortune through speculation, where his quickness, a certain happy instinct and pure luck had stood him in good stead. But he had been unwise, dreadfully unwise, she could see that now, to trust everything to that strange Mr Pluckton in Calcutta, whose eyes had never quite met hers. Oh, if she had only known then what she knew now! If she had only concerned herself with Hector's business affairs, listened when he spoke of them, interested herself in the minutiae of capital and interest, bonds and stock, instead of concealing yawns and turning the subject as she had always done! If she had offered a little warning here, suggested an adjustment there . . . But it was of no use to dwell on what might have been. She had now to make the best of what was to come. And to do that she had to accept that her husband was not the paragon she had once believed him to be, and that the fortunes of the family would from now on rest as squarely on her shoulders as they had done on his.

It would take time, she supposed, to adjust to this new idea of Hector. She was not sure what might replace the parts of protector and protected, of indulgent parent and wayward child which they had always played. Perhaps, she thought wistfully, if she could manage Hector cleverly, so that his dignity did not suffer in the process, she could become more of a partner, a – her mind searched for the word and found it – a friend.

As if in answer to her thoughts, she heard the sound of hooves outside. Hector was back already! And she had done not a hand's turn the entire morning! She jumped up and began to bustle, setting the stew pot on to boil and cutting slices from the large loaf of coarse bread that formed their staple food. She had news of a difficult nature to give him. She was not at all sure how he would take it.

'Fanny!' The door burst open and Hector stood against the light. Fanny sensed something new in him, a stirring of the old power, the electrical force which the past two years had driven out of him. 'I've such news for you! Teddy writes from Wellington in answer to my letter. But I forget, I have kept it all a secret from you! He has found out for me the cost of warehousing which I asked him to enquire about. And Dickson writes from London in the most satisfactory way. All is arranged! I am to receive a shipment of tea and calico not later than April of next year directly from Calcutta! Old Murchison has come up trumps, to my surprise. He is happy to undertake a new venture for once, with the backing of Dickson and the bank in Cornhill. We are to start our business at last and the best of it is that we shall beat the Wellington prices by importing direct from India. Our fortunes are made once more, Fanny! You shall see!'

'Wellington?' said Fanny, feeling suddenly almost faint. 'What do you mean, Hector? You propose to remove to Wellington? But the farm, Duddingston, the town house . . .'

'My dear, that is all to go,' said Hector blithely, coming forward and catching her by the hands. 'You know, our efforts here have richly paid off. The farm will fetch a good price now that we have brought it to such a profitable state, and I have almost clinched a deal with the town property. We shall remove to Wellington as soon as it can all be arranged. Only think, my darling, you shall live in a proper house again, with furniture of your own choosing, and decent clothes, and no more of this hard, rough work! I shall make our fortunes again, I know I shall, in the way I know best, and Duddingston will pay for the first step in the venture! Are you not delighted, Fanny? We will be near to Teddy again and you shall have your little piano once more! Only say something, Fanny! You are looking so doubtful!'

Fanny gave herself a little shake. Why indeed was she not overjoyed? Why could she not respond to Hector, fling her arms around his neck and call him every wonderful name she could think of, as she had always done in the past? It was, it must be good news! Only a few moments ago she had been longing to leave this place and now the chance was hers. Why, then, was she so suddenly full of fear? She leant forward and patted Hector's arm.

'Oh, yes, indeed, it's wonderful, of course, I am sure,' she faltered, and then she burst into tears.

Chapter Fifteen *Otago, December 1844*

1

The knuckles of Jessie's hands stood out white as she gripped the rail of the *Sarah Ann* and gulped great breaths of the rain-laden air. Her hair whipped about her face and she had to brace herself against the pitching and rolling of the small schooner as it lurched on its course southwards. The coast was so forlorn, so forbidding. In the background rose lowering mountains, while in the foreground rocks tumbled from each headland, and the forest, growing right down to the water's edge, was so dense it was plain no human habitation was there. In the livid half-light of this summer night's storm even the gentler hills looked grim.

Jessie shuddered and pulled her shawl closer round her. In a moment she must go below again and face the terrors nearer at hand, the desperation in Meg's eyes, the moaning she gave every few minutes as the pains took hold, the appalling knowledge that her sister's life and that of the baby lay in Jessie's own thin hands.

The boat tilted over, and for a sickening moment she was gazing down into a deep green pit, flecked with foam, like a hungry mouth full of spittle. Then she felt a hand on her shoulder and turned. Malcolm stood beside her. He was trembling. He looked unlike the quiet man she still scarcely knew, even after eighteen months of marriage to her sister. His face, usually withdrawn and impassive, was anguished.

'Go back to her, Jessie,' he said hoarsely. 'She says it's mortal bad. Do what you can. I don't know . . . I can't . . . She needs a woman!'

Jessie looked at the hands he had spread out in a gesture of helplessness and pushed past him. Malcolm was right. Meg needed her. She might not be quite a woman yet but even at fifteen she had more sense than this feeble lump. She cast about in her mind for the advice Fanny had given her two weeks ago, when she had kissed the girls a fond farewell.

'Give her something to bite on if the pain gets bad, and mind you make sure there's plenty of padding on the mattress or it will be ruined. A posset of herbs will help to stem the bleeding afterwards. Mind now, what I've told you about cutting the cord, and make sure the baby's wrapped up warm afterwards for fear it should take a chill.'

Jessie had nodded, round eyed. The birth had seemed unreal then, a remote, unlikely eventuality. How she longed for Fanny now!

A whistling scream greeted her as she opened the cabin door. An unfortunate pitching of the ship coinciding with a particularly cruel spasm had tossed the suffering Meg half out of the tiny bunk, which offered wretched accommodation at any time but was wholly deficient on such an occasion as this. Jessie crossed the cabin with one step, picked up her sister's feet and heaved her legs back on to the mattress. In doing so she made a discovery.

'It's all wet here, Meggie. I suppose it must be what Mrs Jamieson said. Aye, the waters have broke for sure.'

Meg did not answer her. Jessie turned to look at her sister's face. It was scarlet with effort. She seemed about to burst.

'Oh, what is it? Oh be careful, dear Meg! Don't die! Oh Meggie, don't leave me! What can I do? I cannot bear it!'

Meg let her breath go in a great sigh.

'Shut up, you daftie! I'm not dying, I'm trying to give birth!'

The force in her voice shot through Jessie like a tonic. She went to her sister's head and cradled her newly plump shoulders in her arms.

'That's right Meg, all right now, easy now,' she chattered, as Meg pushed again with all her might. 'Hold my hand, squeeze it as hard as you like, never fear of hurting me, go on, darling, go on!'

'Look, will you?' panted Meg. 'Is it coming yet?'

Delicately, Jessie lifted the hem of Meg's heavy cotton nightdress and looked beneath it. She had never seen her sister's naked body since they were small children, and her face flushed with embarrassment. But there was no doubting that the end was near. In the fitful light of the swaying lantern she could see the mound of the baby's head, covered with dark, wet hair.

'Oh, yes!' she cried. 'It's coming! And it's all red, and there's black hair on it, and you're bleeding, Meg. Don't push so again! Oh, Meg, Meg, Ma . . .'

She took a shuddering breath. She was alone now. Oh, how she was alone!

'Ma!' she whispered again, but all that came to her was the memory of phosphorescence dancing about on the water in the stifling, tropical night. She had a desperate desire to run away, to seek help from Uncle Joseph, or even her cousin Jem. Her father, poor weak soul that he was, would be of no use at all. Not that any of them could help her now, she knew that. This was women's work, and she was a woman. She had to pretend to be one, in any case. She breathed deeply again. There would be no second funeral at sea. Not if she could help it.

She took advantage of an easing in the ship's rolling, and, outwardly calm and knowing in spite of her trembling hands, she folded Meg's nightgown neatly up on her stomach, laid a towel in readiness between the crooked knees, patted her apron to check that string and scissors were in her pocket and reached out her hands to ease her nephew, pink, slippery and already opening his little mouth to cry, into her waiting hands.

'A boy!' she called out wonderingly, to the suddenly limp and weeping Meg. 'Oh, Meggie, it's a wee boy, and he's got fingernails and all!'

He was born not a moment too soon. As Jessie fumbled with string and scissors, knocking her head a dozen times on the upper edge of the bunk, the ship began to plunge more violently than ever. Jessie looked up from her work and stared at her sister in horror as they heard the frantic running of bare feet to and fro over their heads. A voice boomed out, 'We'll never do it! Cut the ropes! Cut them, man, or we'll be over!'

Jessie thrust her squirming burden into Meg's arms and turned to the door, but slid on the wet floor.

'No, Jessie!' shrieked Meg. 'Don't leave me! Stay with me, for heaven's sake!'

'I was just going to find out . . .' began Jessie, but stopped. Meg was in no state to be left alone and anyway, now she came to think of it, she was sure the hatch had been battened down. There was nothing for it but to hang on and wait on God's and the sea's good pleasure.

It was half an hour before the worst of the storm abated, and then it was over as suddenly as it had begun. The thudding of feet and the muffled orders quietened down, and the lashing of heavy rain on the deck could be heard in place of the thunderous roar of waves crashing down upon it. The girls had held on to the bunk's edge and to each other, white-faced, crying and praying in turns, protecting with their bodies the mewing scrap of humanity that had threatened at any moment to be thrown against a bulwark or on to the heaving floor.

The cabin door opened with a jerk. Malcolm stood there. In one glance he took in his pale unwashed wife and his blood-stained sister-in-law, then had eyes for nothing but the tiny form, wrapped in a flannel petticoat, that nestled at Meg's breast.

'Is it . . . ?' he began.

'Aye, Malcolm, it's your son,' said Meg, and Jessie, feeling solitary and suddenly tearful when she saw the tender, humble look that had come over the young man's face, stood back to let him pass, then slipped out of the cabin.

* * *

Dawn, when it came, seemed as far removed from the storm of the previous night as heaven from hell. Jessie was out of her bunk early. She had slept little. Her mind was still too strung up by the dangers of the night before, and by the extraordinary ideas that crowded in upon her when she thought of the birth of Meg's baby. Was it always like that, so painful and noisy and – and real? How was it that the body could stretch so, and make such a terrible opening? Could she, too, one day . . . Her mind halted there. It seemed wrong, somehow, to think further. She must try to brood no more on it, to put it out of her thoughts. She got up as soon as the first pale fingers of light touched her face, dressed quickly and went up the companionway and on to the deck.

The world had been reborn. In place of the dark clouds streaked with red that had scudded overhead last night, little puffs of white were dotted about in a morning sky of translucent blue, while the sun, barely up, just topped the trees which last night had seemed so wild and threatening.

The schooner's captain had taken his chance on the wind and tide and had crossed the bar into Otago harbour at first light. The turbulence of the open sea behind her, the *Sarah Ann* was now sailing serenely into a vast pool contained within a surrounding bowl of hills. The wall of land was broken in several places at the further end, and it was possible to see that the sound curved on into the distance. To the north-west rose hills covered with dense bush, broken here and there with barer patches of ground vegetation. To the south-east lay the long arm of a peninsula that separated the sheltered water of the harbour from the sea. It was as if, thought Jessie wonderingly, no human being had ever been here before, no foot had ever trodden on those virgin stretches of white sand, as if this little ship and its few occupants had been wafted on a magic wind to a lost, uninhabited world.

Only a slight riffling breeze broke the calm surface of the water in which the ship made a dancing image of itself as it moved in and away from the turbulence of the rolling seas at the harbour's forbidding entrance, where the waves boomed rhythmically against the black rocks and streamed off their slippery surfaces like long white hair. The woods, too, were so perfectly reflected that it was impossible to say where the land ended and the water began, while the few sea-birds resting on its surface seemed to be gazing at themselves in a splintered looking glass. Water slapped gently against the hull and rippled along its side as the *Sarah Ann* glided forward, but the sound of it was almost drowned out by the thrilling, far-away music that poured from the throats of thousands of birds in the deep bush that came down to the water's edge.

Jessie listened, entranced. She could almost believe that deep in the forest a hundred ethereal churches were ringing out a carillon. She knew the bird that made those four melodic, fluted notes, in perfect timing with his fellows. It was a bell-bird. She had, during one of her 'lessons', asked Edward to teach her the names of some of the native birds and he had been delighted to oblige. He had shown her the many life-like sketches he had made from his own observations, and passed on some of the store of ornithological knowledge he had acquired in his conversations with Tame, their nearest Maori neighbour at Duddingston. He had taken it for granted that her enthusiasm for the natural wonders of the bush was as great as his own, and so, of course, it had grown to be.

It was from the time of her first drawing, she thought wistfully, that he had seemed to see in her a special friend, one who knew not to tease him with questions about his pain, or try to help him get up from a chair. He had, in fact, begun to keep his promise to her. He had given her regular lessons, had explained some of the rudiments of botany. He had shown her how to gather specimens, had encouraged her to draw, and had overseen her first tentative attempts at recording her own observations. The few hours she had spent sitting beside him at the table in the Duddingston cottage she would hug to herself for the rest of her dreary, Edward-less life. She had recited his lessons over and over again as she laboured at the washtub or scoured the pots, and the names of birds and plants had become a litany to her, that she would chant secretly in order to bring back the reassuring sense of his presence. Since the dreadful day when he had announced his departure for Wellington, had packed his bags and gone, she had needed every scrap of comfort she could find. Her greatest pleasure now came from holding one of his old notebooks, which he had casually thrown out when he was packing up his effects but which Jessie had secretly rescued. She took it out often and lingered on every page, absorbing the faint smell of sandalwood and old paper, lost in admiration at the beauty of his flowing handwriting and the delicate accuracy of his drawings.

Now, as the chorus of birdsong came clear across the water, she strained to distinguish the sounds. Tui, bell-bird, kaka, pigeon, she said to herself hopefully, but the music was too far away to hear correctly. It did not matter. She would have time, days, months and years of time, in which to love nature as he loved it, to watch, listen and observe as he had always done. It would be her sole consolation. The empty notebook he had given her and the pens and pencils he had carelessly pressed upon her as a parting present would for ever be her most precious possessions. She would use them well. They would bring her near to him, make her a little worthier of him if ever . . . But it was of no use to go down that path. She would never see him again. Every lifting of the breeze that drove the schooner further up the Otago Sound was driving her inexorably and for ever away from him. All she had left was her precious treasure chest of memories, that she could open and savour whenever she wanted them.

There was that sweet and painful moment, so long ago, just after they had first landed, when he had taken the trouble to come to the emigrant barracks (she still blushed to think of him seeing her in such a common, rough place!) to give her back her doll, which, he had said with a smile that made her knees weak, she must have accidentally dropped on their section in Nile Street. Then there was the day when she had run away from old Henare, the Maori potato seller, because he looked so fierce with his tattooed face, and Edward had chided her and told her not to be afraid, the Maori might look alarming but he had found them kind enough fellows himself.

The accident – her thoughts skated over that. It was too terrible to think of. It was still more terrible to remember her own secret joy. She had believed, poor fool that she was, that Edward crippled would be less appealing to ladies of his own class, and that she, an ignorant maidservant, might dare to hope. She had been well served for such wicked thoughts. Edward had gone. He was happily settled, or so he had written to his mama, with the Gibson family, teaching their hurly-burly sons (at least she had not heard of any daughters!) to read their Latin primers, and not one thought, she was sure, did he ever waste on her.

'Jess! You're up betimes!'

She started. Pa and Uncle Joseph were beside her, her uncle beaming at her as he was wont to do when especially pleased, and even Pa with a smile on his face.

'Eh, but he's a fine wee fellow, is he not?' said Isaiah, who clearly took all the credit for the beauties of his grandson.

'He is that,' concurred Joseph heartily. 'And Meg so hale and hearty, eating a good breakfast yon proud rascal Malcolm has got ready for her with his own hands. We must praise the Lord, for he has been great indeed!'

Joseph seemed about to break into prayer then and there, but Isaiah, seeing the danger, quickly averted it.

'What's toward?' he said, pointing to the port rail, around which was clustered the party of surveyors whom the *Sarah Ann* was conveying to the site of the new settlement. They were pointing and laughing at something in the water.

'What's eating at them now?' said Joseph good-humouredly. The sight of his first grandchild sucking at his fist had touched his heart to the depths, and everything was conspiring, on this glorious day, to fill his cup of blessing to overflowing. He took Jessie's arm and steered her to the port rail.

In the distance, to the port side of the little schooner, Jessie could now see a collection of houses and boats drawn up on a sandy beach. She was sorry to see them. They marred the perfect emptiness of this lovely place. She did not like the idea of others sharing it. A long narrow whale boat had put off from the shore with the obvious intention of approaching the *Sarah Ann*. It was occupied by two men, but it was clear, even from this distance, that at least one of them was hopelessly intoxicated. He was standing up, swaying, in the bows, and his shouts could be heard even above the heavenly music of the birds. The other was feebly attempting to restrain him. The standing figure, turning on his companion, lurched forward and lunged at him. The two tiny forms were seen, for a moment, locked in a pugilistic embrace and then they crashed overboard. There was a second's uncanny silence before the sound of the splash reached the few sailors standing in the bows of the schooner, but when it did they broke into a ribald cheer in which Jem Kirkwood's voice rose higher than the rest.

Jessie tugged her uncle's sleeve. 'I thought no one was here yet, Uncle Joseph. I thought we were the first.'

Joseph shook his head. 'No, my lassie. The serpent has already entered Eden. Look on that headland there. See those miserable dwellings? There's been a whaling station here for I know not how many years, and there's still a dozen or so of the villains left though most of the whales have gone. The captain tells me we'll not be seeing much of them though. They keep to this end of the firth. We'll be lonely enough these next few months, till our good Scots folk arrive, never fear!'

Jessie, watching the men's clumsy attempts to right their boat, shivered. She could see the old whaling station clearly now. It had a derelict, forsaken, sinister look to it. It was as out of place in this pristine, fresh-washed world as a midden in a flower garden. She could make out now the blackened shells of burnt-out huts, the rusting masses of scaffolding and trying-pots, the rotting slipway, the debris of huge whale-bones and broken barrels that littered the bright, white beach. A few men lounged near the huts, attracted by the smoke rising from the cookhouse, though how they could eat Jessie did not understand, as the whiff of rancid fat and rotten flesh was turning her stomach even at this distance.

Jessie turned away and crossed the deck to look at the other shore. But even here she could see signs of human habitation. Clearings in the bush, which at first sight she had taken to be patches of fern or flax, she now recognised as Maori potato gardens. A few whares stood by the stretches of sandy beach that lay between each rocky headland, and smoke rising from one or two showed that at least some were inhabited. Now she could see, in a bay straight ahead of them, a cluster of four or five buildings that had all the appearance of a settler's village. It had a neat, domestic look, reassuringly different from the chaos of the forsaken whaling station. The sight cheered her. She would not, after all, be alone with her family for ever. There might be friends here, company, a means by which news of the outside world could eventually reach them.

The captain's penetrating London voice called out, 'Mr Kirkwood! I'm making for the port of Koputai. I'll set you down there if you've no objection. There's a couple of houses there, with an inn an' all, and your young ladies can have a bit of rest like, before they go up into them wilds up the inner harbour. Anyways, I ain't too sure about pushing on no further. Channel's narrow, so I've been told, and we'd run aground like as not.'

Her uncle's back was turned to her, and Jessie, though she strained to hear his reply, could not catch it. Then she noticed that a canoe had put off from the little port. Its Maori occupants were paddling swiftly towards them. Surely Uncle Joseph would see the sense of stopping here and letting Meg rest in a proper bed for a night or two? They would be able to gain information about other pakehas living here and set up friendly relations.

The captain spoke again. 'You sure about that, Mr Kirkwood? You really want to go straight on up? Well, if you say so. It's your business, I suppose, and since it was thanks to you and your lads that the *Sarah Ann* stayed off the rocks last evening I don't mind giving it a try. I've not done it before, mind, but if the channel hasn't changed from what I've got on my charts we should keep clear of the sandbanks. I'll have to set you down and turn straight back, the tides being how they are. You'll be left to shift for yourselves, straight off. Still, if you've no wish to rest up for a day or two, and take it easy, like . . .'

Jessie had no doubt what Uncle Joseph's answer would be. She did not need to see the grimness on his face in order to read his thoughts. She knew quite well that Meg, the baby, Malcolm, Isaiah and she herself came a poor second in Joseph's mind. His set purpose, his obsession, was to save Jem from the evil company which lay, he believed, at the root of his corruption. Even three cottages and a rudimentary hostelry represented temptations too great to be risked. He was riding Jem on a tight rein and at the slightest relaxation of his grip the lad would bolt and be off. Only an absolute wilderness would suffice as the setting wherein the Lord might be prevailed upon to work his son's salvation.

2

Isaiah stood on the beach beside two crates of fowls and a bundle of fruit-tree cuttings and looked about him gloomily. It was as he thought. Joseph had brought them on a wild-goose chase. There was nothing here at all but a wilderness, no comforts, no civilisation, no human habitation even except for one stone house where the surveyor Davison occasionally stayed and a couple of deserted shacks, their roofs fallen in, wherein, no doubt, some escaped convicts or drunken seamen had indulged in their debaucheries. All around was nothing, nothing at all, unless you counted the sky, or the firth snaking away to the north-east, at whose head he now stood, or the extensive mud flats to right and left, or the open land behind, which looked discouragingly marshy and was covered with clumps of flax and clumps of tall toi-toi grass, all of which would have to be cleared before a single vegetable could be planted.

How he had ever permitted himself to be conveyed hither Isaiah could not imagine. It was all very fine for the young people. They had their health and strength. A day bent double tugging at a mass of fern root meant nothing to them. But at his time of life it was surely a different matter. He had a right to some consideration. It was the same old story. His own better nature had led him to give way to the pleadings of the others. Joseph had mooted this extraordinary notion of making for Otago to await the arrival of the New Edinburgh people, the young ones had as ever followed his lead, and he, Isaiah, had been dragged into it willy-nilly against his better judgement. If the Jamiesons had intended to stay on at Nelson he would not have allowed himself to be so lightly uprooted, particularly when his tomatoes promised so well, but he had received his notice from them and what choice had he in the matter?

Joseph was altogether too high-handed, too fond of getting his own way. But this time he had gone too far. Why, there was no certainty even that they would have a roof over their heads tonight. There seemed to have been very little progress made on the shelter Joseph had assured him they would be able to erect in no time. For his part, he could not see why they should not have remained in Koputai for a night or two. There, at least, were some vestiges of civilisation. He looked up at the sky. It was fine enough at the moment, he had to admit, but who was to say that another storm might not blow up during the night and drench them all and ruin their meagre supplies? If their sacks of flour and sugar were to be spoilt, their plight would be desperate indeed. Wet or fine, he was not in such rude health as to stand up to the rigours of a night in the open air and, anyway, there was Meg and her new baby to be thought of. The others might relish the pleasures of the outdoor life, but he felt that an exception on humanitarian grounds should be made for himself and the young mother. But it was all as he might have expected. Joseph's pride would come first, and he had all but forbidden any of the party to so much as mention Koputai, or the possibility of making their way to it along the tracks that doubtless ran thither through the bush.

A hundred yards away, Jessie straightened her back and looked at her chafed hands. She had already cut a good pile of raupo rushes. Uncle Joseph had pressed the knife into her hands and told her to be a good girl and bring him back a load of them if she wanted her wee nephew to sleep under cover on his first night of life. The thought of the baby, his softness and smallness, his tiny kittenish face and sweet warm smell gave Jessie fresh strength, and she bent to work again.

Swish! Swish! She had found a good rhythm of working now. The pile was growing satisfyingly high. She put the knife down, picked up a huge bundle of raupo rushes, and trotted over with it to the level place above high water mark which Uncle Joseph had chosen as the site for their temporary shelter. He was busy now hammering into the ground the first of the long poles which Jem had cut from a nearby tree. Malcolm, who had finished clearing the chosen area of its rough scrub and flax, took the rushes from Jessie's arms and began with his deft weaver's fingers to tie them into the bundles that would form the walls and roof.

Jessie waved at Meg, who was lying, protected from the sun and wind in a hollow, the baby beside her cradled in a nest fashioned from Malcolm's jacket, and saw in the distance, silhouetted against the brilliant blue water of the harbour, the bent figure of her father looking for shellfish along the tide line. Beyond him, the sails of the *Sarah Ann* were already rounding the first curve of the sound. They were now truly alone.

Jessie started back to her patch of rushes, but then stood still in astonishment. A back was bent over in the very place where she had been working, and another arm was wielding the knife.

'Hey!' Jessie covered the last few yards in a burst of running. The figure stood up. It was a Maori woman. She smiled at Jessie and wiped the perspiration from her forehead, but Jessie could not take her eyes from the long blade of the knife that glittered in the woman's hand. How had this woman come here? Were there other Maori hereabouts? She had supposed the area to be uninhabited. How many of them were there, and, most important of all, were they friendly? Accounts of the killings at the Wairau had impressed themselves upon Jessie's mind to lurid effect. She took a step back and looked round nervously, expecting at any moment to see a horde of warriors leaping upon them all, their clubs raised for the kill. How dreadful to have come through last night, to have suffered so much, only to be butchered and eaten this evening!

The memory of the storm brought the baby suddenly to Jessie's mind. The baby! She must at all costs warn the others! She took a step backwards, then turned to run but her foot caught on a stone. She tripped on her petticoat and went sprawling into the waist-high raupo.

Before she could scramble up again, the Maori woman was beside her.

'Eh! Eh! Not to hurt! Taking care!' she said in a gentle voice, and Jessie saw, with a gasp of relief, that she had dropped the knife. She sat up and looked into the face bending over hers. It was that of a young woman, no more than four- or five-and-twenty years old. Her soft brown skin was lightly tattooed on the lips, forehead and chin. Her luxuriant dark hair was drawn back from her forehead and knotted at the nape of the neck. She wore a simple gown in the European style, but her feet and head were bare. Jessie took in these details at a glance, but her gaze remained fixed on the girl's face, on her generous, friendly smile and the curious expression in the wide-open, innocent eyes.

'*Haere mai, e-te-pakeha*,' said the Maori girl.

'Hello,' said Jessie hesitantly.

The girl put a hand under Jessie's elbow and helped her to her feet.

'Moana,' she said and pointed to herself. 'My name.'

Jessie smiled, reassured. 'Jessie,' she said.

Moana pointed to the men working at their rude shelter, then at Jessie. 'You pakeha, come stay here?'

'Yes,' said Jessie, looking warily at Moana. She did not want to start any trouble. She had heard Uncle Joseph say that almost no Maori lived this far south, and that those who did had been paid fair and square for the land for the settlement, but there was no telling whether her new acquaintance had heard the same thing.

'You live here? Build house? Nice big church? Make farm?'

Jessie nodded.

Moana clapped her hands and bobbed her body forward joyfully. 'Good idea, mate,' she said. 'Lotta people coming soon, make new settlement. You come in nice and early, grab nice bit of land, like.'

Jessie nodded, taken aback with this eloquence.

Moana took her hand. 'You and me make friend. I show you nice things. Best oysters, damn good fern roots. Come!'

Jessie looked across at the working men, and at Meg's still, reclining form. Not for anything would she risk offending this strange, compelling person. On the other hand she felt reluctant to leave the proximity of her menfolk, or the urgent task in hand.

Moana followed her glance and quickly grasped Jessie's quandary.

'First we make whare for night time sleep, eh?' she said. 'Moana help you. My people he no come here this time today. He go hunt long way.' She waved in the vague direction of the hills that rolled away to the south. 'He catch two-three pig, sell you one maybe.'

She had bent to work again while she was still speaking. Jessie followed suit, and a few minutes later was leading her new friend across to the rising frame of their shelter, her arms laden with a bundle of rushes half the size of the other girl's.

Malcolm was the first to see them. He straightened up and spoke urgently to Joseph and Jem. To Jessie's mortification she saw Jem bend to pick up a mallet and hold it braced in his hand, ready for action. She ran ahead of Moana.

'No, Jem, can't you see? She's helping us!'

Jem's scowl remained fixed as he let his arm fall again. It was left to Joseph to welcome Jessie's new friend.

'Aye, well, good day to you now,' he said cheerfully, uncertain of how to address the girl.

'Good day to you now,' she mimicked, then put back her head and roared with laughter. Jessie looked at her admiringly. Moana was so confident and open, so friendly and easy.

'You make whare?' Moana said, addressing Joseph.

'Whare? Oh, aye, that's it, a shelter, where we can all rest tonight.'

'I help,' said Moana decisively. She took hold of Jessie's wrist. 'Jessie and me, we go fetch raupo. Make very nice roof. You like it.'

She ran off energetically. Jessie scampered after her.

'Watch out, Jessie! Don't go far!' Jem shouted after her. Jessie ignored him. It was so like cousin Jem to be sour and suspicious. What could she possibly fear from Moana? In the first glance they had exchanged she had known her for a friend.

The next bundle was cut and deftly tied with twined stalks before Moana spoke again.

'Where you coming from?'

'Nelson.'

'No, no. Where you coming from in old country? Bide-ford? Barnstaple?'

'What? Where's that?'

'Dev-on. Best bloody place on God's earth.'

'Oh!' Jessie was sure she should be more shocked. Uncle Joseph, she knew, would tolerate no swearing in his hearing. But somehow, coming from Moana, the words Jessie knew were thoroughly wicked had lost their sting. They carried an echo of sailors' talk but bereft of all malevolence. 'We're from Paisley,' she said. 'In Scotland.'

'Oh,' nodded Moana happily. 'You damned Jock.'

'Where did you learn English?' Jessie had at first spoken slowly and carefully, but she was discovering that she did not need to. Moana seemed able to keep up with anything.

'My man, pakeha sailor from Bideford. He jump ship Port Nicholson, five-six year ago. He whaler, good whaler, Otakou station. Kill big buggers, make good money.'

'Oh,' said Jessie faintly. 'Where is he now?'

To her consternation, Moana's face crumpled and tears spilled over and rolled down her cheeks.

'He die, too much grog,' she said. 'First my little boy with measles, after my little girl, then my man, he go to Heaven to live with the dear Lord Jesus.'

Jessie's brows, which had risen with compassion at the first part of this speech, rose still further at the second.

'Are you a Christian?' she asked.

'Oh, yes,' said Moana, smiling. 'I have accepted Lord Jesus, and he is my saviour and friend.' She squeezed Jessie's arm affectionately. 'Here, I show you,' and plunging a hand into a fold of her dress, where a pocket was concealed, she withdrew a small book, whose scuffed corners and thumbed pages bore witness to much reading.

' "The Gospel according to St John",' read Jessie, wonderingly. 'You can read and write?'

'Eh, eh, you bet,' nodded Moana vigorously. Bereft of speech, Jessie handed the book back. Moana wrapped it carefully in her handkerchief and tucked it away in her pocket.

'We pray together, read together sometime, you and me?' she said.

Jessie nodded, but before she had time to answer, Moana had hoisted her bundle over her shoulder and was trotting back to the slowly growing whare, while Jessie struggled to keep up with her.

In spite of their best efforts it was plain by late afternoon that their little shelter would not be ready for habitation that night. The framework was but half in place, and only one wall out of the four had any semblance of covering. The roof had barely been started. Jessie, looking anxiously up at the sky, was deeply grateful for the clear, unclouded blue, dimming to velvety purple at the eastern rim, promising a dry night.

Moana's enthusiasm for her new friends had grown when she had discovered Meg asleep in her hollow, the baby nestling in a crook of her arm. She had exclaimed; then, struck by an idea, she had tugged at Malcolm's sleeve. He had looked down at her disapprovingly and withdrawn his arm from her reach. He was a man of deep-rooted prejudice, and he did not hold with natives, still less with forward females. Impatiently, Jessie pushed him aside.

'What is it, Moana? You have an idea?'

'Come, Jessie,' said Moana nodding earnestly, 'I show you nice place, one-two night only, keep cold away from the little mother.' She set off swiftly along the beach, Jessie striving to keep up with her, and five minutes later had disclosed, behind a sandy bank, the upturned shell of an old whale boat, twenty feet long and four feet wide, too low to do more than sit under and badly holed at one end, but solid enough to give rudimentary cover from the night wind and the dew.

Jessie exclaimed with delight, then smiled warmly at her new friend. 'Thank you, Moana,' she said.

Moana did not bother to answer. She had scrambled under the whale boat and was flattening an area of sand.

'Now we make bed,' she laughed, and Jessie, seeing her collect armfuls of dry springy fern and twigs of the manuka shrub and lay them on the floor, followed her example.

'Tea-time!' said Moana suddenly, when the bed was made to her satisfaction, and while Jessie ran back over the sand to fetch her sister to her new lodging and introduce the rest of the family to Moana's ingenious arrangements for their comfort, the Maori girl was busy collecting firewood and arranging large flat stones on which to balance the billy can.

The evening meal was surprisingly good. Isaiah's efforts had been successful and a stew of pipis and cockles, made with water from the small river which ran across the sandy beach to pour itself into the waters of the sound, was accompanied by potatoes from the precious store baked in the ashes and a strong brew of tea. Moana helped in the preparations but when the time came to eat she laughingly declined. She had to go home, she declared, before night fell.

She did not say where her home was, and no one cared to ask her. On all except Jessie the idea of a nearby Maori settlement had cast a shadow of apprehension. An uneasy silence settled on the little party round the campfire when she had disappeared into the gathering dusk.

'I thought you said, brother,' began Isaiah, in the high-pitched complaining voice his nephews found so irritating, 'that the land here was empty. The natives all lived further north.'

'Aye, well, it seems I was mistaken,' said Joseph peaceably. He too found Isaiah a sad trial, worse even than he had anticipated before they left home. He had hoped then that Isobel would be there, his tactful, humorous ally, ever able to share a burden and enjoy a joke, and he missed her more as the days went by. Brother Isaiah was a heavy burden, but shoulder it he must, he knew no other way. Unlike Malcolm and Jem, who relieved their feelings with mutterings and disrespectful grimaces, Joseph had turned to prayer, and by dint of dwelling on his own impatience and seeking divine help in overcoming it, he had achieved a degree of forbearance which in Jessie's view was positively saintly.

'Mr Masterson told me there were a good few natives here at one time,' said Jem, spitting out a piece of grit which had slipped accidentally into his tin dish.

'What did you say, boy? Who said it?' said Isaiah impatiently. He could not understand why young people mumbled so indistinctly nowadays. It was a form of rudeness he could well do without. Meg had had the temerity to insinuate that his own ears were to blame, that he was growing deaf. It was nonsense, of course.

'Masterson,' said Jem, enunciating the word with almost offensive clarity. 'There's been a lot of sickness that's carried off all the bairns.' He saw Meg's arms tighten on the bundle within them, and laughed. 'Oh, it was only the influenza and the measles and such like. They're a weak race, not hardy like us Scots.' He spat out another stone. Jessie, remembering how hard Moana had worked to help them build their shelter, felt her fists tighten round her bowl.

'They're dying out, Masterson thinks,' Jem went on carelessly. 'We'll not be put to the trouble of helping them on their way. There's many fewer than there were. Did you not see the old potato plantings near the heads as we came down the sound? Abandoned these many years.'

'I thought they were natural clearings,' said Jessie. Her throat was taut with anger at Jem and pity for Moana. Her feelings had undergone a change. She had been afraid of the Maori at Nelson, sure they were all her enemies, ready to murder her at the slightest provocation. Cousin Jem had explained to her how untrustworthy they were, how they agreed to sell land one moment and claimed it back the next, how they lied and stole and were altogether inferior to the white races. Now she felt confused. The first Maori she had spoken to properly did not fit Jem's picture at all.

Jem was laughing. 'You thought we'd be quite alone,' he said. 'Pioneers in the wilderness. You needn't worry yourself, cousin, we'll be lonely right enough. There's no people of our kind for miles and miles around. But there's not so many savages but we can fight them off if we have to. I have my own gun and I can use it. I'll not make meat for a cannibal's oven!'

Joseph shook his head. 'There's no call for such talk,' he said. 'The natives have done us no harm, lad, and it's my belief the stories you heard in all they Nelson public houses' – Jem scowled in response to the reproof in his father's voice – 'were mightily overdone. The Maori are a fine people, so the mission folk say, and yon wee girl we met today is friendly enough. She's given freely of her help with nothing asked for in return.'

'Spying out our weakness, I shouldn't be surprised,' said Jem, sourly.

'I don't believe so,' said Joseph. 'There's been missionary work these many years even further south than this, and I would not be altogether surprised if the lassie and her kin had heard the Gospel, and turned their backs on violence and sin.'

'Oh, she has, Uncle, she has!' said Jessie eagerly. 'She showed me a gospel of St John she carries about with her. Only think, she has learned to read and write! And she says we might pray together sometimes.'

Jessie stopped, embarrassed. She did not easily share her private communings with God. She shied away from the glib exchanges of hackneyed phrases that so often constituted the prayer meetings she had attended. Prayer for her was a wayward thing, sometimes a flailing of her mind against an empty silence, sometimes a wild flight of the soul into dizzying realms of space and time.

Joseph's face lit up. 'That's grand, lassie, just grand,' he said, and stretched out a hand contentedly towards the fire from which a spurt of flame had shot up, illuminating the outline of Meg and her baby, who were lying comfortably inside the tilted whale boat on the soft bed that Moana had fashioned for them as if it was the most pleasant lodging in the world.

'Just think, will you now,' said Joseph, sweeping an arm round in a gesture that embraced the beach, whose whiteness was fading now in the balmy air of a summer dusk, the flat land covered with fern beyond it, the hills crested with forest, and the rocking waters of the sea. 'Just think how all this will appear in a year or two. There'll be a bonny kirk in pride of place, I make no doubt, and a school for yon bairn, Meggie, and streets and proper built houses, too, I'm sure.'

'Oh, yes, Uncle,' breathed Jessie, her imagination fired, 'and ships coming up the firth and tying up here maybe, at a wharf or something of the kind, and there'll be horses and carriages and proper pavements with cobblestones, and do you think we'll ever see the gas lighting in New Edinburgh, Uncle?'

'No doubt, my dear,' he said, smiling at her.

'And elegant warehouses for bonnets and gowns?'

He shook his head reprovingly. 'Not too elegant, I hope.'

'And a library of books?'

'For sure.'

'And a – maybe a park even, with flowers where people can promenade on fine evenings and children can roll their hoops?'

'It could be.'

'And a hotel?'

'Not if it serves strong drink, girlie. I would not hope for that.'

'But a post office, Uncle, where we might receive letters from – people?'

'That, surely.'

Jessie fell silent. The idea that she might one day, when the empty land behind her had been transformed into a bustling town, hope to receive a letter bringing news of Edward, perhaps even from Edward himself, would sustain her through many long days and nights to come. Joseph, too, said no more. He was remembering with a pang the gaunt child who had stood not many years ago in the circle of his arms, dreaming with passionate intensity of piglets and calves and spiders' webs.

I'll make sure she's never unhappy again, he said to himself, as if in promise to his dead sister. Then, stiff with the exertions of the day, he rose to his feet.

'Let's to bed, all of us, in our fine new abode,' he said cheerfully. 'My, but it's grand. Why, on the *Speedy*, we'd have thought this a royal palace, so we would. You girls can take this end of the boat and the men will go to the other. I'll stay here a while longer by the fire. The Lord has sent us clear weather in his goodness. It'll not rain the night. There's no danger to be feared, of that I'm sure, but I'll wait up a while to watch, just to be doubly sure. And now, before you go to your rest, shall we not thank the Lord for bringing us safe to our new home this day?'

3 *Dunedin, September 1845*

'Hush-a-ba birdie, croon, croon,' sang Meg contentedly, as she tucked a square of blanket round little Robert's shoulders and gave a push to the makeshift rockers on his cradle. He was a good boy. He'd stop his cry in no time and be off to sleep, and then she could get on with her work.

The baby found his thumb, stuck it into his mouth, and began to make the rhythmic sucking noises that always preceded sleep. Meg smiled and looked about the cottage. There was so much to do, she thought happily, and if she was quick she would get through her everyday tasks and have time to cut down her old petticoat into a new cover for the home-made chair that stood by the fire.

She had not foreseen the happiness that housewifery had brought her. All her life until now she had been at the beck and call of others, but now she was queen of her own domain, and was ruled over only by the little tyrant who was fast subsiding into a snuffly milky sleep. Her cottage, she thought smugly, might not be Holyrood Palace, but it was just as fine and handy as the Jamiesons' house at Duddingston. The Kirkwood men had started work on a permanent dwelling a week or so after they had landed at the turn of the year, and their experience in Nelson had stood them in good stead. Stout timber poles formed the framework of the walls, and Meg herself had helped to weave supplejack vines between them and cover the whole with clay. The neat frontage had two good windows, covered over with sacking, and at one end there was a solid chimney, built of sods and lined with clay. Though there was little extra space in the main room when they were all crowded round the table for their meals, it was fine at night when the men (except for Malcolm, of course), returned to sleep in the original fern whare, that still stood alongside and had weathered well the storms of winter.

Meg lifted the rush matting that she had herself woven and laid on the earth floor, reflecting complacently as she did so how much better a housewife she was than Mrs Jamieson, who, for all her grand ways, could never have contrived such a neat arrangement of rushes, laid down and laced tightly to form cushions on the wooden benches which Malcolm had made from branches, set into the floor on both sides of the table.

She shook her mats out, swept the floor, laid them down again and turned her mind to cooking. A bucket of fresh eels, brought home by Uncle Joseph this morning from his traps in the shallow waters of the harbour, stood outside the door and she had planned a stew of them for dinner. She would need to fetch kindling from the pile behind the cottage, which Jessie had promised to replenish. She opened the door and stepped out on to the stones which were laid about the entrance. Mud was her constant enemy, a sticky, pervasive mud that threatened all her efforts at maintaining a decent cleanliness. She nagged endlessly at the menfolk to wipe their feet and, to pacify her, Malcolm had at last paved the immediate area outside the cottage with large pebbles he had carried up from the shore, thus adding an even more permanent aspect to the cottage. Uncle Joseph might forever be reminding them that they were only squatters here, and that when the New Edinburgh settlement ('Dunedin' they now called it) arrived, they would be obliged to hand their land over and start afresh, but she could not believe that anyone would have the heart to take from her and tear down a home so carefully tended.

She rounded the back wall of the cottage and tutted with exasperation. Jessie had not fulfilled her promise. Only a few twigs lay scattered on the ground. Now she herself would have to fetch what she needed and her morning's routine would be upset. She listened for a moment, but no sound came from the baby, so she set off along the path that nine months of constant use had beaten to a hard track. A clump of manuka bushes nearby would provide enough kindling for today. It would not take her long to gather a good armful. But that was still no excuse for Jessie.

Meg pursed her lips. There was no denying that Jessie was difficult. Meg could not understand her at all. She seemed to take no pleasure in the things that delighted her sister's domestic heart. She would, if pressed, bake a batch of bread or patch a shirt or fetch a pail of water from the creek, but ten to one she would mistake the quantity of yeast, or accidentally stitch two sides of a sleeve together, or slop water into the fire. Then, too, her appearance had become so wild. She herself, thought Meg with pride, managed even in this wilderness to keep her mousy locks neat and her aprons perfectly laundered, but Jessie looked a positive fright. Barefoot, brown-faced, scratched and never without a rent in her skirt or a tangle in her hair, she would run off as soon as her sister grudgingly freed her from household chores, and would spend whole afternoons out of sight away from home, sometimes with that strange Maori creature, but more often than not alone.

She had been 'in the bush', she always said, and would give no further details, but Meg had come upon her once, kneeling at a boulder which she used as a makeshift table, writing in a book which she had snatched up to her chest and refused to let Meg see. Sometimes, it was true, she would bring back a poke full of fuchsia berries or a handful of rock oysters as a peace offering, but nine times out of ten she would appear with nothing in her hands and no excuse to offer and slip silently into her place at the table, looking no better than a fishwife.

When Meg tried to reason with her, tried to make her stay at home and complained that she did not help enough with the housework, Jessie would be contrite for a day or two and work with a rush of energy at every task set her, tripping over the baby, upsetting the flour bin and salting the soup twice over, until Meg was secretly glad when the fit of penance was over and she stole off again to the bush.

Meg tried to talk it over with Malcolm.

'She's so restless,' she said in puzzlement, 'so – so unlike a girl.'

'She'll settle,' was all Malcolm said. He did not hold with flights of fancy and had never attempted to understand his sister-in-law. 'She should wed soon. There's Jem and she should wed, and build their own house. They'd make a pair, they would indeed, forever off on some start or other, same as gypsy folk.'

Uncle Joseph was of no more help than Malcolm. He seemed to be blind and deaf to any faults in Jessie at all. 'Let her be young and enjoy the glories of God's creation,' was all he would say, and as long as Jessie attended family prayers, to which Moana often also came, and remained quietly at home on the Sabbath, he saw no cause to reprove her.

As for Pa, it was years since Meg had thought to consult him on any subject of moment. In any case, he cared for nothing now but his vegetable patch. Each morning he set off to the half acre that Jem and Malcolm had cleared of fern and toi-toi by strenuously hefting out the matted roots with pickaxes. Instead of talking to his daughter, Meg thought resentfully, he preferred to pass the time of day with a funny little fantail bird that would wait for him to appear and hop along the path after him, the bright fan of its tailfeathers bobbing up and down as it snapped its beak at insects. Pa seemed to consider his rows of bean shoots of more consequence than the behaviour of his daughter.

'Don't fuss me with your talk about torn garments and the like,' was all he would say. 'If you knew what a worry it was, keeping your pot stocked with fresh things – but women are aye the same. They've no mind to weighty matters. Even your mother . . .'

Meg, who never listened past this point, had nevertheless to admit that, after only nine months and most of them winter months at that, Pa's garden was a credit to him. His hoard of gooseberry, currant and raspberry cuttings, and his grafted stocks of apple and pear had mostly taken in the untried earth, and now that spring was on its way a vigorous budding testified to their strength. Neat furrows showed where his treasured stock of seeds had been hopefully committed to the soil, and he was at present working to construct a fence around the plot, stout enough to discourage the tramplings of wild pigs.

Meg added several dry sticks to her bundle and hurried back to the cottage. She did not like to leave Robert for more than a few moments at a time, though what danger she feared for him she could not say. A little way from the door she heard him whimper, then there was an ominous silence, followed by an outraged scream from his fully extended lungs. Meg dropped her sticks on the path and ran inside.

Malcolm, working at repairing the old whale boat that had sheltered them on their first night in Otago, heard Meg's shriek from a quarter of a mile along the beach. He dropped his hammer and ran, his heart racing, afraid of fire, afraid of the Maori, afraid of he knew not what. Stumbling over mounds of tussocky grass and dodging spiky clumps of flax, he arrived panting and pulled open the door. His wife was standing by the cradle, a wooden spoon in her hand, beating it hysterically about the floor. The combined yells of mother and baby were deafening. Neither of them noticed him.

'Hold your whist!' he shouted at the top of his voice, then reeled backward as Meg flung herself sobbing into his arms.

'Rats!' she shrieked. 'Half a dozen of them, at least! All over Baby! On his face! For sure they've bit him to death!'

Malcolm disengaged himself and strode across to the cradle. He picked up his son and examined him anxiously from every angle. Young Robert stopped crying and waved his little fists at his father. Malcolm found his own arms were shaking and he passed the bundle back to Meg.

'He's come to no hurt,' he said gruffly, covering his relief with a show of irritation, 'unless you've deafened him with your squawking. But mind him well, Meggie. The rats will be a plague till Jem comes home with the dogs. I didn't tell you, but they were awful bad this night past. One ran across my feet, and I was afraid another would tangle in your hair till I shooed it off. We've not felt them bad till now, as the smell of the dogs has kept them away.'

Meg's anxiety had turned to anger. 'It's always the same,' she said, and Malcolm, watching uneasily the red blotches on her face and neck that signalled rising emotion, suppressed the idea that she took a little too much after her father. 'Always after his own pleasure, as bad as Jessie. We have no need of pork meat just now, and why he must be off hunting, or exploring, or whatever, for three whole days on end when there's enough to be done here, leaving us unprotected, never thinking . . .'

'Oh, aye, well,' said Malcolm, backing away to the door. 'We'll be glad of a bite or two of fresh meat when it comes and some hams to salt. Mind you hang them up well to the rafters when you get it, for the rats are here to stay. At least, they'll be a plague till we get one of Bess's next litter and train it for a ratter.'

He made his way back along the beach but the upset had started him off worrying again. Always naturally anxious, the birth of his son had added to his sense of care. He would not share in Meg's litany of complaints, but it was true enough that Jem was ripe for some mischief or other. It was pig hunting he claimed to be after, but Malcolm would not be astonished to learn that the direction it had taken was up the overgrown bush-track to Koputai and that the pigs in question came in green glass bottles or were clad in petticoats. For all that Otago seemed to be so deserted, the scaff and raff of the maritime world drifted occasionally this far south, and when an undesirable former whaler, or a Botany Bay convict, or a runaway sailor made his appearance, Jem was drawn to him like a moth to a candle-flame. Vicious they were, for the most part, Malcolm was sure. He could not see the attraction for his moody, difficult brother. He had tried once, with great diffidence, to ask Jem what he saw in some foul mouthed old peg-leg.

'You wouldn't understand, Mr High-and-Mighty,' Jem had said defensively, then he had muttered under his breath, 'At least a man may breathe free and not be forever taken to task, like in some folks' company.'

To be fair, it was not as if Jem had sunk to their level, thought Malcolm, considering his brother's career of sin. He might drink whenever he found the chance, though he did not unnaturally crave the stimulus of alcohol, and he might take a woman if she was sure to be free of disease, but he would not follow one that scorned him as far as the next street corner. And there was no denying he had a heart in him somewhere. Malcolm had, with his own eyes, seen Jem belabour a loutish sailor who had tied half a dozen penguins with lengths of flax to pieces of timber and had stood doubled up with laughter at the antics of the poor creatures, who, trying to dive for fish, were continually dragged up to the surface again. Jem had left the man dazed and bloody and had walked into the sea up to his waist to free the birds at the risk of savage pecks to his own hands.

Malcolm settled back to his task. The whale boat, under which they had spent their first night three seasons since, had been patched up by Jem, but much use up and down the harbour, many scrapings on mud flats and stone-strewn beaches had caused further damage to the hull, and Malcolm had set himself the task of making it sound again caulking the gaping seams and strengthening the timbers that held the long, narrow frame together.

He was engaged in cutting short lengths of wire to use as nails when he heard a 'Coo-ee!' and looking up, saw his father coming back from his morning's work of clearing a stand of bush ready for a crop of potatoes.

Malcolm's first quick glance turned to a stare. Behind his father walked Jessie. Her habitually withdrawn expression had given way to smiles and laughter. She was holding something in her arms, something pink, something small, something that wriggled. Wild ideas surged through Malcolm's head. It could not be true! It would have been impossible for her to . . . He must have noticed something! Meg would have informed him! Then, as she came nearer, the bundle emitted an indignant howl, and Malcolm laughed aloud. A piglet! She was carrying a piglet! He put down his tools and stood up, then saw his brother not far behind, dragging after him a fat sow. It had been a pig hunt, after all.

When Meg, herself responding to the distant coo-ee, looked out from her cottage door and saw her family approaching from way across the flat, she did not at first know whether to laugh out loud or cry with vexation. Never could there have been such a strange procession. First came Uncle Joseph with a massive bundle of firewood on his shoulder. Then came Jem and Malcolm, both splashed with gore, each one holding the fore-trotter of the pig, which they dragged along the ground behind them. Tam and Bess, following on, licked at the trail of blood that still oozed from the wound in the sow's side, while last of all came Jessie, tattered and dirty, bending her head over a preposterous snout above which a pair of small, cunning eyes peered out from the encircling arms.

Jessie ran forward, overtaking the others, to show off her new possession to Meg.

'Is he not beautiful? He's mine. He's to be named Denis,' she said all in one breath, and Meg, who had opened her mouth to ban the piglet's entry into her unsullied domain, shut it again at the sight of the pleasure she saw in her sister's face.

4

November 1845

Jessie was alone in the bush. She had slipped away early in the day, full of longing for she knew not what. She had felt remote from every member of her family, except perhaps for Uncle Joseph and the baby. But this morning Uncle Joseph had chided her for her sullen looks, and little Robert had pouted when she had tried to wash his sticky face. Even Denis, who usually came on bustling trotters to her whistle, had run off on some porcine ploy of his own. Jessie had not bothered to look far for him, but had set off on her own before Meg could call her back to perform some tiresome chore.

She leant against the vast trunk of an age-old totara tree, stared up its sides to the top hamper of forest creepers, ferns and orchids that trailed from its highest branches, and breathed in draughts of scent from some unseen flower. She looked up to see where the heady smell came from. It was so strong it made her dizzy. The few splinters of light that penetrated the mass of vegetation above held her eyes hypnotically so that she could hardly tear them away. Whether through fear or some other cause her pulse began to beat faster. Blood pounded in her head and she heard a jangle of notes and far-off voices. The light danced, tantalising, inviting, beckoning her into unknown regions.

A sneeze followed by three fluting notes sounded close by as a bird swooped low over Jessie's head. It dragged her eyes down from the bewitching light and gratefully they followed it. But there was something strange about the bird. It was a tui by its song, by its shape and by the white tuft at its throat, yet instead of the tui's black plumage, this bird had white feathers on its head and back. It landed a yard or two from Jessie and preened itself, then with a squawk it flew to a shrub a few yards further away and turned its head to look unwinkingly at her. Jessie took a step towards it. The bird almost seemed to nod, and hopped another yard or two on to a swinging rata vine. Jessie's will seemed to ebb out of her. The bird, which moments earlier had released her from the spell of the fractured light, seemed to be luring her into another kind of enchantment. Nothing seemed real, except for its still black eye. It stared at her for a long moment and under its power she felt hysteria rise. She would fall into the depths of that horrible, deep eye! She would cross a threshold and never return!

Something disturbed the tui. It cackled, slipped off its perch and flew off. Jessie looked round wildly. Though the bird had frightened and repelled her, she wanted it more than anything else. She was frantic to see it again.

'Come back!' she called. 'Oh, don't leave me here alone! I don't understand! I don't understand anything!'

Blindly she crashed after it, stumbling over the massive roots that boiled around the feet of the vast bush trees, unaware of the fronds and twigs that tore at her clothes, listening for the tui's mocking voice and watching for the flash of its pale feathers. She must not lose it! At all costs, she must not let it go! And then her foot slipped on the slimy mess of a rotten branch and she fell.

The bird had dived low across a small pool in a creek and Jessie's fall had brought her within inches of it. As she tried to struggle back to her feet, she looked down into the water and saw herself reflected in it. She gasped with surprise. It had been more than a year since she had looked at her own face in a mirror. Could this wild-eyed, tousle-haired, mad-looking creature really be herself, Jessie Dunbar? She put a hand to straighten her hair, but it was matted and tangled, and she could not smooth it. A shiver ran through Jessie's body from the crown of her head to her bruised feet. It was as if she had woken from a long sleep. She had been travelling down the road to madness. She had been pulled back from the brink of a pit.

A snort from behind startled her. She looked round in time to see Denis crashing towards her through a clump of ferns. The little pig looked so busy and self-satisfied, so cheerful and common-sensical that Jessie laughed and picked him up. He flapped his ears and wriggled and she set him down again. He stood square on his four thin legs and seemed to smile at her, as if he was expecting a delightful snack to be set before him.

Jessie stood up. She felt giddy. In the last few moments everything had changed. The depression of the past months seemed to fall away from her like a bad dream. Follies and fancies, melancholy and madness seemed, like the white tui, to have flitted away into the immense green depths of the bush. Reality, personified by Denis, was all at once attractive.

'I must go home,' she said aloud. 'Come on, Denis.'

The pig took a few steps backwards, then stopped and looked questioningly at her. Jessie, looking round with the clear eyes of reason, saw that she was lost.

'No,' she whispered, and the dream that had flown away seemed to draw back to her again, the dark trunks to look threatening, the rustling of the leaves to contain sinister secrets, the birdsong to be full of menace. 'No, no!'

As if in answer she heard some way off a familiar voice, singing.

'Moana!' she shrieked, and blundered towards the sound, scrambling through boggy patches and thickets alike to the further detriment of her already ruined clothes.

'Jessie! Eh? Here!' called Moana in response, and in a minute Jessie was in her friend's arms, sobbing out, 'Oh, thank God you are here! Oh, I was so afraid!'

For a moment or two, Moana let her cry, then she held Jessie away from her and looked into her face.

'Where you been, Jessie?' she said, her face full of concern. 'You see something bad, eh?'

Jessie's grip on her friend's arm did not loosen. 'I felt so strange here, as if – as if the bush was bad. I don't know – I never felt such a thing before.' She spoke hesitantly, as if afraid of a rebuff, but to her relief Moana nodded seriously, with understanding. 'I felt as if – I knew there were things, voices, magic—' She stopped.

Moana gave her a little shake. 'The bush,' she said, 'it – alive.' She paused, feeling for the words. 'You pakeha people, you do not understand. The bush you must – respect.'

'I saw a bird,' Jessie rushed on, hardly listening to her. 'A tui, it sounded like. But the colour was wrong.'

Moana's arm stiffened. 'This tui, no black colour?'

'No, it was pale. White, almost.'

Moana drew in a sharp breath and grasped Jessie's wrist. She pushed the other girl in front of her, and then, seeing that Jessie did not know which way to go, passed her. 'Follow, quick,' she said.

Jessie turned to make sure that Denis, who had been rooting among the enticing debris of a fallen tree, was following and ran after Moana, who was darting along what Jessie perceived to be an old overgrown track so fast that Jessie could hardly keep pace with her.

Moana did not stop until they emerged from the cover of the bush on to the shore and were standing on a strip of sand that the tide had left bare between two rocky headlands, well away from the trees.

'Listen, Jessie,' she said, and Jessie was struck with her friend's unaccustomed seriousness. 'You been in danger. You been sick this last time. I see. I watch you. I know. You go alone too much, mate. In the bush too much. There are – some things – forbidden. Tapu. You pakeha, you not knowing all what is good, not seeing all what is bad. Go in forbidden place. White tui, he very full of danger. Make you mad dead maybe even.' She shuddered, and looked fearfully over her shoulder towards the trees, which to Jessie's newly sensitive eyes seemed almost to be leaning forward to listen to her words. 'You touch him? Hurt him, eh?'

'No, oh, no,' Jessie shook her head. 'I just felt a kind of – like a madness. I wanted to follow and follow. I heard things, voices perhaps – and then it flew away and I saw myself in the water, and I knew I had changed. Oh, Moana! I look so bad! So wild and strange!'

Moana laughed. 'It is well now,' she said. 'I see you a little sick before, but now you all right. Our Lord and Saviour, he protect you in there, from evil ones.' She turned Jessie round and pointed to the cottage which, a mile or so away, could be seen across the intervening stretch of harbour water. For the first time Jessie looked at it with affection. Today it represented not a prison but a safe haven. A curl of woodsmoke rose from the chimney promising supper. A line of washing, looking no larger than tiny flags from this distance, flapped from a string of flax that Malcolm had rigged up beside the house. Young Robert's clothes were hanging up to dry. She could even make out a distant form that must be Pa, toiling in the vegetable patch.

'You do got to go home, Jessie, eh?' said Moana gently. 'You a woman soon, not a little girl now. Your sister, she need you help. Look after baby, do some cooking, eh? You lonely. Got to see people more. Big boats full of pakeha coming soon, maybe. Build a nice big town here. Friends for you, a husband, maybe. One day be all right, eh?'

Jessie nodded. 'You're lonely too, Moana,' she said. 'Why do you stay alone in your old whaler's hut? Why don't you go home to your people too?'

Moana's broad face split into a grin. 'You clever, Jessie. I tell you, now you tell me. Maybe one day I go. But I like my house, even I am lonely.' The grin disappeared. 'It was not always like this. Old whalers, good people. Do a lot of work, make sing-song, kind to the little ones, clever to read. Good whalers go, all the bad ones left behind, no good for anything but drinking, drinking. I remember too much the good time, my little ones, my man. I see, I remember . . .'

Jessie put her arm round Moana's shoulder and squeezed it.

Moana's pearly white teeth reappeared between her full soft lips as she smiled in response. 'You happy again now, eh? Go home now.' She measured the distance to the little cottage with her eyes. 'How you go?'

'Along the shore,' said Jessie with a shiver. 'I'm not going back into the bush for a while. Not into this part, anyway.' She stared at Moana as a new thought struck her. 'You saved me,' she said. 'I was lost. I might have been in the bush for ever and gone mad and wandered in circles, hungry, like I've heard happens to people sometimes. You've saved my life, Moana.'

Moana shrugged the idea aside.

'Go home,' she said again. 'But you mind yourself now. Keep a good watch out. I see whale boat, two-three hour ago, coming down this a-way. That one-eyed Gabriel, he coming up here. Up to no good, him. He catch you all alone give you big trouble. Meanest old bastard I never did see.'

Jessie nodded and watched Moana disappear back into the bush. She had long ago learned to disregard her friend's warnings of bad men, runaways, no-goods and the like, who were forever, so Moana warned, creeping about in the bush near the site of the new town, waiting to thieve or beg or do something even worse. She called to Denis, but he had long since trotted off for home. She looked along the shore-line. It would be hard going that way. There was more mud than sand and stepping stones were few and far between. She would have to make haste before the tide came in.

She sat down on a boulder and untied her laces. Her shoes had begun to pinch her badly. Her feet had grown amazingly these last two years, and over-large as these shoes had been when Fanny had bought them for her in Nelson, they were too small now. She would not have bothered to wear them today were it not for the roughness of the bush floor. But here, along the beach, she could as well carry them in her hand and go barefoot.

There was the sound of footsteps behind her. She turned.

'Jem? Malcolm?' she began to say, but the words died on her lips. A stranger was coming towards her, a thin, unkempt man. He was barefoot. He wore trousers that ended in tatters below his knees and a grey shirt rent at the shoulders. His hair was long and wild and his red face had the slackness of the drinker. A scar ran diagonally across his cheek and up to his forehead, across the place where his left eye should have been.

Jessie stood up and stepped backwards. Her heart was beating uncomfortably fast. This must be the no-good man Moana had warned her about! What was his name again? Gabriel! What was it that Moana has said? Her mind was blank. She could remember nothing. Why was this man looking at her so strangely? What could he want from her?

The man had come up to her now. He was standing too close. Jessie could smell the liquor on his breath.

'Well, well, a wench begad, and all alone too,' he said in an unsteady, rasping voice, leering at Jessie with his one good eye.

'I can't stop now,' said Jessie breathlessly. 'My – father and my brother and my cousin – they're all waiting for me.'

Gabriel hesitated and looked across to the distant cottage.

'Fathers and brothers, is it? Well, they're far enough off just now and they'll have to wait a little longer, won't they, my pretty, because you've got a little business first with Gabriel, who never lets a bird as sweet as this one flutter out of his hands without he plucks a feather!'

The man's dirty arm was suddenly round Jessie's waist. She could smell the filth of his body and the stink of fermented cabbage tree root on his breath, and underneath it a half-remembered stench of sweat and fresh blood in a close weaver's shop. She whipped her head away from his as a greasy lock of his hair fell against her cheek.

'A kiss, now,' muttered Gabriel, whose one eye, which moments before had been vacant, was now hot with purpose. A tide of revulsion swept through Jessie. With a burst of energy she freed herself from his clawing hands and began to race, shoes forgotten, along the beach. A curse burst out behind her, she heard him give chase, she felt him gaining on her, knew she would feel his loathsome hand again at any moment. The moment came. He caught her, he held her. He was feeling her, pawing at her, ripping her clothes. A scream rose in Jessie's throat, and another.

'No! No! Help me! Help!'

The man's mouth was on hers now, his strength was forcing her back and down, on to the ground. Twist as she might, she was helpless, her arms pinned to her sides. She felt her knees buckle and give, she was falling with the creature on top of her. She drew all her strength for one last effort.

'Moana!' she screamed. Then, unknowingly, 'Edward!'

A second later the body on top of her jerked as the man was struck a mighty blow. He rolled off, unconscious. Above her, his face contorted with rage, stood Jem.

'Jessie! What is this? What are you doing?'

Jessie gave a shuddering gasp of relief.

'Jem! Oh, thank God! How came you to be here? Oh you have saved me from – from this . . .'

'Get up,' said Jem roughly. 'Cover yourself.'

Jessie looked down and blushed furiously. The brute had ripped her dress. It hung loose, away from her bosom. Good heavens! What must her cousin think!

'He came at me, he pulled me about,' she said, with what little dignity she could muster. 'I tried to save myself.'

'I saw you,' said Jem, and Jessie could see now that he had been running and was still short of breath. 'I warned you. I told you yon Maori wench of yours would lead you into trouble one day. Malcolm spied the boat on his way to cut wood. He told me this fellow was lurking around here. I came to see that you were safe. By God, I was nearly too late.'

He fell silent, but Jessie, herself trembling with shock, hardly noticed how his own arm was quivering under her hand.

'You called out, you called a name,' he said at last.

Jessie hardly heard him. She was staring down with disgust at the inert form of Gabriel who lay on the sand in a heap, his eye closed.

'He's dead,' she said.

'Not he.' Jem kicked the man brutally in the ribs. The body flinched, and a groan erupted from the slack lips. Revolted, Jessie turned away.

'That'll teach you,' muttered Jem savagely, and he raised his foot to kick the man again. Jessie tugged at his arm.

'Don't, Jem, please,' she said. 'Take me home, oh please, just take me away, now.'

For a long moment, Jem stood looking down at her.

'You called a name,' he said. 'You called out someone's name!'

'Did I? I don't remember,' said Jessie, shuddering. 'Come on Jem, please, before he wakes. I cannot bear him to look at me again.'

'You called his name,' repeated Jem, stubbornly. 'You called for Edward.'

Jessie dropped her eyes and turned her head away. 'How can you talk such nonsense?' she said. 'How can I have done?'

'You called out for Edward,' said Jem. He grasped her arms above the elbows and shook her, forcing her to look at him. 'You love him, don't you?'

Jessie tried to tear herself away, but could not.

'Yes,' she whispered at last.

'No!' the word seemed to be wrenched out of Jem. 'You were meant for me! You've always been meant for me! You're mine, not his! I'll not let him take you too! I've been waiting, I've not said a word, I wouldn't speak till you were a woman grown, but now this beast has shown me you're a woman right enough, and you must listen to me! Listen to me!'

He had loosened his grip and Jessie, unable to bear any more, backed away from him, and was walking, almost running, towards home, but she could not stop Jem from speaking. He was beside her, his pace matching hers, his strength threatening her, his torrential speech overwhelming her. Usually so silent, she had never heard him say so much before.

'Jessie, listen, for heaven's sake. Don't you know what you've been doing to me, this past year or more? Don't you know why I've stayed here in this wilderness, when I could have got work as a shepherd any time in the north? I've watched you every day, I've watched you all the time, when you thought I wasn't there, when you were out in the bush looking for birds' nests . . .'

Jessie turned towards him, shocked.

'You've been following me? Secretly? Without telling me?'

'For your own sake! To keep you from harm! How would you have got on today if I had not been near at hand?'

She shuddered again.

'I love you, Jessie, don't you see that? I want to wed you, live with you like Malcolm and Meg, have our own wee house, bairns . . .'

Jessie quickened her pace. The pleading in Jem's voice frightened her almost more than the anger had done. Infuriated, Jem grasped her shoulder and twirled her round, catching her in his arms. She was trembling again with pity and shame as well as fear.

'Don't, oh, Jem, please . . .'

He had never before seen so much of her body, the swell of her firm young breasts, which she was trying now ineffectually to hide with one shaking hand. He had never before seen her vulnerable, at his mercy. His longing for her, for love, overcame him. Hardly aware of what he was about, he crushed her to him, and pressed his lips into her hair.

Jessie's rage shocked them both. She fought him like a cat, scratching, spitting, biting. Wounded, he dropped his arms and stepped back, but she was beside herself with fury.

'I hate you! You're hateful! You're cruel and ignorant and mean! I never want to see you again as long as I live! Do you hear me? Never!'

She turned, picked up her skirts and ran, choked with sobs, her hair flying wildly behind her, her shoes left forgotten in the mud, and Jem looked after her, his face pale, his fists clenched.

'I'll kill you, Edward Jamieson. You've stolen what was rightfully mine.'

He heard a groan behind him. Gabriel was staggering to his feet. With an oath Jem rushed at him, caught him a crashing blow on the jaw, and sent him reeling back into unconsciousness.

Chapter Sixteen

Wellington, January 1846

1

Miss Honoria Gibson was particularly pleased with herself this morning. Her dear kind mama had excused her from her usual early morning duties, and had allowed her to sleep late. She stretched herself like a satisfied kitten and smiled. She was sure to be the prettiest girl of all at the picnic. The chameleon silk, bought not six months ago in London, was far in advance of the colonial mode. Mama would frown, she knew, for clothes seemed to tear to shreds as soon as one looked at them in this wild country, but Honoria did not care what anyone said. She would not, this once, fit herself out in drab, serviceable garments such as the other ladies would be wearing. It would be the chameleon silk today, no matter how many hours of squinting in the lamplight it would take to mend the tears. It was the prettiest of all her gowns and she would break hearts in it.

Honoria flung open the sash window of her bedroom, and leant out to enjoy the perfumed air of a glorious January morning. It was only two months since Aunt Taylor had brought her out to join her parents, and she was still not used to the heady smell of the jasmine growing up the posts of the verandah that ran right along the sunny north and west walls of the wooden house her father had recently built. The place had seemed queer to her at first after the roomy old Queen Anne house at Stanton Parva in Dorset. She had been quite shocked, in fact, when she had first set eyes on it. It was so small, so queer, like a poor rectory or farmhouse, with only five or six bedrooms upstairs and a drawing room hardly bigger than the breakfast room at home. Her father, too, in his fustian coat and plain boots was quite different from the English country gentleman he had been at home, where he was used to ride to hounds with Lord Stanton. And it was strange to see her mother actually sweeping floors and baking bread like a servant. For all that Honoria could see that this was quite the style here, even among the best people, she could not repress a shudder when obliged to plunge her lovely white hands, of which she had always taken such good care, into a greasy mess of dishwater, or rake out the embers of the kitchen fire. She could not get used to the chronic shortage of servants. She was not at all sure that she approved of colonial life.

Of one thing, however, Honoria did wholeheartedly approve. She had never before met such an assemblage of energetic, good-looking men, who all seemed anxious to make her acquaintance, and never had there been such a delightful absence of other females, who at home had always been inclined to cast her into the shade. Here, as never in Dorset, she had found herself the object of admiring eyes, and the experience had gone to her head like wine. If she had a complaint, she supposed it would be that the men seemed too absorbed in their endless talk of sections and ploughs and wool-clips, their eternal stock-breeding and house-building and experimental crop-raising, and that they had insufficient skill in – her mind chose the word 'flirtations' and shied away from it again – *elegant* conversation, in which the county set of Stanton had been delightfully adept. She had on more than one occasion formed the impression that Mr Jack Randall and Mr Henry Lawrence were more interested in their new patent saws and the cost of hired labour than they were in her scintillating conversation. It was a lowering reflection.

Voices sounded round the corner of the house. Honoria leant out as far as she dared to watch their owners come into view. A young man with a limp was laughing at two young gentlemen in their early teens. Mr Edward Jamieson had taken Honoria's brothers down to the beach for a practical demonstration of yesterday's lesson in geology. His two pupils were leaping about him, not wishing to run on yet impatient with the slowness of his pace, and ravenous for their breakfast.

Honoria pulled a chestnut curl out from the artless mass that fell about her shoulders and twined it thoughtfully round a finger. For the past weeks she had been closely observing Mr Jamieson. She was not quite sure at which point she had ceased to regard him as a mere tutor, but it was undeniable that his good looks, his air of reserve and the grace of his movements had now taken hold of her thoughts. There was, of course, his lameness to be taken into account, but in some ways his disability added to his charm, made him seem more interesting, experienced in tragedy, Byronic even, a person in whom one could confide one's tenderest feelings. At the same time, the fact that Miss Susan Randall had been sighing for him could not but add to his attractions.

Miss Honoria pushed her window up a little higher. The wooden sash, barely seasoned, had swollen in the spring rain in its casement and squeaked abominably. She had never before been grateful for it. As she had intended, Edward heard the noise and looked up.

'Good morning, Miss Gibson,' he said cheerfully, raising his battered hat.

'Oh, Mr Jamieson, how you startled me!' she said, smiling to show off her dimples. 'I feel quite ashamed that you should see me like this, all undressed as I am.'

Edward looked at her appreciatively. He had in the past two years gained some experience of feminine wiles and he was not deceived by Honoria's assumed modesty. Her tricks amused him. He had been well aware of her rosy charms since she had first landed at Wellington, and was delighted to stand for a moment and gaze up at her, enjoying the disarray of her beautiful hair and the charming informality of her betucked and beribboned nightgown.

'You look perfectly delightful to me,' he said.

Satisfied, Honoria withdrew and got quickly to work on her toilet. The horses would start soon after breakfast, and she wished to make quite sure that she would appear to her best advantage in the saddle from which she could beguile Mr Jamieson in flirtatious conversation as he rode alongside.

The idea of the picnic had first germinated in the hospitable brain of Honoria's father. Mr Gibson, a gentleman of substantial means and incurable optimism, had come to New Zealand with high hopes. The life of an English country squire, though congenial, had proved too dull for him and he had with a rush of enthusiasm committed himself, his fortune and his growing family to the colonial adventure confident that they would, given good health and a following wind, be bound to succeed. He had quickly built for his family a handsome house on The Terrace, and was looking about at his leisure for promising ventures in which to invest his capital. Sheep, he fancied, might prove profitable in the long term, but he would bide his time until the present unfortunate contretemps with the Maori die-hards had blown over, as he had no doubt it would. He did not, like some of his new fellow citizens, find cause for panic in some of the regrettable incidents which had marred the peace of Wellington for the past few months. It was sensible, no doubt, to take precautions, to avoid known danger spots, to take pains not to offer provocation, and to follow the advice published in the newspaper, but he saw no reason why, if they chose their venue carefully, his family and friends should not enjoy a day of fresh air, exercise and convivial company in perfect safety.

It had needed a little patience to persuade Mrs Gibson of the wisdom of the idea, but she was a complacent and practical woman, whose chief concern at present was controlling the fits and starts of her naughty daughter. It had been a mistake, perhaps, to leave the child with her over-indulgent aunt and uncle at home in England while the roughest part of the adventure was borne by the rest of the family. She had been thoroughly spoilt and was not finding it easy to exchange the frivolous mode of an English miss for the more energetic style demanded of the colonial female. It was marriage that she needed, and Mrs Gibson saw in the picnic the means of fostering Honoria's matrimonial prospects. She deliberated over the list of guests, put her fear of native attack aside, and embarked on the culinary preparations with a flurry of energy.

It remained only to select an appropriate place, and furious discussions between Honoria, Charlie and Frank over the best possible site for the treat had enlivened family mealtimes for weeks past. The boys favoured the beach but Mrs Gibson had objected. It was too windy, she declared, and besides, the litter of broken glass and the nuisance of disreputable persons made it unsafe for humans and horses alike. Honoria wished to ride out to a wild and beautiful dell along the Khaiwharawhara river. It would be unusual and river parties had been quite the thing in Dorset. Then, too, the blossoms of the many trees that grew along the road would add colour to the festivities. But Mr Gibson had squashed that idea. The valley, though romantic, was too remote to be sensible and too rugged to be a practical proposition. It was precisely the place to attract undue attention from warlike natives, and besides, there was no stretch of ground flat enough on which to set out the food.

It was Edward who unexpectedly came up with the answer. He had, he suggested diffidently, while on a recent expedition in search of botanical specimens, come upon a delightful clearing in the bush in the direction of Karori. He guessed that some would-be colonist had begun the work of cutting down the trees, but had all too obviously lost heart and given up the struggle. He had talked to one or two settlers further up the valley. There had been no reports of Maori movements thereabouts, and they all protested that it was safe, being so close to Wellington and far from any earlier Maori habitation. He had thought, at the time, how perfect such a spot would be for an al fresco entertainment. It was sheltered from the wind, offered both sun and shade and had the attraction of a sparkling creek in which the wines and lemonade could be set to cool. If Mr Gibson cared to ride out with him to inspect the place, he was pretty sure he could remember the way.

Mr Gibson was charmed with it. A pleasant hour's ride away, a good track for the bullock cart that would be despatched earlier with the baskets and trays of food, easy paths negotiable even by a lady of Mrs Gibson's girth – it was exactly what he had had in mind. He clapped Edward heartily on the shoulder as he congratulated him, reflecting, not for the first time in the past two years, how fortunate he had been in his sons' tutor. He had not thought either of them would have shown such a bookish disposition. It was thanks to young Jamieson that Charlie had at last mastered the rudiments of mathematics. He had been impressed, too, by Frank's greatly increased ability to converse intelligibly and even with enthusiasm on the subject of crustacea. If things went on as well as this, they would both be badgering him in a year or two to dip into his pocket and send them home to Oxford to study for a degree.

In the meantime, he had no objection to the growing fondness his difficult daughter was clearly developing for her brothers' tutor. In the normal way, of course, a schoolmaster was not to be thought of, but young Jamieson was a gentleman, no doubt of that, and his father a decent enough fellow, a little hearty and vulgar perhaps, with more than a touch of the tradesman about him, but a successful man for all that. Since he had come to Wellington no more than two years ago, he had established a bustling, go-ahead import business that was the talk of the waterfront. Young Edward, his only son, could only be marking time at this schoolmastering business until he took over from his father. It looked as if, when that day came, he would have a fair fortune to call his own. If Honoria took a fancy to the fellow he would not stand in their way. There were others better born and better bred perhaps, but few as steady. It would be a step up in society for Edward, of course, but it did not do to think too much in that stuffy way in this bright new land. In any case, he would rather see his daughter settled comfortably in Wellington, surrounded by all the amenities which the fast-growing town already had to offer, than stuck out in some huge, lonely station, at the mercy of hostile natives, working her pretty fingers red and raw as so many of New Zealand's young women seemed destined to do.

As the picnic party stepped into the forest glade and gasped with surprise and delight, Mr Gibson congratulated himself again. Everything had worked according to plan. A fire had been lit near the stream and a billy of tea was already steaming over it. Cushions had been scattered around on the ground and a rough and ready table had been contrived from a couple of boards placed over the stumps of two gigantic totara trees. The young people, nine young fellows and three delightful girls, were already exploring the place with shouts of delight. There was no doubt, thought Mr Gibson, watching complacently as two young men assisted his squealing daughter to leap from one slippery stone to the next as she crossed the stream, that Honoria was the matrimonial prize of the infant colony. Birth, beauty and fortune were all hers, and in a society with so few unattached females and so many splendid, vigorous young men, it was not surprising that the flattering attentions she received sometimes went to her head and caused her to behave with the kind of noisy silliness which brought a reproving frown even to her mother's indulgent face.

The picnic was a great success. The fresh air and exercise had induced sharp pangs of hunger in the company, and the sheep's tongues, potted oysters, roasted pigeons, cold hams, pickles, green peas, rich tarts, junkets, raspberries and strawberries disappeared with remarkable speed.

In the impromptu games that followed, the high spirits of the young people were given full rein. Their shouts of laughter echoed through the bush as their elders sat in comfort to digest their meal, exerting themselves only in conversation. Jamieson alone, poor fellow, seemed a little out of things. It was a damned shame, thought Mr Gibson, about that wooden foot of his, though he was remarkably adept with it. He would otherwise no doubt be larking about with the best of them, scrambling over fallen trunks, pushing through the undergrowth or jumping over the stream with the others who were following with mad enthusiasm a treasure hunt got up by young Charlie. Instead he was poking about in the foliage by the water's edge, seemingly absorbed in some infernal plant or other, making, Mr Gibson felt sure, a brave pretence of caring nothing for the others' sport.

Edward had, in fact, enjoyed the picnic very well, especially the raspberry tart, and he was now pleased that he had the time to take a close look at the enticing growth along the river. His duties in the Gibson house, though he was hardly overworked, gave him too little time for botanising. As for the games, he did not at all mind missing them. He had nothing against the crowd of young blades, who were vying with each other to show off their muscles to the three giggling young ladies, but he had nothing to say for them either. They were good fellows, he supposed, but not one of them seemed to have the slightest notion of the fascinating things to be found in this lovely wild place. Their only interest in the trees that surrounded the clearing was in how high up them they could climb. Their response to the call of a bird was to boast of how many of its kind they had brought home in their last bag. Their interest in the stream was restricted to the distance they could leap across it.

For a long time now, since his accident in fact, Edward had cultivated the habit of withdrawing from those of his own age. The men had at first riled him with their pity. The women had shamed him with their kindness. He had come to see himself as a person apart, an observer, an outsider. Increasingly, he had retreated into the less complicated world of science. Plants could not pity or patronise him. Insects did not care if he had one foot, or two, or none.

Occasionally, when he plunged into one of his rare depressions, he felt angry and resentful at the hand life had dealt him, but much of the time he was able to push such feelings away, and present to the world the calm detachment of the dedicated scientist. As time passed the resentment decreased. The sense of detachment grew.

There was in fact much of real interest in this clearing in the virgin bush. A mass of small white flowers sprouting from dense leafy stems caught Edward's eye. It was not quite the same as the one described in Forster's illustrated volume, whose pages Edward had practically memorised. He bent down to pick a leaf. Yes! It might – it could be a real find! A new species! He turned the small heart-shaped leaf gently over in his hand and began to search further along the bank for a more vigorous specimen. He must make haste. Mrs Gibson had already risen from her cushion, signalling the end of the party, had shaken out her skirts and was supervising the packing of plates and glasses into the half-dozen capacious baskets in which the picnic had been transported. It was almost time to go home.

Honoria was piqued. A cluster of young men was hovering around her, begging for the privilege of escorting her from the picnic glade to the spot on the timber track where the horses were tethered. Perversely, she wanted none of them. How provoking it was that Edward, the one who amused her most, was standing in a bog, gazing with rapt attention at some tiresome plant and ignoring her speaking glances as he had ignored them throughout the day! She looked round at her ring of admirers. There was nothing to choose between them. They were all dull and stupid. She made up her mind, cut a path through them, went up to Edward and touched him on the arm.

'Will you rescue me, Mr Jamieson, from all these ruffians?' she said, allowing her dimples to show. 'I would be so glad if you would give me your arm as far as the road.'

Startled, Edward looked up from his study, saw the row of indignant young faces turned towards him and Honoria's charming smile upon him and forgot his plant at once. A spark of triumph lit his eyes. She had chosen him, by God! This was a surprise! The most sought-after young woman in Wellington had left her beaux standing and come out after him! Elation made him almost laugh out loud. But then a dreadful thought struck him. Did Miss Gibson really prefer him to all those other fellows, or was it pity she was offering? Or was she, perhaps, using him, flirtatious as she was, to drive some other poor soul out of his mind with jealousy? He scrutinised the heart-shaped face turned up to his. She smiled at him with unclouded admiration, a frank invitation in her eyes. He swept off his hat.

'Nothing would give me greater pleasure, Miss Gibson,' he said with relish, and tucking her hand into the crook of his arm, he gave it a meaningful squeeze that thrilled Honoria to the depths.

The track leading back to the road where the assemblage of carts and ponies was waiting was one of several which intersected the bush, but it was some time before Edward became aware that his preoccupation with

Miss Gibson had caused him to pay too little attention to their direction. They had taken the wrong track.

'Stop!' he said, in consternation. 'I am sure we are mistaken. I know we did not pass that lacebark on the way in. I would certainly have noticed it.'

Honoria, who knew very well the exact point at which they had gone astray, clung to his arm in mock terror and shuddered.

'Oh, do not say so, Mr Jamieson. How very dreadful! Surely we cannot be lost in the bush, a prey to savages, doomed to wander helplessly like the Babes in the Wood?' She clutched him even more tightly, and Edward could feel the rise and fall of her bosom as she breathed.

He looked down at her. He had a strong suspicion that she was playing with him, but it did nothing to reduce her charm. His pulse quickened. He was captivated, flattered, disorientated. This lovely girl was unmistakably casting out lures to him. He was not the same raw stupid boy who had so cravenly run away from – what was the name of that girl who had pursued him with her talk of nightingales at the Enfield ball? Miss Harper! Aye, Letty Harper, that was it! He would not be the same callow fool again. He had only to reach out and claim the lovely creature whose heady violet scent was so strangely affecting him. Honoria was so close to him now that he had only to turn slightly, lay his free arm about her waist, and she was in his embrace. She raised melting eyes to his and closed them, ready for his kiss.

Edward, pushed helter-skelter down a road not of his choosing, whose destination he could not perceive, nevertheless responded instinctively. His senses reeling, he too closed his eyes and bent his head to hers, but in that moment a sudden picture rushed into his mind. He was back once more in the deserted house at Duddingston, reliving an old dream. He saw a woman at the end of the table, the slight, graceful form, the vague outlines of a face . . . Only this time the outlines were clear, the features visible. Good heavens! It was Jessie! Jessie Dunbar! Why the devil did he have to think of Jessie Dunbar just now, of all people!

He opened his eyes and saw Honoria staring at him, flushed and very cross.

'Mr Jamieson, are you quite well? What has come over you?'

He stepped back and began to fan his face with his hat.

'I'm so sorry,' he stammered, 'the heat, you are too good, I beg your pardon, I cannot think . . .'

Her face had snapped shut, the charm fading out of it like a setting sun, leaving nothing but petulance.

'You should not attempt to exert yourself so, Mr Jamieson,' she said spitefully. 'No doubt today has been too much for one of your invalidish disposition.' She turned and ran quickly back the way they had come towards the loud cries of 'Coo-ee!' with which the rest of the party were searching for them.

Edward hardly heard her. He did not see her go. His mind was full of another face, his heart singing to another name. Jessie, Jessie, he repeated to himself wonderingly as he limped back to the main track.

As he came out into the open once more the embarrassment of his predicament came over him. How dreadful! What must everyone be thinking? How angry Miss Gibson's parents must be, how shocked the older members of the party, how curious the younger! But he need not have worried. Honoria, practised in deception, had no wish to have her humiliation exposed.

'Mr Jamieson mistook the path,' she announced airily to her mother, then whispered audibly to a pair of admirers, who had sprung forward with alacrity to help her mount her pony. 'The poor lame fellow, one must show him a little kindness, you know.'

That night it was a long time before Edward fell asleep. He lay on his back on his narrow cot, his hands behind his head, gazing out through the uncurtained window at the stars that wheeled, cold and brilliant, across the velvety sky. For once he was unaware of their constellations, so different from those of his boyhood. His mind was racing with questions, alert to new, extraordinary feelings. He was filled with a sense of peace such as he had never felt before. It was as if he had come home after a long, arduous journey to a place of light and warmth that he had lost long ago and had never thought to find again. It was not simply that he loved Jessie, though he knew without doubt that he did. It was rather as if he had recognised her, known her in a moment of insight for what she was, his lover, his mate, the other part of himself. It was almost as if, at the moment when he had been about to commit himself irrevocably to someone else, she had called his name across the gulf of space and time that separated them.

The idea occurred to him that she might not be free, that she might be married already. He considered it, and dismissed it. She was too young to have formed a permanent bond! And besides, there was no one outside her family at Otago. It was true that Jem might take it into his head – but no. Edward had seen the kind of females Jem preferred, flash and foolish. He had never looked in Jessie's direction, nor was he likely to now. All must be well. He felt sure he was quite safe.

He dwelt wonderingly on every memory of her that now came crowding into his mind. There was no room tonight for practical considerations. Tomorrow he would have to think and plan. From now on everything was changed. He could not go on as a poor tutor, that was sure. His desire to open his own school, his resolve to pay his own way without recourse to his father, his plans for studying and writing – he would think of none of those things tonight. He would dream only of her, his love, as he had last seen her two years ago. He would call to mind her dear, anxious face as she sat on her battered chest on the bullock cart at Duddingston, and listened to Fanny's last hasty words of advice, he would try again to see her eyes, drowned in tears, as he brushed her cheek with his lips in a gesture of brotherly farewell. How could he not have known? How could he not have seen then who she was? But it was of no use to regret that now. The past was over. The future was all that mattered. And the future belonged to both of them, of that he felt sure, to have and to hold, until death one day would part them.

2

Fanny looked round her drawing room with satisfaction. Her new house at Thorndon, a bare ten minutes' walk from Hector's premises on Lambton's Quay at Wellington, though hardly large compared with the Heriot family home in Edinburgh or the splendours of Bushy House in Enfield, gave her more satisfaction than any home she had ever lived in. The delight of treading on proper floorboards after the hardship of beaten earth, the luxury of being bathed in the light that poured in through windows paned with glass instead of forever peering about in the gloom that had barely penetrated the calico over the windows at Duddingston, were joys she still did not take for granted.

Those hard, painful years had not however been wasted. The skills she had learned so painstakingly in Nelson had come to fruition here in Wellington. She had finally mastered the art of bread-making and had even developed a good hand with a fruit cake. Her roasted meats, after years of experience, were now more succulent than any a servant had ever produced for her. The very sight of one of her pies on the table brought a sparkle to Hector's eye when he came home to his dinner, and the scent of the polish she had contrived from a mixture of beeswax and turpentine made her new circle of friends sniff the air appreciatively as they entered the house.

They had been fortunate, of course, reflected Fanny, to buy a section so near to the centre of the new city, and with a house already finished. Its builder had been an anxious kind of fellow, who had first taken fright at experiencing a Wellington earthquake, and had then been thoroughly alarmed by the manifestations of Maori unrest. The reports of the massacre at the Wairau, the troubles in the Hutt valley and the threatening behaviour of the warlike Te Rangihaeata had led him to dispose of his property at a knock-down price and sent him scurrying off to New South Wales, where the land was said to stand still and the natives knew their place. The house he had barely finished had been a model of good building. It was not one of those flimsy pre-cut constructions, brought out from England in numbered sections, that had proved such a disappointment to their optimistic owners. It was a proper, solid, New Zealand villa, made from pit-sawn kauri pine, with a handsome parlour, dining room and study downstairs, as well as convenient kitchen quarters at the back, and three commodious bedrooms upstairs. A shady verandah ran across the front of the house, and the garden, in which a lawn and rudimentary flower borders had already been laid out, was well fenced in against the depredations of passing droves of cattle.

Within a few weeks of their arrival in Wellington Fanny had arranged things entirely to her satisfaction. Her possessions, so long divided between the strictly practical life at Duddingston and the rented-out town house at Nelson, had at last come together. In pride of place, near the drawing-room window yet out of the damaging glare of the sun, stood her dear little piano, its strings tuned at last, its brass brackets furnished with a pair of beeswax candles, its panels positively brilliant with polish.

With an almost voluptuous pleasure, Fanny had unpacked her china and silver and arranged them in the plain, though handsome, sideboard made by Mr Habgood, an enterprising cabinet maker, from beautiful local rimu wood. Fanny had taught her maid to polish the floors assiduously and had laid out on them her bright rag rugs, made at Duddingston with Meg and Jessie by the light of the evening lamps. She had hung curtains of a showy gold brocade, salvaged from the auction at Enfield, at her long bay windows, which gave on to a panorama of the utmost magnificence, the brilliant blue water of Port Nicholson lying jewel-like amid the steep bush-clad hills, whose green crowns shone in the sunshine with an almost tropical lustre. The view, indeed, cast into the shade her pictures, which now graced every wall: a gloomy and romantic etching of Edinburgh Castle, a prospect of Chowringhee, a pair of artless pencil drawings of Edward and Justina in their early teens, and two pretty watercolours of the ghats at Benares from across the Ganges. In pride of place were the portraits of herself and Hector, unrolled from their swathes of green silk, and opulently framed by Mr Habgood.

Fanny had stood back when these were first hung, and uttered an exclamation of delight. How very distinguished Hector looked, still with the pride of wealth upon him! And how elegant, she had to admit, had been that low-cut gown of watered silk and that delightful way of dressing her hair that had brought so many fulsome, if insincere, compliments to Captain Blakeney's lips! That was all in the past now, of course. She could hardly bear to compare her present appearance in the glass over the mantelshelf, so dowdily was she always dressed, so simple was the fashion of her hair, and so horridly brown and weather-beaten her once perfectly white skin. There was no time now to spend on perfecting the arrangement of ringlets and no money to fritter away on expensive confections of ribbon and lace. Besides, here in Wellington extravagant attire was not at all the thing.

But it would not do to think on those melancholy lines, Fanny told herself. In any case, she would not change one day of her new life for a month of the old. There she had always been bored, out of sorts, tired, pitifully ignorant of her own capabilities. Here she was busy, full of energy, proud of her new skills and knowledge. What poor creatures English ladies were, she thought, with their endless charity bazaars and their nonsensical chatter! Not one of them could put a decent meal on the table, or grow a row of beans, or milk a truculent cow. And few of them either, mused Fanny with a secret smile, could spend their evenings keeping the accounts of their husband's business and nudging him every now and then in the right direction. They were too busy vying with each other in petty snobberies.

Fanny's eyes went back to her portrait again. As to snobberies, she could not deny that the pair of portraits conferred on her drawing room a splendid air of distinction. Anyone could see that she and Hector had been persons of quality. She would not at all object to her neighbours admiring them and speculating on the very different kind of life the Jamiesons had been used to at home.

In the infant society of Wellington, barely five years old, the English habit of making afternoon calls had quickly taken root. Fanny had at first felt a little resentful of the valuable time taken up in this way. She could never, in the early months, find enough hours in the day to see to the hundreds of domestic details that had absorbed her, but as her domestic arrangements settled into a rhythm and the fitting up of her new house took less of her time, she had come to look forward to more leisurely afternoons. Perhaps, after all, she could afford to take time now to sit back a little, and enjoy the fruits of her endeavours with other matrons who had become her friends.

Fanny's circle of acquaintance had at first been limited to a couple of close neighbours at Thorndon, but it had quickly grown, both through Hector's business associates, with whom he spent a vast deal of time in the club-house atmosphere of Barrett's Hotel on the quay, and with the better class of person who attended Sunday worship at the Scottish church. Once embarked on the half-forgotten pleasures of a sociable life, Fanny had jumped back into it with relish. Her parties quickly became eagerly anticipated events. The dear piano, brought into service early in the evening to accompany favourite old Scots songs, usually ended the evening going at a furious pace to keep up with the dancers, for every party, however formally it began, had the happy knack of turning itself into a ball. Even Edward, who though he lived with the Gibsons was usually enlisted for his mother's parties, had relearned the art of dancing, and though he shuffled for the most part, stumbled a little at times, and was less nimble than the others in the reels, his partnership was courted by young and old ladies alike, who were attracted as much by his firm yet gentle touch as by his famous lack of susceptibility to feminine charms.

On the afternoon that followed the Gibsons' picnic, Fanny awaited her callers with pleasure. An interesting, if slightly cryptic, conversation with Maria Gibson the week before had led her to suspect that certain developments might be coming to a head. Honoria, Mrs Gibson had hinted, was not wholly indifferent to Edward and the young man had so far shown no signs of being averse to her charms. Fanny's impulsive heart had leaped with joy at this revelation. She liked the pretty, flirtatious child, who put her so strongly in mind of how she herself had been at that age, and she could not imagine that Teddy was not in love with her. The dearest wish of her maternal heart was perhaps about to be fulfilled. Teddy would bring home a captivating little bride, renounce his foolish independence, and take his place at his father's side. Jamieson and Co. would become Jamieson and Son, and the family would be properly settled at last.

A bell by the front door tinkled. No sound came from the kitchen.

'Alice!' called Fanny in exasperation. Her new servant, the sixth girl in two years, must be deaf besides being distressingly adenoidal. Fanny would be relieved when she, in her turn, found a husband and the Jamiesons would be thrown back on their own resources once more.

A shuffling trot was heard in the hall. Alice had responded at last. Fanny settled her skirts about her on the buttoned armchair and smiled expectantly. The smile became broader when she saw her visitor.

'Mrs Gibson! Oh, I am so glad you are come! How are you, my dear, and how is dear Honoria?'

Mrs Gibson smiled back. Though she could not but agree with Mr Gibson that the Jamiesons were not quite *comme il faut*, and though she never caught sight of those dreadful, showy portraits on their drawing-room walls without repressing a shudder, she could not dislike Mrs Jamieson. No one could help but be warmed by her sparkling energy and by the sheer exuberance of her personality. Honoria would deal with her famously, she knew, and as for Edward, Maria Gibson had come to love the boy for his own sake.

'Honoria's very well, thank you,' she said, subsiding on to the sofa and fanning her plump cheeks vigorously. 'A little tired, perhaps, after our picnic yesterday.'

She spoke without conviction. Honoria had not been tired so much as sunk in a fit of the sulks, whose cause she would divulge to no one. Mrs Gibson, less indulgent than her husband, had wished to give the child a good shake, as she would have done ten years ago. The folly of spoiling that good silk dress that should have been made to last for years! But Fanny was speaking. Mrs Gibson brought her mind hastily back to the conversation.

'A picnic?' Fanny was saying. 'Is it quite safe, just now? The news of the native unrest is so . . .'

'Oh, as to that, your son found us a perfect spot, a mere mile or so from our own house, and Mr Gibson was quite satisfied that nothing of that kind was to be feared.'

Alice's entry with the tea-tray curtailed discussion of the picnic. Fanny endured her laboured breathing in resigned silence, but when the girl had at last handed the cups of tea and plates of cake and retired to the kitchen, she could not repress a peal of laughter.

'The sixth! In two years! Whatever is one to do? And yet, believe it or not, even that poor creature has two suitors, both perfectly presentable young men, desperate for a wife.'

'Only two?' Mrs Gibson had caught the infectious laughter. 'I thought that any unattached female could have the pick of half a dozen or more. Why, Charlotte Vane's maid, who came out in the forecabin of the *Tory*, is actually to marry poor Matthew Hadfield.'

'No!' Fanny was gratifyingly shocked. 'Society here is free and easy, one knows, but a servant to marry a gentleman – really, it does not do. Hadfield, did you say? Are they not a Middlesex family? Near Enfield, I believe. My daughter, Lady Dunstable . . .'

Maria Gibson sighed. A penalty of enjoying Fanny's conversation was putting up with frequent references to her daughter, Lady Dunstable. It was a main topic of Fanny's conversation, for much as she had disliked her son-in-law, she could not help basking in his reflected glory. Today, however, Mrs Gibson's patience was not to be overstretched. A topic nearer at hand and of much greater interest to both of them was on Fanny's mind. She approached it in a roundabout way.

'How are young Charlie and Frank progressing with their studies?'

Mrs Gibson responded enthusiastically. 'Oh, Edward has done so well with them. He is an unusually brilliant teacher, Mr Gibson thinks. And, of course, his scientific pursuits are so very . . . I believe he is to have a paper published in a forthcoming journal in Edinburgh – some botanical society or other, I think he said.'

Fanny laughed with ill-concealed pride. 'Oh, Teddy and his plants! He is forever with his nose in some clump or other. It has been the same with him ever since he was a child. His professors at Edinburgh predicted quite a career for him, you know. But he is such a dreamer, head always in the clouds . . .'

She pulled herself up suddenly. This was not the character Mrs Gibson would wish for in a son-in-law.

'Of course,' she went on hastily, 'all that will, no doubt, change when he joins his father in the business. Hector is so busy, his affairs seem to become more involved every day. I am sure I don't know how he keeps his hands on the reins. He will soon be master of quite a little empire, I feel sure! I am – that is, *he* is – forever bent over his accounts, and the balance sheet looks more – I mean, I believe, he tells me, that all looks to be going on in a very fine way. Tea, you know, so reliable an import, do let me give you some more,' and Fanny, quite flustered with the idea that she had been about to betray an unfeminine knowledge of business affairs, bent the silver tea-pot solicitously over Mrs Gibson's proffered cup.

Ten minutes later, when Maria Gibson rose to leave, the two ladies had come to a pretty fair understanding. Much information had been surreptitiously given and received. Mrs Gibson had a better idea of Edward's prospects, and was well satisfied that the young couple would be comfortably provided for. Fanny had a clearer idea of Honoria's strength of purpose, and now had some inkling of the settlements her papa would be prepared to make. As they shook hands in farewell, both ladies read in the smile of the other an implicit pact. No impediment from either side would be placed in the way of the fortunate young couple.

Fanny could settle to nothing for the rest of the afternoon. She leafed through a sheet of tea prices, which she had promised herself to work over before evening, but the numbers jumbled themselves in her head. She began to write a letter to Aggie, but stopped after the first paragraph. It was too absurd to write about musical evenings, and Alice's dripping nose, and the Empress Josephine rose she had grown from a cutting from Mrs Fairfax's bush which was showing bud already, when she might soon have news of far greater interest to impart. It was with a sense of relief that, after running to the window for the umpteenth time, she at last caught sight of Hector, puffing up the steep incline that led to the house. She wrenched open the front door, picked up her skirts in both hands, and ran down the path to meet him.

'Oh, Hector, you are here at last! Wherever have you been?'

Hector looked down at her with surprise. His business in Wellington, though risky and liable to unlooked-for ups and downs, was not arduous, and he had formed the habit of spending at least part of every afternoon with his cronies in Barrett's on the quay, imbibing moderate quantities of ale and discussing the affairs of the new colony with others of his kind. He was not conscious of its being later than usual.

'I have been engaged in negotiations with Pagett,' he said, mustering what dignity he could. He did not quite like the peremptory tone he had recently begun to notice in her voice. He felt sometimes a little uneasy when he thought how much of the paperwork of his new business was in Fanny's hands. He was at the helm of course, there was no doubt at all of that, and it was important for him to be in constant touch with the businessmen of Wellington, to spend his time in congenial surroundings where he could exercise his flair for contacts and deals, and keep his ear to the ground in case advantageous opportunities should present themselves, but there was no need to explain to Fanny that he and Pagett had been happily engaged, for the last hour at least, in comparing the merits of Redland Jewel and Baron's Bolter, two prime specimens that were due to show their paces at the race at Petone on the following Sunday afternoon.

Fanny shook his arm. She did not like the strong aroma that clung to his breath. She was not at all sure that these long hours at Barrett's were good either for Hector's health or for his business. She would have to think the matter over and see if she could contrive a change in his routine. But that could wait. There were more pressing matters at hand.

'Hector! Maria Gibson called on me this afternoon!'

'Yes?' Hector did not see why this mundane event should have produced so much excitement.

'She was so particular in her remarks! I believe she is in daily expectation of an interesting announcement!'

'What? Breeding at her age? Surely she is a little old for that sort . . .'

'Hector! How can you be so absurd! Not a birth, an engagement!'

'An engagement?'

Fanny stamped her foot in exasperation. 'You are so slow! Teddy and Honoria! She expects Teddy and Honoria to become engaged!'

She had succeeded at last in astonishing him, and smiled at the expression on his face.

'Are you telling me that Teddy is proposing to marry that little minx with the brown curls and the saucy eyes?'

'Chestnut curls, and she is a very charming and well-brought up child,' said Fanny, reprovingly.

Hector stood still on the path that led up to his front door, and burst out laughing.

'Hector, for heaven's sake, I am perfectly serious!'

'Aye, my dear, so I perceive. But is our dear Teddy equally serious? That is the question!'

'Of course he is. How can you be so provoking? How could he not be in love with such a sweet girl? You must know that he has been given every encouragement, and the settlements, Maria Gibson tells me, or rather has hinted, of course, are to be very handsome indeed.'

Hector stopped laughing and looked down into Fanny's face.

'Little matchmaker,' he said teasingly. 'You may wish for wedding bells, my dear, but I don't hear 'em.'

'Why ever not? How can you say so?'

'She is not at all the right kind of girl for Teddy,' said Hector positively. Fanny stared at him.

'Whatever can you mean? She's the prettiest . . .'

'Teddy don't care for looks, Fanny. He hasn't stayed aloof from every pretty girl who's cast herself in his way, and believe me, my dear, a deal of them have, just in order to fall for a few dimples and a mop of ringlets. I don't know what it is he's looking for, but I'll lay you any odds it ain't Miss Gibson.'

'Oh.' Fanny was greatly put out. Her excitement had vanished. She led the way disconsolately up the shallow wooden steps on to the verandah, and pushed open the door. A strong smell of roasting mutton met her nostrils.

'The joint!' she cried. 'Alice! Have you burnt it again, you foolish child?' and she sped down the passageway to the kitchen, to gather the reins of household management once more into her hands.

Chapter Seventeen *November 1845*

1

When Jessie left him standing on the shore, Jem stared after her for a long time. The immediate heat of his passion had extinguished itself almost as soon as it had flared and the flames had died down to a smouldering hard core. He felt dull and heavy. At the same time he was aware that a purpose had formed itself in his mind. He let it slowly take possession of him without excitement and his movements were deliberate and steady as he set himself to carry it out.

He put two fingers into his mouth and whistled. Tam and Bess came flying out of the bush and raced towards him. Jem took no more notice of them, but went back to the inert body of Gabriel. He put his hands under the man's shoulders and began to heave him to the rowing boat. Gabriel stirred and his eyelids fluttered but he remained unconscious and the ghastly pallor of his face was unrelieved by any tinge of colour. Jem looked down at him, wondering what to do. He would, on balance, have preferred to have killed the man, but since he was still alive he could not be left unaided, to drown when the tide came up. He tipped the thin body into the boat, and pushed off. He climbed in, ignoring the water that slopped into his boots, and his dogs scrambled in after him.

He rowed for several hours. His shoulders ached and the hard skin on his hands reddened, but he ignored the discomfort. Several times, in the middle of the long harbour, he had been inclined to toss the stinking whaler overboard and let him drown. It would, he reflected, have been doing the man a favour. But he could not bring himself to touch the unconscious body. When at last he reached the burnt out and almost derelict remains of the whaling station at Otakou, he beached the boat, dragged Gabriel from it, and dumped him unceremoniously against a rusting trying pot, whose days of rendering down whale blubber were long since past. A shout attracted his attention. Jem looked round warily. This godforsaken spot had a reputation for lawlessness. The hard-working, respectable men had gone, following the whales, and those who remained were the vicious and pathetic remnants, their brains so addled on an unholy concoction of fermented cabbage tree root adulterated with turpentine that they had degenerated almost to madness.

The man lurched across the beach and looked owlishly down at Gabriel's recumbent body. Jem waited no longer. He had returned the swine to his sty, and felt himself free of him. He strode back to the small boat and headed out across the harbour to Koputai, the embryo port on the far side.

By nightfall Jem had hired himself on to the crew of a French schooner, which, by great good fortune, was heading for Cook Strait and due to sail the following day. A squall off Akaroa had resulted in the loss of two men overboard and the captain was pleased to add another to his crew.

It was not until Jem lay, well fed but exhausted, in his narrow seaman's bunk in the company of ten incomprehensible Bretons, that he had time to think. Through the past hours he had tried to drive from his mind a picture that would rise unbidden to it, however hard he pushed it from him. The sight of Jessie's bosom, peeping from the ripped dress, would not leave him be.

He screwed up his eyes and rolled over in his bunk. He had never before thought of her as a grown woman, ready for love. He had always supposed that one day he would marry her. It had never occurred to him that she would not simply come to his bidding, submissive, ready to do whatever he thought best. He would have expected, had he thought about it, that she would marry without fuss, without demanding the pretty speeches and silliness that other women seemed to find so necessary. But never, until today, had he thought of her in *that* way.

Now that he had glimpsed the perfection of her young body, so different from the raddled flesh of the women he had, from time to time, paid to possess, he could never again see her as the child she had always been to him. Her wildness, too, her passion – but he must not, must not think of it any more! The idea of it would drive him mad. What had, this morning, been an unspoken assumption of a future domestic arrangement had this evening become a torrent of emotion, a desperate desire.

He must plan. He must be clever. He must find a way to win her. He knew for sure that she had had no communication with Edward since they had parted at Nelson eighteen months before. Why, then, had the idea of Edward as a rival stabbed so painfully at his heart? The more he thought of it, in a considered, reasonable way, the more ridiculous it seemed. So fine a swell as Mr Edward Jamieson, with his fancy talk of science and his drawing-room manners, would not look to take to wife a weaver's daughter, born in a hovel and bred in poverty. In Nelson there had been young ladies enough, not many, it was true, but daughters of colonists like the Jamiesons themselves, rich people who gave themselves airs, and looked through a body when they passed him on the road as though he were not there. Edward had noticed none of them. He would not look twice at a girl he had been used to command as his mother's maid.

Jessie, he felt sure, was fooling herself. She had taken a fancy to her mind such as women were prone to do. She needed only time to forget it, time to see things in their proper light. He had been a bit hasty today, perhaps. He had not picked his moment well, coming on her so soon after . . . He would see what absence would do. She would come round to him in the end. There was, in any case, no one else for her in Otago, no respectable man who could offer her a decent home and a handful of bairns, such as every woman wanted. When the New Edinburgh colony at last arrived it would be another matter, but no news had come of their arrival. For all he knew the scheme might have been called off. The Kirkwoods and the Dunbars might be destined to pass the rest of their days alone, eking out their lives on wild pig and a handful of vegetables, waiting for a city that would never be built.

No, Jem told himself firmly, he had no real need to fear a rival. It was safe enough to go away for a while and make himself a man of substance. Jessie would be there when he returned. He might as well take precautions, however. There was no harm in putting Edward off, in letting him know that Jessie was already spoken for. He owed it to Jessie, in any case. There was no saying what kind of ideas a gentleman might have. Edward might take a notion into his head to have his mother's maid as his fancy piece. At this point in his thoughts, Jem's hands balled themselves into fists and his heart began to pound. With a great effort of will he dragged his mind away from the passionate jealousy that threatened to engulf him. He must not think of Jessie. Not now. Not yet. He had first to make his fortune, to find a flock, build himself up a little, show his family that he was a man to be respected.

In the meantime he could not regret running away. Indeed, he felt for the first time in months, even years, that a load had lifted from his heart. Never before, in his entire life, had he acted so independently of his father. He was master of his own fate at last. Grinning up at the boards a few inches above his bunk, he relished the thought of the anxiety his family must have felt when he had failed to appear at the supper table. He hugged himself as he imagined his father's grieved sighs and Malcolm's worried frowns. Jessie would give them some kind of story, he was sure. He would not be altogether sorry if some of the heavy weight of disapproval fell, for once, on her. But he would not think of her. Not now. Not yet. In the mean time, it was just fine to be on his own at last, not obliged to look over his shoulder for fear his father should see him every time he chose to take a drink with the crew of one of the rare ships that had reached the head of the sound. It was intoxicating to be free to speak as he liked, use strong expressions if he so wished, say what he meant to say without forever provoking sermons and head shakings of disapproval. Tomorrow he would decide, tomorrow he would . . .

Quite suddenly, he was asleep.

It was not until ten days later, when Jem reached Nelson and stepped ashore at the busy port, that fears for his future beset him. But when he stood looking about him, his pockets empty, his dogs hungry, and with no idea as to where he might find a bed for the night and no friend on whom he could call, he felt suddenly as lonely as he had ever felt before. At that moment he would even have welcomed the sight of his father, whatever preaching he might have had to endure.

Unwilling to stand any longer in case he attracted comment from the loungers who, while directing streams of tobacco juice about them, watched him from their perches on discarded barrels along the beach, he called his dogs to heel and set off into the centre of town. He looked about him, astonished. It was hard to believe that so much had been accomplished in so short a time.

Everywhere new roads had been laid out, buildings had grown up, fences had broken up the land, drainage gulleys had been dug. Jem's heart felt suddenly lighter. Where so much bustle and energy were to be seen, there must, somewhere, be work for him to do. True, he could see groups of emigrants standing idle, their hands in their pockets, their boots down at heel, about the doors of the many new hostelries but such men had always been there since the first ships had docked, idlers, rascals, spongers off the New Zealand Company's bounty. And everywhere else he looked a hundred small scenes demonstrated the vigour of the town, which seemed to have recovered itself from its scare over hostile natives. Here was a lively fellow splitting posts for fencing in a newly taken-up town section. Beyond him, a group of labourers was at work, digging the foundations for what was clearly to be a handsomely proportioned house. At the corner of two streets a young man, not much older than himself, was at work in his garden, his blue woollen shirt dark with sweat. Jem paused for a moment and looked enviously at the wooden house and the rows of currants, gooseberries and raspberries in its garden. Just so would he one day wish to work on his own place. A woman came to the door of the house, a baby in her arms, and called to the man. He straightened his back, saw Jem looking at him and smiled, but Jem ducked his head and marched on. He had grown unused to the friendly, open way with strangers that was so much a part of life in New Zealand's colonies. The solitary style of Otago had suited his humour better. He could not easily shake it off.

He found himself soon at the hotel he had liked to frequent on his few jaunts from Duddingston into Nelson. He scrutinised the knot of loafers standing about its doors. All the faces were new. He recognised no one. His heart sank again. He knew he must go up to them, talk easily, show a little friendliness, and start to enquire about work, but he hesitated. Shyness held him back.

At that moment he became aware that Tam and Bess were no longer at his heels. He looked round for them. They were standing several yards away stock still, their ears cocked, the hair on their necks raised. Their noses quivering with concentration, they were watching a flock of sheep approaching in a cloud of dust along the road from the harbour. Jem walked up to them and put a hand on each rough back. 'Whisht now. Lie down.'

The dogs obeyed. Jem watched the flock approach. There were no more than a dozen or so ewes and a score of yearlings. He ran a critical eye across them. They looked to be in rough shape, thin and scraggy. Several had ugly abrasions on their legs and noses. The shepherd was having a hard time of it. The road was too busy to make his task easy. There was a constant toing and froing of people, horses and bullock carts. The sheep were nervous. They would bunch, stop still, then scatter in all directions when their shepherd urged them onwards.

Outside the hotel a bullock cart was pulled up, and two men on top of it were unloading barrels and crates, sliding them down a chute-like arrangement of planks from which they were received at the bottom by an aproned fellow worker. A greeting from a friend in the distance caused the men on top to turn their heads. The barrel they had been holding poised for the descent slipped from their hands, bounced awkwardly off the sloping planks and careered into the path of the oncoming sheep. The crowd of idling men laughed and cheered to see the sheep race off in all directions while their shepherd capered after them. Several good-naturedly joined in, and ran hallooing in fruitless pursuit.

Jem could watch no longer. He lifted his restraining hands from his dogs' eager necks, gave them the word of command for which they had been pricking their ears, then tensed in an agony of suspense as they streaked off into action, chasing, darting, swerving, rounding one panic-stricken animal after another, back into a recognisable flock. Within a few minutes it was all over. The sheep stood wild-eyed, panting but still. The dogs lay watching them, their bodies taut, hugging the ground. The onlookers cheered and whistled their applause.

Jem found that he was shaking. He had willed his dogs every step of the way. For months past he had been afraid that in these years away from their work Tam and Bess might have unlearned all that he had so patiently taught them, back in the old days on Lord Eglinton's hillsides. Now he knew that all would be well. He closed his eyes for a moment as the tension eased out of him, and opened them to see the shepherd coming towards him, his hand outstretched.

'Man, I don't know how to thank you!'

His eyes, under the wide brim of his rowdy hat, were crinkled in a warm and friendly smile. His voice had the accent of a swell, but there was a Scots tinge to it too, and Jem found himself almost smiling in return.

'Tom Black, at your service,' the man said.

'Jem Kirkwood,' said Jem, taking the proffered hand.

'I'd drink a glass with you,' said Mr Black, 'but I dare not leave these rascals standing. They're fresh off the boat from Sydney, and I've to get them as far as Richmond before nightfall.'

Jem saw that, for once in his life, fortune had shone on him.

'Would you be needing any help, like?' he asked diffidently. 'I'm just up from Otago myself, and have no plans just now other than to look for work.'

'Is that not the luckiest thing you ever heard of?' Tom Black pushed his hat to the back of his head, pulled a large handkerchief from the pocket of his moleskin jacket, and was wiping the sweat from his dripping forehead. 'I've been looking about for a shepherd these three weeks or more. I've not seen such work with dogs since I left Hawick. I'm a Borders man myself.'

'And I'm from Ayr,' said Jem, still hardly daring to believe in this miracle.

'Well, what are we waiting for, Kirkwood? If work is what you're looking for, work is what you've found, you and those dogs of yours. Let's get them back on the road, and we'll settle the terms of your employment when these beauties are safely penned up for the night.'

A week later, Jem was back in Nelson. His luck had held. Mr Black had taken him on at the princely wage of two pounds and ten shillings a week, all found. Browside Station, near Motueka, was closer to the centre of the town than most. At present the ground was rough and only partly sown with English grasses, and the lodging was no more than a bunk in a wooden shed, but Jem did not care about that. He could not but feel well satisfied. At this rate, after no more than a year he would have a tidy sum to put by, enough maybe to invest in a few ewes of his own, the nucleus of the flock he intended to return with, in triumph, to Otago.

He had come to such a good understanding with his new employer that

Mr Black had sent him almost directly back to Nelson. A prize ram, due to arrive from Taranaki, was expected on the packet from Port Nicholson. Kirkwood should take delivery of it and shepherd it back to Browside.

It took Jem the better part of a day to cover the twenty-mile track to Nelson, and he went directly to the harbour. He need not have taken the last five dusty miles at such a clip. The packet was not yet in. Jem looked along the foreshore. He could now meet the stares of the onlookers. He had found himself respectable employment. He had a position, a secure place of work, the respect and confidence of a property-owning man. He sat down outside the custom house on a whale vertebra, worn smooth and shiny in its long service as a seat. The packet was visible now. The pilot was being rowed out to meet it and bring it in. He would not have long to wait.

A man came out of the long wooden customs shed and looked out to sea, shading his eyes with his hand as he gauged the time it would take for the packet to arrive. Jem recognised him. It was Mr Townshend, the crony of Mr Jamieson in their Nelson days. At once he knew what he would do. He stood up.

'Good day to you, sir,' he said. He had not spoken all day and his voice croaked. He cleared his throat.

Mr Townshend looked puzzled for a moment, and then he smiled. 'Jamieson's man, is it not?' he said. 'Well, well, I thought you had all gone south a year or more ago.'

'Aye, we did, sir, but the Edinburgh colony has not arrived, and I came up here to find work as a shepherd. I'm on Mr Black's place at Motueka. My family have all stayed down there. Do you have any information – are you in correspondence with Mr Jamieson, sir?'

'Certainly I am, my dear fellow, and I shall write in my next that I have seen you. Tell me all your news.'

'There's no so much to tell.'

Under Townshend's friendly gaze Jem's sunburnt face was slowly changing to a deep, brick red. 'My brother's a father now. He has a boy. The rest of us are well, though tired enough of waiting for the colony to arrive. It's my belief they'll never set sail at all.'

'Oh, they will, they will! You must have patience, man. There are so many considerations, the political situation – in short, it is all in a fair way to be settled and your brave compatriots will be with you in their promised land by the end of next year, I am sure!' Mr Townshend's optimism was undimmed after years of colonial experience. The romantic view had ever prevailed with him. His enthusiasm for New Zealand, even after the severe reverses that the colony in Nelson had suffered, was untarnished.

'As for me,' went on Jem doggedly, his face now positively suffused with colour, 'I'm about to be, that is, I am to be . . . I'm wed.' The last syllable was spoken so deep it came out almost as a growl.

'Eh? Speak up man, I did not rightly hear you.'

'Wed!' said Jem desperately. 'My cousin Jessie . . .' He spoke with such unintentional force that a seagull, inspecting the remains of a crab close by, flapped off in fright. Embarrassment overcame him. He fell silent and dropped his eyes. Mr Townshend regarded his confusion with an amused smile.

'Splendid, splendid! Just as it should be! Your brother, I seem to recall, married the sister, did he not?'

'Will you tell Mr Jamieson?' said Jem abruptly, daring once more to look directly into the other man's face. 'Will you tell him about me and – and Jessie?'

'Of course I shall! There is nothing easier! He will be delighted to have news of you. He can have heard nothing, of course, from Otago, you are so cut off in the south, so I have no doubt he will be most interested—'

'Is Edward wed?' Jem broke in on Mr Townshend's loquacity with dogged desperation.

'Edward? No, I do not believe so. That is, I have not heard of it. He is tutor, you know, to a family of boys and hardly in a position to support . . . but I don't doubt his time will come! You young fellows—'

'Aye, sir, thank you, sir, I must away to my dog,' and Jem, suddenly desperate to make an end of it, stepped back, cutting off Mr Townshend in mid-sentence, and fairly ran towards Bess, who was lying peacefully on a sun-warmed boulder in no obvious need of her master's attention, while Mr Townshend shook his head after him and smiled at the honest rawness of the young Scotsman's manners.

Chapter Eighteen *Wellington, February 1846*

1

Honoria regarded Edward steadily across the breakfast table. He was attacking his second mutton chop and the grating of his knife on the plate grated even more powerfully on her nerves. How could she ever have fancied herself in love with him? He was handsome enough, she had to admit, but stupid, wooden, and certainly no gentleman. She would never forget her humiliation on the afternoon of the picnic at Karori. It had been enough to make an angel cry. She looked up the long expanse of white linen to where Mrs Gibson sat among the teacups. There was no comfort to be had there. Mama had been tiresome these last few weeks. Her smiles and hints and meaningful glances were too much to bear. She had got it firmly into her head that Edward and she were – oh, it was impossible! She had not come to New Zealand to be persecuted, to be bothered with schoolmasters who should know better than to look so far above their station! Now she would have to tax her brains to think of a way out of this muddle.

Edward finished his breakfast, set down his cup and stood up.

'Excuse me, sir,' he said, addressing the newspaper which obscured the features of Mr Gibson from the contemplation of his loved ones. The newspaper was lowered.

'Yes, my boy?'

'May I speak with you at your convenience? After breakfast, perhaps?'

A sharp intake of breath from the direction of the tea-pot alerted Mr Gibson to the importance of the request. He beamed.

'My dear Edward! Of course! Nothing would give me greater pleasure. Let us go at once,' and taking Edward's arm he left the room, pausing only at the door to turn and wink at his unaccountably astonished daughter.

It was some time before Mrs Gibson, who had been hovering in the passageway outside her husband's sanctum, was rewarded with the sound of footsteps within and the opening of the door. She stood back to let Edward pass, darted into the room and shut the door behind her with a click.

'Well?' she said.

Mr Gibson was mopping his brow with a large cotton handkerchief.

'Maria,' he said sternly. 'I should have learned by now not to be led astray by these wild schemes of yours. Edward has no more idea of marrying Honoria than of taking a caravan of camels to Cathay. I stopped myself just in time from making a most unfortunate gaffe. As it was, my inappropriately jocular manner sorely puzzled him. You can imagine my embarrassment when I realised that he had no notion of Honoria, and wanted to consult me on a very different matter! You must try, in future, to restrain the child's more fanciful starts. I myself have never observed the least sign of lover-like behaviour in Edward. He has never conducted himself in less than a perfectly proper manner. I believe the whole thing has been cooked up in Honoria's over-heated imagination!'

Mrs Gibson's eyes had grown round with indignation and her massive bosom had begun to heave before this speech was half finished.

'Well!' she burst out. 'Good God! It's disgraceful, Alfred! To lead the poor child on to suppose . . . And then to bring it to nothing at all! What a shocking disappointment! She will suffer greatly over this, I am afraid. You will have to take Edward to task, Alfred. He cannot be allowed to betray in this way the trust we have shown him! Why, he has been treated exactly like a member of the family!'

Mr Gibson ignored most of this speech.

'I have not been aware of Edward leading anyone on,' he said firmly.

'But the walk in the bush at Karori! It was such a particular attention! To take her out of sight, so long away from the rest of the party . . .!'

'Whose idea was it, Maria, to go off together? I seem to recall that Honoria made the move. I thought at the time that the minx was doing no more than teasing her many swains by singling Edward out in such a marked way! As for the length of time they spent alone, I fancy you should question your daughter. I cannot and will not believe that Edward has any idea at all of this business. In fact I am sure of it.'

Mrs Gibson was a fair-minded woman. She thought for a moment, and then she sighed.

'Well, maybe you are right, Alfred, and if you are then I can only be sorry for it. I would have dearly liked Edward as a son-in-law, and he is of all young men the one I would most trust to care for Honoria.' She sighed, and then, to her husband's surprise, giggled. 'I shall have to call on Fanny Jamieson again, and what I shall say to her I really cannot imagine!'

Edward walked briskly down the steep path that led from the Gibson homestead to the main Wellington track. He was not at all displeased.

Mr Gibson had been decent, very kind indeed. His promise of support, both moral and financial, was more than Edward had dared to hope for. He had at first thought something was amiss, as the older man had been so exuberant. Indeed, the thought had crossed his mind that Mr Gibson must have been imbibing something stronger than tea with his usual breakfast of porridge and mutton. But the suspicion had been quickly forgotten. As he had outlined his scheme, Mr Gibson's manner had returned to normal, and they had enjoyed a thoroughly satisfactory discussion.

Really, thought Edward, it was astonishing how much could be fitted into the day, now that he had so much urgent business to attend to. Today he had as usual spent the first hour before breakfast in strenuous physical activity. He had long ago resolved that, though he was bound always to be lame, he need not be correspondingly weak. He had formed the habit of rising early and he liked to put in an hour or two of steady effort on the as yet untamed parts of Mr Gibson's town section. Sawing, chopping and digging as energetically as he knew how, he had noticed his muscles hardening and his shoulders filling out. He took pride in the increasing weights he found himself able to lift, and smiled at the thought of how Jessie would stare when she saw the change in him.

His morning sessions with his pupils had been as rewarding as usual. Edward had promised Mr Gibson that, in spite of his new scheme, he would not leave his present employment until Charlie had been fully prepared for entrance to Oxford University. He had come on amazingly, Edward had assured Charlie's gratified parent. Six months ago Oxford could not have been thought of. Now Charlie would be very likely to distinguish himself.

Edward turned a corner and the wind, blowing strongly from the south-west and unusually cold for the time of year, forced him to turn up his collar. Low clouds were scudding in across the bay. There would be a downpour before long. He increased his pace. He must see old Jarvis before nightfall. The building he had for sale, so near the Wakefield Club in the very centre of Wellington, would be ideal. It was too good an opportunity to miss. And now that Mr Gibson had actually offered to put up £200 and enrol young Frank as his first pupil, he felt sure that other financial support would be forthcoming.

The picture that had dominated his waking hours for the past two days rose in his mind again, so real as to block out the threatening sky. He saw the sturdy two-storey building and the handsome board outside it. How would the lettering read? 'The Wellington Academy'. No. 'The Wellington Institution'. Or perhaps . . . At any rate, the second line was clear enough. 'Principal, Edward Jamieson (University of Edinburgh)'. He envisaged the pleasant rooms filled with industrious youths, the intelligent teachers he would gather into his team, the group of older students that he would take under his wing, the afternoons they would spend in the open air in practical studies of natural history. He heard already the chorus of thanks he would receive from grateful parents, who would find in his establishment the perfect education for their sons. Many, he knew, had been at their wits' end trying to educate their children in these Antipodean climes, so far removed from the recognised seats of learning.

The picture shifted. He saw the little house beside the school that he would one day build. He watched the door opening, the maddeningly indistinct form of Jessie, Jessie waiting for him, Jessie . . . But not yet. He could not go to her yet. He must establish himself first. He had to assure himself of an income, build a proper home. Only then could he claim her. In the mean time, he knew – he could not say why – that she was waiting for him, that she knew everything, understood everything, and would be ready when he came for her.

The summer rain had filled every pot-hole with water and turned the cart tracks into mud, and the light was already dimming to dusk when Edward at last arrived at his parents' house. He had intended to call on them earlier but an unexpected encounter with Mr Toomath, an enthusiast for educational schemes, had delayed him.

Hector opened the door to his dripping son.

'Who is it?' Fanny called.

'A drowned rat!' said Hector, over his shoulder.

Fanny came out of the candle-lit room into the dark passageway and peered out at Edward's shadowy form.

'Teddy! Whatever has brought you out in such weather as this?' Excitement rippled through her. Hector had been wrong, she felt sure. It was just as she had hoped. Teddy was coming home with momentous news.

Edward shook himself, took off his sodden jacket, removed the soaked boot and sock from his one sound foot and limped into his parents' drawing room.

'I have something to discuss with you,' he said.

'Oh, Teddy!' Fanny could not restrain herself. She clasped her hands under her chin, and screwed up her face in delighted expectation. 'I knew it! Hector would not have it, but I knew I was right! I could not be mistaken in something so near to you.'

Edward frowned at her. 'How did you know, Mama?'

Hector clapped an arm round his son's hard shoulders.

'I would not believe it my dear boy, but your mother was right all along. Well, well! A prettier pair of eyes I never saw, and ankles so daintily turned . . .' and he prodded Edward playfully in the ribs.

Edward had stiffened at his father's words, and now looked down at him, unsmiling.

'I beg your pardon, Father?' he said coldly.

'Come, my boy, don't pretend with us. We were once young and in love too, don't forget!'

Edward's face turned red with vexation. 'How could you possibly know? I have spoken to no one of my feelings, nor do I intend to.'

'You cannot hide these things quite so easily, my dear,' said Fanny happily, trying to pass her own warm arm through his unyielding one. 'Why, Maria Gibson saw through the pair of you weeks ago. We are so pleased, so happy for you, my dear boy. Honoria is so exactly . . .'

'Honoria!' The name burst from Edward with such force that Fanny and Hector were startled. 'For heaven's sake, Mama, Father, you cannot believe that I am in love with Honoria Gibson! Why, I would as soon fall in love with a – a powder puff!'

Fanny took a step backwards.

'But you said – you meant . . . You *are* in love, Teddy?'

'Yes, yes!'

'Then who . . . ?'

Edward, thoroughly agitated, had started to pace up and down the room, his one bare foot leaving wet stains on the floorboards. His manner was so like Hector's that Fanny was momentarily silenced.

'I suppose you'll have to know,' he said grudgingly at last, 'though I had no desire to disclose my intentions until I had taken steps to . . .'

'Just tell us, Teddy, please!' Fanny could contain herself no longer.

'Oh, very well! You will have to know soon enough, I suppose.' Edward paused, then spoke quickly. 'I love Jessie, Jessie Dunbar, and I mean to marry her, and I'm warning you, Mama, that anything you say against her, now or at any other time, I will never forget and never forgive and it will come between us for ever!'

He stopped pacing and stared at her fiercely. Fanny was too shocked to speak.

Hector broke the silence. 'Son, you have not seen her for years. How can you be sure of your feelings?'

'I have not seen her for two years and forty-three days, Father.'

He took in the consternation in his parents' faces, and some of his stiffness dropped away. Abruptly he sat down.

'Oh, I know, it's absurd. I do not myself understand how it can be. I have known it for only a few days. But you cannot believe – never before have I known myself as I know myself now! Never before have I felt . . . I am hers, and she is mine, and that is all that is to be said.'

Hector had turned away, and was staring out of the window. Fanny could not take her eyes from Edward's face.

'She is just a child, Teddy,' she whispered timidly.

'She's seventeen, Mama. One month older than Miss Honoria Gibson. A few months younger than you were when you . . .'

'But . . .' began Fanny helplessly.

'I know what you wish to say, Mama, and I shall say it for you.' Edward's voice had recovered its usual tone but Hector and Fanny heard a new vigour in it. 'Jessie is the daughter of a destitute weaver. She has no birth, no breeding, no education to speak of. Her family was in service to ours. She was our maid.'

Over by the window Hector had not moved. Fanny looked imploringly at his back.

'You have to admit, my dear,' she said, turning her eyes back to Edward, 'that the circumstances are unusual.'

'Unusual, perhaps. In England unheard of, but impossible, no. In this country such things occur every day. And even if it were impossible, even if we were living at home, with all the Dunstables of Middlesex breathing down our necks, I would not care a jot. You must understand me, Mama. I have never loved another woman, I have never even looked at another woman and I never shall. I am going to marry Jessie. I shall be sorry for it if you do not wish to receive her, but it will make not a ha'penny worth of difference.'

Fanny gave a shuddering sigh. As Edward had spoken she had seen her hoped-for elevation in Wellington society, by way of the ladder held out by the Gibsons, crash to the ground. She had blushed in advance at the gossip and laughter this marriage would provoke. She had read the stinging letter she was bound to receive from Justina. But she had also recognised in her son a new hardness, a new purpose. Just so had Hector looked when he had swept aside all opposition and carried her off as his bride to India. Just so had she felt, when she had discovered, in the Heriot dining room in George Street, that no other love would ever match this one. Her child was hers no longer. He belonged heart and soul to another woman. Fanny bent her head, and groped for her handkerchief.

'Oh, my darling,' she said, 'I hope you will be very happy.'

Hector moved at last. He turned suddenly and crossed the room to Edward in a couple of quick strides.

'Don't – don't say any more,' he said. 'I hardly know what to say – how to tell you. I had no idea of this. My poor boy . . .'

Edward, relaxed at last, laughed shortly. 'You need not be sorry for me, Father. I'm happier now than I've . . .'

'No! Stop! Wait!' Hector's hand was in the pocket of his coat. He was tugging at a letter.

'Teddy, I would not for the world have wished to bring you this news, but you must know it. I may not have told you that I am in correspondence with Townshend in Nelson. I received a letter from him only today.'

Fanny sat up.

'Today? You told me nothing of this, Hector! And anyway, what has it to do with the matter?'

'I forgot to tell you of it, my dear. I did not think it was important.'

Edward's face was pale. 'What are you trying to tell me, Father? You have some news of Jessie?'

'Yes.'

'What is it? For God's sake, hurry up, Father! Is she well? Ill?'

'She is perfectly well as far as I know. It's just that . . .' He had been leafing through the pages in his hand, and now held one of them to the light of the candles that stood on Fanny's worktable. 'Here is the place. Read it for yourself.'

Edward snatched the letter, and his eyes ran down the page. Then he threw it down impatiently.

'I can't see – I can't take it in! Just tell me quickly what he says!'

'Townshend has run into young Kirkwood, Jem. It seems that he has tired of the pioneer life in Otágo, and has given up waiting for the New Edinburgh colony to arrive. They had expected it long before this. He has taken it into his head to seek employment as a shepherd. He has returned to Nelson where he sought out Townshend, in order, so he says, to gain news of us.'

'Yes, yes! But Jessie? What of Jessie?'

'Townshend writes . . .' Hector spoke with difficulty, his eyes lowered to the letter, his voice gruff. He could not look at Edward. 'He says that all seems well with the Kirkwood and Dunbar families – ah, here is the place. "The youngest daughter, Jessie, is, it appears, promised to Jem, our stalwart shepherd, and they are either wed or soon to be so. He was not entirely clear on this point. I offered him my hearty congratulations, and teased him not a little on leaving his fair one so far away, but he brushed my levity aside in the plain, brusque manner of the simple Scotsman. Words, I fancy, are not his forte! However, he begged me most earnestly, two or three times, to apprise you of his marriage, and seemed anxious to know whether your young firebrand had as yet also found his fate! I could not . . ." etcetera. The rest is all news of an explosion of gunpowder at the quayside – but I need not tell you of that.'

Hector at last brought himself to lift his eyes from the letter, and look at his son. Edward had sunk down on the sofa, and hidden his face in his shaking hands. With an effort, he lifted it again.

'It's not true. I will not believe it,' he said, making an effort to speak in a normal way. 'No, it cannot be true. There's a mistake.'

He sprang up again, and almost snatched the letter from Hector's hand. He read it greedily, then stabbed at it with a rigid forefinger.

'She may not be married yet! You see? Here! He says "soon to be so"! She is not married, I am sure of it. ". . . soon to be so . . . not entirely clear on this point"! You see? Whatever has led her to agree to this, whatever loneliness, or compulsion, or despair . . . I will find out at once. There is no time to be lost. At any moment he may return to Otago!'

He was pacing the room again, while his parents followed him with anxious eyes.

'The *Lucia* sails for Nelson on the next tide, I heard Mr Gibson remark on it this morning. The tide does not turn until dawn. Father, I will borrow a dry coat from you and a few necessities for a couple of days' stay. I am without funds at present. All I have is at the Gibsons. I would be very much obliged for a loan of some twenty pounds.'

Breathlessly, Fanny interrupted him. 'Teddy, you cannot be serious! You are surely not proposing to set sail tonight, in this frightful weather! Only think of the danger! The sea is sure to be very high, and the channel is so treacherous! In any case, is it not a wild goose chase? Jem is probably far away on some remote station by this time. And the Gibsons! You have obligations there. You cannot leave without arranging it first with them. At the very least you must inform them of your intentions!'

'You will do that for me, Mama. You seem already to enjoy a delightful intimacy with Mrs Gibson.' Edward's voice was dry. 'Tell them what you please – that I am sick, I have gone off my head, whatever you like – only do not, I beg of you, tell them the truth. This matter must remain between us until I have it settled.'

He left the room. They heard him clatter up the wooden stairs and move about in the rooms above. Hector started after him.

'The rascal's in my dressing room, making free with my shirts and stockings. Fetch a roll of banknotes, Fanny, from the pigeon hole in my desk. I'll take down my travelling bag for him. No, do not try to throw in any further objections, my love. The boy will not rest until he has had his way and you will only irk him unbearably by trying to prevent him.'

2

The passengers who landed on the newly completed jetty at Nelson Haven two days later were without exception pale from the rigours of the voyage. The force of the wind had been such that only the utmost exertions of the captain and crew had prevented the *Lucia* from being blown off course and far out into the Pacific. Almost everyone, including Edward, had been sick. And yet no sooner had he set foot on the familiar beach on which he had danced with such ecstasy on his first landing in New Zealand, than he forgot his sickness and was ready for action.

His first thought was to hire a horse – no easy matter in a settlement where beasts for hire were still in chronically short supply – and he spent the better part of three hours in an agony of impatience, following up reports of a man who knew a fellow whose mate sometimes let out a flea-bitten roan for a princely number of guineas. The sun was already setting when at last he threw his leg over the bad-tempered creature's back and forced it to an unwilling trot in the direction of Mr Townshend's house on Hardy Street. He was destined to be disappointed. Mr Townshend, he was informed, was away from home, on business.

Edward, looking down at the timid child who had vouchsafed this information, bit back an oath, limped back to his nag, snatched its head away from Mr Townshend's prize lilies which it had been steadily consuming, and mounted, feeling as if he was caught in a bad dream and was doomed to rise and plunge for ever on this see-saw of hope and frustration until he would, in the end, drop with exhaustion. He might as well give up for the day. It was twilight already, and there was nothing more to be done. He knew of no one else who could furnish him with information about Jem's whereabouts. He would resign himself to waiting until the morning, and would look about for somewhere to put up for the night.

It was at this point, when he had given up the struggle, that good fortune began to favour him. He was in the act of dismounting in front of a lodging house on Collingwood Street when a loud 'Halloo!' close at hand made his horse skitter sideways and prance.

'Easy, whoa there,' he said, landing on the ground with less than his usual grace.

'Edward!' said the same voice. 'I am so sorry, I almost unseated you! How delightful to see you, my dear boy! How are you? What a pleasure to meet again so unexpectedly!'

Edward turned to see the familiar features of Dr Monro beaming at him from under the wide brim of an old beaver hat.

'Your foot, man, how does it?' was Dr Monro's first question, and he smiled with approval as Edward stretched out the shoe which encased his wooden foot, and made a few hops and steps to show off his agility. 'You see? I told you how it would be. Was I not right? And what of the pains? Do they bother you still?'

'Oh, well, you know, a few twinges from time to time,' said Edward, anxious to turn from the subject. 'How are—'

'Your parents, are they well?' interrupted Dr Monro. 'Are they in Nelson?'

'No, I—'

'Alone, eh? Where are you putting up? Surely you were not thinking of stopping in this place? How fortunate that I am in town for a few days, for in the usual way I am out at Waimea, on my farm, you know. But I still have my place at Trafalgar Square – you visited me once or twice there, did you not? – and I insist, no really, my dear Edward, I absolutely will not take no for an answer – you are to dine with me and lodge the night. I must and shall hear all your news, and tell you our gossip, which is considerable, I do assure you!'

'Dr Monro!' burst out Edward desperately. 'You are very kind but I am in Nelson on urgent business. I am seeking out, that is, I have come to find Jem Kirkwood, my father's man at Duddingston and I must not lose any time in the search!'

'I see.' Dr Monro looked curiously at him. 'And have you any idea where he is to be found?'

'No, except that he is engaged as a shepherd.'

'But you might as well look for a needle in a haystack! We are no poor village now you know, but quite a town and there are flocks on all sides. Have you no other clue?'

'I believe Mr Townshend knows where he is to be found. It is he I must find first.'

Dr Monro laughed. 'Why then, you have come to the right person! You shall ask him all you wish to know over a leg of mutton, for he is to dine with me this very evening. Come now, unhitch that sorry beast of yours, and I'll send a boy straight back with it to Tom Salter, who fleeced you too many guineas for it if he is still up to his old tricks. If you need a mount while you are here, you shall have your father's old Firefly, for I bought her off Simon Jenkins that your father sold her to when he left Nelson, and a better creature . . .'

Edward was no longer listening. Borne along on the flow of his companion's eloquence, he was assailed by a pungent bouquet of memories: of the first days in Nelson, of the last carefree rambles before he lost his foot, of fear, pain, hunger and exhaustion, but above all of Jessie, whose elfin image rose in his mind more clearly here than ever it had done in Wellington. He felt as if at any moment she might appear at the end of a street or round a corner. Several times he was sure he had seen her, his heart pounded, his palms sweated and he craned his neck for a better look, only to find himself deceived by a similarity of figure, or a familiar carelessness with a shawl.

Such was his abstraction that Dr Monro, shooting sidelong glances at him, wondered if the poor young man was, after all, as well recovered from his tragic accident as he seemed. There was no doubt that he had changed. His face still bore the same sweetness of expression, but there was now a hardness behind the eyes that had not been noticeable before. He had filled out and matured. His voice was deeper, his manner more decided, and his shoulders and chest under the loose-fitting canvas jacket were surprisingly, in fact splendidly, muscular. But there was a desperation, a want of attention in his manner that Dr Monro found disturbing.

The Trafalgar Square house was soon reached, and Edward was able to put aside his immediate preoccupation for a while and look around with interest and pleasure.

'Why, how nice it is!' he exclaimed. 'So many books, and so much music! How much you have achieved! Surely you were not so fine when last I came here?'

Dr Monro rubbed his hands with satisfaction.

'Splendid, is it not?' he said, looking round his cluttered room with pride. 'But, of course, I am not here very often. I am almost entirely in the Waimea, where I insist that you visit me. Surely you are not in such a rush to be away that you cannot spare time to come out to Bearcroft? Company is always welcome, you know, and I could show you all our progress, take a close look at that stump of yours, and we could spend a few evenings over some music . . .'

Edward's rejection of these proposals brought an enquiring lift to Dr Monro's brows. Whatever was the matter with the fellow?

'What is it, precisely, brings you to Nelson?' he asked.

'I am come – that is, I wish to see a person who . . .'

'I know. You told me. Kirkwood, your father's man.'

'Yes, that is . . . I hear he has recently been married, to a – a person I was acquainted with, and . . .'

The blush that now spread over Edward's face and the embarrassment that threatened to impair his speech combined to give Monro a slight inkling of the truth. He took a risk on it, and nudged Edward with his elbow.

'A woman, is it? Why of course, you need say no more! I perceive some dark intrigue! I take it that your interest in this man is not wholly unconnected with his nuptials? A fair lady who caught your roving fancy? No, no! Do not say more! I shall not ask any questions, and do not fear, my lips are of course sealed!'

He winked, and Edward, made acutely uncomfortable by his host's jocularity and scarcely understanding his hints, said merely, 'Thank you, you are very good,' and took a violent swig at the glass of claret the other had pressed into his hand, while listening out for the clatter of the door knocker that would announce the arrival of Mr Townshend.

Jem woke feeling uneasy. He had intended that day to ride up into the back country in pursuit of a pair of wild dogs which had already accounted for two ewes. Once they had a taste for the sport there was no saying what damage they might not do, and Bobby Jones, who was running a small flock on the next section, had warned him that no sheep ever recovered from the bite of a wild dog however small the wound. Doctor it how one might, death was unavoidable. And yet as Jem swung himself out of his bunk and threw open the shutter to clear the foetid air of his hut, he knew he would not be hunting only dogs today. Some instinct, the same kind of feeling that last week had led him to the gully where a lamb had fallen into a cleft from which it could not clamber out, told him that he must not stray far from the station.

He ate his breakfast in the homestead kitchen alongside Mr Black and the two other hands in his usual unsmiling silence, and did not even look up when Nancy, the energetic maid-of-all-work, flicked her duster across his shoulders and remarked airily to the company at large that she might as well treat his worship as a piece of furniture for she'd get as much notice from him as from a table or a stool. She watched him finish his third chop, wipe the back of his hand across his mouth, push back his chair and go without a word, then, hand upon her hip, she stood at the kitchen door and looked after him, wondering why it should always be the moody, difficult ones who were so good-looking, and what a girl would have to do to get a smile from that one.

Jem walked fast towards the creek that ran along the main track to Nelson. He had been working here a week before, fencing in a paddock, and the mixture of English grasses sown last spring were well up now. His eyes scanned the posts. None were down or damaged. There was no sign of theft or visits from wild pig or indeed anything at all untoward. Why then should he be filled with this sense of foreboding?

He came out on to the rutted track and looked down it in the direction of Nelson. The day was fine, the view of mountains, forest and sea one that would have satisfied the severest critic of the picturesque, but Jem had eyes for nothing but a cloud of dust a mile or so distant that betrayed the approach of a horse, ridden at speed. He stood motionless under the shade of a kowhai tree and waited. This must be what he was waiting for. The horseman must be coming for him. The cloud approached and the horse could now be clearly seen ahead of it. It was Firefly! But Firefly had been sold long since, to strangers! A prickle ran up the back of Jem's sinewy neck, making the short hairs stand on end. Surely this could not be some kind of apparition, some visitor from hell come to plague him?

The horse came abreast of him. Jem stepped out from under the tree, frightened Firefly and made her shy. Edward pulled her head round while Jem caught at the bridle. Edward slid to the ground. Without a word Jem led the horse to the tree, tied the reins to a low branch, and turned. The two men faced each other.

There was a long moment of silence. Not a bird called. Not a breath of wind stirred the rushes by the creek.

'I hate you,' said Jem, in a conversational tone.

'I know,' said Edward evenly.

The contempt in his voice stung Jem to an anger that the wildest insults could not have aroused.

'You need not look down your skinny beak at me, Edward Mighty Jamieson,' he growled. 'I'm a man o' means myself now, not your feckless father's servant. You've no call on me now. I'll not do your bidding, no, nor any of yours ever again. And I'm a married man, too.'

He saw Edward flinch and his eyes widen. So the danger was real from this quarter! There was more here than he had thought. It was not just a foolish girl's daydreams that were against him. His enemy had daydreams too. But he had the advantage and he pressed it home.

'Jessie's mine,' he said. 'We've been married two months or more.' He watched with satisfaction the muscles harden around Edward's jaw as he clenched his teeth.

'You'd never think it,' he went on with relish, 'such a timid wee girl, and not pretty like in the face and all, but a woman all right – oh, man!' he shaped a woman's form in the air with his hands. 'You wouldna believe how—'

He got no further. Edward had brought his wooden foot forward in a kick that almost splintered Jem's shin. He found himself sprawling in the dust.

'Get up,' said Edward, 'and fight.'

Jem leaped to his feet and took a step towards him, bunching his fists. Then he turned his head aside and spat.

'I'll no fight a cripple,' he said.

The ferocity of Edward's onslaught astonished him, and for a moment it seemed as though the fight would be over almost before it had begun. Edward's first punch landed well, pulping the corner of Jem's mouth and splitting his lip. Jem staggered back and Edward lunged forward for an upper cut on the chin but he was too awkward on his feet to land it in time, and he plunged into the empty space from which Jem had dodged, saving himself from falling only by landing painfully hard on his stump. Jem rushed at him, aiming a blow at the stomach to wind him, but Edward moved more quickly than Jem had expected, and as Jem missed his target, Edward caught him from behind in a vice-like grip and locked his right arm behind his back.

Jem was taken by surprise. Until this moment he had taken his superior strength for granted. He had always despised Edward for a weakling, even before he was lamed. Now, as his right arm was being inched up towards breaking point, he recognised that he could be beaten, his arm might be broken. Fear added an extra edge to his strength and he braced himself to break free.

Edward sensed the change in him and tightened his grip. His only chance, he knew, lay in wrestling close to the man. In a boxing match he could not hope to dodge about as nimbly as the other surely would. He could rely only upon the power of his arms and shoulders. He revelled in their strength. The months of early morning work had paid off. He was the match of anyone! He could give any man a fair fight! He levered Jem's arm up a notch and wondered how soon it would break.

'No man talks of his wife as you talked of her. You're not telling me the truth. I'll not believe it! You're not wed!'

Jem grunted with pain. 'Believe it or not, it is the truth.'

'You're lying. Tell me it's a lie!'

Drops of sweat were running into Edward's eyes. He shook his head to dislodge them. Jem sensed his opportunity and suddenly, with a supple twisting motion, wrenched himself free. Edward stepped back awkwardly, tripped and was on the ground. In an instant, Jem was upon him. He pinioned Edward's arms above his head, and fixed him with bloodshot eyes.

'I'll talk of *my wife* as I like, and I'll talk of you as I like. You fool, d'you think a woman would look twice at you? You're not fit for this country. Feeble! Soft! Bugs and flowers! Pah! Too daft to catch a cow or mend a fence! Too scared to climb a mast . . .'

He had gone too far, and he knew it. With one wild heave, Edward rose from under him, freed himself and scrambled to his feet.

'I don't know' – he was panting with effort and fury – 'how you persuaded Jessie to marry you, Jem Kirkwood – by some foul means I cannot even bear to think of – but I tell you this – if I ever hear that you have hurt so much as her little finger – or done anything to her but your sacred duty – it will be my supreme pleasure to kill you, and make no mistake – I shall do it.'

He turned his back and walked unsteadily over to Firefly. There was no more to be feared from Jem. The fight had entirely gone out of him.

Edward slung himself painfully back into the saddle and looked down at his rival.

'A woman would be desperate indeed to marry such as you,' he said, and touching Firefly's flanks with his heels, he was away down the track, feeling suddenly as sick, empty and full of pain as if he had lost another limb.

Jem stood for a long while, looking after the diminishing cloud of dust. He could let Edward go now. He had convinced him that Jessie was lost to him for ever, that he, Jem, had married her. Edward would stay away from Otago now. Jem could put his mind at rest on that score. And yet the revenge he had long dreamed of had lost its savour and he was left with a sense of loss. He kicked at a stone savagely and washed his face in the creek, crouching over the water for a long time. Then he went back to the homestead to fetch his gun, and set off into the hills to shoot wild dogs.

3 *Wellington, March 1846*

Edward stood in the centre of his new domain and looked about him gloomily. Two weeks ago the acquisition of this disused warehouse, whose unlined weatherboarded walls gave minimal protection from the Wellington gales, had filled him with joy. Now his interest had waned. The simple building, no more than forty feet long, occupied a small section of land just above the beach at the Thorndon end of Lambton Quay, the principal thoroughfare of Wellington, and Edward had been jubilant at the bargain he was getting. Jarvis, its former owner, whose confidence in the colony had been shaken by renewed reports of Maori hostilities, had closed on Edward's first offer with relief and had taken ship for Van Dieman's Land, leaving Edward the owner of one large shed, whose door opened onto a fine view of the beach and the sea, several bales of canvas, and a couple of sacks of sugar.

Edward paced across the rough floorboards and looked out of the window. He could see the corner of his signboard from here, on which was written the legend, 'The Lambton Academical Institution. Principal Mr Edward Jamieson, M.A. University of Edinburgh'.

The words which had for so long been running around in his head caused him no flutter of excitement now. His eyes strayed past the board towards the dozen or so vessels at anchor in the bay and beyond them to the sweep of the harbour and its encircling hills, broken by the channel through which the ships must sail to the open sea. The dreams he had spun were shattered now. There was no promise awaiting him to the south, no prize for which he could strive. The hard work remained to be done, but without the reward he had hoped for at the end, and he was sickened by the thought of it.

The opening of his school, to which he had looked forward with such anticipation, was a bare three weeks off. Everything remained to be done. There was as yet no furniture, no equipment, few books, pencils or pens. He had not so much as acquired a clock to hang upon the wall, or a ball and a bat for games of cricket. He should be in a ferment of activity and yet he was sunk in a lethargy from which he could scarcely rouse himself. One thought only preoccupied his mind. Jessie was married. He had not recognised his love in time. He had not taken his chance when it was his. He had been tragically, stupidly blind. He was destined to pay for it for the rest of his life in solitude and drudgery.

'Hello, is this the new school, then?'

Edward turned. A large, grinning boy, about fourteen or fifteen years old, stood at the door. His wrists stuck out too far from the jacket he had long outgrown, his hair was an uncombed thatch above his spotted face and one of his bootlaces was broken.

'Where's this Mr Jamieson, then? You know him?'

'Certainly I do. I am Jamieson.'

'Coo, that's rich, that is!' The boy looked Edward derisively up and down, and his grin widened. 'You ain't no schoolmaster, as far as I can see. Where's your cane?'

'I do not have a cane.'

'Not have a cane? How does you beat us, then?'

'I do not beat boys.'

'Wait till I tell my pa that. He won't like it, he won't.'

Edward stepped out of the shadow by the window, went over to the door and looked down at the boy.

'Are you joining my school?' he asked pleasantly.

'Pa says I must,' said the boy sulkily. 'It's not what I want, mind. I've got all the education I need, with writing and algebra and all. But Pa says he can't be doing with me in the shop, getting into mischief all day long, and I'd better mind my books. He wants me to be a clerk, same as my uncle. Not likely! You won't turn me into a clerk, I'm telling you straight, I am.'

Edward, engaging the speaker's defiant eyes with his own, felt his heart sink. In his carefully worded advertisement in the *New Zealand Gazette* and *Wellington Spectator*, he had undertaken to impart a knowledge of natural philosophy, astronomy, chemistry, anatomy, physiology and natural history, as well as a thorough grounding in the usual elements of an English education, allowing special prominence to the study of both classics and mathematics. The enquiries he had so far received had not, as he had hoped, come mainly from those independent gentlemen such as Mr

Gibson, who wished to school their own sons for Oxford or Cambridge, but from families who, having enjoyed little education themselves, hoped that Mr Jamieson's Academy would provide the means of economic betterment for their unruly adolescent sons, or, at the very least, keep them out of mischief. To hold the attention of half a dozen unwilling boys such as this one would, Edward knew, be a far harder task than educating a score of young Gibsons, thirsty and eager for knowledge.

'What's your name?' he asked.

'Blundell. Dicky Blundell,' said the boy, and Edward knew at once that the absence of a 'sir' had been a deliberate challenge. For the time being he chose to ignore it.

'And which school have you attended up till now, Blundell?'

'Hetherington's.'

Edward nodded, and looked at the boy thoughtfully. The methods which Mr Chas Hetherington employed to instil the rudiments of learning into the thick heads of his charges were remarkable only for their brutality. Floggings were as regular a part of his curriculum as the multiplication tables. Fear and violence were the only weapons in his armoury, and none of his pupils had, up to now, been known to acquire a love of learning for its own sake.

'And why do you wish to leave Mr Hetherington's?'

Dicky's grin broadened. 'Mr Hetherington's give me the boot. He won't have me back in his schoolroom. I'm too bad for him.'

'I see.' A smile suddenly swept across Edward's face, disconcerting Master Blundell more thoroughly than the most alarming ferocity might have done. It did nothing to allay his conviction that here was the easiest touch he had ever met in his life, and that there would be more fun to be had with this simpleton schoolmaster even than with the hunchback who lived at the back of Barrett's Hotel. Did he but know it, Edward was taken aback as well. He had unexpectedly warmed to this deplorable child. It would be no easy task to stimulate a brain long since dulled by repression but it would be a challenge.

'Do you read, Blundell?'

'Course I can read.'

'I did not ask if you *could* read, but *if* you read.'

The boy looked uncomprehending. 'I read all right if I have to.'

'Can you reckon?'

'Better than most.'

'Good.' Edward stepped out of the warehouse, looked about on the ground for a moment, then picked up a stone. 'What kind of rock is this?'

Dicky looked at it suspiciously. 'It's a pebble.'

'It is usual,' said Edward gently, 'to address one's schoolmaster as "sir".'

Blundell looked belligerent and the 'sir', when it came, was accompanied by a sneer that robbed it of respect.

'Well, then. What kind of rock is this?'

Dicky squinted at it. 'A muddy one – sir.'

'Hmm. What is your opinion, Blundell, of the French Revolution?'

'My what?'

'Your opinion.'

'I don't have no – opinion.'

'You will, Blundell, you will. Now go home, and inform your father that this school will open three weeks from today. You are to present yourself at nine in the morning in a washed condition, and with a readiness to form opinions.'

The boy gaped at him and ran off, eager to spread the news to his cronies. The new schoolmaster was a rum cove and no mistake. He wouldn't last long. They'd make mincemeat of him soon enough, and when he'd packed his bags and gone that would be an end of this education lark for good and all. There was no other school for boys of their age in Wellington. They'd be free.

Edward watched the lad scamper along the beach, pick up a pebble and hurl it at a gull, then run to a knot of sparring lads, elbow his way to the centre of it, and engage them in eager conversation. He had a pretty fair idea of the kind of devilry they would hatch up between them. It would have to be forestalled. Every move would have to be anticipated, every strike pre-empted. There would be no cane or similar instruments of punishment in his schoolroom. His pupils would be led by the light of reason or not at all. He squared his shoulders. Today's encounter had done him good. Master Blundell had put him on his mettle.

'Edward! So you are here! I have been looking all over town for you.'

Approaching him was Mr Gibson, hand held out in greeting, face beaming. He was even more excited with this scheme than Edward himself and he had been only too happy to invest some money in the venture. He had, for a little while, wondered why Edward had not turned to his own father for funds, but a moment's reflection had shown him that a desire for financial independence was very natural in a young man, and he could not but respect him for it.

'How are you progressing? You have taken possession of your premises, I see.' He stepped into the empty warehouse and looked about approvingly. 'But this is excellent! A healthy situation, plenty of space, good ventilation, natural lighting – you could not have done better!'

Edward was relieved. He had been afraid that the spartan appointments of his shed would not meet with his patron's approval.

'I'm very glad you like it, sir,' he said. 'But, of course, there is still a great deal to be done.'

'Aye, naturally, desks, and a platform for yourself and the like. How are you to set about . . . ?'

'As to that . . .' Edward hesitated. 'I have some ideas for the arrangement of the furniture which I have already – I was hoping to discuss this point with you earlier, sir, but was obliged to act at once. I have, I am afraid, laid out some more money.'

Mr Gibson looked enquiring but said nothing.

'I was offered an excellent opportunity,' Edward rushed on, 'and could not pass it up. The *Catherine* docked last week, as you know, and as it was an emigrant ship I guessed that the steerage fittings – planks, you know, that could be used to line these walls, benches, tables and the like – would be knocked down to the highest bidder. I asked the captain, and he was in haste to leave for Nelson where he is to pick up a cargo of whale oil, and – well, the long and the short of it is, sir, I persuaded him to forgo a public auction and bought the lot from him on the spot.'

'For how much?'

'Twenty guineas. I am awaiting delivery now – that is why I am here this afternoon. And I am obliged to settle with the captain tonight as he sails on tomorrow's tide.'

Mr Gibson burst out laughing. 'My dear Edward, what an excellent businessman you would make! There is more of your father in you than you suppose. To line your schoolroom walls and fit it out with all its furniture for twenty guineas when there is a shocking shortage of timber in the colony is enterprising indeed! I shall, of course, advance you the money, if you will call at my house on your way home. I have a growing certainty that this venture of yours will be a great financial success. You will be overwhelmed with pupils, all eager to pay fees for the privilege of sitting at your feet. How many have enrolled so far, by the by?'

'Fifteen, but I am receiving more enquiries by the hour.'

'Excellent. I perceive that Hetherington is doomed, and not before time. If ever a boy learned aught from that old villain it would astonish me. Your school will become famous, Edward. I foresee, in future years, a veritable Eton, a noble pile of grey stone buildings, rolling playing fields, a dignified staff of masters, a list of distinguished former pupils . . .'

'That would be wonderful indeed, Mr Gibson. However, in the mean time, I am afraid I must impose even further upon your generosity.'

'What is lacking now?'

'I have sent to Sydney for certain exercise books, works of reference, drawing materials, manuscript paper and the like, but the agent demands cash in advance.'

'The devil he does. They are all rogues in New South Wales, my boy. It pays to take care when you do business there.' He looked round the room once more and an idea struck him.

'A clock! You will need a reliable clock to mark your lesson hours. You shall have the old one from our schoolroom, for which we will have no need now that the boys will be down here with you for their lessons. And a bell! What about a bell?'

Edward chuckled. 'There is no need to concern yourself with that, sir. The captain of the *Catherine* had a gong to spare. I persuaded him to throw it in with the timber.'

On the way to his new school at the start of his second week, Master Blundell was pleased with himself. He had, during the previous week, found no difficulty in establishing himself as ringleader of the dozen or so of his twenty-two fellow pupils who shared the same riotous disposition, and resented as much as he did the infringement of their personal liberties perpetrated by the school system, and he was as sure as anything that he had got the better of poor, feeble Mr Jamieson. The fellow was scared, it was easy to see that. Why, old Hetherington would have beaten him black and blue by now. When Johnny Briggs had accidentally made an offensive smell in the course of a scripture recitation, old Hetherington had flogged him unconscious, and even Johnny's father hadn't dared to complain, he was that in awe of the schoolmaster. But Mr Jamieson hadn't dared lay a finger on any of the boys, even when a paper pellet, aimed by Blundell himself, had landed full on the fellow's nose. He had only looked the other way, and had pretended to feel nothing at all.

It was quite plain that Mr Jamieson had no notion of proper schoolmastering. He did not make you learn by heart and repeat your Latin grammar and your twelve times table, as real teachers did. Instead, he talked to you, and showed you things, and made you draw them, and asked you questions. Some of the fellows were soft enough to be taken in. Dicky had almost suspected, by the end of the week, that his own authority was beginning to ebb away. Walter and Harry had even begged him to be quiet when Mr Jamieson was recounting some story or other out of history as they wanted to hear the end of it, but after school Dicky had banged their heads together good and proper, and they'd promised not to give in to any more of the schoolmaster's cajolery. They'd lain in wait for those toadying Gibson boys, too, and bashed them about a bit, though it hadn't gone all the right way, Dicky had to admit. He fingered the bruise on his shin, but deferred thoughts of revenge. There was too much to do before the fruits of victory could be safely plucked. He was, after all, engaged in war, war on the schoolmaster, war on the school, until he and his poor suffering friends had won their freedom.

Dicky stepped gingerly over a washed-up spar as he made his way along the beach to the schoolhouse, nursing a small box in his hands. He was smiling. Today, he was sure, would be his last spent in hated confinement. He had hatched a plan of such devilment that his expulsion must be the consequence. It could not fail. Anyone could see that Mr Jamieson was a coward, easily panicked. All cripples were easily scared. Everyone knew that.

It had cost Dicky nearly all his small hoard of money to prepare for this trick, but the reward would be worth it. The katipo spider, at present lurking in the recesses of the box he so carefully carried was, the Maori boy had assured him, extremely poisonous and anyone unfortunate enough to suffer its bite was certain to be very ill. Dicky did not wish to kill Mr Jamieson precisely, simply to scare him out of his already enfeebled wits, and though it had made him shudder simply to take the box from the Maori boy's hands into his own, he had no doubt that it would work the trick.

The expression of unnatural calm on the faces of his most obstreperous pupils warned Edward that some peculiarly unpleasant prank was in the air. He had spent the Saturday half holiday and the Sabbath rest day in deep thought. His methods, he had to admit, had so far met with mixed success. He had expected those of his pupils who knew nothing of education beyond beatings and rote learning to react a little wildly to their first taste of academic freedom, but he had hoped by now that the initial phase would be over and some genuine enthusiasm for the feast of intellectual pleasures he so diligently prepared for them each day would have become evident. He had, it was true, detected the dawnings of interest in some young faces but no sooner was their attention engaged than Dicky Blundell made haste to divert it. Blundell was, without doubt, the focus of the trouble. If he could but win him round, the rest of them would follow.

There had, however, been no sign of softening from that quarter, and Edward had come regretfully to the conclusion that, at the end of another week of similar behaviour, he would have to ask Mr Blundell to remove his son from the school, much as he disliked the idea of expelling the boy.

A small box lay on his desk. It was obvious to Edward that this was the focus of the mischiefmakers' rapt attention and an inkling of the truth dawned upon him. He picked the box up and turned it round.

'How interesting,' he said. 'A gift, perhaps? I am touched by your thoughtfulness. Now who could have been so kind . . .' His gaze swept the room and came to rest on the smirking face of Dicky Blundell.

'Blundell! How surprising! Shall I open it now?'

A crack of laughter almost broke from Dicky's tightly pursed lips, but he heroically suppressed it, and turned a deeper shade of scarlet in the process.

'I am sure you would like to share in my pleasure, Blundell,' said Edward smoothly. 'Come and stand beside me.'

Dicky's desire to laugh suddenly left him. Reluctantly, he went to stand at Edward's side, but was careful to keep his distance.

'Closer, please,' said Edward, 'or you will not be able to see what is inside this delightful box.'

He pulled at Dicky's arm, and the boy was taken aback by the steeliness of his grip. He had had no notion that the schoolmaster was so strong.

'Now,' said Edward, and he opened the lid of the box. The katipo, startled by the light, ran on to his hand, tucked itself into the hollow of his palm and cowered there. There was a gasp from the rows of watching boys, and a whisper ran round the room as those privy to the secret passed the information to those who were not. Edward, turning his hand, studied the creature with interest.

'Be careful, sir, it's poisonous!' said Frank Gibson in a low, urgent voice.

'Oh, I know, Frank, I know,' said Edward, looking up with unconcern to smile at his old pupil. 'But it's an excellent specimen. I have not seen a finer. Blundell must have gone to some trouble – or, perhaps, expense? – to find it for us.'

His left hand was still closed firmly round Blundell's elbow and he now brought his right hand, containing the katipo, closer to the boy's face. The room was quite silent now. The tension was palpable. It was as if, by keeping still themselves, the boys were willing the spider not to move.

'Tell me, Dicky, where did you find this jolly little fellow?'

Blundell's flush had faded and a pallor had succeeded it. He was looking at the katipo with fascinated horror.

'I – I bought it.'

'I have already reminded you,' chided Edward softly, 'that it is courteous to say "sir" to one's schoolmaster.'

The hand was slowly approaching Blundell's own. Sweat now stood out on the boy's brow.

'Yessir,' he said, licking his lips.

'Would you like me to return your property to you, now that I've had a chance to examine it?'

'No – thank you – sir.' Blundell's voice was jerky.

'Then I suggest we immobilise it, ready for further study.' Edward released his grip on the boy's arm, and gave him a little push. 'You will find in my desk a packet of pins. Bring it to me. I shall return our friend to his box,' and he dropped the spider with a deft manoeuvre into its former place, and closed the lid. 'Ah, the pins. Thank you, Dicky. I shall now slide a piece of thin paper under the lid but over the cavity so that we shall see him without him being able to escape again. So. Now, Dicky, do you open the lid. Why are your hands trembling, boy? There is no need to be afraid. Look, I've pinned the poor fellow to his box. He need not bother us any further. There. He will twitch on his pin for a little while, but I'm afraid he has spun his last web.'

The exhalation from the score of throats that followed this simple act made the papers laid out on each desk positively flutter. Edward, enjoying the first complete silence his pupils had so far vouchsafed him, took advantage of it.

'You may sit down, Dicky. Thank you. Now before we proceed to our morning's study of geometry, there is an announcement I wish to make to you. As you know, Wednesday is our half holiday, but it has long been my custom to use my leisure hours in the search for items of interest to the student of natural history, and I propose to start a collection for this school. It will consist of shells, ferns, grasses, flowers and plants of all kinds, insects, spiders' – he paused to look humorously at Blundell, who seemed to have shrunk into his seat, and whose face was once again red, this time with embarrassment – 'rocks, creatures of the sea, and any other items peculiar to the islands of New Zealand. In time, who knows, our collection might have some wider interest to scientists at home. Can you not imagine it, gentlemen? A showcase in one of the great museums of London or Edinburgh, with the legend "Collection by the pupils of Lambton's Academical Institution, Wellington, New Zealand"?'

He felt with triumph the surge of enthusiasm that was rising all about him. 'I would like to invite those of you who are interested to come on a nature ramble with me in the direction of Evans Bay, Saturday next. We shall, perhaps, have time to light a fire and cook up a billy of tea, when we have finished our collecting work. I shall rely on the more agile among you to scramble up on the rock faces, as I am somewhat hampered by my right foot, which, as I am sure many of you already know, is made of wood.' He hitched up a few inches of trouser leg, and his pupils craned forward with fascinated curiosity to look at the unwrinkled sock which descended into the unnaturally smooth leather of his right boot.

'I have ordered a pair of display cases to be made in which to house our finds. They should be ready within the week. I am sure, Dicky, you will be proud to donate your spider to our collection, of which it will have the honour to be the very first item.'

Chapter Nineteen *Dunedin, 1846*

1

Jessie had been the first to see the fully manned whale boat pulling up the harbour early on a brilliant summer's evening, but she had not at once realised its significance. She had intended to look for pipis and cockles in the tidal flat, but the tide was rising fast so she had decided to fill her pail with fuchsia berries instead. They would make a tasty pie, and since she had taken over much of the cooking from Meg she had developed a pride in her culinary achievements.

It was certainly hard to contrive without milk, butter or cheese, and the want of a kitchen cow, or even a goat, was felt by them all, but it was surprising what a little ingenuity could produce. Isaiah provided an increasing variety of fruits and vegetables. Uncle Joseph and Malcolm often came home with a pig or a brace of wild fowl, while the eel traps in the creek and the rich beds of shellfish kept them plentifully supplied. It was true that their sacks of flour, oatmeal and sugar were now sadly depleted, and that tea had long since disappeared from the stores. Rats had helped to diminish their stocks until Malcolm, in imitation of the Maori, had constructed a cunning platform too high for the rats to reach. In the meantime Moana had shown Jessie how to brew manuka leaves, and the resulting beverage was a passable substitute for tea.

Jessie set her pail down beside her, shaded her eyes against the late afternoon sun with her raised right arm and tried to make out the details of the approaching whale boat. Since her encounter with Gabriel five months ago, she had kept a weather eye out for strangers. She had been more careful in her ramblings and though she was still drawn to exploring the bush, she gave it the caution and respect it was due.

The whale boat was coming nearer. It was unlike any other craft that had come this far in the last two years. It was a larger vessel, but so laden with men and goods that it rode low in the water. A thought struck Jessie and her heart missed a beat. Perhaps it was the surveying party, the advance guard of the new settlement, come at last to measure and dig and lay out the new city! Was it possible? Was their solitude over at last, and the longed for moment here? She stepped back and nearly tripped over Denis, who had craftily stolen up behind her and was about to plunge his shiny snout into the mass of berries in the pail. Jessie shooed him aside and then, filled with shyness in case the men should see her, she darted behind a huge clump of flax, and peeped through its fleshy leaves as the whale boat came ever more clearly into view.

Her guess became a supposition and then a certainty. There could be no doubt! These men were no whalers, no run-away sailors, no escaped convicts from Botany Bay. They had a calm, well-fed, disciplined look to them, the appearance of men embarking on a lawful and pleasurable enterprise. For a moment Jessie felt a pang for the land and its emptiness, for the ancient bush, the untouched shore, the lonely fern flats she had roamed on her own, for the nesting swamp hens with their long gangling legs, and the wading stilts with their nervous, jerky gait, whose age-old peace was about to be shattered for ever. Then she felt only excitement. She grasped the pail, picked up her skirts and ran, not caring who saw her, towards the little cottage yelling at the top of her voice, 'They're here! They've come! It's the surveyors!'

'Jessie, have you not mended my shirt yet?'

'I'm sorry, Uncle Joseph, I . . .'

'Jessie, will you put up some bannocks for me? I'm away up the ridge with the surveyors today.'

'Just a minute, will you, Malcolm? I've only the one pair of hands.'

The bustle in the cottage was so unlike its usual calm that wee Robert felt disturbed. He was not used to being ignored in this way. He opened his mouth to protest, then saw Denis's face peering in at the door and gurgled a welcome instead.

'Will you get that pig out of here?' called Meg in exasperation, but no one heeded her, and for the next half an hour Denis and Robert occupied each other to their mutual satisfaction while the men of the house prepared to leave for their day's work.

'Would you believe it now,' said Meg petulantly, when the two girls had the cottage to themselves at last. 'Uncle Joseph has promised Mr Kettle we'll feed the survey party this evening!'

'It's only the six of them, Meg,' said Jessie, in the placatory voice she reserved for her sister and her father. 'The others are away up at Koputai, buoying the channel.'

'Six! How are we to make enough bread and roast enough meat for so many? We'll be busy all the day long, and my back is aching already fit to break.'

Jessie shot a suspicious look at her sister. Meg had certainly been unwell these past few months. This pregnancy seemed to be exhausting her more than the first and she had been greatly troubled with sickness, but this last week or more her cheeks had become rosy again and her step had regained its old elasticity. Jessie was beginning to suspect that Meg's complaints had become a matter of habit. While she had been unwell Jessie had shouldered an increasing share of the domestic burden, and Meg had enjoyed a respite from the chores which, through repetition, had lost their early charm. She had grown used to having Jessie at her beck and call and was reluctant to take up her share of the work again.

'I'll fetch in some of the flour from the new sack and you can knead it,' said Jessie firmly. 'You've a better hand with the dough than I have and, besides, it will take me all my time to fetch in enough firewood and make a stew. You rested most of yesterday, Meggie, and you can surely manage the bread today.'

Having thus silenced her sister, Jessie worked through her immediate home tasks and set out to find some firewood. Since the surveyors had arrived seven months ago, this task had devolved upon her. Joseph and Malcolm had hired out their labour to the survey and every penny they earned, as well as the generous remuneration for the meals cooked by Meg and Jessie, was going towards the precious hoard which, as soon as the main body of settlers arrived, would be exchanged for land. As he saw his dream coming close to fulfilment at last, Joseph's old fire, lost for a while after Jem's disappearance, had returned.

Jessie ran up the well-trodden path to the nearest trees. She met a young man encumbered with a theodolite coming down it and stepped out of the way to let him pass.

'Good morning, miss,' he said politely, and Jessie could not but notice the appreciative glow in his eyes. She felt the ready blush rise to her cheeks. Even after all these months of company, she was shy of the men who had invaded her solitary world and who spent their days split between their base up at Koputai and the site of the new city of Dunedin, making tracks through the bush, measuring, marking and cutting lines through swamp and fern. In the preceding two years of solitude she had quite got out of the way of conversing with strangers, and before then had been too much of a child to command admiration from the male sex. She returned a murmured 'Good morning' to the man's greeting and bolted on up the hill, and the young surveyor, watching her go, set his mind to wondering how regularly she passed this way and whether he could get that taciturn fellow Kirkwood to put in a word for him with his dashed pretty sister-in-law.

A surprise awaited Jessie beyond the next rise. The trees she had been aiming for were no longer standing. They had succumbed to the surveyors' axes and were lying about, waiting for the bonfire and the saw. Sitting dejectedly on one of the fallen trunks was the Maori girl.

'Moana!' called Jessie, running forward. She checked at the sight of her friend's tear-stained face. 'What's wrong? Why are you crying?'

Moana stood up. 'Jessie,' she said flatly. 'I am glad to see you. I coming today to your house. Eh, I do not know – my news, how I am to tell you?'

'What news, Moana? What do you mean?'

'I too much sad, long long time, Jessie.'

'I know. Your . . .'

'You know something, not all. You pakeha, you not knowing how is our life, Maori people life, before. When I am a child, my mother and my father, my little brothers and sister, all our big family – eh!' She squatted down again among the fallen branches and Jessie could find nothing to say as Moana distressfully rocked backwards and forwards. 'So happy, in that time. We have big village, then, many people, good hunting, fishing, feasting . . . Eh, Jessie, you never see our big potato field, our strong pa, our canoes, like the great ones from the old times. My grandfather, he tell such story, better than missionary one, Rangi and Papa, Sky-father and Earth-mother . . . So happy then, Jessie. No sickness, no liquor, no fighting. My mother, aiee, she love us too much. We play like little children, then we help her, cooking, washing, growing our food. So big family, all my brother and sister . . .'

'Where are they now?' said Jessie. 'Why can you not go and stay with them, Moana?'

'Dead, all dead, only my brother living, he gone down far away with the whale boats' – she waved her arm vaguely towards the south – 'I don't know, maybe he all right. Maybe he dead too.' She shook her head. 'Pakeha coming, bringing sickness, so bad sickness. Even our wise people do not have medicine for pakeha sickness. Many die, too many. Some running away.'

'I'm sorry,' whispered Jessie, stricken.

'Not you blame,' said Moana. 'Some pakeha bringing good things, learning us reading, bringing blankets, and needles, and our Saviour. Some good people. My man, he kind, he a good man, but only drinking, drinking all the time. So much lost . . .' She appeared to be sinking even further into her distress.

Jessie touched her arm. 'You have news, you said?'

Moana roused herself. 'Yes. I married,' she said simply.

'Married?' gasped Jessie.

Moana nodded. 'No good here for me, Jessie. My family all gone, all dead. Soon many pakeha come. They will break our tapu, holy places.

They will cut the trees. I cannot see it. I meet a good man in Koputai. He pakeha man, survey man, John Macdonald, his name. No liquor, no swearing, no working Sabbath. He love me, truly.' Tears welled up again and spilled down her cheeks.

'Then why are you crying, Moana? You should be happy.'

'I am happy!'

Jessie could not decide whether it was a sob or a chuckle that interrupted Moana's speech. 'With John, I am happy. But I am sad Jessie, eh, sad to say goodbye. It is very sad.'

'Goodbye? Surely you are not going away?'

'Yes. Tomorrow.'

'But the surveyors have only been here a few months! They have work enough for years!'

'John not staying here. He has land near Waikouaiti. Now he is married man, he say, want to go back to his own place. We are going together there. I will not see your new pakeha town, all your church and shop and houses. I will not see the trees fall down and the birds fly away.' She stopped.

Jessie was urgently shaking her arm. 'No, no, you cannot go, Moana! I won't let you! Please!'

Moana looked surprised. 'My husband go, I go,' she said. 'You love a man, Jessie, you go to him. All woman do that. One day you do that too, eh?'

'But you don't love him! You don't want to go! You're crying!'

A smile broke out over Moana's soft features.

'I not crying any more, Jessie,' she said. 'I finish to say goodbye now to my old home, to the spirit of my people, and my man and my little ones. Now I start a new life. Be brave again. Maybe other babies. Only when I say goodbye to Jessie, then I am sad again.'

For the rest of the day Jessie was distracted. She worked mechanically through her chores and while she responded in monosyllables to Meg, or answered Denis's insistent requests for food, or obeyed Robert's peremptory commands, her mind circled round her conversation with Moana.

It did not take her long to accept the idea of her friend's marriage. She had, perhaps, always expected something of the sort, and though she felt immediate sorrow at losing her company, she knew that the worst was to come. Her loneliness would grow and deepen in the coming weeks and months. Greater than the pain, however, was her shock at the vision of her friend's past history, of the depths of her suffering, of the tragedy of her losses. Moana had referred to her circumstances before but always with such stoicism and cheerfulness that Jessie had been deceived into thinking that the Maori girl was somehow immune from suffering, that she was, perhaps, a little lacking in sensibility. For the first time Moana had allowed Jessie a glimpse of her anguish, and though she had cast no blame, Jessie could not but feel guilty for what the pakeha had done.

For the first time, too, Jessie realised how much she had to thank Moana for. In all their time together she had been but a babe, while her friend had been old in wisdom and experience. Jessie had felt they were equals. She had felt they were girls together, thinking and feeling together, but now she began to guess, when it was too late to thank her for it, how exquisite had been Moana's tact, how delicate her guiding hand, how subtle her teaching. If Jessie was ready to become a woman now, where before she had been a child, it was Moana's doing, and Jessie had not known it.

As she scrubbed the table top to a milky whiteness, peeled a peck of potatoes and butchered a pig's hindquarter, her friend's words rang in her ears: 'You love a man, you go to him. All woman do that.'

She was still wrapped up in her own thoughts when the men came in for the evening meal. Such was her preoccupation that she was blind to the young surveyor who had smiled at her that morning and who was smiling even more broadly now, nor did she notice the half-ironic sighs and flirtatious looks that were making him the butt of his fellows. She did see, as she passed his heaped plate to him, that Malcolm was scowling but she supposed vaguely that he was suffering from a headache.

Of this naïve assumption she was disabused as soon as the meal was over and the surveyors had returned to their own quarters. Malcolm, having shifted restlessly from one task to another for a quarter of an hour or more, turned on her and burst out, 'I'm warning you, I'll not have it in my house. I know what you're after! You're to stop it, do you hear?'

Jessie and Meg, who had been disposing themselves about the candle with their sewing, turned astonished faces upon him.

'Whatever can you mean, Malcolm?' said Meg at last, looking from her husband to her sister and back again.

'You stay out of this,' he shouted. 'What she is and what she does is not fit for a decent woman even to think on!'

Jessie's face had lost its colour and her needle was suspended in mid-air.

'What can you mean? What have I done?' she said, looking at him with amazement.

'You know fine!' Malcolm was working himself up into a rage. 'Turning the heads of men, flirting, leading them on . . .'

Jessie's hand dropped, and her sewing fell to the floor. She did not pick it up. Malcolm's voice rose.

'I'll not have it! Carrying on and waylaying the men as they go about their work! Accosting them! Interfering . . . You drove my brother to run away, with your cunning tricks! It was you destroyed him! You can take that innocent look off your face, miss, for you can't deceive me. I saw you come home the day he left with your gown all rent and your face red and your – your flesh exposed! You're no better than a—'

'Malcolm!' The deep voice from the door of the cottage made all three of its occupants turn. Joseph Kirkwood had come in unheard and now stepped into the circle of light cast by the candle.

'What are you saying, man? Beware of how you speak! These are serious matters, and you must not bear false witness.'

In his father's presence Malcolm seemed to shrink. He lost his unaccustomed eloquence and stammered out, 'I'm not lying. Look for yourself. She's ripe and ready to drive a man mad with her mischief!'

Joseph did not at once turn to Jessie, but looked for a long moment at the sweat beading his son's forehead and the tremor that shook him.

Jessie did not wait for him to speak. 'You're mad,' she said contemptuously. 'I've never looked on a man that way in my life and you know it.' She stood up, ignoring Malcolm, and spoke to Joseph.

'He's accused me of driving Jem away. It's a lie, though I've not told you all the truth of what happened that day, for I knew you'd grieve over it, Uncle. The fault was mine at the start maybe, but I didn't will it so.'

'Go on, lassie.' Joseph's eyes did not leave her face.

'I wandered too far and got lost in the bush, and Moana found me and showed me the way home. She warned me – she told me to look out for a man, a drunken whaler on the prowl. But I didn't understand what she feared for me. I didn't know what men—'

She broke off, and Joseph nodded reassuringly.

'He attacked me,' she said, shuddering, 'and tore at my clothes, and I fought as hard as I could but he was stronger than me.'

The candle guttered in a draught from the door and flickered on the faces of the three listeners.

'I – I screamed, and then he pushed me over on to the ground, and just then Jem came up and pulled him away and hit him.'

'Killed?' whispered Joseph.

'Oh, no, for I heard him groan. Then – then Jem, oh – he . . . ' she stopped and turned away.

'Jem did what? What?' said Joseph, grasping his niece with unusual roughness above the elbows and shaking her.

'He – he tried to kiss me, and said he wanted to marry me, and – and he wouldn't let me go!'

'Then?'

'We quarrelled, and – and I ran away home, and I didn't know he wasn't coming back, he never said . . . '

'That was all he did?' Joseph removed the shaking hands that were covering Jessie's eyes and forced her to look at him. She returned his gaze innocently, and sniffed.

'Yes, Uncle. I – oh, please . . .'

She stopped. She had mistaken the frown that creased his forehead for anger, but she now saw that it was concentration. To her relief, he smiled at her.

'Oh, girlie,' he said, 'I wish you'd told me this tale long since. You'd have saved my mind a deal of anxious dread. If it was love made my poor daft laddie act so . . .' He shook his head as if at his own folly. 'And I was afraid it was for pure wickedness and in the pursuit of sin that he'd left his own kith and kin, and fled to the flesh-pots of Sydney, maybe, or Auckland, or one of they cities where a man may sell his soul for no more than a glass of gin. But love! For love of a fine lassie! You've given me hope again, my dear.'

He shook his head fondly at her, then turned on Malcolm. 'As for you, you great lump, with your wild imaginings, and your slanders, and your accusations – but I'll say no more tonight. There's things to do before we sleep and we'd best keep our tongues from hasty words till we've waited on the Lord and begged for pardon and peace. I'll need to stir myself if I'm to leave on the morning tide.'

'Leave?' Meg and Jessie spoke together.

He smiled at them, serene again. 'You don't think I would stay here, do you? Now I know my poor laddie is not lost to all hope? I'm away to search for him, and tomorrow's none too soon.'

'You can't leave us, Father!' Malcolm was experiencing for the first time in his life an emotion which he did not understand and over which he had lost control, and he could not foresee without a sense of panic the absence of his father, whose side he had never left before. 'And besides, you have no idea where he's gone.'

'I think I have, son,' said Joseph. 'If Jem was leaving for a short time, intending to come back soon, just to go away for a bit and build himself up as a man of substance before coming home again and trying his suit once more . . .' he twinkled at Jessie and her heart sank, 'he'd be away to find a flock of sheep, and not too far away either. Nelson's where he'd go, where he's known and could easily find a place, and that's where I'll start my search.'

'But you might be away for months!'

Joseph shook his head. 'I doubt that.'

'But the survey, the new settlement, all our plans . . . you cannot just leave us, Father.'

'You'll manage fine without me. You have your Uncle Isaiah,' said

Joseph with finality, and Malcolm, dismissing the idea of his uncle with an impatient gesture, was forced to recognise that there was nothing he could say that would make his father change his mind.

It was now that Jessie, in a moment of inspiration, knew what she had to do.

'I'm coming with you, Uncle Joseph,' she said.

Joseph's face lit up. 'You do love him, then! Oh, I knew you'd be the means of his salvation! I knew the Lord would not—'

'No!' she spoke more violently than she had intended to, and was sorry to see his smile fade. 'I'll not deceive you, Uncle. I don't love Jem and I'll not marry him, not ever. I'm coming with you because – because I have to leave this place. I can't bear it any longer. The talk of the men, the way they look at me . . .' She looked angrily at Malcolm. He said nothing but his colour changed.

Meg stepped defensively to her husband's side, slipped a hand through his arm and stared at her sister with hostility.

'Yes, you go, Jessie,' she said. 'Go on! Leave me here alone, with all the work, and another bairn on the way, and have a fine time in Nelson, like a lady! That's right! Go and enjoy yourself! Don't think about me! Don't—'

'Peace, woman!' growled Malcolm, but his eyes were fixed on Jessie. With an effort he dragged them away. 'You'd best make all right with my uncle and take her with you, if you're bent on going, Father, for I'm sick of brawling in the house.'

'Malcolm, that is not fair—' began Meg, but Malcolm turned on her.

'You'll shut your mouth now, Meg, and do as I'm telling you. I'm fed up with your whining and complaining. You'll get on without your sister and not one more word do I want to hear on the matter.'

He turned to his father. 'You'll be going up on the schooner with the supply party, I take it? They're leaving tomorrow for Wellington and Nelson on the first tide, I heard Mr Kettle say.'

'The first tide!' Meg could not restrain her disapproval, but a look from her husband quelled her, and Jessie, breathless with elation, her brain reeling at the word 'Wellington' and the disturbing ideas it conveyed, watched a grin spread over her uncle's face as he saw his son stand up at last to his shrewish wife, and had to stifle a giggle as he gave her a broad wink.

2 *Wellington, October 1846*

'Am I doing it right, missus?'

Blundell held out to Fanny the blood-dotted strip of canvas he had sewn and watched her face anxiously. She looked at the wavering line of stitches.

'Well . . .' she began, and then she looked at his face. 'It'll do fine,' she said, smiling. 'Your own mother couldn't do better.'

'No, she couldn't,' said Blundell, chuckling at his own witticism. 'She's dead.'

Fanny patted his shoulder kindly and Blundell squirmed with pleasure.

'I've done it, sir! She says it's fine!' he called out to Edward, who was supervising the loading of stores on to a mule cart.

'Excellent, Dicky,' said Edward, without looking up.

Fanny smiled at him fondly. She had never dreamed that this venture of Teddy's would turn out so well. In less than a year her dreamy, impractical son had become a Wellington institution. In a town where dame schools came and went, and where any half-literate person could set up his sign and open a schoolroom, Jamieson's was the only educational establishment with any reputation for excellence. 'Jamieson's boys' were a force to be reckoned with, known for their punishing efficiency with a cricket bat as much as for their intellectual attainments, and they were more than ready to defend with their fists and their tongues any who dared to express doubts as to the excellence of their school or its principal.

Numbers had swelled to forty and Edward had been obliged to seek assistance. He had held out against employing the services of a permanent usher, but had approached any person he knew in the colony with some special academical interest whose enthusiasm could be counted upon to inspire young listeners and who would be willing to spare a few hours each week.

He had not been disappointed. Mr Blakie had agreed to share with Jamieson's young scamps his observations on Caesar's Gallic wars, Mr Mountford had been willing to devote two hours a week to imparting the principles of drawing and even Mr Gibson had been more than happy to make a weekly visit to the schoolroom in order to give the pupils the benefit of his expertise in the French language. The parents had been more than satisfied. Edward had felt able to raise his fees and was in a fair way to paying off his initial debt to Mr Gibson.

The idea of a scientific expedition with the senior boys had occurred to Edward at the very start. The bales of canvas he had bought along with the warehouse had at once suggested the idea of tents to his fertile mind and as autumn turned to winter, and winter to spring, his plans had slowly matured.

For a while he had put them aside. The daily running of the school, the planning and organising, the growing collection of objects of natural history – all this left him with little time to spare for extra schemes, while continued talk of Maori unrest made the notion of taking a group of fifteen boys for a three-week expedition into the wilderness seem foolhardy. But Edward was restless. His school was a success. It was universally admired, financially sound and popular with pupil and parent alike. Yet it did not satisfy him. He felt a need to surmount further obstacles, to conquer greater difficulties, to feed the hunger that gnawed at him.

When he finally set to work on his plans it was with such energy that the difficulties melted from his path. He decided on Otaki, a destination some three days' journey from Wellington, as the site of the camp, and he spent his first vacation from the school visiting the place and making plans with the mission there for the cooking and other arrangements. He examined the supply of fresh water, and noted with satisfaction the variety of bush and the combination of sea-shore and river bank that should provide a cornucopia of specimens for collection and study. He made the acquaintance of missionary and Maori, and received their consent to his plan. He hired a mule cart, arranged a horse for his own use, assembled sacks of flour, potatoes and sugar, camp ovens, cups, plates and other necessaries, set the boys to making tents and persuaded their parents to lend him their support. Swept along on the tide of his will-power, the expedition had now arrived at the point of departure.

Fanny had watched the preparations with unease. She had learned to admire her son's efficiency. She had, indeed, been astonished by it. And yet, while she could not but applaud his success, she felt troubled by it. She could not help suspecting that Teddy was driven less by ambition than by unhappiness. He had withdrawn from her into a secret world of his own, and she feared that its guiding star was the image of that strange child Jessie, who was no doubt the mother of a child of her own by this time. His tenacity surprised her and made her impatient at the same time. Was he intending to waste the rest of his life in useless longings? The thought of it grieved her.

She had done her utmost to turn his mind into more positive channels. She had filled her drawing room with attractive young people more times than she cared to remember. She had cultivated the acquaintance of persons she hardly knew simply to encourage their daughters, and she had lost no opportunity to divert Edward's attention away from his wretched schoolboys and towards more worthy objects of a young man's interest. She had even, she thought a little guiltily, entertained the possibility of introducing to her son a married woman of doubtful reputation, who might distract him in a wholly frivolous way and start the process of a cure. She had schemed in vain. He had frustrated her every effort.

Fanny glanced up at the school clock. It wanted but ten minutes to nine o'clock, and the boys were due to leave on the hour. She stepped out of the schoolroom and looked along the beach. It would be too tiresome if her latest plan miscarried before it had even come to birth.

'What now, missus?' Blundell was tugging at her sleeve.

She looked impatiently at the canvas he still held in his hands. 'That will do,' she said, removing the material. 'I will secure the seam for you' – she made a few deft stitches – 'cut the thread and there! Your tent is finished. Fold it up and put it in the cart, then take your place with the others. They are nearly ready to set off.'

The cavalcade was lined up, ready for departure. The laden cart took pride of place along with Edward's horse, which Frank Gibson was holding for him at the head of the procession. The fifteen boys, each with a blanket strapped to his shoulders and a bag of extra clothing in his hand, were in a state of high excitement. News of the expedition had spread and a crowd of parents and well-wishers had come to the schoolhouse to watch them set out.

The junior boys were to be left in the tender care of Mr Jacob Streeter, a young settler newly arrived from Scotland who had presented himself to Edward with a letter of introduction from Professor Jamieson in Edinburgh, and whom Edward had taken on as his assistant. He stood now like a scrawny crow in his black stuff coat, while his young charges, deeply envious of their seniors, darted about him saying, 'It's not fair, sir. Why can't we go too?' 'Will you take us on a day out, sir, same as Mr Jamieson does?' 'Will you read to us from *Gulliver's Travels*, Mr Streeter, sir? Mr Jamieson promised you would.'

Fanny stood on tiptoe and looked over the heads of the crowd. There she was at last, and charming too, with a lace-edged parasol that should cause even the most shortsighted to blink with surprise. She pushed her way through the crowd towards this vision.

'Helena, you sweet child!' she said. 'How delightful of you to come!'

'I've put up the box of comforts you asked for, Mrs Jamieson,' said Miss Streeter with a smile of such dimpling artlessness that Fanny, not for the first time, wondered how a brother as earnest and callow as Teddy's new employee could have come by such a delicious creature for his sister.

'Oh, don't give them to me,' she said airily, waving away the basket that Miss Streeter was holding out to her. 'Take it to Edward himself. Look, there he is beside the mule cart. Oh, and' – she pulled Miss Helena back by the sleeve as the young woman began to push her way through the crowd – 'make sure to tell him how you made the fudge yourself, my dear! Such a delightful idea! I know he will be pleased with it.'

Edward was too preoccupied to notice Miss Streeter's astonishing parasol until it had all but poked him in the eye. He had been assailed by a sudden doubt as to whether the medicine chest had been packed, and was wondering if it was worth the trouble of unloading the bullock cart to check, with all the waste of time that would ensue. He turned sharply to ask Frank Gibson if he remembered seeing a long brown box going in with the specimen cases and found his face buried in a mass of perfumed lace.

'What the . . . !' he exclaimed, trying to step away from it. The lace lifted and Helena Streeter's coquettish eyes looked up at him.

'For you,' she said dramatically, and thrust an impractical basket into his arms. Out of the corner of his eye, Edward saw the flash of cherry-coloured ribbons that adorned his mother's bonnet, and knew that she was watching.

'How kind,' he said curtly, taking the basket and dumping it on top of a bundle of cheeses. It slipped and he did not straighten it.

'I – the fudge . . .' she began.

'I am much obliged to you,' he said, and thrusting her aside he worked his way through the crowd towards Fanny, whose expression of hopeful anticipation was wiped at once from her face.

'You are never – I repeat never – to play such tricks on me again, Mama,' he said, and she winced at the fury in his voice. 'You have understood nothing, and I fear you never will.'

For the benefit of the onlookers he planted a hasty farewell kiss on her cheek, then forced his way back to the head of his cavalcade, took the reins of his horse from Frank Gibson's hands and blew a blast upon his whistle.

A cheer rose from the fortunate departing, and a groan from their envious fellows as the mule-cart driver cracked his whip, the axles creaked into unwilling motion and the boys, marching two by two, stepped out along the road to the Kaiwharawhara gorge, and, led by Edward's ringing baritone, broke into the rousing strains of 'When to New Zealand first I cam, Poor and duddy, poor and duddy . . .'

Fanny watched the procession for a long time and chewed at her forefinger until the skin was red and sore.

'I have some excellent news, my love,' said Hector, passing a hand over his shock of still black hair in order to check, as he did several times a day, on the progressive thinness on his crown.

Fanny put down her starched napkin and turned her head towards the dining-room door.

'Nellie!' she called. 'You may clear away now!'

She rose from the table, tucked her arm through Hector's and led him into the parlour.

'I bought you some of your favourite cheroots,' she said, in the manner of one offering a treat to a child, 'and you can tell me all about it while you blow a cloud.'

Hector settled himself comfortably in his favourite chair.

'I have received mails from home today. Dickson has surpassed himself!'

'I knew it!' Fanny interrupted. 'He has done well with the flax! I was certain it would make a handsome profit, Hector! I told you—'

Hector sat up and stabbed at the air with his cheroot in a decisive gesture which Fanny had not observed for some time.

'Not the flax, my dear.' He could not help smiling at her crestfallen face, but this was his moment of triumph and he was determined to enjoy it. 'I am afraid you were a little too optimistic in your predictions. I should not have allowed you to argue me out of my own view of the matter. The fact is that the flax you persuaded me to buy has brought us a substantial loss, while the wool, which you tried to dissuade me from taking, has doubled all expectations! The reception from Dickson, his comments on the quality – oh, it passes all bounds! I think you must in future allow me to be the judge of such matters.'

Fanny tapped her foot impatiently. 'That's all very well,' she said crossly. 'Perhaps you have been lucky this time. But I am sure, Hector, I feel it here' – she pressed a clenched hand to her bosom – 'that there is no money in the end to be made from wool.'

'No money to be made from— ! Fanny! Have you gone mad?' Hector jumped to his feet and went to look out of his window at the magnificent vista of sea and mountains. 'I tell you, the very first clip has exceeded all my forecasts and Dickson begs me to invest further.'

'But there are sheep everywhere you look in Scotland,' protested Fanny. 'Why should the people at home go to the trouble of buying it from half-way around the world when it is to be had so near at hand?'

Hector smiled indulgently at his wife. 'These are not matters which females can be expected to understand,' he said.

'Hector! How can you be so . . .'

'So what?'

'So – unkind? After all I have done these last two years for the business!'

He saw that he had hurt her, and though not understanding the cause, strode across to her chair and took her hand in his.

'I am very grateful to you, my dear,' he said. 'I think – I do not quite understand why, but I think I have been not altogether myself since the – the Calcutta crash.'

Fanny said nothing. It was, as far as she could remember, the first time he had referred to his financial disaster since they had arrived in New Zealand. The subject had been tacitly avoided by them both. She now saw, for the first time, a spark of the old energy in her husband, and perceived more clearly than she had done before how deeply the wound had cut.

'I have not been quite able to – that is, I have found it difficult to decide easily upon things, to bring my mind fully to bear on the business. But now . . .' He gave Fanny's hand a last squeeze and dropped it. 'Now I feel quite differently. Today's news has altogether invigorated me! Oh, Fanny, Dickson writes in such terms, says we have hit upon the very thing! It is the way forward, I know. I feel it in every muscle! I am certain I will succeed in this! By the end of next year I am sure there will be enough to take a share in my own vessel and, with a few successful shipments, I should be able to buy out my partners and do as I have always intended, set up a three-way trade! Wool from New Zealand to London, manufactured goods from London to Calcutta, and muslins and even teas from Calcutta to Wellington!'

Fanny felt a little chill enter her heart. Hector misread the expression on her face.

'Oh, do not be afraid, my love. I have learned my lesson and this time I shall take care not to leave my affairs in unworthy hands! This fortune, once made, will be ours for ever! I know what I owe you. You have done more for me, my sweet Fanny, than any man has the right to ask of his wife and sometimes I have felt as if the burden of what I have done to you has been almost too great to bear! But soon, never fear, you shall be a fine lady again!' He squared his shoulders and smiled down at her, and the look in his face was exactly that of the young man who had swept her off her feet in Greyfriars Churchyard twenty-seven years ago.

'Now I am myself once more! I am on my feet again, Fanny, and do not intend to be knocked off them again.' He pinched her chin. 'I am sorry if you have come to enjoy being the wife of a poor man, my dear, for I will, within ten years from now, be delightfully rich!'

'But the accounts, the books . . .' stammered Fanny.

'You need not worry your dear head over such things any longer,' said Hector delightedly. 'I have drafted a notice today for the *Gazette*. I am advertising for a clerk. I can well afford it and the work will soon be such that only an experienced person will be able to undertake it. I don't need you in the business any more.'

His smile told Fanny that he believed he was removing an onerous burden from her and giving her pleasure. Her pride prevented her from correcting his misapprehension, but she felt tears prick behind her eyelids.

'Well,' said Hector, rubbing his hands, 'I will have to leave you to enjoy a peaceful evening with your sewing and your books, for I have business with Harper which I could not complete this afternoon, and I have engaged to see him at eight o'clock. There is so much to be done I hardly know how I shall manage it all!'

The prospect of being too busy once again seemed to delight him, for he beamed at Fanny, dropped a perfunctory kiss on her hair and left the house.

Fanny stood at the window and watched him go. The promised tears had not been shed but she was irritably aware that a headache was coming on. It was a sensation she had almost forgotten. She had hardly suffered from it since Enfield, and the idea that she had not, after all, left her headaches behind at home depressed her. She waited till Hector's springy step had taken him out of sight and drifted back to her work table. How was she to pass the hours until bedtime? Teddy had been so cross this morning, she did not dare pursue any of the delightful social plans she had concocted for his return. Indeed, she did not see how she could justify the parties of young people she herself enjoyed so much if promoting Teddy's happiness was not to be their real purpose. She could, of course, occupy an hour or two checking through the columns of figures she had looked forward to this morning but there seemed now to be no point in it, if the books were soon to be taken out of her hands. 'I don't need you in the business any more,' Hector had said, and as she remembered them, the words stung her afresh.

She opened her workbox and looked at the half-finished mass of crochet lace. She had promised to supply a table cloth for the church bazaar, and had worked on it happily until this evening. Now it held no attraction for her.

A pang shot through her temple and she sat down. She supposed she would have to take a composer and retire to bed early. Tomorrow, perhaps, she would have a clearer head. She would be able to hit upon some notion to relieve the accumulated depression of today.

A loud rat-tat at the front door startled her. Fanny sat up and thought rapidly. If the Streeter child had come to call she would have to think of some means of putting her off. She had been a little hasty perhaps to encourage the girl quite so openly, to foster hopes in that susceptible breast. She heard Nellie's footsteps pass down the corridor and a murmur of voices in the hallway. Then the door of her parlour opened.

'It's a man and a female,' said Nellie baldly, and it was clear from her tone that she disapproved of the callers and did not wish her mistress to encourage them. 'They says they wants to see you.'

'Haven't they got names?' said Fanny with asperity. Nellie's small pretensions never failed to irritate her. The maid sniffed.

'Scots he is, mum, and I can't catch his name. And if the young person's got one she speaks so low I can't hear it.'

'Well show them in, girl!' said Fanny, full of curiosity, then leaped to her feet with amazement as Joseph Kirkwood and Jessie Dunbar shyly entered her parlour.

3

Such was Jessie's apprehension at entering the Jamieson house that she could hardly control the trembling of her limbs. The schooner had docked at six o'clock, and Joseph had at once enquired about a passage for Nelson, but it appeared that no ship was sailing until the next day and he would be obliged to kick his heels in Wellington. Jessie had spent a good part of the ten-day voyage in trying to think of a way of suggesting a visit to the Jamiesons while they were in Wellington, but the boldness of the idea, even now, terrified her. In the end, to her great relief, the matter was taken out of her hands. Uncle Joseph, scanning with interest the buildings of Lambton Quay, had seen a familiar name.

'Jamieson and Co.!' he said, and her heart bounded in her chest at the name. 'Look, Jessie, do you not see, beyond the wee jetty? I'm sure as sure it must be our old friends.' Without more ado, he set off along the muddy track with Jessie at his heels.

Almost to Jessie's relief, the building was locked and barred. Mr Jamieson had clearly left his premises for the day. Joseph shook his head with disappointment, then turned as he heard a call.

'Hey! You there! What are you doing?'

The speaker was a well-dressed man of middle age with a woman on his arm. Joseph approached them, and took off his hat.

'You need have no fear,' he said serenely. 'I'm no thief. I was once in Mr Jamieson's employ and I wish to pay him my respects. Do you have any knowledge of where he's lodged?'

The man looked narrowly at him for a moment, then nodded. 'Yes, he's over in Thorndon. If you walk along this road for half a mile and turn left at the end of it, you'll see the house on a knoll ahead of you, painted white with a cabbage tree by the fence.'

Joseph thanked the man and turned to his niece. 'Is that not wonderful? It will be a fine thing indeed to see them all again. Now then – it is this way, is it not?'

He turned in the direction of Thorndon and would have set out then and there to walk the short distance if Jessie had not tugged at his sleeve. Now that the moment was so close she wanted only to flee. The sight of the woman on the man's arm had made her feel worse than ever. The dress she had been wearing, though plain, had been so good! Her hair, smoothed down on the crown, had been coaxed into a mass of ringlets that peeped out from below a bonnet whose trimmings, though they would hardly have turned heads in Paris or London, seemed positively opulent to Jessie. Her own appearance had been a matter of almost complete indifference to her during the years of solitude in Otago. Her gown was patched all over and her head was wrapped only in a simple shawl. She felt wretchedly ashamed. How could she present herself at the Jamiesons looking the poorest drab, the most complete fool? Why had she not foreseen this moment, and, at the very least, added another petticoat to make her skirts stand out a little? How foolish she had been to expose herself hatless to the sun, so that she was burnt to a coarse brown colour!

'I – please, Uncle,' she said weakly. 'I'm hungry.' It was untrue. She had never felt less like eating in her life, but as a tactic for delay it served its purpose.

'Aye, you're right,' he said. 'It would not be kind to arrive hungry for our visit and put Mrs Jamieson to the trouble of feeding us. We'll find ourselves a bite of supper first, and then we'll set about finding the place.'

The meal ended and the hour of confrontation approached. Jessie felt more and more desperate. As they climbed the rise that led to the house, she prayed that it might be the wrong one. When her uncle raised the knocker on the front door, she had to force herself to remain standing beside him, so great was her desire to turn and flee, and as she followed him and the haughty maid into the parlour, the grandest room she had ever entered in her life, she felt that after this experience not even death itself would have the power to terrify her.

She was at once relieved to find that Fanny was alone. It would be easier to slay her dragons one by one. She accepted Fanny's fleeting embrace, then stood looking about the room as Joseph answered their hostess's tumbling questions.

'What an extraordinary . . . Such a surprise! You can have no idea of how often I have thought of you these last three years! How is Meg? The baby?'

'A fine boy, ma'am, and growing well. There'll be another before many months are past.'

'Oh, I am very pleased to hear it. I was so concerned to think of the poor child all alone at such a time! But Isaiah! And Malcolm! Jem! Tell me everything! Why, Jessie, have you left your husband behind, or is he with you?'

Jessie's eyes, which had been passing wonderingly from the portraits on the walls to the satin-like sheen on the polished wooden furniture, flew in surprise to Fanny's face.

'My husband?' she said, and blushed furiously at the word. 'I am not married!'

'Not married?' Fanny's voice rose on the question, while her face fell. 'But we were told, that is, Jem informed our friend Mr Townshend in Nelson that you and he were . . .'

'Oh, no, no,' said Jessie imploringly, and Fanny, seeing that she was really distressed, forbore to press the matter further.

'You have heard from Jem then?' broke in Joseph eagerly, and Jessie, as her uncle explained something of his mission to Fanny, had time to recover her feelings, and wonder if Edward might not at any moment come through the door that led out of the far side of the room.

Fanny's attention, though claimed by Joseph, was only half on the subject of Jem. Her eyes wandered again and again to the extraordinary creature beside him. She could hardly recognise in this wild young woman the timid little girl she had known so well three years ago. She had at first wanted to laugh out loud at the girl's preposterous dress. The gown, cut and sewn from coarse cloth by an amateur hand, was ludicrously ill-fitting. The lowliest servant in Wellington would have scorned to wear such a garment. The shawl which had covered her head in place of a bonnet had fallen back on her shoulders to reveal a mass of soft, tangled hair, hastily tied in an amateurish knot at the nape of her neck.

And yet, Fanny could not say how it was, there was something magnetic about the girl's appearance. She had the unfettered grace of a wild thing, poised to flee at a hint of danger. There was in her every movement a swiftness, a lightness, a freedom that was almost shockingly natural. She walked as boldly as if she had never felt the hampering weight of a multitude of petticoats. She swept the hair from her eyes with the directness of one who had never given a moment's thought to bonnets and curls.

'And how is Mr Edward Jamieson?' said Joseph Kirkwood at last. He was thoroughly enjoying the visit. He rejoiced to see Mrs Jamieson so comfortably situated, and though he could not but deplore the worldliness of her attire he appreciated the comfort of her parlour, and was happy to see her relieved from the necessitous circumstances of Duddingston.

His question was a cue that both women had been waiting for. Their eyes flew to each others' faces.

'He is away just now with a party of schoolboys. We are not expecting him home for at least three weeks,' said Fanny with relief. She had seen enough in Jessie's face to tell her the worst. The girl was in love and could not hide it. A temptation presented itself to Fanny's mind and she tentatively explored it.

'He is so very busy,' she said with a little laugh that sounded false even in her own ears. 'You must know that he has opened a school! It is the most delightful enterprise. He has forty pupils and is becoming quite well known, even beyond the limits of Wellington! He is in some haste to build himself up and make his way in the world, for, as I am sure you must guess, he will soon be thinking of adding to his domestic responsibilities.'

Joseph smiled innocently. 'He's to be wed, then?'

The lie hovered on Fanny's lips. An engagement between Edward and Honoria Gibson, or Helena Streeter, or half a dozen others came almost tripping off her tongue. Then she looked into Jessie's eyes, read the agony in them and could not go on.

'No,' she said baldly.

Jessie was too agitated to listen to the remainder of the conversation. She hardly heard her uncle announce his intention of leaving for Nelson in the morning. She did not take in Fanny's halting invitation and Joseph's eager acceptance of it until she kissed her uncle goodbye, and followed her old mistress out of the parlour, and up the stairs to a well-appointed bedchamber.

'You must be very tired, my dear,' said Fanny, playing for time. 'If you have everything you need for the night you can retire now, and we will have time to talk in the morning.'

Fanny had acted on impulse and she spent the night regretting it. Whatever could have persuaded her to invite Jessie to stay while Joseph was away at Nelson? A marriage between Teddy and Jessie was the last thing she wished to promote. She scolded herself, wondered at herself, and tossed and turned beside Hector's peacefully slumbering form while the clock on the dining-room mantelshelf chimed the night away.

When morning came, she knocked at Jessie's door and peeped in to find the bed made and the room empty. The sound of raised voices led her to the kitchen. Nellie was giving vent to her feelings while Jessie stood by the kitchen table wide-eyed with anxiety. Nellie turned to Fanny.

'It's not what I'm used to, mum! I'm telling you straight I am. In all the gentlemen's houses I've worked in I've never had no young persons coming into my kitchen, taking the work out of my hands and the bread from my mouth as like as not. Saying as how she "only wishes to help"! A likely story!'

Jessie started forward and tried to speak but Nellie thrust out a ladle towards her.

'Don't you give me any of your lip, my girl. I seen your kind before, working your way in here, spying . . .'

'Nellie,' said Fanny wearily. 'That will do.'

Nellie stared at her mistress mutinously.

'I got my rights, same as anyone else,' she said.

'Yes,' said Fanny, 'and so have I. A week's pay in lieu of notice, Nellie. You may pack your box at once.'

A flash of triumph passed across Nellie's face, which she concealed by turning with a flounce to the door. She had been planning for some weeks past to convey herself and her few possessions to Nelson, where dwelt a labourer who had taken her fancy on the emigrant vessel. She had not left the Old Kent Road and braved the perils of the deep, she said to herself with a toss of the head, to spend the rest of her life serving other people in their fancy dining rooms. It was time to set up her own home and the extra week's wages would not come amiss.

Jessie and Fanny were left face to face in the empty kitchen.

'I am sorry,' stammered Jessie. 'I did not mean . . .'

Fanny laughed. 'I'm delighted to see the last of her,' she said honestly, 'for a more foolish creature you cannot imagine, and though I have shown her three times how to make a custard she cannot get the trick of it.'

There was another silence. Fanny sat down at a chair by the kitchen table, and pointed to the other one.

'Tell me, my dear,' she said. 'Was it very dreadful in Otago?'

For answer, Jessie dropped her head on her arms and burst into tears. Fanny allowed her to sob for a few moments without restraint, then, as Jessie hunted fruitlessly about her clothes for a handkerchief, extracted her own and pressed it into Jessie's hand. This simple act of kindness threatened to bring about a fresh attack of weeping. Dread of meeting Edward, dread of not meeting him, love and guilt towards her beloved former mistress had combined to make her quite overwrought. She controlled her tears with an effort.

'It's – it's not so bad,' she said, applying the handkerchief to her eyes. 'We have the cottage all nice and tight, and now the surveyors have come . . .'

'Tell me,' said Fanny. 'Tell me everything.' She had, ever since they had said their farewells, longed to know the fate of the lonely band of pioneers, adrift on their far-distant southern shore. She had tried to follow them in her imagination time and again, surprising herself with the extent of her interest. The Kirkwoods and Dunbars had, after all, been woven into the very fabric of her life in their years together at Duddingston.

Jessie began to talk, haltingly at first, and then with increasing fluency. She was unused to putting her thoughts and feelings into words and she was even more unused to the charm of a fascinated audience. Fanny gave her her entire attention, gasped at the narrative of little Robert's birth, exclaimed at the loneliness of the tiny cottage at the head of the long sound, and shook her head sympathetically at Jessie's account of Moana's plight. Some parts of the story Jessie omitted. She did not mention Gabriel or her cousin Jem except in the most general terms, nor did she describe her own attempts to observe and draw the wild birds and plants she had discovered in the bush.

By the time the recital had come to an end, Fanny had made a decision. If Teddy wished to marry this girl, she neither would, nor could, stand in his way. She could not, if asked, have explained this *volte-face*. She only knew that it was right and, as soon as she had accepted it, she felt a lifting of anxiety, and with it a pleasurable feeling of expectation. She made a rapid assessment of the situation. It was fortunate indeed that Nellie had so speedily removed herself. She would not have to fear servants' gossip in the work she was about to undertake. It was an excellent thing, too, that no one in Wellington knew of the Jamiesons' past connection with the Dunbars. The fact that they had at one time been master and servant could easily be concealed. It would, of course, have been a great deal more awkward if the girl's family were living within easy reach, but they had committed themselves to the new settlement at Dunedin and would doubtless remain there, as remote from the gossips of Wellington as if they had been in China.

Fanny's eyes sparkled. Jessie had presented herself at an excellent moment. She had been in need of a project, and here was one ready to hand, at this very moment vigorously blowing its nose at the far end of the table. It would be delightful to dress the child, to take her under her wing, to teach her some of the feminine arts of which she appeared so woefully ignorant. Young as she was, she would be easy to mould, might even in the end be perfectly presentable. A dozen plans rushed into Fanny's head but with uncharacteristic caution she checked herself. There was something unpredictable and headstrong about the girl. She possessed the same kind of intensity Fanny had recently noticed in Teddy. She had not succeeded in managing him very well of late. Indeed, she rather feared she had set his back up. It would not do to range this child against her too. She wished, after all, only to become Jessie's friend, her guide, her mentor. It was, on reflection, a positive advantage to have such unformed material from which to create a daughter-in-law, a blank sheet, as it were, on which she could draw a design of her own choosing.

She jumped up from her chair. 'Now, Jessie my dear,' she said happily. 'We have a great deal to do.'

Jessie looked puzzled. Then her face cleared. 'You mean now that Nellie has gone?' she said. 'Is it your washday today, or your baking day? I have not brought my pinafore . . .'

'No no, child,' said Fanny impatiently. 'Your clothes!'

She smiled at the startled look in Jessie's eye. 'We must make you a little more presentable before we can go abroad together in Wellington.'

'Go abroad?' said Jessie. 'But . . .'

'Now,' said Fanny kindly, 'you know and I know that at Nelson, when you were nothing but a child, you were employed in our service, but that is not the case now. You have come to visit me as a guest and, I hope, a friend. And I shall take it very amiss if you do not let me entertain you.'

Jessie was bereft of speech.

'After all,' Fanny went on happily, 'we must make sure that you show yourself to your best advantage when a certain . . . But I shall say nothing on *that* head!' and as she congratulated herself on her discretion, she remained unaware that she had not only betrayed a knowledge of Jessie's heart, but admitted her own acquiescence to its most secret desires.

Jessie was so astonished by Mrs Jamieson's extraordinary hints that she could only suppose she had misheard. It could not be true that her old mistress, so rich and grand as she was, could actually be encouraging her former servant to love her son! She decided that she was too stupid and ignorant to understand Mrs Jamieson, and followed her obediently up the stairs and into Fanny's bedchamber, determined to show her gratitude during the course of her stay by assuming as many domestic duties as she could.

As the morning progressed Jessie's astonishment increased. Fanny, possessed with a ruthlessness that would brook no objections, seemed to have taken a fancy into her head to dress up her one-time maid as one might a doll. She first made Jessie discard her old brown gown, then dived into trunks and boxes, drawing out cotton petticoats, fichus, trimmings of gauze and knots of ribbon until her bed and chair actually disappeared under a display that would not have disgraced a modish dressmaker's establishment.

At last she made a pile, and held one gown after another against Jessie, shaking her head over some, hesitating over others, and eventually swooping on a simple cotton stripe dotted over with a print of blue anemones.

'Just the thing!' she cried with delight. 'It does not do to be too elaborate, after all, for the roads are so muddy that one is forever being splashed. Now try this, my dear, and I will fasten it for you.'

Jessie did as she was bid, then stood obediently while Fanny fussed about her, shaking out a flounce here and nipping in a tuck there. She stood back at last and exclaimed, 'Quite, quite charming!'

Jessie, perfectly tongue-tied with embarrassment, stood stock still, hardly daring to breathe.

'Well, go on my dear,' said Fanny impatiently. 'Pirouette about a little.'

Jessie took a couple of awkward steps.

'Shoes!' said Fanny. 'Those ancient boots are fit only for the back country, and they must be of little use there for I see they are holed in the soles. We shall provide you with something more becoming this afternoon. In the mean time, I have a pair of half-boots that I believe will fit you perfectly. I shall be glad to give them to you for they pinch my toes abominably.'

Fanny was ransacking an old cabin trunk as she spoke and she emerged breathless, the boots in one hand and a complicated arrangement of net and ribbon in the other.

'Is not this a charming headdress?' she said enthusiastically. 'I would have liked of all things to see you in a large straw poke, but it is no use to think of such things in Wellington. No one wears them here, for the wind is so very . . . But with a trimming such as this, even the plainest cap would be charming. Sit down here, on the corner of my old cabin chest, and let me fix it for you.'

Jessie, still silent, did as she was told and submitted to Fanny's fingers until that lady pronounced herself satisfied. Fanny stood back at last, looked at Jessie, and almost caught her breath with surprise. 'Why, you are quite, quite lovely!' she said.

Jessie stood up, and treading warily between the tumbled piles of clothes upon the floor, stepped over to the pier glass and looked at herself. She saw a tall young woman gowned in a deceptively simple robe of white cotton patterned in blue. Her hair, brushed to a glossy sheen, was parted in the centre and looped over the ears. A diminutive cap trimmed with a mass of silk flowers and net had been arranged over her hair to stunning effect by Fanny's experienced fingers. It was the face and form of a beautiful stranger.

The sight of herself frightened Jessie. 'I can't – it's not . . .'

'Don't be absurd, my dear,' said Fanny bracingly. 'Oh, I know it will take a little time to accustom yourself to a new way of dressing, but you must remember that gentlemen expect – that is, they are accustomed to a certain way of – and besides, you have such a natural grace, a charming figure! You are a positive delight to gown.'

Into Jessie's mind rose the image of another woman, a thin, gaunt figure with work-roughened hands who had once clothed her in a plain brown dress with a white kerchief round her neck, and called her a rosebud. She felt ashamed.

'Mrs Jamieson, you are very kind,' she burst out awkwardly, 'but I cannot, I mean – I do not feel able . . .' With trembling fingers she pulled the trimmed cap off her head and laid it on her bed.

Fanny saw that she had gone too far, and moved to correct her mistake.

'You are very right,' she said matter-of-factly. 'A plain style will become you better.' She worked quickly at Jessie's hair, removed the loops and pinned it into a simple knot. 'As for the dress, it is the simplest thing imaginable, and the colour becomes you to perfection. You will do me a great favour by accepting it, as I have no use for it any more, and had intended to give it to Nellie. Now, if you will help me to clear away this disorder we have made, I will lend you a pinafore, and we will see how fast two pairs of hands can complete the work that Nellie never seemed able to finish in a day.'

4

Jessie found that she had stepped into a world so different from the one she had always known that she might as well have been upon the moon. She had never before known such pampering, such idleness. Here in Mrs Jamieson's house the sheets were so smooth, the beds so soft! Each meal was a banquet, each conversation a labyrinth of intricate meanings. She felt caught in a lovely web spun by Fanny's deft fingers. At times she luxuriated in it, but more often it filled her with terror.

Fanny had been careful. After her first attempt to dress her young friend she had sensed the danger of rushing things and had planned her approach carefully. She had refrained from seeking a new maid to replace Nellie. She preferred, at the moment, to have the house to herself and, in any case, Jessie seemed to gain satisfaction from performing domestic chores. They were a support to which she clung as a drowning woman might hold on to a life-raft. To boil up the linen, bake a batch of pies or polish the candle brackets on Fanny's piano seemed to give her more pleasure than any of the more conventional treats that Fanny suggested.

Dressing the child had not been an easy matter. Fanny had at last persuaded her to accept three simple gowns, a patterned shawl, a couple of plain caps and two pairs of already used boots, but the reticules, fichus, fans and earrings which she sought to press upon her guest had all been refused with such growing embarrassment that Fanny had learned to desist. In any case, she thought, looking with approval at the sleek head bent over a pile of mending, it was undeniable that simplicity was the best adornment for the girl. The bows, ribbons and ringlets that a Honoria Gibson delighted in, and used to such effect, would only serve to dim the natural grace of a Jessie Dunbar, whose unusual beauty seemed to radiate from within.

It was not until a week had passed that Fanny felt ready to expose Jessie to her first small taste of Wellington society. She had planned it all most carefully. Several promenades along the quay in search of everyday necessities had passed off well. Jessie had been introduced to one or two passers-by, and had responded shyly but with self-possession. Fanny had had no cause to blush. Jessie's manner was neither pert nor obsequious but open and natural. Her voice, too, was quite acceptable. It was clear and low, and although it was strongly marked with the lilt of Scotland, it reflected the gentle speech of her mother's native Ayrshire rather than the coarser patois of the city dweller.

'My dear,' said Fanny one morning after the breakfast dishes had been cleared away, 'we must bustle about today, for I am expecting one or two callers this afternoon.'

Jessie looked up without alarm. 'When would you like me to bring in the tea?' she said.

Fanny laughed a little too loudly. She was unsure of Jessie's response.

'You will not need to worry yourself over the refreshments. We shall contrive somehow. You, of course, will be sitting with us in the drawing room.'

Jessie dropped the duster she was plying round the ornaments on the mantelshelf and turned to stare at Fanny.

'I – I can't,' she said.

'Don't be ridiculous,' said Fanny. 'Why, I have promised everyone the chance of meeting you.'

'Of meeting me?' repeated Jessie stupidly.

'Of course! It is not everyone who goes off to live in the wilds when a mere child, as you have done, and who returns years later as a grown woman! It is a story that excites the greatest interest.'

Fanny turned back to the papers she was sorting on her little desk. She did not quite wish to meet Jessie's eye. The curiosity of her friends, though real enough, had not been altogether spontaneous. Fanny had hit upon the clever notion of presenting Jessie as a curiosity, a child pioneer, an intrepid explorer of the wilds of Otago. This would serve to account for any little irregularities of speech or deportment that might otherwise have been difficult to explain away. She had thrown out enough hints as to storms at sea, weeks of near starvation, forays into the bush, Maori magic and desperate whalers to create a romantic feast at which her friends were only too eager to sup. Though it contained the germs of truth, this picture would have surprised Jessie very much indeed if she had heard Fanny describe it.

'Please,' said Jessie wringing her hands. 'I don't think – that is, it would not be right . . .'

'I shall not hear another word on the subject,' said Fanny firmly. 'You shall wear the striped cotton, for though it is plain it becomes you admirably, and I insist – no, this time I will not take no for an answer – that you accept the seed pearl necklace I showed you on Thursday. It is exactly the thing for a young girl, and I positively will not let you refuse it a second time.'

She got up and left the room, and Jessie, who had at first wished to run after her to beg to be let off, stood thoughtfully, twisting the duster she had retrieved from the grate in her hands. Her mind was in a turmoil. This visit to Fanny was her chance, her one great opportunity to win all that she most ardently desired. If she was ever to marry Edward (and the idea that had once seemed no more than a ridiculous dream now appeared less impossible as each day passed) then she must somehow find the courage to enter his world. She would have to learn to meet and converse with the people he knew as his equals. The idea of sitting on a chair and sipping tea from one of Fanny's best cups was not so momentous as it would have been a week ago. She had learned to do it every day. But to be introduced to her friends as an equal, to be asked questions, to be forced to speak – the idea of it made her tremble with fright.

Jessie was still trembling when, a few hours later, the last of Fanny's visitors arrived, and yet a merciful sense of unreality had come to her aid. She felt divorced from herself. This was not Jessie who sat here, smiling and nodding at the gracious Mrs Franklin, exchanging 'how de do's' with Mrs Gibson and Miss Honoria, and passing the milk jug to the austere Mrs White. It was another creature altogether, a strange being called Miss Dunbar, who somehow, from some prompting of an inner self, seemed to know what to do and what to say. This Miss Dunbar was actually the centre of all these ladies' attention.

'Oh, do tell us,' said plump Mrs Franklin, whose husband owned one of the finest town sections but whose skirt was reassuringly splashed with mud, 'how did you live so long down there without the company of another white woman?'

'My sister – she and her husband, that is – we were together.'

'Ah, your sister? She is a married woman, then?'

'Yes, she has a little boy.'

'A baby! Not, I trust, born in the wilds?'

'Oh, yes. At least' – Jessie's brow wrinkled as she sought for strict accuracy – 'on the schooner as we approached Otago.'

'But you must have been entirely without the support of . . . ! How very . . .' Mrs White's nudge reminded Mrs Franklin just in time of the presence of Miss Honoria, and she checked herself, saying only, 'I trust at least that the weather was calm.'

'No,' said Jessie, paling a little at the memory, which she was not used to dwelling upon. 'There was a storm.'

Further questioning was impossible, but the minds of the married women raced as they watched the expressions crossing Jessie's sensitive face. Mrs Gibson, who was much amused by Fanny's protégée, leant forward to tap Jessie's knee.

'The wild boar,' she said.

Jessie's eyes, suddenly turned on her, looked so huge and startled that Mrs Gibson was irresistibly reminded of her husband's nerviest hunter at home in Dorset.

'I beg your pardon?' said Jessie.

'Mrs Jamieson informs me that you tamed a tusker,' said Mrs Gibson, 'which, I must confess, seems a feat quite above the ordinary.'

Jessie curled inwardly at the teasing note in her voice, as she tried in vain to understand.

'A – a tusker?' she said.

'There,' said Mrs Gibson happily. 'I knew it was all a hum. I have found you out, my dear Fanny, for a shocking story-teller. There is no pig in the case at all.'

Jessie's brow cleared. 'Oh, you mean Denis,' she said. 'But he is quite a little pig, and very tame.'

Honoria Gibson, who had felt herself very much left out in the cold by the attention paid to this dubious young person, gave a spiteful titter.

'How singular, to be sure! I myself have never, I must confess, been tempted into an intimacy with a pig. Hardly the fit companion for a lady.'

Her mother frowned and Fanny flushed, but Mrs White, who had noted the restraint of Jessie's costume with approval and had from the outset frowned on Honoria's showy headdress, leaped to Jessie's defence.

'You are quite wrong, Miss Gibson,' she said, stabbing a finger towards that young lady. 'Pigs are second in intelligence only to ourselves and their reputation for dirt is quite undeserved. If,' she turned graciously towards Jessie, 'you have indeed managed to tame a wild creature of that sort it is greatly to your credit. I myself have devoted some study to the care of goats. Their milk, you know, is so much more digestible than that of cows, and I have found . . .'

Fanny relaxed. The breeding of goats was a passion with Mrs White, and she enjoyed airing her expertise on the subject. The older ladies listened politely and covered their yawns, but Jessie leant forward, fascinated. This was the kind of talk she could understand. There was a proper subject, real information was being exchanged. It was more to her taste than the subtle fencing that seemed to be the style between the other ladies. She had felt all at sea with them, as if she were stumbling blindly through invisible curtains. With Mrs White you simply had to listen to what she was saying and try to understand.

It was clear to Fanny that Honoria was not amused. The pout on her face was growing more pronounced by the minute. She had only agreed to accompany her mother on this visit because she had been promised a freak, a child of the wilderness who had survived nameless adventures. Instead she had found this plain creature, whose lack of social grace would have caused waves of laughter at home, and who, worst of all, seemed to cast her inexplicably into the shade. And on top of all this she was obliged to endure the tedium of Mrs White's horrid goats. Her foot began to tap ominously and Fanny, with the instincts of a good hostess, sought quickly to put matters right.

'Perhaps,' she said, breaking into the flow of Mrs White's discourse, 'Miss Gibson would care to entertain us with some music?' She stood up and went towards the piano to look through the pile of songbooks on the lace-covered table beside it. Honoria flushed. She was aware of being patronised, and her temper would not stand for it.

'Why does Miss Dunbar not play for us?' she said, putting fractionally too much emphasis on the 'Miss'.

'I don't know how to,' said Jessie simply.

'What? You have not learned the pianoforte? How very odd,' cried Honoria. She caught her mother's furious eye and clenched her fists with vexation. This odious girl had made her betray herself into unladylike behaviour. Now she would have to endure yet another homily from Mama on the long road home. It was so unfair! In Dorset one was not expected to converse with jumped up nobodies, and one certainly did not have to listen to persons who lectured one on the subject of goats. She longed more than ever for London, and vowed to herself that sooner rather than later she would make her papa send her home.

Fanny closed the door after her departing guests with delight as well as relief.

'A great success!' she said, clapping her hands. 'You were delightful, my dear. And Mrs Gibson was so cross with that minx Honoria! I had not the least idea that she was so ill-natured. How glad I am, after all – but never mind that. She is dreadfully spoilt, of course, and there is a want of openness, of naturalness that one cannot but compare . . . And Mrs White was so pleased with you. She is a person of consequence in Wellington, for although she has her oddities she has great strength of character and is equal to any emergency, and that of course counts for everything in the colonies. "A very good sort of young woman," she said to me, and coming from her that is praise indeed.'

She put an arm round Jessie's slender waist. 'I feel quite – quite proud of you!' she burst out, 'and I'm sure I should not say it, but I could not be more fond of you, my dear Jessie, if you were my own daughter.'

* * *

Three days later, Joseph Kirkwood came back from Nelson. Jessie saw him from the parlour window. He was walking up the slope towards the house, his head bowed, his gait slow. He looked weary.

'Uncle Joseph!' she cried, and ran out of the door and flew down the path to meet him. He held her away from him and looked her up and down. He shook his head over her grand appearance, but his eyes twinkled.

'Eh, but you're as fine as fivepence,' he said. 'Too grand for the likes of us now.'

'Oh, no, no,' she cried, distressed at the thought. She saw that he was no longer thinking about her, and although she did not wish to mention Jem she asked the question that would most please him.

'Did you find my cousin, Uncle?'

He nodded but without a smile. 'Aye, my lassie, I found him.'

'And is he well?'

'If you mean in the body, he's well enough. But if you mean in the soul, I couldna say.'

Fanny appeared round the corner of the house with a trug in her hand, deposited it hastily on the stump of a tree, and came up to Joseph with her hand held out in welcome.

'Why, Joseph Kirkwood! What a delightful surprise! We had not looked to see you until the end of the week at the earliest!'

'Good day to you, Mistress Jamieson. I see you have been at work to turn my niece into a fine lady.'

Jessie flushed at the dry note in his voice, and stepped back a pace, but Fanny appeared not to hear.

'You will come in, and drink a cup of tea with us, Joseph,' she said firmly. 'We wish to hear all about your progress in Nelson. Jessie, run on, my dear, and set the kettle to boil, for I'm sure your uncle wishes to refresh himself.'

The kitchen fire had burned low and the wood needed fetching from outside, so that Jessie took longer than usual about the task. When at last she came into the parlour with the tray and set it down beside Fanny's chair, she could see at once that her uncle and her old mistress had not been engaged in a mere exchange of pleasantries. His face was stern, and hers was flushed. Jessie's heart missed a beat. Had they, perhaps, been talking about her? Had her new gown and modishly dressed hair offended her uncle's strict principles? She need not have worried. The talk had all been of Jem.

'But you say Mr Black speaks highly of him, says he is an excellent shepherd, and will soon be in a way to set up his own flock?'

Joseph nodded doubtfully. 'Oh aye, he'll have lucre enough, and flocks and herds, I've no doubt of that, for his mind is set on worldly wealth. But his heart is still froward, and there is no repentance in him. Stiff-necked! Stiff-necked!' The old man, sitting uneasily on the edge of Fanny's brocaded chair, clasped his hands together between his knees and heaved a great sigh.

Fanny saw her chance and she seized it. She had long wished to talk to Joseph Kirkwood of his son and now she sat forward on her chair, took a deep breath and began. She talked well and at length. She spoke of the boy's sensitivity, of his unexpressed desire to please his father, of his excellent qualities, of a young person's need to cut free from the parental hearth, of the harm that constant carping could do to a certain type of man.

Joseph heard her out in silence but it was clear that she had made no impression on him, and when at last she paused, he burst out, 'What for do you talk of love and understanding and all the rest of it, as if I did not love him so much it well nigh kills me? Don't you understand woman? It's his eternal soul I'm fighting for! If the boy does not repent and turn to the Lord and take the priceless gift of salvation, then he is doomed to everlasting damnation! Can you not see it's that which haunts me, to be tormented in the flame, the great gulf fixed . . .'

In spite of Aggie's training in religious matters, Fanny had never acquired the absolute certainties of her sister. Her faith, though real, was elastic and she had always enjoyed a comfortable vagueness on the subject of damnation. Joseph's prophetic agonies were not of a kind that she could share and she fell into an uncomfortable silence for a moment or two, then looked round for a more cheerful subject. Her eyes fell on Jessie.

'Well,' she said, with an attempt at brightness. 'We must not forget another young person. I have so enjoyed Jessie's visit that I must ask you to lend her to me for a little while longer. Surely she need not return to Otago just yet?'

Jessie sat up with a start. She had been lost in a brown study and had heard very little of the conversation. Her uncle's appearance had given her a shock and she had needed time to assimilate it. She had never before noticed how very rough and calloused his hands were, so unlike the smooth white hands of Mr Jamieson. His clothes, too, though clean, were worn and threadbare and he could not be taken for any but a working man. She had not before had cause to think critically of his speech or his manners. He had always seemed so far above her, so unassailable in his authority, but now she noticed that he sat with awkward stiffness, plying his teacup with clumsy fingers, and she missed the easy grace with which Hector and his friends lounged and strolled about the room. Then, too, his speech was so very Scots, so uncompromisingly Biblical!

It had always sounded rich and sonorous in her ears but now she found it embarrassing. She saw the yawning abyss between her world and the Jamiesons', and was appalled. She had made herself ridiculous these last two weeks, a servant girl pretending to be a lady, a fool who thought she could reach out and pluck the forbidden fruit! She wanted to go away into a corner and cry, to tear off this pretty gown that she had been so happy to wear this morning, to don her old brown homespun again and disappear for ever, to a place where she would be far from the mocking laughter which she imagined must even now be ringing round the homes of Fanny's friends. She was too overcome to speak.

Joseph spoke for her. 'It's kindly meant, I don't doubt,' he said heavily, 'but we must be away in the morn. There's a schooner leaves for Otago, and I've secured places for the two of us. The weather's fair for the voyage, and I'm not wishful to bide longer. Jessie comes with me.'

'Oh, but really,' protested Fanny. 'Why can the child not remain—'

Joseph stood up, and shook his head with such decision that Fanny was silenced. 'She comes with me,' he repeated. 'Jessie, you'll meet me at the quayside at eight o'clock, for the tide won't wait for us.'

Jessie nodded. 'Yes, Uncle,' she said.

Chapter Twenty *October 1846*

1

Jem needed to think, and as usual the exercise did not improve his temper. It had taken him many days to recover from the effects of his father's visit. He had been knocked back by it. The unexpected sight of his father had initially elated him, but at the end of only half an hour he had realised that nothing had changed and the disappointment made him angry. He had worked so hard, done so well, gained respect from the boss and the hands alike and now it would all be for nothing when they saw how his father treated him, scolding him like a child, warning Mr Black to keep him away from the taverns of Nelson and throwing dark looks at Nancy, whose saucy talk he took very much amiss. Jem had kept his temper with an effort, had listened in silence to his father's exhortations and even suffered himself to be prayed over. There was nothing he could say or do, he knew quite well, that would remove from Joseph's mind the notion that he was one fallen from grace, a lost sheep, a prodigal son. He had doggedly refused to leave his employment and return to Dunedin, as Joseph had begged him to do, and would not budge from his declared intention of remaining in Nelson until such time as he could buy a flock of his own and lease a stretch of land to run it on. Joseph had had to be content with that, and they had parted at last, puzzled and sore, each one convinced of the pig-headedness of the other.

It was only when the impact of his father's presence had faded a little that Jem began to remember in detail some of the news he had given him. At the time he had found it hard to listen, hard to take anything in. But on the next day as he tramped about the hills, his gun over his shoulder and his dogs at his heels, checking and rechecking on the welfare of the sheep, snatches of conversation returned to him.

'Jessie? Oh aye, you were too hasty, you young fool. She's shy, that one is, easily startled. You'll need to give her time. It's my belief she'll come round to it in the end, if you show her a repentant heart. But no respectable woman will take a man that drinks and breaks the Sabbath and . . .'

'Och, yes, she'll be coming back to Dunedin with me. I'm away to fetch her from the Jamieson house. Edward? No, I didn't see him, and nor will she either. He's away off on some wonderful scheme or other with those boys of his. It's a pity, so it is. A grand lad, and you would do well to look at his example . . .

'If you'd only come home and settle down and put your mind to making a wee place for yourself, and showing her how canny you are with building and the like . . . There's not a woman alive can resist a home of her own and a good man who shows he's sober and honest and diligent. If you'd only . . .'

That evening, as he sat with the other hands around the kitchen table, he heard nothing of the conversation and had to be nudged twice by Dickie Turner for failing to pass the salt. A new man, Vanwijk, had arrived on the station and though he was Dutch and could not as yet speak much English, Jem had noticed that he had not felt himself at all handicapped in joking with the irrepressible Nancy. The banter was not to Jem's taste. He himself had never responded to the girl, but somehow he had got used to being the object of her loudly expressed admiration and the butt of her affectionate raillery. Now she was leaving him alone and turning more and more of her attention to this daft foreigner, who could not even say her name without it sounded wrong.

A burst of laughter made him raise his head from his plate, which he had piled high with potatoes and chops. The damned Dutchman had caught the girl as she was passing behind the bench, had pulled her to him and was trying to kiss her lips while she laughingly beat at him with a ladle and the other hands shouted encouragement. The sight of them disgusted him. In any case, his appetite had gone. He pushed the remains of his dinner away, stood up and went out into the yard. Then he whistled up the dogs and set off along a footpath to an outcrop where he could sit in peace and watch the sun sink towards the bush-clad hills in the distance.

The fresh air cleared his head and a train of thought at the back of his mind now rose to the surface. Jessie had been staying at the Jamiesons. His deception must now be discovered. Edward would soon know, if he did not know already, that Jessie was not wed, nor even promised, to her cousin. The danger was real again. There was nothing now to prevent his rival from pursuing her to Otago and snatching her away, and Jem, remembering the look in Edward's eyes when he thought she was lost to him, knew suddenly that that was what the man would do. He knew, too, that he must prevent it. He could no longer feel that Otago was comfortably inaccessible. The surveying party needed constant resupplying and ships from both Wellington and Nelson were now calling regularly at Koputai. It would be easy for Edward to get himself south. He might, indeed, be on his way already.

Jem could sit still no longer. He jumped to his feet and stood irresolute. He would have to change his plans. He had not intended to act yet. He had meant to put by a much greater sum from the wages he was so carefully saving. He had meant to have enough capital not only to buy a section near Dunedin but to stock it also. Now he must think again. He could not sit idly here while that cripple, that dominie, that *gentleman* robbed him of his woman.

There was only one thing he could do. His father and Jessie would be transferring from the Wellington packet to the Otago supply vessel in Nelson tomorrow, or the next day at the latest. He must retrieve his savings, collect up his few belongings and sail home with them. His decision would, he knew, call down the wrath of Mr Black upon his head and he would be obliged to bear the usual tirades of his father, but he must, somehow, make Jessie see reason, he must wed her, have her, before her fancy lover got to her first.

He set off purposefully down the hill and back to the homestead.

A flock of pigeons, nibbling peacefully at their plumage, were the first to hear the cacophony of the cavalcade that wound its way down the Kaiwharawhara gorge, and they cocked their heads to peer at the strange sight before flapping away in alarm. Jamieson's boys were returning to Wellington in cheerful mood and full voice, their singing enhanced by a number of bullock horns pressed to several pairs of inexpert lips.

'Louder than that, boys! Let 'em have it!' shouted the first in the train. Blundell was determined that no citizen of Wellington should fail to be aware of this triumphant return. It was he, indeed, who had insisted on a proper order for the entry into town. Edward had seen to it that the packing cases, with their precious collections of specimens, were disposed in the mule cart in such a way as to minimise the effects of bumping over the appalling roads, but it was Blundell who had made sure that every boy had his blanket strapped to his shoulders, and had even given them practice in marching step by step, in the way that his uncle, a sergeant in the Thirty-Seventh Foot, had taught him.

His classmates were experiencing various degrees of euphoria. Patterson could not wait to show his mother the impressive number of sandfly bites on his legs and demonstrate to her how little he cared about them. Higgins was dying to present to his startled parents the brace of quail he had shot with Mr Jamieson's gun under the latter's guidance, while Rogers, who had always distressed his father by fighting shy of water, was looking forward to astonishing that gentleman by diving off the jetty and demonstrating how well Mr Jamieson had taught him to swim.

The first boys reached the bottom of the gorge and came out at the waterfront on the road that ran along the shore from Wellington to Petone. Enthusiastic cries rang back towards Edward, who rode at the back of the column.

'Sir! Sir! I can see the first houses!'

'There's a new ship in, sir! It's standing off the quay, sir!'

'There's the school! Look, they're out playing cricket! Hi! Hey! We're back!'

Ear-splitting shouts and blasts on the horns broke out, and it was all that Blundell could do to rally his men and get them back into the orderly column on which he had set his heart.

Edward, smiling at his efforts, lifted his broad-brimmed hat and mopped the sweat from his brow. The last three weeks had been extremely taxing. There was no doubt that the experiment had been a success. Most boys had gained in confidence, self-reliance and stamina, and all had benefited from the companionship which had forged them into a united and purposeful band. At the same time, it had been a constant strain. He had been filled with a dread that some real harm would come to his young charges. He could not without a shudder think of the moment when Frank Gibson, climbing up a rocky ridge in search of a bird's nest, had almost fallen and broken his neck, nor of the moment when Blundell, foolishly teasing a bull on the track through Johnsonville, had very nearly been gored. The swimming lessons, though in the main successful, had also kept him constantly on the alert.

His eye moved over the bobbing heads in front of him as he made one final count. Yes, they were all there, and there was now not one boy he did not know well, whose strengths and weaknesses, virtues and faults he could not easily have described. This new knowledge had not been without surprises. He had found unexpected fears in the boys who had seemed the most independent and hidden resources of endurance in those who had not shone in sporting pursuits. He had also, he had to admit, been surprised by his own reactions. There was only one word that could describe the feeling he had for this ramshackle assortment of adolescents. It was love.

Edward was the last to emerge from the gorge on to the Wellington road, and by the time he was in sight of the town, his pupils had already managed to alert its citizens to their approach. People were standing at the doors of various houses and business premises that made up the colony (now as large as a good-sized fishing village) and some had already set off along the road to meet them. He saw with a smile that the game of cricket in progress outside his schoolhouse had been interrupted, watched a boy run inside to impart the news, then saw the door burst open and a wave of children pour out of it, while Mr Streeter stood overwhelmed among them, gesturing with his long black arms, vainly attempting to restore order.

Soon they were passing the Thorndon house and Edward looked up at it a little guiltily. He could not see his mother and he did not look forward to meeting her. Though she had been trying of late, he had not been quite kind when they had parted, and he was afraid that she might have been upset.

The noise generated by the mob of schoolboys penetrated into the warehouse in which Hector was inspecting a consignment of wool that he was about to ship to London on the *Mary Dee*. He went to the open door and looked along the beach. Aye, there he was, the rascal, with his damned young hooligans, and it was grand to see him home again. He had not been anxious over the boy precisely, but he had spared him a thought or two. It was a major enterprise to lead a party of mischievous schoolboys away into the wilds and he had looked forward to their safe return. A fine fuss Fanny would be in, now that her one chick was restored to her. She would be all on tenterhooks over this love affair with Jessie, and he would hear of nothing else for weeks to come. Hector smoothed back his hair. It was a strange business, he thought, and Fanny's behaviour was one of the strangest parts of it. She had done a right about turn over the girl. He had thought she had set her heart on a much grander, or at least, more conventional bride. But that was Fanny, he thought affectionately, forever plunging after the most unexpected thing, investing all her enthusiasm in one mad scheme after another, and opening her eyes with disbelief if you so much as hinted at any inconsistency in her behaviour.

He himself had been so busy these last weeks that he had had few thoughts to spare for the quiet young woman who had flitted like a shadow about the house, but he could see how she had caught Teddy's fancy. There was about her a curious stillness, yet beneath it a man could sense a strong will, an independent mind and a well of hidden excitement. She would not make Teddy an easy wife, he was sure of that, but she would not make a dull one either.

It was a magnificent day, hot and sunny, the bottomless blue of the sky reflected in the lapping waters of the harbour. The notorious Wellington wind was today no more than a pleasant summer's breeze. Hector's eyes lingered over the view. There were a score or more vessels in port, some unloading, others taking on bales and barrels and an assortment of Antipodean spoils. There was here but a pale reflection of the turmoil of the London docks and, Hector had to admit to himself, he was often nostalgic for that. The society of entrepreneurs in Wellington, though congenial, was on a very different scale from the milling throng of merchants, sea captains, men of affairs and brokers of all kinds among whom Hector Jamieson's had once been a name to reckon with. On most days, of course, especially when the sun shone as it did today, he was keyed up with the excitement of his expanding business, with the satisfaction of watching the balance in his ledgers increase month by month, with the notion that he, a gambler, an adventurer, was riding a winner once again. And yet whenever he saw the wind fill the sails of a laden barque and blow it out through the heads to the open sea beyond, he felt a sense of depression; he knew that he was stranded in a backwater, excluded from the centre of things, and homesickness attacked him.

He shook it off now before it had time to work upon him. He would take an hour or so away from his business (he had earned it, after all) and go to greet his son. After all, he had news for the boy which should bring a smile to his face, and there was nothing more pleasant than to be the bearer of good tidings. He turned his head, shouted an instruction to the two men in the warehouse loft above and set out along the beach.

The crowd around the schoolhouse had grown. The heads of excited boys bobbed up and down. Hector could hear Edward's voice. He had not realised quite how penetrating and authoritative it could be.

'Careful with that box, Higgins. It contains the ferns. No, Blundell, you may not ring the school bell to apprise everyone of our return. The news seems to have spread quite satisfactorily. Ah, Mrs Patterson – your son is quite well. There is no recurrence of the cough you feared.'

Edward disappeared into the schoolhouse and was lost to view. Hector was about to follow him when he felt a hand on his arm. He looked round to see a tall stranger standing beside him.

'Excuse me, sir. Can you inform me of where I might find Mr Jamieson?'

'I am Jamieson,' said Hector with a small bow. His hand was grasped immediately, and pumped up and down.

'Excellent! Excellent! I am Stanwick, Charles Stanwick, from Edinburgh. I have read your latest paper on molluscs and I must congratulate you. A very fine piece of scientific investigation! I have messages for you from various members of the university, and an invitation to send some cases of specimens to . . .'

He was fumbling in the pocket of his coat in search of a letter, but stopped as Hector said, 'I fear there is some mistake. I am not in the habit of writing scientific papers. Perhaps my son, Edward . . .'

'I beg your pardon! Of course! E was the initial. I have then the honour of speaking to Edward Jamieson's father?'

'Yes, indeed. My son is by now in his schoolhouse. He is a schoolmaster, as perhaps you know already. He has but half an hour ago returned from an excursion up country with some of his pupils. You will find—'

'Thank you, thank you very much,' said Mr Stanwick hastily, and he began at once to push his way through the crowd towards the schoolhouse door.

Hector watched him go. He felt disinclined to follow him. This was not an auspicious moment in which to convey tidings of a romantic nature. He would wait until later, or allow Fanny the pleasure of acting the part of Mercury. In any case, he felt a little shaken by the encounter. He was accustomed to being a personage in his own right, of being Hector Jamieson of Jamieson and Co. He had never until now been reduced to the mere status of Edward Jamieson's father, and he did not much care for the experience.

When Fanny returned from an afternoon visit to Karori to find Edward already at home, she was mortified to have missed his arrival. This was a moment she had looked forward to eagerly for days past, and she intended to relish it. She kissed him soundly, remarked on how brown and how thin he appeared to be, exclaimed over the deplorable condition of his boots, and following him up the stairs to his room, embarked at once on the task of making him happy.

'You will never, never guess, my dear, who has been visiting us while you have been away!'

Edward, intent on extracting a pile of dirty shirts from his travelling bag, did not answer.

'Someone you would most particularly have liked to see! Someone who lives a long way – to the south!'

Her words penetrated Edward's abstraction and he turned a wary look upon his mother. She was gazing at him, hands clasped under her chin, with a look of sparkling mischief in her eyes.

'Mama, please,' he said wearily. He need not have bothered to feel guilty over her. She was teasing him with another of her silly games and he would not be drawn into it.

Fanny saw that she had made a false start and worked hard to repress her exuberance.

'I'm sorry, my love,' she said. 'I do not mean to tease you. It's just that my news is so very . . . But I will not beat about the bush any longer. Jessie Dunbar has been here, staying with us. She—'

He was in front of her in one swift movement, his hands painfully gripping her shoulders, his cheeks whitening.

'If this is some kind of joke, Mama, I will . . .' he choked.

She laughed a little awkwardly. The intensity of these two young things was incomprehensible to her, and they somehow had the knack of making her feel uncomfortable. She knew, of course, the strength of a great passion. Had she not been madly in love with Hector? But she had always kept her sense of fun, had always been able to laugh, and add a little spice of extra drama to the whole affair. Edward and Jessie were so alarmingly serious.

'Stop crushing me to pieces, Teddy,' she said, removing his hands from her shoulders, 'and sit down on your bed and listen.'

It was years since she had addressed Edward as a child, but the trick worked. He obeyed her. He listened in silence, his colour changing from white to red, and back to white again. When she had finished speaking she was touched by the pleading look in his eyes.

'Tell me, Mama, swear to me, that what you have said is true? She is not married? She is not promised to anyone else?'

'Ask your father,' said Fanny simply.

Edward stood up, dazed, and began to stuff the linen back into his bag.

'What are you doing, you silly boy?' cried Fanny. 'Give all that to me! It needs a thorough boiling.'

'I must go to Otago at once,' said Edward.

'Have you taken leave of your senses?' said Fanny sharply. 'You have a school to run, matters to attend to. Mr Streeter has managed the juniors very creditably in your absence but he could not possibly control the senior boys as well. You cannot leave until the holidays start. It is only two weeks until Christmas, when school will be out in any case. For heaven's sake, Teddy, have a little sense! And besides, where is the need for hurry? You do not want to come upon Jessie when she is just returned home. Allow her a little time to recover from her journey! Two weeks can make no difference, after all.'

Edward pulled a shirt slowly from his bag, looked at it and passed it across to Fanny.

'You are right, I suppose,' he said reluctantly. 'I should not leave the school just now. Though how I am to wait so long I really can't imagine!'

Chapter Twenty-one *Dunedin, December 1846*

1

Jessie could not believe that life in Otago could have gone on so mundanely during her six weeks' absence. It seemed as if she had been away for at least a year and she half-expected, when she stepped out of the whale boat into the two feet of water by the Dunedin shore, that she would find young Robert already learning his letters and Denis a fully grown porker.

'There's no use for fine ladies here,' Meg had sniffed when she saw her sister dressed in a new shawl and gown, and with unpatched boots on her feet, but she had been mollified when Jessie unpacked her bag, for Fanny had put up for Meg a great supply of clothing, shoes, small items for the household and garments for little Robert as well as the new baby, and though Jessie had refused more than a handful of things for herself, she had felt no scruples in accepting them for Meg.

'Will you look at this now?' Meg gasped, pulling out a frivolous lace cap (which, had she but known it, Fanny had rejected as hopelessly outmoded). 'When does she think I'm to wear such a thing down here?'

Jessie, too busy to answer, was extracting a pair of kidskin gloves and holding them up for inspection. The idea of mincing about in the solitary mud of the Otago harbour in such fine garments as these made both girls burst out laughing, and in the prolonged fit of giggles to which they succumbed, Meg's old jealousy and Jessie's resentment were forgotten.

The best things were soon packed carefully away against the time when the colony would finally arrive from Scotland and there would be some society to admire them, and the days fell back into their old routine. Outwardly it seemed to Jessie as if she had never been away. The men went off sometimes for days at a time with the surveying party, with the exception of Isaiah, who would not move from his vegetable patch. Meg and Jessie cooked, baked, washed, cleaned, mended and minded Robert.

And yet it seemed to Jessie as if she had begun a new life. She looked on the wilderness in which they lived with fresh eyes. The curiosity of Fanny's

Wellington friends had shown her that they were indeed embarked on an extraordinary adventure, that Uncle Joseph had a vision for them and for their future quite outside the usual order of things, and for the first time she felt proud of her family. She could see that even her father had played an admirable part in taming this little area of the original creation and making it bear fruit. She felt, too, more patient with her sister, bearing the burden of motherhood with no older woman to help and guide her.

At the same time, Jessie had never before felt so distant from them all. She was waiting. Though she often doubted and sometimes despaired, she knew that soon there would be a change, that he would come or that she would receive word from him, that one way or another her fate would be decided. She spent many hours trying to remember the exact words that Fanny had used when she spoke of Edward. Her hints had been so strange! At times they filled her with the wildest hope. At times she believed she had imagined them all. Sometimes she was angry with herself for not accepting Fanny's invitation to stay in Wellington, where she might have continued to learn how to become the kind of young woman Fanny seemed to think that Edward preferred. And yet an instinct told her that she had been right to come home. She was not an Honoria Gibson and no amount of trying would make her into one. She was herself, and if he did not like her as she was he would not like her at all.

The hardest thing to bear was the assumption of all the members of her family that it would be only a matter of time before she agreed to marry Jem.

'I'll put that by for you and Jem when you set up your own house,' or, 'Here's Jem's stockings to darn – you might as well get used to it,' Meg would say fifty times a day, and Jessie no longer bothered to remonstrate with her. Since no one listened to her denials it did not seem worth the trouble of making them.

Jem observed this increasing complaisance with satisfaction. He took it as a softening towards him. He had not been much in the habit of observing other people, but he now watched Jessie's every action and listened to her every word. He noticed the way she withdrew from raised voices and demonstrations of anger into a kind of inner stillness where no one could follow. He saw how silent and bored she became when the talk turned on small domestic matters, and how she became animated, her cheeks delicately flushed and her slim hands gesturing decisively when she spoke of the finds of natural objects she had made in the bush or on the shore. An unusually shaped shell or a rare fern brought a spark to her eye more readily than the gift of a new ladle, which Jem had taken some trouble to whittle for her from a piece of driftwood. She had even seemed to prefer the present of an albatross feather to a carefully worded compliment on her cooking, which he had succeeded in delivering with painful gruffness after half an hour of agonised thought.

Even when it came to her precious specimens, however, she was still unpredictable. Jem had spent the better part of a night in hunting one of those strange, wingless creatures with long stabbing beaks that the Maori girl had called a kiwi. He had trapped the thing at last, killed it so neatly that the body was scarcely harmed, and presented it to Jessie with every expectation of receiving grateful thanks. She had expressed an ardent wish to see such a bird close to, and he had made it possible for her. He could not understand why she had seemed so irritated. She had looked at it with disgust and asked him to take it away. He had put her reaction down to the well-known changeableness of the female mind and undeterred had, on the following day, at some risk to life and limb, climbed a forest giant to fetch a bunch of flowering orchids, which had had a warmer reception.

By the end of the fourth week in Otago Jem could not, in spite of some small gains, feel that he had made all the progress he would have wished. He could not say that Jessie showed him any liking or disliking. In fact, she seemed not to notice him at all. He had redoubled his efforts. He had marked out a site for the cottage he intended to build. He had talked in her hearing of the size of the flock he would one day bring down from Nelson. He had showered upon her shells, pebbles, flowers, fern fronds, feathers and a dead lizard, all to no apparent effect.

All the time, Jem's longing for her had grown. He could think of nothing and no one other than her. Wherever he turned, there she seemed to be. If he spent a day cutting fern with one of the surveying parties, he would catch sight of her solitary figure in the far distance, pegging out the washing by the shore. If he went off to the bush to hunt pig, he seemed to see her form in front of him, slipping away between the trees. And even when he rowed up the harbour to Koputai, her reflection appeared to shimmer out at him from the glittering surface of the water.

It was on one such trip to Koputai that Jem received bad news. A consignment of supplies for the surveyors had been delayed by bad weather, and the ship had been forced to put in at Waikouaiti, some way up the coast. The vessel had been too badly damaged to complete the voyage, and the sacks of flour and sugar, affected by damp, had been sold off cheaply to the Waikouaiti settlers. An urgent request for a fresh consignment had been dispatched, and the gossip at the port was that within the next day or two a ship from Cook Strait would be arriving in Otago. This news made the hair at the back of Jem's neck rise, and his heart thump. He knew as certainly as if he had received a letter that Edward Jamieson would be on board.

From this moment a kind of madness seemed to possess him. As he rowed the long distance back to the lonely cottage at the head of the harbour, he felt physically different. His head was clear, plans forming and refining themselves almost without his volition. His muscles were more taut and vigorous, his ears and eyes more sharp and keen than usual. He could see now that he had been foolish and weak these past weeks. He was facing the most serious challenge of his life and only swift and sudden action could avert defeat. He had allowed himself for too long to be held in thrall by his father's over-strict morality and the romantic folly of a dreaming, untried girl. The present state of affairs called for boldness and ingenuity.

By the time he stepped ashore, Jem knew what he would do. It was late afternoon. The men had returned from their labours, and a curl of smoke rose from the chimney of the cottage and the surveyors' camp fires. He could smell from yards away the eel stew that the girls had prepared for supper. He dragged the boat ashore and disposed the oars, neatly as a seaman, then ran his fingers over his unruly hair and tucked the ends of his shirt into his breeks. He had never been in the way of thinking of his looks, but he had begun to care that Jessie should not be disgusted by any disorder in his appearance, used as she now was to the fine ways of Wellington.

The following night Jem slept badly. The plan that had come to him so simply with the rhythmic motion of the oars seemed in the small hours to be unrealistic and fraught with peril. But towards dawn he slept and when he woke the problems seemed to have smoothed themselves away. He felt himself a little distanced from reality, superior to the others, who went about their daily business ignorant of what was about to take place. He felt immensely powerful, all-seeingly wise, and tolerant even of his father, whose vision seemed now so small, so hedged about by the petty restrictions of convention.

The main surveying party was working towards the south-east of the Dunedin site while several smaller groups were engaged near the harbour or out on longer expeditions along the coast. Jem, who was in good standing with Mr Davison, the director of the surveying operation, had requested and received permission to absent himself from his normal work and to take his gun off after wild dogs, whose night-time raids on the surveyors' camp had become a real nuisance. After breakfast, therefore, he picked up his gun and made for the door of the cottage.

'By the by, Meg,' he said, turning at the door and studiously addressing his sister-in-law rather than Jessie, 'there's a grand pile of firewood ready cut and bundled for you up the burn. It's not two miles from here. You could bring it down easy in a couple of trips.'

Meg looked at him crossly. 'Two miles! Do you think in my condition

I could go half a mile with one of your loads of wood on my back? Why did you not lift it home yourself?'

Jem's smile held no shadow of his customary surliness. 'I laid it up for you last week, and forgot to tell you of it,' he said. 'I was away off in a great circle round the hills and you'd hardly expect me to take it along too.'

'I'll go for it,' Jessie said. She knew it would fall to her lot sooner or later and, in any case, she did not in the least mind a walk on this lovely summer morning, though it would be hot work on the way home with a bundle on her back.

'I'll be away, then,' said Jem. He ducked his head under the low lintel of the cottage and went out before either girl could read the satisfaction on his face.

Jessie set out on her walk later than she had intended. Meg had relapsed into fretfulness again these last few days and a tiresome number of domestic chores had piled up, waiting for Jessie's attention. The sun was high when she eventually felt ready to go. She fortified herself with a scoop of cool water from the brimming cask by the door that Malcolm filled each morning from the burn, and left the cottage thankfully, glad to swing her arms in freedom and breathe in the clean balmy air of this glorious, cloudless day.

The cache of firewood, as Jem had described it, lay to the west in the opposite direction from the surveying parties and Jessie met no one and heard no sound of human life as she hurried along the path cut through the fern of the shore flat. She paused for a moment by the bridge of lashed branches that the men had laid over the burn and looked down into the clear water, wondering if there were elvers in the shade of the stones on the bed. But she saw nothing move except for a couple of brilliant green and gold feathers that spun round and round on the eddying water as if propelled by a will of their own.

She arrived at the edge of the bush and looked about for the bundles of wood. She saw no bundles. Instead, she saw Jem emerge from the cover of the trees.

There was something about him, an eagerness, an air of excitement, that alarmed her.

'Hello,' she said warily. She wanted to ask what he was doing there, but somehow the question did not come out.

Jem studied her face. He had watched her so closely these last weeks that he could now read her every expression, and he knew he must take care not to frighten her further. He assumed his customary gruffness.

'You've come round by the wrong path,' he said shortly. 'The stuff's away over there.'

Jessie tutted with exasperation. 'I can't get along there for it,' she said. 'There's a gully that's too deep to cross and no path. Anyway, I'd cut my clothes to pieces on the bushes.'

He pretended to consider. 'You'll have to follow me, then,' he said. 'There's a track through the bush I've been along many times. I know it well. It comes out just above the gully. You can get to the wood easily enough from there, and there's an easy way down home from there too. Come on.' He turned and started to go back into the trees.

Jessie hesitated, uneasy. She had not come this way in her previous ramblings. Moana had discouraged it. There was something to avoid in this area, some grave or stone or ruined house, something *tapu* to the Maori. Moana had never told her precisely what it was but since she had seen the white tui, Jessie had learned respect for Maori prohibitions. And, besides, she did not like to be alone with Jem. Since the confrontation on the beach, when he had held her so strangely and talked so wildly, she had avoided him as best she could, taking care not to look at him or talk to him in any way that might arouse his passion. Above all, she had made sure that she was never alone in his company.

Jem stopped and called back to her. 'Are you coming or not?' he said, with his usual irritability. 'I've things to do today. I've to get away up the ridge before mid-afternoon if I'm to have any chance of a shot.'

His impatience reassured her. There was nothing lover-like in his behaviour. It was quite the reverse, in fact. Jessie held her skirts away from the grasping fingers of a vine and followed him into the bush.

Half an hour later she was hot and distinctly cross. She had addressed numerous questions to Jem's swift-moving back, and he had not deigned to answer half of them.

'Are we not nearly there yet? Surely we should have come out ages ago? Are you lost, Jem? For goodness' sake, where are we going? Why don't you say something?'

Her suspicions began to grow. Jem must have mistaken the path, but he was too proud to admit to it. They must be lost! It was of all things what she least wanted. She looked about anxiously. Every way she turned she could see no more than a few yards distance into the matted tangle of trunks, vines, ferns and bushy undergrowth. Men had been known to wander in circles for days in terrain such as this and die at last of thirst and despair.

'Jem!' she called again, and the urgency in her voice was such that he turned at last to look at her.

'We're there, Jessie, we're there!' he said, and she saw with an unpleasant shock that the expression she had mistrusted was back in his face, a naked eagerness which he did not now try to conceal. She stopped on the path, not wishing to advance by another step, but to her surprise, Jem went on a pace or two, then suddenly disappeared. She looked about wildly for a moment, then heard him laugh and call to her.

'Here! I'm here!' came his voice, from somewhere near the ground. She looked down and saw a fissure in a long slab of grey rock.

'What are you doing?' she said helplessly. 'Come out! Where's the firewood? I want to get out of the bush. I want to go home!'

He reappeared like a jack-in-the-box in front of her, grasped her hand firmly, and before she knew what had happened, had pulled her after him down a short, steep incline to an area of flat forest floor, behind which opened the mouth of a cave. In spite of her fear she looked round in wonder. This secret, beautiful place would at any other time have filled her with delight. Soft banks of moss made brilliant green cushions outside the cave, whose interior seemed dry and coolly inviting on this hot day. A spring, coming from somewhere higher up, trickled in one single stream of crystal water at the edge of the glade, and the scent of some bush flower, far out of sight in the great canopy of the forest roof above, drifted through the air, while a bell-bird on a nearby branch chimed away in full-throated song.

Jessie's eyes swept quickly round and fastened themselves on Jem's face. The intensity in it made her catch her breath. She stepped back.

'What are you doing?' she said. 'What is this place? Why have you brought me here?'

He did not make the mistake of frightening her further by moving closer to her. He had not handled nervous sheep and hunted game for years past without learning how to manage a wild one.

'Is it not lovely here?' he said soothingly. 'I found this place for you. It's your place, Jessie, our place. It was made for you and me, for us to be here together.'

'What do you mean?' she said. Her fear was growing but she was angry now too. She wished most of all that he would stop saying her name, dwelling on it as he did in that caressing, silky tone. He had never called her anything in the past.

'You're mine, Jessie,' said Jem, speaking steadily and low. 'You've tried to deny it, but you cannot. You were made for me, my cousin. You're mine by rights, everyone knows that. You and I are to wed. It has to be. We're to be man and—'

'No!' Jessie's anger had surpassed her fear now. Her eyes blazed with it. She stamped her booted foot on the mossy ground and her breath quickened. 'Will you never listen, Jem Kirkwood? I'm not yours! I won't marry you! I don't love you – in that way – and I never will! Can you not understand when a body speaks plain and clear? We never will be man and wife. Never!'

'But we will, Jessie, we will.' The quiet certainty in Jem's voice sent a shiver down Jessie's spine, and impressed her more than any outburst of anger would have done. She felt her legs begin to tremble and tried unsuccessfully to control them.

'What do you mean?' she whispered.

'This is to be our first home,' said Jem with dreadful gaiety. 'I'll not hurt you. I'll not make you cry. But you'll stay here with me.'

'No!'

'You'll stay here with me until you agree to wed me.'

'I won't! You can't do this! You can't force me!'

Jem ignored the interruption.

'We'll go home when you've promised yourself to me, body and soul, given yourself to me of your own free will—'

'I'll die first!'

'Oh, we'll not die,' said Jem. He intended his manner to be reassuring. 'We've water here, and a good supply of food. Look . . .' he pointed inside the cave, and Jessie could see a bulging sack on a ledge at the far end of it. 'If you want for fresh meat I've my gun, and there are pigeons enough to feed an army. And you needn't fear to be cold in the night, for I'll keep you warm, I'll—'

'No! No!' The words were so faint she could hardly hear them herself. She took another step backwards, conscious of a dreadful paralysis that had crept upon her. Somehow she must escape, she must find a way out of this nightmare. 'Leave me alone!' she pleaded. 'Let me think.'

Jem looked at her measuringly. He did not think she would take flight, and he knew she would not get far if she tried it.

'Sit on yon rock,' he said, 'and I'll wait by the burn. You can take your time. There's nothing to hurry us. We have all the time you want. All the time in the world.'

2

Under other circumstances, Edward would have relished the opportunity offered by the voyage down the east coast of the South Island to Otago but from the moment he set foot on the supply vessel at Lambton Quay he was filled with an apprehension he did not understand. This feeling of dread was so strong that he could not summon up interest in any of the sights and sounds along the way. The bush-clad shores, the beaches, the sweep of hills and mountains in the interior and the vista of swelling waves held no fascination for him. Even the sight of a royal albatross, dipping its vast wings over the mast, did not really interest him. He turned away from it to look back to the shoreline, straining to catch the first glimpse of Otago.

There were maddening delays. The wind was contrary and the little schooner was obliged to butt against a strong southerly, making each mile a weary labour to the sailors. Off Banks Peninsula a leak in the bows became too dangerous to ignore and the captain was obliged to put into Akaroa, where the carpenter took two full days to patch up the hole. Even with journey's end in sight, their luck did not turn. Heavy seas made the captain nervous of attempting to cross the bar into Otago harbour and the heavily laden craft tossed and pitched for eight frustrating hours before he felt confident of getting safely through.

It was almost two weeks after he had left Wellington that Edward at last found himself in a whale boat being rowed up the inner harbour to the site of the new city at its head. His presence had excited some curiosity on the part of his companions. Most people who took the trouble to visit these remote parts had a good reason – a region of virgin bush to survey, city streets to lay out, supplies to ferry, or some financial speculation to pursue. This tense young man gave the strangest of reasons for undertaking the long and uncomfortable journey. He had come, he said, to visit friends, for all the world as if he were on a jaunt from London to Brighton.

Edward had been aware of no other person on the schooner and he noticed none of the crew manning the whale boat now. His thoughts were in a turmoil. The dream of Jessie that had sustained him for so many months past seemed no more than that – a foolish, insubstantial dream. What, after all, did he know of her? How could he trust mere memories? Supposing his feelings had played a terrible trick on him, created an unreal love for an imaginary woman, and driven him on this mad adventure only to land him in disappointment and embarrassment when at last he came face to face with the real Jessie? This anxiety, bad as it was, was yet not the worst. His dread had intensified. He was now desperately afraid, afraid for Jessie, afraid for himself, afraid of Jem. Why had he not raced at once to Otago when he had learned that she was still free? How could he have let any other consideration stand in his way? As a man in a nightmare who finds when he tries to run that his legs are shackled, he felt a bursting sense of frustration.

It was a still grey morning and the sea was as calm as a millpond. As the whale boat approached the shore, Edward saw the little cottage, the fern whare and the surveyors' tents standing in brave solitude in the vastness of the landscape all around, and felt suddenly self-conscious. There would be others apart from Jessie whom he would have to face, and on whose hospitality he would be dependent. He had no speech prepared, no reason to give for his unexpected arrival, and it was with a sinking sensation that he splashed ashore and walked up the well-worn track to the cottage.

He need not have worried about his reception. Meg was alone, engaged in plucking a brace of quail, and so preoccupied was she with the events of the past twenty-four hours that she hardly seemed surprised to see him.

'Mr Jamieson, well, well, now, whatever can have brought you all the way to these parts?' was all she said by way of greeting, and she could not even shake hands with him as hers were all over feathers.

He looked round the cottage with the greatest interest, wondering, with a catch of his breath, if Jessie might not at any moment come through the door, and looking with some astonishment at the sight of a toddler feeding potato peelings to an affectionate pig.

'You'll not find any here but me,' said Meg, mistaking his glance. 'They're all away off hunting in the bush for Jessie.'

Edward started at the sound of her name.

'And there's no use asking me what it's all about,' said Meg in a complaining tone. 'No one tells me anything. They'll only say that Jessie's lost somewhere in the bush, but they're sure to find her today, and it's all the fault of Jem, though I do not understand how. I thought for sure they were to wed, though she's been that set against him you wouldn't believe, never thinking of my feelings in the matter. It's too much to expect a person in my condition to have the care of a younger sister, and why she should turn up her nose at a respectable man who's her own kin I cannot understand. And now it seems he lost his patience at her, which I cannot wonder at, and took her into the bush to push her into making up her mind, and she ran away and is lost. And Jem came running home in a bother calling out to Malcolm and his uncle to help him find her because he's scared she's lost for ever, and my uncle in such a taking he's scarce ate his breakfast. Jem is as surly as a bear and Malcolm is not much better, and even my father's gone off, leaving me here on my own, and if I should be taken bad they'd neither know nor care. It's all a fuss about nothing, I am sure, for Jessie knows the bush better than any of us and many's the time she's been out for days together, though never all through the night before, I must admit, and found her way home in perfect safety.'

'Do you mean,' said Edward, straining to follow this rambling discourse, 'that Jessie has been lost in the bush all night?'

'Well, she was not lost precisely, not at first in any case, for Jem was with her.' Edward did not seem to find this information reassuring, but Meg, bending to recover a knife which young Robert had picked up from the table when her back was turned, did not notice the grim tightness around his mouth. 'She should have stayed with him and promised what he asked, and made herself engaged all right and proper as he wanted instead of running off wildly on her own when his back was turned. It was no wonder he lost her at once for the trees are very dense hereabouts and I would not care to penetrate far into it for anything, still less at night. But there's no telling Miss Jess what she should and should not do. Headstrong – aye, and full of secrets too. Why, I mind when—'

Edward could remain silent no longer.

'In which direction did she set out?' he said. 'Is there a track, any landmarks, any way of showing me . . .?'

Meg looked at him with disfavour.

'It's a wild goose chase,' she said. 'She'll come back in her own time and she'll let no one near her until she's good and ready. Besides, it's nigh on two miles to the place where she went for the firewood and a long way, says Jem, into the bush from there, and with your crippled foot and all—'

'I can walk very well, thank you,' said Edward, through set teeth. 'I will set off now if you will be so good as to point out the direction.'

Outside the cottage the low cloud was beginning to lift and a few patches of blue were appearing. The track Meg had pointed out lay over a rudimentary bridge, then cut through a wide, flat area of scrub and fern which ended at the dull green edge of the bush. Edward's heart was pounding and his palms were clammy. What dark things had been going on here in this wild, remote place? What turmoil of feelings, what depths of longing and despair? What passions and rages and acts of violence? Above all, what had that madman done to Jessie? He forced himself to think, to plan, to pace himself. He had learned to walk well enough with his wooden foot, though it was a wearisome business after the first hour or two. In normal circumstances he preferred to walk without a stick, which served to announce his infirmity. Today, however, he would need all the help he could find. He stopped by the first good-sized shrub, cut himself a staff and then went on again, covering the ground at a steady pace, his mind racing eagerly ahead, scanning the bush, memorising the gullies, the hills, the slopes, the angles of the ground. It would be impossible to see the lie of the land clearly from under the dense cover of the trees.

He stopped for a moment by the creek, his mind working furiously to unlock a memory. He and Jessie had stood by such a creek once, near Duddingston. What was it they had talked of? He knew it was important. Yes, that was it! They had talked of getting lost, of the impossibility of finding one's way. He had boasted (how could he have been so arrogant?) that the bush held no terrors for him. The trick, he had said, was to find running water and follow it. Sooner or later it must lead to a larger stream or to the sea. He looked up again. This small rivulet debouched from the trees not far from the spot Meg had described to him, where Jessie had disappeared. There was a chance, just a chance, that she might remember his words and stumble over it, and follow it out into the open. At least it offered him a plan. He would keep beside the creek into the bush and work his way systematically along it until he either found her or dropped with exhaustion. He did not rate his chances very highly. The Kirkwood men, he knew, must have combed the area with their usual thoroughness. They had probably now abandoned their search on this side and penetrated further into the bush. But it was his only starting point and he would have to take it.

3

As the long afternoon turned to evening and twilight fell, Jessie was sustained only by anger. She moved restlessly about, pacing the small flat area outside the cave while Jem went quietly and steadily about the business of making camp, fetching firewood, gathering dry branches and leaves for bedding, and cooking a creditable meal from the simple ingredients he had hidden away days before. Sometimes Jessie watched him in incredulous silence. Sometimes she ranted at him or jeered at him, but to no avail. There was only one subject he was prepared to discuss, he told her, and that was their future together, the life they were destined to share.

By nightfall she was wrung out, and as darkness fell she began to feel more frightened than angry. She kept away from the mouth of the cave, not wishing to see the bed Jem had so carefully prepared. She ate a few mouthfuls from the plate he offered her, and when he told her with the hint of a threat in his voice to lie down beside him and sleep she had no choice but to obey. She avoided looking at him, and stretched herself out on her back, arms crossed on her chest, as cold and discouraging as a marble effigy on a tomb. To her great relief he did not attempt to touch her.

Rest, however, was impossible. She had set out that morning with no shawl over her cotton gown as the day had been warm and sunny, but here in the cave it was cold and she had to grit her teeth to stop them from chattering. With considerable effort she lay absolutely still and pretended to sleep. She was afraid that any movement, any confession of discomfort, would rouse Jem, lying motionless nearby, and bring him to her side. She could not abide the thought of hearing his voice or feeling the touch of his hands.

At last, in the small hours, nature's demands could be ignored no longer. She got up and started to creep outside. In an instant he was standing up, his hand on her arm.

'Where are you going? You're running away!'

She shook him off roughly. 'Oh, for goodness' sake,' she burst out. 'Will you leave me be now? There's things a body must do in private and I'll not have you standing over me while I do it!'

He grunted and went back into the cave. For the first time since this adventure had started, Jessie found herself alone and the sensation went to her head. The call of nature was forgotten. She *could* run away! She *could* creep behind a bush, and wait there in the dark, moving slowly and quietly till she melted into the trees! He would never find her. The faint gleam of moonlight that penetrated the forest canopy was enough to prevent her from colliding with the great trunks that rose up all around, but in the play of shadows it created it would be easy to remain out of Jem's sight. For a moment she thought of the danger of losing herself, she thought of Moana's warnings of *tapu* hereabouts, of the white tui. She remembered the old terror of the dark she had known as a small child when Ma had blown the candle out, but the longing to be rid of Jem was stronger than everything. Almost without willing them to move, her feet began to glide over the bush floor, down the hill, away from the direction they had come from to this place, away from the cave and the fire whose red embers she could still see between the trees.

Within a few moments she knew she had succeeded. It had needed only a dozen yards' distance to put her out of reach of her cousin's madness. She seemed to possess new, unfamiliar skills. Her feet seemed to glide safely and soundlessly over sticks in her path, and chose out soft, quiet ground. For once, too, the infuriating tangle of thorny vines did not clutch at her. She felt almost as though the bush was friendly and was aiding her escape.

After a few minutes she heard Jem's anguished voice and she smiled in triumph.

'Jessie, oh, Jessie, where are you? Come back!'

'I will not,' she whispered under her breath.

'Jessie, I'll not harm you! You must come back! You'll not find your way out of here alone! You'll be lost! You'll die!'

Jessie stood quite still, listening as he crashed about through the undergrowth near the cave, desperately searching for her. Her heart was pounding so loud it seemed to her that he must hear it and she took deep breaths to try to calm it. After a few minutes she heard him move away from where she stood and she stole a few steps further into the trees.

'Jessie!' he called. 'I'll take you home, I'll take you back now. I'll not make you promise anything. Just come back, do you hear me?'

He sounded so passionately sincere that she was almost tempted to trust him. She took a step back towards the cave. Then she remembered how he had deceived her before. He had been so cunning with Meg over that business with the firewood. He had planned all this so carefully. She would be mad to go back to him. She stole on, step by careful step, until after half an hour or more the sound of his cries and his clumsy search had faded into the distance. Now she was truly alone and truly lost. Shivering uncontrollably, she sank down at the foot of a tree, whose mass of twisting roots and huge trunk seemed to offer a strange kind of hospitality, put her arms round her knees, laid her head upon them and waited for the morning.

She must have dozed a little after that for when she opened her eyes fully and came to her senses it was already nearly light, and the birds were well into their thrilling dawn chorus. She stood up and looked around, and as a full realisation of her situation came to her in the cold light of dawn her skin prickled with fright and her stomach constricted. During the hours of darkness she had been lulled into a kind of dreaming, half sleeping, half waking, in which fear and pain had been dulled, but now she could not disguise the truth from herself. She was absolutely lost, in a region of the bush she had never been in before, with no clue as to where she was or how she could find her way out of it. She did not even have the benefit of the sun to guide her. The morning sky was grey and overcast. Jessie reached behind her and put a hand out to the great trunk against which she had sat all night. It had seemed a safe haven in the hours of darkness. Its strength had comforted her, but it had lost its power to do so now. It was just another tree, no better or taller or wider, no different in fact from any of the thousand upon thousand of others that stretched away into infinity.

Jessie looked about her, trying to remain calm. Which way should she go? No one direction seemed any more promising than another. She shut her eyes for a moment. She must on no account fall into the strange, demented state she had experienced once before. Moana had saved her then, but Moana was not here to protect her now. Not even Denis would be able to find her this time. She must, above all, avoid the temptation of falling into a panic, of dashing about wildly and exhausting herself. She must hold back her imagination, must not allow herself to see things, must not surrender to madness. She must close her heart to the white tui.

She stood irresolute, trying to think. And then she caught a sound above the deafening din of the birds. Someone was brushing stealthily through the undergrowth, making twigs snap and leaves rustle! It could only be Jem! He must have changed his tactics, have decided to move quietly, as he would if he were hunting pig. For a moment she almost wished to call out to him, but she resisted the temptation. She would not ever allow herself to be held powerless by any man, ever again. To be caught in his trap would be far, far worse than to be lost in the bush. Somehow she would find her way out again. But she would do it alone.

Since Jessie had left the cave, Jem had passed a night of miserable suspense, and since first light he had been systematically searching in ever-widening circles round the cave. The enormity of what he had done was slowly dawning upon him. This adventure, which had seemed so right and good when he had planned it, had turned into a nightmare. He had not thought sufficiently of how she would respond to him. He had expected tears, which he was ready to wipe lovingly away, and reproaches, which he would have gladly borne. He had thought she would have been frightened, and he would have reassured her; full of questions, to which he would have known the answers. He had not for a moment doubted that she would submit. Her contempt, her rage, her defiance and her absolute determination had taken him by surprise, and he realised as he, too, lay stiff and sleepless in the dark, that he had failed. He had then begun to cudgel his brains to think of a way out of this muddle, but the cold had seemed to numb his mind.

From the moment she had disappeared from the cave he had known she would run away, and when she had failed to answer his call he felt sure that she would be lost, that she was doomed to die. He searched with a feeling of hopelessness, feeling himself to be a murderer.

He had almost decided to go home and ask for help in the search when he came close to finding her, but she had wedged herself a little way into the crease between a giant rimu trunk and its parasitical rata vine, and he did not see her. He passed within an arm's breadth of her. She saw him clearly. She could have put out her hand and touched him. She smelled his sweat and it made her shudder. When he had gone she felt almost faint with relief, but then, remembering the tortured expression on his face, she shivered again. How dreadful to be the cause of such pain! It must have been something in her, something she had said or done, that had driven him to this madness. She felt sick with herself, unclean, guilty.

She waited for a long time until she could hear him no longer, and then thought carefully about what she should do. Her earlier panic had gone. She was steadier now. She talked out loud, reassuring herself. She had a fair chance of finding her way home. She could not be more than a mile or so from the edge of the bush. She had only to think, stay calm and make a plan, and she would be saved.

Edward, she whispered to herself, as if the name were a talisman.

It did, indeed, work like a charm. Her memory stirred. There had been a conversation once at Duddingston. Edward had been telling her of some poor runaway sailor who had been lost in the bush and almost died of hunger and thirst. At length – how was it now? – he had come upon a creek and had followed it, knowing it would eventually lead him to the sea. And so it had! And he had been saved! Surely, any spring in these hills could only flow in one direction, to the basin of Otago harbour! And once she stood upon its familiar shoreline she would instantly see her way home. Only one problem remained. Where would she find running water? She cocked her head to listen, and for the first time ever wished that the birdsong would cease. Above this din even the sound of a torrent would be inaudible. She looked about her. The ground sloped away steeply and she guessed it would fall to a gully in which no doubt a stream must wind its course. She would see if her guess was right. It was the only thing she could do.

Four hours later, Jessie was exhausted and tormented with thirst. She seemed to have been stumbling for ever over fallen tree trunks, black with decay, through dense masses of fern and thickets of all but impenetrable scrub. She was dirty, and her face and arms were stinging from dozens of cuts and scratches. That first descent had been a waste of time. She had slipped down a virtual ravine only to find herself in a dry ditch. At that point, the sun had come out. It had gone in again almost at once, but Jessie had had time to see from its position that she was heading in entirely the wrong direction, south-west instead of north-east! She had been badly frightened by the discovery and the urge to bolt too hastily back the way she had come had had to be resolutely resisted.

As the hours passed, her thirst and exhaustion grew. Disgust for herself grew at the same time. She had not only lost her way in the bush, her whole life seemed to have lost its way. Every person she touched was hurt by her. Wherever she went, she left in her path a tangle of violent feelings.

She was making slower progress now. She had lost her sureness of foot and had begun to stumble, and when finally she tripped over a protruding root and fell heavily on her hands and knees she gave way to tears and could scarcely struggle back on to her feet again. At last she did so, and then remained poised, her tear-stained face motionless with concentration. Was she imagining it? Was that rushing, whispering sound only the breeze playing in the leaves, or was it, could it be, the sound of running water? She forced her way through the matted undergrowth to the place from where the noise now unmistakably originated, then burst through a clump of tall ferns into a glade where a fallen tree had torn a gap in the dense green roof overhead, fell on her knees beside a dancing creek, plunged her hands into the cool water and drank a deep, refreshing draught.

When she had slaked her thirst she sat back on her heels and looked about her. The creek was larger than she had expected. It welled over rocks to tumble in a series of sparkling cascades down the tangled hillside. Jessie felt as if she could go no further. She sat down on a fallen branch, leant her back against a boulder and gazed up into a welcome opening between the trees to the sky above. The low cloud of early morning had long since dispersed and the sun was out again. She watched the movement of fern fronds overhead as the faint breeze ruffled them. Why had she ever been afraid of the bush? She was not any longer. It offered escape from the turmoil of life outside. Perhaps here she could find a permanent peace, forgiveness for the pain she had caused, relief from the vain longings that tore at her. She closed her eyes, and as she allowed her mind to soar wordlessly up into the glittering light that danced over her head, she felt her guilt, her loneliness, her secret desires float up, like the smoke of a sacrificial fire, and in their place came a kind of peace she had never known before. She lay still and savoured it. She felt now no sense of urgency. She was not even hungry any more. To find her way home was not important. She could die here.

'Thank you,' she whispered, and fell asleep.

When Jessie woke up, she was still filled with joy. She stretched herself as if she had been in her own bed in the cottage on the shore and sat up. All would be well now, she knew. Everything would be well now. She knelt by the stream again and washed the blood and dirt from her face and arms. Then she caught sight of something spinning round and round on the eddying water. Was it a leaf? No, it was a green and gold feather. Jessie frowned at it for a moment. She felt that it was immensely important but could not at once think why. Then she remembered. Yesterday, on the way to fetch the firewood, she had seen a couple of feathers, just like this one, floating down the burn that led past the cottage. Was this the same creek? It must be! She had only to follow it down the hill and she would be home! Such was her sense of inner peace that this discovery did not even surprise her. It seemed normal. She knelt forward to drink again, but her hair fell over her face and into the water. She sat back on her heels and threw back her head. Droplets of water showered from her hair making it sparkle in the sunshine. Arms raised above her head, she gathered up the heavy strands and knotted them at the nape of her neck.

It was thus that Edward came upon her. He stepped up into the sunlight and saw her kneeling on a bed of moss, as simply as a wood nymph, her long hair thrown back over her shoulders. She had grown taller in the intervening years. Her body, though slim and still as graceful as that of a child, had rounded into womanhood. She was as natural and without artifice as the white orchid on the branch above her head, whose creamy flowers exhaled a heady fragrance. He recognised her instantly.

She had heard nothing. The sound of the water cascading over the rocks had covered the scratching of his boots on the rocky ground. But, like an animal with the sixth sense of the wild, she knew that she was being watched, and turned her head and saw him. He was not the same raw, wounded boy she had known at Duddingston. He had broadened and hardened into a man. His face was leaner, weathered by sun and wind, the eyes more watchful, the mouth more powerful. And yet she knew him at once.

It seemed to both of them as though the moment lasted for ever. She, in the elevated state of mind from which she had not yet descended, believed momentarily that he was a vision. He, who had almost given up hope in the long weary search that had lasted all day, feared for an instant that she was a mirage. Then she leaped to her feet. He stepped forward.

'Jessie,' he said.

She stood motionless, and he was afraid that she would take fright and bound away into the bush like a startled hare. But she stood still, and took a shuddering breath.

'I love you,' she said.

The words had come from her without her knowing it. She had spoken instinctively. Drawn by her great eyes, he stepped across the few yards of ground between them, his doubts, his fears, his disbelief swept away in this one great reality.

'Jessie, my love,' he said, and drew her into his arms. She stood still within their circle, hardly daring to move in case this dream should vanish away, feeling through her whole being the bliss of a perfect homecoming. Then she put her arms around his neck and, as simply as a child, lifted her face for his kiss.

4

The evening sun was beginning to dip over the horizon when Edward and Jessie at last reached the cottage. They had not consciously dawdled on the way. Indeed, Edward had remarked more than once, 'We must make haste to put your poor family out of their misery,' but it had not served to hurry them.

They had found their way out of the bush soon enough, doubling back along the stream, and when they emerged from it the landscape lay spread out before them, the colours dyed deep by the brilliance of the late afternoon sun. Every nearby leaf and stem, every distant stretch of blue water and expanse of dense trees seemed to pulsate in the intensity of light.

Edward and Jessie, hand in hand, brushed through the fern alongside the stream as blissfully unaware of anything outside themselves as Orpheus and Eurydice in another age. Sometimes they spoke. Often they were silent. He pushed ahead of her where the going was rough, and held her hand to guide her where the path was obscured with a tenderness he had never known he could feel. She leant on his shoulder when she had to jump down from a steep place, and placed her bare feet where he instructed with a trust that filled her whole being with contentment. By the time they came to the cottage door, and Jessie, lifting the latch, invited him with a smile to follow her inside, both felt they had been together for a lifetime, and neither could imagine that they could ever be parted again.

It was clear, however, from the range of emotions that crossed the stricken faces of Jessie's family, that they did not share this view. The events of the last twenty-four hours had taken their toll of everyone. The menfolk, drained from their long day and very angry with Jem, had returned from their fruitless search a little ahead of the happy couple and though their relief at finding Jessie safe and well was obvious, their reception of Edward was less than cordial. They were too intent on weathering the storm that seemed to be driving the family apart to welcome the intrusion of an outsider. Only Joseph managed to offer the unexpected guest a hearty greeting. He clapped his hand on Edward's sturdy shoulder and shook it with affectionate roughness.

'Well, well, this is a surprise indeed! And a grand one too! I never thought to see a Jamieson in these parts, but you're most welcome, lad! Very welcome indeed, and I trust you'll remain with us for a time? Is it in search of your scientifics you are? Your ma was telling me – she'll have informed you of our visit to Wellington – that you're as busy as ever, investigating the wonderful works of Creation! Aye, aye, sit down, sit down, and Meg will have some tea ready directly, eh, Meggie?'

He seemed to become aware of the heavy silence into which his greeting had fallen and fell silent himself. Then he shook his leonine head.

'Eh, lad, it's a strange time you've chosen to visit, for there's family matters we must think on just now. You'll have heard, mebbe, Jessie has told you, why she . . . how she came to be . . .'

Edward bowed his head. His own face was so ablaze with happiness he felt ashamed to show it to this broken old man.

'Yes,' he said. 'I've heard.'

Joseph looked round behind him, searching with troubled eyes for Jem. Malcolm was drawing himself a bowlful of water from the kettle that hung on a hook over the fire for his evening wash for all the world as if nothing out of the ordinary had happened all day. Isaiah had sat himself with a groan of relief on a bench by the table, and was addressing himself to a cup of tea which Meg had set before him. Jem was not there.

'If he was but ten years younger! I'd take a belt to him then, right enough. I'd chastise him for his folly. For it *was* folly! He's not so lost in sin, sunk in depravity . . . You said yourself, lassie, he did not lay a finger on you to hurt you! You must not believe . . .'

The latch clattered and Jem himself came into the cottage. He stood looking round the hostile faces, lingered for a moment on Jessie, who had turned away towards the fire, then fastened his eyes on Edward.

'Bastard!' he said with vicious emphasis. Then he crossed the room, unhooked his coat from a nail on the wall, picked up his boots and went out again without another word. Joseph followed him.

The silent listeners within heard Joseph's cry, 'Son! Son! Where are you going?'

For answer, there came only the familiar whistle Jem used to call his dogs, and the grating of wood on shingle as he dragged the boat down the shore and into the water. They heard the oars click into the rowlocks and their rhythmic splash as Jem began to row away. Then Joseph's voice, thin with apprehension, came again, 'Son! Jem! Where are you going?'

And faintly, over the sound of the oars, the listeners heard a voice from across the water. 'To the devil!'

Then there was silence.

It was a long time before Joseph returned to the cottage, and when he did, darkness had fallen. The flame, guttering in the shallow oil lamp that stood on the table, flickered on the ring of faces that sat around it. The hour he had spent in prayer had brought Joseph a small measure of comfort. A phrase had come to him through his passionate pleading. 'He who endures to the end shall be saved.'

It had resounded in his mind, taken possession of him. There must be some new meaning in it that God intended him to discover. He must wait and pray and it would be revealed. He had watched the little craft until it was swallowed up in the gathering gloom, and waited a while longer until he felt able to face his family. Then he sighed deeply and walked back towards the glow of light that shone from the cottage's open door.

Even before he reached it, he heard his brother-in-law's voice raised in unusually emphatic tones. 'No! I will not be gainsaid! There's no use in taking that wheedling tone with me! I am your father, Jessie, and you would do well to remember it! You owe your obedience to me. I will not have you marry and move away from your family! It is a strange idea, a most unusual idea. And outside your station in life too! You should know better than to think of such a thing! You owe your duty to us here. It's a child's place to consider their parents first. Who is to look after me in my old age and infirmity if you are a thousand miles away? Meg will be too much taken up with her bairns and, besides, she has my own delicate constitution. You take after your mother. She was a strong woman until she took it into her head to weaken herself. And your mother, I am sure, your poor dead mother, would wish you to remain here, where you are needed—'

'But, sir,' broke in Edward, 'surely you do not wish – Jessie's future – her happiness . . .'

'Oh, her happiness!' snorted Isaiah scornfully. 'It's a fine thing to talk of happiness! Young people these days think of nothing but their own selfish whims. What of duty, that's what I say! What of obedience, and righteousness? We were taught to do our duty first, to honour our father and mother, and think of our own happiness last! Jessie's duty lies here, to me. And to her sister, of course.' His hands were waving agitatedly, and the red patches that had appeared on each cheek showed he was moved by no common emotion. He looked towards his oldest daughter for support.

'Well, as to that . . .' said Meg doubtfully. She had been so startled by Edward's declared intention to marry her sister that she had not had a chance to examine her own feelings. On the one hand, she felt a strong sense of ill-usage. It was not fair that Jessie should have all the luck, that Jessie should have attracted such a magnificent suitor and would now be whisked off to a life of luxury in Wellington, while she, Meg, was obliged to remain in perpetual servitude in this forsaken desert. But then she had glanced at her husband, and had caught him staring at Edward. The jealousy in his face had frightened her. It was time, indeed, that Jessie was away, far away from them all. She had not known a moment's peace of mind since Joseph and her sister had returned from Wellington. She made up her mind.

'I do not see why she should not go, if she's so set on it,' she said, with a little toss of the head. 'I can manage as I did when she was gone before. I'm sure I have no wish to stand in the way of—'

She did not have the chance to finish. Jessie had flung her arms round her sister's neck. 'Oh, Meggie, thank you! Oh, Meggie, you do understand!'

Meg patted her perfunctorily. In spite of herself she was touched. Come to think of it, it was noble of her to relinquish her sister in this way. She looked at Edward, saw the gratitude in his smile, and preened herself. She had always been magnanimous, she told herself, and now she would show them just how great was her heart. She leant across the table.

'Now then, Father,' she said firmly, in a tone that expected to be obeyed. 'You know quite well we can get along fine without Jessie. You have me, and Uncle Joseph, and Malcolm. And it's not so long now but what the settlement is sure to arrive. And in any case, you have time to get used to the idea. They cannot marry yet for there's no minister nearer than Nelson to tie the knot.'

Edward and Jessie looked at each other in dismay. This aspect of the matter had not occurred to either of them. 'Surely,' said Edward, 'at Waikouaiti or at Koputai . . .'

'No,' said Meg triumphantly. Bearing bad news had always been a particular pleasure of hers. 'Nowhere nearer than Nelson, and I know what I say, for we could not have Robert christened until the minister visited Koputai six months ago. He was already walking!'

'What was that? What did you say? Don't mumble!' said Isaiah irritably, but when the matter had been loudly explained to him he smiled approvingly at Meg.

'There,' he said, 'that settles the matter. You see, Jessie, how little you know of the world. Now let us, for heaven's sake, forget the whole subject. It has been a wearisome day and I am more than ready for my supper.'

Joseph had stood silent by the door during this exchange. The young people's love for each other had hit him like a hammer blow. He saw the truth of it in their faces, and his heart sank. Why had he not seen it before? The answers to countless small puzzles were now perfectly clear to him. Jessie's desire to visit Wellington, her alarm as they approached the Jamieson house, Edward's sudden appearance at Otago – all were now explained. Above all, he knew now why Jessie had been so set against Jem and why his poor boy had shown such hatred for Edward. Joseph felt an ignoble desire to slip from the cottage and seek his bed in the whare next door where he could slowly accustom himself to this painful knowledge. But he knew where his duty lay. There was work for him here, for a healer of wounds, for a judge among the people, for a peacemaker. He stepped forward into the circle of light and five pairs of eyes turned anxiously towards him. Isaiah seemed the least pleased to see him.

'I am looking to you, brother,' he said hastily, 'to uphold my rightful authority as a parent. This foolish child has made some hasty promises to that young man, without so much as a hint of it to me, and is actually proposing to wed! I have told her, naturally, that there is no question of it. I am strongly opposed to the match, and it is of no purpose your trying to persuade me into it, for I will not change my mind!'

Pleased with this speech, he stared belligerently about the room. The response was disappointing. His audience ignored him. Their attention was fixed on Joseph.

Joseph sat down heavily, and laid his great hands upon the table.

'Well, well, my lassie,' he said, shaking his head fondly at Jessie. 'There's many a thing now I understand that I did not see before. How long have you been sighing over this rascal?'

Jessie turned her eyes on Edward, and her face was so ablaze with happiness that Joseph could hardly bear to look at it.

'All my life,' she whispered.

'Jessie, how can you be so daft?' broke in Meg impatiently. 'You did not know him in Paisley. We knew nothing of the Jamiesons until we saw them on the ship, and then they were cabin passengers.'

Jessie shook her head, but her smile did not diminish.

'Ma knew them,' she said. 'Ma was grateful to them. They saved her life once.'

'What is this nonsense?' Isaiah had moved uneasily on his chair, and his eyes wandered uncertainly between Jessie and Edward. For answer, Jessie stood up and went to her narrow bed under the window. She picked up the quilt that lay carefully folded upon it and brought it into the light.

'It's the first thing I remember,' she said. 'We were hungry, and Ma wouldn't get up, and a tall man came with very long legs, or maybe there were two. And he brought food and put this quilt on Ma. It was like a dream!'

'Aye, that was Mr Armstrong,' nodded Meg, 'though what this has to do with . . .'

Jessie was turning the quilt over in her hands. She pounced on a corner of it with a little cry of triumph. 'Here! Look!' she said.

The others craned forward, but seeing no more than an old patch, sat back disappointed.

'It was Edward made this hole with his scissors when he was a wee boy,' said Jessie, watching with delight the mystification on the faces of her family. 'It was his aunt mended it. When the bad times came in Paisley, she gave it to the minister with a parcel of food.'

'Mr Elliott,' said Edward. 'I remember him. I liked him. He used to . . .'

'Elliott!' Isaiah, distracted by this strange story, was shaking his head in wonderment. 'It was Mr Elliott came with yon bedding. I mind him well. He was aye a good friend. He was our own minister before the cholera struck and he went away to preach to the grand folks of Edinburgh. Ah, lad,' he pointed a thin forefinger at Edward, 'you should have known us in those days! A joint of fresh meat every day, and the laundry sent out! I mind well, Mr Elliott. I can see him now, a-sitting in our parlour on one of the good chairs, drinking tea from a fine china cup. We were not reduced to earthenware then!'

Meg had closely examined the darn. 'It's strange,' she said. 'It's like a sign, or a spell. And the stitches so small they could have been set by the wee folk.'

Joseph frowned at her. 'Now, Meg,' he said. 'There's no call for superstitious nonsense and heathenish talk! We're no ignorant savages, bemused by signs and wonders. We're children of God, walking in the light. However' – he too looked closely at Aggie's handiwork as if the stitches could reveal a momentous secret – 'there's no denying it's passing strange. And if yon good woman who sent poor Isobel this timely gift in her hour of need was indeed this young man's aunt, then wc all have cause to be thankful. But,' he paused, and Jessie saw to her great relief the old twinkle in his eye, 'it does not mean you two can run off together without your father's consent!'

'No, indeed!' Isaiah bridled at the thought.

'Nor, even if he gave it, could you marry without a minister.'

Jessie and Edward looked at one another in dismay.

'Of course,' went on Joseph, musingly, 'there's ministers in Wellington—'

'Brother!' burst out Isaiah indignantly. 'You're not intending to support this match? I won't have it – I tell you! You'll never wheedle me into—'

'But,' said Joseph, ignoring the interruption, 'it would be impossible for you to travel together unwed.'

'Ah, you see,' Isaiah sank back into his seat. 'It needs an old head to—'

'That's why you'll need a person to accompany you.'

'No, now really, brother! This is too much!'

'A person of years and wisdom, to whose keeping a young girl could safely be entrusted.'

'You are not to do this, Joseph. I will not have you take my daughter away to Wellington a second time! I should never have allowed Jessie to accompany you in the first place. I was overruled! It is ever the way! Against my own judgement! Besides, you have been away for long enough. We can ill spare you.'

'I was not suggesting myself, Isaiah. Who better to perform such a task than the girl's own father?'

Isaiah's mouth, opened already for further remonstrance, remained suspended. The idea was too novel for him. Before he could speak, Jessie jumped up from her chair and ran round the table to lay her cheek against his.

'Oh, Pa! Oh, it would be of all things wonderful! Say you'll come, Pa! Only think of the plants you could bring home for your garden! The seeds, the cuttings—'

It was a blunder. Isaiah seized upon it. He shook himself indignantly from her embrace. 'My garden! That's it, miss. You've hit the point! Who is to care for my garden? You cannot expect me to leave my sprouting beans?'

Edward on the other side of the table observed the cavalier manner with which Isaiah had shaken off his love's embrace, and was exasperated beyond bearing.

'Come, sir,' he said hotly. 'You are not proposing to sacrifice the happiness of your daughter for a mere row of beans?'

Isaiah's protuberant eyes seemed to swell further with indignation. 'A mere row of beans? A *mere* row . . . ? Do you know what you are saying? It's all very fine for you, young man, bred in the lap of luxury, never knowing hunger and want, but for us plain folks the provision of our daily bread is no small matter. I . . . ' he paused and tilted his head backwards to squint down his nose at Edward. 'I am the principal provider of this family' (Meg and Jessie exchanged incredulous glances) 'and I know where my duty lies. My duty, sir, is to a row of beans!'

For a moment, the room was quiet. Jessie's heart sank. She knew that her father, weak though he was, could be unexpectedly obstinate when he felt driven into a corner. From behind Isaiah's chair she signalled to Edward to say nothing more.

And then, into this pregnant silence, there came a strange noise. There was a snuffling at the door and the sound of a heavy weight being repeatedly nudged against it. Edward looked round. No one else seemed to find the occurrence at all remarkable.

'Denis,' said Jessie obscurely. She went to open the door, and Edward gasped as a large amiable pig trotted composedly into the room at her heels.

'Jessie!' shrieked Meg. 'Will you mind what you're about? Don't bring him in here! Look, he's been rolling in dirt, he's covered with something! What is that over his ear? Oh!' She stopped and put her hand to her mouth.

Isaiah rose to his feet with a cry of rage. 'My beans! My spinach! My garden!' He crossed the room with unusual energy, plucked the bean seedling from Denis's guilty ear, and raised his foot.

'No, Pa, don't kick him!' cried Jessie. The pig darted behind her skirts on nimble trotters, and peered round at his aggressor, flapping his ears apologetically. Meg stifled an undutiful giggle. Isaiah stamped his frustrated foot angrily and disappeared into the night.

'Quick, Meg,' said Jessie, 'help me get him out. We'd best tie him up tonight.' A moment later they were outside. Joseph and Malcolm turned simultaneously to look at Edward. He was still staring in astonishment at the door. Father and son caught each other's eye. A slow smile crossed Malcolm's face, erasing momentarily the lines of worry that habitually criss-crossed it. An answering grin from his father seemed to tickle his humour even further. A rare laugh bubbled up inside him and erupted in a gust. Joseph and Edward caught the infection, and when the girls, breathless and tousled from their exertions, came back inside, they found three great helpless creatures rocking, convulsed, in their seats.

'Will you hush now!' hissed Jessie urgently. 'My father's coming back!'

Joseph wiped his streaming eyes and turned to face his brother-in-law, who stood, woebegone, a broken raspberry cane in his hand. 'Wanton!' he was saying, shaking his head in disbelief. 'Wanton, wild destruction!'

'Not so, brother,' said Joseph, wagging his finger at him. 'There's not one leaf falls from its branch without it is the will of God. It is a sign, so it is. You have sought to put a row of beans in the path of his will, and he has shown you the error of your ways.'

He stood up, took Jessie's slight hand in one great paw and Edward's in the other. Then he clasped them together, and his white brows almost met over the bridge of his nose as he glowered at Isaiah. His voice, when it came, resonated powerfully around the small room.

'What God has joined together, let not man put asunder.'

Chapter Twenty-two

1

George Street, Edinburgh
December 29th 1846

My dear Fanny,

You will shortly be celebrating your sixth Hogmanay in your adopted country and I hope for your sake that its prosperity improves. We read alarming accounts in our newspapers of the poor prospects for the settlers and the fearsome activities of your natives with such outlandish names as I cannot pronounce them. You say nothing of this in your letters. Do not, I beg of you, conceal distressing intelligence from me. I would always rather know the worst. Effie Macfarlane says you are probably not in the affected areas, and that in any case it is always worse hearing bad news from a distance, for when you are there it never seems the same. I know what she means for I recall how vastly different were the lurid newspaper accounts of the collapse of a house in the High Street last month and the actual truth, which was that two arms were broke, and several crowns, and a lot of dust and rubble made. By the by, Jamie Burns was not killed, whatever the circulated reports have claimed. He was dead drunk in the Cowgate at the time and knew nothing of the matter until two days later, so do not trust what you read. Though I do not suppose this sort of local news from Scotland is given any prominence in your Wellington papers, so you probably have not heard of it at all.

I have received Teddy's latest and am writing to him separately with this mail. He is very regular in correspondence and writes a good hand, very neat and clear. Mr Simmonds taught him well, I own, though he charged too much for his services as a tutor. I told him so at the time. I detect a little sadness in Teddy's last. Is he well and happy? You know I have never been quite easy about his constitution, and beg you will make sure he wears flannel when the wind is strong. He has done very well to set up his school in so short a time but you must see he does not overtax himself, sister. Young men are so careless of these matters. There was a hint of reserve in his letter that made me fear in case he has some secret worry and could fall into a melancholy.

The weather here is most inclement but you must not think that I am dull. Mr Elliott has charged me with the arrangements for the Relief Society Bazaar and I am run off my feet with the work. He has not yet recovered from the demise of Miss Alison Fyne from an inflammation of the lungs, but I believe the spring will aid his recovery. In my opinion it is all for the best for she was not good enough for him.

We have so far a great deal of netting, some purses, a few watercolours and a handsome embroidered tablecloth ready, but the small useful items, which sell quickest and make the largest profit, are the least popular to make and I have set Lily to the task of helping me. She does so gladly, poor child, for she is touchingly devoted and if I could only persuade her to use her handkerchief instead of her sleeve and breathe through her nose instead of her mouth I believe she would have quite a normal appearance.

There was a deceptive patch of ice on the pavement last Thursday forenoon and I took a little tumble as I was on my way to market. It has strained my hip somewhat but old Dr Brown, though needing more attention now than some of his patients, has assured me no lasting harm is done and a little rest in my bed is all that is needed. It is a pity that such things always take place when one is busiest for I have no time for my bed just at present. Do not, I beg you, get into one of your fusses, Fanny, for by the time you receive this letter it will be quite healed.

Justina writes happily. She has no news of an increase to her family and is I fear a little cast down by it. I have advised her to take plenty of rest and make sure she includes enough sustaining nourishment in her diet. This fashion for tight-lacing has done her no good I fear. I told her as a child how it would be if she took liberties with nature. She has invited me to pay her a visit this coming summer and so I plan to do.

Effie begs me to send you her particular regards, and so does Mrs Hamilton, but I would not set any store by that.

Your loving sister,
Agnes Heriot

Port Nicholson
January 1847

Dear Patterson,

Further to my last of Nov 6th 1846 I write to confirm as I promised that the shipment suggested can now go ahead. You will be hearing in due course from Dickson of Cornhill, an excellent man and fully conversant with the Bengal trade.

At present tea and calico (bleached and unbleached) also cases of prints (assorted) are our primary requirements. As you may know, most imports come to these islands via New South Wales, but by shipping direct to Wellington we can cut costs and add up to ten per cent on our profits.

Prices are holding up well at present, and the market is recovering satisfactorily from some recent political disturbances. I hear you say 'Strike while the iron is hot!' as you were wont to do many times on the Calcutta Exchange.

I attach to this sheet a list of the prices I promised you, and the quantities I can accommodate.

Yr obdt servant,
H. Jamieson

P.S. By the by, the good air and excellent climate of this country have worked their spell upon my son Edward, whom you may recall as an infant in short coats. He is but today returned from the wilds of Otago with a lovely bride upon his arm, and is to enter the matrimonial state a week from now. Fanny begs me to inform you that the circumstance of preparing for this event has drawn to her attention the chronic shortage of fine silk, ribbons, thread, muslin, etc. in this country. If you wish to include a small quantity of such and any other more luxurious items I will try whether or not they will find a market here.

Thorndon, Port Nicholson
January 1847

My dearest Daughter,

You will be surprised to receive another from me so soon after my last, but I have news that will, I know, interest you extremely.

Your brother is about to enter the bonds of matrimony, and in the most romantic way, for he has plucked his bride from the heart of the forest (to be precise, from Otago, at the southern extremity of the Middle Island) and has brought her hither to his parents' house, where the wedding takes place on Tuesday sennight.

I fear you will be a little startled when I disclose to you, my dear Justina, that Edward's bride is none other than Jessie Dunbar, whose family was for a short time in our employ at Nelson. It was not precisely the match I would have chosen for Edward, but I have come to believe that she will suit him very well. Indeed, they are so vastly in love there is no sense to be had from either of them, and if their sighings and gazings do not soon abate, I own I shall be heartily relieved when they remove to their own house, which details Edward is at present arranging.

You must not think, my love, that the connection is one to blush for. In the colonies, you know, we see things in a very different way and the daughter of a respectable weaver, who has had the misfortune to fall upon hard times, is by no means an unacceptable bride for the son of a merchant who ditto. Jessie herself is a ladylike young person with considerable beauty of face and form and manners of an open simplicity one cannot but approve. She has little formal education but a naturally enquiring mind and will rapidly make herself a fit companion for your brother on the intellectual plane, while in all other matters she is content to follow my guidance. In short, my dear, your father and I have given our whole-hearted consent to the match, and though at first it was Edward's determination that overruled us, we have come to love Jessie for her own dear sake. She will make a charming wife for your brother, and they will deal extremely together.

I venture to give you a little hint, for you may not think of it, but I know your new sister would be most happy to receive a message from you, a few lines perhaps, to reassure her of her welcome among us. She is a little shy in some ways and quite afraid of pushing herself forward, and a kind word from you will, I am certain, give her much joy.

You will of course know how to break our happy news to the Dunstables. A respectable Ayrshire family – prominent citizens of Paisley – pillars of the Presbyterian church – I am sure you will contrive very well.

Your affte,
Mama

P.S. That we are not quite living in the sticks you will understand when I tell that we have managed very cleverly for the wedding day. Such is your brother's impatience to secure his bride that his unhappy mother has been vouchsafed but two weeks to make all ready. You may rest assured, however, that Jessie will be charmingly arrayed. She is dark of complexion, tall and graceful, and her dress will be an elegant fawn silk trimmed with blond lace. I have pricked my fingers all to pieces in the construction of a delightful bonnet, and am only sorry that silver ribbons are not to be had in this corner of the Antipodes for any money! A sweet reticule and veil of chiffon will complete the picture, which must, I am sure, satisfy the severest critic.

Thorndon
January 1847

My dear Aunt,

Mama is at my elbow wishing to snatch the pen from my hand to write you of our momentous news, but I insist on being the first to tell you that I am the happiest of men. I am to be married Tuesday next, here in Thorndon, and my joy would be overflowing were it not that you will not be here to join us at the feast.

Jessie Dunbar is no new acquaintance to our family. She and her parents, her sister, an uncle and two cousins were our fellow travellers on the *New Zealand*, and worked with us at Duddingston in our pioneering days. Since our removing to Wellington their family group has lived in the wilds of Otago, where she has suffered greatly from loneliness and a total absence of society, and has learned to rise above adversity with the greatest heroism. I cannot begin to describe her virtues to you – I can only write that never before have I known such perfect harmony with another human being.

Mama will furnish you more accurately than can I with all the details of our nuptials. She is not to be deterred by shortness of time or the erratic availability of supplies in Wellington, but is planning a great blow-out. She has sent out invitations to I know not how many of our acquaintance, and my poor Jessie and I are likely to be well nigh dead with exhaustion ere we begin our married life. The ceremony is to be conducted by the Reverend Mr Macfarlane, and will be followed here at home by a great feast. The talk is of nothing but marquees, strips of bunting, sucking pigs, roast fowls, puddings, pies and cases of French wine, so you will see that it is to be a splendid affair indeed.

There is a strange circumstance regarding a quilt which I know will interest you greatly, but Mama insists absolutely that I leave the telling of it to her, and since I have had the privilege of breaking our happy news to you, I feel that it is only fair to comply with her request.

I have arranged living quarters for us in a neat cottage a short way from our schoolhouse on the beach, but we do not intend to remain there for ever. My educational experiment has succeeded so well that I will one day be obliged to provide better accommodation for my hopeful pupils, and when that day comes I shall build alongside the school a house fit for such a bride.

Dear Aunt, be so good as to convey my best regards to Mr Elliott and inform him of our happiness. He will be doubly pleased for he was a frequent visitor to Jessie's parents' house in Paisley before she was born.

Mama is giving me a nudge to pass the sheet to her, so I must conclude by sending you the loving greetings

of your devoted nephew,
Edward

Friday

Dear Mr Jamieson sir,

I would not write you but thatt my pa has said I must. I wanted to see you myself but he says I must stop in till I have truely learned better. It was me what broke the schoolhouse window sir, though it was axidental as I could tell you better myself if my pa would but let me out but he will not. It was Hetherington's boys fault tho' I do not try to excuse my own part in the matter. They said such things as could not be bore regarding our school and I felt obliged to chastise them for it sir. Thatt is how the stones was thrown. It was mine hit the window but not by my wishes and the first one got Smithers good and proper on the ear so he bled like a pig which served him right. I will pay for it what it costs sir if you will send me word to my house where my pa is keeping me in all day long and then I will pay you. I seen the missus yesterday from the window and she looks a right one so I wish you happy you can expect my wedding gift when my pa lets me out. It is a pair of good kiwi eggs thatt I blown myself like you shown me nice an big and not a single crack.

Yr respectfull pupil,
D. Blundell

Chapter Twenty-three *Wellington, January 1847*

1

Fanny was too well versed in the ways of the world not to know full well the risks involved in marrying beneath one. It was all very well for colonial society to pride itself on its democratic style, to air the view, as many frequently did, that equality was a fine thing and the snobberies of the Old Country greatly to be deplored. It was quite another to overlook the indiscretion of a young man of good family and excellent education, the son of a rising merchant and brother-in-law of a baronet, who had travelled to New Zealand in all the comfort and dignity of a cabin, to foist on to society a bride reared in a weaver's hovel with no pretensions to good breeding or education, who had travelled steerage and had actually been in his mother's service. The community of Wellington was small enough for privacy to be impossible, and Fanny knew full well that tongues were busy over the affair.

She had, she felt, been right to introduce Jessie to the polite world in the character of a pioneer heroine. It was a role she would easily be able to sustain for it was not a sham. The child had indeed lived a life more eventful than many, young though she still was. It would be important, however, to build on this foundation, to take the high ground and hold it.

It was to this end that Fanny had decided that the wedding should be as splendid as any Wellington had so far seen. There were difficulties. Two weeks was all the time that Edward would allow her. He wanted to be married all right and tight before school opened again, he told her, and no wheedling would budge him. Then, too, the lamentable lack of supplies was tiresome in the extreme. She had managed to secure a fine piece of silk for the wedding dress and had put it tenderly into the hands of Miss Treager, no mean dressmaker, who promised faithfully to have it made up in time, but gloves, slippers and bonnets were not to be had anywhere and she was obliged once again to sift through her trunks for old things to refurbish. As for ribbon from which to fashion favours for the gentlemen's lapels, there was not a yard of it nearer than Sydney.

These, however, were minor problems compared to the matter of the bride's father. No manoeuvring on anyone's part could pass Isaiah off as a gentleman, and though the bride herself, beautifully gowned and robed in youth and her own natural grace, would be acceptable to all but the highest stickler, Isaiah could hardly fail to raise eyebrows.

Fanny pushed the thought to the back of her mind. There was too much to do to tease herself over matters outside her control. From morning to evening she fussed and planned, ordered and cajoled, her mind concerned with a hundred details.

The object of all the bustle, however, remained oddly unmoved by it all. Jessie felt as though she was living in a dream. She was borne along by an almost painful rapture, and though she submitted to every demand of Fanny's and concurred with every suggestion, it was clear that her mind was elsewhere. When she and Edward were together they had room in their thoughts for no one and nothing but each other. When Edward was absent she was prey to an absurd anxiety that some accident might befall him, so that she might never see him again.

'What a pity that we have had no time to assemble a trousseau!' sighed Fanny for the hundredth time.

'Yes,' said Jessie, gazing out of the window and wondering if Edward would appear over the brow of the hill.

'You have no linen, no handkerchiefs, no chemises – it's as well Aggie doesn't know. She would be quite shocked.'

'No,' said Jessie. She sensed she had given the wrong answer, caught Fanny's eye and blushed. 'Yes, I mean.'

Fanny laughed indulgently. 'There's no doing anything with you today,' she said, 'and I'm not surprised you are distracted. The night before one's wedding after all . . . I remember I almost died of anticipation.'

Jessie smiled at her. She had heard several times a complete account of Fanny's runaway marriage, and it still made her gasp with sympathy and admiration. Then she turned back to the window.

Fanny put the finishing touches to the last display of greenery with which she had decorated her drawing room in readiness for the morrow. It consisted entirely of ferns and she considered it a masterpiece. Each frond differed in size and shape from its fellow and the effect, thought Fanny, looking at it with pleasure and pride, was certain to call forth cries of admiration from the wedding guests.

'There,' she said. 'Is it not charming?' There was no answer. Fanny turned and saw that Jessie was back at her old post by the window.

'There's nothing to be gained by waiting for Teddy, my love,' she said composedly. 'He will not return here tonight. He is to remain at the Gibsons and will go from their house to the church. You will see him next standing before the altar. It would never do, after all, for bride and groom to pass the night before their wedding under the same roof! Did he not explain how it was to be arranged?'

Jessie sat down abruptly on the window seat, which Fanny had cleverly fashioned from packing cases and covered with a pretty chintz.

'Yes, I suppose – that is, I did not realise . . .'

Fanny shook her head at her. 'Come,' she said, 'we had better make sure that the men have hung the bunting correctly about the trees, for there will not be time to do it again tomorrow. It is of the greatest importance to secure it firmly, in case the wind should veer round to the west again during the night.'

The bunting required more time and energy than Fanny had predicted and the sun was dipping over the horizon when at last she was satisfied. She sent Jessie inside to rest before the evening meal and stepped out of the gate and walked a little way down the track in order to view the effect of the house and garden from a distance. This was the first impression the guests would receive, and Fanny was determined that it would be a good one.

A man was coming up the track. The setting sun in her eyes, he appeared to Fanny no more than a dark shape against the sky.

'Good evening, ma'am,' he mumbled.

'Good evening to you,' she said absently.

The man stood still. Fanny became aware that he was staring at her. She shaded her eyes to see him better. He was a total stranger. She waited for him to pass on up the road but he did not move.

'Is there any way I can help you?' she said at last, beginning to feel a little uneasy.

He shifted from one foot to the other. 'Are you from Edinburgh?' he asked diffidently.

'Yes,' said Fanny.

'Were you living once in George Street on the south side?'

She peered at him more closely, her interest aroused, but not one glint of recognition came to her.

'You would not be related to Mistress Heriot, would you?'

'Who are you?' said Fanny urgently, stepping closer to him. 'How do you know my sister?'

'Oh, I didn't know her precisely.' The man stepped back awkwardly. 'I was caddy to Blair the grocer, and I used to hump her basket for her. You'd be the sister now, who went off to India? I mind well the day you came home. A yellow-bodied coach. I watched you leave again for Greenock when you emigrated. Miss Heriot was with you, I remember, but she came back to her house a few days later.'

Fanny moved so that the sun was no longer in her eyes.

'No, but who *are* you?' she said. 'What's your name?'

'You wouldn't remember me, missus,' the man smiled. 'Wullie's my name. Wullie Gordon. I wondered if maybe I'd come upon you sometime over here. It was seeing you leaving like that, so gay and full of life, made me think of emigrating myself. I couldn't get you out of my mind. It's been years since then but I never forgot, and I finally took the plunge last summer. I've been here but a month and not once hungry. I've not regretted it.'

'You left only last year? Oh, this is wonderful! Wonderful!' said Fanny. She wanted to cry and laugh at once. 'My sister, you have seen her? Quite recently?'

'Oh, aye, missus. Six months ago, before I left. I told her I was going to New Zealand. She looked at me awful strange. "And have you a mother?" she says. "No," says I. "Not since I was a wee boy." "And a father?" says she. "Aye, but he is not one to stand in my way," says I. I thought she'd burst out crying, she looked so sad, but you know how Mistress Heriot is, ever ready with a sharp word. Oh, I meant no offence, missus. She was often kind to me when I was a ragged boy. She just poked in her reticule and said, "Oh the weary, weary colonies. They break hearts, Wullie, so they do," and she put a sovereign in my hand.'

Fanny, less restrained than her sister, gave a sob and fumbled for her handkerchief.

'I'm sorry, missus,' said Wullie, looking down. 'I had no wish to. . .'

'No, no!' cried Fanny. 'You cannot believe how extraordinary, how wonderful – but tell me, tell me everything! How does she look? Well? Happy in a general way?'

'Och, yes, I would say so,' said Wullie. 'She's ever at the kirk, you know. I've seen her often with the minister, Mr, er . . .'

'Elliott, Mr Elliott,' said Fanny, gulping tears.

'That would be him, aye. And she's a mother to him, so they say, forever giving him possets for his cough and the like.'

Fanny chuckled shakily. 'Oh, Mr – Mr Gordon, will you come and see me soon? There is so much I wish to ask you. You cannot imagine – it is so strange, so marvellous to speak to someone who has known – who has seen so recently . . .' Tears threatened to overcome her again.

Wullie Gordon twisted his cap in his hands. 'Aye, I'll come right enough. But I'm away to Petone tomorrow. I'll be in these parts again next week. I'll call on you then, for sure.'

He set off, and the gathering shadows swallowed him up. Fanny looked after him for a long time, then she went slowly back into the house.

2

Afterwards Jessie could remember almost nothing of the marriage ceremony. Wrapped in a cloud of happiness, she walked in her silken gown and practical brown boots on the arm of her father down the rough track from Thorndon to Lambton Quay. At the door of the wooden Presbyterian chapel she felt Fanny's touch on her arm, and obediently changed her boots for satin slippers. Like a sleepwalker she passed up the aisle to stand by Edward. As one in a dream she repeated her responses. She heard nothing of the coughs and fidgets, the rustling of flounces and the scratching of hobnails on floorboards. She heard nothing, either, of Mr MacFarlane's sermon, did not, like everyone else in the chapel, wonder at its inordinate length, but sat with a beatific smile on her face, clutching her bouquet of jasmine and roses as tightly as if it were a lifeline.

It was clear from the bemused expression on her bridegroom's face that Edward's case was much the same. He appeared to be dazzled. On their first walk together as man and wife down the aisle to the church door, they smiled at each other once, then did not dare to exchange looks again. It was as if they were afraid that something might burst. The babble of voices all round passed unheard.

'Your boots, Jessie dear! Give me your slippers. I will carry them back to the house for you.'

'What a charming bride! Fanny, this is your work I am sure. I congratulate you, my dear. As pretty as a picture!'

'Forty-seven minutes for the sermon! It is too much for a wedding. I confess I heard not a word. My mind was firmly fixed on the sucking pig Fanny has promised us.'

'Poor MacFarlane is used to seeing only six or seven in his pews. The opportunity went to his head.'

'Mr Dunbar, you are to take the arm of the groom's mother. You must follow directly after the bridal pair. Mr Dunbar! Do you hear me?'

The procession began its slow progress along the quay, and Fanny was silently blessing heaven that the thick mud which usually marred the thoroughfare had been dried to a manageable hardness by two weeks of fine weather, when she was startled by a loud halloo and a stinging sensation on her cheek. She looked round. A gang of about twenty boys had appeared as if from nowhere. They stood in an orderly line, and raising their hats in unison gave cheer after cheer, conducted by Blundell, who had had them practising for days, and was now directing the youngsters in the correct manner of throwing rice.

Edward and Jessie, rudely brought back to the real world, burst out laughing, then Edward, receiving a sharp hail of rice in the face, scientifically aimed by an expert small thrower, charged at his boys with a roar of mock rage making them scatter in delighted terror.

The incident had so amused the wedding party that they did not at first notice a bustle further along the quay. A brig in from New South Wales was unloading its cargo of cattle. The beasts, nudged overboard by the unsympathetic flicks of a sailor's knotted rope end, were splashing into the shallow water and swimming to the shore where a lone cowman was trying to muster them into an orderly herd. It was unfortunate that the boy's hilarious cheers broke out at this precise moment for the cattle, which had been cooped up in dark cramped quarters for several weeks and were now in a state of high excitement, needed no more encouragement to stampede. A medley of tossing horns, bucking hooves and waving tails came careering down the quay followed by the hapless herdsman, who was vainly waving his stick and succeeded only in adding to the confusion.

The wedding party, used to such vicissitudes of colonial life, stepped smartly out of the way of the oncoming rush, which would have passed without incident had not Isaiah, confused by the half-heard sounds and made more clumsy than usual by the tight boots which Fanny had forced upon him, stumbled and fallen over a stone. It seemed for a moment as if he must be trampled to death by the flailing hooves but Jessie, separated from Edward by the stampede, saw her father down on the ground in the path of the herd and herself rushed into the mêlée.

In a few seconds it was all over. The watchers saw only the white crown of Jessie's bridal bonnet as she stood over her father's body and thrust her only weapon into the maddened faces of the cattle, who, afraid of the large white bouquet waving in their eyes, veered away from her. By a miracle she was not touched. One moment she was in the thick of the charge, the next it had passed her by and the stunned observers saw the bride, regardless of her silk gown, kneeling in the dirt beside her father.

'Are you hurt, Pa? Open your eyes! Look at me!'

Isaiah did as he was told, opened his eyes, saw the danger was over, and sat up. Then he shut them and fainted.

Edward was at once by Jessie's side. His hands were trembling so violently he could hardly lift her to her feet, but when she was finally standing he clasped her to him, almost crushing her in his relief, oblivious of the commotion all around.

Fanny took command. She looked round for an ally and found one.

'Blundell,' she said. 'Run to your father's shop and bring a wide board. Anything that will do for a stretcher. And hurry!'

She bent down and patted Isaiah's hand. 'There, see, he is coming round again. A nasty fright but no harm done. We will have him home and lying down in comfort directly.'

The wedding guests, roused from their shock, were buzzing with talk. Mr Gibson reached Jessie first. She had been released from Edward's embrace and stood quietly by her father, waiting for Blundell to return from his mission of mercy.

'My dear Miss – Mrs Jamieson, I *should* say,' he said, squeezing her hand in an avuncular fashion. 'You are a heroine indeed! Such gallantry! And on such a day as this – to face those brutes with nothing more than a posy in your hand! It beats everything!' He shook his head wonderingly and prodded Edward in the ribs. 'You're a lucky dog, Jamieson, by God you are!'

Behind him, his daughter and Miss Streeter, disgusted by the turn of events, stood in silence. They had formed an alliance for the occasion and had enjoyed an exchange of whispered malice in their pews at the expense of the bridal couple. But there was no running counter to the tide. Jessie had won all hearts with her demonstration of courage. The two girls looked at each other sympathetically and Honoria Gibson passed a wilting hand over her forehead.

'I declare this heat is too much for me,' she said faintly. 'I must make haste to find some shade or I shall feel quite unwell. I am not accustomed to the alarms of the farmyard.'

'I feel just the same,' said Miss Streeter quickly. 'Allow me to accompany you back to the house, Miss Gibson. I am sure *Mrs Jamieson*' – she looked spitefully at Jessie – 'will excuse us if we steal a march on her and arrive ahead of the wedding party? To avoid the headache . . . a glass of lemonade . . . a little peace and quiet . . .'

Arm in arm the two young ladies walked off, unnoticed by everyone. All eyes were on the groaning figure of Isaiah, who had recovered consciousness but seemed on the point of further collapse. Blundell, with miraculous speed, had reappeared. Surpassing himself in enterprise he had not waited to consult his father but had torn from its flimsy hinges the door to his irascible parent's shed, reasoning that it would be worth a beating to act the hero in front of all the nobs of Wellington.

By the time the wedding party reached the Thorndon house, Isaiah, carried by four stalwarts on his makeshift stretcher, was feeling very much more himself but on standing up he tottered, and said in a quavering answer to Fanny's kind enquiry that he would do better to lie down on his bed. She sent Hector up to see to all his wants, feeling relieved. Isaiah had been providentially removed before anyone had had time to be disgusted by his follies. At the same time Jessie had won universal admiration. Things could not have been better arranged, thought Fanny a little guiltily. Now nothing remained but to bask in the approval of her guests and revel in the happiness of her children.

She ran up the stairs to her bedchamber. She needed a few moments in front of her mirror, to rearrange her hair and lay down her reticule and gloves. From the drawing room below she could hear the tinkling of her little piano and a chorus of pleading followed by Hector's fine voice singing 'Jock o' Hazeldean'. She went across to the big bay window and looked down into the garden. The bunting had held up well against the wind. It fluttered gaily about the trees that fringed the lawn. The grass was partially covered by a striped marquee in which the lavish breakfast was laid out. The guests were moving in and out of it and around the paths of her garden, admiring her flowers and standing in brightly coloured knots to look out over the magnificent panorama of Port Nicholson.

A little apart from everyone, with eyes for no one but each other, stood Edward and Jessie, her creamy dress forming a focus of brightness against the greenery of a rustic trellis. Fanny was surprised by a tightness in her throat and a rush of tears to her eyes. They seemed so young, so unarmed against the world! Then, too, they were so lost to everyone else, so intent upon each other! Fanny had to admit to a little prick of jealousy. She had relinquished her daughter to Sir Andrew Dunstable without a pang but she could not give Teddy over to another woman so easily.

Just then, as if she had heard her mother-in-law's unspoken thought, Jessie turned her head and looked across the expanse of lawn up into Fanny's eyes. For a moment they regarded each other. Then Jessie lifted her fingers to her lips and blew Fanny a kiss.

'You dear, dear child,' said Fanny, wiping her eyes. Then she turned away from the window and went downstairs to her guests.

Hours later, Jessie and Edward were alone at last in the bedchamber of their own small cottage. They moved about uncertainly for a few moments. Jessie admired the pegs that Edward had fixed to the wall the day before. Edward demonstrated the clever catch to the door. A suffocating shyness had come over Jessie, while Edward seemed afflicted with breathlessness. He loosened his cravat, then took it off and folded it with unnecessary care. Jessie bent to pick up a dead spider from behind the chest of drawers and made much of opening the window and dropping it out. She stood so long there, looking into the darkness, that Edward's courage grew. He took off his jacket, hung it over the back of a chair, and went to stand behind her. He slid his arms around her waist. Slowly she turned in his embrace until she was facing him.

'I don't know . . .' she whispered.

'No more do I, sweetheart,' said Edward, his confidence growing as hers waned. 'We're no more than babes, either of us, when it comes to this.'

He smiled down at her, then the smile faded as his eyes held hers. He felt his heart turn over but the trust in her face held him back. He was afraid of hurting her or frightening her. Slowly, he bent his head to kiss her lips and his arms tightened around her. She seemed to stiffen, and he sensed a withdrawal. He loosened his embrace and buried his head in the deliciously soft skin of her neck. 'Don't be afraid. It's only me, your husband,' he whispered.

To his relief she chuckled, and he felt her melt against his chest. 'You should say "It's only I,"' she said, 'and you're the schoolmaster and all.'

'Well, then,' he said, with infinite tenderness, 'if I'm the master, it's I must tell you what to do. Get into your nightgown now, Jessie, and come to bed.'